WICKED NINNISH

ALSO BY MICHAEL SCOTT CURNES

2017   *Coping with Ash*, ISBN: 978-1-7772988-1-4, Fiction
       Winner, Royal Dragonfly Book Awards and the New
       Apple Book Awards. Bronze Medal Fiction Winner,
       Independent Book Publisher Awards

2012   *Living Artfully, Reflections from the Far West Coast*, ISBN:
       10-1926780140
       Contributing Writer to this anthology

2011   *For the Love of Mother*, ISBN: 978-1-7772988-2-1
       2012 Green Books Fiction Award Winner, Finalist for
       International Book Awards

2008   *Writing the West Coast: In Love With Place*, ISBN: 10-1-
       55380-055-9
       Contributing Writer to this anthology

1996   *VAL*, ISBN: 1-885487-19-3, Brownell and Carroll
       Publishers, debut fiction novel

For more information, please visit www.michaelscottcurnes.com

WICKED NINNISH

A NOVEL BY

michael scott curnes

CONTENTS

Bay
2
Dunlap
59
Epper
sage 20
Morfee I
(117)
Robert Pt
Eugvik Rk
Lone Cone
753
Maurus
Elbow
Bk
Channel
Rassier Pt
2
Kakawis
Lagoon
10
RGAS
LAND
10
Opitsat
2 (24)
10
Heynen Channel
5
Moser Pt
Stubbs
56
Duffin Pass
Tofino
Browning
5
2
(1)
(1)
76
(61)
2
46
R
46
(43)
87
Rk
20
82
5
(1)
Templar Channel
2
McKay Rf
09
5 (10)
(4)
(1)
(15) (3) (27)
(50)
Wickaninnish
(50)
10 (5)
Surprise Rf
(43)
37
Nob Rk
(2) (7) 27
(50)
Lennard
(4)
09
(27)
Cox
Bay
Fl 10s 35m 17M
82
30 27
42
16
Vargas
Cone
Cox Pt
131
31
30

Mosquito
Harbour
5
(7)
Plover Pt
100
Fortune
Channel
EARES
LAND
Mt Colnett
802
20
70
Dark I
(67)
50
Kirshaw
Its
40
60
Gunner
Inlet
2
Dawley
Passage
Island
Cove
Sea Pk
416
(34)
5
Mc
(62)
10
Windy
Bay
30
Warne I
142
60
Auseth Pt
40
40
Almond
It (21)
50
McBey Its
40
Indian I
224
40
Indian
Bay
Grice
Bay
Kootow
ISTA PENINSULA

CLAYOQUOT SOUND

Wickaninnish.

It was one of the few words in the Wakashan tongue that was spelled exactly the way it sounded, according to the half-native half-Caucasian seaplane pilot, who rattled off the island landmarks passing beneath them like green-dusted sugar cookies on a blue conveyor belt. His lone passenger, occupying the co-pilot seat but not performing any flight function beyond ballast, registered the names silently to himself committing what he could to memory and refreshing what he already knew about Clayoquot Sound. For the first time, with his nose out of books and maps, absolutely vibrating from excitement and the bouncy flight, the widely grinning passenger surveyed the vastly rugged 350,000-hectare area of fjord-like inlets and islands that were situated around the mid-point along the wild west coast of British Columbia's Vancouver Island. The two men, outfitted with matching mint-green earphones with padded microphones they could adjust to fit close to their mouths, had still been half-yelling at each other for the past hour, trying to be heard and understood over the single de Havilland engine.

Though Wickaninnish may have sounded the way it was spelled, it still took some lingual gymnastics to say, given its twelve letters and four syllables. The passenger straightened some and leaned forward, calling upon his spelling bee days.

"Wickaninnish," he said. "W . . . I . . . C . . . K . . . A . . . N . . . I . . . N . . . N . . . I . . . S . . . H," he recited, before pronouncing the full name again, in perfect competition form.

The pilot nodded and smiled as he eased the plane into a slow, right-banking turn. "It means *nobody sits or stands before him in the canoe*," he said. As they neared their destination and flying about as low as he could, he told his passenger of the revered Chief Wickaninnish, who had presided over the coastal Nuu-chah-nulth people nearly a century ago.

"That island down there is named for him," he said, pointing, taking his hand off the yoke momentarily. "High in those ancient trees are platforms that still hold the bones of my ancestors—well, the native ones anyway. My Norwegian ones are buried over there on Morpheus Island." His arm swept the width of the cockpit to point ambiguously in the opposite direction. He could probably sense his passenger was studying him. With his long black hair in a ponytail, his wide, angular face set off by washed-out blue eyes behind aviator sunglasses, he knew that he presented as a bit of an enigma; a local native kid who had excelled in school and had trained to become a pilot. He proudly went on to explain how his people called themselves the Nuu-chah-nulth, which meant *all along the mountains and sea*, referring to the location and size of their home territory. "For thousands of years, they made this place home and at one time, they numbered 30,000 inhabitants, maybe more," he added. "That was of course before smallpox and place names in other languages arrived on southeasterly winds, to change them, their territory and their history forever."

The pilot's passenger—Heritage Warren Carter III—had made the arrangements to charter that pricey one-way flight almost a month earlier. Since taking off that morning from the seaplane base on the Fraser River, adjacent to the Vancouver International Airport, Heritage had been drinking in the pilot's commentary like he was coming off a sacred meditation on thirst. But the moment the plane's elevation began to drop and the town of Tofino rushed up to greet them, the passenger found himself suffused with enough adrenaline to float an object twice the size of their seaplane. The suspense and anxiety of the two-month assignment he was about to begin, at his grandfather's behest, had commandeered most of his waking moments (and many of his sleeping ones, too) for much of that summer. The stakes in this mission could not have been higher for Heritage professionally, personally, and financially. He needed to calm his nerves and tame his excitement in order to deliver results that would unlock his reward; an expected, though conditional, inheritance worth millions. If someone had asked him what his pilot's first name was, or if he remembered leaving Vancouver at 10:30 that morning—just about fifty-five minutes earlier—he would have drawn a blank, as there were so many thoughts currently ricocheting about his brainpan like pinballs. But party trick of party tricks, he could damn well spell *Wickaninnish*. And *that* was something.

The pilot—it bugged Heritage he couldn't remember his first name—veered the plane right a second time for his final approach over the blue-green runway, chattering mostly to himself about how he wasn't bitter over the region's history, like so many of his native family and friends were. "It's our lot," he stated. "Besides, you can't fix in a single lifetime what's taken a dozen lifetimes to screw up."

The plane began to skip like a flat rock thrown underhand across the choppy water, before the engine throttled down to a sputter as they taxied toward the dock. Heritage was migrating—not unlike a hundred different species of shorebirds; or the gray, humpback, and orca whales that stopped by Clayoquot Sound, at least twice a year. Like them, he'd come to feed, rest and grow stronger for the trip he was expected to eventually have to make back. Looking around, though, he was instantly mesmerized; transfixed by the otherworldly beauty of the place. He didn't think he'd ever seen so much green in so many different shades. Already, the thought of leaving an Eden so lush, tranquil, and pristine, to return to the uninspiring rhythm of his noisy urban rituals, sent a thunderbolt rattling down his spine.

So, this was Tofino. Heritage's head was bobbing in a nod of recognition. He was finally arriving in the small, fabled town at the westernmost point in Canada that could be reached by paved road. It had recently become a bit more famous as the gateway to Clayoquot Sound and near the epicenter of what became known as the "War in the Woods," which had pitted loggers against tree-huggers the summer before. Aside from being there on assignment for his grandfather, Heritage had long wanted to experience Tofino for himself, but he just hadn't found the time until the time and opportunity found him. He was finally there, responding to a feeling, his own call of the wild, answering some howl that emanated from deep inside the moss-dripping rainforest that the antenna of his soul had intercepted and that he now desperately needed to decipher in order to survive. Corny and New Age as it all sounded, Heritage just knew there was some higher reason he was supposed to be there. This also marked the first time in thirty-two years that he felt as though he was spiritually in tune and listening to the universe. Now, *that* was something, too.

He had held off his arrival until after Labour Day—after the swarm of several hundred tourists had thinned, after the never-quite-guaranteed good weather had passed, and almost a full year after nearly a thousand protestors had been arrested and hauled away for blockading a bridge and logging road in a valiant attempt to save the rainforest. Heritage suspected it was easy to get lost in such impassioned swells of humanity, so he mostly avoided crowds; no concerts, sporting events, Pride parades, or protests. As a pragmatic non-joiner, he hadn't kicked up any real dust in his lifetime and he lately wondered what it would take to knock him off the fence and bring him out as an activist. He wondered and yet he knew the answer: his grandfather's death. That's what it would take for Heritage Warren Carter III to strip off his disguise, step from the shadows, and exercise an independence he'd only imagined.

On the water, the cockpit windows began to steam up and Heritage realized he had been sweating beneath his barely wrinkled Mountain Equipment Co-op wardrobe. He was all nerves and suddenly self-conscious in the tight space. The pilot flapped open a vent window and cooler air whooshed inside the plane, bringing gas fumes with it. Heritage coughed then excused himself, mumbling some excuse that he hadn't realized how overdressed he was. He looked down at his fancy Timberland boots with instant embarrassment—they showcased not one single scuff. He felt like a fraud, and wished he'd thought to tangle with a blackberry thicket to give his costume a more authentic look. He was going to stand out in this place; the polar opposite of his preferred strategy, which would have been to blend in with the surroundings and maintain an incognito status for as long as possible. The extent to which he had miscalculated his appearance and underestimated his below-the-radar-detectability in a village of maybe one thousand inhabitants were about to be graded as naively negligent. All he could do now was work to minimize the fuss and fanfare of his arrival. There were other measures he had taken that should still serve him well. He wasn't going to rely on his grandfather's gold-letter-embossed introduction, and he would downplay his role as the loyal emissary of the Toronto family empire, if possible. He would work hard to minimize the number of local residents who knew the details of his mission and he would instead bolster the architecture of a backstory that he was really there to learn the hospitality business and, if he had time, maybe write a crime fiction novel. Heritage had also decided to abbreviate his pretentious names by dropping some letters and syllables—something Chief Wickaninnish might have considered. He would be introducing himself to the occupants of this emerald edge of the continent, just as he had to his seaplane pilot an hour ago, as a streamlined and counter-version of himself—as *Tage*.

For years, he had treasured the nickname like a royal title, and there was a reason for that. It had been bestowed on him a few years earlier by a celebrated West End drag queen who went by her own rules and moniker—known after dusk, onstage (or on an upturned barstool) as Imogene Mantoya (AKA Michael Rozzeau according to his daylighting Royal Bank of Canada mortgage broker nametag). Heritage had tumbled for Imogene's glittered eyelids over cheeseburgers at Hamburger Mary's one autumn weeknight when she and her entourage burst through the diner door with baritone audacity, demanding a table for eleven. The waiter closest to the door arched a single eyebrow, gave a bitchy shrug, and suggested the traveling drag ball improvise with the tables as he had no intention of fussing with the furniture. Heritage had been four bites into his Proud Mary double-patty jaw-stretcher when Imogene's black-laced butt cheeks whoop-ee-cushioned down on the red vinyl next to him. Seconds later, telescoping one plum-painted fingernail, she pinched a French fry from his plate, and the rest was herstory.

The pair introduced themselves to each other. Imogene explained that in her court, only she could command a name of three syllables, so she then decreed that *the tall, dark-haired hottie formerly known as Heritage-blah-blah-blah, would henceforth be called Tage.* And with that, Tage was knighted. Blushing, he responded by ordering a round of milkshakes and French fries for Imogene's crew. Given that the already irritated server was in the last throes of his work shift, this labour-intensive order pushed him into SRO (stark-raving overload)—a term he'd coined and fully expected would catch on if he just kept using it.

After half an hour and a ruckus of twelve final straw slurps, Queen Imogene sashay-dragged Tage and the rest of her court (none of them kicking nor screaming) a full five blocks to the Odyssey dance club on Howe Street. It wasn't too long after that first royal tryout that Tage, the trust-fund brat formerly known as Heritage Warren Carter III, could be regularly spotted on his own at the Odyssey—and at some random point in the evening, shirtless and glistening—practically every Thursday night. Armored in black eyeliner, he'd commence marathon-dancing his privileged ass off—showcasing his leanly muscled, nicely abdominal-ed, thickly dark-haired torso—to hours of house-techno-pop, all the while being admired and showered by endless cruising attention and comped cocktails. None of this weekly routine, not the eyeliner, the gay clientele or being inducted into a drag queen's court was meant to telegraph that he was gay. Oh, no. It just meant he liked to dance—a lot, with his shirt off, to the delight of mostly male horndogs on the hunt. What was gay about that? And besides, he nearly always went home alone to add to his sexual intrigue and all-around-general sexiness. Heritage wasn't ready to sew on any permanent labels or cast his identity in bronze—at least not before his inheritance got sorted.

The pilot bumped the dock with the seaplane, before cutting the engine and hopping out of the cockpit to lash it, front and back, to the cleats that had been bolted there for that purpose. The moment had arrived for Heritage to present his reinvented self again—like some espionage character springing unrecognizable from the plot of a Cold War spy novel, complete with a new outdoor wardrobe and the rugged start of what was sure to become a disguising beard.

There, on the First Street Dock in Tofino with the red-painted railings and a modest sign adorned with a pair of breaching killer whales that heralded the unofficial terminus of the Trans-Canada Highway, Tage inflated his lungs with sea air while his heart drummed more noticeably than normal. He had rehearsed his arrival in Tofino. Make no waves, leave no wake, and cover every last one of his Carter tracks—that was to be his modus operandi for this mission. Considering the unscrupulous reason behind why he was really there, he couldn't be too cautious. He had already sacrificed the first three decades of his life trying to please and appease his grandfather for the sole purpose of preserving what he believed would be a sizeable inheritance. He was closer now to a payoff than ever before with his grandfather ailing as he was, in and out of hospital with alarming regularity. Heritage had never been comfortable with his family's questionable, resource-gobbling history and the source of their wealth—the Carter Pulp and Paper Company—and so was only waiting for his grandfather to keel over so he could do something good with the blood money instead.

Getting a thumbs-up from the pilot, Heritage unfastened the dial at his sternum to release the three-buckle seat-belt harness and realized for the first time how he must have been riding with nearly every muscle tensed in anticipation. He expelled a snort of laughter, stretched his limbs, and relaxed some, before twisting his body to climb out of the plane. His ears had been pinched and sweating under the headset and he massaged the cartilage there before patting his still mannequin-perfect wavy hair. The pilot, with his legs braced between pontoon and dock, held out his hand to help the city slicker down the short ladder. From the pontoon's storage hatch, the pilot retrieved Tage's backpack, lugging it to the bottom of the ramp that led to the main road deck of the wooden dock. The luggage handling reminded Heritage he should tip the pilot, but he wasn't exactly arriving with fistfuls of cash. In fact, after making the last payment on the sleek kayak that was strapped to the top of one of the seaplane's pontoons, and chartering that seaplane to the island, Heritage, heir occasionally-not-so-apparent to his fickle grandfather's multi-million dollar estate, was functionally broke and momentarily cashless.

"No matter," the pilot indicated when Heritage apologized. "You can buy me a beer at the pub when we run into each other again." Awkwardly, Heritage reached out his hand so they could shake on it. "I'm just going to check at the office to see if you can leave your kayak here for an hour or two while you get provisions in town." The pilot let go of Tage's hand. "I'll be right back."

Heritage kicked himself for not having at least a twenty-dollar bill that he could have given the pilot to show his appreciation. On second thought, he supposed, appearing in public without cash could aid his image-building as a struggling writer at the crossroads of poverty and creative genius—but he would still need to rough up his thousand-dollar wardrobe. How believable was his ruse going to be, he wondered as he roughly scraped the toe of his right boot under the raised rail timber on the weathered dock? Could he even command the fortitude and commitment to write a novel? *Probably not,* he concluded, and chuckled to himself.

The missed gratuity did remind him that visiting the local bank to open an account was on his checklist of arrival tasks. Like always, his allowance and expenses would be paid under the table and magically show up in his Vancouver bank account, but he wanted to create a separate account for local buying. One day—and he sensed that it would be coming any moment—he wouldn't need to worry about money anymore; not where it came from, nor how he chose to spend it. But to twist the ratchet on Heritage's nuts another notch, his grandfather's senior solicitor had recently reminded him that HWC Sr. hadn't yet announced a successor to the family business. That threw the matter of his inheritance under a speeding and out-of-control question mark.

Heritage lowered the backpack from his shoulder and set it on the dock. He jogged up the steep ramp to get his bearings. Under a sun-blocking hand, Heritage surveyed the necklace of islands from left to right and spoke their names softly from memory: Meares, Morpheus, Stone, Strawberry, Stockham, Stubbs, Felice. When he squinted to gaze beyond the in-between spaces, he thought he might be glimpsing portions of Wickaninnish and Vargas islands, too. These islands punctuated navigation channels that beckoned his paddling exploration with invader-names like Lemmens Inlet, Father Charles, Heyman, Van Nevel, and Duffin Passage. His nostrils brimmed with pungent whiffs of drying kelp, a cedar campfire, and a nearby deep fryer that was possibly already cranking out halibut and chips for an early lunch rush. There were traces of less pleasant things too: offal mixed with diesel fuel and a not-so-distant sulphur smell that threatened to expose the village's underwater, raw sewage outflow, which was less than half a kilometre away from that First Street Dock. All of this was accompanied by the staccato, high-pitched screeches of two bald eagles, arguing with each other from atop the aging crowns of cedar trees on two separate but adjacent islands. Tage could also detect the mosquito-hum of distant fishing, whale watching, water taxis, and motorboats. Just minutes earlier, the whine of their own seaplane had disrupted the morning calm as just one more reminder of the progress that had ended maybe a dozen centuries of peaceful, symbiotic isolation for the Nuu-chah-nulth.

Just then, a hovering raven dropped a clam from a height sufficient enough to crack its shell on the creosote-soaked planks of the dock, a short distance from Heritage's newly scuffed boots. His body jerked at the noise, then stepped quickly backward as the bold and hungry black bird dove for his opened treasure. In the morning sea air, Heritage could imagine what the raw clam brunch felt and tasted like on the beak and tongue of the clever creature.

Taking in the vista with the widest grin on his scruffy face, using every one of his senses, he marveled that he was finally standing there, in the middle of what until now had only been a nautical chart facsimile. Rising mystically into an animated, three-dimensional utopia, Clayoquot Sound formally introduced itself, in its green and blue finery. The pleasure to make its acquaintance at last set his heart on high-thump. No matter what this adventure would resolve or reveal, it had finally begun.

Tage had been somewhat forceful in his negotiations with his granddad and had succeeded in building-in an eight-day kayaking holiday he'd nicknamed his "orientation" before beginning his grandfather's latest and possibly last assignment. Heritage hadn't taken a real holiday in years. The notion of real holidays when you didn't have a real job—one he'd earned or was even good at—had seemed altogether frivolous. He had been ostensibly working five days a week as an elevated paralegal while attending law school, but he was really just his grandfather's on-call errand boy, mostly hanging around to see if loyalty and shared DNA would pay off in the end. Sure, he had a downtown office to report to, the wardrobe, frequent travel to and from Toronto, and regular meetings to attend, but he felt few expected him to ever produce or say anything that would add value or change the course of business. Now that he was out of the city, out of his dry-cleaned button-down shirts, and standing on the porch of paradise, Heritage, Jr. could easily make the case he was overdue for an adventure vacation. In truth, he wished he were solely there to upgrade his kayaking skills, and maybe find inspiration and space to write that crime novel one day. Instead, he had been given the inconvenient task by his ailing boss-slash-grandfather, to execute a high stakes and quite possibly hostile takeover of the Headlands Lodge.

It had been Heritage, Sr. who, with hindsight and maybe a shot of sodium thiopental, could admit he had been swindled into becoming an investing partner in a risky, high-end hotel operation. Perched dramatically on a cliff above the crashing

Pacific surf, just a short way from downtown Tofino on acreage long-owned by Heritage's grandfather, the Headlands had been purpose-built with local rainforest timber to attract and cater to the wealthy—and those pretending to be. Why his grandfather, some years earlier, had decided to expand his portfolio of assets to invest in a hospitality venture at the end of the road on the other side of the country, was likely to remain a question that neither of them could ever answer or properly defend. It had been a family acquaintance and Toronto businessman who had talked his grandfather into the deal—a shyster (to use his grandfather's terminology) by the name of Brad Fraser, who had apparently been a University of Toronto graduating classmate and close friend of Tage's since-deceased father. As the story had been told over and over again by his bitterly resentful grandfather, Fraser had grossly over-represented everything—from the extent of his relationship to Heritage Warren Carter II, to the cost of construction, to the grand opening date in the project's feasibility study. Even so, feeling both sick and sentimental about the tragic loss of his only son—Tage's father—followed shortly after by the passing of his demented and ultimately institutionalized wife of sixty-four years, his grandfather had agreed to finance and front forty-five per cent of the project's start-up costs, in exchange for forty-five percent of the lodge's profits. While his grandfather still owned the land and had already recuperated his original investment in the lodge, and should have perhaps been satisfied with the arrangement, he had become convinced that Brad Fraser was cooking the books and skimming hundreds of thousands of dollars a year—maybe more. Normally, Tage's grandfather would have just wanted to be bought out of the deal and made whole, but because the Headlands had been lucratively exceeding revenue projections, he had made the decision that he wanted Brad Fraser out of the deal instead. In pursuit of this ouster, he was dispatching his grandson to personally audit the hotel operation, try to catch Fraser in the embezzling act, and then—with evidence or without—present his shady business partner an exit clause he couldn't refuse.

Tage already knew this would not be an ordinary work assignment. This would push him. It would get uncomfortable and test his loyalty to the family. A job was a job, he'd always heard others say. He'd maybe said as much himself when he was a little younger and more idealistic than realistic. But that was also before his vision for the future and his grandfather's expansion plans for the company had begun to diverge—and radically so. Over a period of five years, working and living in Vancouver had transformed Tage into a future-concerned, bleeding soul, dyed-in-the-green-wool environmentalist . . . in principle.

In the beginning of his new career, after law school, when he put on the monogrammed cuff links that had belonged to his father and began really working for the family company, it had been remarkably cushy—posing in a Vancouver or Toronto board-room, shuttling paperwork back and forth between the company's dual headquarters, and being called Mr. Carter by the company underlings. As the frequent flyer miles and other perks added up, he hadn't given much thought to forests he'd never seen, which supported habitats and species he hadn't ever bothered considering. But there must have been something magical and accumulative in that *Super Natural British Columbia* glacier water, though. After years of drinking the pure stuff, surrounded by those jagged, snow-capped Coast Mountains at the sea's lapping edge, he'd gotten irretrievably drunk on existential guilt over what was happening to the planet and began to crave a sobering redemption that only inherited and repurposed money could buy. His own grandfather had triumphed from the destruction of life-giving forests. Tage was spoiled and trust-funded by the proceeds of this raping. As he grew older and more principled, it just didn't sit well with him. He knew his new outlook would not jive with his grandfather's capitalistic and resource-destroying ways, so he'd kept his green-leanings and his fairly new resolve to become a vegetarian out of sight, tucked away in a secret shoebox on a high shelf in the same closet where he also stored his avant-garde pansexual orientation. Sure, depending on the methodology used, he was probably way more *homo* than *pan*—but he liked having options and didn't want to get backed into any particular corner.

Everything began to change for him the previous summer when his grandfather confided to his tight inner circle that his off-again, on-again cancer was back on and at long last deemed untreatable and terminal. Heritage couldn't help but straighten up his posture, tighten his corporate suspenders and begin to fly right through his grandfather's final stretch. At the same time he was ingratiating himself, he was closely following a news story that just wouldn't go away about a Vancouver Island anti-logging protest camp that had attracted hundreds of environmentalists from all walks, who were willing to risk arrest to halt the destruction of the rare, temperate coastal rainforest. That camp had swelled to over one thousand impassioned activists—many getting their first taste of civil disobedience as they got deputized as brand-new rainforest defenders on the spot. Located in a clear-cut not far from Tofino, the protest camp became a magnet. Before that summer of '93 had ended, more than 900 conscientious objectors had gotten arrested and hauled away with permanent criminal records for everything from trespass to defying injunctions to contempt of court—but not before capturing the attention and imagination of the world. Even Tage had felt inspired and compelled to anonymously send a $5,000 Canada Post money order to the *Friends of Clayoquot Sound* to assist the arrestees with their legal expenses.

High-ups at Carter Pulp & Paper were paying attention, too—to their bottom lines. The protestors' beef was with the logging company, and by extension with the government that had continued sanctioning the deforestation regime. Carter Pulp & Paper somehow dodged the ire, and continued cranking out toilet paper and newsprint as though the pulp magically came from someplace

---

else that wasn't endangered—which just wasn't true. Heritage had thought about joining the resistance, but couldn't see subjecting himself to the unsanitary conditions of the protest camp, nor the confrontational posture of the escalating blockade. His larger fear, of course, was getting discovered as the likely heir to Canada's largest forest-devouring paper company. With his inheritance on the line, he knew he had no business at the summer-long blockade, but he sure respected those who endured great personal sacrifice to bring the world's attention to that War in the Woods.

"Hey! Wanna give me a hand with the kayak?"

It was the pilot, shouting up at him from the water just as the untethered and tightly loaded boat splashed into the water. Heritage spun around having momentarily forgotten about his kayak. It would be a while before his wallet forgot the added $800 tariff that the morning's commute from Vancouver had cost him just to transport the boat there since everything was based on weight and the kayak was loaded. But he didn't doubt that it would be worth every penny the moment he braced his knees and plunged his paddle into the cold Pacific waters of Clayoquot Sound for the first time. Almost daily that summer, he had paddled False Creek, English Bay and around Vancouver's Stanley Park to Coal Harbour and back, getting into shape for this assignment, learning balance and endurance and on at least one outing—humility, when he dumped in front of a throng of tourists. He was at last ready to graduate from shore-hugging to open water, and now that he was there—in Clayoquot Sound in the shimmering emerald flesh, he couldn't wait.

"Of course!" Heritage hollered down as he broke his trance and loped toward the steep ramp that connected to the lower dock. He had placed his first boot step on the pathway of metal mesh just as a projectile clipped him from behind and a blondish streak of lightning tried to bolt past him, knocking him off balance.

"Who the hell are you?" the kid demanded without stopping.

"Besides in my way?" he yelled over his shoulder with a voice that seemed deeper than his age.

"Heri . . . Tage," he stammered still recovering from the side-swipe, before remembering to use his alias. "I'm Tage," he repeated, "and you are—?"

"I'm Aidan." The good-sized kid, who presented as a mannerless teenager, stopped at the bottom of the ramp, folded his arms below his chest, and instantly sized up the newcomer. "What kind of name is Tage?" he asked suspiciously.

"The kind of name that belongs to me," Tage replied. "I'm sorry, but I didn't make out your name. Tell me again?"

"*Ai-dan*," the boy repeated loudly and slowly, exaggerating his pronunciation like he was speaking with a foreigner, before turning to resume his getaway. "Like *Satan*, but with an *A!*" he shouted back before hopping into a small, aluminum skiff at the end of the dock, untying it from a wooden cleat. He ripped the cord on the outboard motor and the boat lurched, then sputtered away from the dock. Heritage figured if he was old enough to drive a boat, he must be in his teens and was possibly just over-developed for his age. The California surfer-looking kid gunned the loud engine, momentarily pointing the bow into the sky until he could settle it onto a plane as he waved back at Heritage unapologetically.

The pilot jerked his arm in the air as though he were about to throw the kid the finger but then, possibly realized that he was still dealing with a child. "Hey! No wake! You're going to kill somebody someday, Aidan!" he shouted instead.

"Fuck off, Jason!" the kid volleyed back with a defiant voice that bellowed across the water. That was the pilot's name! Jason, Heritage noted.

"Or someone's gonna kill you, is more like it." The pilot completed his thought as Heritage approached to help him with the kayak.

"Ninn-ish!" A woman's shrill voice suddenly sailed out and

into Clayoquot Sound from one of the sea-facing decks in the line of weather-worn buildings situated on the bench of land above them. Tage turned in time to see her shoulder-length white hair as she tossed her arms up disgustedly before disappearing back through the open sliding glass door.

"You okay?" the pilot asked his passenger.

"Sure. I'm a survivor," Tage boasted, turning back to take the lead rope tied to his kayak from the pilot's hand. "So, what did you find out about me leaving my kayak tied here for an hour or two?"

"You'll have to clear that with Dottie Bard. It's her dock. It's practically her goddamn village." The pilot glanced around to make sure he hadn't spoken too loudly. "Anyway, that was her," he jutted his chin to point up the hill," and it looks like she might be on her way down to tell you that you can't park your boat here. Don't take it personal," he advised. "It's how she welcomes most newcomers." Using the hand holding his sunglasses, he pointed toward the white-haired woman, already charging down the hill. "Look, I'm outta here. My breakfast is calling." He started up the ramp before turning back around. "Nice having you aboard."

"Yeah, you too, Jason," Heritage joked. "See you around for that beer at the pub, maybe."

"Near impossible not to, since I practically live there," the pilot revealed before he began his march up the hill, whistling what sounded like an *ABBA* tune trailing behind him in the warming morning air. Heritage watched him tip his head as he gave a wide berth to the portly woman with that shock of snow white hair heading toward the dock's ramp. While Dottie Bard may have intended to intercept him on the dock as the pilot had predicted, Heritage could see she had gotten waylaid by another local resident and he could tell by her flying arms and hands that their conversation was spirited if not confrontational.

So *that* is Dottie Bard, Heritage registered, fussing with his kayak as he filed the visual record into his cerebral card catalog of characters he had been prepped he would either encounter, need to defuse, or have to collaborate with in order to achieve the family's business objectives that had been set out for him in this mission. He already knew her name and a fair bit of her reputation from conference calls he'd been on with the co-owner of the Headlands earlier that unseasonably dry summer, when, at full occupancy, the lodge and much of the Village had suddenly run out of water. Tage recalled the backstory that Dottie Bard had been the not-so-silent fiscal and negotiating agent that had brought about a modernization of the village water system in 1984—part of her much grander architecture to build an eco-tourism economy at the end of the road. Listening to his grandfather, Brad Fraser, and his grandfather's lawyer hammer things out during the series of problem-solving calls that explored ways to get water trucked to, stored and flowing at the Headlands again, Tage also learned that it seemed Dottie's true objective with the waterworks had not been altruism, but an attempt to bolster her struggling trio of summertime money-makers: Clayoquot Sea Kayaking, Road's End Bookstore, and The Sounder Hostel—all of which operated under one roof that quite possibly stretched over the very sea-facing deck from which she'd just shouted minutes before. That water deal usually delivered gravity fed rainforest-filtered fresh water from a lake high up on Meares Island—a good ten kilometres across the inlet—through giant pipes running along the harbour seafloor. But it also brought a considerable measure of notoriety and civic indebtedness to Dottie Bard. According to Brad Fraser, this engineering achievement alone had transfigured a relatively unknown but tough-as-cedar woman from Alberta into a living local legend which also helped her get elected and re-elected to Tofino's Village Council during each of the municipal elections that had occurred since.

Dottie had tamed the rainforest's most persistent resource—the up to five metres of rain that fell there annually—but Fraser seemed pretty confident that it had also been Dottie Bard who had been behind the first environmental protest that jammed the chainsaws from getting onto Meares Island in 1984. Just a handful of years later, with eco-tourism ramping up nicely and the ground-breaking and construction getting underway for the Headlands in 1988, there was the Sulphur Passage blockade on Flores Island that stopped another of grandpa's subsidiaries, Carter Challenge, in its logging truck tracks. And then there was last summer's whale of a blockade that most assumed Dottie had conceptualized and financed which signaled that perhaps the heyday of timber clear-cutting was running out of political and economic gas. In a related turn, not the least bit coincidental, any market hit to the timber industry also devalued the stocks and earnings in the family paper company. Protests and blockades were always bad news for his grandfather and Brad Fraser had convinced him that Dottie Bard was the scheming mastermind behind the anti-logging movement with her own special knack for making bad things even worse. *She is like Midas, that one*—Fraser had said on a recent phone call—*except that everything she touches turns to shit*. His commentary was probably meant to give the pair of capitalists a common enemy to defeat, but Tage's grandpa trusted nobody and that included his partnership with Brad Fraser even though together they had erected the magnificent four-star, 48-deluxe suite Headlands Lodge—stealthily grabbing a high-end stake in Dottie's new eco-tourism economy.

Heritage had known for months that he would need to make her acquaintance and gain her tacit trust right away. He also knew that the first impression he gave would make or break his chances with this gatekeeper to the town, and determine his success in Clayoquot Sound. He watched her spin around at the top of the ramp and leave that animated conversation in a huff to stride back toward the building she had emerged from a few moments earlier.

It was time to throw the toggle on his charm offensive.

DOTTIE'S DILEMMA

Having secured his kayak front and back with practiced half-slipknots, Heritage hefted his thirty-kilo pack onto his left shoulder and trudged up the ramp, already second-guessing himself. Perhaps he should be bolder and more forthright about his newfound environmentalism—tell Dottie about his somewhat symbolic but well-intentioned financial support of last summer's blockade. There was no question he would have preferred to face this particular family adversary with some proof of his better character—a green badge or ID of sorts that proved he could belong there and be trusted. It would have been handy to present an arrest record from the previous summer's blockade had he not been too chicken to give up a weekend and show up to be counted among the more than 900 forest defenders that had been carted away and booked as criminals. That would have been the right credentials to lead with, certainly, but instead he'd cooked up a whole different story—that he was there to write one—a novel, if he had it in him. And while he was at his opus, he would make himself available to the greater eco-cause. That would be his introduction to Dottie Bard and with that maybe he could finally chart a new course to make up for a mostly wasted life of goody-two-shoe passivity. But his complete caterpillar-to-butterfly metamorphosis would have to wait for the ailing grand patriarch to kick off. This, if Heritage predicted the grade correctly, would trigger the inheritance avalanche that would surely swoop down the ravine toward him from his grandfather's mountaintop of cash. Of course, in the meantime, that meant pretending to be someone he wasn't—someone not out for himself or there to take advantage of the natural riches of the place. But Heritage liked to think he had become quite accomplished at faking that he was someone other than Heritage Carter's grandson. He'd been trying to live the namesake down much of his adult life. He wouldn't have to much longer, he'd calculated. Biology would determine the recalibration of his new world order any minute. That assignment, at the request of his recently bed- and cancer-ridden grandfather, would surely be his last for the family empire—a short-term show of family force to settle past-due accounts.

Pausing to steady his breathing and readjust the ridiculously weighty pack onto both shoulders, Tage got his bearings at the corner of First and Main Streets, next to the House of Himwitsa Art Gallery, and across the intersection from the Maquinna Motel. Foot, skateboard, bike, car, and RV traffic was picking up for the noontime rush-hour guaranteed to produce at least one honking horn likely from or aimed at a German tourist not at all skilled in maneuvering his oversized rental camper. Waiting for a shirtless biker to clear the intersection, with a surfboard stowed in a custom metal tube frame welded to the side of his bike, Heritage fixed his hazel eyes on a baby-blue painted building, half a block to his left. It housed the three primary pillars of Dottie

Bard's empire: kayaks, books and lodging—all under a cedar shake roof that looked and probably was almost a century old.

The building and Dottie Bard had both seen better days, as he was about to discover. He walked through the propped open door and through a small forest of decorative windsocks and spinners. The driftwood-and-glass-topped coffee counter, behind which she was standing, had multiple purposes by the look of things. Beyond being the landing pad for lattes and cappuccinos, it housed the cash register for book, clothing, and kayak gear purchases. It was also the hostel registration desk, the notary desk if you had papers requiring a witnessed signature, the kayak tour or rental desk, and the weather station for those taking to the water.

The high counter also served as a precautionary barrier—like an outer reef that kept Dottie more than an angry arm's reach away from her blowhard enemies but also gave her something to lean into—not if, but when she regularly received or dispatched gossip. Not only was Dottie Bard the village notary, she was a two-term city councillor, ran the village's only and semi-affordable hostel upstairs for visitors under thirty years old, and was at one time the only licensed real-estate broker on the West Coast of Vancouver Island. She'd mostly retired that last shingle, now that others were catching on to the lucrative notion of selling paradise. She was also a mother to an adult daughter, but since she'd never really put a lot of time or effort into motherhood, it scarcely got a mention on the list of things she had either achieved or currently had on the go. She'd made it her mission to create a one-stop mercantile, where nearly anything in Clayoquot Sound could be monetized and she had succeeded for at least three summer months of every year for a little more than the past decade she'd been at it.

According to Brad Fraser at the Headlands Lodge, Dottie had written her own rules on several occasions, and only fools or newcomers would challenge her authority to do so. Heritage was vibrating at the opportunity to size her up for himself. He had a track record of aligning himself with powerful women—or, in the case of Imogene Mantoya, a man who dressed and acted as a powerful woman. Heritage liked to think of himself as a lady's man—not in the romantic sense, but as an advocate, automatically downplaying his gender-flexing to theirs if he sensed an opportunity for gals to take the wheel, set a course, and drive. The way his too-early-departed mother had helped him see things in this testosterone-fueled world, was that women birthed the monsters. So, it seemed only appropriate to give them first crack at taming them into mannered submission—or, if need be, slaying those who were spineless or worse, hopelessly macho and misogynistic. His fancy footwork and habit of always, *always* putting the toilet seat back down had kept him off most slay lists.

At first, Dottie didn't look up from her fortress counter. She was frantically engrossed in what appeared to be an arts and crafts project. All Heritage could see was a mop of straight white hair and a glue stick that seemed to have a mind of its own.

"Pardon me—would you happen to be Dottie?"

"Right now, I'd say I was anyone but me if I could." She looked up and changed her tone. "Yes. I am Dottie. Got a deadline, that's all."

Heritage smiled one of his let-me-get-you-on-my-hook smiles, and extended his hand. "I'm Tage. I've just landed."

"From which galaxy?" She momentarily launched back into her project, accustomed to dismissing transients for what they were.

Heritage withdrew his hand, burying it deep in the cargo pocket of his embarrassingly still-pleated outdoorsy pants "That's a fair question," he offered weakly, "but I come in peace."

She slowly looked up, pulling her hair back from her face. "Nobody comes to Clayoquot in peace, my dear. In pieces, maybe. But peace is what they come here expecting to find. Most do. Everyone arrives here running from something. And you're no different, if you're honest with yourself. Now—what can I do for you? Then I'll tell you what you can do for me."

She pulled over a high stool and perched to let him know she was finally ready to allocate some attention. Heritage momentarily teetered from one leg to the other, as if about to pee himself from adrenaline. Dottie smiled warmly, putting him, he already suspected, falsely at ease.

"Well, a couple of things actually." He freed the strap cutting into his shoulder and gently lowered the pack to the beige-linoleumed floor.

"Oh, a couple of things, huh? Then you'll really owe me. Not the way you probably wanted to start things out, is it?"

"I don't mind making good on my debts." Heritage winked at her and counted with his fingers as he spoke. "I need ask if I can leave my kayak tied to your dock for a few hours while I do some banking and grocery shopping. I need paddling directions to the Headlands Lodge. And," he said, looking around the shop, "I might as well pick up a good book to read while I'm here. I don't suppose you have coffee on, do you?" He pretended to ignore the imported Italian Espresso machine behind her under the window.

"It's Thursday. Bank's closed today. And I can't think why in the world you'd want directions to that monstrosity-of-a-lodge on the rock. Name your poison, greenhorn. *Canadiano*, latte, or cappuccino?"

"I will take a *Canadiano*, please . . . with room, and thank you." Originally from Toronto, Heritage had taken a while and several reprimands to get used to not ordering an *Americano* in British Columbia, where folks were particularly sensitive to the influx of Americans . . . first the fishermen, next the Vietnam draft dodgers, and then the refugees from Reagan and Bush. You couldn't swing a bat and not hit a Yankee in BC. It had become statistically impossible.

Dottie turned her swivel stool around until she faced the window. Without getting up, she ground the beans and began drawing two shots.

"What kind of bank is closed on Thursdays?" Heritage asked in a voice loud enough to be heard over the espresso machine.

"The same kind of bank that is also closed on Tuesdays. You're really not from here, are you?"

His nervous chuckle was the confirmation she didn't really need. "Toronto, originally." He was still yelling when she stopped the machine.

"I'm sorry to hear that," she replied in monotone.

"No need for sympathy." He grinned. "I said *originally*. I'm redeemed."

"Says who?" Dottie placed a clear glass-pedestaled coffee cup on the counter. "Creamo is behind you—unless you take soy or almond, which I keep in the fridge."

Heritage thought it should have maybe been the other way around, with the dairy not sitting at room temperature, especially that early in September. But he didn't say so. He lightened the hue of his espresso by at least eight shades and drifted toward the bookshelves while Dottie half-washed utensils in a sink that seemed better suited for a camper trailer. When the clanking stopped, she came out from behind the counter, tugging down on an oversize cable-knit sweater to conceal hips and a butt that might have given away her age faster than she'd intended— another reason she may have preferred to operate from behind her driftwood barricade of a counter.

"How 'bout we shortcut your browsing and I will just recommend a book for you? How long you staying?"

"Uh, okay," he said, tentatively. "Not sure. Thankgiving? Maybe Christmas."

"Monsoon season. You'll need a thick one. Here," she proclaimed. "*The Discovery of Heaven*, by Harry Mulisch . . . just came out."

"Sounds great." They were collaborating already, he thought. She was back behind her fortification, ringing up his purchase as he finished his coffee. "Delicious. Thank you." He paid using a debit card, since the rest of his plastic carried his full name. Dottie Bard might be tipped off, and his alias shattered.

"Tell me your name again." She handed him the receipt.

Tage tucked the receipt inside his new paperback. No such thing as a welcome coffee on the house, he noted. He looked up. "Uh, Tage. My name is Tage."

"So, let's get right down to what you can do for me, shall we, Tage? I need to lock up to run an errand, and your kayak will fit on the back of the herring skiff, so we can talk on the way."

"On the way to what?" he asked before wondering if it might not be wise to question Dottie Bard.

She shot him a glare that affirmed this hunch before transforming it into a sly smile. "It's not you who has to trust me, remember," she said. "It's me who needs a reason to trust you, now, isn't it?"

Heritage raised his eyebrows and smiled back at her with chiseled movie-star teeth that normally disarmed would-be challengers. When she didn't melt, he quickly and wisely determined she might be a few years beyond flirtatious manipulation. "Tough town," he assessed out loud, deciding to downplay his raw physicality to address her intellectually.

"Tough city, indeed. Follow me." The tall-ish woman, who was probably dragging her Birkenstocked heels through her own sixties, lent the impression that she might have raised her share of hell in the turbulent Sixties. You don't get facial lines like that unless you've cheated life and gotten away with it, was one of the last things his mother had told him.

That was just months before she was murdered by her husband, his father, eight years ago, on Christmas Eve. Heritage Warren Carter II then shot himself, while his only son slept fitfully on a red-eye flight home from college, for the ill-convened family holiday celebration. The murder-suicide had been an unspeakable act; one that he and his grandfather agreed—for the good of the company—could only be referred to as an unfortunate family accident, period. Money kept the story hushed and out of the papers. There would be no elaboration or analysis of his father's mental illness, nor any mention of the frequent episodes of rage and jealousy. Grief ensured that neither grandfather nor grandson would ever address the herd of elephants in the family living room—his father's perpetual feelings of inadequacy. He'd been set off, Tage was certain, by a lifelong inability to please his own, over-achieving father. Tage's grandfather would have none of that introspection, and chose instead to spend the rest of his years in unresolved denial.

Four days after that Christmas, Heritage had stared deep into the casket that held his mother's cosmetically repaired body. In that moment, he came face to face with the second edge of her wrinkle theory: when you leave this world with no lines on your face, it's because life has cheated you and badly. He would have liked to see aspects of his mother in Dottie—or in any older woman for that matter—but he did not and had not since she died. She was gone, and so far, he felt the truly cheated one and missed her every day. But he was in Clayoquot paradise now and was anxious to transform the sadness his father had sowed. He was ready to earn his lines, railroad tracks and interstates.

Tage and Dottie cut diagonally across an empty lot to access the coin-operated copy machine just inside the entrance of the grocery store locally known as the Co-op, at the corner of Campbell and First streets. A service call she'd made on her own office Xerox a full three weeks earlier had failed to produce a repairman—something she chalked up to living in the last pothole on the road less traveled. She reached into her front pockets for the change she'd advanced herself from the tip jar on the coffee counter. Dottie didn't like defeat or making concessions, so she invented workarounds, like making her call-to-action photocopies at the Co-op. It was a simple matter of fact that living at the end of the road required improvisation. This adaptability, especially when fused with her unique brand of stubbornness, had served her well. She could number the big battles she'd conceded using one hand, and that wasn't counting her ring finger, which had never known compromise and never would. Bard was her maiden name and Bard would be her dying name—something she figured many of her soft enemies secretly wished would get realized sooner than later. While it was melodramatic, even Shakespearian, Dottie suspected her hard enemies weren't just wishing anymore. For years now, she had felt them closing in, likely choreographing her demise and possibly even growing impatient which kept her on guard and constantly looking over her shoulder. Being solitary and self-sufficient kept things simple and uninvolved, and as a notary and town gossip, Dottie knew how vitally important autonomy was—since most personal relations, in her experience and observation, eventually turned legal and nasty, though rarely in that order.

Heritage scanned the grocery store from where he stood, smelling a combination of bleach and rotisserie chicken. He took a step toward the closest aisle in search of something quick to snack on while Dottie arched over the copy machine like a church organist in the throes of a fugue. His mostly-vegetarian brain tried to override the smell of chicken and instead had him in dire need of a buffalo mozzarella, spinach and heirloom tomato panini, olive oiled and freshly pressed. Or maybe he could get by with a multi-grain ginger and lemon-zest scone. But of course, these were city extravagances he'd have to live without here in the boondocks. He took solace in this rural transition knowing he would eventually adjust, but momentarily he was having some difficulty recalibrating his urban palate and shaking his big-city impatience. He withdrew a handful of coins from his outdoorsy pants and examined the balance of his worth, which appeared to be fifty-five cents. The unmistakable glimmer of currency caught Dottie's eagle eye and she swooped down to peck the quarters and Bluenose dimes from his palm with talon-like precision.

"Think of this as your arrival tax; your contribution to the greater cause; an entry fee to the real fight." She raised her fist in solidarity. "This will buy us eighteen more media opportunities and you just can't put a price on that exposure." At last she handed him a warm photocopy as it emerged from the green glow of the machine.

Heritage's eyebrows grew closer together in a concerned prelude to his first crisis in Clayoquot. "This flyer asks people to boycott the future development of a floating wilderness recreational outpost by my new employer," he said. "This is the hand that is supposed to feed me and teach me the ropes of the hospitality business over the next few months. I'm not sure I can play any part in this counter-propaganda." As soon as he blurted this out, he realized he had abandoned the agenda-free stance he had hoped to convey. Neither his grandfather nor the company lawyer had mentioned anything about Brad Fraser's expansion plans for the Lodge. That was surprising news that he would need to report back.

"The hand that feeds you," she corrected him, nearly spitting, "is Mother Earth. Mess with her and she'll see to it you starve in the end. Brad Fraser is nothing but a marionette for an American timber-buying consortium. Once he pulls his wooden head out of his wooden ass and gets all his strings untangled, you can bet he'll dance a number for them as our giant trees fall one after the other. That man is evil, by gender and by deeds, and I will bring him down with the thud of an ancient cedar." She paused to evaluate how much she might be frightening her recruit and then clinched her induction ceremony. "You either grab an ankle to take him down with me or you lend your arm to prop him up, but you must decide now. We're late—or at least, I am."

The copy machine gave a mechanical sigh as the lights faded and the last photocopy emerged. Dottie gathered the leaflets and plucked the one back from Heritage. His brain scrambled for a way out of this quandary. They both wanted Brad Fraser out of the picture. Surely, Tage thought, there was some way to collaborate there. Too late. She had taken his silence as rejection.

Heritage stammered at first—something he rarely did around anyone—and then weakly muttered, "I have to start work at the Lodge in eight days, or I won't be able to afford to stay here. It's not a matter of choosing sides."

"That's just fine, then." She turned to leave the store.

Heritage was flushed, fearing that he had alienated the one person even Brad Fraser, on conference calls, had warned him against pissing off. She glanced back over her shoulder, white strands of hair aloft in chaotic animation. "Or," she deadpanned, "you can start working for me, immediately. Starting right now, I'll pay you every bit as much as the Headlands and provide housing—not to mention a conscience you can actually live with. If, in eight days, it doesn't work out, you can hand your soul over to the Devil."

Heritage let slip a smile—seeming to accept her proposal before even he realized what he had done.

"Well, let's go!" she cheered.

Heritage craned the backpack onto his shoulders and followed her out of the store. This would be his first wrinkle, he acknowledged, touching his face. Let the collection begin, he conceded in his mother's memory.

His first task under Dottie's indenture was to pick up a dozen loaves of banana bread and a ten-litre urn of coffee from the Sun-Ryes Bakery while she locked up her waterfront mall for a day of ecological hell-raising—apparently, that was her specialty.

Mona Rye, who had owned and operated the bakery since its first misshapen loaf in 1979, introduced herself and then revealed her surprise that Heritage had been taken under wing by the one woman in town considered absolutely wingless when it came to nurturing—a regular emu among mother hens on the unsanctioned village welcoming committee. Heritage shrugged his shoulders, smiled and offered his name with a wink. For an instant, Mona forgot her middle age, her physical liabilities, and even that fresh batch of cheese buns still in the oven, and lost herself in his square-toothed smile.

"There's more where that came from, Tage," she yelled after him down the sidewalk outside the bakery. In the midday sun, Mona squinted in the direction of his lumbering image, smoothed the apron across her lopsided chest, and silently cursed Dottie Bard for no particular reason.

At the dock, he stowed the bags of bread and the plastic coffee urn in the white and blue trimmed boat that Dottie had pointed out, and waited for her as she spoke with a rotund man on the waterside deck of her building. The conversation appeared to be somewhat hostile, once again punctuated by the movement of their arms. Tage tried to busy himself by fiddling with his kayak—but out of one eye, he managed to see the man point toward him just before Dottie lost patience with the discussion and walked away. No waves, he reminded himself. No waves. He pulled the kayak along one side of her boat and awaited directions from Dottie the skipper and his new temporary employer, who strode with a whole new determination down the hill toward him.

"What was that all about?" he dared ask once she was within hearing range. "I only ask because that man seemed to be pointing toward me."

Dottie deliberately paused, set her stance, and responded. "I suppose it would be nice to think that within your first hour of arriving in a totally new town, someone else's conversation could revolve around you. I will grant you that you were one of ten topics we covered in sixty seconds of general ranting at each other. But what you witnessed up there is all about me and the years I've spent carefully curating my enemies. Grab the other end of your kayak and we'll lay it crossways."

"It's loaded."

"With what?"

"My books."

"Your books," she repeated, trying to stay calm while coming up with a quick solution that wouldn't delay them further. "Out with them. Come on. Out with them. Stack them on the dock."

Heritage didn't question her and began the process of unpacking the watertight compartments. Laying his personal library out on the dock invited an inspection he hadn't anticipated. Getting past this customs lady was going to be a *Midnight Express* affair that forced Heritage to reveal much more about his character and motivations than he would have liked. His wonderfully disguised neutrality was about to get splayed out on the dock as contradictory. Dottie seemed amused by this undressing of his soul, as Tolstoy and Gandhi and Rachel Carson and Edward Abby all found their individual reckonings on the thick-lumbered dock. Dottie pretended to tinker with a stubborn knot, but could not conceal her gratification, as her newest foot soldier's impressive reading list revealed both that he was a thinker and that she still commanded impeccable judgement of character. He added his newest purchase, *The Discovery of Heaven*, to the top of the pile.

"Now, pick one," she said. "You can stash the rest in this milk crate and I can keep them for when you get back." She passed him the yellow milk crate that had a frayed blue rope tied to it.

Heritage couldn't help but feel violated, as he began filling the crate. It was as though he had been required to strip one garment at a time until all his secrets had been uncovered. He had always felt that way about books and the intimacy they held. He had heard of criminal investigations that had subpoenaed library records to build a case against suspects based on their most recent reading. *The Catcher in the Rye* had been suggested as an example of literary incitement to kill a public figure like the Hinckley assassination attempt on Ronald Reagan or even John Lennon's killer who just sat there, after firing four shots into Lennon's back, reading Salinger's novel until the police arrived to arrest him. From what Tage remembered of American politics in the mid-eighties, he didn't know anyone who hadn't thought of killing Ronald Reagan themselves whether they'd read Salinger or not. Still, Tage had read the novel precisely because of this notoriety, but by the end he found the only person he really wanted to kill was J.D. Salinger for not bringing Holden out of the closet more explicitly.

Why he was feeling vulnerable and suspected Dottie might be building a case to use against him could only be measured by the ways in which he was collecting information about her for exactly the same reason—to get an upper hand he could use to his advantage. Heritage was a master at assimilating adversity and Dottie seemed a pro at dispersing it, so it was simply a matter of time before their symbiosis kicked in. Perhaps minutes.

They pulled away from the dock and began motoring north. He yelled over his shoulder and over the sputtering engine. "Am I on the clock now?"

She smiled even as she strained to navigate a course between crab trap floats and shoals of sand and rock looming just beneath the surface.

"May I inquire as to my current job description?"

"Dead weight," she answered. "Your job is to hold the bow of the boat down so I can see over the top. You're doing fine, by the way, in case you needed some feedback."

"And when we get where we're going—"

"What?"

"I said, *And when we get where we're going—*" he yelled even louder.

"You'll be serving as my loyal representative at the Bawden Bay Blockade, that is, until the RCMP runs you off—which should be sometime tomorrow afternoon, if I gauge their pre-emptive movements correctly. I can't stay. I'd love to, but I have a house showing at four and a council meeting tonight at seven-thirty. Someone needs to deliver the banana bread to bolster the troops. That someone's you—my new envoy. Rain's forecast by nightfall. They'll need all the encouragement you can give. Can you handle it?"

"Of course, I can handle it. And when I get back . . ."

"*If* you can find your way back."

"I can navigate back just fine, thank you! And then we'll discuss our mutual future and a strategy for allowing me to serve out my employment obligation to The Headlands—maybe work for you on weekends or evenings?" He was operating on the principle of keeping his friends close and his enemies closer.

Dottie seemed to be pretending not to hear him—which, considering the loud motor, was not altogether implausible. He persisted with a scowl until finally she answered him. "Yes, yes—we can take care of all that, but don't worry about Brad Fraser. He's been taken care of."

"What do you mean, *taken care of*? Rubbed out? Silenced?"

"Don't I wish I had a bite to go with the bark?" she confessed under the deafening sputter. "He already knows. I told him I was stealing you away—right off the dock."

"You did what?" he asked, miffed by the audacity of her interference.

"Don't worry," she said. "I told him I'd have you back in a week's time—so you can tell him then that you'd prefer to work for me, if you want to. You weren't even scheduled to start working for the monolithic swine until the seventeenth anyway. You'd be surprised how much could happen to change your whole life in that time. What's your rush, Tage?"

"I'm a man of my word, that's all."

"A man of his word, in my experience, can nearly always be made to choke on it!"

"I see." He didn't.

Through Father Charles Channel and around the west-facing slope of Catface Mountain, Dottie plowed the skiff toward their destination. As they entered Millar Channel, prevailing winds tried to hold them back, but she ducked into Bawden Bay and escaped the worst of it. A good hundred metres from shore, where Bawden Creek emptied into the sound, she brought the motor to an idle and moved up front, where she began stuffing the banana bread loaves into Tage's kayak compartments, where his books had been. She rattled on about Brad Fraser trying to punch a service road through the ancient forest somewhere over there, she'd vaguely pointed. She said he had made a special use license application to site a floating wilderness lodge with something like a half a dozen rooms, a kitchen, living and dining area, so he could attract wealthy sports fisherman and hunters to the middle of nowhere to empty their wallets. Maybe that was where the missing money from the Headlands had gone, Heritage hypothesized, thinking about his grandfather's suspicions that Fraser had been embezzling. Dottie let Heritage secure his own hatch covers and told him he would have to paddle with the coffee urn between his legs and then, without further directive, the two of them lifted and extended his kayak onto the water next to the skiff. Tage was busy scaling down his pack to the overnight provisions he thought he would need to see him through the next few days, like his tooth brush and fancy hunting knife, placing excess items into the milk crate with his books when the first raindrops began to hit his face and arms. He snapped the two pieces of his primary paddle together and pulled his spray skirt up to his waist. He stared through the blowing rain to shore, which he calculated to be 150 metres away.

"And they're expecting me?" he asked.

"No, silly. They're expecting *me*. It's your job to convince them you're just as ornery and loaded for loggers as I am. Now, scowl. No, I mean really *scowl*."

Heritage made an angry face. It was surprisingly easy, given the circumstances of her manipulation and meddling. "So, I'll see you in a few days, then."

"Absolutely you will. Now give 'em hell." She was about to head off, when she remembered the balance of her morning exertion. "Shit! And make sure the press gets these flyers." She handed him the large Ziploc bag of flyers they'd copied earlier. "We don't score unless we dunk these fact sheets through the media hoop."

"Gotcha. Thanks, Dottie—I think." He smiled as the rain peppered his face.

"Give it a few days, and you'll know if this is right. Now aim for the mouth of the stream. Camp is just to the left, on reserve land."

Heritage eased himself into his kayak. The rudder foot mechanisms had been set at just the right length for his long legs months earlier in preparation for his first opportunity to ply Clayoquot waters. He took a deep breath just as a swell moved him away from the skiff. It was like watching the Apollo 14 command capsule separate from the lunar module, before returning to earth. Heritage wondered when and where he'd be returning. He adjusted his life vest to give himself more room under the arms. Acknowledging just the right measure of ceremony, he dipped the right end of his paddle into the gray water of Clayoquot Sound, and shoulder-muscled his way toward shore. A dozen strokes later, the monotonous roar of Dottie's boat motor had disappeared around Clifford Point, as the sand and pebble beach rose up beneath him. In more ways than he could imagine, he had arrived. *This* was the Clayoquot Sound his spirit had been seeking.

Dottie arrived back at the dock below her building, soaked and harried by a squall that had been crouching behind Catface Mountain waiting to pounce on her busy afternoon plans. An unrelenting wind from the south had turned her fifteen-minute sprint back to town into a forty-five-minute haul that made her appreciate what driving a snowplow must have felt like. Her years on the West Coast had taught her there's no such thing as foolproof rain gear when you live in a rainforest. *Gore-tex, Schmoretex!* she liked to say to tourists who complained about the rains, though in that drenched moment, it wasn't nearly as colloquially cute-sounding as she had thought. Eventually everything there, including the proverbial frog's bottom, leaked. Her yellow raincoat, already patched in several places with duct tape as old as the hardware store where she'd bought the roll on opening day, was no exception. She knew she'd have to change completely or at least throw her underclothes into the dryer before continuing on to her house showing. Heading up the ramp, she looked toward her building and instantly detected that no lights were on anywhere. Normally, her place looked like a used car lot, with festive spinners, windsocks, and lights strung everywhere to draw the tourists in. The skies had certainly darkened enough that electronic eyes should have automatically turned on the exterior light show. This brought her to the second most predictable aspect of West Coast living—the hydro tended to go out just about as often as the frog's bottom got wet. So much for drying her clothes.

"Mum!" Her daughter's shrill, familiar voice caught her off guard, and she spun around on the wet incline. In that second, her balance suddenly swooshed forward while her feet slipped back, and she hit the deck with a not-very-ladylike *smack* and skidded about a metre down the steeply angled ramp—made even steeper by the low tide. It wasn't enough to knock the air out of her, but she would be bruised, all right. And on her kneecap—the only place she hadn't been able to count on the extra cushion of cellulite yet.

"Stephanie?" she yelled. "Why aren't you at the blockade?" She did not get up, thinking it made her predicament appear more intentional—as though she had freely elected to kneel down on all fours to have this exchange with her daughter.

"And why haven't you had asphalt shingles nailed to that ramp for traction like you keep promising?" Stephanie returned, rushing up the ramp to give her mother an arm up. "We had to move camp to Matilda Inlet over on Flores Island. Got chased out by black bears. I was trying to catch you before you came out."

Dottie thought for a moment, brushing the wet grit from her wetter pants. "Black bears? They shouldn't be aggressive this late in the year. They've had plenty to eat."

"Well these boys must've been sick of berries and grubs, then, because they were all over us like . . . well . . . like *bears*."

"Tage!" Dottie said, righting herself from the slippery ramp using the rickety railing before bursting into laughter. "He's going to think this is some initiation ritual. I suppose it is."

"What are you talking about?" Stephanie, frustrated with her long, curly rust-red hair in the wind, grabbed at it with both hands, stuffing handfuls into her hooded raincoat. "Who's Tage?"

"Your blockade reinforcements, that's who Tage is . . . or was," Dottie amended. "Hired him fresh off the seaplane this morning." She cleared her throat. "And I've just dropped him off on a bear-infested beach, with—get this—a dozen loaves of sweet, sticky banana bread from SunRyes. He's going to kill me—if the bears grant him his one wish, that is."

"You've hired a man? I'm shocked! To do what?"

"Oh, to do whatever—you know. There are a thousand things that need doing this time of year now that the tourists have started to clear out—like replacing this ramp and fixing this railing." She kicked at the loose support using her good knee. "And then there's me. *I* need doing from time to time, too, if you must know." She watched her daughter's face. Her statement had gone unchallenged, which meant Stephanie hadn't really been listening. There was nothing new there, and this made her wonder why she even bothered trying to shock her anymore. Their relationship had been on mechanical life support for the past decade and a half. Stephanie had turned away to stare out at the water. Dottie followed the direction of her gaze and could see that Meares Island had been swallowed by the clouds that had been shoved into the sound's fjords and channels like packing

Styrofoam. There was still a good measure of weather out there and she felt bad having left a newbie in the wilderness to sink, swim, or become bear food—but he was a man, so she didn't feel all *that* bad.

Stephanie was temporarily lost in her own little world, trying to decipher her attachment to the place. She couldn't wait to go and yet she knew that a minute after leaving she wouldn't be able to wait to get back to Clayoquot Sound again. It was always that way. She was only leaving Clayoquot now because she'd been convinced by her handful of dope-smoking casual advisors that it was time for each of them to move on to their winter gigs, either down under for surfing or to Whistler and Banff for skiing, or to Patagonia—where Stephanie was headed to work as a kayaking guide. Once again, she'd chase other adventures until Clayoquot tugged her back. As always, she would justify it, like the others did, by saying that she was only going to where the jobs were. Even though her heart and the opportunity to work year-round for her mother could have easily held her here, it was usually her mother who drove her away.

Stephanie had been born four blocks away in the Tofino General Hospital and was forced to grow up too fast in a place where time hardly moved at all. There had been events in her thirty-two years that should have destroyed her. There had been events in her life that should have destroyed her mother too—like when teenage Stephanie made Dottie a grandmother—but they both somehow survived that ordeal. And to cope with the day-to-day guilt strung like a worry-bead necklace she wore as a permanent choker, Stephanie liked to make believe all three of them— grandma, mom, and son had survived that ordeal to flourish and lead decent, productive lives. But on her mother's advice, she had surrendered her child at birth without seeing or holding him, so she could never be sure she'd done the right thing by him—wherever he was and whomever he had become.

Stephanie wet-blinked herself back to the present, then

smiled, wiping an eye, returning to the iceberg she usually imitated when interacting with her mother. She was secretly sentimental and occasionally revealed evidence of it to Dottie. The latter kept believing they could one day settle into a more traditionally caring mother-daughter accord but for Stephanie, this was permanently off the table.

Dottie sensed her daughter was back from her daydream and possibly listening again. "Wick could certainly use a handyman to repair boardwalks and clear trails and—"

"Wait," Stephanie said. "You, Dottie Bard, are going to allow—no, make that *accommodate* a man on Wickaninnish Island? Penis and all?"

"Well, let's hope so." It wasn't the first time Dottie had leveled with her daughter. "You're not the only one who can have it when she wants it, you know. We could all use a little François in our boudoir, if you know what I mean."

"Believe me, Mother. There is nothing little about my François. But you probably already knew that. You usually have first crack at the newcomers, don't you?" Stephanie looked down at the clay on her gumboots. "It doesn't matter, Mother. François humours me, even though he doesn't love me."

"There's nothing wrong with a little humour, dear. Oh, pardon me—a *large* humour." Dottie knew she was pushing her daughter's buttons. This was verified and followed by a very awkward moment filled with rapidly shifting postures between mother and daughter as they tried to right the former back onto her feet. Stephanie had long been suspicious of her mother's flirtatious behavior around her on-again-off-again boyfriend. Stephanie had always assumed her mother to be a latter-day lesbian, except when it came to competing for the men in whom she happened to have an interest. There was really no other explanation but lesbianism for her tightly-woven island coven of similarly shaped earth-mother-goddess-minded women. So it generally pissed

Stephanie off to see her mother vying for a stake in the drastically limited supply of available penises in the sound.

The break in the rain was finished and the two of them scurried to get under the overhanging metal roof of the kayak shed just as hail pellets began pinging overhead. Dottie had to raise her voice. "In my experience," she said, "love in a relationship can be overrated and as long as your other needs are being addressed—"

"Let me stop you right there, Mother." Stephanie was not in the mood for a lecture. Birds, bees, and biology had never been a family strong suit.

"And where do you think you came from, my dear? Not to disappoint you and all, but it sure wasn't from love, darling."

"I know, I know. You've made that very clear. While the rest of my friends can make the claim that they were love children, sprung from the loins of a rebellious decade, I have to find my place among the bad jokes."

"Don't be bitter, Stephanie. Just because you didn't spring from love doesn't mean you weren't born into it."

"Whatever, Mother." The feisty redhead glanced away suddenly, finding it very difficult to look her mother in the eyes. Dottie hadn't exactly denied carnal involvement with François before he and Stephanie had started dating, and since he had made no small boast about the fact that he'd made it with nearly a dozen *womens* (as he put it, in his Quebecois vernacular) since his arrival, Stephanie supposed it was not out of the question statistically. It was time for her to leave Clayoquot's drama, and its dangerously limited gene pool.

After the hail stopped pinging the roof and shapeshifted into rain, and after a ridiculous moment of silence where neither mother nor daughter had anything nice to say, Stephanie switched topics. "So, let me see if I understand this scenario." She was practically yelling to be heard now above the rain, in what was shaping up to be a first-class westerly, well in advance of the winter storm season. "You've just left a total stranger to these parts, alone on a beach crawling with bears, and, as we now see, in the middle of a torrential downpour?"

"He has gear and provisions, I think," Dottie yelled back, defensively.

"He has banana bread, Mother. Have you ever fashioned a lean-to from banana bread, in a downpour? He's practically a walking concession stand for anything with four legs and half an appetite."

"He'll survive one night. He's a big boy, Stephanie."

"Well, that is how you like them, isn't it, Mother?" Stephanie was not amused by her mother's hobby of collecting people in one moment only to discard them in the next. She was mostly disturbed by the premonition that with her rapidly approaching departure she was becoming more and more throw-away like her mother every day, casting off love and security just because she got bored or irritated. Here she was, bailing on the relationship she had been the one to initiate with François, even though she knew from the start that he would be unable to anchor her in any one place. "Look, I've got to get back to the blockade camp before nightfall, you know . . . take advantage of the slack tide while I've got it. I'll see you in a couple days then, before I leave for Patagonia."

"I should hope so." Dottie grumbled as she turned to face the hill again.

Stephanie paused in the persistent rain long enough to make sure her mother had gotten most of the way up the muddy slope, before climbing into her aluminum hulled, inflatable zodiac. It was raining much harder now, nearly giving the day a sense of night. Stephanie untied her boat and puttered away from the dock into zero visibility. Rainforest rains, like grudges, could last for days around here. She took a deep breath, set her determined jaw, and gave the high-powered inflatable some gas.

BAWDEN BAD

Five minutes of qualified panic passed on the sandy, pebbled beach while Heritage nervously scuffed a rut nearly deep enough to garage his kayak. It quickly filled with rain and beach runoff. Just because he didn't see or hear a camp didn't mean it wasn't in there somewhere, he thought as he scanned the dark and imposing tree line. Dottie had no reason to mislead him. He hollered toward the trees as the rain suddenly doubled in volume. He dodged for the salal bushes and hunched there a moment before remembering to move his kayak higher up on the beach. He darted back into the open rain. His fiberglass, Seaward-Tyee kayak—signal-yellow on the deck, and white on the underbelly with black hatch covers and black bungees—was so new it didn't yet have any scratches. That bothered him, so he took advantage of the stony beach to drag his boat roughly toward the brush. Nobody was going to take him seriously as a paddler or out-doorsman if he couldn't showcase a few scrapes and bruises. He sat on the back of his legs and adjusted the collar on his fleece jacket. So this is what it was like to be a wet sheep. He briskly rubbed the rain into his absorbent sleeves. He evaluated his situation, crouching there, and realized he looked too clean-cut to be taken as anything but the city boy he was. Suddenly, the JFK Jr. look he had spent years perfecting irritated him to no end. He took a handful of mud and somewhat ceremoniously smeared it into his fancy Mountain Equipment Co-op wardrobe. *That's better,* he thought with a dirt-under-the-nails satisfaction. But then he took the masquerade a dangerous step further by unclipping the multi-blade Gerber pocketknife from his belt, opening a longish looking blade, and carving what looked like a grizzly bear gouge across the top of his right hiking boot. He rubbed some sand and dirt into it to make it appear as though he had barely escaped with his life.

Heritage chuckled in a crazed way that startled him back to survival planning and sent his heart racing. He hadn't seen a soul at this so-called outpost—so who'd be thinking one way or the other about his appearance anyway? The panic pried its way into his brain again, so he stood and took a few steps in each direction to see what he could make of his predicament. Because the rain had taken on the viscosity of crème of celery soup, he couldn't see more than a few metres beyond the shore—so that ruled out kayaking back to the village. He experimented with a series of quick shouts.

"Hey! Hel-lo? Anybody here?" And then, "HELP!"

There was no reply—just the sounds of rain dripping and drumming and the waves lapping on the pebbled beach. He didn't hear or see anyone nor could he smell a campfire, which he thought would have been a necessary creature comfort in that weather. And he certainly wasn't getting any drier standing out in the open. He returned to the salal and under the mixed canopy cover of Sitka spruce, Doug fir, alder, and cedar trees to think. In a way, the situation was pretty similar to the solo kayak-camping plan he had envisioned for his first eight days in Clayoquot Sound, anyway. He had all the equipment. He had a pristine beach all to himself. While he hadn't provisioned up at the grocery store, he had banana bread and coffee, so breakfast was sorted. With his attitude readjusted, he naively thought he'd wait out the rain.

He lasted ten more minutes.

The rain only came down harder. He worked his wedged pack and tent bag back and forth, trying to free them from the rear kayak compartment so he could get at his rain jacket, which was stuffed in a different dry sack. The robust odor of thermos coffee swirled out of the kayak and helped him relax. He poured about a cup's worth from the large plastic urn into the tin bowl of his mess kit, and balanced it on his knees. The steam rose to trace the contours of his face and reminded him he didn't have it so bad. He laughed explosively, feeling he looked very much the rugged type—straight out of a Marlboro cigarette ad—again, not that anybody else was around to notice his modeling.

From where he hunched, he identified two trees that he could tie a tarp line between. Once that was secured, he could set his tent up underneath, where he could get and stay dry—theoretically. He hadn't yet realized that common sense wasn't rainforest sense—dryness was as fleeting as it was subjective. His outdoorsy expertise would improve through lots of trial and plenty of errors, he figured—but at last the learning—like the rains—had started. Despite the awkward start with Dottie, he was exactly where he wanted to be on his first night in Clayoquot Sound; camping on a remote beach, all by himself, communing with ancient trees, lulled to sleep by the ocean waves, giving the rainforest a chance to imprint on him and vice-versa. There hadn't been any preordained urgency or instruction from headquarters that mandate he needed to meet Dottie Bard within an hour of arriving in Tofino. He could have kept to himself, minded his own business, grabbed a few groceries and paddled out of the harbour with nobody giving one shit who he was or why he was there. He'd definitely bungled that plan . . . or had he? Maybe it was better this way to have that introduction already ticked off his list. Normally, he would have steered clear or dashed away from a woman like Dottie, who presented as frazzled and disorganized as she did and who juggled people and projects-in-progress like beanbags that didn't shatter if dropped. Inside his skull not nearly as thick as it looked was a hardened nucleus of wisdom that Heritage usually kept on high alert for female booby traps like hers. He'd needlessly rushed that first encounter, but it landed him here, in this pristine place. He couldn't stop smiling.

His bowl of warmish coffee finished and now collecting raindrops, Heritage searched the front hold of his kayak for matches. He wiped the rain out of his eyes and set about establishing his first camp in Clayoquot. He set off to find dry wood as the rain pooled and intensified making his search for anything not already wet both ridiculous and comical. He hadn't wandered a dozen metres before he spied a torn triangle of white cardboard tacked to a sea-facing tree. He smoothed it out and deciphered the running ink:

> Attention Friends. Have moved camp
> east of Ahousaht Sep 4, 1994.
>
> This spot overrun with black bears . . .
> acting most aggressive!!!

"Shit!" Heritage said before instinctively looking around to see if anyone or anything had heard him swear. "Shit, shit, shit," he repeated, in a lower register, scrambling for his kayak. He tossed his unpacked belongings into the larger opening of the cockpit and tugged the boat toward the water. Then he realized that, first, he still couldn't see more than a few metres beyond the shore, and two, he hadn't a clue where this place named *Ahousaht* was. Faced with this new, rather pressing matter of life and death, he decided this was not the sort of survival play he had fantasized. He had anticipated something more moderately inconvenient, maybe, like running out of drinking water or discovering his matches had gotten wet. He didn't recall any scenarios involving bears during Wilderness 101—a beginner class that Mountain Equipment Co-op had offered the previous spring, mostly—as far as Heritage could tell—for new immigrants to Canada from Hong Kong. That class—spread over three Saturdays—had succeeded in making its students feel comfortable purchasing loads of pricey, outdoorsy gear and survival equipment but seemed to gloss over any real circumstances in which their individual survival might practically and actually get called into question.

He half-strapped his pack to his kayak, momentarily stowed his bowl and the coffee urn, and then shimmied into his sprayskirt. Standing there, he trembled, paddle in hand—almost frozen in this combative stance, until a bit more of the shit got scared out of him. As long as he stood still, he reasoned, he would be blending in, just like a chunk of driftwood—or, given the rainforest downpour, like a drowned rat . . . except this rat had to pee. He quietly lifted his skirt. As long as he didn't attract the attention of something with teeth, he would be okay. In the middle of his urine stream and self-coaching, there was a definite jostling in the salal and salmon berry bushes. Twigs and branches snapped and crashed until finally, that sea of green foliage parted, and out walked the Moses of black bears, his snout twitching in the air. Heritage awkwardly stepped into the kayak backwards, and when he found no place for his legs, he swiveled his waist and threaded them inside the boat without turning or taking his eyes off the bear, which was maybe ten metres from supper, by the look of his eyes and panting mouth.

"Shit! Shit!" Heritage chanted under his breath, like the word was a Buddhist mantra. He slowly pushed himself backward across the saturated sand with his paddle, not quite realizing how far away his kayak was from water, flotation, and escape.

The bear edged further out of the forest until four paws were in the sand. The rain slowed to an aggravating drizzle, but Heritage was barely aware of it now as he muscled down the beach like a freshly hatched sea turtle trying to negotiate a shell more cumbersome than protective. When he looked again, there were now eight paws and forty claws in the sand, as another black bear emerged from the brush. The bears grunted at each other, or maybe at Heritage, before moving closer to the awkwardly moving kayak-man who had broken a sweat beneath his fancy, though not claw-proof, Gore-Tex. He glanced over his shoulder when it seemed it was taking way too long to reach the water.

"Fuck!" he shouted back at the bears. They lunged toward him a few metres and then stopped abruptly. He waved the paddle madly in the air as he struggled out of the cockpit, calculating he had a better chance if he closed the distance to the water by foot. He jerked the kayak toward the ocean—adding plenty of authentic scratches to the rounded hull for sure. The bears rushed him in spurts until he splashed backwards into the low surf and climbed back into his kayak. He must have seemed out of reach or beyond their allotted caloric expenditure for such offensives, because they just stood there sniffing and snorting, their fur spikey in the rain.

With his heart beating so high in his chest he couldn't swallow, Heritage's eyes watered, until the tears overflowed his lids. He coaxed his shoulders down and tried to relax his face and upper body. It wasn't that he felt he had won the engagement or that he was past the grip of danger as much as he was genuinely astonished that wilderness and nature were real. He'd just seen proof with his own eyes. Even with the bears now turning away from him to check out the area where his tarp and rope had been left behind, and with his silicone-protected hiking boots filled with ocean water, Heritage just had to smile—admitting to himself and perhaps to the bears that he hadn't fully anticipated all the challenges of this new territory. It was small consolation to imagine that the big city retailers who had sold him his equipment and insisted he buy the silicone *and* the Gore-Tex—and the bear spray, too, he just remembered, probably hadn't put their products to the test either. Recalling their spiky gelled hair and that homogenous, leftover late-80s look that he had once or twice aspired to duplicate, Heritage now felt reformed, converted, even delivered from his urbanizing ways. The last of his own hair gel slicked its way down his neck and back, to join sizeable tributaries of bear-induced sweat. It all pooled, ironically, inside the same silicone-sealed boots—which were just as efficient at keeping moisture in as they had been money-back-guaranteed to hold it out.

With one last moment of respect paid to his carnivorous welcoming committee, Heritage dropped his rudder and turned his boat to head into the fogbank. Kneading the elastic-rimmed spray skirt around the combing, he suddenly smelled coffee again just as he felt a startling hot liquid rush between his legs. He'd forgotten to secure the lid on the coffee urn. Over his shoulder, he noticed the bears were cultivating a renewed interest in him or more likely the smell of his coffee. One of them seemed to growl good riddance.

"Yeah, yeah—I'm leaving," Heritage yelled back uneasily, while the fog wrapped about him like a soggy face cloth. When his paddle no longer dragged on shells and sand he paused to assess his predicament. He undid the spray skirt to confirm what his java-marinating genitals already knew. The uncomfortably high temperature of the coffee in which he found himself sitting sent a most distressing signal to his bladder. Suddenly the dire need to relieve himself a second time became paramount. But where?

Heritage shifted his butt to relieve the sensation, but it was not going away. He un-bungeed his bailer and began pumping the coffee over the side. In his growing desperation, he paused to examine the design of the pump. It occurred to him that he could urinate directly into the out-take hole of the device if the pump's plunger were completely depressed. Then the waste could be sanitarily ejected overboard by pulling on the plunger.

Thrilled by the real-life opportunity to use yet another of his kayak implements in a dire survival situation, he unzipped his pants and docked with the pump. But soon, he feared he might overfill his reservoir and have an even bigger mess. He decided to increase the pump's capacity by pushing the plunger even further down—but that created a vacuum-like seal on the head of his penis. Stuck, and embarrassed, he threw a glance in each direction to make certain he wasn't being watched—though the uncontainable laughter of anyone witnessing his dilemma probably would have been audible by now.

With his circulation and his urine stream suddenly cut off, Heritage began to fear permanent damage or at least a menacing hickey. An internal pain told him his bladder had not been fully relieved, but he pulled off the pump as though it were a leach, and then sprayed the contents overboard. He wasted no time in returning the pump for a second fill-up. This time, he wasn't overly concerned with spillage. He flushed the pump with half a dozen cups of coffee still swirling about the bottom of his boat, and then attended to his manhood, holding it gingerly for inspection. Fortunately, a little redness was all he could detect, so he tucked matters back inside his still-warm, still-wet pants.

Heritage resecured his spray skirt and got a firm grip on his paddle—but in the tidal drift, and surrounded by fog, he'd lost sight of land. He was now at the mercy of the currents. At first, he paddled with determination. The sea quickly turned to a series of deepening swells that told him he must have floated into a main channel. He wasn't sure if the tide was coming or going—so he couldn't ascertain if he was being pushed further into the island matrix of the sound, or being flushed into the open sea.

Heritage ruddered his kayak to face the swells so they came at him head-on. But he could only see them seconds before they affected his balance. He must have spent fifteen minutes paddling this way before he was overcome by a feeling of doom and helplessness. He stopped long enough to notice that the rain had subsided. That was something. He wasn't cold. He still had energy, and he wasn't hungry or thirsty. Everything beneath the spray skirt had turned into a sweltering terrarium. He relaxed some. He leaned forward to retrieve his lifejacket from the cross-hatched bungee cords just as a swell caused him to wobble a bit too much to one side. He corrected his balance, and before the next swell, he had threaded the PFD over one arm and then the next. The blood slowly returned to his head and after a cleansing breath, he reached into the forward hatch to extract one of the two flares he'd been talked into buying—along with a first aid kit and the bear spray he'd momentarily forgotten about.

He held the flare's wire cage and tried to figure out how to ignite it. He wondered about the efficacy of a rescue device that depended on somebody watching the sky at the precise moment the person in distress signaled for help. In this fog, in this remote part of the sound, Heritage knew the odds weren't good, but he tried to think positively. He unscrewed the red cap on the orange stick, grabbed the plastic red ball threaded through the ignition cord, and tugged. There was a rush of air followed by a flame that made more noise than light. When it didn't rocket into the sky like he thought it should, he tossed it up, only to watch it arc a few feet above him before splashing into the water. Down, down, down the still-burning orange orb sank, taking his positive attitude with it. That gave him an idea of the dark depths that churned beneath him—but it also allowed him to calculate his drift by the distance he had traveled in seconds, away from the slowly disappearing glow on his starboard side. Confident in what he felt was the confirmation of a landward drift, he shifted his bum and began paddling with the current.

It hadn't really looked like a flare to Stephanie, but she had been wiping the rain and saltwater splash from her blue eyes and couldn't be sure. She knew every inlet, channel, and rip tide in the sound—she'd been the lead kayak guide with her mother's business for most of her life. She unzipped her rain slicker and pulled the hood off her hair, allowing the velocity of the open boat to add volume to her natural curls. If her admirers ignored her stubby fingernails and unusually broad shoulders—built by years of paddling—she could be mistaken for an attractive woman. That wasn't ego. It had been commercially verified by the few modeling stints she'd been able to pick up with the various sports-oriented retail catalogs and one car commercial that traveled like a carnival to the forest highway and Clayoquot beaches for a four-day shoot. She'd been told on more than one occasion that she possessed an almost masculine-femineity that embodied a sensuality that resonated with both the male and female markets. She had inherited those traits from her mother—the coarse hair, the rugged beauty, the negotiation skills, and the ability to turn these assets into what she really wanted to get ahead—plus, she was offered as much sporting gear as she could ever desire in lieu of pay.

Stephanie knew it was at the junction of these many similarities, where the resentment could sometimes fester like a bacterial infection, between Dottie and her. They each took turns picking at a scab that never had a chance to heal. When the opportunity to billboard her mother's has-been status presented itself as richly as it had today, Stephanie could only lodge the scent in her perfectly proportioned nose and follow the pheromone trail. A new man in the sound—however overrated, as she'd found most men to be—was a lead to be investigated, a notch to be chiseled, an example to be made. Plus, she wanted to one-up that no-good-but-gorgeous-summer-tryst-of-a-boyfriend of hers for cheating on her behind the hanger at the airport dance last Saturday. She gunned the twin forty-horsepower outboard engines and passed between the navigational beacon on Monks Island, and the reefs off the Chetarpe Indian Reserve.

Heritage thought he might be hearing a motor, but the wind had picked up and it was beginning to rain again and he couldn't place the direction of the sound. He held his paddle still and listened. It was a motor, all right, but it seemed to be receding. At first, he yelled—about as effective as winking his eye, given the rebuilding volume of the storm. Then he waved his paddle— nearly tipping the boat as a sneaker swell passed beneath him. He jerked forward and snatched the final flare from the hatch, this time electing to take advantage of its hand-held design. He popped the cage and began slowly waving the flare in an arc above his head. The rain began pelting him sideways. "Shit!" he grumbled, getting a better grip on his paddle while maintaining the flare that was seconds away from a fizzle. He squeezed his eyes shut to force the rain off his thick eyelashes that were more nuisance than decorative. When he opened them again, the motor sounded closer, but his flare had gone out. Still, he couldn't see much more than the tip of his kayak. The craft passed him on the right, several metres away, with no indication of slowing down. He yelled. He was unprepared for his first shout, and it came out muffled by phlegm. He cleared his throat and tried again. Just as his shoulders dropped in defeat, the motor cut. He yelled again.

"Hey—!"

"Hello—?" a woman's voice volleyed back at him through the fog.

"Over here," he said. "Over here!" A softer motor hum loomed closer, and soon, the outline of her watercraft came into view.

"Hello there," she greeted, more personally once they'd made eye contact.

Heritage straightened his posture and tried to appear more in control of his situation than he was—the Marlboro Man's rescuer being a woman and all.

"Was that your flare I saw a minute ago?" she asked, a bit tongue-in-cheek, pulling the zodiac alongside the kayak. Heritage reached for one of the guide ropes threaded around the bumper of the inflatable craft.

He gave her a smile and came clean. "No use pretending I'm out here because I want to be, huh?"

The woman pulled a few strands of long hair out of her mouth and smiled back.

He went on. "I, uh—this afternoon I was dropped onto a beach that turned out to be infested with black bears, so taking to the water appeared to be the lesser of—you know—two evils." He was trying to appear attractive and calm all at once when another swell lifted one edge of her zodiac over the bow of his kayak, pushing the nose under water. He yelped.

His heroine tried to act as though she hadn't noticed. "Sure. I know the beach—up round Bawden Bay, right? Are you looking for the blockade, then?" She leaned down to help him steady his kayak. She had already unzipped her Patagonia slicker to the point of provocation, and she knew that her life jacket, which always crammed her ample breasts together, would exaggerate the effect if she leaned over.

The effort was lost on Heritage, who was still struggling to transform his helpless flare-waving antics into a more dignified and manly display. "Yes," he finally said. "The blockade. I have coffee and banana bread—or, rather, I *had* coffee when I started out."

"You're not what I'd call your typical take-out deliveryman." Stephanie fiddled with the ropes until her face was very near his.

"Yeah, well—" Heritage felt he was about to tumble over his words again. "What can I tell you?"

"How about your name, for starters?"

<hr>

"Oh yeah. Sorry. It's Tage." He held out his hand before realizing it still gripped the spent flare.

"Tage," Stephanie repeated, licking her bottom lip. "I'm Stephanie. Care to come aboard?" She raised one eyebrow just enough to add frosting to her innuendo. Another rolling wave swelled beneath him, buoying him closer to her face—inadvertently, they brushed noses.

"Whoa, boy!" he responded, a bit embarrassed.

Stephanie smiled. She seemed to enjoy studying him—toying with his nerves. Mostly, he figured, she liked being in control—and clearly, as far as he was concerned, she had the upper hand. She repeated her offer, and finally Heritage released the spray skirt with a tug on the release tag and handed her his paddle. As she steadied his boat with both hands, he rose slowly until his coffee-stained britches were right in her face. She giggled.

"West Sumatra Indonesian Blend from SunRyes would be my guess. I know it well."

Heritage placed a hand firmly on her shoulder and stepped over her arm and around her until he was inside the boat. "Yes," he responded, lowering the spray skirt to his ankles and examining the damage for himself. "I tipped the coffee urn over, getting into the kayak as I was being chased from the beach by two grizzlies." She seemed to have locked her eyes on his crotch, making him think his zipper was down. He checked. It wasn't.

"Grizzlies? Really? My, how this harrowing tale of yours grows. First the beach was infested and now they're grizzlies—which, by the by, we don't have on Vancouver Island." She lashed the kayak along one side of the zodiac with a free rope.

"All right—black bears. But they were bears, okay?"

The rain kicked up again with a sudden gust of wind that lifted the bow of the inflatable, knocking Heritage to his seat—of course, he tried to make that look intentional. Stephanie told him that was a good place for him, and to hold on while she maneuvered their boats closer to land and out of the wind. So, he sat there. She made it sound as though getting a boat closer to land was the easiest maneuver in the world, after he'd been paddling without success for the better part of an hour. He watched her, admiring how kinky her long red hair became in the rain, and how the blush rushed to her cheeks each time either of them smiled or tried to flirt. He waited for the storm to diminish her authority, her attractiveness. He waited for his fear of the high seas to register on her face too. It didn't. The more the sea and the storm challenged her, the more beautiful she became. And the more he watched her, the more he found he couldn't turn away. He had been a lost-at-sea mariner for no more than twenty minutes and already he had urges and impulses this siren seemed Poseidon-bent to explore. He needed first to exert himself, to re-establish his faltering dominance. Strangely, his other needs at the moment seemed to be manifesting sexually. Was he getting turned on by this fantasy of a female rescuer while the rescue was still in progress? The scenario was playing out like a one-handed read from the pages of *Penthouse*. He just stared, thinking the intensifying rain should act like a cold shower and dowse the spark of his own lust, any minute now.

Stephanie was aware of his stare, and she allowed it. It played into her little seduction scheme nicely. It certainly helped that he wasn't bad-looking, as human sacrifices went. In fact, he was quite a nice catch and this surprised her, even though she had intentionally gone driftnet trolling for him. From behind the console where she stood piloting their course through the chowder, she admired the natural waviness of her victim's dark hair, and how well he'd been put together. With his broad shoulders, he looked like a kayak guide himself, except that his square-jawed face had not yet been etched to sandpaper by sea spray. He was tall and lean, but not at all frail. She could tell that about him even before he had hauled his wet pants and presumably hairy legs out of the kayak. Stephanie was mad about hairy legs. Her own François was a yeti down there. She had always considered it unfortunate that a man's legs came connected to the rest of his body, since she usually couldn't bring herself to value anything above the waist. She would try to make an exception with Heritage, but a man's die was usually already cast with her. His ocean-reddened fingers were long and narrow, attached to great, meaty palms. His forearms and biceps too looked substantial inside the clingy raingear—she could tell that when he held something, that something knew it was being held. When he climbed onto the zodiac from his kayak, she had made note of the way the straight black chest hairs peeked above his neckline—casually, so that it wasn't lumberjack gross. She liked how his expressive eyebrows grew almost together across the bridge of his narrow nose, and how his long black eyelashes set off a pair of eyes coloured more cedar bark than hazel. All things considered, she had to acknowledge that the task before her might not be as unpleasant as she had thought.

She reduced the throttle as a rocky outcropping seemed to thrust its way toward them through the fog. She eased the zodiac around to the leeward side of the headland, where it was calm, no swell and no surf, and the rain began falling vertically for a welcomed change. She lobbed a small anchor over the side and pulled each of the twin motors up just as the rain intensified for at least the twentieth time that afternoon. She handed Heritage a bucket and instructed him to start bailing rainwater out of the zodiac. She reached into the hatch next to the steering console and extracted a blue tarpaulin. She quickly threaded a thin rope through every other grommet, and knotted guidelines to form a tent over the top of them, ingeniously directing the rain outside the boat. In little more than sixty seconds they had a shelter. Heritage leaned over the side of the zodiac to secure his hatches, and to cover the cockpit of his kayak. He thought to grab what was left of the coffee, and one of the shapelier loaves of banana bread, and presented them under the blue tarp as a gratitude offering to his rescuer and heroine.

"It's the least I can offer. After all, I was charged with bringing provisions to the blockade." He smiled widely, showing off large, impeccably white teeth that looked blue, like everything else under the tarp. His cheeks dipped into identical dimples, completing a Bermuda Triangle of sexy potholes with the cleft in his chin. When Stephanie refused to look away, he played a bit with his hair—only to the point of demonstrating how futile it was to seem groomed under the circumstances. "So, short of finding the real blockade, what shall we protest?"

"How about this weather?" she suggested. The rain hitting the tarp sounded like they were trapped beneath the membrane of a drum during a U2 concert. "Say, how old are you? I'm curious."

"Thirty-two."

"Hey, me too! Sagittarius . . . Jupiter rules my need to roam, Man."

"Taurus, and no idea about the rest," he admitted. "Shouldn't we try to make the blockade before it gets dark?"

"No use striking out in this mess. It will pass soon enough. What's your rush? So we play shipwrecked for half an hour or so." She climbed from the back of the raft over the main seat pontoon to join him in the center of the boat. Their heads beneath the tarp formed the peaks of their floating coffee shop. Heritage began to break into the banana bread when she intercepted his hands.

"Come on. Let's get those wet pants off."

Staring into his rapidly darting eyes, she directed his hands to the waistband, and together, they unbuttoned and then unzipped them. Her hand was heavy against him there and he began to stir. He managed to laugh a little awkwardly, protesting as she tugged at his shorts. She relented, settling for the full removal of his pants. His legs were just as deliciously forested as she had expected.

"Well, well," she said, appraising his choice of red underwear boxer briefs. "How trendy of you."

"What can I say?" Heritage offered blindly in his useless defense. Some things were already stepping up to the podium to speak for themselves, he figured.

"What can you say, indeed?" she responded, her eyes now fixed on the outline that protruded the all-cotton weave. Shoulders weren't the only broad things on this boy, she thought, folding at the waist to plant her blue-tinted face boldly between his legs.

"Oh, no," Heritage said—more of a resignation than a denial. She forcefully rubbed her cheek against him there, and his hips involuntarily convulsed. He gently grabbed both sides of her head and simultaneously pulled and pushed. Her breath was comfortably hot and when it seemed there was no blood left to run his brain, he grunted his surrender and shut down all cerebral function. She pushed his shoulders back until he was lying down. Then she climbed onto him, peeling off her slicker and life jacket in the same motion. Heritage supported her weight by cupping his long-fingered hands over her T-shirt, thumbs hooked under each of her breasts and fingers extending under each arm. Her hair dangled like a beaded curtain on his face and he smelled the morning's shampoo, the scent revived by rain. She rhythmically teased him by pressing her pelvis against his underwear, and by dragging a knee up between his hairy legs to pin him to the floor of the raft. She didn't kiss him, though, and when he craned his neck to kiss her, she drew back, just out of reach. He couldn't know that Stephanie didn't like kissing—just like she couldn't know that his weathervane had historically tended to veer more homo than hetero. Neither of them was expending emotions nor exhibiting resistance—all of this was strictly mechanical, with all their parts merely doing what their parts were designed to do.

Heritage began to arch his pelvis under her, taking full advantage of the ultimate waterbed to amplify his enthusiasm. He snuck his hands up under her shirt to investigate and cradle her authentic fullness there, which he found remarkable since he was more accustomed to congress with drag queens. He felt he needed to show his appreciation, somehow, for the way she'd rescued him, and the way she was resurrecting the dormant vestige of his heterosexuality—something he'd been convinced had been exorcised by Vancouver's West End gay scene. It was the recompense she seemed to be wanting. She seemed to be enjoying herself.

The more handsy her captive became, the more invasive and clumsy the whole thing seemed to Stephanie. She needed to stay in control—otherwise, this revenge on her mother wouldn't be grudge-alleviating. She took his wrists and lowered them to the fastener on her pants—and together they shoved her pants and underwear at least as far her knees; she shimmied out of one pant leg in pursuit of greater leverage. Next, she grabbed the elastic waistband of his boxer briefs and jerked them down, causing his snagged erection to suddenly release and slap violently against his flat stomach.

"Sorry 'bout that," she said—too matter-of-factly to be sincere. He looked into her eyes, which she diverted elsewhere. Her cold hand snatched his manhood to stand at a more perpendicular orientation, and then she walked on her knees until she was positioned to accommodate him. When her attempt at coupling kept missing the mark, he took hold of himself with a hand that knew better than she did which angles were comfortable and which were not, and momentarily held her off with the other.

"Wait! I've got a condom somewhere in my kayak." He tried to scramble out from under her, but he couldn't get traction on the wet rubber floor. It was like being on a Slip 'n Slide. "Come on," he implored, "let me get to my things."

"Not to worry. I'm on the pill. And besides, I'm closer to Tierra del Fuego than I am to ovulation right now."

"It's not just that, you know." Heritage knew he was blushing, even under the blue tarp, but in the other half of his world, legions were dying from unprotected sex. She lacked the patience for a lecture and reasserted herself so relentlessly that Heritage was completely inside her before he realized what had happened. "Fuck!" He cursed her as much as the circumstances that would prevent his conscience from enjoying a minute of this if she continued—and she did.

Her face went flush with surprise of its own. She couldn't tell if it was his girth, his resistance or the angle, but she could tell he was right up there. She tried to mask her discomfort with a breathy *oh-h-h* and experimented with movement.

"Look, Stephanie," he sounded out her name as soon as it came to him. "I have a few rules—God!" He clamped his eyes shut and gritted his teeth to mask how good it really felt. He didn't breathe again until he was sure he had controlled the sensations and the involuntary spasms. He opened his mouth to say this wasn't a particularly smart idea, and then she flexed and shifted. The rollercoaster car arched over the top of the first climb, and in that second, Heritage sucked a quick breath before the descent knocked it out of his chest. Without slipping out, he bucked her onto her side and then onto her back, where she bumped her head on the housing of the motor. He thrust into her once, then again. He was beyond the gully, through the blackout tunnel, and heading into his first loop-de-loop, still searching for air. She groaned and he shoved again and again—neither realizing his roughness nor that he was disrespectfully clutching a fisful of red hair, immobilizing her against the pontoon seat while he careened through the ride of his life. Hurtling into the second gravity-defying loop, his breath just couldn't catch up and he went into it with a jolt that nearly caused him to pass out.

Rain machine-gunned the tarp as their bodies rose and fell in synchrony with the Pacific swells. He could feel the dangerous beat of his heart pulsating through his groin. His head arched back until he clenched a fold of the musty tarp in his front teeth just as pent-up glob after glob cannonballed into her vastness, muffling any plan to pull out in time. He shuddered as though a rickety wheel had come off the coaster track, as everything but the rain slowed to a brake-squealing stop.

She disgustedly pushed him off her and scooted away. She held the back of her head, having hit it solidly against the motor. She felt dizzy ill now, between the undulation of the boat and the sudden disdain she felt for the reflexively twitching man, with his pants down and his erection still cumming. She thrashed at the tarp for an air hole and vomited over the side of the zodiac. Heritage stared at her bare butt and the creases embossed there by the seams of the boat. He caressed himself like you'd trace the sleek fender of a sports car that had just performed well in a Grand Prix. Then, without thinking, he used the same hand to try to comfort her. She jerked her shoulder away from his touch, and spit-coughed into the sea.

She wasn't quite ready to admit it to herself, but Stephanie had started resenting him before she'd even met him—and that could only pale with the way she felt about him now. She felt raped, but not by him—by her mother, for some screwed-up reason. He had merely been the queen's brainless emissary, suckered in by her mother's power-hogging antics. But Stephanie had turned him into the dragon of the month, attempting to slay him with a foil she'd intended for her mother—or maybe for François. That was the rape. That was the skewed justice and missed mark of her plan. She'd cried *en garde!* to a wrong and hapless opponent. Where was the victory or gratification in that?

Heritage chose to speak, unwisely. "Look—I'm sorry if I hurt you . . ." He pulled his underwear and then his pants up, already looking for his shirt. He jostled the tarp, which irritated her. He rocked the zodiac, which irritated her. He had given her what he thought she wanted, and *that* irritated her. It reminded him that he was much better at teasing women than pleasing them. He should stick to what he knew and preferred. There were a lot of factory extras that came with the heterosexual model, and he wasn't exactly nuts about that.

"You know, the rain's letting up and I can see a clear course now," he said. "Maybe I should just hop back in my death trap and . . . you know, paddle. Whadyasay?"

"Do what you want to. Why spoil your record?"

He objected. "Hey—that's not what I wanted, just then. Your hand was on the control from the beginning."

"Is that what you call it? Your *control*? Jesus!" She held her arm toward him rigidly. "I'll take you and your banana bread to the blockade and then we're even. Rescue debt cleared. You understand me?"

"Whatever you say."

Heritage busied himself with the tarp and began readying the boat for a getaway. He'd rather be exposed to the elements than have to face the consequences of his hormones. And in keeping with a longstanding tradition following such romps with less-than-sane women—or men, for that matter—he silently issued a proclamation to swear off sex for good (or at least a fortnight), until he could figure things out again. God—he was a mess.

The two of them muscled his kayak to sit crosswise and precariously—at least from his standpoint—behind them, resting against the front edge of the outboard motors. He kept fussing with the balance, just not satisfied his boat was secure.

"Can you sit down, please?" Stephanie snapped, as she edged the zodiac away from the rocks. The motor sputtered and then lurched, knocking Heritage to his inflatable seat. She gunned the boat into the channel, and he extended his long arms to clutch the guide ropes on either side. She set her course into the wind. The rain stinging her cheeks and freezing her forehead would not impede a woman serially scorned who needed a quick and dirty getaway. Her eyes watered but she ignored the tears. It wasn't like they were being forced out of her head because she was happy or even sad. If she cried for any reason these days, it was indifference.

She had no more feeling for this Tage-cum-lately than she had for her mother, or for François—or anyone anymore, for that matter.

Actually, that wasn't true at all—the more rational half of her brain appealed. She recklessly banked the zodiac into a high-speed right turn that nearly dumped the kayak and its paddler into the drink. Stephanie knew she had broken every last one of her own rules when she ended up feeling too much for François. That's why she was trying to hurt him, like he'd hurt her with his stunt at the airport hangar dance. She was a fighter and usually highly competitive, but after catching the two of them in the act and learning the identity of the latest Tofitian to win François' sexual affection, she knew she could no longer vie in his arena. Her only course was to broadcast that she was rebounding with a conquest of her own, and to downplay that she was even bothered by his philandering. Well, that, and leaving him and Clayoquot Sound again should deliver a clear message that it was over between them. She bit her lip and bounced the zodiac into a fog bank, where she'd have a chance to pull herself back together. She couldn't just hurt people at will. She wasn't her mother, after all. She wasn't François, either. The problem was, she hadn't really been Stephanie lately. She didn't know *who* she was anymore. She figured she'd find herself in Argentina—the land of Patagonia, Tierra del Fuego, and time. She needed space and a new perspective to sort things out, and to finally grow up, like her mother had often chided her. But make no mistake about it. She was not leaving Clayoquot for her mother or to get back at François. She was leaving it in spite of them.

The zodiac caught air at the top of a swell, and for a second, Heritage didn't breathe or look, fearing that his kayak had either been launched or snapped in two. The rigid hull of the inflatable boat slapped back down on the water's surface, jamming his vertebrae and expelling his air. What if he wasn't cut out for the ruggedness of Clayoquot Sound? Sometimes his powers of persuasion had worked best when he used them on himself. And this wouldn't be the first time he'd gotten out ahead of his abilities or his comfort zone. He stretched out his long legs and crossed them at the ankles, signaling to Stephanie that he was in control again. She jerked the steering wheel so suddenly he nearly tumbled right over the edge of the boat. She half apologized with a smirk. "Dodging a crab trap float," she lied.

The fog began to give way to a blur of green, and soon, a coastline appeared. Heritage figured he could swim to it if he had to—given Stephanie's postcoital mood, he took nothing for granted.

"What's that?" he asked, pointing with his chin toward the land.

"Matilda Inlet," she answered, yelling above the motor as it transitioned into a lower, louder gear. She was doing her best not to be irritated by everything he did or said, but she couldn't help being short. She was mostly angry with herself, for using sex like her mother might have done a few years back. Now that she had captured this strategic ace, she didn't know when (or if) she'd even get a chance to play it. With mere hours left before her departure, the damage she'd have time to wreak would be limited, but if she knew anything about her small village, it was that rumours grew legs and would make the foot-blistering rounds on their own. She supposed the prevailing question should have been—what did it matter if she were leaving anyway? What was the point of packing grudges or plotting revenge? Wouldn't it be cleaner to just superficially reconcile with her mother, make-up with her enemies and lovers, and move on? Of course it would. But there wouldn't be enough time to make all those repairs.

She would miss that aspect of the sound—knowing everybody's business and watching everyone's little dramas play out. Lord knows she should bawden passed out popcorn for folks who turned up to watch the many moments when she'd been the one acting dramatically. Maybe she still had one more cliff-hanger up her sleeve, maybe not. The thought occurred to her that she might just leave a note and disappear early—pack up and go in the night, high mystery and no goodbyes. She knew she could lie low at her Uncle Lyle's Gastown loft in Vancouver until it came time to fly to Santiago and then on to Punta Arenas. Lyle, who wasn't very fond of his evil sister, wouldn't volunteer that he was harbouring a refugee—not if Stephanie asked him for cover. This flee-by-night plan, of course, would mean she'd just wasted a shag—but there were worse things, she supposed. It was decided, then. She would jettison Tage at the blockade camp, slip back to her cabin on Wickaninnish Island after dark, grab her things, and hitchhike to the ferry terminal during the night. She knew the refrigerated trucks, loaded to the gills with fish guts and filets from the BC Packers processing plant, would have room for her in the front seat if she worked her red hair in the headlights just right. Already, she was doing it again—the watermark of a true pro and an apple from her mother's rotten tree. It was not a proud moment.

FETCHING FRANÇOIS

Stephanie was gauging the weather and the amount of daylight she had left, with one foot on the zodiac and the other on the dock at Ahousaht Village, where the solitary, public Chevron gas pump was situated. She was topping off the tanks for her escape when François swaggered up behind her and tried to plant a kiss on her cheek. Her hair, much frizzed by the storm, got in his way.

"Christ!" she scolded him. "Don't sneak up on someone unless you . . . oh, jeez—never mind." She realized his command of English couldn't keep up with her command of bitching, so she let it go. "Listen, this is Tage—I don't know your last name." She didn't apologize for that or give him the opportunity to fill in the blank. "Can you get him and his kayak to the camp and introduce him to everybody? I can't stay."

Heritage reached out his hand, unsure what to make of this stranger's romantic posturing with the woman he'd just been . . . what? Accosted by, he supposed. She did start it, right? He express-reviewed the sequence of events to bolster his defense, in case Stephanie tried to claim that it was he who had come onto her. He subconsciously readjusted his crotch with the other hand when the wet pants didn't stretch with the rest of him as he rose, but instead pinched his traumatized nuts.

"Eh? What do you mean you can't stay?" François asked. "We need to get Sennan back to da dock at 'esquiaht. Did you remember?" François smiled, flashing a mouth of long white teeth—but for one right in front that was discoloured and a bit misaligned. It was perhaps because of this single imperfection that his other hand rose to wipe his mouth in the next movement—almost as automatically as he'd smiled in the first place. His accent was East Montreal and thick. He was every bit as tall as Heritage, whom he'd helped< onto the dock. François didn't let go of Heritage's hand right away—not that it was uncomfortable for either of them.

"Shit," Stephanie exclaimed, insulted by the sight of her boyfriend holding hands with the newcomer. "Hesquiat's another thirty minutes beyond Hot Springs Cove. It will take a good hour each way." She moped, returning the nozzle to the pump. "Isn't anyone else going his way? Why not take him in your boat?" She fumbled the gas tank lid and it bounced off the rubber pontoon and into the water. "Fuck!" She snatched a fish net from the floor of the raft and scooped it into the gray-green water, chasing the fading glimmer of chrome like a Coho chasing a lure, as it went down, down . . .

"Got it!"

François flipped his straight long, dark brown hair behind a shoulder. His olive-green eyes narrowed into a smile that didn't show his discoloured tooth. "Over at da blockade camp, we are orphans of da revolution and refugees of dis wedder."

Stephanie jerked her head around to face him. "What?" she snapped.

"*Nous sommes les enfants da la guerre*," he repeated, in a voice so velvety laden with foreign cinematic tones that it squashed her resistance, just as it had the first time she had swooned for him and his accent. Even Heritage shifted his weight under some Francophilic trance. Stephanie usually turned into a kirsch-soaked fruitcake every time François spoke French—precisely why he did so, she was sure, on an annoyingly regular basis. "Yours is da only boat wit a fast motor. I have had no had time to scrape da barnacles off my skiff and Sennan has an important meeting tonight with his band council. He cannot miss dis."

Stephanie stalled, threading the cap back on the tank. François smiled at Heritage when she wasn't looking, knowing that he would win this debate. "If you're too tired, you know Tage and I could take Sennan. I know da way and wit your Zode we could be flyin'. You could even take my boat back to town if you didn't want to wait for us."

The thought of those two collaborating and navigating on the high seas, with less than a gram of marine sense between them, suddenly exhilarated her. It was all she could do to keep from breaking a bottle of champagne over the bow for their maiden-less voyage. "Okay," she answered, almost too quickly. "But be careful. Best to leave Tage's kayak here just in case." She threw her pack on the dock.

"Just in case what?" Heritage asked, hearing an ominous tone in her voice.

She smiled at him in a way that confirmed his trepidation. He wasn't exactly thrilled about going back out on the water, especially if it was going to take a couple of hours. He glanced at his fancy waterproof diver's watch and noted that it was already getting late. He found it intriguing that François would invite him along, though—and decided in that moment to prolong his first adventure by a few rugged and action-tossed hours. He hitched up his kayak to the dock and threw his pack back into the zodiac.

"We have time for a washroom break, don't we?" Heritage suddenly felt unclean—what with the scent of sex inside his coffee-stained pants. That was Stephanie's cue to shift her belongings to François' nearby skiff and make her exit.

"You'll have to wait for Sennan. He's in der now." François pointed toward the Chevron. "Tinks he had some bad oysters last night. Not feeling well." He laughed, punching Heritage on the arm and making eye contact until Heritage thought his own eyes might melt to jelly and run out of their sockets. "After Sennan comes out, you might not want to go in right away, you know?"

Heritage laughed and began to massage his arm where he'd been play punched. Still, François didn't look away. Finally, the washroom door exploded open and a thin native emerged, literally gasping for breath. François doubled over, laughing.

"What?" Sennan hollered, defensively. He walked down to the dock, obviously uncomfortable and embarrassed. "That is the last time I eat your cooking, Frenchie!"

Heritage tipped his head to the native fellow in acknowledgment as they passed each other on the long dock as Heritage made his way to the washroom. He appreciated François' suggestion he give the washroom a chance to air out, but elected instead to take his chances. He needed to face himself in the mirror—to take an accounting of what he'd been through and where he was now, given that he had woken up that morning with his head on a Vancouver pillow. He opened the washroom door and was instantly repelled by a wave of volatile gases. He heard François laughing again at Sennan's expense. Feeling sorry for the bloke, Heritage forged ahead, shutting the door behind him. Inside, he thought about lighting a match to kill the stench, but he feared he might take the whole Chevron station up with him.

Quickly, he took off his jacket, his fleece crew neck, and his T-shirt, until his chest was bare. He splashed cold water on his face, waiting for it to warm up. When it didn't, he braced himself for a cold bath from the sink. He pushed the dispenser for a palm full of watered-down soap and rubbed it into his chest and under his arms. The smells of sex—of Stephanie—were still evident, despite Sennan's lingering bowel work, so Heritage scrubbed even harder. He opened his jeans and shoved his underwear down around his kneecaps. He took more soap and began handling himself in a tender way until quite a lather had worked itself up in the density of his pubic hair. He pivoted a few steps to the left until he was facing the only toilet in the closet-like room, and he peed through the middle of the metal toilet seat. He didn't mind looking at himself naked. He had always been proud of his attributes. He was an attractive man, and he knew it—not in a conceited way, but more like a storeroom clerk who was confident in his inventory.

He flushed, then began to rinse the soap from his body, creating quite a puddle around his boots. It wasn't the type of soap that rinsed away easily. He persevered. François yelled something inane outside: "Ya fall in or pass out?" Heritage didn't bother answering. The food-poisoned native had suffered enough. He finger-styled his hair quickly, sensing he'd already been in there long enough to raise questions from those obsessed with monitoring the washroom from the dock. He pulled his pants to his waist, threw his shirts back on, and popped the door open— emerging, at least in his estimation, a new man.

On the dock, he saw François embracing Stephanie and instantly looked away to take in the vista. Beyond the hand-lettered *Welcome to Ahousaht* sign that leaned against a framed building that no longer had its front walls, past the gutted motorboat that had been abandoned halfway up the shore next to an equally derelict Ford Bronco with all the windows broken out, Heritage saw dirt roads and houses squeezed next to each other with a tangle of cedar wood ramps and staircases, with a television satellite disc on each building. Out of the corner of one eye, he watched the pair on the dock as their embrace turned into a rather impassioned kiss. What the hell? He kicked a pebble into a mud puddle that probably never ran dry. It was then that he took a moment to appreciate that it actually wasn't raining, and the wind had stopped too. While he was looking up at the dark grey clouds that had snagged on the surrounding hilltops on the east side of Flores Island where the village was situated, a collarless dog that looked ferocious as a fairy-tale woof, ran up to him at full speed. Skidding to a stop, it turned over onto its back, exposing its belly for a rub. Heritage obliged, making an instant friend.

Sennan was already sprawled out in the front section of the boat, under a pile of blankets. As Heritage neared the zodiac, he flashed Stephanie a narrowed-eye look of disqualification that only she could see. She rolled her deceitful blue eyes as though she couldn't care less about what he thought, or that she might have hurt him with her sudden callousness. As she climbed into François' boat further down the dock, he helped François lift the kayak off the zodiac. "What do you have in der?" François asked after finding the boat to be much heavier than its featherweight design might have suggested.

"Coffee and banana bread," Tage replied. "Plus my camping gear."

"Is da coffee fresh?" His fulsome dark eyebrows raised into the bunting of dark hair that parted in the middle and was loosely gathered behind his ears.

"Do you have a cup or a thermos? Heritage asked. "I was supposed to deliver those supplies to the protest camp." With some effort, they lowered the kayak to the water in the space between the zodiac's motors and a half-sunk fishing boat named *Salty Lips*. François hopped aboard the neglected vessel and secured the kayak to its portside. "Is that your boat?" Heritage inquired.

"Nah," François replied. "It is clearly not going any place soon, so your kayak will be fine for a couple hours here. We should take some coffee and banana bread for our trip, eh?"

Heritage flashed a smile and then introduced himself to the gut-preoccupied Sennan, who could scarcely lift his hand and groan back at him. "Would some coffee and banana bread help?" Heritage asked Sennan, while he filled François' thermos with the last of what was left in the bottom of the larger container. "You know, put something solid in your tummy?" The bundle of blankets seemed to be shaking its head *no*. Heritage positioned his belly on the zodiac's pontoon and leaned overboard to reach the front hatch of his kayak to retrieve a wrapped loaf of bread and then he waited for François to stop fiddling with ropes and other things so they could get underway. In the time he had to think about it, Heritage recognized he was feeling something like jealousy about Stephanie and François—not because Stephanie had used him to cheat on a boyfriend, but because quite possibly he already liked the boyfriend, who was exotically handsome and friendly, and seemed equally at ease with him, even though they'd just met for the first time. This was strange to him. And yet it wasn't—he'd felt these odd vibes and mostly harmless attractions to other straight men before. They rarely amounted to anything beyond insomnia-fueled jerk-off material when he'd had too much caffeine. Thinking of which, he glanced down at his coffee stained and java-stinking pants that looked positively broken in now and no longer fresh off the rack.

François suddenly hopped out of the boat and jogged down the dock to have a quick exchange with another arriving boatman he knew that looked around the same age. Heritage watched their body language, as their arms seemed to do most of the talking. He wasn't the only one watching. Stephanie, too, had stopped what she was doing to monitor and perhaps judge their brief exchange. The two men were definitely friendly—that much was obvious from the one-armed, cheek-nuzzling hug they gave each other when they departed. François hurried back, jumped into the zodiac and Sennan moaned from the sudden movement of his universe. The lanky replacement pilot turned the ignition key and the engines sputtered then stopped.

"You're engaging the throttle too quickly," Stephanie yelled back at him from his boat as she pulled it away from the dock.

"Yeah, yeah," he muttered, waving her off, suddenly back in

the company of men, where different facades were maintained, and women generally weren't listened to. "Don't worry about us."

"As if I would," she lobbed back across the water. François waited for her to clear the dock before he pulled away from it himself and headed back out and into the inlet at first following then overtaking Stephanie's wake like a daredevil as they sped past her.

"Here we go," François hollered, reaching down to squeeze Tage's thigh above the knee. Tage looked up at him with a smile and straightened his posture from where he sat next to the steering console. François took the lid off his thermos and slugged back some of the lukewarm coffee that had been through more than a grinder in the past several hours. Inside Heritage's grinning head, he was content replaying this madcap comedy of errors and revisiting the clowns he'd encountered so far: Dottie, Stephanie, and now François. What would this act reveal, he wondered?

With the kayak off the zodiac, Sennan's riddled mass holding down the bow and François at the helm, they were soon flying like a hovercraft around the southeastern tip of Flores Island. It was all so thrilling that Heritage could not stop smiling, even though the cold wind on his teeth made them ache. He was getting to see the length and breadth of Clayoquot Sound upclose and personal in his first hours in the territory. He couldn't have planned this introduction and his orientation any better.

The raincloud ceiling was lifting, and the sun began poking through the cumulonimbus lace to promote what could be a show-stopping sunset if the weather held. The swells seemed almost pedestrian given the seaman at the helm. It was sexist and likely not at all warranted for Heritage to feel like he was in better hands with a man driving the boat. François had migrated to Clayoquot, just as he was doing now—a total novice in these waters, whereas Stephanie had likely been plying these inlets and passages her entire life. But as a man, himself, he still felt safer with François driving—maybe because François hadn't double-crossed him yet as Stephanie had, so he settled in and owned that. He did his best to concentrate on pointing out the hazards in the water ahead of them, which kept him from studying François outright. Still, the men leaned into each other as gravity and navigation allowed. Lost in his thoughts and the exhilaration of flying, Heritage briefly felt diabolically tempted to casually mention that he had earlier banged François' girlfriend in that very boat. That would give them something immediately in common—something they could quarrel or bond over. Yet Heritage knew that was silly, and he didn't want them to connect on that level. He didn't want to triangulate his way through Dottie or Stephanie anymore, either. They'd both betrayed him and shouldn't and wouldn't be trusted again.

François' weather-reddened hands wrapped around the dinner-plate sized wheel with a white-knuckle grip that might have worried any passenger paying attention (or not suffering from shellfish poisoning). Heritage had been watching Sennan constantly readjust his position under the blankets with nearly every slap of the hull and just knew the poor man was going to be sick for a while. Plowing into the open channel that separated Flores Island from a peninsula jutting out from the jagged coast of Vancouver Island in the distance, the trio encountered a bit of a crosswind—the remnants of that westerly or southwesterly that hadn't quite blown itself out according to François—and the boat was responding awkwardly over the choppier water. Sennan stirred and groaned on the rubberized canvas floor in front of them. Rough seas were not sitting well atop the toxic shellfish he was desperate to evict from his body. Heritage crouched forward and more snuggly tucked the blankets around him. Sennan narrowed his eyes, focusing on the kind stranger who was trying to tend to him—but it would not make him feel better. Heritage gave him an uneasy grin and returned to his bench seat near the console.

"Hey, shift it to da left, will ya?" François yelled into the wind. "I'm going to move closer to you so we can hold this boat down."

He switched hands on the prop and moved to the windward side next to Heritage. The closeness was necessary to redistribute weight, but Tage also welcomed it. His body suddenly tingled with a thousand little itches that he could never hope to relieve. He took a deep and obvious breath that François was obligated to acknowledge.

"You okay?" François asked, speaking directly into his right ear.

"Fine," Heritage responded curtly, looking straight ahead, not daring to look him in those green eyes in that cozy proximity. François smiled anyway. Heritage was rapidly learning that between François' French extraction and his clowny Quebecois edge, he had probably always been able to bend the rules of masculine sexuality. Heritage was positively feeling the tension of that tightrope on which François seemed completely comfortable bouncing up and down on without the aid of a balance pole.

Then, François shot his left arm nearly out of its socket and pointed, "Over der!"

Tage squinted and was sure he was seeing killer whales, but François corrected him saying they were Dall's porpoises. Black with white spots and white-tipped dorsal fins, they seemed to be racing the zodiac as they got closer, keeping up with the boat until they lost interest and peeled off the chase. François rested his still pointing arm across the back of Heritage's shoulders and kept it there until a chunk of driftwood in their path required a last-second jerk of the steering wheel to avoid a collision.

As they neared the Hesquiaht Peninsula, the winds began to ease. François stood, widening his stance to expertly weave the boat in and out of rocky outcrops with dexterity—the speed and the risk of which puffed up his manhood as the zodiac zigged, zagged and darted toward their destination. Both of their eyes watered in their widened, unblinking glee. François yell-talked over the motors boasting that he wasn't still the marine dope Stephanie had him figured for, and that he'd made a lot of progress with his boating skills since arriving in the sound just seven months earlier.

Stephanie may have taught him how to interpret chart maps, anticipate weather, and read the ever-changing surface of the sea, he explained—but it had been his buddy, Marcel, another French-Canadian, who'd taught him the stunts. "You will meet Marcel," François predicted as though he would make that happen. "Dat's da guy who I was talking to at da dock in Ahousaht, by da way."

Heritage was pleased that François was that comfortable with him, already talking about a future where he would be introduced to François' friends. He took that moment on the bench to ask him what had brought him here and what kept him here. François chuckled, then pointed out that Stephanie had never asked him questions like that. She also never asked why it was so important for him to learn boating, or why he'd come to Clayoquot Sound in the first place. According to him, she seemed always too busy to be bothered by his details or background. Listening most intently, Heritage vowed in that moment, to never be like Stephanie.

François filled the next fifteen minutes explaining that his quest to follow in his father's gumboots hadn't really panned out like he'd hoped. Growing up, like most kids, his dad had been larger than life, handsome and fit— "just like me," François added, patting his abdomen. Captain Lucien, as he was pretty much known by everyone south of the Laurentian Mountains, had been this fearless mariner who owned a small, licensed fishing fleet that operated on the St. Lawrence Seaway; a business that he'd taken over from his father and his father's father before him. And so, by longstanding family tradition, Lucien had selected François' older brother as his successor to take over the fleet. "Shortly after dat, when his relationship with da ol' lady hit da rocks, my fadder, he decided to travel as far west as he could get in Canada to escape my mudder. So," François tried to wrap up the story before Tage became bored, "he made it here to Clayoquot Sound, where, as da story sort of ends, he found dis boat dat belonged to nobody—a 19-foot Boston Whaler wit da name *Polly* that was just floating empty wit nobody and nutting aboard near some outer rocks not far from Tofino."

"What do you mean, the story sort of ends there?" Heritage asked, demanding a better ending than that.

François shrugged his shoulders. "Dat's as far as I get. Every time I ask people about my fadder or dat boat, everyone pretends they know nutting. I know dat's not true, but what can I do about it?"

François braced his left leg against Tage's right shoulder. Heritage flexed, lending him more support than was probably necessary. Blurs of green and gray hurtled past them as the boat veered further away from the shore heading north again through more open water. The bow gradually lowered as they picked up speed until they were mostly hydroplaning across the top of the water, and no longer plowing ramshackle through it. François tried to explain the difference between hydrodynamic lift, which they'd just achieved, and hydrostatic lift, which would deliver them a fair bit more rattled and leave Sennan more sicker than he already was. But it was all Greek to Heritage, who never expected to achieve an optimal speed with his paddling for either lift to make a bit of difference. He could appreciate, though, that the feeling was maybe as satisfying as a horse settling into a full gallop after an annoying trot. Even Sennan looked more at peace with the boat skipping across the tops of troughs—less green, less dead. Everyone's comfort aside, Heritage wasn't yet willing to let go of the urgency of their medical plight, and when the wind blew one of Sennan's blankets down, Heritage, like a trained medivac attendant, pounced to raise it back up around the man's shoulders.

The wind blew through his Kennedy hair—and for some reason, he could not resist pushing his fingers through it, over the crown of his head, and through the waves that tumbled to the base of his neck. It was some strange, autoerotic manipulation that heightened his tactile awareness to an almost insupportable level. He went for a second pass.

"Wonderful, isn't it?" François noticed. Like a cat two paw-steps from a rolling purr, Heritage could not answer, and instead, just closed his eyes jutting his chin into the rush. It *was* wonderful.

Heritage settled back on the seat bench near the steering council and focused on the pressure of François' hip as it found balance against his shoulder once again. The heap of blankets atop Sennan lifted and fell as the pale man breathed laboriously. Fighting his own chill that had come on with this new velocity, Heritage envied the warmth Sennan must have been feeling under all those blankets, tucked in as he was just out of the wind. But he didn't envy the persistent knots that must have been twisting his guts. Heritage caught a gulp of sea air and suddenly found it necessary to concentrate on something else before the power of suggestion made him queasy. Of course, not thinking about it was practically impossible. As a kid he had been highly susceptible to motion sickness in the car or at an amusement park. Even as a grownup, if he dwelled on it or watched someone else under its grip, it could be curtains for his tummy.

Shit! He couldn't stop thinking about it as the first icy fingers of nausea jerked at his esophagus, just above the stomach. Frantically, he tried to recall the sensation of wind through his hair, or revel in the touch of François' leg, still pressing hard into him. But nothing could override his preoccupation with what he feared might be the coming mutiny of his last meal which had been a soggy fistful of banana bread. Suddenly petrol fumes swilled about his head and he burrowed his nose inside the flaps of his jacket. In there, he distinctly smelled a melange of borax soap, coffee, and sex. He forced his face back into the onrushing wind and took huge swallows of air. When he realized that wasn't such a good idea, he tried quick slurps of air, while trying to talk his revolting body into abandoning the insurrection. The zodiac glided across a smooth patch of sea—and for a moment, Heritage believed he had gotten things under control. Then Sennan bolted from his fetal position and flopped his head over the side, barfing what must have been half his body weight. The zodiac in that moment might as well have been the back seat of the family car Heritage remembered from childhood, and he lunged into a competitive match of monkey-see, monkey-puke. François had to quickly maneuver himself to compensate for the human bilge pumps spewing off both sides of the craft.

"I didn't realize da water was dat rough on you two," François hollered, trying his best not to laugh. "I'll take her in some and we can hug da shore."

Heritage's embarrassment prevented him from feeling better after that cleansing. When he'd returned to an upright position, François reached his thumb and index finger to Tage's chin and gently turned the newcomer's face upward for inspection.

"It's green, all right," he verified. "Like da wicked witch from da Wizard of Oz."

Heritage plunged his hand overboard, splashing his face and mouth with seawater before François could caution him otherwise. The arresting taste of salt sent Heritage back over the pontoon to eject what he could on the frothy crest of a dry heave. François reached for his canteen. Steadying the steering wheel with one raised knee, he held the fresh water in front of his new friend's face. Heritage took the cap off the canteen and thoroughly wiped its neck after each swig, spitting out the first, gingerly swallowing the last.

This first day in Clayoquot would be his baptism and he vowed he would live the rest of his life unable to forget it. That was saying something, since he couldn't even remember waking up that morning—on a thin inflatable mattress on the floor of a friend's Cardero Street apartment in the West End. He didn't recall having any premonition that today, of all days, would change his life, though it clearly had. He tucked his fingers beneath the guy ropes of the boat and clenched his teeth. He could take it. A day was only twenty-four hours—the balance already behind him. He bore down on his stomach, flexing the muscles he'd worked hard to put there, and reasserted mind over body.

TAGE TUMBLES

Not more than a half hour later, François and Heritage had left Sennan safely retching in the comfort of his own home in Hesquiaht Village, and the pair was back on the water headed south—when François suddenly cut the powerful, side by side motors in open water. As the propellors sputtered in idle, Heritage shook his head to jar his hearing back into place.

"You feeling better now?" François asked trying to suppress what Heritage took as the beginning lift of a snide little smile.

Heritage leaned over the side and spit out a chewed wad of licorice fern and wild ginger roots that Sennan had tucked into his palm wrapped in a white cotton cloth that he had tied into a small satchel. The chief, who couldn't have been much older than they were, had assured Tage the roots would work for sea sickness though he doubted they held had any power over foul shellfish. Whether it was mind over matter or there really was something medicinal at play, Heritage did feel much better and said so, nodding, though he found it odd that they'd stopped in the middle of the ocean just for this question to be asked and answered. "I'm fine now. A little embarrassed, but fine." Heritage opened the sachel and took another generous pinch of plant roots into his cheek. "Thanks—really, I'm fine."

François was nodding back and his smile grew to reveal that crazy-coloured front tooth of his. "I was tinking dat perhaps if you were feeling, you know, a little better, we could stop at da 'ot springs and take a wash—you know— if you want to, dat is."

"Sure. Yes, definitely I would," Tage answered, feeling instantly revived by the thought of extending his one-on-one time with his new buddy—plus hot springs meant land, and land meant the cessation of ocean travel. No arm-twisting was necessary. The need to bathe suddenly took precedence over everything else— except maybe brushing his teeth, thanks to his coffee-doused, bear-infested, sex-laced, and seasickness-spiked marathon of an afternoon. "Let's do it," he added, even more enthusiastically.

"Right on," François said, restarting the motors. "Right on."

Heritage continued to chew on his medicinal cud deciding that François' accent was as seductive as it was comical. It helped that Heritage had been exposed to Québécois Frenglish all his life since Quebec and Newfoundland were the two provinces from which the totality of Canada's comedy originated. If it hadn't been for those two good-humoured regions, Canada, well, she would have been just as fuddy-duddy as the UK.

In hardly no time at all, they were motoring back into the cove, this time hugging the shore opposite Hesquiaht Village where they had just deposited Sennan. It had started sprinkling again but wasn't sustained, though neither one of them cared about that since their plan was to get wet anyway. Minutes later, on a rudimentary boardwalk winding through ancient cedars to reach the springs, Heritage counted his footsteps, thankful for each time his soles met the solid boards and earth beneath him. It was approaching dusk on what had perhaps been the longest, most adventuresome day of his life. He breathed deeper now; no longer afraid his guts would ambush him. "How do you say dusk, in French—you know, this time right now after the sun has gone down?" he asked his companion.

"What sun?" François poked him in the ribs and jogged a half step ahead to be just out of reach should Heritage try to retaliate. "*Le crépuscule*," came the answer to his question at the end of a menacing laugh. Silently to himself, Heritage repeated the term so he could remember it, too tentative with his pronunciation skills to attempt it aloud, even though he had attended several years of French Immersion school as a young child growing up in Toronto.

Continuing to advance at a cautious gait and still needing to make constant corrections to keep from walking off the elevated path as his eyes inventoried every detail of the forest, the urbanite became transfixed in a trance of verdant euphoria. The most giant trees with their even more gigantic shadows, grew thicker and towered taller than he had ever seen, each with a trunk as big as an upended school bus. The forest with its drooping cedar fronds, ferns and fiddleheads nearly swallowed up the metre-wide plankway that wound its splintered and rotting way through the last vestiges of twilight toward what he hoped would be hot springs and not the scene of his own grisly murder without witnesses. Had he been with any other total stranger he'd only met just hours before, he might have actually been concerned about his safety in these darkening and spooky woods. But he already sensed his gentle guide—who had gotten a few metres ahead of him when the width of the trail narrowed to the point they could no longer walk side by side—was this sensitive, intelligent, fun-loving soul that he giddily wanted to trust immediately.

When the silvered cedar and snot-slippery boardwalk ahead appeared as though it dead-ended at the largest cedar tree Heritage had encountered so far, he paused a moment to catch his breath. He reverently placed his hands on the reddish-orange cedar bark that was layered vertically in narrow strips that looked like petrified locks of hair with whimsical chartreuse streaks. Rapidly, his fingers read the ridges like Braille in search of a swashbuckling story that had to easily have been more than a thousand years in the making. Heritage marveled. For someone who had been able to palm a basketball since he was a teenager, his hands suddenly looked the size of a doll's when laid on this monolith. The self-transplanting urbanite felt he wanted— no, *needed*, to pay homage, like the original tree hugging Bishnoi women of India, so he spread his arms out as wide as he could to hug the trunk but could not find its curve. He expelled the breath from his lungs to stretch even further and still he could make out the tips of his outstretched fingers on either end of his already impressive wingspan without having reached the places where the enormous trunk began to round. Through his chest, Heritage expected to detect a pulse from this living beast that he could synchronize with his, and through osmosis, he would have liked to tap and syphon the wisdom from the ages it must have known. The only thumping heart the tree revealed belonged to him but in their fusion, his existence was validated, and his embrace got returned. He slowly tilted his head and long neck backward, panning his gaze up the trunk like a freight elevator that could have easily fit inside the tree's circumference. Though his eyes traveled through a dozen or more stories of articulating spokes overhead, he could not see its crown. Heritage turned to press the spine of his 187-centimetre frame flat against the trunk like his height was about to get measured at the doctor's office but next to this yardstick, his stature was laughable. He chuckled out loud thinking François would hear him and maybe double-back, but the forest, in that spot and for a moment, had become a dead calm. He'd been left behind. His hearing sharpened. His hazel eyes widened. His pupils dilated and had surely become the size of an owl's as the last of the day dimmed in that shadowed glen, while a full battalion of muted orange tree trunks that had stood at attention all day, all century, seemed to be stepping backward at ease into the shadows of the night descending. The colour-leaching scene reminded him of a Seurat or a Monet painting accomplished by thousands, maybe millions of points or brush strokes. Only when he pulled his eyes back and slightly out of focus, could he begin to truly fathom the sacredness of the place. Just beyond those dots, and the sky-scraping strokes that dwarfed him, he was overwhelmed by the towering evidence of more history than he'd ever learned in school, and it stopped him still.

"Dis one's a CMT. She's a beauty, eh?" François had quietly double-backed once he realized he'd lost his sidekick.

"CMT?" Heritage asked, needing more of an explanation.

"Yeah. A culturally modified tree. See dat long strip of bark dat's missing?" he said, pointing to a 3-metre-long shallow gouge that was about a foot wide at the bottom but tapered to a single apex higher up the trunk, revealing the orange flesh beneath. "Da First Peoples here used cedar bark for everything . . . weaving baskets, hats, clothes and even walls and roofs."

Nodding his head and glancing around, Heritage now realized that most of the cedars in that grove were CMTs which is why he'd mistaken their trunks for orange.

"Da First Peoples, dey only took what dey needed and left da rest of da tree standing. Now, we take da whole tree witout tinking and turn half of it into TP just to wipe our butts."

Heritage could sense he had either just blushed or gone flush from the arresting guilt-flash that came over him but figured there wasn't enough light left for François to have noticed. His grandfather's generation had tragically operated as though resources were unlimited and there for the industrial taking. It made him queasy to imagine what François would think of him if he only knew his connection to such short-sighted wastefulness.

François mentioned that it wasn't hard at all for him to remember falling instantly in love with the temperate rainforest the first time he walked through it like this. "Take your time,"

François encouraged him, before turning to continue down the boardwalk. "Da springs are just a hundred metres furder."

When Heritage stumbled out of the forest at the boardwalk's end some minutes later, he felt and possibly looked overcome. François, already waist deep in one of the thermal pools, laughed at him. "Are you completely high on da rainforest now?" he asked. "You look high."

In truth, Heritage had never felt more spiritually awake or solidly grounded, emerging from that forest cathedral as though he'd just had a full-on, spirit-filled, holy ghost epiphany—which he supposed, it was. His grandfather's ways in these ancient woods needed to cease, but Heritage knew his grandfather needed to cease first before any real change could be possible. Like a train he could hear rumbling in the distance, the change-locomotive was getting closer now, the tracks had begun to vibrate. Heritage would be the engineer and the brakeman of his generation.

"I have to thank you for bringing me here," he said, leaning down to unlace his Timberlands. The ocean raucously tossed itself on a mostly lava-rock beach maybe five metres below them and a decent sized waterfall that Heritage could see was steaming, tumbled over a slight cliff face that was located just behind them. Stepping out of his boots and coffee-dyed socks, he had to carefully negotiate some sharp rocks to get to the spot where François had shed his clothes. Heritage began removing the layers he'd put on that morning inside his modest but completely paid for Yaletown condo without an accurate clue what his first day in Clayoquot Sound would hold. In the scant moonlight playing peek-a-boo through a short-lived teaser of a cloud break overhead, he took note of François' white underwear half-folded on top of a pair of jeans that sat on top of his suspender bib rain pants and coat—which confirmed the undress code. Heritage had already assumed they would be naked, and that it would be no big deal— something he'd been looking forward to since he didn't mind stripping down in front of strangers. Between his natural gifts and those he'd honed from a fanatical obsession with abdominals, he had ensured there was nothing to hide in situations like this. He turned around to beam his confidence to François, whose eyes were already shut anyway. Heritage eased into the pool without a splash or discernable ripple—ignoring the possibility that the space would be too small for both sets of long legs.

Without opening his eyes or shifting to give Heritage more space in the pool, François said, "When my time comes, I want it to be right here, just like dis, when I take my last breat." Heritage could think of no way to respond to a poetic statement that made such complete sense. Instead, he issued a satisfying groan from the back of his throat as the temperature of the water reached inside him to touch his bones. After a moment of silence, François whispered that theirs wasn't the hottest of the pools and that the next one up at the waterfall was the hottest as it was near the source of the springs where it bubbled out of the earth. Heritage could extrapolate that the series of smaller pools below them must be gradually cooler, until the lowest one became overtaken by the ocean waves. The suggestion seemed to be that Tage could move to a cooler pool if this one was too hot or crowded for him. The heat had brought a sweat to Tage's brow, but he was enjoying the crazy intimacy of that moment and didn't want to budge. In the next minutes, though, he started to wonder if François might be one of those people just not comfortable with silence (Heritage's own mother had been that way) when he went on to describe in detail the first time he had experienced the medicine of these thermal pools. Of course, it had been with Stephanie and of course they made love right here under the stars, not that Heritage needed her to barge back into *his* private time with François or to be reminded that he also wore the mark of the she-beast, having been with Stephanie, too.

Heritage maybe could have done with less detail regarding François' priors. He crossed his arms and closed his eyes. One minute went by, and then another, without a word or a stir as the two of them just floated together completely deaminated. Soaking naked in that steamy gurgling utopia—a refuge from the rain, the zodiac motors, the nausea, the black bears, the banana bread, and the manipulative woman the two of them now had in carnal common—Heritage was pretty certain he was making a memory with François. It seemed the perfect, dynamically natural spot on the planet to make one, too; where two guys could unknot and unwind. He was understanding what François had meant about wanting to die here, up to one's neck in water that had fallen from the clouds perhaps centuries ago, percolated through boggy layers of time to penetrate deep into the core, where it was heated by tributaries of subterranean lava, to expand and bubble back up to the surface, spill over the waterfall behind them to rejoin the ocean, evaporate and begin the whole cycle over again. Definitely, a slow, gentle boil here would be the ultimate way to slip the surly bonds of earth. There was no debating that.

With the weight of his first day in Clayoquot, Heritage involuntarily yawned, turning his head to the side, hoping his pool-mate hadn't noticed. He next boldly stretched his legs and tried with his butt cheeks to scoop out a more comfortable position on the pebbles and sand. He grazed François' leg in the maneuver and instantly apologized. François hopped up, moving to stand beneath the thermal shower.

"Can you reach da soap over der on top of my tings?" François asked, pulling his long, wet hair off his face.

Heritage was on a ten-second delay—still analyzing whether he had provoked his friend's exodus from the pool.

"Got it," Tage hollered over his shoulder. François' clothes were folded very neatly at the edge of the pool they were using, so Heritage didn't really need to clamour out of the water, but he did anyway, wanting to cool off. After crouching over the rocks with his butt facing François, he retrieved the bar of soap—noting that it seemed coarsely homemade—at the bottom of a grungy shaving kit that had seen better years. When he turned back around, he wanted to think he'd caught his new buddy watching him through the long fingers he rubbed on his unshaven face. Heritage figured that would have been too convenient a setup for what he was already fantasizing might happen next, given that the two of them were naked, alone in the middle of nowhere and at least one of them was primed, having already had sex once that day. Heritage chuckled to himself thinking he would need to travel back a decade or so to his early twenties for the last time a double header had happened in the same day, but it wouldn't be unprecedented. He stretched the soap bar toward the other man without making eye contact, as though he were ridiculously trying to afford him some measure of decency. That modesty amused François, who grabbed his hand and pulled him under the waterfall with him. The water tumbling off the overhang was shockingly hot, and Tage squealed, stepping right back out of it to recover at the side. Then he felt stupid just standing there like a washroom attendant. So, he plunged down in the pool near François' feet and faced the ocean.

"You get used to it," François spoke, before beginning to wash his hair.

"Don't use all the hot water," Heritage responded, thinking that was a damn funny thing to say. He then waited a few seconds before readjusting himself to sit at a different angle that kept François visible from the corner of one eye. Once the Quebecker's eyes were under siege by soap, Heritage did a full scan of the tall, handsome, soapy man standing in the waterfall. Unlike his own furry torso, François's upper body was smoothly bare, but below the waist, the man was practically a centaur! It excited Heritage to realize that his feelings for this guy were wandering beyond voyeurism and teetered somewhat awkwardly close to desire. It shouldn't have surprised him, he supposed, and of course it didn't. He'd had sexual encounters with about as many women as men, and so far, neither gender had measurably pulled ahead in his orientation race. That should have made him functionally bisexual—except that Heritage preferred to avoid the label game altogether. He certainly had not fallen in love yet—and this he believed would be the jolt to lodge his pendulum fast, one way or the other. But just then, on cue, the head of his pendulum began its rise through the black water to betrayingly bob on the surface, like some cautionary, neon-reflective buoy. Unknowingly, while François performed his regimen, Heritage had started rubbing his hairy chest with the water he'd cupped in his hand. He stopped that auto-eroticizing nonsense at once— shifting brain gears, in a futile attempt to tame his budding tumescence. But it was too late. He clumsily flopped over in the pool to conceal the special interest François was beginning to inspire and stared instead toward the entrance of the cove.

"It's your turn."

François lobbed the soap into the pool by Tage's butt. The splash startled him, and he flinched. François laughed. Heritage waited until François was hunched down over his belongings before he climbed out of the water—and even then, he showered with his back to the pools at first. The more he thought about needing to lose his calling card, the harder—not to mention redder—he became, as the geyser-hot water gushed in perpetual sputters over the slimy rocks overhead. He worked the soap under his arms, unable to shake the knowledge that the homemade bar had just traveled every byway and crevice of François' lean body. He started to wash the sex, the coffee and the residual borax soap off his genitals a second time and found that the slipperiness of the mineral water with soap only made matters worse. Desperate, he began to dwell on the physical attributes of Dottie Bard, who had gotten him into this mess in the first place. Lo and behold—for the second time in maybe four hours, he conquered his arousal. Granted, the first time had followed an orgasm that had gone sideways so he had deflated quickly—but any recovery he could walk, swim, or paddle away from was still a recovery. He turned around, because he suddenly found he could, and asked François flat out, "What do you know about Dottie Bard?"

François had just lit a joint he'd rolled with wet fingers and he was in the middle of holding in his first toke. Heritage was rinsing off the last of the soap and faced him head-on so the two could converse and Heritage could show off, just in case anyone cared to pay attention. François was reclined on the side of the pool, his crossed legs thrusting his ample uncut penis into the air atop his scrunched but well-packed scrotum. He looked disturbingly Christ-like—posing for the Pietà.

"Dottie Bard?" François asked, exhaling. "She's one crazy witch! If I see her walking down da street on da days I am in town, I walk four blocks da udder way—which is difficult in a town dat doesn't have dat many blocks." He took another drag but exhaled immediately. "Da same goes for her daughter anymore. I've just decided dat."

"Come on," Heritage protested, turning back around to rinse the last of the soap from the pelt that was his torso. "Dottie can't be that bad. Of course, I just met her for the first time this morning. There's probably a lot I don't know about her." There was a sudden touch on his shoulder, and he spun around to find himself face to face—in fact, erection to promising erection—with François, who steadied him and brought their lips together, gently but effectively forcing a stream of marijuana smoke into his mouth. Tage reflexively tried to pull back, but François would not allow it, placing his index finger on Tage's lips, motioning him to be still. Heritage looked into the green eyes of this god-descended-incarnate for something he could grab onto or trust. Gripping François by his biceps, he went in for a daring kiss—thinking he might lose his mind, but that it would be worth it to find his soul. François did not resist the kiss—in fact, returned it. The smoke Tage was still holding in his lungs began to sting. Turning slightly to the side, he issued a straw of white smoke. He was hyper-aware of his soapy erection as it fenced with François'—and all at once, there was nothing left to hide or withhold. François' hand reached around the small of Tage's back to press them more firmly together. Neither man closed his eyes nor turned away as their mouths explored what their minds had wondered that whole afternoon.

François slow-motored the zodiac from Hot Springs Cove through the dark back to Ahousaht Village, while Heritage, riding in the front for the past forty-five minutes, had trained a handheld spotlight on the water from the bow until his forearms cramped—scanning for rocks, logs, and land that he could warn François to steer clear of as they shore-hugged Flores Island through intermittent fits of rain and a persistent headwind.

They retrieved Tage's kayak, remarkably still tied to the gradually sinking *Salty Lips*, and topped the fuel tanks of Stephanie's zodiac when a light still burning inside the Chevron station at the end of the dock, suggested someone was there to take their money. When they inquired after Stephanie's whereabouts, shrugged shoulders sent them to the second boat dock at Marktosis where François spotted his aluminum skiff. Stephanie hadn't used it to head back to Tofino after all and must have decided to stay the night at the blockade camp waiting for her own boat to be returned. Oh, joy, Heritage whispered to himself when considering the prospects of that reunion—even more awkward now that he'd shagged her boyfriend too.

When the soggy, worn-out pair finally reached the dwindling protest camp on the beach at Marktosis, it was raining steady and hard. The camp had been bleeding numbers for days even before getting evicted from Bawden Bay by bears, as students had begun peeling off after Labour Day to return to their colleges and universities for the fall semester. To Heritage's relief, Stephanie had neither been seen at the Marktosis camp nor leaving

Ahousaht—which hatched the mystery of her disappearance among the five diehards sitting under tarps around the campfire.

Without discussion or coordination, Tage and François pitched separate tents—some distance apart, whether for appearance's sake or because they each had their own sets of camping equipment—Heritage was unsure. Perhaps what had happened at the hot springs, stayed at the hot springs, Heritage supposed. Not long after they had arrived and had downed a beer and a hastily half-roasted bratwurst each, the rain intensified, driving everyone into their separate tents. There, Heritage Carter III spent his first night in Clayoquot Sound—metres away from the man who had rocked his boat, delivered him from the mother-daughter shenanigans of the Bard welcoming committee, and perhaps revealed the beginning of a future path they might journey on together through that ancient, tangled, coastal temperate rainforest.

Maybe? Maybe not.

Heritage had probably been through these motions and emotions before—though, in his end-of-a-very-long-day fog, the questions of when and with whom he couldn't immediately recall. The beam of his flashlight, propped upright in one of his hiking boots, illuminated the orange and yellow panels in the gabled ceiling of his brightly coloured tent. None of the other rebel-rousers had a shelter that fancy–which only advertised what an outdoor newbie he was. It wasn't that he was acting or faking it; he just hadn't logged enough experience at it yet. It was really no different when it came to sex, he thought, caressing his genitals inside his sleeping bag. He wasn't really a sexual being, mostly because he couldn't figure out which emotions to bring or which lessons to take away. Perhaps if he had been wired to have sex more frequently—monthly, weekly, or even daily—he could be more nonchalant about it, plant his flag of virility wherever he pleased and just do it without strings around the clock. That must be the playboy high life, he thought—just jauntily stroll away from serial encounters without feeling a thing, except worn out and maybe a little raw.

As things stood in Clayoquot Sound, at the end of a very long first scrimmage, his personal scoreboard charted fumbles and touchdowns and maybe even an end-over-end high-soaring kick through the goal posts at Hot Springs Cove that could decide the game. With the heady lavender scent of François' homemade oatmeal soap wafting out of his toasty sleeping bag, and only seconds remaining on the clock before tumbling fast asleep, Heritage found he needed to contend with one last erection that needed to be intercepted and vanquished.

And score!

STEPH ESCAPE

Neither Heritage nor François could have known that the moment she reached Marktosis, across the narrow inlet from the Ahousaht Chevron, Stephanie had hatched a new plan. No sooner had the two men in her zodiac disappeared from view and she had tied up François' boat at the dock, she had waved down Marcel, the driver for Turtle Island Water Taxi, as he slowly motored past with another passenger heading out of Matilda Inlet. Marcel wasn't her favourite person in Clayoquot Sound—due to one quarrel, grudge, or another—but Stephanie was desperate to get the hell out of there. She offered to share the fare with the female passenger, one of those government social-worker types, with the first name of Kari. The pair chatted about everything and nothing, as the driver motored them around the calmer backside of Vargas Island to reach Tofino before the storm really whipped up again. But Stephanie didn't stop there. She next talked the water taxi driver into popping her over to

Wickaninnish Island, so she could grab a few things. He was headed that way anyway, to pick up one of the Stewart brothers on Echachis Island, just south of there. Stephanie was eager to avoid any future involvement with her mother and the pair of men—her lovers—who she'd dispatched an hour earlier in the opposite direction. So Marcel, who really owed her anyway, made a useful accomplice. The time had come for her to leave Clayoquot Sound so she could get on with her sub-equatorial disappearing act.

Stephanie knew she would soon be losing daylight, at least in the forest, as she sprinted along the trail like a white-tailed deer being chased by a cougar. The trail was roughly half boardwalk and half mud once the rains started each year—and with the day's precipitation, the ratio had already become more the latter.

The cross-island trail on the south end of Wickaninnish Island led from Stephanie's mother's cabin on the east side facing Tofino to her own cabin perched above the island's only decent beach on the wilder west side, open to the Pacific Ocean. Wickaninnish served as a barrier island that slowed down the really big storms and calmed the harbour waters on the Tofino end of the Pacific Ocean's frequent winter tantrums. Oriented longitudinally—looking like a misshapen kidney bean—the sixty-four-hectare island was permanent home to nobody. Privately owned by a dozen shareholders as an environmental sanctuary, really only one extended family—the Greenes—could claim year-round residency. But even they had an on-the-grid second home in Tofino, or perennially disappeared to the American Southwest to escape the rains, which could annually top four metres and usually arrived sideways on gale-force winds.

Stopping briefly at her mother's cabin, the wayward daughter had left a hastily scribbled SOS note on the back of a co-op grocery sack. Following the SOS block letters, she had written in parentheses *Save our Stephanie*—thinking she was being clever. She rolled it up to stick conspicuously out of one of her mother's many empty wine bottles that had a tendency to multiply and accumulate on her kitchen counter. Stephanie moved the bottle with the note to the dining-room table to make it even more obvious. The empties—epitaphs of countless boozy self-therapy sessions—also lined both sides of the pathway leading from the cabin to the outhouse. Dottie had half-buried years and years of wine bottles there to catch the full moonlight, or a flashlight beam—like runway lights to aid her many after-dusk navigations to and from the loo.

Over the years, Stephanie had worn her own shortcuts into the spongy forest floor, traversing the narrowest point of the island to access Big Beach. She'd lived more than half her young life in a cabin there that she'd designed and mostly built herself on a rock cliff ten metres above the angry surf at the north end of the beach. As she leapt across logs and bogs and creeks that she never managed to find the time to span with bridges or boardwalks, she raced the clock, visualizing the water taxi's movement as Marcel continued south another nautical mile or so to Echachis Island for his next fare. Echachis was technically its own island—though at low tide, a good jumper could get to it from Wickaninnish without getting too wet. For centuries, Echachis was a whaling haul-out and blubber-rendering spot for the Tla-o-qui-aht First Peoples. These days, it was considered a sacred burial site and home only to the identical Stewart twins who resided there as the band-appointed custodians.

After twenty-seven years growing up in their attentive shadows, Stephanie still couldn't tell the always-smiling twins apart. She had frequently commuted (her mother called it running away) to Echachis from Wickaninnish during summer low tides, to hideout or get stoned with one or sometimes both of the brothers in their cedar-hewn bachelor pad, which doubled as a carving shed. Their place certainly looked like an anthropological museum or art gallery, but it never opened to the public, since Echachis was off-limits to *mamałn'i–m'inḥ* unless personally invited by and accompanied at all times by one of the Stewarts. Both men, accomplished carvers and storytellers, had spent their lives pre-serving their traditions and heritage by transfiguring cedar wood into dugouts, totems, bowls, masks; and cedar bark into clothes, woven hats, baskets, and medicines. Their hands were muscled, meaty, and arthritic from nearly five decades of this—but their arms always welcomed Stephanie warmly. The same welcome was not extended to her mother, whom the twins wrongly or rightly perceived as possessing some manifestation of evil.

The sound of the water taxi's motor had faded with distance and the density of the forest as Stephanie emerged into a new soundscape—the low thunder of the surf breaking against the outer rocks at Big Beach. That sound grew louder, until it was all she could hear. It would take just a couple minutes to grab her things and race back, so that Marcel and whichever of the twins he was grabbing from Echachis didn't have to wait for her too long in the small cove in front of her mother's cabin. Ambi-tiously, she'd been packed for a month as she scaled down her provisions and revised the gear and outfits she would need for her South American adventure. Stephanie had self-banished to the island's west side shortly after her first period at age thir-teen, which coincided with her first major blow-out, drag-down fight with her mother. The two had been at each other ever since, but for the past decade, Stephanie had lived these safe, couple dozen tree lengths from her mother's cottage and for the most part, this had brought about a tenuous détente between them. Before that, Stephanie's bedroom and general living quar-ters, had started out as an uninsulated play fort they called the First Mate's Cabin. That quirky little A-frame had been slapped together behind her mother's place by one of her mother's suitors to give the copulating adults a measure of privacy in the main cabin—but with each birthday, the First Mate's Cabin seemed to shrink until it became much too cramped and close for adolescent comfort. As the daughter of an original island shareholder, Stephanie was afforded the opportunity to acquire her own share when she turned eighteen, and she had been saving her summer kayak-guiding money for this eventual emancipation. She had needed to lobby the other shareholders to bless her selected site above Big Beach, and while everyone could appreciate her need to get as far away from Dottie as the island confines allowed, several—including the nearby Greene Family—had not been in favour of spoiling Big Beach with a cabin on the northern promontory. Being her pushy mother's pushy daughter, Stephanie had mounted a campaign to wear her dissenters down. In the end, she got her way, because Bards always win.

She couldn't dispute that Wickaninnish Island had been good to her—had given her the skills and backbone she needed to survive in her mother's world. But over the years, Stephanie's resistance to her mother's rather unusual way of life had caused more friction than either of them could handle. Stephanie had been weaned on her mother's practice of witchcraft, but didn't really believe Dottie had any real powers, other than the gift to alienate. It hadn't taken long for their mutual resentment to become their strongest bond.

Stephanie was more than independent. She was rebellious, sure. What child of a morally pretending political parent wasn't? She'd long since outgrown any need for Wiccan pageantry and potions. She instead preferred to poke all kinds of holes in her mother's practice and belief system. It had been no picnic being a witch's child. No matter how integral her participation had been in her younger, introductory Wiccan years—and no matter how much her divine and sacred vagina had factored into her mother's grand design for a full-on feminist coven island community—Stephanie was no hippie. She was a flunkey at spell-casting and skeptical of other such outdated nonsense. Relocating to Big Beach had given her mother plenty of hocus pocus room to hex her guts out while Stephanie was spared the obligation of participating or ascending to something she was not and could not become. Still, this was paradise on earth and even though she was leaving now, she knew it was seasonal and only temporary. All of a sudden, though, the weight of her departure and the uncertainty of her immediate future manifested in a pair of tears that stung her wind-chapped cheeks. She windshield wiped her face with a forearm and willed herself back together. For goddess sake, she wasn't leaving Wick forever. Stephanie didn't see how she ever could, since the island had always been a part of her anatomy, just another vital organ she would perish without.

The trail veered left when it came to an upended ancient cedar that had thrust up a two-story wall of roots perpendicular to the ground that for centuries had contained it. This was the last forested stretch of path before abruptly petering out to dump her onto the sand of Big Beach. In the open, she sprinted across the beige-wet sand like a plane leaving a runway and leapt halfway up the rockface with renewed energy and purpose. She threw open the door to her triangular cliff house.

She was met by a scream which provoked her own.

"Shit!" she shouted. When she managed to focus and the wind had returned to her chest, she saw the two boys on the futon, both with their pants and underwear pulled down to their knees, apparently looking up each other's buttholes with flashlights. She first recognized Mason's kid, Rowan, who dropped his flashlight and scrambled past her in a bolt, out the door and into the forest, hiking up his pants in flight. Rowan had been birthed on Wickaninnish Island in a forest clearing, smack in the middle of a candlelit summer solstice incantation ritual. Somewhat miraculously, he was delivered alive, though prematurely by a doting trio of ceremoniously robed priestesses turned midwives on the spot without one clue what there were doing. They did have the communal sense to transfer mother and infant by motorboat to the hospital in Tofino and the pair recovered under properly trained expertise. Always this bright, nautical-minded child—Rowan fashioned his own boats and surfboards almost from the moment he first held a paddle. He had showed such promise, and so Stephanie was surprised to catch him in such a compromising position. But the other teen didn't run, bending over, instead, to give her a full moon before fastening his jeans around his waist, and standing his ground defiantly.

"Dammit to hell, Ninnish! I've warned you about breaking into my cottage before. What the hell is going on here?"

"Fuck you! You're not my mother. Quit acting like you own the whole goddamned island." The boy—who didn't look like a boy in or out of pants—grabbed the flashlight off the floor and moved toward the door, which she blocked.

"Maybe your mother should know that you're running around with your pants down again. Maybe I should walk you home right now and let Mona know what I found you doing in my cottage."

The boy compressed his face and his eyes narrowed into slits. "Maybe you should fuck yourself with this flashlight." He brandished it in her face.

"Is that what you were trying to do, Ninnish?"

"Don't call me that! My name's Aidan." He tried bumping her to see if he could get past. He couldn't.

"Everyone calls you Ninnish. Why do you suppose that is?" When the kid, who was already taller than Stephanie, just stammered there, about to explode, she volunteered her theory. "Is it because you act like a ninny? Because you like boys, Aidan?"

"Shut up, you junior witch! Look, it's Rowan who dared me, okay? It wasn't my idea." He shuffled from one Converse-sneakered foot to the other. "I've gotta go." He pushed his way by her, and now she allowed it.

"This is the last time, Ninnish! I catch you in my cottage again, I'm telling Mona!"

That didn't matter one bit to him, and she knew it. Wasting her energy trying to put a fifteen-year-old boy in his place was pointless—or was he sixteen already? She knew nothing of kids, and sometimes even less about adults. Why she wasted her time with either was for the psychoanalysts to work out. She had a taxi and a future to catch.

She stood on her front porch above the rocks and surveyed the open ocean for what she knew would be the last time for a while. When she came back to Wick again, Ninnish would probably be in jail, or maybe dead. It wasn't her watch anymore. She'd leave it to the others in the coven to raise that child to adulthood, and then it would be society's problem. It was safe to presume they would fuck things up without her around—but what the hell, right? Nothing lasted forever—not Aidan's juvenile delinquency, not her own bitterness, not her mother's dominion. The two things a person could count on—and the two things Stephanie would miss most about Clayoquot Sound—were that new hope always sprang from decay, and that no mark was so indelible it could endure one season of hard rain in these parts.

WICKED NINNISH

The non-stop rain hadn't aided Heritage's whimpering state of abandonment as he holed up in a miniature A-frame shack alone on Wickaninnish Island for the past two-and-a-half days heading into his third night. He figured he must be serving some universe-imposed and Dottie Bard-sanctioned solitary confinement—but for what unpardonable offense, he didn't know.

In any case, Wickaninnish Island is where he found himself. He'd so far passed the endless time counting and naming the spiders; reading from his newly purchased book, *Discovery of Heaven*; and regularly dumping out the indoor pots that collected the rainwater the shabby pitched roof couldn't keep out. To sustain himself, he nibbled on rations of salmon candy, the non-moldy remnants from a package of goat cheese, a few dozen Kalamata olives, and a loaf of SunRyes ancient grains bread that had to be at least four days ancient, by his count—and that was if it had been fresh when it had arrived at the protest camp.

This limited bounty wasn't Dottie's catered hospitality. These supplies had been his share of the remaining food when the camp had hastily disbanded for good, following his only night with the activists. This got washed down with collected rainwater from a pot he'd placed outside under an opening of the trees. After 3 p.m. each day, he allowed himself a special treat—a few measured sips from a 1.5 litre jug of Chile's finest *Gato Negro* that he'd found stashed and unopened on its side in the rafters.

Now that he was physically there, the island's name had added meaning by becoming his first Clayoquot Sound address. Every so often, he speed-drilled himself on spelling *Wickaninnish* frontwards, then backwards, until he'd drift off to sleep or have to pee. Subjected, as he had been, to a rainforest water torture that had lasted more than sixty hours so far and sounded like a shower head stuck on its massage-setting and trained on the metal colander of a roof over his head, he began to wonder what going crazy would look like. He already knew what it sounded like. Trickling noises, and window streaks, and overflowing pots, and puddles expanding to connect to even larger puddles, all made him have to pee constantly—and each time he'd ventured out to use a tree or the outhouse, he checked the bay to see if he could see beyond the fifteen feet in front of him. For two-and-a-half days, he couldn't.

He had been unceremoniously dumped there by Dottie on the driftwood-strewn beach in a small bay she had said belonged to her, since it was in front of her cabin. His stint in law school had taught him better—he knew that any land along any of Canada's three ocean coasts, and which could be covered by saltwater at high tide, belonged to the Queen of England. But Heritage didn't say anything and figured he'd let Dottie take that up with the Crown.

The dumping had been literal. Dottie had been in such a careless rush that she had shoved the nose of his kayak off the back of her boat, before he'd had a chance to baby it, causing the first set of dings and scrapes when it hit some underwater rocks there in the shallows. Her apology had been "it looked too new anyway." She next pointed from her boat toward the trees, saying he could make full use of a smaller out-building behind her house that once belonged to her daughter—like she was deceased or something instead of enjoying a Patagonian holiday. Then Dottie used the same already-raised hand to wave goodbye. With no more formality than that, he'd been dumped. She turned her motor back on and pointed her boat back into the sheets-of-rain, yelling over the rev of her motor, that he should "lay low" until the weather cleared or she came back for him—not indicating which she thought might come first. That had been almost three days ago.

If Heritage had suspected he was being played and manipulated by everyone he'd met so far in Clayoquot Sound, he would have been close to right. As one day followed another, this hunch—unlike the weather—was becoming clearer with each bucketful of rain. If you hesitated at all to reveal your purpose in a place like this, your purpose got assigned to you. He'd for sure hesitated with Dottie and look where that got him! But if he was going to play gullible enough to accept her explanation— that there had just been a misunderstanding about the blockade location—then he needed to understand his endgame with her. There were things he would need from her. His grandfather had told him that much. As the senior ranking village politician, she could pave the way for (or stand in the way of) the Carter Family takeover of Headlands Lodge. He'd need her on his side if this mission was to succeed without the costly headache of added litigation, bureaucracy and public opposition.

Heritage had been able to piece together—from the shouted conversation they'd shared during the twenty-minute lift she gave him across the weather-tossed channel from town—that Dottie believed her daughter, Stephanie, had gone missing and that she already had the RCMP looking into her disappearance. Heritage elected not to volunteer that he had met Stephanie—more-than-met-her, actually—that he may have been among the last to see her alive, and that his spermatozoa might or might not still be detectable inside her female parts. He had learned just enough in his thirty-two years to not unnecessarily complicate the already really crazy shit.

That it hadn't stopped raining in the days since the throw-away sex with Stephanie and the sex that had been more than sex with François, didn't help defuse the melodramatic nature of Heritage's new isolation. Every time a new leak developed in the tin roof of the one-room cabin, requiring another cup or stock pot or gumboot for collection, Heritage flashed back to that last kiss with François in the rain as they were motoring out of Hot Springs Cove. Between emptying these collection vessels when they neared overflowing; keeping the dollhouse-sized cast-iron stove stoked; and alternating between sit-ups, push-ups, and chin-ups (until the rafter he'd been using snapped from his weight, or perhaps dry rot); Heritage was moderately content in his cabin fever. Earlier in the day, he had contemplated paddling his kayak across Templar Channel to see if he could pick up a scent of François in town. But visibility was nil. Dottie had urged him to stay on *Wick* (her time apparently so precious, she'd taken to abbreviating the chief's and the island's name) until he heard from her and besides, François had already told him he was starting a new eight-day rotation at the remote oyster farm on the other side of Meares Island where he worked.

In his stuck and obsessive state, Heritage couldn't help but replay the newsreel of the past seventy-two hours over and over, to be certain he hadn't missed anything and to remind himself it hadn't all been a dream. He'd been slingshotted from one end of Clayoquot Sound to the other in that time since the float-plane had delivered him like fresh meat from the butcher last Thursday. In the first twenty-four hours, he had had some degree of sexual relations with two different people of two different genders—more sex than he'd tallied in the previous three summer months. He had dodged bears, Dottie Bard's insistence that he cancel his arrangement at the Headlands to start working for her instead and the RCMP who had apparently arrived twenty minutes after he and François had packed up their tents and left the camp at Marktosis—according to Dottie who sadly pronounced the blockade washed-out and dead. And that was just the first twenty-four hours. Day Two and Three had felt like he was being quarantined, isolated, and cut off from the world—ostensibly, again according to Dottie, for his own protection.

Heritage stepped outside to unfold his body and stretch under the eaves in the rain as he telepathed his feelings and growing distress into the sound. From the narrow deck that ran the five-metre length of the A-framed cabin, he stared into the fog bank, which continued to mask any view he might have enjoyed. W, I, C, K, A, N, I, N, N, I, S, H, he spelled out loud, as though he were projecting his voice from an auditorium stage. How to spell it was all he knew about the place, and this had begun to frustrate him.

While he couldn't see much beyond that rotting porch, he could make out the architecturally unimaginative shape of Dottie's one and a half story loft cabin—maybe twice as big as the shed she was lending him. The boredom, his growling stomach, and his curiosity got the best of him, and he decided to see if he could learn more about her while he was exiled here. He reached inside and grabbed his raincoat off the hook on the back of the door, and a flashlight that wasn't his from a small table. Surprisingly, he'd found the batteries in it were still good, though he was certain he'd drained them down a fair bit the past few nights while reading his hefty paperback novel well after dark—which in this dreary weather and time of year, began sometime between 3:30 and 4 p.m. if he was lucky. A working flashlight did suggest to him that the cabin's last occupant maybe hadn't vacated the premises before the start of the Vietnam War—contradicting the place's hippie décor and vibe.

He dashed the ten metres, leaping puddles and skidding onto the algae-slimed decking outside the sliding glass doors. Dottie's place wasn't locked. The cabin shed he occupied hadn't been locked either. It may have been a Wick Isle policy or a break-in-reduction measure that saved on broken windows, jammed locks rusting hardware, and splintered doorframes.

Dottie's cabin didn't smell any less musty or any more lived-in than the shed. Like his hovel, there was no electricity, which gave the flashlight an immediate purpose. He trained its beam to reveal the dimensions of an austere layout. Against the north wall without windows, a curved staircase traced the bend of the primary chunk of driftwood that had been upended and set into the wooden floor on its wider bottom end and attached to the loft railing to provide a low banister on its tapered top end. These dusty stairs led to a sleeping loft with a double mattress on an open upper floor half the size of the main level. Under this overhang, was an appliance-less kitchen, a faded Polynesian curtain that partly concealed a shelved pantry the size of a telephone booth to the left of a single back door—the upper half of which had a curtained window in the same fabric as the pantry, and the remaining space seemed turned over to a combination living and dining room. On the south wall without windows, a flying saucer-shaped wood stove painted in bright orange enamel grew out of and seemed to hover above a cement-and-pebble patterned floor with embedded shells and blue-green glass Japanese floats of varying sizes and shapes. A soot-bottomed olive-green tea pot with an unraveling rattan wrapped handle sat on top of the wood stove inside a cast iron pan next to the stove pipe that grew like a bean stock to disappear through the roof. Large single-pane windows were stacked atop the side by side pair of sliding glass doors to form the nearly all glass east-facing wall and provide a view from both downstairs and the loft—though the view was theoretical as it was currently masked by fog that refused to lift.

From the top of that window wall, the highest point in the cabin, a steeply pitched cedar-shaked roof sloped down toward the back of the building. A comma-shaped deck that Heritage had nearly slipped into the splits crossing, seemed to grow out of the cabin on the waterside, with a circular cut-out large enough to accommodate the trunk of a towering western red cedar tree that had been there long before Dottie. The cabin, from what Heritage could remember, was positioned maybe fifteen metres back from the beach, which consisted of rock, pebbles, and a tangle of drift-wood that had a good-sized passage chainsawed straight through it. Beyond that squatted the petulant fog bank—or maybe more technically, the rain cloud so fat and heavy it could not get its ass off the water. If Heritage's orientation was correct, the Templar Channel—the narrow finger of land that the Village of Tofino occupied—and Meares Island must be out there in that grey muck. And François, too—thinking about him, maybe.

Who knew what was out there, really?

Heritage continued snooping. The northern wall next to the staircase was all bookshelves. He had to feel sorry for those books, molding away in the dampness. Slightly off-centre from one of the shelves was what looked like an old fish aquarium, with a clear plexiglass-hinged front panel. Inside were large editions of star-tling titles: *Buckland's Complete Book of Witchcraft*; *Book of Shadows*, by Gerald Gardner; another book by Gardner: *High Magic's Aid*; *Aradia, or the Gospel of the Witches*, by Charles Godfrey Leyland; *Living Wicca* by some author named Cunningham (he couldn't make out the first name that wrapped around the spine); *The Spiral Dance*, by another writer who went by the name "Starhawk"; *The Witch's Way*, by Janet Farrar; *The Book of the Law*; *The Encyclopedia of Magical Herbs* and the fattest volume housed within this sort of air tight, waterproof collection was a burgundy velvet bound edition of *Malleus Maleficarum*, by Heinrich Kramer and Jacob Sprenger.

That last book looked to be the oldest in this creepy collec-tion, and Heritage decided to examine it outside its glass coffin enclosure. He lifted the lid and carefully extracted the volume. Originally written in 1487, it had been translated into English as *The Hammer of Witches*. Heritage started through the yellowed pages when a few coloured index cards dropped out from between the ones that hadn't been damp-glued together. He picked three off the floor and started putting them back inside the book when he noticed writing on the cards. Recipes? But for what?

For spells!

He put two and two together. There were dozens of these cards—all in the same pencil-lead handwriting that seemed to be a form of coded shorthand. Some of the writing he could make out—numbers signifying quantities, and references to *enemies, revenge,* and *fertility.* The rest were abbreviations, broken up by symbols and dots that he could not interpret. Heritage tucked the fallen ones back into the ratty book toward the front section from where he thought they had resided.

Was Dottie Bard a witch, then? He slowly lowered the plexiglass door to the collection and used the sleeve of his raincoat to wipe away his fingerprints. His stomach growled again, reminding him he was hungry—or that there was a limit to the amount of salmon candy one man could ingest before falling ill. Dottie had examined his book collection on the dock the other day—now they were even. Of course, if he were caught, she could place a spell on him. What could he do to her?

He moved to the kitchen and combed the pantry shelves, finding a can of pork and beans, a corroded saltshaker, and six tins of smoked oysters stacked on top of each other that when removed, Heritage learned had been holding up the corner of the tippy shelf above them. It would be Thanksgiving tonight, he thought as he prepared to borrow a few provisions. On the top shelf behind the Polynesian curtain, Heritage found the mother-lode: another unopened bottle of Gato Negro Cabernet Sauvignon and a decent supply of half-spent pillar candles, in more shapes and sizes and colours than he could catalog by flashlight. He moved the wine, beans, and oysters to the table, along with two of the larger candles. On the center of the table was another wine bottle with candle drippings—this one empty, except for a large brown paper note, rolled up and stuck in the opening. He pulled it out and walked it to the windows where he could read the writing:

Mum: I would date this, but I don't know what day it is. I'm sorry I am leaving Clayoquot for Patagonia without saying goodbye. It has been a shit-show couple of days and I just need to shake my head of these cobwebs and get on my way already. I told you I'm guiding for a kayak outfit for a few months near Punta Arenas. Depending on how that goes, I could be back for Christmas, but more likely by early spring, so that I can get some traveling in while I'm down there. I have this unexplainable need to visit Montevideo—don't ask me why. I will try to call you when I get a chance but don't worry if that doesn't happen for a couple weeks or more. I will send postcards every chance I get. Love, Stephanie.

P.S. Your new fellow, Tage, is adequately hung, it turns out, and can't be bothered with condoms. Goddess, let's hope I don't get pregnant again. That would fuck things up, wouldn't it? At least this time, I would be able to decide for myself what happens with the child.

Heritage lowered the note and let his gaze drift in disbelief out the window. "Well, that conniving bitch," he whispered to himself and any eavesdropping spiders.

It looked as though the rain might have stopped. Heritage opened the sack that the note had been written on and gathered up the provisions he intended to raid from Dottie's place and placed them inside, which he also intended to remove from the premises. Nobody else would read Stephanie's note to her mother—least of all, her mother. She had said she was on the pill—plus she'd bucked him off her—right after he'd started to climax. Or maybe he did the bucking? He couldn't recall. The truth was he couldn't remember the sequence of who did what, or where he'd ejaculated. Why in the hell would she brag about that to her mother? Theirs had to be one twisted relationship—somehow, he'd parachuted right into the middle of it.

Feeling suddenly dirtier than he was, Heritage returned with the groceries to his cabin and stoked the wood stove with a dry split of cedar he'd liberated from Dottie's fireplace. From the nail on the inside of his cabin door, he grabbed the green sweatshirt with satiny yellow collegiate letters that spelled OSU. It had been hanging there by its hood when he arrived and he hadn't thought much of it, but it would double nicely now as a bath towel. He brought the fabric to his nose and was pleased it didn't smell moldy. He gave it a shake out. He had needed to use François' towel at the hot springs, since he had forgotten to pack one of his own.

He rooted through his pack for a bar of Irish Spring soap that he knew he'd remembered and then ambled down the path past Dottie's place to the water. More afternoon light seemed to be filtering through the trees, but he might have been hallucinating, since the fog bank still seemed wedged in the channel. He took off his boots and socks and tested the water temperature with a toe, and then his whole foot. More or less convinced the ocean was just as cold as the rainwater he had been collecting, he stripped down and began walking into Dottie's shallow bay. It was really more like a bite that had been chomped out of the island's eastern coastline, rather than a full-fledged bay. *Dottie's Bay*—he scoffed at her arrogance as he braced himself for the shock to his system that would reach in and yank the air from his lungs the second his genitals became submerged in that ice water. He stood on his tiptoes to hold that moment off a bit longer, before grabbing his nose and dunking his 187-centimetre frame beneath the surface. He hadn't bathed since the hot springs, hoping to preserve François' scent, but now he felt filthy after having snooped through Dottie's cabin and finding Stephanie's missive to her mother.

The soap lathered quickly in the dark hair on his chest and stomach. It was certainly exhilarating, he thought as his legs began to cramp. The soap slipped from his hand, but it floated in the saltwater and he retrieved it with his long arm, bringing it to his head for a shampooing he'd remember. There was an ache in his nut sack from the cold, but it egged him on to get the job done so he could live with himself again. He got some suds in his eyes and cupped his hands to bring seawater to his face. That stung as much as the soap, so he submerged completely under again to rapidly work the soap out of his hair and eyes. When he surfaced, he was facing Dottie's place, his hair partly covering his eyes. He thought in that second that he had just seen a face in the driftwood. He pulled his hair back with his hand to comb the shore with his squinting eyes. He felt his heart thumping madly inside his chest. The face wasn't there anymore, if it had been there in the first place. You only had to look at the age of the trees, both those standing and those strewn about, greying on the beach, to just know without any doubt that the place was haunted by spirits—maybe even Chief Wickaninnish, himself!

Just then, a sea otter loped across a horizontal log, right there on the beach in front of him, pausing to reposition its flexible spine to better examine the sudsy creature it had just detected in the water. The two studied each other a moment before the otter undulated out of view. Heritage dispatched the soap bar underwater to scrub his shriveled parts. Heritage began walking up the pebbled slope, rinsing away soap as he moved until his kneecaps were above water. Then he saw the face again. Human, not otter. White, not native. Male, he thought, not female, not flinching. But when Heritage blinked, the face was gone again. He reflexively covered his nether region with both hands, one still holding the soap.

"Hey," he shouted toward the logs but there was no reply. He dunked down again for one final rinse to get the soap out of his ass crack, and then, following the slope underwater, he pulled himself along until his air gave out. He popped up suddenly much closer to shore to see if he could startle his watcher into revealing himself or his hiding place. The green sweatshirt was gone, he realized—and with it had vanished any trace of the face. Ghosts and otters notwithstanding, Heritage could no longer make believe that he was holed up alone on Wickaninnish Island.

Smelling all bergamot and citrus clean, beginning to feel toasty again with the pot belly wood stove stoked to slow burn for hours, Heritage was wary and tuned-in to every sound. The wind had picked up outside which seemed to have startled the rain to come back from its break and the treetops to commence their all-night dance-a-thon. Under the cot on which he was trying to relax, wearing only his underwear and lying atop his sleeping bag, he had just noted with some distress that the height of the growing stack of dirty clothes was about to overtake the height of the stack of clean camping clothes he had remaining. This was how Heritage kept track of time and it was about to tip the balance of his roughing-it enthusiasm. He wondered why in the hell he was accepting being stuck and uncomfortable in this teepee of a shed when he could have been living it up at the posh four-star Headlands Lodge somewhere on the other side of that immoveable fog bank. He had a reservation and was expected later that week but surely he would be accommodated if he decided to show up early. He was agitated and spooked even before it became dark. With intermittent wind gusts swishing the branches of nine-story tall trees in every direction overhead like a pom-pommed cheering squad at halftime, he was becoming a tangle of nerves the Gato Negro couldn't touch. How he pined for another marijuana kissing session with François. Every creak and snap and whoosh took on new spookiness and for some reason, now, three days into fog arrest, there was suddenly a foghorn out there in the sound, wailing from somewhere south of his position. Why it hadn't been warning ships around the clock before now was another mystery Heritage wasn't going to stick around long enough to solve.

Plied with so much wine his toothpaste spit was crimson—Heritage's mind ping-ponged off every angle inside that mini A-frame asylum. He could be a chain thinker that way, becoming so analytical he couldn't stand his own company. He obsessed about the face in the driftwood and where the green sweatshirt had gone. He wondered about the damage Dottie may have already done with Brad Fraser at the Headlands Lodge, and whether this would jeopardize his obligation to his grandfather. He fretted all over again about what had become of François after he had delivered him and his kayak to Dottie's dock before nosing his skiff back out into the weather and heading across the harbour to Meares Island. Somewhere out there was a floating oyster farm that François had said he worked at—eight days on and four days off. But was he working now? Or was he off work, sitting at a pub, drowning himself in a pint, and kicking himself for letting that handsome hottie at the hot springs get away from him?

Heritage wondered if anyone was curious or even looking for Stephanie, whose zodiac was still tied at the dock in Ahousaht—though evidence suggested she had been in her mother's cabin since then. Where was that note again? A little fuzzy from the Gato, Heritage got off his butt to re-examine what she'd written. He had started reading through her scribbled good-bye when he noticed the bag had been ripped and the P.S., along with the whole bottom of the paper sack, was gone!

Something or someone had been inside this shack while he was bathing . . .

Wait. That face! There had been someone there, watching him—perhaps stalking him still. And in their possession was the postscript that had implicated him by name and, well, by description. "What the hell?" he blurted out to nobody. On second thought, how did he know nobody was listening?

He blew out the candle closest to the window and then

sat down on the only chair in the place and noisily scooted it more into a shadowed corner that the other two candles hadn't exposed. The wind, his heart, his breathing—they were all audible in a world he was trying to hush so he could concentrate. Someone was out there. An otter wouldn't have had a need for an OSU sweatshirt, or the bottom quarter of a paper grocery bag. Someone was fucking with him. He reached for his book as a prop to broadcast he wasn't bothered or amused by the intimidating antics. He tried reading to calm his mind and stuck with it for maybe ten minutes. He lifted his head from his book to stare blankly inside the cramped space. He automatically moved the bookmark a small pinch of pages backward—a habit he'd picked up in law school—whenever he couldn't remember what he'd just read. This told him his brain was trying to work out something else. He closed the book, stood up and moved to the rain-streaked window, where only the candle lit half of his reflection stared back at him. It occurred to him in that moment that Stephanie may not have disappeared herself and that, there were decent odds she might still be there, stalking him and plotting her revenge—but for what? Had he really hurt or wronged her in some unforgiveable way? And without her zodiac, how in the hell could she have gotten from Ahousaht to Wickaninnish—unless of course, she was a witch too?

"Maybe she just flew here on her broom," he blurted out loud, his breath steaming up a patch on the window. He turned around to examine the empty picture frames arranged on an otherwise useless bookshelf. What had happened to the subjects imprisoned in these half-dozen frames? Had they been eliminated by wicked spells and then ritualistically removed from all memory? Was the same fate awaiting him?

In the next second, there was a particularly ferocious gush of wind followed by a sharp *crack* overhead—a falling tree branch hit the shed roof with a cranium-splitting *thud*. Looking up, Heritage saw a jagged spear point penetrating the ceiling, not quite directly above his head.

"Fuck me!" he screamed.

He threw the cabin door open with a slap and hopped outside onto the deck to look up with the flashlight. The tree branch, easily taller, quite possibly waterlogged and heavier than he was, stuck dead perpendicular into the angled tin roof. It could have killed him—maybe it should have killed him. As he stood there, his body getting lashed by rain, that ridiculously tardy foghorn sounded its two-tone dirge and another option wandered into his brain. Perhaps that tree—that javelin through the roof was meant to kill him according to the prescripts of some wicked spell. Was this a Wiccan warning? Maybe this scare is what he needed to get the hell off this island before he went mad—or worse. Using a hand to deflect the rain from hitting his eyes, he trained the flashlight beam way up into what had to be the origin tree. It was a contorted red alder that seemed to have started out growing straight and narrow snuggled up right next to the cabin, but at some point in its development had sent the majority of its trunk and limb weight into the open airspace directly above it. Heritage was only able to identify the species as an alder, and know it was a deciduous variation of the birch family, because of his family background. He and his grandfather had taken countless walks through forests all over Ontario and the senior tree-know-it-all had always insisted that any heir to the family empire needed to know his trees, too. When his grandfather diversified from pulp mills into logging and later built the Headlands Lodge, trees became the lexicon by which he spoke and operated. Heritage knew that red alders were usually the first chutes to spring up in a clear-cut, and through some symbiotic relationship involving nitrogen-fixing bacteria, the trees roots became an essential ele-ment in restoring the top layers of soil that typically got wrecked, washed out or carted away in the earth-destroying practice that was clear-cutting.

He scratched his scalp through his thick hair and remembered something else, too. Alders had the dubious reputation among loggers as *widow makers*. Their dense wood made branches heavy and prone to snapping off at the trunk to drop straight down like a weighted dart.

He pulled his hair back off his forehead and held his hand there like a barrette, sensing that something around him was different. Something had changed. It had stopped raining—that was it—and when he looked back up through the trees, he could make out the waxing crescent of the moon. The foghorn sounded its two-tone dirge—paused—then repeated. Heritage dropped his gaze to peer through the darkness in the direction of the water and to his delight, in the distance, he could see a cluster of lights—illumination above the water that had to be coming from Headlands Lodge and civilization itself! He let go a *ya-hoo!* feeling like Noah must have felt after forty days and nights of continuous rain. This development in the weather seemed equally biblical, positively epic! This, and the clearing sky overhead startled him into action. In his underwear briefs and bare feet, he gingerly climbed a metre up the wet alder trunk to get a height advantage and a measure of leverage as he tried to rock the roof-piercing branch back and forth like a loose tooth. His efforts were useless and the battering ram wouldn't budge. As a hardwood, alders weren't much good for making paper, his grandfather had lectured. But Heritage also remembered his grandfather saying that most of the lobby furniture at the Headlands had been locally made from red alder—that there was something sleek and classy about that wood's grain when its lacquered red hues reflected the dancing flickers and flames of the giant river-rock fireplace in the lodge's grand sitting room.

The thought of such cozy opulence, finally within his sights, prompted Heritage to start packing his things to make his channel crossing at sunrise. He would revel in paddling out of Dottie's possessed little cove to check himself in early at the Headlands.

Sunrise, he romanticized, having not seen glimpse of the orb in days, couldn't come quickly enough. Now, if only the rain held off, that fog bank didn't return, and he survived the night . . .

Heritage had slept like a chunk of driftwood after gorging on beans, smoked oysters, and what had been left of the salmon candy like it was his last flipping supper—washing it all down with the body of Augusto Pinochet (the 1.5-litre balance of that newfound bottle of Gato Negro). He had more passed out than fallen asleep, but so what if he had needed to marinate his brain in order to come to life and death terms with that near-fatal spire through the roof, or to neutralize his nerves after realizing someone or something had been inside his cabin and had made off with half the note Stephanie had left her mother?

Heritage awoke renewed, decisive and just a tad bit hungover. He was not at all clear about how he'd explain to Dottie Bard that he couldn't stay on Wickaninnish Island—that he couldn't work for her or shirk his obligation at Headlands Lodge—but he was absolutely positive that he was leaving that jinxed shed of a lean-to, and that today would be the day he got sprung from summer witch camp. He sat up in his sleeping bag, and new pressure on his bladder magnified an already overwhelming need to urinate. He pulled a fleece over his head and stood in the open cabin door in his long flannel bottoms and flip-flops, trying to prepare himself for the muddy clomp to the outhouse. He thought he could just pee there off the porch—or all over the building for what he cared—and be on his way, since he wasn't coming back. But then his lower gut grumbled and cramped, suggesting an outhouse sit-down might be necessary.

He splashed and skidded along the muddy path toward the stubby outhouse that was located a good six metres away, equidistant from the main house and the satellite shed he'd been utilizing. As he hopped onto the short boardwalk leading up to the boxed hole in the ground, he simultaneously lowered the front of his pants to minimize the time he'd have to spend inside the ripe shithouse. When he jerked at the driftwood-handled door, he immediately discovered the can was already occupied.

"Hey, don't you knock?" the kid asked, without stopping or even slowing his hand.

"What in the hell are you doing?"

Heritage shrieked the question from adrenaline shock, and not because it wasn't already obvious that the child, with the front of his t-shirt hiked over his head and behind his neck, was masturbating in his outhouse. Rather than answer him, the boy, whom he recognized from the side-swiping collision on the dock ramp that first morning, stared wide-eyed at the goods Heritage's still-lowered pajama bottoms revealed. The boy's tongue jutted out one side of his mouth and the concentration on his face suggested the whole exercise might become life-threatening for him at any moment. When the kid didn't stop—but, in fact, accelerated—Heritage turned his back to him and peed into the salal bushes off the edge of the boardwalk, trying to think of what to do next. The spring hinge of the outhouse door sent it clapping back shut against the frame of the hut, causing Heritage to jump a bit—but nothing was going to interrupt the flow he'd held back overnight. He could hear the child panting inside the outhouse, and what sounded like a wrist bone cracking from the violent repetitions. A smile edged across Heritage's face—not that he would allow anyone to see it. He'd been a boy just as desperate once, too.

The outhouse door was flung back open again as the teen gasped for air.

"I can shoot cum already and you can watch for yourself if you don't believe me," the kid boasted in a breathy voice that found its way through the generous ventilation gaps in the cedar-and-driftwood design of the shitter.

"No, that's okay. Thank you." Heritage had to laugh at his own politeness, given the delicacy of the situation. His urine stream was nowhere close to diminishing anytime soon. Then, making conversation, he asked "how old are you, anyway?" suddenly trying to recall the age of his own sperm debut.

"Uh-h-h-h . . . just . . . turned . . . fif-teen." He could tell the boy was surrendering every cell of his teenage being to achieve the feeling.

"What grade is that in school, then?" he inquired over his right shoulder. Curiously, Heritage needed to verify the boy's claim, thinking his first wet dream seepage didn't happen until maybe he was in seventh or eighth grade, and he'd always assumed he had been the first in his group of jack-off peers to achieve emission around the middle of secondary school.

"Going . . . into . . . Nine," the boy moaned, long and delirious.

"That's bullshit." Heritage still did not turn around. "You must be the biggest guy in your class, then, unless you were held back a year or three for being dumb."

"Fuck you! Check it out if you don't believe me." The child's groaning intensified most dramatically, and Heritage couldn't help his perverted smirk. He didn't believe the bragger but was finding it a challenge to dismiss his insistent boastfulness. Aidan took a sharp inhalation and kicked the swinging driftwood door back open with a gunshot-like slap. "Look, dammit! Here it comes," the kid said, expelling his lungs.

Heritage shook the piss from his dick and tucked himself inside the flimsy flannel. He was immediately uneasy about the way the thin fabric failed to conceal his adultness and why his adultness wasn't going away even after he'd peed. He turned around to face the outhouse with his hands folded in front of him. "Look." Heritage paused. "I can't remember your name."

"No. You look!" The boy said, shooting the orgasm onto his stomach before extending a sample toward him on his fingertip. "Told you I could cum."

Heritage tried to act anything but impressed, though he was amazed by the feat—not to mention the swollen girth and length of the teenager's parts. The kid was not at all shy and had no shortcomings to be embarrassed by that Heritage could see, though he now felt compelled to look away. A breeze shook a few residual rain or dew drops from the branches overhead and Heritage wiped his face, forgetting in that instant that his hands had been part of his nether camouflage. "Now it's your turn," the child bargained, staring below his waistband.

"Hardly," Heritage responded indignantly, replacing his hands.

"Hard-*on*'s more like it," the boy said, pointing at the man's protruding pajamas. "You either cum for me now or I'll tell people you did anyway, and that you watched me jacking off."

"Whoa, now wait a minute," Heritage protested. "That's not what happened, and you know it. Besides—you're on my property anyway. Now get off."

The kid grinned sarcastically. "I did already. It's your turn to get off, or I tell. That's the deal." The not-so-little devil wiped his mouth where some drool had been glistening, and leaned forward, placing elbows on bare kneecaps to wait.

Satan with an A!—the adult suddenly remembered. "Your name's Aidan," Heritage said, calling him out. The boy's blondish straight hair had been cut in a layered way, though it appeared that someone had used a bowl (or maybe several) to partially achieve that asymmetrical look. Maybe he'd just slept on it funny. The freckled and youthful face his hair framed dared not reveal a smile while deep in negotiations. Heritage shifted about nervously, placing his hands on his hips in exasperation.

"What—you don't think people would believe me?" the teenager demanded, in a voice still soprano-tinged, though everything else about him functioned like a tenor or worldly baritone. "How 'bout when I tell them you're circumcised, that there's a mole on one side of your dick, and a scar on the front of your hip that disappears into your pubic hair?"

"I don't fucking believe this!" Heritage stammered, subtly tracing his appendectomy scar through the hiked-up flannel with his finger. "Who are you?"

"Your worst nightmare. Isn't that about right?" The kid started to reveal a smile, but took it back lest it compromise his ultimatum. "So—you cumming or not? What's it gonna be?"

"I think you're bluffing," Heritage told him before turning to walk back to his cabin. He sensed the kid probably wouldn't let him off the hook that easily—and he was right.

"I think I'll go home and tell my mum first. Her name's Mona, and she runs the bakery in town. Next, I'll tell my Aunt Dottie, who really owns this property you say belongs to you." His voice grew louder, to make sure it reached the man who continued walking away from him. "I figure the RCMP will probably take things from there, don't you?" He was finally yelling when he pulled his jeans up and walked after the newcomer. Heritage stopped on the cedar walkway just short of the cabin door and thought a moment. His own breathing was now erratic, and he wouldn't have been surprised if steam were coming off his body—he was becoming that angry.

"Well?" the brat taunted him. "I may be a kid, but I don't have all day. I have things to do."

Heritage stepped inside the cabin, snatched his jeans from the chair where he'd left them to dry—which was a joke, as the breached ceiling had dripped on them all night—and emptied a spare pair of gumboots he'd been using to capture the rainwater. Dressing as he went, he marched back outside, where the kid was still waiting.

"Come on," Heritage ordered without stopping. "Let's go."

"Go where?"

"Let's go and tell Mona the news together. I think that will have a much bigger impact. That way, she can ask me any questions she might have about your story—right there on the spot, face to face, adult to adult." Heritage forced the excess flannel into his wet jeans before stepping barefoot into cold rubber boots. If ever a variation on the cold shower trick was going to work against residual arousal, bare feet in clam-cold gumboots had to be the way, he figured. "Come on! I don't have all day either."

It was not the way Aidan wanted things to go and while he wasn't sure he wanted to back off his demands, he did. "Never mind, then," he said. "I was only joking, anyway." He reached his hand toward Heritage—without realizing that the hand he'd just finished masturbating with might not be socially appropriate for formal apologies or introductions. "Friends, then? Welcome to Wicked Ninnish Isle."

Heritage grabbed his hand and shook it. "Look, the name's Tage, in case you forgot—and I'm probably more embarrassed by this than you are. So, no worries, okay?"

"I'm not worried," Aidan said, fastening his jeans. "I'm not embarrassed either—just the opposite. Until next time, then—see you around."

With that, Aidan disappeared into the woods on a pathway heading north, leaving Heritage standing on the porch with his mouth hanging open. *Wicked Ninnish*? Was that what the kid had just called the place? Heritage shook the bats from his belfry, and cracked his own devilish smile, thinking about what had just transpired. During the eleven-minute standoff, he realized he hadn't thought about François or Stephanie or witchcraft or hexes or spells—not once. It was probably premature to accept this as a sign of deliverance from what had been a self-obsessive, three-day funk. He did find it reassuring that under pressure he had been able to think clearly and function morally and responsibly—that he hadn't lost his mind or his principles during this bizarre isolation. But now the time had come to re-enter normal society; leave this child-run *Lord of the Flies* island, catch his first shower since the hot springs, and sleep in proper, high thread count bedding again.

———

SIGNAL DISTRESSED

It took less than twenty minutes to gather up his possessions, repack the kayak, and point its scuffed-up bow east toward the Headlands Lodge. His entranced eyes, thrilled to have something to view at any distance, surveyed the ridgeline of Meares Island as it rose up behind the narrow isthmus of land upon which the village of Tofino was stretched. He stepped into his spray skirt and hoisted the straps over his shoulders. He dropped his polarized sunglasses from his forehead to the bridge of his nose and climbed inside his boat. He walked the boat into the water using only his arms, paddle balanced across the spray skirt, life jacket zipped up tight. He gently tugged the toggled cord to lower his rudder as soon as the water was deep enough for it not to drag or hit submerged rocks.

With a half dozen strokes on each side, he emerged from the slight bay—Dottie's Bay—into the main channel. To his left he spotted a navigation beacon sitting atop a welded metal tripod that was bolted to the top of a column of white-painted concrete that had been fused to the very rock obstacle it was meant to warn mariners to avoid. Heritage could see another cabin on the shoreline—maybe this was where Aidan had come from to torment him. Maybe that was Mona's place, too, since he now knew that Aidan and Mona were connected. Heritage wouldn't have thought Mona could be the mother of a child—well, a teenager that young. She had seemed quite a bit older but maybe he had misread the lines on her face. That, of course, made him think about his own mother, and what she'd always said about face wrinkles—so good on Mona!.

To his right and a distance away, in the ocean opening up beyond Echachis Island, Heritage spotted the lighthouse on Lennard Island. That must have been from where the trippy foghorn warnings were originating—better late than never, he chuckled. The water then transitioned from chops to swells and he could feel the current moving on a diagonal under him, pulling him off his straight-as-an-arrow planned crossing. He began to pull stronger on his right side to stay the course. He smelled coffee at the same moment he had the sensation of sitting in it again. He pulled a few more hard strokes, since he was in the thick of a current that seemed to insist on carrying him north. Was it his imagination, or was he sitting lower in the water than he should have been? He lacked the experience to say for sure, but when the sensation of sitting in water didn't go away, he stopped paddling and lost all forward momentum. It was like he was driving a car sideways as he watched the Headlands sneak further and further away from him on his right. He released the spray skirt by pulling on the looped strap in front of him and stared with terror into the cockpit–now half-filled with sea.

Panicked, he quickly gauged his distance from either shore and began paddling erratically to regain control of his course. He must have a crack in his kayak somewhere. The evidence was rising about his hips. He pinned this on Dottie in the split second that followed. She'd dropped his boat in her haste to get rid of him a second time. He cursed her with each stroke but hadn't committed to a shore he could reach quicker. He was at a disadvantage in the swells sitting so low in the water—he couldn't judge distance as he kept sinking into one trough after another. As much as he wanted to make a break for the Headlands on the other side, it appeared further away than Wickaninnish Island behind him. *Wicked Ninnish*, he remembered—no slight intended to the chief.

In that indecisive moment, Heritage was being pulled by the current toward what looked like a wall of water that seemed to stand straight up, about a metre high. He took on the first of several whitecaps sideways—they broke over the top of the open cockpit. That's it, he decided, tilting the rudder and paddling into a wide turn in the swells, to head back to his starting point— but even that had migrated further south and away from him. When he paddled out of the swells and had gotten his kayak back into the choppy water again, nearer the shoreline, he was almost even with the navigation beacon. There, standing on the deck of the two-level cottage behind it, was Aidan, his blond hair lit by the sun and looking like one of those troll doll fiber optic filament lights. Heritage had bigger problems than a teenager at the moment. He paddled south, hugging the shore, trying his best to make his frantic strokes look leisurely.

The psychological setback of drifting more like a submarine than a kayak back into Dottie's Bay was beyond upsetting but he wouldn't let that, or a broken boat, destroy him. He'd leave it to Wicked Ninnish to finish him off, he supposed.

With Heritage's unfurled tent, sleeping bag and every piece of clothing he owned—dirty or otherwise—draped over rocks and driftwood to dry in the sun, Dottie's Bay looked like a neighbourhood yard sale about to open for business. His upturned kayak rested on a gurney of boulders for inspection or autopsy—revealing a dent he hadn't noticed before launching that had shattered into a spiderweb of microscopic fissures in the fiberglass that gave in when he applied pressure with his finger. He would be escaping nowhere soon—at least not in that craft. He stood atop the sturdiest log in the pile and surveyed what looked like a crash site. The more rapidly drying pages of *The Discovery of Heaven* flapped loudly in the breeze nearby. There was an occasional boat that went past, but content to be soaking in the sun, Heritage was oddly in no hurry for a rescue. He needed to dry out too, and the day was shaping up to be radiantly glorious for just that.

Surely, he and Aidan couldn't be the only humans here. He glanced down at his sandaled feet and decided the time and weather had come to verify that. Hopping off the log, he browsed the selection of drying goods for a pair of shorts and a t-shirt. He filled his water bottle from the rain bucket he'd placed in the clearing not far from the alder that had tried to kill him in the night. He popped his head inside the little A-frame that might have been his coffin to inspect it in full light, sun streaming through the triangle of windows and through the puncture hole in the ceiling. Now the spiderwebs were really visible and Heritage felt a shiver rumble through his body. How could this have ever been the best choice of available accommodations? His eyes narrowed as his opinion of Dottie Bard grew another thorny tendril already climbing up the trellis of his disdain. She had tossed him to the bears, broken and bloodied the nose of his kayak, and then attempted to feed him to the spiders. He thought about the good, working relationship he was told he would need to have with that woman—and how rocky the start had been between them. Sure, in a glass half full, they could still become tried and true friends—that is, if he didn't end up tossing the glass at her head the next time he saw her.

He remembered a ratty, empty nylon backpack—the type kids

used to carry their books to school—that had been hanging on the back of the cabin door, on the same hook as the now missing OSU sweatshirt. Thinking he might be able to repurpose it, he reached around to grab it, and that's when he saw more of Stephanie's faded handiwork, drawn with a black marker on the inside of the cabin door. It appeared to be a rudimentary facsimile of the island, as it was set off by giant scrawled capital letters *W* and *I*. The map featured a simple trail network in dashed lines, along with what Heritage took as the marked locations of thirteen other cabins, all drawn using square shapes, except for one that had required—for some odd reason—a triangle. There was also an upside-down star inside a circle, which Heritage had at first interpreted to mean YOU ARE HERE, but after further examination, and correlating where Dottie's cabin had been depicted on the map, he realized that couldn't be correct.

The triangle interested him simply because it was different from the other icons used on her map and he wanted to understand why. It was positioned on the opposite side of the island which he had yet to explore. A dashed-line made it look like a trail began on the other side of the same outhouse he (and now, Aidan) had been using that seemed to link first, to the upside down star in the circle, and then continued north past a concave indentation in the island's coastline that had been labeled with the initials *B.B.* There were four boxes drawn relatively close together in a pin-wheel cluster formation below the star, but there was no dashed line that connected to or between these squares. Instead, a row of hashmarks appeared to carve off this entire southwest node of the island from the rest of the map and just so there would be no mistaking it, a very amateurly-drawn skull and cross bones had been added to indicate this was possibly out of bounds. Beyond the triangle, the dashed line continued north, paralleling the outer coast to connect two more square icons, one located on either side of what looked like the midpoint and widest part of the island. There, the trail had a Y-junction where it either continued north to the top of the island to reach another three boxes or it turned right to return—more or less in a straightly drawn dashed line back to the east side. This line had been labeled *T.I.E.* and either terminated or started just below where another box had been drawn—the only place Heritage thought Mona and Aidan's place could be on this map, based on where he'd seen Aidan watching him from a cabin deck. There was one final box, the thirteenth icon, that he couldn't account for that was not that much further north of what he believed was Mona's place on this map. There was no dashed line leading to it or away from it, so perhaps it was only accessible by boat or maybe broomstick.

Yelling over her boat's motor in a persistent rain on the way over to dropping him off, Dottie, in her scattered way, had tried to give Heritage an express orientation of Wickaninnish Island. She explained that the private island had been cooperatively purchased in the late 70s by a group of loosely organized shareholders that had pretty much stopped cooperating with each other not long after the ink had dried on the purchase and sale agreement. Dottie made it a point to let him know that the others—celebrated and esteemed just like herself—were all diehard, tree-hugging, anti-war, peace-loving environmentalists of some renown. (Heritage made note). In exchange for their pooled financial investments and by lottery, each of these charter shareholders had drawn a chit from a bucket that corresponded to a pre-determined building site that measured roughly four hectares along the island's coastline on which they could construct one primary, off-the-grid cabin. The interior of the island's pristine rainforest was designated as property in common to be managed in perpetuity as an ecological sanctuary preserve—or so mandated the quickly penned constitution brought forward by one of the hippies in the group (who claimed to possess a law degree). After a flurry of site-trading, so friends could build adjacent to friends, this manifesto was ratified by consensus at their first annual general meeting—which, as Dottie described it, had been this clothing-optional, pot, LSD and boozy bacchanal on the beach that first summer.

And that's about all Heritage could remember, either because he couldn't hear over the motor or hadn't cared enough about what she had been telling him to retain the rest. Dottie did emphasize that the other island shareholders were beginning to age out now, meaning they had become fair-weather weekenders or summer cottagers at best, and now that summer was over, he shouldn't expect to run into anyone. Now that he thought about it, that was akin to saying *nobody will hear you scream*. And as he'd discovered, he was hardly alone on the island. He shook his head and wondered why he should believe anything that woman told him.

Equipped now with a treasure map of the place that had already expanded his command of the island's geography, it was like Heritage was a budding anthropologist, all of a sudden, with a whole new civilization to discover. He rummaged through his things, looking for a pen or pencil and a piece of paper onto which he could copy the map. When he found none, he decided to repurpose Stephanie's *SOS*—which he had stupidly left behind, face up on the table. He had a quick word with himself about that bit of carelessness, thinking he'd covered his tracks when he bolted out of there earlier that morning. He reached to the belt holding up his cargo shorts, and—happy to be using another of his fancy MEC gadgets for his wilderness survival—he carefully unfolded his Gerber pocketknife to cut the folded seams of what remained of the sack using the retractable scissors. Folding back the blank side of the brown paper into a serviceable canvas, Heritage was almost set. For want of a pencil, he settled for a burnt piece of kindling with a charcoal tip that he extracted from the long-since-cold wood stove, and then did his best to copy the details from the backside of the A-frame cabin door onto his paper.

The start of the trail was so overgrown with salal that Heritage had trouble finding it. Salal was remarkable that way. Most people knew the waxy leafed plant as the greenery florists used when arranging or wrapping a bouquet of roses, but any hiker in the Pacific Northwest could tell you that salal is so prolific it could conceal a body or even a mass grave after just one rainy season of unbridled growth. Heritage had already ventured a few metres into the woods in several spots only to realize that he wasn't on a trail yet at all. When looking down didn't work, he decided to look straight ahead—like a magic trick, the trailhead revealed itself as a break in the trees. He was on his way across the island, striding and hopping over and around stretches of rotting boardwalk that had once attempted to span mossy bogs. Occasional cedar treads spaced closely together like the ridges of a pair of corduroy pants helped him get over muddy spots, and chain-sawed cuts into fallen tree trunks provided reassuring evidence that other people had been this way, too. After falling through a section of boardwalk, though, Heritage no longer cared if his sandals got wet or muddy. He sucker-splashed through the streamlets and mud that every so often suction-grabbed hold of a sandal, forcing him to step right out of it and then have to back-track to extract it.

Jurassically massive cedar trees regularly arrested his travel and demanded his touch and admiration. As though his palm were a stethoscope, Heritage laid his hand on each of the giants. He even ventured off trail to reach and commune a moment with the grandest of these monoliths. The forest in the middle of the island blocked light and muffled sound but also entombed history—along with the smells of fungi and bearded moss and water-logged plants in various stages of suspension and decay.

The trail veered left—or at least he thought it did—and poured him into a large clearing that for some reason instantly reminded him of standing in the middle of a large geodesic dome like when he got to go inside the U.S. Pavilion during Expo 67 in Montreal. He'd been five years old at the time, one hand in his grandfather's and the other in his father's—both men steadying him so he didn't fall over as he arched back, trying to take it all in. Heritage felt just as dwarfed and insignificant now standing in that voluminous space. The tree in the clearing's center was a colossal, ancient cedar—hands down, the largest tree of any kind that Heritage had ever seen—larger than the one at Hot Springs Cove. He walked widely around it with his lower jaw unhinged. Its trunk had the girth of three or four upturned school buses strapped together—and this base seemed to have pulled up the earth along with it like a green turtleneck sweater as it hydraulically pushed its way through the centuries into the troposphere.

Like Jack and his beanstalk, Heritage harboured a belief that if he climbed to the top of that tree—a top he couldn't see from where he stood—he would be able to survey creation and possibly discover heaven . . . giving a nod to the title and theme of the doorstopper-of-a-novel he had started reading days earlier. Maybe three elevator stops up its trunk, the tree split into a dozen trees from its candelabra centre, each remarkable on their own. It had likely been this growth spurt, this massive expansion of the tree's biomass, that had created the clearing's dome effect, with its lush, dark-green canopy draped over an infrastructure of gravity-defying limbs that looked like the ribs of a hundred umbrellas. Not even salal, skunk cabbage, or mountain huckleberry received enough sunshine to make a go of it underneath this imposing lid.

On a particularly comfortable, cushy-looking bed of thick moss on what he took to be the eastern side of the trunk, Heritage paused, kneeling reverently. Then he lay face-down atop this inclined pillow at the base. With seven deep inhalations—his maximum attention span for meditation and the length of a blessing ceremony that seemed appropriate to him—he sucked in the essence of the nutrients that had been accumulating, decomposing and recyling there for eons. Heritage was becoming One within the sacred rainforest and he wanted—no, *needed*—the sacred rainforest to become One within him, too. He daydreamed of falling forever asleep on that verdant spot, a la

Rip Van Winkle—and imagined his body being assimilated into the forest floor. Every scrap of DNA, every corpuscle of his existence, the codes and nuclei from his cells, would all get carried high up into the cadmium columns where the microscopic bits of Heritage Warren Carter III would gently heave to and fro on the boughs and fronds of this unbelievable specimen of a tree, if he could just stay still long enough—which, of course, he could not.

He felt a bug on his neck, and in the time it took to gasp and swat, he was out of the sacred and back on his feet—using magical levitating propulsion, his own superpower, reserved for emergency situations just like this. How ridiculously shallow he felt next—obviously not at all ready to become one with the forest if it involved bugs to break him down into useable bits.

He'd recently read an article in the *Vancouver Sun*—scientists were starting to find salmon DNA inside core samples of trees on Vancouver Island and further north in the same narrow stretch of rainforest, along BC's Central Coast. Some of those trees were more than a thousand years old and several hundred metres away from fish spawning streams. The brainiacs in their lab coats were able to surmise that over the centuries, half-eaten salmon carcasses had been carried deep into the forests by bears and birds, and the scraps decayed and dissolved to become absorbed into the future, locked inside these living giants. Heritage was, and of course couldn't help but feel, insignificant in its towering presence. He wanted to mean as much to this tree as the tree was meaning to him in that moment, but how? Maybe he was just being silly, but he felt empty, irreverent, like he was rushing this communion much like he barrelled through life as though he only had so much time he could waste on being philosophical or introspective and that maybe he could adequately get by with just a half-blessing from this giant, before pressing on to whatever came next. He needed to sacrifice next for now, for once in his life, and just be still. So, bugs or no bugs, Heritage got down on the moss shag carpet again and spread out his arms and legs like he was da Vinci's Vitruvian Man, this time on his back, training his watery gaze up the trunk from a different perspective to its diminishing point where the trunk itself disappeared in the pyramidal and sky-scraping foliage. A raven cawed in the distance as Heritage allowed his body to sink in the sphagnum moss, surrendering his resistance to perhaps the most organic moment of his life. Behind shuttered eyelids, he imagined legions of Lilliputian-like sprites and nymphs linking their fairy wings to dance a protective ring around him that would keep the witches and demons and, of course, the bugs at bay, too.

It had probably only been a minute when a snapped branch sounding alarmingly close-by jolted him from his trance. With every one of his muscles statue-still, his hazel eyes blinked open as wide as he could get them to enhance his listening. His heart thumped a war drum behind his sternum as he held his breath imagining he was sufficiently camouflaged at the base of the trunk. His eyes came into sharper focus, tuning from the distant widescreen kaleidoscope of every imaginable shade of green to a close-up, almost cross-eyed examination of a beige protuberance that was sticking out from the feathery orange bark of the trunk, and almost touching the end of his nose. Was it fungi? He sniffed. Then he saw that there were replicas of the first specimen spiraling in what had to be a man-made pattern around the trunk. They weren't mushrooms—he touched the closest one, and when it boinged back into place, he thought it must have been rubber or plastic.

Heritage slowly hinged at the waist and then twisted his upper body around to examine the trunk's many anomalies on all fours. He pulled his head back to more clearly identify what he thought he was seeing, and when his brain confirmed it, he lurched his torso backward even further. The dirty, rubbery protrusions were disembodied limbs—the legs and arms from baby dolls, each attached to the trunk's flesh with a tiny, rusted nail, to complete one continuous circumnavigating ring. As he scratched off the accumulation of dirt on a little hand with his finger, the arm detached, just as another tree limb snapped somewhere nearer by. Heritage froze—half-paralyzed by the prospect of an approaching stranger and half-scared shitless by the creepiness of the baby parts that formed a belt wrapped around the base of this epic tree. In an instant, that peaceful clearing took on a ceremonial or ritualistic element that spooked the fuck right out of him. Heritage flashed back to the Wiccan library in Dottie Bard's cabin, as the concept of sacrifice—human sacrifice—suddenly barged its way into his contemplative meditations. Could this site be the spot on the map that had been marked with the upside down pentagram inside the circle? A discernable chill clamoured through his body like a marble had been dropped down the chutes and ladders of his skeleton. What the hell was this place?

Tentatively, Heritage raised himself up to a standing position, scanning the woods for anything or anyone who may have joined him. Seeing or hearing nothing new, he tried to find the trail that had delivered him into this clearing. The problem was that there were several, and he didn't know which one he needed. Lying in the moss had been like being blindfolded and spun around at the start of a pin-the-tail game. He was now disoriented and unsure. After his second nervous lap around the edge of the clearing, and after accepting he had no landmark or memory to rely on, he chose a trail he thought would carry him north and maybe west.

Were there bears on this island? Wolves, maybe? He didn't know and hadn't been told. The madwoman who had delivered him there had plopped him into a snarling, drooling bear trap once before—and he had been diabolically strapped to twenty-five kilos of banana bread, to boot. He wouldn't put anything past her. Heritage grabbed the next branch off the ground, figuring he could weaponize it if he needed to, and then picked up his long-legged pace.

Within another ten minutes loping through the woods, Heritage noted the forest composition begin to change. The giant cedars grew further apart until they had been replaced by towering coastal Douglas firs, and the in-between spaces were filled with scrub pines that were contorted into frozen backbends, as though a prevailing wind was holding them that way, even though the air was still, but cooler now. Something else was new—the sounds of crashing surf grew louder, as though a DJ were tinkering with the bass and treble knobs of a stereo trying to find a soothing balance. And there were new smells too—wafts of fishy ocean spray, an aerosol that permeated that part of the forest.

Heritage knew he was getting closer to the ocean but he hadn't been able to see it yet through the trees and the ground foliage that grew thick and taller than he was. Just at the moment the roar grew loudest, the dirt trail beneath his feet transitioned into the shaved and well-worn top of a long log that quite literally dumped him out of the forest and facedown onto a white sand beach. Lifting his head out of the warm sand, he gazed upon an almost tropical mirage so real he could swear he heard ukuleles and smelled spit-roasting pig. How other worldly, the scene struck him after being pinned under forest, fog and rainclouds for three suffocating days. He pulled the grocery sack map out of his back pocket and figured this beach must correspond to the rough indentation of the coastline that Stephanie had marked *B.B.* If *B.B.* stood for Big Beach, and he was only guessing, he'd seen beaches that were bigger, though none that looked more welcoming and beautiful to his marooned, castaway eyes. Maybe the first *B* stood for *beautiful*, which would make even more sense, since it was, plus he had it entirely to himself.

Black, jagged rocks that looked obsidian from a distance, rose into formidable cliffs on either end of a beach that was shaped like a scallop shell. From where he stood throwing no shadow onto the sand in the mid-day sun, Heritage assumed he was facing south. When he climbed to balance atop a silvered specimen of bleached driftwood the size of a sedan, he could see the tops of a partially submerged archipelago of black rocks that curlicued like an arthritic index finger from the bottom of the beach into the sea to form a natural jetty. This seemed to be absorbing the brunt of the Pacific's assault on the continent by deflecting wave after wave straight up into the air. Beyond this low, rocky break, the ocean opened up to the horizon—and Russia, Heritage guessed—where a skyline of voluminous thunderheads also seemed to stand straight up in the sky to lord themselves over the expanse.

At the far end of the beach, where the finger of barrier rocks almost, but not quite connected back to the island, was an opening between the rocks and the adjacent cliffs, where white foam floated on top of calm water like a feather down blanket. Heritage was thinking that the opening seemed about the length of his kayak or maybe just wide enough to scoot a zodiac through, but in either craft, you'd have to time the surf just right to not get munched. He had walked halfway down the beach toward the water to get a better look when he spotted a cabin on top of the cliff to his right. It looked as though it could have been another A-frame, but the sleek, almost modern looking structure was painted black to blend in with the rocks. Had it not been for the sun's glare bouncing off the triangle of windows, he might have missed it, but as an extension of the black cliff below and with the sun illuminating only the glass at the top, it reminded Heritage of the pyramid with the eye of providence on the backside of a US dollar bill. Then again, this being Wickaninnish Island and this pyramid being all black, it was uncanny how it also looked like a witch's hat.

He folded the makeshift map and stuck it back in his pocket. He took that moment to celebrate the sun, which he hadn't seen in a week. He stretched his arms overhead, and let the heat warm his face. He peeled off his two upper layers of clothing next, needing the sun to kiss every square centimetre of his skin. He hopped off the driftwood to land his feet in the sand. Then off came the sandals, revealing moisture-wrinkled and dirty feet and toes that he wiggled and buried in the warm sand. It was a

September sun, so not nearly as hot as his vitamin-D-deprived body craved—but it was his first solar blessing since arriving in Clayoquot Sound. He'd been warned about the rainy season, so he didn't know if this would be among the last showings of the giant star he would experience before fall caved into winter's relentless bullying.

Heritage spun slowly around like a solar panel riding a merry-go-round, his arms outstretched and his city-white feet tamping the sand. Out in the open, in the sun, on that pristine beach, he felt fantastic—the opposite of the fright that had washed over him ten minutes earlier, in the dark shadows of the forest that with the doll limbs, was growing creepier by the minute. On a lark, he shoved his pants and underwear below his knees, clumsily kicking them past his ankles as he began a lanky jog down the beach toward the frothy, churning Pacific. In the last few metres, he constricted every muscle, bracing for the ice water he knew would steal the air from his lungs and snatch his testicles from their suspension. Submerged. Washed. Baptized. Repeat.

He didn't know how long he'd been asleep in the sand and basking in the sun. It could have been an hour and it might have been fifteen minutes, but it wasn't twenty years. The dark hair on his chest and stomach had always served as sunscreen, but he was feeling the first tinges of a burn on his face and shoulders. He readjusted his toasting genitals and flipped over on his stomach. Sand had stuck to his backside, and he brushed off the spots he could reach. A breeze coming off the water pushed a ball of dried seaweed past him and up the beach like a tumble weed. He propped himself on elbows and his eyes followed the seaweed's path into the accumulated driftwood at the edge of island's the tree line. In the sun, the island made itself out to be a pretty sweet utopia—and Heritage even found himself flirting with the idea of building his own house in a place like this one day. In the next synapse, however, he remembered the tree ring of doll appendages, and this gave him a shutter in the sand that brought him back to his better senses. The wind picked up, and sand grains chased bits of sea foam and other dried seaweed balls up the slope of the scalloped beach.

Heritage was hungry, so he woofed down a squished power bar, washing it down with beaver juice—his new nickname for the rain-barrel water. On the wind, he thought he might be hearing voices—maybe hollering and hoots, and the bass beat of dance music, like you would hear at the Odyssey. Could this be another hallucination of his ever-twisting imagination, too? He sat up, and out of modesty, pulled his daypack and clothes closer to his naked body. This was followed by immediate paranoia and a sensation that he was being watched—that the forest had eyes and ears and a heavy breathing hunger that spooked him, regardless of whether the beast that stalked him was cerebral or truly carnivorous.

But the forest also had exquisite taste in dance music. The unmistakable banjo-and-violin stanza from Rednex's "Cotton Eye Joe" hopped from tree to tree, just as catchy and hypnotic as it had been when it pulsed out of giant speaker stacks at The Odyssey every Thursday night that previous summer. Heritage cocked his head and gauged that the music seemed to be coming from the other side of the headland, beyond where the black cottage was perched on the rocky cliff. He put his clothes back on sheepishly—just in case he were being observed, since he couldn't convince himself he wasn't—grabbed his mostly empty daypack, stuffed his outer shirt inside, and bounded up the beach in his shorts, flipflops and tank top toward the black basalt rockface that grew taller and more sheer the closer he got to it.

At its base, Heritage reached up to select his first handhold and promptly cut open his right palm on a mussel shell—just one jagged edge in a wallpaper sheet of mussels clinging to the lower rock that in his enthusiasm he had mistaken for the rock itself. Blood dripped from his clenched fist which he instantly submerged into a tide pool near his feet. He splashed his hand around until it seemed the bleeding had stopped. It was eerily calming to watch his blood swirl around in the saltwater but he recoiled when his blood appeared to activate the mint-green tendrilled anemones to awaken. He withdrew his hand before creating a *Little Shop of Horrors* sequel and returned to the wall in front of him. The black rock might have been a volcanic remnant but it wasn't obsidian. It was more likely part of the geological upheaval in the Cascadia subduction zone, that he'd read about, where the Pacific continental shelf was sliding and grinding under the much larger North American continental plate.

While scrambling straight up the six, maybe seven-metre high rock wall had seemed the most direct route to reach the cabin, it certainly couldn't have been the most practical or safest approach, but halfway up, Heritage was already committed to the ascent and determined to get on top. When he was maybe twice his height up the face of the rock, and too far to lower himself back down, he had to coax his limbs—and especially his throbbing, cut hand—to finish the job. Despite the bleeding that hadn't stopped, Heritage couldn't provide first aid mid-climb, though he did pause to marvel a moment at the contrast between the blood, his white hand, and the charcoal-black rock face, before pulling his body up the cliff even further.

Heights hadn't bothered Heritage as a rule, unless there was a very good chance of metal fatigue (roller coasters, ski lifts, observation decks, and airplanes) or a dangerous fall—but by the time he realized he was in trouble, it was usually too late. It was too late again. He was committed to reaching the top, and kept pulling, weight-shifting, clutching, and awkwardly turning-out his steps to stay tight to the wall until he succeeded. With one last knock of a kneecap on a rock that was jutting out further than the rest, and one last staccato expletive, he made it to the top. After inspecting his knee and his palm, he surveyed the comfortably safe height above the ocean on which the cabin was pinned, making the perch quite possibly untouchable by waves even in a bad storm. There was a reason the cottage had been the only one on either version of the island maps to be drawn using a triangle. There were only three sides to it, plus its floor—all triangles that when assembled, formed a pyramid. No, wait, he re-examined, as he walked around the outer deck. Since the cabin only had three sides to it, Heritage had to revise his descriptor. He was sharp enough to know that three sides made it a tetrahedron, technically. There was a triangular deck, an interior triangular loft, a triangular floor plan, and a triangular roof. The windows were salt-glazed, as he discovered when he cupped his hands to peer inside. He walked around to the forest side of the structure, where, true to apparent Wick protocols, he found an unlocked black door at the end of a more approachable boardwalk that extended out from the forest. He lifted the cast-iron hasp lock with his bloody palm and crossed the threshold for another opportunity to snoop, since these island cabins so far had each held a trove of clues for him. And with so much of his future, professionally and personally, hanging on the success of this mission, he believed that the more he knew, the more he could triumph.

Inside the cabin, he made several quick deductions. This was, or had been, Stephanie's cabin. A weathered slab of driftwood that was hand painted "First Mate's Cabin" was the first clue. In that second, he remembered that Dottie had referred to Stephanie's cabin by this name; had even said he'd see a sign with that name to know he was in the right place. Now, Heritage was thinking maybe this was where she intended him to bunk, and not in the garden shed he had been squatting in. In this cabin, painted black inside and out, photo frames had photos—of Stephanie, of Stephanie with her Mum, of Stephanie in a group photo with other women (one of whom Heritage thought could have been Mona from the bakery, but at a much younger age). There was a frame that had either fallen over or been turned over on the countertop, and when he lifted it, he saw it was a portrait of Stephanie and François during happier, more carefree times. He placed his thumb on the glass to cover Stephanie's egotistical smirk and studied François' face and his smile with that off-colour tooth. He leaned back against the angled wall, yearning to be delivered from his melancholy when it came to his feelings about that man. With his straight, long, brown hair and expressive eyes, François looked as though he were happily in love or at least smitten with Stephanie when the photo was taken. But Stephanie looked bored, almost irritated. She had appeared bored and irritated during her brief encounter with Heritage, too—and that's *when* they were having sex, so maybe François and Heritage were equally good at pissing her off. Some people were oddly that way—trudging miserably through their lives and wanting to be anyplace other than where they stood. Maybe Stephanie had already been plotting to run away to Chile or Argentina in this photo. It was clear she didn't want to be photographed. Heritage set the photo on the shelf standing back upright. François was too beautiful a specimen to be left face-down. And that's when he noticed the thumb print and a pad of blood he'd just left on the glass. He lifted the front of his tank top and gave it a clean or at least a good smear. He looked around for a band-aid or a cloth he could wrap around his hand but his search was commandeered by the stunning view from the large windows to the open ocean beyond the outer rocks and the waves that had traveled across the open Pacific from Hawaii—or maybe Kamchatka, more likely.

Now *this* was a cabin and perched strategically on this cliff—it was modern and with its double pane windows and clearly solid construction, it felt fortified. Heritage decided to lay claim and seize the castle; to sleep there tonight as a trial and maybe the next couple nights too, before shifting to The Headlands. He could get used to this view and the constant rumble of the surf below that he was feeling in his feet and legs as much as he was hearing outside. He climbed a sturdy ladder to a triangle-shaped loft open to the main floor below. This added height revealed an even more impressive view and explained why the windows went all the way to the peak of the roof on two sides of the steeply vaulted walls that culminated at a point and not a ceiling. He couldn't stand or even sit fully upright on the double-size mattress that commandeered the entire loft, without knocking his head—but the view was euphorically mesmerizing—he imagined that at night, under the stars, it would be like the cockpit of a space capsule. He could definitely be convinced to stay another night or two on Wickaninnish Island now, at this new base camp. Maybe if Dottie hadn't been so rushed and distracted, or maybe if she cared about him, she would have taken more time and provided more specific directions to ensure Heritage had landed in the right place. He could already appreciate how Stephanie must have needed to create more distance away from her mother, as she had gotten older and more independent. She must have daydreamed of this island-wide separation since she had even diagrammed it on the back of the door to her little cabin shed. Staking her cabin there on this cliff, above an otherwise pristine beach, must have been a gutsy move, and was likely met with some opposition by the other island shareholders who might have wanted to keep the beach common, undisturbed. Not that Stephanie struck him as a woman who gave a shit about what other people thought, but he bet she had made concessions in her design to ensure her building blended into the landscape and didn't take anything away from it. Even Heritage hadn't seen it during his first ten minutes on the beach.

It was swelteringly warm in the loft at the peak of that pyramid of a cabin, and the heat begged Heritage to crash a while on the mattress, gazing out over the ocean from atop his own private lighthouse. Cleverly repurposed, there were two side-by-side built-in air vents in the headboard side of the loft on the only wall of three that wasn't windowed—both of these vents were recycled turn crank venting windows from the ceiling of a camper or travel trailer. He had to put in extra muscle on the first turn to unstick the seals, and a few pine needles dropped to the pillows below, followed almost immediately after by his own head falling to the pillow. Heritage could really hear the music now with the square windows cranked open—the song now playing from somewhere on the other side of that promontory was *What is Love* by Haddaway. He would check that out next, but first . . .

The smells and sounds of the surf slamming into the rocks was a masterclass in pure method relaxation and the sea breeze freshened the loft to the optimum degree for a quick catnap.

DOCTOR FEELGOOD

Stephanie had never been crazy about air travel, though she did it at least perennially since jet engines tended to be the best way to get far away fast from her overbearing mother and the Clayoquot Sound brand of island life that—while pretty damn idyllic—could sometimes feel suffocating and had always been entirely too gene-pool shallow where she craved a deeper end. Bali, Sri Lanka, Tasmania, Belize, Madagascar, Fiji, Thailand, Vietnam, Croatia were all stamps in her passport, but this would be her first foray into South America and the caballeros who inhabited it.

Given the way she'd slipped out of the sound leaving so much unresolved with her mother and with François, Stephanie was already having second thoughts about this year's migration. She was sitting in the gate area at Vancouver International Airport, anxiously bouncing her right leg looking like a junkie or a drug runner, waiting to board the first of four flights that would deliver her as far south of the equator as she was starting out north of it, before the end of a very long day. She'd just spent three unsatisfying days laying low at her Uncle Lyle's townhouse in Gastown. Normally, she would have been able to debrief the summer season with her Uncle Lyle and embark on her next adventure with a scrubbed mental slate, but he'd apparently been tied up with some ballet troupe from England all week and hadn't really been around to function as her couch-side analyst. In his defense, she had shown up days earlier than he'd been expecting her. In almost all of her previous years, she had counted on Lyle—who wasn't really her uncle—but always seemed to know just how to help detoxify her at the end of each summer so that she wouldn't leave British Columbia so angry. His wise counsel had been the key to her returning home each spring, sufficiently missing her rainforest and with a reborn willingness to try once again to reconcile with her mother so they could amicably tackle yet another busy summer together in business in Clayoquot Sound. When he was on Wickaninnish Island, Lyle was the miracle worker living next door just a stone's throw north of her cottage at Big Beach—the one who could gently patch up anything that needed mending. Except he was never there on Wick, when she really needed him. As Uncle Lyle aged, Stephanie, in recent years more often than not, had needed to steal away to Vancouver for her tune-ups. She guessed it wasn't meant to be for this trip and she'd need to find another way to get her oil changed.

Stephanie loved her uncle and had adopted him as her surrogate family—not because he needed adopting, but because Stephanie sure did. When Lyle Hudson wasn't playing uncle, psychologist, and father figure to Stephanie Bard, he was a very busy, in high demand medical professional. For decades, he'd been the licensed doctor of choice by rock and movie stars who found their concert stops or filming gigs in Vancouver were made less painful and usually much more psychedelic after a visit to his Gastown office or an occasional backstage house call by *Doctor*

Feelgood, as those in the know had addressed him throughout the '70s. A drug-scene pioneer, himself, just a decade earlier, Lyle had volunteered for LSD acid tests while in medical school, and later became revered by those whose lives he'd saved inside the free medical tents he would voluntarily set up at rock concerts and festivals to treat overdoses. He became a sought-after underground expert on LSD dosage, and his nickname stuck through the '80s, just as the Vancouver movie scene and Hollywood North came into vogue.

He'd told Stephanie so many dose-and-tell stories, she couldn't keep the celebrities straight, but she knew every one of his tales had been accurate and true. He never let his own celebrity go to his head and stayed out of trouble, always true to his principled, organic Manitoba upbringing. You just knew that about Lyle, though you would never suspect he had been a dealer—facilitator had been his preferred title—by looking at him. Stephanie loved that unsuspected edge the most about her humble uncle. There was some evidence on display in his cabin on Wick but much more cramming the shelves and bulging out of the drawers in his Gastown home in the form of autographed mementos from *the grateful cured*—as he called his clients. That collection of signed photos and thank-you notes was probably worth a fortune and Stephanie had jokingly convinced Lyle to leave it to her so that she could set up a trendy little curio museum after he passed. The rock legends and movie stars and starlets were impressive, but Stephanie had always been much more impressed by the other little-known aspect of his earlier life as one of the original founders of Greenpeace. Most people weren't aware of those credentials either, and Lyle never boasted about them. He drifted in and out of people's consciousness just as he had always drifted in and out of his own—courtesy of the hallucinogens and sundries he prescribed others and regularly skimmed for himself. Long before Stephanie had realized she needed this quirky old man in her life, even before Lyle became a Wickaninnish Island shareholder, he had been a maverick chemist-turned-pharmacist, putting himself through med school.

There had been two stories in particular that he told her that made her wish she had been around as an adult contemporary of his in that cerebrally enlightened, patchouli-doused transition between the late '60s early '70s. Apparently, back then, Lyle had been one of three recently graduated single doctors who banded together with a lawyer named Curtis McLeod to purchase an upscale house in Deep Cove. After their swinging bachelor pad became infamously known as the *Party Mecca* and began drawing disciples as well as the scorn of the North Vancouver Police Department, the four began casting around for more remote investments into which they might sink their pooled salaries and playboy mentalities. The lawyer had just helped a California client acquire an entire island offshore from Tofino—and thought the other bachelors should buy into it. But of course, they needed to see it, get a sense of its energy vibe first. So in March of 1969, into an aqua blue Ford Mustang Boss 302 they piled—destination: Wickaninnish.

Lyle told Stephanie that after driving for hours over a gravel logging road, they finally reached the coast in the middle of an horrendous wind and rainstorm that had knocked the power out and washed out the road in several spots. Curtis had been driving, as it was his car, and mistook a sign he had barely seen in the headlight beams as the turn-off to Wickaninnish—which happened to be the name of the island they were headed for, but was also the name of an already rustic-looking beachside inn, though it had only recently been erected. When they pulled up in that Mustang out front, the innkeeper—a guy by the name of Robin—invited them inside and told them they couldn't get any further on the road in that storm. Lyle had taken one look around the place and agreed on the spot to buy into it, thinking that inn on the beach had been what Curtis had driven them all that distance to see. To celebrate what Lyle had thought was happening,

Dr. Feelgood opened his black leather doctor bag and passed out large LSD tabs to everyone—including the other dozen-or-so guests who had huddled in the main open-timbered space around a massive fireplace to wait out the storm. Lyle couldn't exactly remember what happened next, but said he managed to climb up into the rafters of that massive room and spent the night up there tripping while an acid-fueled orgy broke out on the furniture and floor below him.

Stephanie loved to romanticize that story and longed for a renaissance of free-loving times that she had missed. That mystical nirvana was really what she had been chasing her whole adult life. In reality, she was heading to Patagonia now to look for it there. Unfortunately, she was leaving without the attitude adjustment her uncle usually helped her achieve before any big change in her life. Just thinking about him and replaying his stories in her head gave her enough connection to know she would be okay. Stephanie twirled the bracelet on her left wrist—a woven lanyard of old sailcloth that held indescribable sentimentality for her. It always reminded her about the second most fascinating thing about her Uncle Lyle—the tale she truly cherished—and that was his Greenpeace creation story.

In 1971, after buying into Wickaninnish Island and building the first floor of his cabin there just north of Big Beach—with the help of his new hippie buddy, Robin, from that other Wickaninnish-named establishment, who also happened to be a carpenter versed in West Coast timber-framing—Lyle had gotten himself sweet-talked onto a mackerel fishing boat headed to Alaska. The fisherman captain who had been so persuasive was the now-dead, ex-husband of Sharon, the Californian who had first purchased Wickaninnish Island before being convinced by Curtis McLeod she should sub-divide it. Stephanie could never remember what his first name had been and never met him as he'd died while she was very young. Anyway, the captain and a few of his fishing pals had decided something had to be done to stop a planned five-megaton nuclear test in the North Pacific. His quickly recruited skeleton crew of radical ecologists had decided they needed a doctor onboard—and a pharmacist would come in handy to combat the seasickness, or to ease the discomfort of hangovers and bad trips. Bearded and longhaired, prairie-born Lyle hadn't thought twice about signing on to the adventure even though he'd never really been on a boat in his life—except for BC Ferries or to cross the channel to Wick from Tofino. He threw a *Gone Nuking* sign on his medical practice door and set sail from Vancouver on the *Phyllis Cormack,* on September 15—a member of the crew of hippies who dubbed themselves the Children of the Campaign for Nuclear Disarmament.

Along the way, the boat's name got changed to *Greenpeace*— and an international environmental movement was forged. Lyle and his fellow sailors didn't stop the nuclear test, but they did unintentionally delay it. In an attempt to raise morale among the energy-sagging crew as they navigated a series of nonsense coordinates they'd been counter-fed by the US Navy to send them off-course, Lyle had been playing Beethoven's Fifth and the Moody Blues at full volume on a battery-powered cassette player positioned too close to the compass in the boat's helm. Doctor Feelgood's all-night pep rally on the floating Party Mecca caused the compass to malfunction, knocking them even further off course by another fifty nautical miles. This maneuver confused the pair of US Coastguard ships that had been tailing the *Phyllis Cormack* at a distance, and they lost track of her while working to sweep the detonation zone clear of civilian boat traffic. The nuclear blast was delayed by several days as a result, until a Hercules transport plane was scrambled to locate the trawler confirming it was far enough out of the blast zone that the test could proceed.

Stephanie knew that the Greenpeace Foundation had been formally established in Vancouver eight months later, prompting Lyle to take even more time off from his medical practice to open a sister office in England before jumping back on a Greenpeace ship headed for the South Pacific—this time to protest French nuclear testing. It had been this dashing in and out of danger—and the drugs he took to cope with the fear and stress of getting caught—that had aged his face faster than normal living, though he kept his boyish haircut and was often mistaken from behind as a teenager. Her Uncle Lyle still thrived on adrenaline, real or synthetic, and he wasn't out to win any beauty pageant. He could be as nurturing as he was aloof, and since Stephanie hadn't gotten many breaks in her young life, he fawned over her, making sure she had a hideout when she needed one, and money for her travels, her clothes, and her boats.

She sure could have used one of his pep talks now. Where in the hell had he disappeared to right when she needed him most?

Heritage sat bolt upright, smashing his head against the steeply angled wall. He had dozed off for ten, maybe twenty minutes on the sunlit mattress in the loft of Stephanie's cabin. He had been dreaming that he was being chased through the woods by an angry mob of villagers. It took him several seconds to remember where he was, and how he'd arrived there. He wiped the drool from his forearm, rubbed his forehead with his cut palm, and checked for blood on the pillow before heading back down the ladder to the main floor of the cabin. He thought to check the cupboards for food before departing, in case he didn't make it back. He shop-lifted a few cans of tuna and a package of dried seaweed used for—he didn't know—making rice-less sushi, he supposed. He tossed the provisions in his daypack and stepped outside.

Distant clouds had gotten closer, and a stronger breeze had arrived. With it, autumn seemed to have hitched a ride. How could it have gone from summer to fall during an afternoon cat nap? And then, there it was again—the music. This time, he recognized George Michael's "Freedom" sailing over the rocks and through the trees. Still holding his head and detecting a slight bump starting to emerge, Heritage left the triangle cabin, secured the latch, and this time, used the level boardwalk that linked the cabin to the treeline that fringed the edge of the island.

There, he ducked back into the forest, traveling on a steeply inclining trail that immediately veered north paralleling the coastline toward the music and the celebratory hooting he could now pick out from among the music, surf, and wind sounds. Humans, Heritage deducted like some hopelessly optimistic Gilligan, meant rescue, and he perked up quickening his stride. The composition of trees changed again—the trail climbed under a canopy of more dwarfy and contorted Sitka spruce across a forest floor that was mostly dried pine needles. Salal didn't grow there, perhaps on account of the salt spray or maybe the tree litter. Light streaming through the trees and the sound of rock-stopping waves intensified on his left, informing him he was on a cliff at a good height above the ocean.

Heritage could make out the sounds of male voices by the time he rounded a curve in the trail, and realized he was no longer in the forest, but exposed on the edge of a steep rock face. He crouched down. His position was high above the ocean and next to a rim of a canyon gouged in the rocks to his right. The sea gushed through this gap to inundate tide pools and a lagoon, catching the sun's glare on the other side. As he looked up the cliff he saw, across the canyon at roughly the same level— seemingly hanging from the rocks but possibly safety-cabled to trees—another cabin. It was painted a disguising shade of green against the forest backdrop but still it perched there, however precariously, all by itself, out in the open.

Heritage scissor-stepped backward until he was under tree cover. There, to his astonishment, he took in the sights and sounds of a beach party at full tilt, but without a beach. A half-dozen men, most lanky and tall like he was, climbed on the rocks and hung from the cabin deck rails—none of them wearing more than briefs, and a few prancing around completely nude. Heritage wished he had a pair of binoculars or even better, an invitation. Had his favourite dance club, The Odyssey, gone on location in the rainforest for a special jungle-themed event or was some pop star recording a music video in the absolute middle of nowhere?

Suddenly he was distracted by a movement behind a tree trunk higher up the slope, above the cabin. What he spotted there seemed even more out of place than the dance party. He stared until his eyes watered. And just when he was about to blink, a creature jiggled some salal and darted between tree trunks—a creature that looked about the age and stature of Satan with an A.

Heritage was brand-new to island surveillance and neighbourhood watch—whereas any evidence of humanity departing from or landing on the shore was not likely to escape Aidan's adolescent attention. Heritage consulted the map from his back pocket. It appeared there was a trail that quite possibly led straight from Mona and Aidan's place to this cabin. At least from his drawing it also looked like the trail he was on continued down the cliff to pop up on the other side of the gap near the green cabin. Heritage scanned the shore and couldn't see any evidence of a boat. He took that to mean the shirtless crowd that both he and Aidan were staking out had crossed over land from the other side of the island. The teenager had probably followed the arrival of these latest invaders with his pirate telescope and had then scrambled out of his cabin and escaped his boredom to track the all-male platoon as it marched across the island. Landing any boat between the rocks in ocean surf struck Heritage as daredevil foolish. Looking straight down from the elevation of her pointy black loft, Heritage was even more certain that Stephanie might have been able to time a break in the waves to scoot between the rocks at the top of her beach with her zodiac, but he would have to see that stunt to know if it were possible.

There was one man in the group, milling about the deck, who

didn't have his shirt off—a white breezy number that looked like a Cuban guayabera with its untucked, straight hem. When he turned around to gesture to one of the other attendees with an arm that swept the horizon from left to right, his face was visible to Heritage and revealed, even from that distance, that he was quite possibly twice as old as those he entertained. He must have been the cabin's owner—why else would he be so different from the others, who all looked like GQ models? Heritage thought he could even make out the man's wrinkles, suggesting he had probably gotten the maximum out of life as this successful dance party in progress only bolstered. Heritage grinned, gave a little salute from under his tree cover, and sent him a silent cheer from the cliff—for earning his lines and for being interesting enough that so many beautiful creatures would want to be around him.

Had Stephanie been there to act as Heritage's guide as he toured around the island, she could have scanned this scene and instantly explained it for him. She'd have told him that Lyle Hudson didn't drive a boat, didn't even care to learn how, but certainly had the means to hire any driver who was open to his brand of tender since he never carried cash. Usually they got paid in mushrooms, cocaine, ecstasy, LSD, occasionally strong painkillers or some other fancy, city-sourced pharmaceuticals. This compensation also usually guaranteed there was no shortage of volunteers who would take the navigational risks to get Lyle on and off the island while putting up with his eccentricities, not to mention his hypochondria. Though he would eventually see it for himself, Stephanie might have also pointed to a good-size tree growing out of the cliffside just below the cabin, where she would have recognized a local. She would have explained that the day's boat driver, Marcel, was a case in point. For the past decade, Marcel had been Lyle's favourite high seas chauffeur—next to Stephanie, of course, who had also boat-pooled Lyle and his ever-changing entourage back and forth, or shuttled them to the Hot Springs. She'd suggest that Marcel, who was lying buck naked in the sun, draped like a napping cheetah over a low limb of that fir tree, had probably passed out from Quaaludes.

To Heritage, that tree looked as though it had grown out horizontally from the cliff for its first fifty years before shooting straight vertical in its second fifty. Stephanie would postulate with some accuracy that Marcel must have been easily persuaded by Lyle and his half-dozen British guests (Heritage could hear the accents for himself) to join them for a lazy, druggy, Sunday afternoon dance party. It wouldn't have taken much arm-twisting, either. Marcel, Stephanie would add, was a money-grubbing workaholic and had probably needed a day off after the summer he'd had, and so instead of dropping the passengers at the cut on the island's east side, he'd anchored his boat not far from Mona's place, and helped porter the party supplies across the Trans-Island Express Trail—or the *TET*, as Stephanie and the other islanders called it. Marcel had surely been rewarded on arrival at the cabin, most likely with a "ten-strip"—1000 micrograms of LSD, the scientifically precise dosage that Lyle would have said he had personally calculated for a man of his body weight, stature, and metabolism. As part of his flirty examination routine—though her Uncle Lyle falsely claimed to be of no particular sexual orientation at the same time she knew he had long nurtured a crush for Marcel—it would have been absolutely essential to the dosing for Lyle to first see the boat driver as naked as his modesty would allow. This is why both Aidan and Heritage, behind their individual blinds, were able to admire the tanning nude cheetah with an arm and leg dangling on either side of his branch. This was also why nobody else at the party, except Lyle, was wearing much more than a sun visor or a beach towel. And that might have been the extent of the general explanation that

Stephanie could interpret at a glance from Heritage's spy stoop had she been there. Heritage was glad she wasn't.

As for the pedigree of this mostly naked and cavorting cliffside crew—from the curly haired one in a mini-skirted sarong liberally applying sunscreen to their boat driver's unresponsive body, to his four friends on deck who appeared obliged to interpret with dance whatever song came next in rotation, to a slightly shorter, compact-muscled blondie already passed out inside the cabin who Heritage could not see from his vantage—these flawless, athletic creatures comprised the male dance corps of the Royal Ballet Company. They had either been rescued or (depending on who was writing the police report) kidnapped by Dr. Feelgood at the donor reception that followed their two performances of *Le Corsaire* at the Queen Elizabeth Theatre. The company had been given a free day before departing Monday morning for the next stop on their North American tour, which is the only opening Lyle—already a generous patron of the ballet and opera—would have needed to overwhelmingly convince six of the finer males to make a day trip with him. He would have promised them an all expenses paid and all muscle aches medicated drive to his cabin located in the middle of a real rainforest, vaguely promising to have everyone back to their hotel rooms by midnight (but more likely sunrise). So, into his Lincoln Continental the six dancers had piled. Lyle's dispensary had been thrown open during the ninety-minute ferry crossing from Horseshoe Bay to Nanaimo, which insured that nobody would complain of cramped anything during the three-hour sardine-packed road trip that followed from Nanaimo to Tofino.

"Why don't you take a picture? It'll last longer," Aidan blurted out after creeping up on Heritage from behind, dislodging him from his crouched position. The sudden startle nearly launched Heritage over the side of the cliff, but he snatched a shrub with his cut hand, just in time.

"Shit, Aidan!" Heritage whisper-yelled, his heart still kettle-drumming within his ribcage.

"You seem to be enjoying what you're seeing down there. Betcha wanna join them, don't you?"

Heritage fixed a stern, squint-eyed stare into the eyes of the kid—who, while not as tall as Heritage, had an upslope advantage. "Nothing escapes your watch, does it, Aidan? Why aren't you in school, anyway?"

"Because it's Sunday, you dork!"

Heritage had lost track of the days. "Where's your Mum? Does she know you are running all over the island?"

"Where's *your* Mum?" Aidan fired back.

"She's dead," Heritage said, sinking to a fourteen-year-old level of discourse. There was silence for a moment while Satan with an A came up with his next move.

"Hey! Up here!" Aidan yelled, standing directly behind Heritage and waving his arms in giant arcs—which appeared, from the distant dance party, to be Heritage's arms, waving for attention.

"Heya!" came an enthusiastically shouted response from across the rock canyon that temporarily separated them. "Come join us!" It was one of the British males bellowing from the deck, while the other dancing men launched into a re-energized round of *woot-woot* in time with the disco beat.

Before Heritage could turn around to strangle Aidan, the teenager had disappeared back into the darkness of the forest. Heritage reluctantly waved, using his own arm, and began descending carefully down the skinny cliff trail. He dropped the last metre when the trail abruptly ended, and he splashed down into the streamlet below. His timing was synchronized with an ocean wave surge that came up the narrow rock canyon at the same moment, drenching his cargo shorts. The surge retreated and Heritage ran across the pebbles, seaweed, and sand to gain elevation on the rock wall on the other side—pulling himself, embarrassed and soaked, up the rock, to a landing about ten metres below the cabin deck.

"Come on up," one of the men hanging over the balcony encouraged, with his enticing British accent. As Heritage came into reach, the dancer extended his shirtless and well-defined long arm to pull the new arrival onto solid construction. When the fellow didn't let go of his hand, Heritage rushed out an introduction.

"I'm Heritage," he announced, absent-mindedly using his full name and turning the grasp into a handshake.

"I'm Benji," the man still attached to his hand responded, oddly not offering to introduce the others who had joined in a dancing circle around them. "We're from London, baby!" He cheered and the dance floor exploded, compelling Heritage to join in. It would have been rude not to, as it was also apparently rude to keep his shirt on—his only dry article of clothing. He was aided in the shirt removal, and all the hairless dancers gasped, then fawned over his hairy torso but nobody seemed to know what should be done about the wet pants. Heritage was still leaving wet sandal prints where he danced on the deck, which prompted another dancer, who was only wearing his pouch underwear, to remark,

"You're soaked, mate!"

"And circumcised," said another, licking his lips.

Heritage started to explain. "Misjudged the depth of—"

And then a pair of hands were working to release the button at the waist of his shorts. *And isn't this just how half of all gay porn movies begin?* Heritage was thinking, as he stepped out of the lowering shorts. He was blessed by genetics and hard work and so never minded stripping down. He looked down to the naked man draped over the tree branch and then up to the tree line on the cliffs that surrounded the cabin, keenly aware that there was a pair of adolescent eyes up there watching everything. Instead of choosing shyness, Heritage decided he would become part of the show. He knew he stood out, whether up close or at a distance—and he reveled in a bit of exhibitionism from time to time. He could slip into this batch of beautifully formed adult bodies and be instantly accepted—while Aidan was likely masturbating himself raw in the kiddie section of the woods. Heritage figured that, as Sundays went, this one was probably banner for the kid, providing memories and jack-off material to last maybe the rest of his formative years.

That's when the older guy in the Cuban-looking shirt awkwardly dance-walked his sixty-something body through the open French-style doors of the house. The arrival of a prom chaperone might have killed the gyrations and the dirty dancing at any other venue, but here, the host was incorporated into the choreography as the belle of the Ball. He instantly cozied up to Heritage—who was bouncing around in his white Calvin Klein briefs like a taller, much hairier Marky Mark.

"I don't remember stuffing you into my car this morning," Lyle said, lifting his mirrored sunglasses high into his full head of straight, brown-and-gray streaked hair. Heritage didn't understand, and so smiled quizzically back at him. Lyle continued. "This is my cabin—I'm Lyle Hudson and welcome to the Party Mecca. And you are . . . ?"

The dancer named Benji who had welcomed Heritage to the party squeezed his sweaty body and banana underwear pouch between them, and took over the introductions. "This here is Heritage," he said, stretching out every one of his vowels.

Lyle placed a cigarette-stained hand on the dancer's right pectoral, and groped him there for a creepy five seconds before using the same hand to push him aside, in one connected movement to reach and shake the hand of the newcomer. *"Enchanté,"* he said, taking and examining Heritage's hand in his own. "Let me give you a tour." He practically sang the words, still not letting go of Heritage's hand.

"Don't tie this one up too long, now," warned another of the British dancers, who had momentarily stopped dancing, took a drink from his water bottle, and was looking Heritage up and down. "Something this beautiful absolutely needs to be shared."

"Oh, do hush," Lyle reprimanded, sounding as though he were affecting a London accent of his own. He led Heritage inside the opened doors, and once on the other side of the speakers that had been angled outward to the dance deck, the two could actually hear each other much better. Heritage's eyes adjusted to the darkness as he looked up to the steeply pitched ceiling. It started low in the back—near the kitchen with its counter and shelves crammed with mismatched dishes, stacked coffee cups, and pots— and rose to the open second story that was filled with a giant, suspended cargo net. Just then, the day's catch in that net shifted and turned over onto his stomach, adjusting his half-hard penis to stick through the links in the rope. Lyle reached up and gave the uncircumcised handle a tug. "Go ahead. It's good luck." Heritage—wanting to be a respectful guest in Lyle's home—followed suit to demonstrate he wasn't shy. The netted treasure groaned in ecstasy—which is what he was on, Lyle revealed a second later, though it was also "cut with Viagra. I don't see the point of being on MDMA without being able to get a hard-on, do you?"

"I don't have a ton of experience with drugs," Heritage said— but might as well have just put his tongue out, since his admission in front of a free-wheeling pharmacist almost begged for more experience.

"What is your mood right now," he asked, "and what do you want to do with that mood—say twenty minutes from now? Surely you want to be totally in a party mecca mode like the rest of us, no?"

"Uh, my mood right now is curious, but cautious. I suppose I wouldn't mind feeling a tiny bit more uninhibited in life generally, but that likely requires a lengthier analysis and perhaps a lon-ger-term prescription than what you're offering." He scrunched up his face indecisively.

"Atta boy! It's your lucky day! I am a doctor and a pharma-cist, so you are in good hands. What are you, eighty kilos?"

"About that."

Lyle opened his antique and very worn black doctor's bag while Heritage scanned the few metal-framed and faded photos propped up on the shelves around the kitchen. There was one of a much younger Lyle with his arm around what looked like Yasser Arafat. That was random, Heritage thought. But then a dance party on a cliff on a mostly uninhabited island at the western edge of Canada was also random.

"What's your story, Heritage?" Lyle said while he opened the pharmacy. "And whatever you say, just don't tell me you're here because you have ties to Dottie Bard."

"Uh—" Heritage managed an empty syllable before Lyle cut him off.

"I see. Well—tell me more, and maybe I will just overlook that."

Heritage appreciated the pass. "You can call me, Tage. I go by the shortened version of my name among friends," he flattered the host but wasn't sure why.

"Why don't you go by Heri, then?" Lyle asked, placing both of his aged hands on his newly arrived guest's torso. "Because hairy, you most definitely are!"

Heritage knew he was blushing. "I arrived from Vancouver last Thursday. I am here to consult over the next four to six months with Brad Fraser at the Headlands Lodge."

"Shit!" Lyle wailed dramatically. "That was the other name you shouldn't have mentioned in my presence."

Heritage chuckled on the outside, panicked on the inside. "Strike two then?"

Lyle screwed up his wrinkled face. "I don't even know what sport that is, but you'll have to do better at playing it if you're going to win me over." The doctor's head nearly disappeared inside his bag, but he kept talking, albeit muffled. "Being adorable may not be enough to save your ass in this wilderness, Darling." Lyle carefully closed his bag with his right fist clutched and took an exaggerated look around to Heritage's backside. "Though even your ass is adorable, so you could still get on my good side if you have a sense for adventure."

"I . . . I do," Heritage stammered, not even sure what he was trying to qualify for anymore, though he certainly had no intention of having sex with Lyle. He couldn't contain his shudder at that thought.

"Okay, then." He held out his closed hand, indicating it held the medicine. "This should un-inhibit you, but there's a test."

"I usually excel at tests."

"That's good. Here, you will see that Doctor Feelgood has prescribed two pills." Lyle opened his weathered hand. In it, Heritage could see three pills—one blue, two pink. The pink pills each had a heart-shaped stamp. Lyle clenched his fist and said, "Follow me." Heritage did, back into the open living room space where they stopped underneath the snoring lump in the cargo net. Lyle pulled on the guy's uncut dick and carefully tucked the pills, one at a time, within his foreskin.

"Time for Heritage to go fishing," Lyle commanded. "With your hands tied behind your back."

Heritage knew what Lyle intended—he had put his mouth onto similar trophies before, and now he took this challenge as a modified pin-the-tail-on-the-donkey without the blindfold and only a facsimile of a donkey. He stepped up and vaguely apologized to the volunteer medicine cabinet. He was tall enough that he only needed to crane his neck to get under the prize. Watching the old doctor watch him, Heritage smiled, opened wide, and took the man's full penis, coming back into arousal thanks to the doctor's fiddling, into his mouth. His tongue went to work. It was a little like tying a knot in a cherry stem. The pills were neither hard to find nor difficult to extricate, and with one swallow after the other, Heritage had taken the doctor's orders. But he didn't stop there. It turned out, surprisingly to him too, that Heritage enjoyed being watched performing fellatio on a passed-out stranger, so he kept at it just to prove how uninhibited of a good sport he could be. The cargo began to moan and thrust. Benji and the other dancers had wandered in from the dance deck to see what had become of the new arrival, and Heritage's eyes grew wide, recognizing he was now pulling an audience along with him, but he had already committed himself to the hazing if it meant being accepted into the Party Mecca.

The blond man in the cargo net continued to squirm his beautiful body back to life. The next thing the highly focused Heritage could register about his own body was Benji's hands pushing down his Calvins, which dropped to the floor planks about the same time as Benji's knees. There, the Brit commenced a reciprocation on Heritage that the others cheered on. Lyle fumbled to light a cigarette, showing his large yellowed teeth in a big smile that couldn't be tamed.

Another of the dancers couldn't take observing one second longer, and surely but forcibly moved Heritage off his spot beneath the net, taking over the chandelier erection by saying, "Step aside, honey! I have wanted to get a taste and a bitter load out of this nasty, stuck-up prick since last season." The corps of ballet dancers gasped, as sexual relations between company members were a big no-no—but not one of them seemed able or willing to look away.

Lyle was so delighted that he couldn't stop grinning. Then he remembered he'd stashed a couple other pills—not in someone's foreskin, but between the ass cheeks of Marcel the water taxi driver, who was splayed over the tree trunk below the cabin. He clapped his hands quickly together to get everyone's attention. "If anyone is coming down, there are at least two more pills the Easter Bunny has hidden in the ass cheeks of our water taxi driver." Three of the dancers broke away and scrambled onto the deck and down the stairs like it were a screaming fire drill.

"Remember, no hands!" Lyle hollered after them.

Meanwhile, Benji took Heritage by the cut hand and led him out the back door and a ways into the woods behind the cabin, where the two kissed and pleasured each other for what seemed like languorous hours, during which Heritage's meds kicked in. The sounds of music and chattering accents became sublimated under the wind that had strengthened the sway of the branches overhead that let strobe flashes of sunlight dance about the forest floor all around them like a mirror ball had been suspended from the treetops. The nearby heave and crash of the ocean rocked the pair—Heritage and Benji—into a spooning, post-coital stupor. Their whole world had become stoned, courtesy of Doctor Feelgood.

Lyle had taken his cigarette out of the house and onto the deck above the churning froth that swelled like lungs wedged between the rocky, mussel-covered channels in the rocks below. With his afternoon sex party in its penultimate throes, he knew exactly what he needed before the long trip back to the city. He gathered some kindling, an old Georgia Strait newspaper, and a towel, and made his way down the rocky trail to the metal bathtub he and some hippie friends had cemented into place a decade back above a shallow grotto in the rocks. The tub was fed by an ancient garden hose that continuously diverted fresh, forest-filtered water from the tiny creek that emptied into the sea on the other side of his cabin. Lyle fished a chunk of driftwood out of the tub, and coaxed a small fire to life in the empty space under the tub, cigarette dangling off his lower lip the whole while. Sometimes it took forever for the water to heat, but Lyle's nerve receptors were mostly fried from decades of drug use, and the afternoon was hot enough already, though clouds were conspiring overhead to fix that in short order. He stripped down and took the plunge, releasing a string of curse words into the atmosphere.

Aidan hadn't stopped looking for the best seat in the amphitheater. At least once every summer he could count on Uncle Lyle—the ultimate impresario and curator of freaks—to bring at least one worthy spectacle to the island. When most of the afternoon's action had momentarily moved inside, Aidan had daringly crept into the open, keeping behind rocks, but getting closer and closer to the naked water taxi driver, whom he of course recognized as Marcel. He'd had plenty of run-ins with Marcel on the water and in town, but had never seen him naked, so this was an unexpected treat. He snuck right up close and could see him breathing. His skin glistened bronze with oils and his shoulder-length hair had mostly slipped out of its usual ponytail. Aidan followed the topography of his back over his butt and down his legs. He crouch-walked a few steps to get some height so he could see Marcel's nuts that looked like kiwis scrunching out from between his thighs. Aidan didn't need to coax his own erection, since he'd arrived with one. He was thinking he wouldn't mind seeing the rest of Marcel's equipment now that he'd gotten close enough to touch it—if only Marcel hadn't been lying, passed out, on top of it.

There was a sudden celebratory commotion coming from inside the cabin. It spilled onto the deck as three nearly naked men rushed down the stairs toward Aidan and the tree. He slipped back and behind a rock at the last possible second so as not to be detected. When he raised his forehead and eyes over the top of the rock, he could see the trio of men barreling over the rocks toward him. Aidan watched as they descended on Marcel like a pack of hyenas that hadn't eaten in days. *What the hell?* The three men seemed to be sticking their tongues and faces into Marcel's butt. There were grunts and shoves and a general frenzy happening less than three metres away from Aidan's hiding spot, and the teenager could not understand what he was seeing. Were they eating him alive?

All the attention on Marcel's crack proved to be the magic button that reanimated him—he was beginning to respond with his hips and pelvis to the pressures and tongue-probing underway. And then, as quickly as the men had descended on Marcel's ass, they cheered and retreated up the hill to disappear back inside the cabin. Aidan didn't know what kind of game they were playing, but he was jealous of all the fun they seemed to be having. He was jealous of Marcel too, though he didn't know why exactly. Maybe because he was naked, maybe because he'd just gotten his bum played with by strangers. One thing was for sure—Aidan was becoming more frustrated by the minute, feeling left out of the adult reindeer games. But he wasn't giving up. A naked Marcel was still within reach, and just needed to be turned.

Aidan looked around for a tool. He'd watched plenty of animal films at school and observed wildlife for as long as he could remember. As easily as other primates used sticks or blades of grass, or ravens dropped mussels and clam shells from a sufficient height onto rocks or pavement to break the shells open, Aidan, too, evolved on the spot to figure out how to get what he wanted. He started lobbing pebbles at first, trying to startle the sleeping man awake and into an upright position. But his projectiles either fell short or too lightly. The teen turned to larger pebbles and a piece of driftwood, which required more precision and heft. Fortunately, during the entirety of his summer holidays just ended—when he wasn't jacking off or religiously using the penis pump his Uncle Lyle had smuggled him for this last birthday—he had started lifting a set of iron dumbbells his Mum had picked up at a yard sale. He had been determined to return to school a bit more intimidating and physically developed than he had been, so that he could be the one pushing the scrawny, nerdy kids around, rather than being one of the pushed. He was already taller than anyone else in his class. He'd often been teased for getting held back a year or two in school, though that hadn't been the case. He was just physically maturing quicker for some reason. He'd just turned fifteen at the end of the summer—though he was still getting used to telling people his new age. He had started ejaculating after all, just as he'd started shaving, though he hadn't really needed to yet. His Uncle Lyle had casually mentioned in passing earlier that summer that it was never too early to start training your whiskers just like your desires—hence the thoughtful and timely penis pump birthday gift.

He lobbed another fair-sized pebble at Marcel and hit the side of his head. The boat driver swatted a hand at his face, but didn't jump up or turn over.

"Ninnish! Stop throwing rocks before you hurt someone," Lyle reprimanded from where he sat up to his neck in tepid but warming bath water. Aidan hated being caught, but he was red-handed, so he put his next rock down and scampered over the barnacles and tide pools below the cabin to greet his Uncle—who wasn't actually related to him.

"What were you trying to do?" Lyle said.

"I don't know," Aidan said. "I'm bored, and there's nobody my age to play with today."

"Where's Mason's boy?" Lyle took off his glasses to examine how dirty the lenses were. They were always dirty. He could barely see without them, and couldn't see well enough with them to know when they were dirty. Being red-green colour blind since birth (unless he was on acid), he recently hadn't been able to distinguish a set of traffic lights while driving on Pacific Boulevard because they had been mounted horizontally rather that vertically, and he hadn't committed the colour order of lights in that configuration to memory. This had landed him a traffic violation ticket, and because of his advanced age, an order to retake a driving exam.

"Rowan went to Vancouver this weekend with his Mum. Hey, that's Marcel hanging over that tree, isn't it?"

"Why—do you have a crush on him?" Lyle liked teasing the kid about his indeterminate sexuality, theorizing that if he normalized the homosexual option, the teenager wouldn't be consumed by thoughts that he was alone.

"No!" Aidan's denial was a bit too emphatic to be believable. "He's the only guy up there that I recognize. Well, and that newcomer, Tage, or whatever his name is."

"Tage?" Lyle took a few seconds to realize he must mean Heritage. "Right. What do you know about him? You usually have your ear to the ground for island gossip." He needed to keep shifting his ass cheeks now that the metal was heating up. Soon he would need to hang his ankles and wrists out of the tub to avoid touching the bottom with his bottom altogether. In winter, when storm tides were higher, his hot tub would be inundated by surf, that eventually dowsed his fire and cooled the water extending his bath.

"Well, I know he banged Stephanie," Aidan blurted out.

"She told you?" Lyle couldn't believe this, given the rather expert blowjob he'd just watched Heritage give to a complete stranger hanging in the net from his ceiling.

"She bragged about it to Dottie. Makes no difference to me," Aidan lied twice in that response.

"Where is he staying on the island, then?"

"How should I know?" Aidan snapped. "I'm not his travel agent!"

"Touchy subject with you, I can tell." Lyle moved into the ankle and wrist bum-suspension position as a breeze kicked up, supercharging the fire under his butt. He stared at the last patch of blue sky being swallowed up by clouds the colour of steel wool. "Weather's changing," Lyle announced. "Time to think about getting off this island and back to the ferry. I promised my guests to have them back to Vancouver by midnight."

"Yeah, I gotta go, too." Aidan was lying again. His mum had gone to Vancouver with Mason and Rowan for the weekend, but were expected back in Tofino before dark. He'd gotten out of the back-to-school shopping trip by faking a stomach-ache—like he had any use for new clothes. His mum had only agreed to let him stay behind, on the conditions he stayed home, cleaned his room, and didn't take the boat out—he'd violated all three conditions of his parole so far, plus some she hadn't even thought to spell out for him in advance. He'd been driving his Mum's boat since he was twelve, and the coast guard no longer bothered stopping or citing him anymore, since he was such a smart-ass, every bit as tall as most of them. Attempts to correct his behavior only made him more defiant. Raised without a father by a single, working mother was the usual explanation for Aidan Rye's juvenile rap sheet, which already included petty shoplifting, graffiti-related mischief, and exceeding the harbour's speed and wake limits. He wouldn't do hard time for any of these offenses, since his life without a father figure was usually considered by the authorities to have been hard enough.

Aidan bounded over the rocks like a mountain goat, paused to pick up another pebble that he tossed at Marcel's sunburned bum but missed, and disappeared up the cliff and into the trees in the direction of Big Beach. Lyle raised his pruned body out of the tub, dried off, and threaded his skinny limbs into clothes he had worn most of the previous week. It was time to gather up his ballet troupe for the long migration back to the city.

MARCEL'S MAYDAY

Heritage had no recollection of how long he had been standing there with his arms wrapped around that ancient cedar tree. There was a wet line of drool that traveled several centimetres down the trunk and he could feel the indentations on his cheek from having pressed his face into the contoured cedar bark. Had he been trying to make love to the tree? His arms, when he released the trunk, ached from cramps he tried to shake out, as he coaxed the feelings back into his numb hands. He was all questions and no answers. He looked down at his bulging underwear—stained by dirt, cedar, moss, and who knew what else. He smiled. He quite likely had experienced a wild and uninhibited romp, though he couldn't remember the better parts of it. Good for him! But now he had to be serious, because the situation called for seriousness. The weather had changed for the worse. He wasn't sure where he was, or where everyone had disappeared to, or whether what he thought had happened, had even been real.

He was pretty sure he had been abandoned in the woods, with a belly full of Ecstasy and a hard-on full of Viagra. The swelling in his briefs; his heightened sense of colour, sound, and smell; and the realization that despite being mostly naked, he wasn't at all cold, left no question about what he'd ingested. What was left of his wits told him it was to time to find his way back to his cabin before it got much darker. He stumbled a few steps in every possible direction—trying to pick up the path that had delivered him to that tree on that island in the Pacific Ocean somewhere in the Northern Hemisphere of a spinning planet that disoriented him. He was suddenly overwhelmed and sliding into a fully activated panic attack. Where was his map? Where were his shorts that had the pocket that contained the map? Where in the hell was that teenager?

"Fuck!" he yelled in frustration until his lungs emptied. Where was the sun? Where was the sound of the ocean? Where was his day pack and his shirt?

He turned to face the dim light in the trees, and guessed that direction to be west. He ambled off, zagging and zigging his nakedness through the underbrush and trees, until he reached a cliff and was able to spot the boardwalk a short distance to his right, bridging the rock ravine to Lyle's cabin. Relieved to recognize the landmark, he scurried toward it. There wasn't a soul or ghost. Doors and windows were closed though not locked, speakers had been brought back inside, the cargo net was empty, the tree branch was void of cheetahs, and the photo of Lyle and Yasser had toppled off the shelf, to lay face-down on the grimy counter. His pants, shirt, and daypack were all hanging from a single, crucifixion-size spike, sticking at an angle in an upright driftwood column that supported the roof, and higher up provided an attachment point for the cable that held the net in an opened and irresistible shape.

Heritage pulled on his shorts and shirt and added the 2nd shirt he'd balled up in the bottom of the daypack with the cans of tuna. The power bar wrapper was stuck to the back of his shirt, but he didn't notice it. Looking out over the dark grey water, he guessed the sun was about to reunite with the horizon behind those storm clouds. He wouldn't be able to go anywhere that involved dexterity or navigating the forest after dark—so he climbed the ladder to the net in the loft, curled into a fetal position, and swayed his still-altered self, fast asleep.

"Mayday! Mayday! Mayday!"

Heritage tried to sit upright, but the cargo net didn't give him enough leverage—which wasn't helped by his groggy inability to remember where he was. Outside, strong winds lashed the cabin, jiggling the entire structure on its posts. Heritage flailed and crawled in the net, trying to grab the fixed ladder along the wall. Beams creaked. A strip of metal flashing must have peeled back and was slapping against the metal roof like applause. The few branches he could see through the sliding glass door had bent and were being pinned backwards by wind. The much-amplified din of the breaking surf was louder than any sound Lyle's speakers could ever crank out—and all the while, it seemed as though a fire hose had been trained on the windows.

"May Day. . . May—" The moment he moved toward the radio in the kitchen, it crackled and went silent. Without a flashlight or candle, Heritage could not see a thing in the kitchen area, which was away from the front windows at the back or forest side of the cabin.

He wasn't dreaming—at least he didn't think so. He was pretty sure there must be a marine radio that had been left on somewhere in the cabin —but where? He knocked something off the counter with the protrusion in his underwear. And why in the hell did he still have a hard-on? It was chilly, like the inside of a walk-in cooler, and he didn't have any other clothes. He grabbed a musty Hudson's Bay blanket from a basket next to the wood stove and wrapped it around his shoulders. The insides of his nose began to itch instantly.

The radio crackled every once in a while, but not frequently enough that he could hone in on its location. He saw a beam of light bouncing around through the rain-streaked window—far away, he figured. But how far? He couldn't tell in the dark, without landmarks that would have been new to him anyway. If a boat were in trouble, he rationalized, there wasn't anything he could do—except perhaps toss it a life-saving boner. He pressed his unwavering manhood against the glass of the French doors as his eyes peered into the storm's abyss.

"This is the coast guard . . . to the vessel in distress, state your coordinates!"

Finally, Heritage found the radio and its microphone attached to the wall right next to the French doors—opposite the kitchen where he thought the radio sounds were coming. There was no response to the dispatcher's question. Heritage muscled one of the double doors open and held firmly to the handle in the strong wind to see if he could make out the source of the beam of light, still cutting through the airborne surf and fog like a lightsaber. The weather rushed inside. He could make out a small boat, maybe the size of François' aluminum *Lifetimer*. He heard the thud and scraping of metal against the rocks. *Oh, god*, he thought as he grabbed the microphone and pushed the transmit button.

"Coast guard—come in! Can you read me?" He tried to remember the right lines from all the *Airport* movies, plus *The Perfect Storm*.

"Yes, I hear you. This is the Tofino Coast Guard Station. What is the reason for your mayday? Give me your coordinates."

"I'm not in the boat—I'm in a cabin on the west side of Wickaninnish Island."

"Repeat—where?"

"Wickaninnish Island. W, I, C, K . . ." He started, then paused but didn't release the transmit button while listening for a response. Without acknowledgment, he continued. "I can see what looks like a boat near the rocks, and its searchlight is bouncing all over the place. I hear loud bangs and metal scraping. I think this is the boat that sent the mayday."

There was silence for another twenty seconds. Heritage wondered if he'd even pressed the microphone button before talking, and realized he had, but that he hadn't let go of it when he finished speaking.

The coast guard dispatcher came back on the radio. "This is Tofino Coast Guard Station trying to reach the boat in distress with the mayday. Please squawk your position. Repeat, please squawk your position."

Heritage stood there, holding the door open with a bare foot that was getting wet, the radio microphone in one hand and anxiously clutching his erection in the other. Maybe he should just butt out of this. Maybe he wasn't even able to transmit from that radio and it was just there to hear weather reports or—another explanation popped into his head—he was just doing it wrong. Maybe he was still high and hallucinating up in the cargo net, and this was part of his trip. The boat wasn't answering—or if it had, Heritage wasn't hearing it over the radio. A few more seconds went by. His eyes watered staring into the storm, trying to spot the boat or its searchlight, but both seemed to have been swallowed by the darkness, if not by the sea. Then, finally, the radio popped to life again.

"This is the Canadian Coast Guard Tofino Station attempting to reach either the vessel in mayday distress or the individual on Wickaninnish Island's west side. Do either of you read? Over." The male dispatcher voice sounded more frantic now. Heritage gave the boat a chance to respond first—but in the silence and with his heart racing, he pressed the microphone button and identified himself.

"This is Tage Carter. I am not on the boat in distress. I am in a cabin on the west side of Wickaninnish Island, just north of Big Beach."

"Carter—this is the Canadian coast guard station in Tofino. Can you see the vessel in distress from your vantage point? Over."

"I *could*," Heritage responded, getting used to the microphone. "At least I think I saw the light bouncing around from a boat. But I no longer see the light or the boat." He remembered to adopt the radio protocol he'd just heard the coast guard use, and added his own "over."

"Can you provide a description of the boat? Over."

"I can't. I can't see in this storm. It is pitch black and raining sideways in this wind. The beam of light and the sounds of metal scraping or hitting rock were the only signs that something— someone was even out there. Over."

"We have a cutter en route. Please stay on this channel and monitor for additional instructions. Over."

"Will do. Over."

And with that, Heritage was once again alone in the dark, in the storm. He began to wonder if a soul or souls had just perished in that tempest tossing itself against this barrier island to the continent. He sneezed twice in a row and cast off the ratty blanket, electing instead to build a fire in the wood stove. When he looked up from his smoldering kindling tower, he spied the red-and-white, well-lit coast guard boat bobbing in the agitated surf like a toy. Its searchlights jabbed about in the horizontal downpour like it was Hollywood movie premiere night. Heritage closed the wood stove latch and stepped outside the French doors to stand in the weather's onslaught at the edge of the deck railing, while his woodstove fire grew and began to illuminate the inside of the cabin like a beacon. A searchlight beam traveled up the rocky cliff face until it pulled Heritage out of hiding. He waved, but suspected that was more confusing than helpful. He wasn't a shipwreck survivor—he didn't want to give that impression, when others might really need to be rescued. He decided to jump back on the radio.

"This is Tage Carter again on Wickaninnish Island. The coast guard boat has arrived and is approximately in the last known position of the boat in distress. Over."

He waited. There was a brief crackling but no further sounds came from the radio. The coast guard boat moved south behind the headland and out of his limited range of view—and after five minutes, it had not returned. Heritage was stumped—and he was awake, completely now. If his help was needed from shore, he wondered if maybe he needed to get down there. But without a flashlight and in this storm, he could break his own neck on those rocks and wouldn't be seen or heard by anyone. The fire in the woodstove, on the other hand, might serve some locational purpose—a signal that somebody was there. Plus, he was wet again and shivering. He decided to stoke it full and keep it burning. But neither the coast guard nor the shipwrecked sailors showed or seemed to need his assistance.

Heritage had slipped back to sleep—this time on Lyle's sofa, which in the daylight, had more unidentifiable stains than he would have normally been willing to overlook. At some point during his slumber—likely when the woodstove and the storm outside burned themselves out—he had dragged that Hudson's Bay blanket back on top of his body.

"Hey! Anyone home?"

There was a rapid knocking on the cabin door. Heritage opened his eyes. It was light outside—calm but socked in by thick, immoveable fog. He bounced off the sofa like he'd been spring loaded. Fuck if he didn't still have a hard-on . . . now, that was embarrassing!

"Hello there!" Heritage greeted the intruder, rubbing his eyes with one hand, trying but failing to conceal his crotch with the other.

"Are you Tage Carter?" A dark-haired, dark-skinned, blue-uniformed man was standing there in a navy blue baseball cap with an emblem patch. He was slightly shorter than Heritage but bulkier, built like a gymnast. "I'm Matt Greene, acting captain from the Tofino Coast Guard Station. I also live here, on Wickaninnish Island—grew up here."

"Oh," was all Heritage could manage as he leaned forward to shake the handsome man's hand. "I am Tage Carter. I, uh—I am on the island at the invitation of Dottie Bard." As he spoke, he realized his words didn't explain what he was doing in Lyle's cabin. He also hadn't learned the lesson yet that dropping Dottie Bard's name hadn't been a great calling card so far—he would need to remember to stop doing that. "I was on Big Beach yesterday and heard music coming from Lyle's place. I popped over the headland to check it out and ended up joining a bit of a party in progress here."

"And you were on the marine radio last night reporting a boat in trouble out there on rocks," the captain said, pointing out the windows.

"Right. Yes. That was me—trying to help." Heritage felt oddly intimidated by the man, like this was an interrogation, like he was believed to have done something wrong or suspicious and that he should be very careful with what he said next. Then there was the boner factor. "Do you want to sit down?" he asked, grabbing the blanket off the couch to hold it in front of the scene-stealer as he sat down first.

The uniformed man kept standing despite the invitation and Heritage thought, with that square jaw and broad forehead, he might be native or Hawaiian. "That's why I am here. We found the boat. We know who it belongs to, but the owner is missing."

"Oh, Jesus!" Heritage felt a chill, thinking he may have seen and heard the final moments of someone's life play out in front of him. "I've been here four—no, five days now, and have only met a handful of people. I'm pretty sure I won't have any information that could help you."

Matt Greene looked around the cabin. "We believe the missing boater was here yesterday, at Lyle's party. His name is Marcel Labbé. He drives a boat for Turtle Island Water Taxi. We are recovering the boat, but we haven't located Marcel."

In a fixed stare out the window, Heritage rewound his memory back to the previous afternoon. The only guy he hadn't met—because the man was so out of it—was the fellow draped naked over the tree branch.

"Uh, I met Lyle here yesterday, and some ballet dancers from London. One of them was named Benji. Those are the only names I remember. I didn't meet any other locals yesterday." Heritage paused. "Wait. That's not true. Aidan was here yesterday too."

"Aidan Rye was at Lyle's party?"

"Not as a guest, no—but I caught him spying on the party from the woods."

"Yes, I see. That sounds like Ninnish, all right."

"Ninnish?"

The captain grinned, using only one side of his mouth. "Aidan is known as Wicked Ninnish around here. He can't keep out of trouble."

"Wicked Ninnish," Heritage repeated out loud. "Like Wickaninnish. Clever. And yes, I've already noticed that about him."

"So, you can't say as though you saw or met a Marcel Labbé here yesterday?"

"I'm sorry. I can't—at least not without a picture. And even then, well . . ." Heritage stopped short of incriminating either Lyle or himself.

"We have a statement from Jason, a floatplane pilot from Megin River Air—"

"Say," Heritage interrupted him. "I know Jason. He was the pilot that flew me here from Vancouver last week."

Matt nodded, then continued. "Jason said he bumped into Marcel on the dock last night, said he seemed to be completely out of it, but not in a drunk way. He said Marcel needed to get back to Wickaninnish Island because he thought he must have dropped his wallet near Lyle Hudson's place."

The mobile marine radio tucked into the leather holster on the captain's belt squawked to life with a burst of static.

"Captain, we've located the body. We are certain it is Marcel, and I am very sorry to report we can pronounce him dead—drowned, actually, here at the scene."

The so-far stoic Captain Matt Greene bit his lower lip, looked out to sea and pressed the microphone button clipped to the lapel of his red floater jacket. "Copy that. I'm coming down."

Heritage was stunned; both men in that living room were. Marcel must have been the water taxi driver that had ferried Lyle, Benji and the others to the island from town. Matt spoke first. "Marcel Labbé was a largely decent friend to me," he said, before closing his eyes a few seconds. "Anyway, this is a small town and I am likely to know the victim of any accident on or off the water."

"I'm sorry," Heritage offered, thinking the captain could use a hug, but with his erection and not knowing the man, he resisted. He was sorry, too, but only because he had been among the last to see a dead man alive—stoned and still. He felt connected and sad by association.

"Uh—procedure here calls for you to stop by either the coast guard station or the RCMP detachment in the next few days to provide a statement." Greene wiped his mouth with the back of his brown hand. "I'd offer you a ride back to town, but looks as though we will now be transporting the, uh, deceased, and procedure says . . ." His voice trailed off.

"Thanks—I understand," Heritage said. After an awkward minute, the coast guard captain tipped his head and backed out of the cabin.

Heritage rubbed the sleep and the drugged hangover from his heavy eyes and watched Matt scramble down the rocks and cliff trail to the cleft in the rocks that had permitted the coast guard boat to get in close at high tide. There, he joined three uniformed and red-jacketed colleagues. It took all four to pull the water-logged victim from the sea and onto the vessel's deck.

The needle on Heritage's freak-out scale had once again bounced into the red, warning him to question what in the hell he had gotten himself into with this Clayoquot experiment. As the coast guard vessel threaded its way through the narrow rock channel, and bucked through the outer waves to disappear into the fog bank, Heritage panicked. He remembered he'd left all his belongings drying on driftwood and rocks near Dottie's place, that his kayak's nose was busted, and that he was still stuck there on that island, unless he figured out a way to unstick himself. He also worried about the story he would tell the coast guard or the RCMP when he stopped by to give his statement. Would he mention the drugs? Would he admit to drugging too? Would his erection ever go away?

He grabbed his day-pack, secured the outer cabin door by dropping the driftwood paddle, and began jogging along the trail he'd assumed the dance troupe had used the previous afternoon. Within metres, he was back inside the gnarly, spooky forest, and panting heavily. Perhaps his lungs weren't ready for this sprint, but his adrenalin kept egging him faster. He came to a fork in the trail and in midair, chose the path leading to his right, believing he needed to head more south than east. Zigging, then zagging, then leaping and stumbling on tree roots, Heritage flew like a bat using sonar. It was exhilarating, until—

Thud!

The wind was knocked out of his chest. He picked moss out of his lips and propped his torso on his elbows to focus on the spot where his sternum had just landed hard. He lay diagonally on top of a rock-and-shell outlined path that was blanketed in a creeping lime-green carpet of mosses in a bit of a clearing in the woods. He slowly recovered his breath, and rose to his feet, where everything began to come into sharper focus.

It wasn't just the trail he had been on that converged there, but a series of five, distinct footpaths he could make out just under the moss and forest litter, that transected that clearing and then continued into the woods in five separate directions. At first, Heritage thought the under-moss lines looked like spokes spanning out from a hub that was the raised mound in the center he'd just fallen on top of, but when he brushed the leaves and pine needles away from a section of path, he found it was much more intricate than that. Scampering about like an anthropologist, he quickly determined that each of the trails were lined with fat, white shells, the tops of which the forest had stained green and brown with the passing of much time and the accumulation of who knew how many decades of debris. These bulbous shells would have at one time stuck out of the moss carpet like runway landing lights, except they had camouflaged with the seasons to blend into and were now disappearing under the forest floor. Heritage picked one of the shells up to examine it, shaking the packed dirt out of its opening. A chambered nautilus came to mind, and he remembered seeing shells just like this—though bleached clean white—on the bookcase at Dottie's place and on every other stair tread at Stephanie's triangle cabin. He replaced the shell precisely back into the moss, careful not to disturb the energy of what was clearly a sacred spot. Concentric circles of surf-rounded rocks wove in and out of the pathway spokes, and when he stood tall and squinted, Heritage could make out the faint outline of a pentagram. It was oriented upside down as he had has stumbled on it, but the paths criss-crossing there formed a star. Once he knew it was there, it was all he could see.

Wait a minute, he thought. There was a pentagram in a circle on the map on the back of the A-frame's door. He reached for his copy of the map in his back pocket, but it was gone. He checked all his pockets and the daypack, but no map. What? Had it just disintegrated when he got swamped by the wave gushing through the rock canyon below Lyle's place? Heritage shook off a shiver of fear.

He seemed to have stumbled into a manmade—or more likely

a witch-made—labyrinth. His heart thumped as he stepped in
to more closely examine that raised mound at the centre of the
clearing. Falling on top of it had dislodged the moss there and
Heritage focused on the point of impact where he could scarcely
make out the outlines of what appeared to be doll-heads. He
peeled back the moss like the skin of an orange to expose several
green Japanese glass floats that were stacked in offering on top of
the pedestal of doll heads. It had surely been one of these hardened orbs that he'd taken in the chest when he tripped there. He
pulled back the moss further to get a closer look at the doll heads
that lined the five sides of the pentagon that was the star's centre.
The largest was the size of his fist, but others were smaller, like
you'd find on a Barbie. Moving slowly around the mound on his
hands and knees, Heritage counted twenty-three doll heads that
had been masoned into the mud in varying degrees of dirtiness,
burial, and decay.

He couldn't resist dislodging one of the heads for closer examination, though he was fully aware it could trip a booby trap or
worse, cue the apocalypse, tinkering, as he was, at what could possible be the entrance to the Hell Mouth. The doll head was filled
with compacted dirt but a white shard of what must have been
quartz, caught his eye. He fingered its edges but quickly replaced
it inside the doll's hollow head along with the dirt, rubbed his
hands on his pants, and took a step backward. Standing too
quickly and remembering in that head-rush of a moment that the
ring of doll appendages sticking out of the bottom of the giant
cedar tree trunk was likely not far from this spot, Heritage knew
he went white.

Adrenalin washed through him again, triggering every flight-
wired cell in his body. A raven on a hemlock branch overhead
issued a low-register yodel, sounding like a wind-chime of broken
bones. Heritage raised his arms in supplication, signaling that he
meant no harm or disrespect to that sacred-to-somebody place,
and that he would be leaving immediately. The raven swooped

down from its branch straight toward him and the centre of the mound. At the last moment, Heritage ducked with his arms protecting his head as the giant black bird extended its eight scaled claws and attempted to snatch something from the disturbed altar of treasures. In the raven's ruckus of screeches and wing flaps, Heritage caught a glimpse of what the bird must have been after, a curious item he had carelessly overlooked during his excavation. The crow cawed in defeat, swooping back up to a different branch, empty-taloned. Heritage took a step forward to examine the treasure the raven appeared to be after, wondering how in the world he had missed seeing it for himself.

Of all the out of place things, he was holding a well-worn but not necessarily old, black leather wallet—that belonged, according to the BC driver's license tucked inside, to one, recently and tragically deceased Marcel Labbé.

MONA'S MALAISE

It was midday before Heritage had found his way back to the familiar, almost-welcoming wine-bottle lined section of Dottie's trail. An enduring downpour had flushed him out of that labyrinth-altar-clearing in the woods and sent him scrambling across the island on a trail the rains had turned to muck. In his delirium, he had not been able to work out what day it was—but he settled on it being Monday and let that reality sink in. He needed to report to Brad Fraser at the Headlands Lodge in two days. With his busted kayak, he wasn't going anywhere without a helping hand that he'd need to shake soon. He had erred that morning, acting all bravado, not admitting he had been marooned, and not breaking down to beg for a ride back to civilization with the handsome coast guard captain. In what he was sure must be the onset of delirium, he no longer cared how he got off that god—or more likely, goddess—damned island—as long as it was soon, and not in a body bag, like poor Marcel.

He'd approached the A-frame muddy, stomping his sandaled toes that were caked in the primordial ooze of a decaying forest floor. His lower legs were badly scratched up and bleeding in places. He would have given his scrotum for a long, hot shower and a shave. He knew he must have looked positively primitive; a distant cry from from the Mountain Equipment Co-op super model he'd been when he arrived six days earlier.

To his surprise and the delight of his growling stomach, there had been two labeled and clear plastic bags tied together and hanging over the doorknob of his loaner shed. On one were the words *Stromboli Buns*, written in black Sharpie pen, and on the other, *Cheese Buns*. Heritage was disappointed to have missed the thoughtful bearer of these baked goods, but he wasted no time shoving a Stromboli in his face. Only after he had swallowed the doughy olive and sun-dried tomato bite did he realize these savoury buns could have been tainted, laced with strychnine maybe? As far-fetched as that sounded inside his head, a normally trusting Heritage was now, officially, a suspicious and anxiety-ridden fellow on high-alert. This unsolicited gift was all but guaranteed to reveal the next life-threatening challenge (or challenger) he would have to overcome or outwit.

Inside the A-frame, he discovered the majority of his clothes, which he'd foolishly left outside in the sun thinking the rains were done, were now dried and folded in neatly arranged stacks next to his rolled sleeping bag. Who had been his angel chamber maid, and would they be back in time for turn-down service, he wondered? He would have appreciated the opportunity to thank her or him, and then immediately demand and negotiate his return to town.

He would have benefitted from the company of anyone who would listen and possibly help him decipher the events and island landmarks he'd discovered in the past few days. Had Dottie redeemed herself and returned for him? He didn't see her boat out front and a quick dash to her cabin revealed nothing. Heritage was perplexed. He walked down to his still-upturned and broken kayak propped on the driftwood at the foreshore. Once there, he spotted his submerged tent in the shallow waters of Dottie's Bay. He threw his arms into the air in surrender, thinking nothing had gone right or according to his overly romanticized notion of the place. While he felt he could squarely blame his tent-turned-submarine on the winds that had carried the overnight storm, he couldn't dismiss his hunch that other, more devious forces may have been afoot. He tentatively waded into the cold water, which stung the cuts on his lower legs, hoping the tent wasn't any deeper than his thighs.

It was. His next carefully placed step sent the water level above his waist and it felt like an icy dagger plunged through his groin. He gasped, then laughed out loud, sure the cold water would thwart the semi-to-full erection he'd been sporting since yesterday. Stretching his leg, Heritage grabbed the nylon with his toes and started to pull the tent toward his hands, but part of the fabric was clearly snagged on rocks. He didn't want to rip it, but he also didn't want to dive under the surface or return to the beach without his tent. His teeth chattered as he stood there trying to coach himself out of his indecisiveness. He realized he was already committed, and the ache behind his ball sack had subsided, so he sucked in a giant gulp of air and under he went, following the stretched tent fabric hand over hand until he reached the points where it had snagged on what seemed to be an old anchor, about the size of the end of a pitchfork. The saltwater stung his eyes and the bit he'd swallowed going under, lingered to burn the back of his throat.

Heritage tried to move the anchor, but it was wedged fast between the rocks. He was nearing the end of his breath but stubbornly continued to work the fabric off the part of the anchor it had twisted around. At last, success! He burst above the surface of Dottie's Bay like a trident missile, and dog paddled back to the beach, pulling the tent between his legs.

He emerged from the water with his clothes and the tent clinging to his body. The fog had moved out of the channel, only to reveal the resident dark rainclouds reorganizing overhead. Heritage pleaded for them to hold off or go someplace else. He grabbed the bag of tent poles and stakes still strapped under bungees to the top of his kayak, and started to set up the tent in front of Dottie's cabin, when he realized the tent held an unintended bounty from the sea: a Dungeness crab about the size of a stool seat. The orange and blue of the crustacean had blended with the coloured panels of his tent, and Heritage hadn't seen the little guy at first. He was sure hard to ignore now, pincers waving like he was at a football game.

Before getting dumped on this island and even though he had intended to go hard-core vegetarian the moment he arrived in Clayoquot Sound, Heritage didn't mind crab, had even ordered it occasionally at Joe Forte's on Thurlow Street in Vancouver's West End. Ordering one and killing one and cooking one were three very different things . . . two, if you killed it by cooking it, he supposed, but that struck him as even more cruel. He was certainly getting sick of canned fish and he would feel bloated if he just chain-ate the buns one after the other, so he found a crab pot in Dottie's kitchen without even having to hunt for one. He filled it outside by dunking it in the barrel of Beaver Juice, then he cobbled together a campfire at the edge of the beach and set up his tent close by, crab captive inside, while the water took forever to boil.

With the water bubbling and starting to roll, it came time to corner the crab in a corner of the tent. He tried to reach for it, but it was all claws. He zipped his captive inside and lumbered over the driftwood to get his kayak paddle. Back inside the tent, on his first try, he slipped the blade under the crab and lifted his many legs off the tent floor, continually having to adjust the paddle so that the feisty guy couldn't scramble off, and airlifted him to the waiting pot of heated rainwater while the boil got going. Then, the two of them had a stare-down, Heritage trying his level best to put *The Little Mermaid* out of his head. In the end, he couldn't do it. This new Sebastian was released back into Dottie's Bay to sing for another day with Ariel and all the other critters under the sea.

All the tent flaps and zippers were now open and beginning to flap in the breeze that was kicking up. Heritage figured his tent should be dried out before bedtime. But then, "dried out" was one crazy term and a fleeting physical state in a rainforest. To help the tent along and maybe signal his distress to a boater who happened by, he had built a fairly large campfire and stick-toasted a few of the cheese buns. When those laden clouds started to sprinkle again, Heritage collected his clothing with his sleeping bag from the shed and situated himself inside his new bedroom. What he couldn't find was his novel, *The Discovery of Heaven.* This puzzled him most, since the book weighed a good couple of kilos and wasn't about to be blown away anywhere. It wasn't in the shed. It wasn't in any of the drybags. He double checked the hatches of the kayak once more before the heavens unzipped flaps of their own and began to piss all over him.

While he might have passed the remainder of his daylight hours wondering who had left him the baked goods and whether they'd taken his book for payment, Heritage could not stop obsessing about the drowned water taxi driver. The contents of his black leather wallet displayed atop his sleeping bag reconstructed part of the story, but not enough of it. There were four twenty-dollar bills, a BC driver's license (he had died a young man), a bank card, an empty Trojan condom package, a Vancouver Island Regional Library card, a creased photo of himself and an abundantly tattooed woman in a tank top, and a Canadian one cent penny with a date stamp of 1969—his birth year. The latter had left a permanent ring in the leather pocket. His lucky penny? Given that Marcel was dead, Heritage concluded that it hadn't worked. None of these contents—not even the cash—seemed worth jumping back into a boat in the middle of a storm to retrieve. But as a water taxi driver, Marcel likely lived on the water and had little fear of it. For him, zipping back to Wick may have seemed like driving across town on an errand. Heritage, on the other hand, felt skittish about the ocean—well, about most everything, now that somebody had been killed.

Heritage put everything back into the wallet exactly the way he'd found it—or how it had found him. There was enough in there to begin to construct the basic scaffolding of the man Marcel must have been. It wasn't so much the missing bits—the foundation or cladding—that Heritage found himself wanting to know more about as it was the significance of that empty Trojan wrapper. That, and how the drowned man's wallet had ended up wedged in a mossy altar at the center of some witch's ritualistic labyrinth, in the middle of the rainforest, a good distance away from where Heritage had last seen him alive? Why had the twenty-five-year old risked death trying to return to the island by open boat in the middle of a nighttime storm? It made no sense. Nothing in the wallet seemed worth dying over—not even the cash.

And yet he *had* died, and someone had deliberately placed that wallet in the woods—unless it had been the raven that carried it to that spot, which seemed even more preposterous. Heritage tucked the wallet under his pillow where he lay stretched on top of his sleeping bag listening to the rain begin to pelt the nylon overhead more steadily. He had alternated between Stromboli and cheese buns, baffled and now overstuffed, too. He rubbed his stomach and instantly grew another bothersome boner. He flipped over on his front and dozed off to the sounds of a rainforest hellbent on earning its name.

When he awoke from his nap with his nose buried in his left

underarm, Heritage was jarred by a whole new awareness of how ripe he had become. He sniffed his other underarm. The smell reminded him of vitamins. He had an earthy, metal pungency to his body aroma, like perhaps he had been sweating out the pharmaceuticals. He poked his head out of the tent and was pleased to see the rain wasn't all that sturdy. Heritage was coming around to accept that breaks in the persistent precipitation was the best he could look forward to it as it never seemed to let up completely.

The water in the crab pot was lukewarm, the embers beneath it not glowing, but not finished emitting heat either. He tossed a few branches and a boomerang shaped piece of driftwood on top of the ashes and used his mouth as bellows to direct oxygen under the stack. Satisfied that the fire would pick up, he grabbed his bar of soap and popped inside Dottie's cabin to retrieve a tea towel he'd remembered seeing on a shelf in Dottie's pantry that had cradled the last unopened bottle of Chilean vintage he'd polished off a day or two ago, then he dashed to the cove. When he had finished rinsing all the soap off his body and out of his hair, he did a quick sniff test, and decided he needed to soap up once more, even though his hands were turning blue and his teeth were chattering. At last, satisfied, he dashed back to his tent to towel dry in front of the campfire, which he restoked. He borrowed a wooden chair from Dottie's dining-room table. With the pot of water sufficiently warmed and the chair scooted under the eaves of the roof's slight overhang, he commenced shaving, using his own reflection in Dottie's sliding glass door as his guide. It felt as though he were getting ready for a date night, which made him pine for the pleasure of François' company again. There was so much he wanted to tell him and so many questions he suspected François could help him answer. But that would have to wait until they managed to run into each other.

The weather witches cranked the shower handle and it began to pour on him again, full pressure, but at least it was a warm rain compared to the ocean he'd just bathed in. Heritage hustled to secure the side window flaps of his tent under a rain fly that would only be functional if the precipitation was falling vertically, the smallish towel around his waist falling off twice in the frantic maneuver. It was raining so furiously that he abandoned the tent and took cover in Dottie's cabin. He hadn't managed to grab any clean clothes, so tea towel it was! The open two- story space was musty, damp, and cold. Heritage built a second fire in the orange spaceship of a wood stove as his outdoor campfire had been completely doused. It seemed to take forever, but within fifteen minutes he and the space were warming up nicely. It was getting dark, so Heritage lit some candles he'd found on counters and in cupboards. Still resolved not to spend the night inside Dottie's spooky cabin—with all her witchcraft books and residual curses and spell recipes and ingredients—Heritage was resigned to stay put until the rain lessened.

The woodstove and candlelight lent a healthy glow to his cleaned skin and Heritage was content that he could live with himself again . . . like he had a choice. What a difference a bath and fresh shave made. Maybe he was surviving off-the-grid isolation after all. He had surpassed the need for telephones and electricity and plumbing. He'd never, in all his years, cultivated a need for companionship, so that wasn't about to trip him up—though he found himself constantly thinking about the people he'd encountered in Clayoquot Sound so far. Particularly François. The notion of eventually sharing his life with someone was usually a harmless hypothetical thought that kept curled up in a corner in the very back of his mind, but he sensed an awakening since arriving in Clayoquot Sound—a stirring that he hadn't experienced in the city. He caught himself smiling—his own reflection in the sliding glass door, looking back at him, letting him know it was okay to have these thoughts.

With the cabin approaching toasty, Heritage was becoming drowsy where he sat on the futon sofa—still in front of the stove, still naked but for the towel around his waist, still content to simply be still. The demands of his work schedule and secret family mission would become apparent in another 48 hours, but for now, not one muscle was required. Remarkably, he couldn't find a single window in Dottie's cabin that opened, except for the double set of sliding glass doors. He got up to check the rain, which he could hear on the roof, and to crack open one of the sliding doors a few centimetres to let some fresh air in to cool his sauna down. He glanced at his wristwatch—6:30 and it was already dark outside. Being inside Dottie's place after dark wasn't as creepy as he'd made it out to be, and the thought of climbing into a cold sleeping bag didn't appeal. He was missing his paperback but had plenty to read inside the wall-mounted fish aquarium, if he could convince himself to get in the mood for a little occult.

"Oh, what the hell," he declared out loud, in his deepest voice. "Unleash the demons." He reached inside the glass case to take another and closer look inside the thickest and oldest looking book in Dottie's collection: *Malleus Maleficarum*. Lifting the hefty volume from the shelf with both hands, a book that Heritage already knew was full of bookmarks, he was careful this time to handle it with care. Even with this extra caution, a yellow-aged index card fell from the weighty compendium and cart-wheeled out of his reach under the futon sofa. He went flush, suddenly fearing he wouldn't be able to put things back exactly the way he'd found them and that, Dottie, if she were a witch, would intuitively know he'd violated her inner sanctum and then sic her flying monkeys after him.

In that moment, a new noise startled him just as the towel around his waist loosened and dropped. He lowered the witch book out of modesty and remained still as a statue—his eyes darting around the cabin ceiling and walls. After another creak in the flooring, he sat on the futon, with his knees to his chest and that residual dance party half-erection pressing into his abdomen. The fire in the stove had almost exhausted the last of its embers, and a few of the candles had burnt out, but the rain had not diminished. The candles that were still burning caused a reflecting glare against his side of the sliding glass doors, preventing him from seeing anything on the other side. It was silent but for the drumming rain and the beating of his heart which felt lodged in his esophagus.

Heritage reached for the towel on the floor, and slowly raised it up his long hairy legs and fastened it around his waist again. He had begun to calm down just as there was a rapping at one of the windows. He jumped, already wrestling with the creepy sensation of being watched. He stood, more tightly secured his towel and moved a few steps to the closest sliding glass door. He was straining his eyes and fully expected to be eyeball-to-eyeball with that damned kid, Aidan. But to his surprise and then horror, it was the woman from the bakery, Mona—Aidan's mother.

She appeared in full hunter green rain gear with yellow gumboots. She looked as though she had been crying. What had that brat told her? Heritage free-fell into a panic. He opened the sliding glass door. Her mascara had run down her face through the many wrinkled ravines that delta-spread from the outer corners of her large brown eyes—lines crisscrossing lines like lattice must have eroded her youth away a few decades or more ago. This was a woman who must be expert at cheating life, Heritage reasoned, thinking of his own mother.

He smiled. "Hello there—"

"It's Mona," she supplied the name in case he didn't remember, "from the SunRyes Bakeshop in town. We met last week briefly when you picked up the banana bread for the protest camp."

"Mona. Yes. I remember. I'm Tage. Come in!" He felt any colour he had in his cheeks drain away to reveal a complexion white as a movie screen, on which Heritage worried the baker would see his guilt projected in stop motion animation. Whether he was guilty or not—and for what transgression exactly, was something he didn't quite know himself.

———

"What brings you out on a night like this?" he asked, nonchalantly, motioning her inside.

Framed and dripping in the dim candlelight, he could tell by Mona's gaze that she had seen everything when the towel dropped, but that she knew even more, and that was likely why she was there. He was ashamed, then defensive—all before she'd even opened her tiny mouth to answer him. Observing her silence as she removed her rain hood, Heritage thought her old enough to be the grandmother of a fourteen-year-old, but not the biological mother of one. She'd looked younger in the sunlight on the sidewalk outside the bakery. He supposed everyone did—look younger in the sun, that is.

"Oh good," she said, glancing at the half-empty bag on the table. "You received the buns I left."

"Oh my god—your Stromboli buns may one day be credited with saving my life!" he said. She smiled, though uneasily. In that second, he realized she may have also been the one who had gathered and folded his drying clothes. "Thank you for the baked goods, and I have a feeling it is you I should also thank for collecting my scattered clothes and putting them in the shed." She gave a single chin nod, and he went on. "Thank you. It was sunny when I left for a walk-around yesterday, but a storm snuck in before I could get back."

"Storms here will do that," she said, "especially this time of year as we head into our rainy season."

"Say, Mona." He rushed to take advantage of what he hoped might be a more casual reason for her calling, and asked, "You didn't happen to come across a thick paperback novel that I may have also left outdoors, did you? It's called *The Discovery of Heaven*."

Mona shook her head. "I'm sorry, I didn't." She was wringing her hands either out of nervousness or in an attempt to warm them up.

Heritage tried to discern how truthful she was being just as he was anxious to learn why she was really there.

"This is a bit awkward for me," Mona finally confessed, wiping the hair off her face with bony hands quite possibly as white as the flour they manipulated into freshly baked treats every day. Heritage had allowed his shoulders to slump when he thought this might have been a social call, but her rather ominous introduction caused them to scrunch up around his neck again, like predator-provoked quills. "It's about Aidan, my son," she said. "I think you know my son."

"Yes. We, uh . . . we met each other the other morning in town, as a matter of fact. Is there a problem with Aidan?"

She looked Heritage in the eyes rather coldly. "The problem," she said, "is with Aidan's mother . . ." She paused. "With me."

Heritage froze. His quills had begun to cramp from tension. He was lousy at confrontation, and even worse when forced to shift from offensive to defensive and back again. "Please sit. Let me grab some clothes, I'll get some more wood for the stove, and light some more candles. Would you like some tea, perhaps?"

"That would be nice," she admitted, beginning to shed the layers of rain gear and wet underclothes like a Russian nesting doll, until she reached a dry one. Heritage dashed outdoors to his tent for a quick change but struggled to see in the dark without a flashlight. He couldn't find underwear and ended up putting on his fleece jacket without an undershirt and threaded his legs into his thin flannel pajama pants—neither of which chromatically went together or could girdle his barely flagging semi-erection. The pointlessness of covering up now after he was sure Mona had already seen all there was to see, was not lost on him, and putting his vanity aside, he hurried to gather kindling and recycled cardboard. With the rain and having been away overnight, he hadn't had much opportunity to forage for new driftwood and though he didn't feel completely right using up all the bounty of someone else's wood-chopping labour, he pinched a couple wedges of cedar from Dottie's pile next to the back porch. Despite his feelings toward her at the moment, he would try—if he had time—to replenish it the moment the weather cleared—however flimsy that promise or the notion of improving weather might be. Feeding the flying saucer with cedar, he reached for his last chunk of driftwood to place on top before closing the hatch.

"None of my business," Mona paused, "but you probably shouldn't be burning driftwood in the stove. The salts in the wood tend to corrode the stove pipe."

Heritage raised his eyebrows and made an oopsy-daisy face as he hadn't thought about that and tried to remember if he'd used driftwood in Lyle's wood stove. He clanked the half-filled teapot from the counter to the top of the woodstove, then sat awkwardly across from the baker who had plopped down on the futon sofa next to the antique book. He was sitting on a wooden chair with its back between his stretched open legs. When her focal point seemed to wander between his legs, he lifted off the seat, spun the chair around, sat back down and crossed his legs so suddenly, that he squished his stuff uncomfortably together. He didn't let the sharp discomfort show, but instead, used it to brace himself for whatever she had come to discuss with him.

"Aidan tells me that he explained things to you about our situation. That you know about my condition." She paused when it seemed he wasn't catching on. She crossed her arms, and continued. "I have been fighting this . . . this cancer of mine, for several years now. For a while it had gotten better, it seemed. But lately, this last year, it's been getting the best of me. I mean that literally. It is robbing me of the chance to raise a son, to run my business, to live my life. It's killing me." Heritage could tell she meant that literally, too. He got up to hunt for tea bags among his provisions. "I don't suppose you have herbal, do you?" she said.

"Actually, I do—uh, *she* does," he assured her, referring to Dottie's provisions.

"Aidan said he told you about this new chemotherapy session my doctor thinks I should try in Victoria, starting as early as this coming Sunday." She stopped to make sure he was tracking, but Heritage sat there having not yet lowered his raised eyebrows and didn't know what to say. Aidan hadn't mentioned anything about anything, really. It was curious that he'd told his mum they had discussed something they clearly hadn't. He was relieved, however, that the little bugger apparently hadn't set out to frame him after all. Heritage leaned in and worked at appearing more focused, more concerned. Mona continued. "I told my doctor I didn't feel I could leave my son with anyone for two weeks like that. But you know doctors and their sense of urgency." Heritage was attentive but reached over to add another small cedar branch to the wood stove.

"I had pretty much decided against the treatment until Aidan told me you had offered to watch him for the next two weeks while I'm gone. Well, of course it sounded too good to be true. But I thought it might be worth coming over here in the rain to find out for myself. I'd tried to catch you yesterday afternoon before the storm."

Heritage didn't know what to say. The shock of finding himself still wriggling on Aidan's manipulative pitchfork must have been wallpapered all over his face. He tried to compensate. "I can only imagine how difficult it must be for you to be facing this—to have no real options but to leave your son in the care of a total stranger. Wouldn't, uh, maybe Dottie Bard be a more logical guardian?" He was grasping, and it showed. "That way, Aidan could stay in town after coming home from school. He goes to school, right?"

She managed a short giggle. "You must not know Dottie Bard. She is far too busy taking care of all of Dottie Bard's interests to be bothered with a child—and that includes her own, who has just run off to South America. Oh, and yes, Aidan goes to school. He is just starting his first year at high school."

"Well, I only have a kayak, it's a single, and thanks to Dottie—" Heritage stopped himself, not fully aware of alliances, but then continued. "The nose of my kayak is busted, and I have been waiting for a lift back into town to get it repaired. Dottie hasn't been back for me after dropping me here—without provisions, I might add, five or six days ago, so thank you again for the baked goods." The tea kettle whistled, and he got up to play host. He poured the hot water into two mugs as he plotted, wiggled, and improvised in his head. "Plus, I am starting my new job at the Headlands on Wednesday."

He was grateful that Mona couldn't read his true mind. If he could have read hers, he might have realized she was scared and just as reluctant to ask this favour of him—as he was someone who she knew nothing about. Surely, he had to be her last choice after having asked every other standing adult in Clayoquot Sound, he supposed. It certainly wasn't entirely Mona's fault that anyone who knew Aidan had probably already declined the impossible task. No, Mona didn't know him, but Heritage knew Aidan and that was more than enough to defiantly stand his ground—there was no way he was going to step into that trap. No way.

"You won't need a boat," Mona said. "And if you do, Aidan's got a permit to drive our boat as long as he is with an adult." Heritage thought that was interesting—as he distinctly remembered watching Aidan speed away from the dock unsupervised and unattended that first day he had arrived by floatplane. Mona continued. "He's been driving motorboats since he was eight, and that's nearly half his life. And another thing, I don't leave for Victoria until Friday morning. That would give you the balance of the workweek to start your new job before you needed to worry about—" She stopped herself short. There was no reason to give any impression that this newcomer needed to worry about everything that could go wrong while she was away. One of them losing sleep over it was enough.

"Aidan's what? Fourteen?"

"He just turned fifteen last month. I know. He's big for his age."

"I'll say," Heritage volunteered before realizing how loaded his statement may have sounded. He quickly recovered. "I figure he can mostly take care of himself at that age."

Mona likely knew otherwise, but instead said, "Exactly. This is why I would be so grateful for your willingness to keep an eye on him starting this Friday. He doesn't need a babysitter. He's not a baby."

"No, indeed." Heritage had certainly seen enough physical evidence to the contrary. "But I still don't think I am the right candidate. I really have my hands completely full at The Headlands, plus, I still need to get off this island, get my kayak repaired, and get in the proper headspace to start a new position." He was rambling now, thrashing about in the water, and knew he would lose his buoyancy any minute. Mona was this sweet lady dying from cancer plus she'd brought him baked goods, folded his tent and clothes and would happily run he and his kayak into town in the morning. Heritage bit his lower lip and just knew he couldn't say *no* to her.

Mona knew that too, which is why she continued. "My treatments begin at the BC Cancer Agency on Sunday and continue for five days. I am told I will need to stay an additional twenty-four to forty-eight hours for observation and follow-up, and if all goes well, I should be back home by the following Sunday." She took a cautious sip from the teacup, testing the temperature of the beverage and the room.

Heritage didn't see any way out because there was no exit. Clearly, Aidan was leaps ahead of him and had cooked up this scheme to entrap him. Leveraging his mother's debilitating weakness, the kid was now playing Heritage for his own twisted purpose. Heritage was more than officially on guard now. More immediately, however, there was a cancer-ridden woman sitting with him in that one-room cabin, and she was screaming out for compassion and begging for relief from her suffering. He had the capacity to deliver some measure of both, so he softened his resistance and adopted a less aggressive, more tea-sipping posture, while Mona continued to butter him up.

"Aidan said you were awesome—his word, you know. There's not much accounting for the vocabulary of a fifteen-year-old. I, on the other hand, don't know what words I should use. I will tell you that I ran this past Dottie and she didn't hesitate in recommending you. She said she could sense you were a man of great character, that you would be great with children, and couldn't understand why someone hadn't already made a father out of you." She raised her mug to salute him with a slanted smile.

Heritage believed she might be flirting with him—had she not just told him she had cancer, she might have tried flirting even harder. There could be no doubt that if she were making a pass, she would know exactly what she was vying for, having most likely window-shopped the merchandise, before rapping on the sliding glass door.

Heritage was stewing behind his curtain of tea steam. So, Dottie had endorsed him for the task . . . on top of abandoning him . . . on top of her attempt to feed him to the bears . . . she was saddling him with Satan with an A. He ruminated on this, not sure whether to be flattered or pissed off. He warily landed someplace in the middle. "I'm sorry I don't have any milk or sugar," he toasted her back, adding, "to your good health, Mona." And with that he won her heart.

Over the next half hour, Heritage learned plenty, plus he'd secured a ride to town with Mona first thing in the morning. Though she'd known Dottie for twenty-two years, this was the first time she remembered ever enjoying a cup of tea in her cabin. The two apparently weren't all that close, seldom saw anything the same way, but Mona felt she couldn't afford to alienate her, and so maintained a tenuous friendship under a guise of sisterly solidarity. Mona said Dottie was manipulative and pushy by nature—not that he needed to hear that newsflash from Mona. Heritage had already been made *Dottie-aware*, and since arriving, had experienced those headlines for himself. His right leg was bouncing nervously, until he saw that Mona was distracted by it, so he stopped. On one hand, he was internally outraged that not only had Dottie presumed then calculated his willingness to take on the Herculean task of playing temporary father-figure to Aidan, but she seemed to be outwardly trying to sabotage his commitment at the Headlands which was the real reason why he was in Clayoquot Sound at all. And then on the other hand, Heritage was not a man without compassion and especially with the woman sitting across from him bravely looking her own demise in the eyes, he hoped to be even half as brave when he introduced Aidan to his rather organic brand of authority. Father or parole officer—Heritage figured that nobody quite knew what Aidan needed—but at fifteen, he certainly didn't need to face his mum's cancer and the high possibility of losing her, all by himself and on his own. Heritage could sense that Mona had probably always been a tackle-it-herself-gal and that her pride would have otherwise and normally prevented her from pursuing a favour this big from anyone, but in the next breath, she explained that Dottie had insisted she get over her stubborn self and learn to rely more on neighbours. And by neighbours, Mona knew Dottie didn't mean herself.

"More tea?" Heritage poured from the teapot while asking. He knew he wasn't out of the rainforest yet. His on-again, off-again paranoia that Aidan could still turn on him had backed him up against the outhouse wall—right where Satan with an A or Wicked Ninnish wanted him. If Heritage didn't agree to teen-sit him now, there could be no guarantee that Aidan wouldn't blackmail him in the future. At least this way, he and the kid might begin again on a different footing, establish some mutual respect, and put their previous encounters and show-and-tell sessions behind them. And if Dottie had personally recommended Heritage for this parenting stint, and Aidan had told his mum that he thought Heritage was *awesome*, what could possibly go wrong, he was thinking facetiously. Considering the character sources of these flimsy testimonials . . . *everything*! That's what. His right leg began bouncing again.

Quirky as it was, its witchiness and Marcel's tragic death notwithstanding, he could admit the island was growing on him—whether fondly or bacterially, he wasn't yet sure. While he was certainly expected and welcomed to live at the Headlands over the less busy winter months ahead, he certainly wasn't obligated to live there. When things grew confrontational or uncomfortable between with Brad Fraser—as he expected they would, once Heritage began digging into his questionable bookkeeping—perhaps a couple nautical miles between them might be advantageous, even strategic. With proper provisions and a working kayak, Wickaninnish Island still held unlocked potential and an allure he wasn't quite ready to write off.

The more he listened to Mona's story, the more he realized he could earn valuable credits if he kept Aidan alive while his Mum was undergoing treatment. And since Dottie had recommended him for the task, she'd owe him too. He hadn't forgotten the advice he'd been given by his grandfather, by the floatplane pilot, or by Brad Fraser. You didn't tell Dottie Bard no when she expected to hear yes. This would make the second time she'd volunteered him for a risky work assignment, though. He was lucky to have emerged alive from the first, and here she was, tossing him into another pair of equally destructive jaws.

Growing more candid during her second cup of tea, Mona billed herself as one self-reliant, self-rising, self-made loaf of wonder broad. She had built her SunRyes Bakeshop from scratch, one measuring cup at a time. From her first bag of unbleached flour in 1972—the same year the logging road got paved and turned into a highway to Tofino—to leasing a double garage in an alley behind the BC Liquor Store in 1975, she had always stayed true to her original recipe for success, surrounding herself with colourful people—her hand-chosen ingredients—who made life and business sweet. She'd been sizing up a vacant village lot across First Street from the post office around the time that Dottie Bard first tracked mud through her doorway, asking how she might invest in her expanding bakery operation. Always a scant too trusting and almost biblically kind to strangers, hippies, and the downtrodden, Mona pitched her business plan, and Dottie wrote the cheque that would become the frosting that held those two misshapen cake layers in business together for the first ten years, until Mona was finally able to repay Dottie's original investment. Even then, according to Mona, Dottie still tried to strong-arm her into letting her keep her hands in the SunRyes cookie jar, but Mona had had enough of her meddling and overlordship. Their relationship and the détente that followed had suffered as a result, but Mona stood by her oven mitts.

He took quick slurps of his tea and said little while Mona proceeded to rattle through the particulars of Aidan's school schedule and the four-pill-a-day timing for his prescription of Ritalin. Heritage sensed all sorts of alarm bells going off but knew this review of the particulars would release Mona's conscience so she could leave her only child in the hands of a relative stranger. This must have so preoccupied her, because she hadn't asked him one thing about his background or what brought him to Clayoquot Sound. There had also been no mention of Aidan's father or siblings—and that seemed to explain much of Aidan's behaviour. Not that Heritage was any developmental expert; he'd already become an adult by the time he'd lost his own father. It hurt his brain to remember what he had been like at fifteen, but he was pretty sure he didn't have Aidan's confidence or independence. Aidan had been dastardly clever in each of their brief exchanges, and Heritage couldn't help but respect that, even if he didn't understand the fifteen-year-old's motivations or endgame.

By the time Mona signaled she was ready to head out back into the storm, Heritage could have mounted his own Riverdance Irish line dance with his growing troupe of second thoughts. As a newcomer, he saw this as an opportunity to become part of the

Wickaninnish Island community, and if the African proverb were to be believed, it might well take the whole damn village of them to raise that devil of a child. Heritage would make his contribution as selflessly and profoundly as he could. Anyway, on an island without electricity, telephones, or cable TV, he figured Aidan would quickly prove to be all the entertainment he could handle.

"Of course—I'll do it," he told Mona. And that blasted her off her futon launch pad and into his arms. Still holding onto him, she explained that crying was something she hadn't been able to control ever since her first mastectomy—well, not really since the late-teenage hysterectomy that preceded it by several decades, she said, adding, if she were being accurate about her waterworks. Even her closest friends never really knew whether or not the plumbing would be on or off with Mona, so they always brought tissues—tucked in pockets or socks or folded under watchbands. Heritage just held her there as she joy-sobbed—the two of them standing in the dim light of the flying saucer of a wood stove. Then, she pulled back, clearly flustered and trying to regain composure. She stepped back into rain pants she'd left to redeploy at the door and her still-wet rain slicker, nervously chatting while the two made arrangements for a 7:30 a.m. pick-up in Dottie's Cove—even Mona called it that—and then she said she'd radio a fellow named Mac Mulligan in town. He was a wiz at fiberglass repair. If he had the time, Mona figured Heritage could have his kayak back on the water in about forty-eight hours.

"One last thing," she reached a hand to his freshly shaven and rosy cheek and she held it there. "Personally, I don't care if you burn the whole beach full of driftwood in Dottie's wood stove—that would serve her right for dumping you here without provisions—but you should know and be forewarned that if she discovers someone has messed with her implements—" Heritage obviously registered a blank. She pointed. "The book you have opened there on the couch . . . if she learns you've touched it, there will be consequences for you that I can't predict. The woman, for all her faults, actually possesses powers I wouldn't fiddle with if I were you. Just take it from a cancer ravaged woman who knows the extent of her wrath."

Staring beyond one last embrace through the sliding glass door, Heritage suddenly recognized he was seeing lights across the channel. They had to belong to Headlands Lodge. He patted Mona gently on the back and said, "Everything is going to work out alright. I am not afraid." In that moment, glimpsing civilization through a silhouette of trees for the first time in five days, he damn well believed it. Mona passed through the sliding glass door and instantly disappeared into the hell-raiser of a stormy night.

Heritage plopped down on the futon next to the intimidating, velvet-covered and wood-bound volume he had extracted from the collection on the wall. He moved a still-burning candle closer in and lifted the cover and opened the first pages on his lap. He read out loud in a dramatic whisper to spook the spiders and test his own mettle:

> Lucifer attacks through these heresies at that time in particular, when the evening of the world declines towards its setting and the evil of men swells up, since he knows in great anger, that he has little time remaining. Hence, he has also caused a certain unusual heretical perversity to grow up in the land of the Lord—a Heresy, I say, of Sorceresses, since it is to be designated by the particular gender over which he is known to have power.

Heritage paused, wondering who had underlined this passage in dull pencil, and why. He flipped to the next bookmarked page that delineated *incubus* (demons in male form) from *succubus* (women victims), and how through *apologia auctoris* both could be explained, justified, and saved by prayers and transubstantiations.

Boring, Heritage thought, growing sleepy. He advanced to the next bookmark, a weathered newspaper article from the *Edmonton Journal* with a date of November 12, 1963, about the persecution of powerful women who were considered consorts of Satan, who could make crops fail and men impotent—especially those lost souls who smelled of sulphur and brimstone. Heritage sniffed his forearm, having not a clue what brimstone smelled like. Holding the snipped article in one hand, he scanned the page it marked with the middle finger of his other hand. It seemed to be a how-to instruction manual for hanging, drawing, and quartering some-one—a step-by-step checklist that started with the guilty being drawn or dragged to a ceremonial spot, hung from a tree or scaf-fold, emasculated, disembowelled, and beheaded before having the arms and legs removed by axe by or the simultaneous lurching forward of four horses in four directions.

Ouch. Heritage squirmed.

He put the newspaper article back and closed the heavy book, thinking that was enough uplifting reading for one night. He placed the volume back in the aquarium on the wall and closed the glass doors. He lifted the tail of his t-shirt over his head to carefully wipe the glass of his fingerprints. He washed the tea mugs with a little dish soap and the rest of the lukewarm water from the teapot. He blew out the candles and cracked the front hatch of the woodstove so it would burn itself out. Then, satisfied that everything had been returned to the way he'd found it, he squeezed through the sliding glass door, took a pee against the cedar tree trunk and through the hole that had been cut in the exterior decking, and scrambled into his tent. He would need to wait until daylight to gather his things and break camp in antici-pation of his boat lift into town.

He would check into the Headlands Lodge a day early, get properly cleaned up and rested for his first big day on Wednesday. He wondered if he would miss Wickaninnish Island, even though he should be able to see it every day from the lodge. With his kayak repaired, he could bop back and forth—and would need to so he could uphold his promise to Mona and keep Aidan breathing and conscious until she returned. He really did need to speak to Dottie at some point about the possibility of upgrading to Stephanie's other cabin, overlooking the beach on the island's outside coast. He would need to steel himself for that encounter, since she wouldn't be happy to hear he was carrying through with his obligation at The Headlands.

HEADLANDS HO!

Heritage didn't know the first thing about fiberglass; fortunately, Mac Mulligan did. But when Mona, wearing her one-piece, head-to-toe red floater jacket, overshot the First Street dock with its weathered red railings, and instead, slowed her boat to pull up to Dottie Bard's dock, Heritage began experiencing low-grade hyperventilation. He had not factored into his morning schedule a confrontation with Dottie. He didn't want her intervening in his plan for the day to continue onto the Headlands Lodge, and he was still ticked at her for the series of drop-and-runs and for not checking on him during the past several days. Aidan, sharing the same bench with Heritage at the mid-section of Mona's boat, had spent the channel crossing in a huff and fuming because she hadn't let him drive the boat when they'd come to pick him up. When Tage had looked back at Mona for insight into her son's clearly foul mood, she had just rolled her eyes. Aidan bolted out of the boat and up the hill without offering to help with the kayak or even say goodbye.

"He wanted to show off his boating skills in front of you, and I wouldn't let him," his mother explained, securing the stern and then the bow to the dock.

Heritage only had one thing on his mind: bracing himself to face Dottie. "This is Dottie's dock, no?" he asked.

Mona bit the inside of her cheek. "Symbolically, maybe?" she offered, diplomatically. "I was under the impression the Village owned all the docks except the First Street Dock, which is federal. That's why it's called the Government Dock." She pointed behind her to the red-railing dock. "And the coast guard dock, which is shared by the RCMP. But, yes, Dottie says this is her dock."

Now Heritage was the one biting the inside of his cheek. He appreciated the look on Mona's face, which told him more than her words.

He saw an older white bearded man striding toward them on the dock, as he transferred his backpack, dry bags, and paddle from the boat to the thick lumbered decking.

"Good morning, Mac," Mona said fondly to the grizzly of a man, who reminded Heritage of the Captain Highliner mascot that he'd grown up seeing on boxes of frozen fish sticks. "Mac, this is Tage."

Heritage reached up his long arm and shook a meaty hand, inside which, his own hand almost completely disappeared. In addition to the Santa Claus beard, Mac had a shock of thinning white hair and eyes that were a blue deeper than the sea on this sunny morning. Heritage supposed him to be in his early sixties—possibly a little older than Mona, though he could see them matched well together had they been a couple.

"Is this the broken beauty?" Mac asked, lifting the nose of the kayak off Mona's boat as Heritage lunged to grab the toggle bar at its stern to lift it to clear the gunwale on the starboard side so as not to scrape or bang up the hull any further.

"Yeah, Mac. It's fairly new," he added, "but it got dropped onto rocks and now takes on water near the bow."

"Well, that's no good," Mac said, gently.

Mona held a hand across her brow to keep the sun from her eyes. "I will leave you two men to this," she said. "I need to cover staff breaks at the shop. Tage, are you sure you don't want a lift back to Wick at the end of the day?"

"No. Thanks, Mona. I'm shifting to the Headlands Lodge for the next few nights, but I will rendezvous with you at the bakery Thursday afternoon around four, like we discussed?" It was both a statement and a question.

"Yes," she waved as she untied her boat from the dock, front and back. "Mac, tell Dottie that we are good for Friday. She has offered to take me down to Victoria. Tage is going to try his hand at taming my beast of a son while I'm away for treatments."

"How very brave of both of you," Mac said, showing beautiful teeth behind his smile. Heritage wondered if they might be dentures.

"Thanks for the lift, Mona," Heritage hollered after her as she turned her boat around to head to a different dock. She waved her arm without looking behind her. He continued walking the kayak the length of the dock and up the hill toward the sheds below Clayoquot Sea Kayaking. "So you work for Dottie, Mac?"

The older man chuckled out loud. "I work for the occasional paycheque . . . I am not one for formal arrangements or com-mitments." He'd set two sawhorses under a clear thick plastic tarp. "Let's flip her over on her belly," he instructed, adding that he was referring to the kayak and not Dottie. Heritage issued his best laugh track as his arms crossed over each other to set the kayak upside-down on the badly worn sponge padding that looked as though it had been repeatedly hockey-taped to the saw-horses. Mac's trained eyes went right to the spiderweb of fissures. "Well, the good news is that it looks to be an easy fix and with your white hull, there will be no problem matching colours and making it look good as new."

"Well, it *is* new," Heritage interjected, feeling a bit sore that it had already been broken. "And the bad news?"

"The bad news is I'm waiting on fiberglass. It was supposed to have been on the bus last Wednesday, but there was a mix-up and then the bus ended up breaking down somewhere around Sproat Lake, so I haven't received the supplies I need to fix this, or the other half-dozen kayaks that are piled up on those racks." He vaguely pointed elsewhere. "The fleet that got banged up this past season."

"I see," Heritage leveled with his disappointment, hands on his hips. He looked out across the harbour toward the native village of Esowista.

Mac registered that wasn't the answer the newcomer was hoping for. "You got places to be, I take it."

"A few obligations, sure, but nothing I can't work around. After here, I'm heading to the Headlands Lodge and can get there without a kayak easily enough, I imagine." As soon as he said that he looked at the significant pile of his belongings down on the dock and cringed. "I might ask Dottie for a lift. The way I see things, she sort of owes me."

"Boy, you *are* new!" Mac exclaimed. "Dottie doesn't think she owes anybody. I should know, since I have been her indentured lover-slash-handyman for the past three years."

Heritage couldn't help it. "My god, what did you do?"

Mac gave a devilish grin without showing his teeth, and nodded his head, seeming to acknowledge his lot. "No explaining the affairs of the heart," the older man said. "And Dottie is out this morning. She's been on a tear these past few days, convinced her daughter Stephanie has been abducted or something. I usually give her a wide berth and stick to my oyster farm."

"Oyster farm? Really?" Heritage perked up. How many oyster farms could there be? "I met a fellow named François who told me he works on an oyster farm." Heritage jumped at the chance to go fishing for François.

"François works for me. It's my farm, my own pioneered system of seeding ropes that dangle deep like windchimes in the nutrient-rich Clayoquot waters."

"Oysters grow from seeds?" Heritage was fascinated.

"We call the larvae *seeds*, about the size of your thumbnail. We tuck these inside of three-strand nylon ropes, drop them in the water from floats, and in a year's time, oysters the size of your hand will grow from these attachments and are ready for harvesting."

"That sounds so cool," Tage said, before suggesting he would be really interested in seeing the operation. That wasn't what he was interested in seeing at all, but he didn't mind oysters . . . and cozying up to Mac Mulligan seemed another strategic move on his Clayoquot chessboard.

Mac gave the kayak a couple quick pats. "Listen, I can give you a lift to The Headlands. I'm just sitting here waiting on a bus anyway. It won't arrive until tomorrow and I've heard the surf is decent at Cox Bay today. Tide is incoming."

"You surf?" Tage asked him, perhaps a bit too incredulously.

"Well, that's what I call it." The two of them had a short burst of laughter.

Mac grabbed Tage's hefty backpack in one hand and a dry bag in the other, and Heritage tagged behind the young-old sea captain, carrying his lighter possessions—his tent and sleeping bag roll. They walked past the side of Dottie's building to a carport that looked as though it was begging the next breeze to topple it over. Mac opened the trunk of a white 1965 Thunderbird. "What a ride," Heritage exclaimed as he pretend-fawned over the vintage automobile. Cars weren't his thing, but men were supposed to act impressed anyway.

"She's a movie star. Andy Griffith drove her in his *Matlock* television series, season two, episode eight." It clearly wasn't the first time Mac had rattled off these facts. "Hop in," Mac invited, before cranking the radio. The front bench seat had enough room for

Mac, Heritage, and Marvin Gaye, who was coolly chant-singing "What's Goin' On?" from at least two forward dash speakers.

"So, besides oyster farming and fiberglass repairing, what else keeps you busy, Mac? And what brought you here if you aren't from here?" Heritage was feeling very comfortable in the man's gentle presence, and this sometimes turned him into an investigative journalist. Like his dearly and tragically departed mother, Heritage struggled with silence in the presence of others and thought it should be filled with constant, curious, and appreciative dialogue. It's what was supposed to make him a great lawyer, but he somehow had fallen short of that finish line, so far.

Mac turned left at the only flashing traffic light in the village, the Thunderbird's windows down and Marvin spilling out into the deserted streets and sidewalks. "I'm from Chicago, originally. Ex-navy navigator on a mine-sweeper and salvage diver, at your service." He was using his barrel-chested voice to be heard over the radio. "Oh, and Vietnam is what brought me here." Heritage acted like he knew what that meant, though it took him another ten minutes before he realized Mac was talking about draft dodging. "What about you? What's your background and what brings you here?"

Heritage gulped, trying to remember what he'd practiced for inquisitions such as this. "Toronto . . . I was born in Toronto but came west to attend law school at UBC. I've been in Vancouver for the past six years." He wondered if he could get away with that. He couldn't.

"So you're a lawyer?" Mac asked, sort of disdainfully.

"Technically, no." Heritage was beginning to divert from the script and needed to flip the conversation back to Mac. "Salvage diver, eh? Any cool underwater finds around here?"

"Well, there's the *Tonquin*—my nemesis. I've been on the hunt for her more than the past twenty years."

"Tell me about the *Tonquin*." Heritage settled into cross-examination mode, where he was much more comfortable.

Mac lowered the radio volume as they left the downtown core of the village on Highway 4. "Well, almost 200 years ago, an American merchant ship named the *Tonquin*, had been exploring this coast as part of the Astor expedition. Just over a year earlier, she'd sailed from New York past the Falkland Islands and around the tip of South America. Coming back up the Pacific coast, she'd spent time in the Hawaiian Islands before she stopped in at Astoria, Oregon. While there, at the mouth of the Columbia River, the captain traded with the Indians who told him the fur pelts they were getting had been obtained through trading with other tribes further north."

Mac paused to take questions. There were none, so he continued.

"With her twenty-three sailors and ten cannons, she sailed north to find the source of the furs—rumoured to be mostly otter but some beaver too. It was mid-June in 1811 when she sailed into Clayoquot Sound and began trading with the Nuu-chah-nulth. When a Tla-o-qui-aht chief set the price for his sea otter pelts too high, the captain of the Tonquin threw a pelt back in the chief's face."

"Was this Chief Wickaninnish?" Heritage asked, trying to impress, and hoping he might be quizzed on how to spell the name.

"I don't think so," Mac answered. "Wickaninnish had been the chief of the Tla-o-qui-aht for at least the previous thirty years but would have been quite old by that time. Definitely, Wickaninnish had not been impressed with earlier Americans he'd encountered who he viewed as cheats and believed had no good intent other than to plunder the coast. No—" Mac seemed fairly confident with the history as he understood it, "—I think it was this younger fellow named Nookamis, that the chief might have dispatched to the ship to attempt to trade with these Americans. The captain of the Tonquin wasted no time insulting Nookamis. He refused to pay what he said were inflated prices for the fur pelts, a few of which he threw back in Nookamis' face. He ordered the *Tonquin*'s crew to prepare to set sail the following day. Nookamis turned, taking his men and pelts with them. The next morning, Tla-o-qui-aht canoes intercepted the ship—right over there," Mac pointed west though Heritage saw nothing but trees, "between this peninsula and Wickaninnish Island, in what we call Templar Channel today."

Mac turned right onto the gravel Mackenzie Beach Road. "Upon their return, the Tla-o-qui-aht said they'd decided to lower their pelt prices and this got them invited back aboard the *Tonquin*. Concealed under the pelts and their clothing, they had knives and clubs and proceeded to attack and brutally butcher the captain and the majority of his crew. Four or five of the crew, with at least one badly wounded, managed to retreat below deck where their guns and munitions were stored, and tried to fight back. The Tla-o-qui-aht retreated."

At the end of the gravel road nearing the beach, Mac turned the Thunderbird right again at the large—almost ostentatious wooden carved sign for Headlands Lodge, and continued along a narrowed, asphalt driveway. He returned to his story, picking up the pace. "When night fell, all but one of the surviving crew members lowered a skiff thinking they would row that open boat back down the coast to Astoria. The following morning, the Tla-o-qui-aht returned, this time in war canoes. When they were met with no resistance, they boarded what they thought was a ghost ship. With more than one hundred natives aboard and beginning to loot the ship for anything of value, the wounded crew member lit the powder keg below deck and the *Tonquin* exploded and sank, killing the last crew member and most everyone else aboard."

Heritage's eyes had grown large. "So there is a shipwreck right out there, between here and Wickaninnish Island."

"There sure as hell should be, but I haven't been able to find her," Mac admitted, coasting the Thunderbird to a stop at the giant timbered entranceway to The Headlands. He put the car into park but kept the engine running. "I have hauled up some odds and ends over the years, but nothing I can conclusively say belonged to the *Tonquin*."

"And what happened to the crew that had escaped in the skiff?" Heritage asked. "Did they make it to Astoria?"

Mac unfastened his seat belt. "Nah. They were captured by other Nuu-chah-nulth not much further south from here, and then they were slowly tortured to death as retribution for the killing of so many Tla-o-qui-aht."

Mac was out of the car and unloading Heritage's things from the boot to stack on the wide wooden boardwalk that led to the lodge. "I really appreciate the lift, and the story, Mac. Thank you."

"I'll contact you, I guess here, when your kayak is ready for the water again."

"Right. Thanks for that, too." Heritage had one last request. "Do me one more favour and say hello to François from me when you see him. Maybe let him know I've shifted here to The Headlands."

"Will do," Mac promised, looking past the lodge to the water below it. "Surf's up!"

"Hang Ten!" Heritage added with a wave of his hand, pinky and thumb extended.

Sitting in an overstuffed armchair in the open-beamed lobby at the Headlands Lodge—cedar fire crackling like gunfire in a colossal stone fireplace—Heritage began to conjure his own theory about the interior design of the grand room. Ralph Lauren, Perry Ellis, L.L. Bean, and Eddie Bauer must have had one helluva four-way love-in to have inseminated their immaculately ejaculated rugged wilderness theme that dripped over every square centimetre, from the hardwood flooring to the cedar-beamed ceiling. Green, red, and blue plaid upholstery; broad red cabana stripes on sailcloth curtains; nautical antiques; ship mast banisters; weathered rope cording and nets; old lantern chandeliers; and lumber. Wood, wood, and more wood, everywhere you looked. What wasn't anywhere, and this stood out like a billboard of unspeakable igno-rance, was any reference to native culture—no art, no iconography, no mention of the area's indigenous history. The interior design of the place, with all its nautical over-sentimentality, had white-washed Chief Wickaninnish and the attack of the *Tonquin* right out of the picture windows that framed—barely a stone's throw away—the site where it was said to have happened, according to Mac Mulligan. This didn't seem right to Heritage, and he was there to take notes, make changes. But so far, the chief seemed to have been right about the Americans and those who followed them . . . they had come to plunder the coast, and the Headlands Lodge was a testament to the conquerors.

Sitting in that Great Room and waiting for Brad Fraser to arrive, Heritage had been wholly transformed, from shipwrecked island castaway to Bay Street financier, thanks to the nearly ninety minutes he'd spent in the steamy shower and at the dou-ble-basined washroom in his corner suite on the third and top floor of the Headlands Lodge. His room featured a king-size feather bed in front of a large picture window view of Dottie Bard's shabby hippie-witch cabin—of all possible vistas, straight across Templar Channel on Wickaninnish Isle. This eyesore alone might have made her Brad Fraser's enemy, had their common his-tory not already forged an unrecoverable animosity long before they had sabotaged each other's views.

Heritage was about to learn that Fraser—an American, him-self—had been Dottie's husband's best friend and logging buddy, long before Dottie Bard had fled west to Tofino from Edmonton. The tree faller and the root bucker duo had been inseparable crewmates after being hired right out of high school in 1968 by MacMillan Bloedel—the behemoth American logging company that had wandered north from Seattle to systematically begin razing the old-growth cedar forests right off the face of Vancouver Island. Fraser had reluctantly agreed to be Johnny Armstrong's best man when he married Dottie in a ringless, rush ceremony a few years later in 1972—but only after he realized he wouldn't be able to convince the groom that his wife-to-be and the mother of that daughter of theirs (born two-and-a-half years earlier) was a witch.

Fraser would also tell Heritage that he had also failed to convince the police investigators that Dottie must have had something to do with her husband's bizarre disappearance after their relationship had suddenly soured a decade and a half later. Mysteriously, Johnny's Boston Whaler had been found stripped empty and out of gas near Wilf Rocks between the northern tip of Wickaninnish and the southern end of Vargas islands. Just the boat—no anchor, grappling hook, lifejackets, nets, buckets, or radio. Neither his body nor any article of clothing had ever been found but most townsfolk, including Brad Fraser, quickly came around to the notion that there had to have been some measure of foul play involved and that Dottie Bard knew more than she was saying. *Somebody* had to have made off with the radio and depth sounder, because they had been screwed into the steering console.

Heritage checked his fancy dive watch. It was eighteen minutes past the start of what was supposed to have been a 10 a.m. appointment, albeit hastily arranged. Heritage was arriving a day early and whether or not Brad Fraser believed this to be a surprise inspection to throw him off balance, he had agreed to move their first in-person conversation a day earlier than they had calendared over the phone. Heritage looked again at his watch and caught the raised eyes of one of the front desk clerks—who seemed to nonverbally communicate from across the Great Room that he was sorry the lodge manager was such a doofus. Heritage smiled back, as if to say he didn't mind waiting. But this bad habit of Fraser's—his notoriously poor punctuality—was on his long list of chronic issues his grandfather had dispatched him to fix. It had been made clear to Heritage III that Heritage I didn't expect him to teach Fraser manners or how to properly run a business. By *fix*, his grandfather had meant get rid of completely. Fraser had to go. It was Heritage's task to make the exit door seem irresistible. If that failed, he would need to push Fraser out of it anyway, then immediately change the locks.

Everybody has their price, his grandfather had stated, but everyone also has an Achilles's heel. The art of the deal was discovering the heel first, to avoid paying the full price or any price at all. The working theory was that Fraser's weakness was alcohol. It was no surprise, then, when the smell of booze arrived a millisecond before Brad Fraser did. His white Oxford button-down needed ironing, and it didn't appear that he had even bothered to shave to meet the grandson of his angel investor—unless this facial shabbiness was the start of an autumn beard or goatee.

"I'm sorry I'm running late today," Fraser said as he sat down on a loveseat opposite his guest.

"No worries, Brad," Heritage returned. "It's nice to finally meet you in person, after all of our conference calls and correspondence. And listen, with the fog and rain we've had this past week, it might have just as easily been me running late—days late." When Fraser looked like he wasn't following him, Heritage added, "I needed to transfer by kayak from Wickaninnish Island to my suite here this morning."

"Oh yeah? What were you doing over on *Wicca* Ninnish? Though I probably don't even have to ask how you ended up there."

"*Wicca* Ninnish?" Heritage probably didn't have to ask either, knowing exactly what Fraser had meant when he emphasized *Wicca* and figuring the long-dead Chief would either by now be flattered by all the conjugations and contortions of his name, or he would be spinning in eternal rage by the disrespect he was still being paid.

"Well, I know you already managed to get yourself tangled up with Dottie Bard, so figure she's the one that got you onto Wick. Nothing but bad news, witchcraft and voodoo over there—but you can figure that out on your own." After a brief pause, Fraser forged ahead and gave Heritage the history of his dead logging buddy and laid bare his litany of suspicions about Dottie Bard.

Heritage listened politely as it was all information and a fresh perspective he could use, one day.

Mugs, cream and sugar, a basket of fresh croissants, and a French press full of coffee eventually arrived on a hunter green napkin-lined tray, delivered by the same empathic desk clerk that likely spent the majority of every work shift apologizing for Brad Fraser's path of managerial incompetence and destruction.

"About Dottie Bard . . ." Heritage began to articulate a defense while tossing up a blind of alibis behind which he hoped he could continue his double-agenting for as long as it suited him. "The seaplane pilot . . ." Shit, what was his name again? Jason! "Jason told me she was the kayaking authority in town, and that it was the generally accepted safety protocol, I guess, or maybe she just liked to have all paddlers register with her first before taking to the water."

"She's just a nosy control freak, a delusional nutcase who has appointed herself gatekeeper to the wilderness. Clayoquot Sound does not belong to her nor does she have any authority over who comes or goes, who paddles or doesn't. That's ridiculous!" Brad had been holding a croissant in the air and the more animated he became, the more its flaky little crumbs flew everywhere.

Heritage let the spittle from Brad's rant settle among the croissant crumbs before continuing. "Well, it turned out," he said, "that she was in the middle of something important and needed an extra set of hands. She asked if I could help out." He paused. "Well, she didn't really *ask*. You weren't expecting me here until tomorrow morning, so I guess I got voluntold how I would spend my first week in Clayoquot Sound."

"You were shanghaied, is more like it!" Fraser stirred his black coffee and gently introduced a stream of cream. That was his mid-morning ritual and a trick he said he learned in Saudi Arabia—it distributed the cream in a way that didn't cool the coffee. "But now I'll play the nosy one and just ask you straight out, did your grandfather send you here to buy me out?"

Heritage giggled at his bluntness, adding cream to his own coffee, though not as

ceremoniously. It was time to pivot to a more ruthless posture—more faked than authentic—but effective when deployed in the right situation, all the same. He sensed in that moment, that it was time to play the big city jerk and make it clear in the most certain terms, that he wasn't there to make friends.

"You ready to be bought out, Brad? Is that it?" He could be just as direct and had excelled in cross-examination. There was a lull in their tête-à-tête, during which Heritage held his tongue. Law school had taught him to set the bait and wait . . . or maybe it had been his mother who deserved the credit there.

"This resort business kills patiently, and I'll admit to chasing the retirement dream of finding a hammock stretched between two palm trees somewhere in the Caribbean. But we've just had a record season, so I think I am just going to pad my nest with a few more summers like this one, build the empire up, hire a few more staff so I don't have to work as hard, and then sell, before it's too late, you know?"

Heritage extended his coffee mug in a toast to Fraser's longevity. "You will likely outlast my grandfather," he freely disclosed.

"But outlasting you may prove the bigger challenge? Is that what you are here to tell me?"

Heritage smiled, pacing himself. Long before his arrival in Clayoquot Sound, he'd spent hours working with his grandfather's chief lawyer, Lonnie, practicing this delivery so he could replicate the rehearsal verbatim when the time came. Neither of them thought that moment would happen during the first meeting, but Heritage sensed his opening. "I am here to learn the business and offer efficiencies where I think it enhances the investment and suggest some changes where it doesn't. When you defaulted on the loan agreement earlier this spring, and my grandfather covered the losses, you forfeited your controlling interest and we became equal partners. My grandfather would prefer that Carter Pulp & Paper take a more active role in the Headlands Lodge, given this new share distribution."

Brad Fraser was becoming visibly uncomfortable. "I wouldn't say *defaulted*."

Heritage couldn't let up. "Well, it is the term the bank used, and the consequences were spelled out in the original partnership and capital offering agreement. You are still a rich man, and on the surface, nothing needs to change, Brad. Publicly, you will still be the owner of this enterprise. I am here to assure you that my family is content remaining a silent partner for the time being, but also know, to protect our own investment, we have to become more intimately involved in operations. We are suggesting an elegant solution here that preserves your integrity." Heritage extended an open hand, the one with the cut that he could see was healing nicely, and raised his eyebrows to solicit permission to continue.

"I'm all ears," said the possibly hungover man with croissant crumbs on his unpressed white dress shirt.

"Okay. It's pretty straightforward. I get named the interim general manager, while we get the finances back in line. This explains my presence here to the staff. Three months from now, you either have the means to buy back your five percent controlling shares or CP&P seizes the advantage." Heritage took a quick sip of his coffee and pressed forward, "At which time a buyout offer—cooperative or hostile—will most certainly be on the table."

"General manager? Don't you think that promotion comes a bit prematurely? You said you were here to learn the business."

"Let's not kid ourselves, Brad. I am here to run the business into stronger profits, and more importantly, if I can be frank, to hold my grandfather's impulsivity at bay. We are both just buying time until whatever comes next, okay?" Heritage extended his hand. Fraser was suspicious and reluctant, but without any choice but to accept the arrangement being offered, they shook on the arrangement being offered. Heritage continued. "And I appreciate the top floor corner suite, but we need to free this up for paying guests before the weekend. I have already instructed the front desk to put it back in inventory."

"And where will you be staying, then—over at Wicca Ninnish, with your new friends?"

"I'm not so fast at friend-making. I am my grandfather's grandson, after all. Trust is never automatic with us Carters. If it doesn't come with bank-backed references, and if it can't be bought, insured, or otherwise guaranteed—well then, I guess I am content being a loner for the time being. I will figure out my housing but will certainly enjoy the suite in the meantime. Let's schedule a staff meeting for tomorrow afternoon when you can introduce me and my role here for the winter months ahead."

"That sounds fine." Brad Fraser finished the last swallow of his coffee, returning the mug to the saucer percussively. "I don't know if your granddad mentioned this, but I am off to the Bahamas a week from Friday for a month of rum and grass-skirt chasing. I take holidays this time every year, so your timing is perfect to cover me off. I will leave you my keys, and you can use my office while you teach yourself the upscale resort lodge business."

Heritage's grandfather *hadn't* mentioned it. But things would be easier without the drunk innkeeper drooling over his inexperienced shoulders—shoulders that were expected to learn the hospitality business and prop up operations and his grandfather's sanctimonious mantel without ever shrugging. It all seemed to be going according to plan thus far.

After a forty-five-minute tour of the main lodge, the kitchen and housekeeping areas, and a few of the duplex forest cabins that weren't occupied, Brad and Heritage split a generously sized tuna melt in the dining room and planned the agenda for what was going to be the first hotel staff meeting that wasn't also its alcohol-fueled annual Christmas Party. Understandably, the alpha male was not comfortable sharing the helm with a new captain, nor did he relish the task of addressing the two dozen or so staff members without drinks in their hands—or one in his own. Heritage assured the anxious owner and burley ex-logger that he was prepared to do most of the talking—but that only seemed to compound the awkwardness for a man accustomed to being the only boss.

"You're just putting me in charge while you are away in the Caribbean?" Heritage simplified matters. He could tell by the demonstrative exhale that this approach and explanation for his sudden arrival was acceptable. It would also help bracket the temporary nature of the arrangement, almost suggesting that things would return to normal once Fraser returned from holiday. That would provide Heritage his *in* and both men, their *out*, when this experiment or inspection or whatever it was, came to an end, and hopefully reached some mutually acceptable conclusion.

"Yes, that sounds good," Fraser said. "That's better." The red-faced man with his bulbous, open-pored nose, took the opportunity to relax his rotund, unhealthy looking body that had seemed otherwise headed into cardiac arrest. In another minute, though, Brad began to fidget at the table and invented a sudden need to tend to business downtown after lunch. The pair stood and walked toward the front desk just as Dottie Bard walked up the wide steps and crossed the threshold into the lobby. Her white hair was animated by the winds that skirted the rocky promontory that jutted into the Pacific Ocean like a disdainful chin.

"Dottie," Fraser said.

She returned the greeting. "Bradley. Tage, I see you managed to find your way behind enemy lines."

"Dottie," Heritage acknowledged, tentatively.

"I will be brief. You may have already heard that my daughter, Stephanie, has gone missing. Her zodiac has been tied to the dock in Ahousaht since Friday, and nobody has seen or heard from her since around noon that day. I am assisting the RCMP in spreading the word, and I am asking for your help in keeping a watch out for her. Oh, and I also have posters for the first annual Clayoquot Oyster Festival." She extended the mailing tube to Brad Fraser who symbolically passed the baton to Heritage. "Since we are having the event here, I expect you will be more than happy to help us promote it among your staff and guests."

Neither of the two men had the chance to say anything. Heritage wanted to blurt out that Stephanie wasn't missing, but held his tongue, remembering that he had misplaced the paper sack note she'd left in her mother's Wickaninnish cabin and wouldn't be able to back up any claim with proof. Brad Fraser couldn't give a shit about her oyster festival and was plenty pleased that he would be out of the country when Dottie's event came to his lodge.

"And Tage, please make it a point of stopping by the store this evening or tomorrow morning for a quick chat about your work schedule, would you?"

"Uh, sure." Heritage sounded like a kid just summoned to the principal's office for a talking-to. He did need to clear the air with her, and check into the possibility of using or even renting Stephanie's cabin while she was away. But he had no intention of working for her—particularly now that he'd gotten saddled with watching Aidan for the next few weeks.

"Heritage has full use of the company truck." Fraser awkwardly upped her ante by exaggerating how much he trusted his conniving financial partner's grandson. "He can pop into town whenever he needs to, for business or otherwise."

Heritage gave both of them a respectful nod. Dottie's white hair whiplashed around as she turned to leave. But instead of making her well-heeled exit, she smacked right into François, just as he loped through the open double doorway carrying a tote full of Clayoquot-grown oysters on ice. A handful of chipped ice slushed over the lip of the tote and onto the wood floor at Dottie's gumbooted feet.

"Dottie!" François said, in more of a yell than a greeting.

"Where have you been?" she demanded. "Have you seen or heard from Stephanie?"

"No. You?" François glanced beyond her crazy white hair and spotted Heritage standing there. His face shifted into an apprehensive grin.

"The RCMP have been looking for you. They want to ask you some questions about her disappearance."

Brad Fraser was used to excusing himself from Dottie's drama cyclone, having walked out of a half dozen village council meetings when her debating and grating voice grew tedious. "I have to make a call," he lied, before disappearing into the offices behind the front desk. "I'll let chef know the oysters are here so he can crank up the barbeque," he hollered back to François.

"Stephanie isn't disappeared," François told Dottie. He locked eyes with Heritage, raising his eyebrows to telegraph their familiarity. "Hello, Tage." He looked back at Dottie. "She is gone to Patagonia. But you know that already."

Heritage would have followed Brad into the back to avoid the awkwardness if it weren't for his desire to reunite with François. He took a half step back and planted an elbow on the front desk to wait this out.

Dottie wasn't satisfied, and deeply suspected the Quebecer knew more than he was letting on. "What do you know about her zodiac being left at the dock in Marktosis?"

"I left it der. She asked me to take Sennan back to da hot springs in her boat. When me and Tage got back to Ahousaht, she was not der."

Heritage shifted. *Great. Implicated.*

"You and Tage?"

"*Ye-e-s.*" François drew out his response, sensing an interrogation.

Heritage jumped in. "Stephanie rescued me from the bear-infested beach you dropped me on, and then we linked up with François in Ahousaht."

"Well, well, well," Dottie said, like she was spinning the crank on her judgment tractor to get it going. "You have wasted no time in making your big splash in Clayoquot Sound, have you?"

"Circumstances have provided me a few opportunities to make myself known, yes."

Dottie was visibly pushed, but she returned to her line of questioning with François. "So, you just left Stephanie's boat at the dock?"

"We could not find her, and nobody at the blockade camp had seen her, eder. I had my own boat der so thought it best to leave her boat for her so she could get back. She knew my boat was der. I bringed Tage with his kayak back to town in my skiff."

"Brought. You *brought* Tage to town." She could see how he might be innocent. But she wasn't a judge, and she wasn't the RCMP, and, most importantly, she hadn't heard from her daughter—so everyone was a suspect. "Where can the RCMP find you, then? Are you back in town, or still out at the oyster farm?"

"Dees days, I am ten-on and four-off. It's da harvest season starting real soon. I am on day six only."

Heritage took note of that. He had thought it was eight days on and four days off for François at the oyster farm.

"Well maybe you could stop by the RCMP detachment and speak to one of the officers before you head back up to the farm." She looked around François to address Heritage. "And you could do the same on your way into town to have your chat with me—since you were also, I presume, one of the last to see Stephanie before she disappeared."

"She is not disappeared," François repeated with an incredulous laugh, but Dottie ignored him, already turning her heavy gumboots to leave.

Heritage, at last alone again with François, was nervously giddy. "Hey," he said.

"Hey," François replied, readjusting the load of heavy oysters to balance on his other knee.

"I was hoping and looking forward to a chance to see you again," Heritage admitted.

"Well, here I am." In the awkward few seconds that followed, both men shifted and stalled. It wasn't quite the reunion Heritage had been thinking about, but at least they were standing face to face again. "I have four more restaurants to deliver to and then I am heading back up to God's Pocket—where da oyster farm is, you know."

"God's Pocket? What a name! Where exactly is it?"

"Up Lemmen's Inlet, in da crotch of Meares Island." François sounded as if everyone should know where that was.

Heritage made a mental note. "So, you are working until this Saturday, then." He wanted to get a plan out of him—something he could look forward to. He wanted to pick things up from where they left off—especially with Stephanie out of the picture—momentarily forgetting that Aidan had taken her place. "You can find me here, where I am staying—or we could meet up on Wickaninnish Island if you wanted to get together."

"I don't understand. What you doing here?" François set the tote on the wooden floor. The Headlands chef rushed up and grabbed it, as though a kidney or heart had just arrived on ice for transplant. François extracted an invoice from an unzipped pocket in his yellow raincoat and slipped it under the grip of the chef's meaty hand as he hefted the tote onto one of his shoulders. The chef turned back toward the kitchen, but paused long enough to extend a free hand to Heritage.

"You must be Mr. Carter. Stu Solberg, head chef. I understand you have already had the kitchen tour, but I was dropping kids off at school—so pop back in anytime this afternoon and I will make us an early dinner while we talk shop."

Heritage realized in that moment that his intended low profile must be confusing to François and Dottie—maybe even to Brad Fraser. They must have all been surprised by his many local connections, made in less than a week. It really came down to circumstances, like he had told Dottie. He hadn't set out to become enmeshed in everyone's personal business, but he was learning quickly that everyone was already tangled up together in Tofino.

"Later," Stu said to François, and vanished into the kitchen.

François' eyebrows seemed to be locked in a permanent arch.

"I can explain," Heritage said, briefly taking François' arm to turn him and lead him through the main lodge doors and out to the covered entrance porch.

"What you doing here?" François asked Heritage a second time as he opened the driver's door to the panel van he'd borrowed for the deliveries. "Brad Fraser is a pig and everybody know dis."

"Well, I know it too, but it is complicated. We haven't had much time together but maybe when you come off the farm, we can talk," Heritage offered just as he spotted the green OSU sweatshirt wadded up in the passenger seat. He couldn't break his stare as his brain sprinted off trying to figure out when exactly François might have been to Wickaninnish Island to retrieve it from the A-frame he'd been using. What else had he seen there? Stephanie's note? Had François ripped the P.S. from the bottom of it? Did he know that Heritage had had sex with his girlfriend? Did François have his paperback novel too? Heritage tried to remember when he first noticed the sweatshirt was gone. Was it before the dance party at Lyle's . . . after Marcel had drowned? His recall was a complete blur. Was it possible that François had known Marcel, another man his age also from Quebec? Of course, they had to know each other and maybe this was why François seemed hurt and was being short, almost dismissive with him. The lanky Quebecer climbed behind the steering wheel and closed the driver door between them. He rolled down the window, but not all the way.

"Maybe I already know all der is to know, eh?"

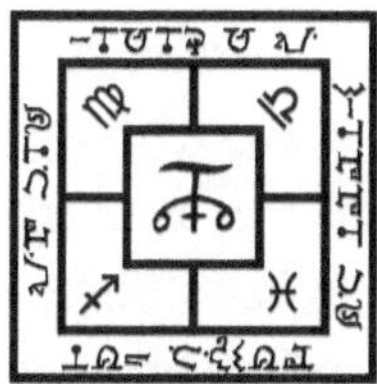

PAGAN PROGRESS

The Tofino Branch of the Vancouver Island Regional Library was helmed on Thursdays and Saturdays between the hours of ten and two (the only days and hours it was open) by a wildly red-headed and delightfully cherubic librarian named Gillian. With quite possibly all the known Celtic iconography catalogued in nine tattoos—four on each arm and one in the middle of her upper chest—she challenged the stereotype of her normally bespectacled profession. She seldom wore a shirt, sweatshirt, or blouse with full sleeves—her tattoos were her identity and her wardrobe as much as they were her heritage.

She often explained her body art for those brave patrons who inquired. Starting on her left shoulder was the Awen of the Three Rays of Light. The Triquetra, sometimes known as a Trinity Knot, was colourfully centered on her left bicep. Below that, stretching the length of her forearm, was a Celtic Cross (upside-down to everyone but her). Beginning at her wrist, a musical harp could be seen on the top of her left hand, looking almost like a henna design. The Green Man covered her entire right hand (again, upside-down to others, but not to her). The Crann Bethadh wrapped around her forearm. The Shamrock adorned her right bicep. A Brigid's Cross perched like a compass honoring the four elements on her right shoulder. And square center on her upper chest, just above her sternum, was the Triskele—a triple spiral spoking out from a hub and representing the three stages of life: life, death, and rebirth.

Heritage had just been the latest patron to ask about her ink. He didn't really have the time to kill, having made a special, mid-morning trip into town expressly to drop Marcel's wallet by the RCMP detachment and to speak with Dottie on her insistence, only to find out from Sarah—her part-time store-sitter—that Dottie was on a daytrip to Nanaimo and wouldn't be back until the town council meeting later that evening.

But this is not what had brought him to the library attached to the seventy-five-seat community theatre and village offices. He was there to see what he could find out about witchcraft, maybe gather a few nuggets of useful gossip if the librarian seemed chatty, and learn if Wickaninnish Island or Tofino or Clayoquot Sound were somehow significant in the greater Wiccan subculture. What he really wanted was intel on Dottie Bard—but he didn't think he could be that overt without Dottie finding out, so he decided to invent the cover that he was interested in witches.

"You're that new guy that I overheard Dottie Bard talking about outside of the SunRyes Bakeshop the other morning, aren't you?" Gillian toyed with her hair flirtatiously. "Here to write a novel—or something like that?"

"Something like that, yes." Heritage slowly blinked his dark eyelashes and then fixed his gaze on her green eyes to bring her under his own mystical powers. "My name's Tage. Tage Carter." His mouth lifted into a smarmy, suspicious smile that women, for some reason, couldn't resist. It was disgusting to rely on such ploys, but he was a handsome guy, and that got him favours and places. It's not like that made him sleazy, he'd often tell himself in a valiant effort to keep his special powers and vanity in check.

"I'm Gillian," she almost sang, blushing and swooning, and pulling her voluminous hair into a ponytail with her left hand as she extended her right hand to greet the newest deity to have found his way to the end of the road. "Can I help you find something in particular?" She hadn't technically surrendered the key to her heart—that belonged to someone else—though Heritage was misreading her enthusiasm and presumed it was telegraphing her interest and availability.

"I'm curious about something." He paused, luring her in closer. She leaned forward on her high swivel stool expectantly. "I remember reading an article, maybe it was in a book, about a Wiccan subculture in Clayoquot Sound—on Wickaninnish Island, perhaps?"

"Interesting."

The librarian leaned back and crossed her inked arms over her substantial breasts. There was probably much on the topic she could tell him, but Heritage was sensing he must have elevated her guard. In that silence, patience mattered, so he waited her out, dangling his charm in the space between them like it was mistletoe. Any useful bit of information could get revealed and link to other information he had already discovered on his own.

"How much do you want to know?" she finally asked, batting her stubby eyelashes. Ah-ha, Heritage thought as he leaned in, celebrating that he had succeeded in getting her onto his hook. His widened eyes and a raised eyebrow nonverbally communicated he wanted to know everything she knew on the topic.

"In the late '60s," she began, launching right into it, "the Coven Celeste was founded near Sylvan Lake, Alberta, by a man named Gordon Bard."

"Wait a minute. As in Dottie *Bard*?

Gillian only smiled and then continued. "He had been the

grandson of London's High Priestess, Lysbeth Turner—herself a devout Gerald Gardner disciple. Now, among the pagan and occult communities, Gerald Gardner is widely recognized as the father of Wicca. Lysbeth Turner had been initiated into his New Forest Coven about the time that Gardner's star had started to ascend in the realms of spiritualism, nudism, and modern witchcraft."

"Nudism?"

"Yes. Gardner, though he was born in England, had been living abroad, and found, when he returned to London, that his health was being compromised by the climate. He went to a doctor who suggested he try nudism. Gardner began attending the Lotus League in North London—an indoor nudist club—and soon concluded that nudism was curing him. There, he heard of an outdoor nudist group that met regularly at a place called the Fouracres Club. Shuttling back and forth between the indoor and outdoor clubs, Gardner dabbled in pagan rituals and druidism, and for a while, aligned himself with the Order of Bards, Ovates, and Druids."

"Wait. There it is again. Bard is Dottie's last name. Is this a coincidence, do you think?"

Gillian smiled. "It doesn't matter what I think."

"Well, go on then." Heritage looked at his dive watch, noting the time.

Sensing he was pressed, Gillian picked up the pace of her lecture—the subject of which she seemed a fair bit more than just familiar with. "Gerard Gardner died in 1964, but fast forward to the '70s. With a number of books under his name and in wide circulation—like *The Book of Shadows* and *Witchcraft Today*—the Gardnerian Philosophy of witchcraft and the occult became the modern framework for most of the Wiccan covens that began popping up all around the world around that same time, including one in Sylvan Lake, Alberta."

"Right." Heritage was nodding, thinking he remembered those very book titles among the collection at Dottie's island cabin. "A coven in Sylvan Lake, Alberta . . ." He began forming details of a theory out loud, remembering that Brad Fraser had said that Dottie had come here from northern Alberta and also recalling the newspaper article clipped from the Edmonton Journal that marked the pages of the weightiest book of all in Dottie's collection.

"The Coven Celeste, like most covens, remained matrilineal, and so to the daughter of Gordon and Heather Bard at Sylvan Lake, passed the athamé, as it will eventually pass to her daughter—each of them becoming high priestesses in their turn, just like their mother and grandmother before them."

"Sorry, what is an athamé?"

"An athamé is a ritualistic blade, usually with a black and decorated handle, that is the primary banishing implement used during Wiccan ceremonial and sometimes satanic traditions. It represents the element of fire."

"And the current high priestess of the Coven Celeste, let me guess, resides here in Clayoquot Sound?" Heritage made a logical leap over the broomstick with that one. But he was right, according to Gillian's slowly nodding head. "And Stephanie?" Heritage asked. Gillian continued nodding. "And you—?" There needed to be some reason the librarian knew so much about witchcraft.

Gillian stopped nodding. She lowered her head and began reciting in a syncopated and robotic way, as though she were slipping into a trance—or deliberately trying to freak him out. "We believe the earth is alive and all of life is sacred and every living thing is interconnected. We see the Goddess as immanent in the earth's cycles of birth, growth, decay, and regeneration. Our practice arises from a deep, spiritual commitment to the earth—to healing and to the linking of magic with political action." She began to fall out of character and cracked a smile, but Heritage encouraged her with a smile of his own and she continued. "Each of us embodies the divine. Our ultimate spiritual authority is within, and we need no other person to interpret or decode the sacred for us. We are an evolving, dynamic tradition, and we proudly call ourselves witches." Gillian glanced up into his eyes and paused. "Should I go on, or have I scared you shitless?"

"Not at all," he lied. "Please, continue."

"Our coven rituals are participatory and ecstatic, celebrating the cycles of the seasons and our lives, and raising energy for personal, collective, and earth healing. We know that everyone can do the life-changing, world-renewing work of magic—the art of changing consciousness at will. We strive to teach and practice in ways that foster personal and collective empowerment, to model shared power, and to open leadership roles to all. We welcome all genders, all gender histories, all races, all ages and sexual orientations—and those differences of life situation, background, and ability that increase our diversity. All living beings are worthy of respect. All are supported by the sacred elements of air, fire, water, and earth. We make decisions by consensus, and balance individual autonomy with social responsibility. Our tradition honors the wild, and calls for service to the earth and the community of all living things. We work for all forms of justice: environmental, social, political, racial, gender, and economic. Our feminism includes a radical analysis of power, seeing all systems of oppression as interrelated, rooted in structures of domination and control. We work to create and sustain communities and cultures that embody our values, that can help to heal the wounds of the earth and her people, and that can sustain us and nurture future generations."

"Where can I sign up?" Heritage sounded enthusiastic and sarcastic at the same time.

"Why, at your local library, of course!" Gillian reached for a giant reference catalog on the corner of her desk, and dramatically heaved the spine open, reaching for a pen as though she were being serious. "Your hypothesis is valid." She patted his hand. "There is a Wiccan sub-culture here, but we are mostly harmless and wouldn't recognize a newt if one ran across our spell books in the middle of an incantation." Gillian's stone-serious face disintegrated into a giggle. "I'm just joking," she paused, then said, "I know what a newt is."

The door to the library opened noisily with the unoiled creaking sound of a haunted house secret passageway and an RCMP officer strode through, looking somber and heading toward the librarian desk.

"Hello Pete," Gillian greeted him.

"A word, Gillian?" the officer inquired.

That was Heritage's cue to move along. He smiled his thanks for the information as he backed away from the circulation desk. Just as he reached the doors, he heard the officer say

"It's about Marcel."

Not only was Dottie Bard an honest-to-goodness witch (though Heritage doubted she was either honest or good) she had a pedigree that she could trace generations back to London. All Heritage had was an eventually dying grandfather and a whole branch between them on the family tree that his father had lopped-off during a jealous rampage. With a surname like Carter, Heritage had always assumed his ancestors came from Great Britain but after his father's fatal stunt just before Christmas that year, any pride from the family crest or interest in his family's origins sort of withered and died too.

Heritage left the library feeling a little stunned about the witchcraft revelations and hearing the officer mention Marcel's name had added another chill to his afternoon. He was still carrying Marcel Labbé's wallet in his own back pocket. The RCMP detachment was located right across Third Street from the library and it had already been the next stop on his errand list even before the officer entered the library to speak with Gillian.

When Heritage arrived at the reception window, there was

nobody on the other side of the glass. The waiting area was sparse, painted a shade of yellow from the late '70s, with one recruiting poster on the wall in both official languages, a self-serve bulletin board with missing person notices from across the country, the 1994 tide chart and a flyer for the first annual Clayoquot Oyster Festival. Heritage scoffed at Dottie's promotional confidence—that her festival was being hyped both as first and annual—before even learning if it would be a success or a flop or even repeatable.

"Hello—is anybody home?" Heritage steamed a patch on the glass with his greeting. There was no response. "Hello?"

He waited another minute and then decided to try the door handle. Maybe the town's only officer was next door at the library. The knob turned and was unlocked. He stuck his head inside and hollered again. He heard a toilet flush and quickly withdrew his head, closed the door quietly, and repositioned himself at the glass. When the on-duty officer emerged from the washroom, Heritage yelled "Hello!" and tapped on the glass. The officer approached him.

"How may I help you?" asked the dark mustached man who looked quite a lot like Freddy Mercury—complete with a gap between his front teeth.

"My name is Tage Carter, and I am hoping I can help you. I was asked to stop by here or the coast guard station regarding that fellow, Marcel, who drowned in the storm Sunday night—or I guess it would have been early Monday morning."

"Right," the officer said, looking around for something. "Wait one second for me, eh? Our dispatcher is home with a migraine today."

"No problem," Heritage responded, content to study the uniformed man.

Frustrated, the officer grabbed a nearby yellow legal pad and returned to the counter on his side of the glass. "I'm going to need to ask you for a driver's license or ID, please."

"Sure." Heritage thought he could have better anticipated

that question, but extracted a wallet from each of his back pockets, placing them on the counter. The officer noted this and commented.

"You that rich you need two billfolds?" he asked.

Heritage looked him in his brown eyes and smiled. "One of these wallets," he scooted the black one under the slot in the glass, "belonged to Marcel." The brown eyes became demonstratively larger. The officer gloved his left hand in latex and opened the wallet for a quick, one-handed pry, before placing it into a Ziplock bag pre-labeled with the word *EVIDENCE* in black block letters and the French translation of the word, *PREUVE*, in red block letters.

The officer stretched his upper body to reach the door and invited Heritage to join him on the other side. Down a short hallway, Heritage followed the officer, who was a good measure shorter, and quite possibly even younger than Heritage, until they reached a desk with a name plaque that read *L. Toren*. The officer motioned for Heritage to sit in the chair opposite the one he was taking behind the desk. Heritage compared the nametag to the desk plaque for a match, wondering what the *L* stood for. *Lance*, he decided randomly. Yes, *Lance Toren*—it sounded like a porn star name, and the good-looking fellow behind the desk in uniform looked like picture-perfect casting for any of the half dozen gay porn movies Heritage had perused.

"Your identification card, please?" L. Toren reached his gloved left hand out without looking up while scribbling on the pad with his other hand. Heritage fished his Ontario driver's license out of his wallet and aimed the piece of plastic between Toren's thumb and forefinger, causing the officer to recoil when contact was made. "You can place it on the desk," he said. "Thank you."

"You're welcome," Heritage said, sort of clearing his throat at the same time.

"And so how do you know—" Toren stopped himself. "How did you know Marcel?"

"I didn't," Heritage responded, not meaning to turn every

question into a riddle. "I saw Marcel for the first time on Sunday afternoon, but I did not meet him."

"How's that?" Toren asked, looking up, presumably to read Heritage's face for honesty.

Heritage paused in that spotlight. "I was staying on Wickaninnish Island—at the invitation of Dottie Bard."

"You are no longer staying on Wickaninnish?"

"That's right. I am now staying at the Headlands Lodge." He decided to try out his new title. "I am the new general manager there."

"Is that so?" the officer asked. "What? Brad Fraser's liver finally give out?" He quickly covered up any inappropriateness in the joke with a follow-up question. "You were on Wickaninnish Island where you saw Marcel but didn't meet him—please continue."

"I was on a hike about the island on Sunday—it being the first day of sunshine in the week that I have been here, and from the big beach on the outer coast, I could hear music. I continued hiking north, up the island's west side to see if I could learn where the music was coming from. That's when I encountered a small party happening at a cottage on the cliff owned by a guy named Lyle." Heritage waited to see if the officer registered the name or looked confused, and then went on. "I introduced myself to Lyle and a couple others, but Marcel, or the man somebody had told me was Marcel, was sleeping in the sun, so I didn't meet him."

"And aside from Lyle and Marcel, who were these other people?"

Heritage smiled. "Uh, almost unbelievably, they were a group of dancers from the Royal London ballet troupe."

"London, Ontario or London, England?"

"England," Heritage answered. "They were the real thing!" Heritage may have been impressed by this, but Toren didn't seem to be.

"And were their drugs and alcohol at this party?"

"I wasn't there very long, I, uh, didn't drink anything—" Heritage stammered, and the tiger pounced.

"Do you have any knowledge of, or did you take any drugs at this party, yourself?"

"I was given some Ecstasy, yes," Heritage confessed into those brown eyes as though he had Wonder Woman's golden lasso coiled around his torso, compelling him not to lie.

Officer Toren looked back down at his yellow pad and made a longer note. "Do you know who supplied the drugs you took, or saw being used at this party?"

"I don't."

"Now, this Ecstasy you said you were given, but you don't know by who—"

"I suppose I should clarify. I was directed to where the drugs were being, uh, stored, and I was encouraged to help myself."

"And you did?"

"I did."

"And so I can assume then, that you've consumed Ecstasy before, and knew what you were taking and the effects it would have?"

"Yes," Heritage answered confidently, suspecting he was blushing, given the warmth he was suddenly feeling in his cheeks. Toren didn't look up from his pad.

"And you mentioned you were shown where the drugs were kept. Where was this, exactly?" He looked up and into Heritage's face.

Heritage was definitely blushing now. "In sort of a little purse," he said.

"Like a coin purse," Toren asked.

"Yes, like a small coin purse." Heritage felt bad minimizing another man's carrying capacity, but he was in a tight spot. It did make him wonder how many coins you could carry in a foreskin purse, though.

"Hmm. Okay."

"Mind if I ask you what the *L* stands for?" Heritage didn't care whether the officer minded or not.

"Luis," Luis responded. Heritage knew not to take that as a victory. He was still in the hot seat, though he knew he'd done nothing wrong, except maybe confessing to taking an illegal substance. "I don't suppose you know whether or not Marcel had taken any drugs—"

"Not while I was there. He was asleep in the sun when I arrived, and asleep in the same spot when I left."

"I wonder if you would have been able to determine the difference between someone sleeping and someone passed out?"

"Could you, Officer Toren—I mean, from a distance—adequately judge if a man were sleeping or passed out?" Heritage didn't mean to get snippy, but he would have objected to that leading and subjective question in court, arguing it as inadmissible.

"You a lawyer or something?"

"I went to law school but I, uh, this is embarrassing, but I failed to pass the bar exam on my first attempt." Heritage hoped that made him sound human and not just incompetent. "Now I have to wait until next February to try again.

"Too many drugs?" Toren had turned antagonist.

"Not enough," Heritage countered, sarcastically. "I became bored by the lack of imagination and the less-than-zero tolerance for creativity in the criminal justice system."

Toren put his pen down. "What would you have liked to see as an alternative to the system we have?"

"Are you serious?" Heritage practically squealed before launching into his scholarly opinion. "In our multicultural society, on lands we have stolen from the First Peoples who were here for thousands of years before us? Who in the hell do we think we are to impose our justice system—our determination of what's right or wrong—our beliefs, our religions, our economies— on anyone else without first understanding that our system of laws and order are not divine or universal? It boggles the mind!"

"But how do you really feel?" Toren at least revealed a smile that broke the tension. He handed Heritage's ID back to him. "I trust I can contact you at the Headlands if I have any further questions or need a lesson in civics or social discourse?"

"Absolutely. Yes." Heritage eagerly stood to leave.

Toren motioned him to sit back down. "We haven't covered how you came to possess Marcel Labbé's billfold."

Heritage lowered his butt back down into the plastic molded chair that may have been easy to clean and disinfect but was really uncomfortable after five minutes of sitting and had made his crack sweat. "As I told Matt Greene from the coast guard the morning after the accident, I was waiting out the storm and fell asleep in Lyle's cabin later that night after the party, by myself, after everyone had left the place to head back to Vancouver. That's how I heard Marcel's mayday on the marine radio."

"Go on," Toren encouraged.

"Matt Greene had mentioned to me that, uh, the seaplane pilot, oh, what's his name again? Jason! Jason had told Matt that he'd bumped into Marcel after dark and that Marcel had said something about leaving his wallet on Wickaninnish Island and that he was heading back there to retrieve it."

"But you had his billfold?"

"No. Not when I spoke with Matt. I found Marcel's wallet on my way back across the island later that day."

"Which was still on Monday—yesterday?"

Heritage had to think a moment. "Yes, yesterday."

Toren was still writing when he said, "there's one more thing, Mr. Carter." He placed the pen on an angle across the legal pad like when you close your dinner plate with your fork and knife after eating. "We haven't been able to notify the next of kin yet, so if you can help us preserve Marcel's identity until we can reach his family, I would appreciate you not speaking with others about the fatal accident that occurred below Lyle Hudson's place. We are working to keep this out of the paper and rumour mill for now."

"Of course." Tage tried to remember if he had mentioned this to anyone already. It hadn't come up with Mona or Mac. His conversation with François had been curt, and he hadn't said anything to Brad Fraser, so maybe the RCMP and coast guard had managed to keep a lid on this accident so far. But that sent Heritage down another mental whirlpool wondering how much trouble the authorities would have if they ever had to contact his next of kin—never mind *next*, he revised—his *only* kin—if something were to happen to him out here. He'd scrubbed his own wallet of any connection to his grandfather and the family company. Brad Fraser knew about their blood-link, of course, but he was hightailing it to the Caribbean by the end of the week.

Heritage had long been lugging around a premonition that he was about to be permanently orphaned in the universe by his grandfather's passing, after which, there would be no kin, no common ancestry left for anyone to contact. He didn't want to be that one tree in a forest that fell down with nobody around to hear if it made a sound or even notice that it had fallen. Heritage needed a confidant and an emergency contact for practical sake, like the trust-relationship he'd once cultivated with a drag queen so similarly abandoned that she'd had to reimagine and rename herself *Imogene Mantoya*. Even the two of them eventually outgrew each other and had fallen silently out of touch.

In that lonely, somewhat self-loathing moment, standing in the sun that would abandon them all in the coming days for months, Heritage realized that he needed somebody in his life who cared, who he cared about and who was paying closer attention. But so far, six days in, he had to admit he had not been all that impressed by the available Clayoquot candidates.

ROAD RAGED

It had been a goddess-awful early start for a road trip, but Dottie knew she had to be back in the village by seven, to preside at the regular council meeting as the acting-mayor. She had learned over the years of chauffeuring Mona to medical appointments that leaving before dawn would usually guarantee that Mona would sleep the first two hours of the journey—which meant a respite for Dottie as well. She couldn't count the times they'd made these sojourns to Victoria or Vancouver for the various tests, surgeries, and treatments her friend's frail health required. It had been one long blurred decade of hair and breast loss, weight fluctuation, nausea, side effects, and radical surgeries that had chiseled Mona into somebody different. Not better, not worse— just not the same. Dottie didn't know who would have been there for Mona if she hadn't been, and Dottie frankly couldn't imagine a life without her priestess and constant companion of the past seventeen years—though the merciless onslaught of the cancer had forced Dottie to face that eventuality, and sometimes daily.

Dottie monitored her dozing passenger as she negotiated the climbing, diving, curving, and slumping road that was Highway 4 through the mountains beyond Kennedy Lake, leading them inland from the Pacific Ocean. The two of them had already been through several lifetimes together—or so they believed and had been told by any number of spirit mediums and so-called-oracles that they had consulted. Their bond was strengthened by the comforting knowledge that this lifetime had not been their first nor would it be their last incarnation together—so they wasted few tears dwelling on what would come next. In her heart, though, Dottie knew what Mona denied, and this drained the colour from the knuckles on both hands gripping the steering wheel.

Without question, she could have used more time with Mona to reinvigorate the Coven Celeste. Grandiose had been their vision for wiccan renewal and bringing the ancient practices of witchery and the black arts to a modern age at the very intersection of planetary ley lines that—during a trance prophecy Dottie had been mystically shown—converged over the southern end of Wickaninnish Island. Just like at the sites of the pyramids, Angkor Wat, Stonehenge and Machu Pichu, Dottie's blueprint for an all-female master planned community, a utopian haven she was already marketing as *Wicca Ninnish*, was on the verge of realization. But Dottie knew that Mona had straddled the fence from the beginning with her dominant leg stuck fast in her own realities and the other leg not quite long enough to reach the ground that Dottie was hellbent on consecrating. Over time, they had become lazy with their rituals and lapsed in their recruiting. Then, this past summer's record-breaking tourist season had been the best economically, but also the worst—depending on whether you were a banker counting the heaps of cash in the back, or a teller on the frontline, drained of all essence, and unable to stand upright by the end of the Labour Day weekend. Dottie and Mona were both the bankers and the tellers in each of their businesses just as they womaned the helms of each of their destinies. Dottie hadn't realized until the frictions and pressures and bounty from that summer lay bare an entirely different future on the way, that for she and Mona, Wickaninnish Island had been their vessel and that both their helms were on the same boat but facing opposite destinations; Mona's terminus rushing up too quickly now to be avoided. Dottie would soon become a sole navigator, the only hand on the broom handle stirring the cauldron of possibilities, and this squeezed a set of tears from her grey-blue eyes.

Neither of them had anticipated the instant worldwide popularity of Clayoquot Sound and Tofino, following the previous summer's War in the Woods. Their hamlet of not quite twelve hundred inhabitants had become this Mecca among environmentalists—and in a new hippie world order, hundreds of thousands of people had made a pilgrimage to the spot where thousands had been brave enough to lay their bodies down in front of an endless convoy of logging trucks, and where more than 900 had been rounded up and taken away by the RCMP, in what became the largest mass arrest in Canadian history. Dottie and Mona had been so busy supporting the blockade camp with food, first aid, cash, and encouragement, that they hadn't even made it to the front line of the barricaded logging road until the last weekend before the rains washed out what was left of the resistance. It was there, on the abutment of that bridge crossing the river flowing out of Kennedy Lake, that the two of them had gotten handcuffed and charged with aiding and abetting civil unrest.

Just driving past the clear-cut that had been christened the Black Hole and had served as the site of the blockade camp made Dottie's blood boil. She thought about waking Mona to point out how the site next to the highway was greening up, since the two had argued over whether anything would ever grow there again after all those people had squatted and shitted there in tents and

Volkswagens and oil-leaking campers. But Mona's wrinkled face looked so relaxed and peaceful that Dottie let her be.

The arrest had been harder on Mona than Dottie. Mona had received a four-month house-arrest ankle bracelet, and a significant fine—since the protestors had been fueled by freely provisioned SunRyes Stromboli and cheese buns that arrived daily at the blockade kitchen. The RCMP didn't know what they didn't know when they arrested Dottie Bard, assuming she was just another Tofino businesswoman moonlighting as an amateur protestor. In fact, two days before her arrest, Dottie had conspired with her Yankee ex-patriot draft dodger boyfriend—an alumnus from the '68 Chicago riots—to blow up the Kennedy Lake bridge, which would sever the only access logging trucks had to the ancient forests beyond. But that was a whole other chapter in the summer saga.

Dottie couldn't avoid a slump in the road and entered the bend at a speed that amplified the jolt. Mona reflexively jumped in her sleep but settled back into a slump of her own, with her chin resting near the top of that brutal scar on her chest—the site where the cancer that riddled her insides had planted a conquest flag. She was one tired fighter, Dottie thought, reducing her speed to make the ride slightly more comfortable.

Highway 4 was really nothing more than a half dozen layers of asphalt that failed to disguise the rudimentary logging road that lay crumbling and, in some spots, washed out beneath it. That was also a metaphor for these two gals, who covered up their herstories, secrets, distress, and battle scars with happy clothes and ridiculously optimistic and unpragmatic attitudes. Dottie thought of the secrets that would go to the grave with her dear friend and wrestled with the relief that thought gave her. Secrets were tricky things, and risks multiplied with everyone who knew or discovered them. Dottie supposed some people shouldn't be trusted with secrets. She'd wondered this about Mona these past few months and suspected she might be clearing out the warehouse of her conscience in preparation for . . . Dottie didn't want to think about it.

She glanced across the front seat and noted the uneasiness with which Mona's sweatshirt lay across that lopsided chest. Dottie made an angry face and squeezed the steering wheel tighter to contain her steam. She wasn't about to whine about how unfair the world was, when she'd caused plenty of its unfairness. Mona was just plain weak, and that's what bothered her most. A stronger woman, like herself, could have staved off the cancer, and never allowed it the torque it wrenched on her unlucky lug nut of a friend. Then again, a stronger female companion could have helped Dottie achieve an even greater power base in the sound. As things had turned out, she'd been held back and, in many ways, betrayed by Mona, compelled as she was to play nursemaid to the only liability in her otherwise flawless ledger of perfectly calculated and easily manipulated assets. Mona's had been the only dissenting voice when Dottie had unveiled her blockbuster development plan for Wickaninnish Island at the annual general meeting on Big Beach three years earlier—and at every AGM since. Dottie could neither forgive nor forget that mortal transgression, which proved nearly as fatal to their sisterhood as this cancer would be—not that Dottie had wished or conjured this outcome intentionally. Still, she was sitting on a brood of plans that would hatch a more exclusive and progressive Wicca Ninnish, and Mona, for the time being, was still this immoveable boulder in her way.

It had long been Dottie's master scheme to incorporate Wickaninnish Island with a hand-selected citizenry of her own, over which she would preside during the day as Her Worship the Mayor, and after dark as the Coven High Priestess. She would personally recruit investors who were either witches or sympathetic practitioners of the occult. She'd already commenced recruitment by courting Gillian the librarian into buying the next share to become available. The only obstacle for civic recognition as an unincorporated municipality within an established electoral district, apparently, was that a minimum of thirty people needed to continuously inhabit the island for a period of no less than 120 days annually. This would qualify them for their place name and a post office. Wickaninnish Island, as it had been originally parceled by covenant, only allowed for twenty year-round inhabitants. Only eleven of these (Dottie included) had managed to calendar qualify, as the balance of the shareholders were seasonal, fair-weather, summer cottagers, and Mason's husband, Clive, was away doing time for involuntary manslaughter in an Abbotsford prison after his run-in with the logging truck a decade earlier. Poor bastard, Dottie felt, but his incarceration hadn't really affected the island's census since Mason gave birth to their son Rowan shortly after and had been persuaded to stay on fulltime. Dottie's uphill, slippery-sloped challenge rested on persuading the others to extend their summer stays, include Wick for their Spring Break and Christmas week getaways despite the predictably inhospitable weather, and, of course, obtain consensus around penciling another ten to twelve land shares on the map to expand the island's population to the thirty residents it needed to qualify for incorporation.

Beyond the librarian, Dottie kept a running short list of eager would-be shareholders, ranked them, and pressured each of them to sign a prospectus promissory contract that she herself had not only drafted but notarized. Plus, she'd collected a twenty-five percent deposit of ten grand from each of them, which she held in a numbered trust account. She was even grooming Tage, the newcomer, into falling in love with the island though she doubted he had the deposit money at the ready plus he was a man, which she was prepared to overlook in order to get closer to the magic census number. Hell, she'd even employ him and garnish the deposit money figuring the stronger women could band together to run the men off after incorporation anyway. She had valiantly tried, at each of the past three AGMs, to table her community expansion plan and secure the votes granting her the authority, as president, to establish and sell these additional ten shares she'd mapped out and featured in a glossy tri-fold brochure she had photocopied at the Co-op. But she kept coming up a few votes short each round, which placed the dissenters on her shit and magic spell list.

Her most loyal opposition had come from the woman dozing in the passenger seat next to her. Mona had been an adamantly convincing campaigner and Mason had been the first to buckle under Mona's canvassing—which surprised no one, since Mason was known as the human weathervane. Dottie was already working Mason and was confident by next year's AGM, she'd turn again, so Dottie could get closer to achieving consensus. Curtis McLeod was another one. He was the lawyer buddy of Lyle Hudson's from the legendary Deep Cove Party Mecca House they'd once shared, and he was the one who had helped Sharon Greene carve up the island into shares for sale in the first place. He was also the architect of the first shareholder agreement and the first to acquire a share of his own that he had yet to build a structure on—and often waffled about selling. Irritating to everyone, Curtis had abstained from voting at each of the previous consensus roll calls.

Sharon Greene, on the other hand, would be an American capitalist to the end, and had enthusiastically supported Dottie's ambitious expansion plan, particularly since the proposed island map re-tinkering hadn't touched Sharon's five-share dynasty at the south end, below Big Beach—where she was ensconced with her second husband, Steve Greene, and their four children. Both parents were rabid environmentalists, Area 51 conspiracists, UFO fanatics, homeschoolers and artists. Steve fancied himself a mystical truth seer and the unofficial caretaker of the island's trail system. He was a transplanted, full-blood Ojibwa from Ontario, and the exotically handsome father of the pair's four children who were coming into age and should soon start having children (future census statistics) of their own. This calculus of Dottie's would begin with the Tofino Station coast guard captain, Matt. As the eldest of the Greene spawn, Matt had been gifted—as each of his younger siblings would be on their eighteenth birthdays—with an island share within his family compound. Engaged to be married next Spring, Matt had already delighted Dottie with his boastful talk of wanting to sire a huge family. Armed with their own and growing voting block, the Greenes had strongly supported Dottie's vision for Wickaninnish Island.

Uncharacteristically defiant on this one issue, Mona was dug in, and the cement of her terminal cancer had cured hard around her resolve. She would die on this hill. Already, the shares and the build-out of cabins had altered the pristine microcosm of the island, in her estimation. Originally divided so that no cabin or house was within sight of another structure, Wickaninnish Island was gentrifying. Gone were the years when she could imagine herself a castaway on a deserted island. Gone was so much of what she had truly treasured. *Gone* was a recurring theme for Mona. She would succumb to it sooner than later, and not only had Dottie accepted this reality, she was constantly recomputing the impact Mona's passing would have on the plans she had for Wickaninnish Island.

True, Mona had defied Dottie and lobbied Mason and the other women on the island against the plan in the beginning, when both the sisterhood and her wise elder influence over it were stronger. Dottie knew that Mona's old guard stubbornness was weakening the conclave at the same time Dottie believed in her heart that she was the only one who could fortify it anew. And except for the last two holdouts of Mason and Mona, everyone had mostly accepted that Dottie had a near stranglehold on consensus and would eventually get her way. She knew that she could compel Curtis to vote her way in the end. What Mona didn't know was that in recent months, Dottie had managed to persuade Mason to reconsider her position—but only after Mona had passed on. Dottie knew Mona could still sabotage her plan by leaving her share provisionally to Aidan when he turned eighteen. And since Aidan hated women, neutralizing this threat early on was a priority. Dottie figured she could convince her godson to also hate Wickaninnish Island—especially if she gave him a taste of the enticing world that lay beyond Clayoquot Sound. Enter Tage Carter. There was no end to her brilliance.

And Mona was no flunky from the school of shameless manipulation either, and even while she slept, she surely schemed, and made lists and calculations of her own. Dottie knew this about her closest friend which is why she preferred to merge their powers against common foes like the multi-national logging and mining companies and the governments that sanctioned the wanton rape of Mother Earth while a perverted world stood by and watched. It was an odd relationship, brokered far more by circumstances than desire or affinity, but neither of them could afford to be caught, even dead, on each other's nasty spell list. Their perennial disagreements over Dottie's plans for the island were as close as either pushed to triggering an irreparable rift, and even then, Mona had graciously amended her stance to carry a "while I'm alive" clause. There had always been Aidan to protect. Mona and Dottie both knew he was the only reason for their unbreakable loyalty to one another. The knot in that little arrangement was that Aidan somehow knew this too—and manipulated them both mercilessly.

Perhaps it was welling anxiety or a curve in the mountainous road taken a bit too recklessly that bounced her from her subconscious wanderings to rejoin Dottie in the front benchseat of the twenty-year-old Riviera.

"You know, Dot, I forgot to mention this to you but that boyfriend of Stephanie's—François, or something like that—well, he was in the bakery the other morning, and you'll never guess who he was asking about." She flipped down the compact mirror in the sun visor and checked her lipstick—one of the few aspects of her dilapidated appearance she could still do something about.

It always amazed Dottie how Mona could emerge from what had appeared to be a completely catatonic state completely ready for conversation. She checked the clock built into the dashboard and silently lamented she hadn't quite gotten her full two hours of solo driving in, plus she was now stuck behind a pair of logging trucks she couldn't pass.

"Who?" she said, impatiently.

"Come on. You didn't even try to guess."

"Well let's see, dear . . ." Dottie signaled her intention to pass. "We've known each other for what, almost twenty years by now? We probably have a thousand or so people in common. You still want me to begin guessing?" She slapped the steering wheel when her attempt to pass was canceled by oncoming traffic. "Where in the hell are these logging trucks coming from? I didn't think any logs were supposed to be coming out of the sound since last summer's blockade, but I've followed this damned convoy for the last hour! Have you heard anything about active logging? I sure as Dickens haven't."

"Lucien Pelletier," Mona said, slapping the visor up. Dottie may have veered away from the guessing game, but Mona hadn't. "Did you hear what I said?" Dottie wasn't responding—in fact, wasn't breathing.

"François asked about him, and you're just now telling me?"

"Pardon me, but I have spent the last couple of days arguing with doctors over how best to extend my life. It slipped my mind, okay?"

"What do you think his interest is? Lucien's been dead and gone from these parts for over a dozen years."

"He said," Mona continued, pouring coffee from a thermos into a cup she was struggling to steady with Dottie's impatient driving, "that he thought Lucien Pelletier might have been his father. Of course, I didn't offer him anything but my blank stare."

"Which you've certainly perfected, Mona." Dottie bit her lip and attempted to pass the logging truck again, this time on a blind grade. The moment she'd committed to the pass, a car appeared over the top of the hill and Dottie gunned it, forcing the oncoming car onto the shoulder.

"Oh for shit's sake, Dottie!" Mona screamed, spilling about an eighth of her pour onto her lap. "You're going to get us both killed and then who do you suppose is going to finish raising Aidan? Huh? Tage?"

Dottie waved an apologetic hand at the driver she'd forced off the road, and then changed the same hand into a bird she used to flip off the logging truck drivers, who honked back their disdain for the SAVE CLAYOQUOT bumper sticker on her rusted rear fender. "This isn't good, Mona. I knew there was a reason I couldn't stand that filthy Quebecer. Oh goddess! I should have seen the resemblance."

"I for one am very surprised you didn't. He's a dead ringer for his father, if you ask me. I told him I hadn't heard of the man and that I'd been around just about as long as anybody."

Dottie concentrated on making up driving time, and hurled the vehicle well over the speed limit, now that the logging trucks were behind her. With someone making inquiries as close to home as that, she couldn't leave the fort undefended for very long. She needed to get Mona to the hospital and race back. In the next four hundred kilometres she would have to figure out a plan to frighten François off the beaten and dead-end path.

"Sweet Lucifer!" Dottie exclaimed, slapping the dashboard.

"What is it?"

"I can only assume Stephanie and François had sexual relations."

"It is the '90s," Mona offered without thinking. "Oh, God!" She just realized Dottie's point. "That's not good."

"None of this is good, Mona. Go back to sleep. I need to think."

That should fix Dottie, Mona thought, leaning her head against the passenger window and shutting her eyes. She couldn't stand the power Dottie derived from playing nursemaid and ambulance driver—especially when there was plenty in Dottie's own house in complete disorder. Mona knew that even with half a chest, a missing womb, and maybe just a few months left in this life—especially if this Hail Mary therapy session didn't take—she still had it better than Dottie Bard, whose karma chit was about to get punched. It's not that she wished her friend ill. It was simply due her—whether Mona wished it, predicted it, caused it, or not. It would come. She sensed it was on its way like a harp-playing celestial winged messenger, but more likely an overloaded logging truck that might come barrelling around the next bend.

And Aidan would be fine. Mona knew this in her heart because it was the bargain she'd made with the goddesses. She and Dottie had delivered Aidan from a broken cradle to the porch of manhood, and if he could just manage to survive puberty, he would find his own way. He could take the SunRyes Bakeshop or leave it. The same applied to Wick. The comfort that he could monetize both and get the hell out of there if he wanted to, helped Mona settle her worrisome breathing and drift closer to her transit across the River Styx she would soon need to be making.

MULLIGAN STEW

Mac Mulligan—nobody truly believed that was his real name—had showed up at the dock with his broken sailboat in the Summer of '87, all grizzled and sea-worn, itching for a scuffle and throwing his weight around like he meant trouble. He had just made a harrowing solo trip from San Francisco, where his motor conked out about 500 kilometres off the Oregon coast. There he sat for days, until the winds resumed so he could begin inching his way northward again. Of course, he and Dottie faced off from the moment he planted his sandaled foot on the planks of her dock. It was her obligation, as the unofficial welcome wagon, to intercept and fleece all newcomers for whatever skills they had. Her first words to him—which was the usual greeting she threw at most strangers—were, "You know you can't park there, right?"

Whether he actually did it or just maintained the rumours about himself, Mac became revered and reviled in the years after arriving in Tofino for spiking ancient groves of trees with metal stakes at chainsaw height or for staging forest fairy raiding parties to remove, rearrange, or just royally fuck-up the ribbons that timber surveyors had placed in advance of the road building and falling crews. Mischief in the woods became an art form with Mac Mulligan—a genuine Houdini, with multiple hideouts, death-defying escapes, and sleight-of-hand tactics deployed to spare the destruction of the precious, pristine and sacred rainforests of Clayoquot Sound.

Knowing nothing about explosives, and at the height of the previous summer's protest, Mac had decided he would blow up the bridge at Kennedy Lake to keep MacMillan Bloedel's logging trucks from reaching the ancient groves beyond. He had needed an accomplice to rendezvous with him at the top of the lake, twenty-two kilometres from the bridge, to whisk him and his borrowed motorboat over Sutton Pass and out of Clayoquot Sound before the Mounties arrived. Dottie had grown accustomed to playing Bonnie to his Clyde by the time he had hatched his latest demolition plan and shared the logistics with her.

In a dress rehearsal the night before, they'd stashed the boat trailer behind a brush pile off Lost Shoe Creek Road and motored the boat to a sand bar about a kilometre from the bridge, but still within jogging distance from the blockade at the Black Hole. Mac had stayed at the camp that evening to convince the leadership to abandon the bridge the following night, as heavy rains would be moving in from a system offshore. He had been triangulating the weather forecast with RCMP movements and the diminishing protestor population for weeks to pick the wettest, least risky night of the summer, and by late afternoon the next day, the prevailing wind began to deliver one of those iconic, horizontal, sideways West Coast rainstorms. It was sure to clear the camp of all but the most rigid diehards, keep the cops in their cruisers, and minimize the bystanders who might have otherwise been on the bridge. No storm would ever deter a real rainforest defender and that's what separated Mac Mulligan from the throngs of eco-terrorist wannabes.

Besides, he had seen far worse storms at sea—and so when the protestors hightailed it back to the camp for cover, he lagged behind, pretending he was taking a pee off the side of the bridge. When everyone had cleared and nobody was looking back, he high-tailed it in the opposite direction, toward the stashed boat. The storm, with its belly-dragging grey clouds, reduced visibility and daylight to the point that Mac needed to use a flashlight just to untie the slipknot. An experienced sailor, Mac could tie and untied knots in his sleep—so this was his first bothersome omen. Getting the outboard motor to start sputtering was his next one. Mac had to remove each of the spark plugs, wetting each of the connectors with his tongue. It worked! He was on his way through the diagonal rain and into the wind.

Checking his watch, he could see that he was running forty-five minutes ahead of schedule. That was a healthy development, he figured, as he would likely encounter some trouble getting a fire to start in that rainstorm. He had brought with him a wooden crate double-wrapped in tarps and filled with dynamite that he had pinched from a Mac-Blo bunker in the Megin River watershed, near a site where a new logging road was being blasted through the pristine terrain. He hadn't bothered with fusing or timers—instead he planned to start a fire on one side of the bridge. It would then spread along an oil stream he would pour across a beam running the width of the bridge to the wooden box of dynamite.

That part of the plan hadn't been thought through in advance, and once Mac had climbed up and into the bridge's under-structure, things weren't quite how he had imagined. In the quickly diminishing daylight, he couldn't spot a timber beam with a clear run that wasn't broken up in regular intervals by the stringers running the length of the bridge. He had to improvise, stashing the dynamite box on a ledge beneath the road surface, then lighting a fire in the crotch of a pair of crossbeams. To ensure the fire reached the box, Mac coated a spare wooden paddle in oil that he'd grabbed from the bottom of the borrowed boat, sticking the handle in and leaning the paddle against the side of the dynamite box. Just as the flame began to climb up the paddle, he dropped into the boat and sped away.

It had been around the start of hour three that she'd been waiting in her car, with the engine and lights turned off, in that gravel turnout below the highway with the boat trailer attached, that Dottie had tightened her grip on the steering wheel as she peered through the windshield into the most crippling darkness. At the time, she was remembering now, the winds and the driving rain had made it difficult to have a window rolled down, but she had wanted so desperately to hear the explosion—or at the very least a gigantic flash of light in the dark sky. But either the terrain was too mountainous, or she had been too far from the bridge. She had just had to wait it out and trust that confirmation was coming. When Mac's headlamp finally rounded the spit of land where she was parked, he was almost two hours behind his own schedule. He'd run into all sorts of problems—floating, even partially submerged logs and other remarkably shallow spots in the lake had challenged him the entire way. Mac had also been waiting for the concussion or a flash from an explosion but had arrived at their rendezvous spot unsatisfied and without evidence that his attack had been successful.

It would be another twelve hours before Mac had slipped back into the swamped-out camp, after ditching the boat and trailer on the other side of Vancouver Island, and even longer for Dottie—who had continued driving into town to very publicly resume her regular activities, before either of them learned that the damned bridge, as far as anyone knew, was still intact. That next morning, the RCMP had discovered some charred bridge deck planking, which led them to the half-burned boat paddle and the wooden case of dynamite that had been miraculously untouched by flames.

In a lovely irony, that made Dottie smile to this day, the RCMP had interpreted the Mac-Blo markings on the case of dynamite as sufficient evidence that some angry logger or loggers had tried to frame the protestors. By that point, the real damage had already been done on top of that bridge—to the lives of the hundreds of arrested protestors and to the logging company's profit margin. That summer's War in the Woods had also taught Dottie and Mac how to trust and rely on each other—once they'd figured that out, intimacy and the other elements of their odd, organic, and somehow symbiotic relationship had fallen nicely into place.

And that's the way it happened. That highway was so jammed with memories good, bad, and even monotonously routine, for Dottie, that they outnumbered the potholes—which was really saying something. It had only taken driving past that rendezvous spot just off the highway on her return trip from Victoria after having deposited Mona in the hands of her new cadre of oncologists, for all the stress and high-climaxing drama of the previous summer's confrontation to come boomeranging back at her like it had only been last week and not already a whole year ago.

She checked the dashboard clock and gave the Riviera a punch of gas. She was just going to make it under the gavel. It was only the third time in nine years that she would have the opportunity to shine as acting-mayor and the power trip was positively exhilarating—particularly given the evening's contentious council agenda. She was anxious to show Brad Fraser who could and who could never plop a floating wilderness sport fishing and hunting lodge in the middle of her precious Clayoquot Sound.

ALDER STAKES

Heritage had risen before the sun since he'd already learned he couldn't rely on its appearance to get his day started. This had also marked his last night at the Headlands before shifting his base camp to Mona's place back on Wickaninnish for the next several days. He'd slept the previous three nights in five-hundred-thread Egyptian cotton bliss in his handsome suite at the Headlands, and he would need to carry that comfort memory with him as he returned to the land of roughing it.

He had wanted to get an early jump on the day for several reasons. He needed to sort and pack his belongings into those things he needed on the island, and those he could stash in Brad Fraser's office that was becoming his office while the fat, drunken cat was away. The task had been as easy as dividing the recreational camping clothes from the business attire since he would be commuting to work by boat or kayak for the next week and a half and he could shower, shave, shit and change clothes when he got there. He wouldn't need his tent at Mona's, but he had decided to bring his sleeping bag along, just in case. Heritage also wanted to get back on the island early enough and long before Aidan got sprung from school for the weekend so that he could master the lay of the land. He also wanted one last chance to triple-check that he had completely vacated the A-frame behind Dottie's place and that he had sufficiently disguised if not covered his tracks inside Dottie's cabin. It had been niggling at him that he might have forgotten to retrieve one of the index cards that had fallen from that volume of witchy hocus pocus and disappeared under the couch. He remembered it falling but he couldn't remember if he had actually retrieved it to put it back. Mona's cautionary warning about messing with Dottie's implements had stayed with him the past few nights and reminded him again each time he glanced across the channel and saw the sun reflecting off Dottie's cabin windows. In addition to these items on his list, it was a workday for him at The Headlands.

He'd fully intended to paddle back across earlier in the week to tend to this, but without a boat, he had been stuck, this time on the side opposite the island he'd been stuck on for almost a whole week. The holdup had been his kayak and a problem with the fiberglass or the acetone or the resin or maybe it was the catalyst. Heritage couldn't really remember what the culprit had been. Mac, who was quite the talker, had methodically reviewed the nine steps in the fiberglass repair process in detail the previous night when Heritage had dashed into town after work in Brad Fraser's Jeep Cherokee to retrieve his boat. Before releasing the kayak, Mac had wanted Tage to know the steps in case Mac wasn't around the next time the boat needed repairing. Mac had also said he would have advised against buying a fiberglass kayak, but since Tage hadn't asked him for his opinion first, it was pretty important that Tage learn how to repair it himself.

What had felt like forty days and nights of nonstop rain had only been ten, with just one glorious half-day of sunshine—that being the last day of Marcel Labbé's life—plus a couple hours reprieve between showers the day that followed. This, Heritage's tenth morning in Clayoquot Sound—would prove positively glorious, with an honest-to-goodness sunrise unfolding from behind Mount Colnett on Meares Island. The sky had been transformed into a tapestry of oranges and reds more brilliant than he remembered ever seeing in the city, and he was mesmerized by the spectacle unfolding overhead as he pulled his kayak across Middle Beach to the waterline. When at last the sun had crested the mountain, he reluctantly looked away—his light-starved eyes had grown overly sensitive to solar light during his short time in Clayoquot Sound, and he felt like a mole.

His commute had been brief, paddling across calm water—a cinch, compared to his earlier attempts to tackle Templar Channel. The waterway had become infinitely spookier now that Heritage knew it covered an underwater grave for most of the *Tonquin* crew plus a hundred-odd Tla-o-qui-aht warriors. With every stroke of his paddle, he wondered what else was down there.

His time on the island would be brief as he needed to quickly scoot back to the Headlands to properly start his third official shift of on-the-job training—the day's focus was going to be on housekeeping, and he certainly didn't want to be late for mastering the basics of toilet scrubbing and hospital sheet corners. His rudder up, he dragged the kayak in the sand until it was several metres above the tide line. He unzipped his life jacket for added dexterity and bounded through driftwood and over rain puddles to check Stephanie's little cabin first, to make sure he hadn't left anything incriminating behind. He laughed out loud at the notion that he was behaving as though he were guilty of something and trying to cover it up, when it just wasn't the case. He was paranoid and anxious about teen-sitting Aidan and definitely already looking over his shoulder. He hadn't patched things up with Dottie and his rendezvous with François earlier in the week had been less than spectacular, so Heritage was coming up short on who he could trust not to impale him in the back with a sharpened alder stake. And speaking of which, Heritage was surprised to see the tree limb had been removed from the little shed's roof and a piece of tin had been inserted under the silvered cedar shakes to patch the puncture. When he went inside the structure, he thought to check the back of the door but found it painted over with an almost eggplant coloured background and ridiculous orange petaled flowers sloppily roughed in before the background had dried. Heritage emerged from the cabin with his hands on his hips, looking around for some *Just for Laughs* cameraman. Now, who in the hell had time or the motivation to do that—and in the three days since he'd shifted to The Headlands? He shook off a shudder.

Heritage checked his wristwatch. 7:50 a.m. He dashed down the wine bottle pathway to take a leak in the outhouse, happy to find it vacant—presumably, Aidan was in school. Then he let himself back in Dottie's main cabin just to be sure he'd put the teapot back and that things were just as he had found them. As for the index card that might have dropped out of the antique book and slipped under the sofa, he didn't see it, at first. He knelt and that's when he saw a lifted corner of the card. He tried to reach it but couldn't get his forearm far enough under the clearance. He had to move one end of the futon to retrieve the card, and that's when he noticed a faint outline—an incongruity in the grain of the floorboards. He brushed the dust bunnies aside. It appeared to be a square hatch cut into the floor, but with no handle. Heritage thumped on the floor to test its hollowness. It sounded like a ripe watermelon to him, but there was no handle to lift the boards. He took two steps to the kitchen area and removed a knife out of the butcher block holder and tried to carefully pry the hatch open. It worked, but what was revealed sent Heritage tumbling backwards and back onto his feet, cussing up his own little storm.

A human skull lay on its side and a wolf spider the size of a loonie tried to scamper up the side of the interior box that the hatch lid had covered.

Hyperventilating, Heritage kicked the lid back into place, tapping it down with his foot. He jerked the sofa and roughly replaced the wooden legs back inside the dust marks where they had been positioned. He returned the index card, without even examining it, into its tomb inside the brittle pages of *Malleus Maleficarum*. Then he backed out of the cabin and sprinted to his kayak.

Heritage's heart thumped madly in his chest beneath his perhaps too tightly bound life jacket. He had been so focused on escaping that witch's lair, that he hadn't noticed the weather change again. From out of who knew where, a rainwater-logged cloud ceiling had begun lowering to take another long nap on the water. Threading his shaky legs into the kayak at the water's edge in the cove surrounded by trees, Heritage noted with much satisfaction that the interior of the cockpit was completely dry, thanks to Mac. In the five minutes it took him to paddle the hundred or so metres to the cove's opening, his visibility across the channel had vanished entirely. He lifted his yellow-tinted paddling glasses to his forehead to make sure they hadn't just steamed up from the heat he was putting off under his gear and the spray skirt, but he still couldn't see much beyond the tip of his kayak.

Another curse?

He continued to drift into the channel from the momentum of his getaway paddling through the cove. When he glanced back, he couldn't make out the opening to the cove he'd just threaded with his needle of a craft. He was in a soup of a mess and it was muffling, completely calm, eerily silent. No motors, no surf, no birds and no foghorn—strangely, since he knew now the lighthouse just south of Echachis Island existed and he had heard it sounding off and on during the previous week of heavier weather. In his adrenalin-charged motivation to get off that island and back to civilization, Heritage was more-than-committed to the crossing. He felt confident he must be pointed in the right direction, because he had studied the line between the lodge and Dottie's cabin. He had the straight-forward orientation clear in his mind, so he began stroking with intention, propelling the boat deeper into oblivion. Gray water swirled into mini whirlpools each time his paddle dipped below the surface. He locked his knees against the insides of the cockpit, determined to hold the rudder in a fixed position, calculating that if he paddled straight and didn't move his feet, he would reach Middle Beach or the rocky shoreline below Headlands Lodge.

He listened and strained his eyes. All the while, he kept paddling, finding syncopation in his rhythm that felt like choreography—except with a measure of terror thrown into the score. He'd left the cove at ten minutes past eight and had been strength paddling for twenty minutes, fully believing he had been transiting the channel in a straight line. Every one of his senses was hyper-focused, as he looked for input that either confirmed he was on course or provided a clue as to how he should correct it. But inside that weather pillow he was deprived. The only sounds were from his paddle scooping him forward and the occasional thump when it knocked the hull as his arms began to fatigue. Why didn't kayaks come from the factory with plastic Boy Scout compasses embedded on the deck of the cockpit? He might have just invented something—if he survived the crossing he'd have to remember to apply for a patent.

He thought he was heading in an easterly course, but without a single landmark other than the bow of his own boat, he couldn't know how wrong he was. He stopped paddling to listen again. Dead. Calm. Silence. He couldn't help thinking that this would be the part in the movie where a killer whale came from the depths of nowhere to chomp off the front of the boat with his legs still inside it. This thought would have done a number on his psyche if the skull spider house hadn't already destroyed his ability to think cognitively.

Suddenly, the blasted foghorn blared, sounding as though

it were coming from directly behind him. Now, he'd studied the charts and he knew the Tofino lighthouse was on Lennard Island, which was south of Echachis Island, which was connected to Wickaninnish at low tide. How in the hell was that foghorn sounding from *behind* him?

The foghorn went off again, and again the long, two tone, blaring seemed to be emanating behind his right shoulder somewhere in that cotton candy. On the third sounding, Heritage relaxed his shoulders and continued paddling for several strokes, correcting the rudder with his left foot to pull his orientation more to the left and northward. If that lighthouse were behind him, then he had drifted way too far south. This was possible, he figured, if the tide was running out of Clayoquot Sound. Mental note: add tide chart to the list of things he shouldn't have forgotten and without which he promised he would never go out kayaking again—conditional (once again) on him surviving this crossing.

He stopped paddling, bracing the two-bladed aluminum pole across the cockpit rim. He noted that the foam rubber drip rings didn't seem to be working well—water was pooling on top of his spray skirt. He reached to the top of the cockpit rim for the quick release on the skirt, to direct the water off one side. He quickly reattached the spray skirt around the raised rim. It was after that and before he'd begun paddling again that he heard the sound of breaking surf on a beach. Maybe it was rocks, but Heritage really wanted it to be a beach.

He began paddling with new purpose, and a good ten minutes later, the shoreline gradually became more and more visible as the ocean got louder. Swells appeared beneath the boat, passing from his right under the boat at an angle to the left. He tried to stay in the grooves of these swells but decided he needed to orient the kayak to be more perpendicular to the swells so that the swells could guide him to where he thought he needed to go—that is, wherever those swells were heading.

His problem—though he was too amped to know it—was that

the tide had been running out of the sound since the high tide mark that had peaked at around 5:45 a.m. Heritage had paddled and drifted in the strong currents a good kilometre south of Middle Beach and The Headlands, then another half-click south of MacKenzie Beach. If he didn't veer left in the next fifteen strokes, he would have either beached on the rocks or gotten carried through the surfers of Chesterman Beach. Fortunately, at that moment, Heritage spotted just that; maybe a half-dozen vertical surfers in the mist, about twenty-five metres in front of his bow. He could suddenly gauge the height of the breaking waves—much too high for a graceful beach landing.

He depressed his left foot on the rudder brace as far as he could stretch it and began paddling like a windmill to avoid getting picked up in the surf that would have surely nose-planted him in the sand. Either his eyesight had miraculously improved or the fog was lifting. Sunshine began to spill through that filter and the coastline was gradually revealed. While Heritage had succeeded in crossing the channel, he had been carried three beaches south of his intended landing.

The paddling was easy now and a reddish hue returned to his knuckles, as he cruised past a large circular house on a rocky point that divided Chesterman from MacKenzie beaches. At the far end of Mackenzie Beach, as the fog elevator continued to rise off the water in front of him, the outline of the massive, three-story timber-framed Headlands Lodge appeared. Heritage recalibrated his trajectory, now able to see back across the channel to Echachis and Wickaninnish Islands. How ridiculously off-course he had paddled in the fog during the past forty minutes! What a novice—still. But at least Mac's fiberglass patch had passed its endurance test.

Despite his early on-the-water workout and the traumatic start to his day, Heritage still arrived for work before Brad Fraser. Heritage needed to compress his workday so that he could be back on the island by four when Aidan was expected home from school. He hadn't actually seen the adolescent troublemaker since the lift Mona had given him back to town with his kayak, and so expected a bit of tension during their first night as bachelors under the same roof. Since the kid had already demonstrated a talent for outsmarting him, Heritage knew he couldn't slip up during the next two weeks. He would have to be on his best behavior, because Aidan would not be.

Heritage showered and changed clothes in his suite, then packed up his things so he would be ready to head back to Wickaninnish Island the moment he thought the lodge was ready for the weekend influx. He greeted the morning shift front desk staff. He moved on to fluff and straighten the pillows in the grand lobby sitting room. That focal point of the lodge was anchored by a multi-ton river-stone fireplace in a space ringed by floor-to-ceiling windows that overlooked the beaches on either side of the promontory. Heritage next constructed a cedar-wood fire in the giant fireplace—already assuming Brad Fraser's tasks, after a mere half-week on the job. More recently often than not, these things had been getting done closer to noon, according to the confidential rumblings of a few employees who'd begun to warm up to the interim general manager following the all staff meeting where he'd been introduced and had said a few words to put everyone at ease. Heritage was subtly taking charge and couldn't help but swell with pride to think that this four-star showcase could one day be his to manage and maybe inherit. He only needed to persuade his grandfather he was competent and ready for the responsibility, and to begin firmly conditioning Brad Fraser to accept a buyout and that his cushy gig at the Headlands was finally up.

The smell of blazing cedar permeated the timber-beamed room and blended with the smells of fresh coffee, croissants, and locally woven cedar baskets brimming with pine-scented potpourri. Heritage slowly pivoted, taking it all in, momentarily ignoring the ocean channel that lay just beyond those windows and could spell the end of him yet.

The kitchen staff were moving about the dining area with purpose, setting up and ready to replenish the hearty continental breakfast that would coax the handful of off-season guests down from their sleeping chambers. Heritage glanced at his wristwatch and realized it would likely be another hour before Brad Fraser showed. This gave him time to check in with his grandfather.

Sitting at Fraser's desk, Heritage made a quick checklist of topics to cover, entered his calling card number and waited for the connection. As the phone rang, he hoped he could accomplish a brief check-in with his assistant without actually speaking to the old man. They hadn't connected since he'd arrived in Clayoquot, mostly because Heritage hadn't had access to a phone with privacy until now. While the junior Heritage needed to remind the senior Heritage that he was still on the job, should still be collecting paycheques, and should still be included in the latest version of his granddad's will, it was one of those maintenance phone calls that would require him to act and possibly grovel. Of course, if he groveled enough, and acted well, he'd get more than his inheritance. He'd finally get even with the life forces that had mostly conspired against him when it came to his family.

"Hello Monica. Tage here." He was off to a good start and recorded a checkmark in his first box he'd labeled *call answered* on the 2-column form. Usually calls went straight to his grandfather's answering machine—this big, clunky reel-to-reel contraption that sat on one corner of his desk and smelled like fried electrical wires. Heritage, the grandson, always listed his goals on a legal pad before each of these phone calls to his grandfather. His grandfather's personal line had been answered by his assistant. "And how's Mr. Carter today?" he asked in a cheerful voice, always counted on to lift morale and be the softer yin to his grandfather's more rigid yang "Oh," he spoke into the receiver. "Okay, sure."

Not a good start after all. He erased the checkmark he'd just made. He was being forwarded to the family lawyer, who was handling Mr. Carter's telephone calls today.

"Lonnie. It's Tage, phoning from Clayoquot Sound in BC. What gives?" He bounced the eraser end of his pencil on the pad. "Perforated? That doesn't sound so good." He put the pencil down as the lawyer explained his grandfather's steadily deteriorating intestinal condition. Heritage next asked if he should rush home, but Lonnie firmly recommended against this, said his grandfather was a fighter and was still insisting on working from the office three days a week, just not today. Tage had a feeling the call was going to end awkwardly with the rest of his boxes unchecked, but he let Lonnie rattle on about shareholder unrest and nervous mill floor supervisors who were being egged on by union reps to escalate grievances. In the meantime, he closed his eyes and listened until Lonnie had finished.

Last year the crisis and false alarm had been skin cancer. The year before that, it was a heart arrhythmia. Heritage the Younger wasn't getting any younger, and couldn't help that he'd become callous over the years, as one medical threat after the other failed to materialize into the final blow. Heritage had sometimes been convinced that his grandfather was mean enough to outlive him. In the intervening years, and then decades, Heritage gambled against time, struggled to behave, lived within his allowance, and waited. Each was the only living family member the other had left, but that hadn't made them closer. They didn't have much in common, except for their genes. Their contradictory duality permeated everything from the board room to the mill floors. Heritage was aware that union bosses had been known to voice the opinion that the day after the senior Carter's funeral, was when life, wages, and the company outlook would take on a more humanistic era at CP&P with the kinder, gentler heir taking the helm.

Tage hadn't let that go to his head for even five minutes, since he fully intended to let the board of directors and shareholders buy out his interest in the mills and logging companies. He didn't dare let his grandfather know this, as he would have certainly been excised from the organization chart. But his mind was made on this, and his conscience would be cleared. He had no interest in paper or deforesting the planet. The presumptive heir was instead presently lining up his future ducks to hold onto the Headlands for himself as well as the valuable acreage surrounding it and suspected he would be met with no resistance as the directors hadn't grasped the reason his grandfather had made that investment decision in the first place. Heritage knew why, and possibly Brad Fraser did, too, since he'd talked his grandfather into letting him build the lodge at the edge of it.

On a whim in the '70s, during a timber survey, Heritage Carter Sr. had purchased the thirty-five hectares on which the Headlands was situated as a placeholder for the retirement compound he'd promised his wife and Heritage's grandmother, Margaret. Multiple sclerosis and dementia had other plans for Margaret's brain and spinal cord. She passed five years before Heritage's parents, and so was spared that gruesome holiday scene, but she never was well enough to travel west to see the property in person. The loss of his only true love made the soft spot that the grandfather had for the property even softer. Enter the opportunistic Brad Fraser, and plans for the Headlands were hatched—at least for his grandfather—in Margaret's memory.

There had been no inheritance from his dead parents, because they too had been waiting for the old man to keel over. With that middle generation disqualified by his father's revolver, Tage fully expected to one day be able to get at the family's wealth. Neither he nor his granddad pretended to be upset by the flimsy, materialistic basis for their relationship, nor acted the least bit bound by it. There were only three things that needed to happen: Heritage Carter the First needed to see that his grandson was worthy of running the Carter Pulp & Paper empire, including the Headlands Lodge and financial stakes in several logging companies; Heritage Carter the Third needed to *be* worthy; and finally, Heritage Carter the First had to be the first to die.

It was a simple tableau that hinged on biology, a spot of good acting and some really grand staging. That was the way Tage saw it, but his grandfather had often pointed out that not only did they rarely interpret or see things the same way—they usually seemed to be looking in opposite directions. Heritage the Third had struggled in his earlier years to learn his role, and in his later years, to stick to it without wildly improvising. The most frequently highlighted example of his under-qualifying was that he had thus far failed to marry or produce a fourth Heritage, which would have clinched the family fortunes much more securely and spared him this life of double, even triple jeopardy. He hadn't married. He hadn't conceived a child. He was, in all probability, gay. Any one or a combination of these three would have gotten him booted from the upper corporate echelon and sent him packing with a consolation prize that would have been a fraction of the whole chimichanga. Though he would never speak his truth aloud, Heritage had never really wanted to have anything to do with Carter Pulp & Paper. He just didn't have the demeanor or discipline for commodities with all that volatility. Making toilet and photocopy paper required zero passion and even less creativity. He was cut out to make a bigger difference. His mother had imprinted that notion on him his entire childhood as she tucked him into bed while his father chronically worked late and eventually, to death.

Though he had lately been turning in a good performance as the loyal grandson, he was an impatient player. For this reason, he'd perked up at the mention of perforated intestines. Something like that could brighten one's day under the right, desperate circumstances. Heritage opened his eyes.

"Uh, Lonnie, I—uh, just started this assignment last week. This is not the best time for me to steal away to be at Mr. Carter's bedside, regardless of how serious you are making this sound, and as badly as I might want to be there. There is a lot at stake right here at the moment."

Heritage whispered the last bit with his hand cupped around

the mouthpiece. His grandfather's attorney explained that his position was not to tell him what he should or shouldn't do—but he was strongly urging him to fly home. His words, to be exact, were, "For the sake of company continuity and public share stabilization, there needs to be a clear and present link between the company's past and the company's future. What's more, this link needs to appear anticipated, calculated, and secure. None of us knows what Mr. Carter will do in the end. He has no fewer than three final will and testaments prepared before him, which chart three very different directions for Carter Pulp & Paper. I won't mislead you, Tage. Not all three include or even provide for you."

Thus forewarned, Heritage hung up, with the understanding that a confidential fax was on its way with a cover page addressed to him that outlined the conditions of the agreement he had been instructed to propose, and that he would gauge the day's meetings with Brad Fraser to see if he could finagle a two-day breakaway over the coming weekend. He'd call Lonnie in the next day or so, with an update and possibly his flight information.

"Ah, shit!" he blurted out as soon as he'd hung up, remembering his commitment to terror-sit Aidan for two weeks. "Shit!" he exclaimed again, grabbing the attention of one of the chambermaids as she passed by the open office door on her way to the reading room, armed with a feather duster and a vacuum.

"Is there something I could get for you, sir?" she asked, poking her head through the door frame with a four-diamond smile.

Heritage relaxed his face. "No. Thank you, but no—unless you babysit, that is." His brow arched in anticipation, then fell. "No, I wouldn't wish that on anyone. Never mind." Heritage winked and then followed the housekeeper as far as the front desk where the fax machine had just whirred into action to signal an incoming transmission. Heritage took the next twelve pages one at a time. The twelfth page was just a blank CP&P letterhead, which got him scheming. He asked the morning's desk clerk if she could sign him onto one of the spare computers momentarily, and once in, he pecked out a one-page collateral addendum to the agreement that he manipulated to print onto the blank page letterhead he'd placed face down in the photocopier paper tray.

Tucking the fresh paperwork into his legal pad leather notebook, he strolled into the grand room. It had started coming to life, with couples who had made the semi-circular wooden staircase descent, following the scents of coffee and freshly baked croissants, on top of which they would shortly slather the lodge's famous salal berry jam. Heritage mingled with the guests, checking on their stays and learning where they were visiting from . . . Seattle, Vancouver, Berlin, and Antwerp. Everything around them, except for those tasteful textile accessories à la E. Bauer and R. Lauren, screamed *wood*. Wood floors, wood paneling, wood window frames and sills, wood furniture, wood beams, wood supports, wood canoes, wood desks and coffee tables, wood key fobs, wood curtain rings, wood banisters, wood doors, wood molding, wood-burning fireplace flanked by two upright wooden canoes with wooden bookshelf inserts. It wasn't inconceivable to imagine Brad Fraser and the front desk clerks all wearing wooden veneer underwear beneath their polo shirts. And into that woody tableau sauntered the timber baron himself: Brad Fraser.

"Good morning, Brad," Heritage said, greeting his slightly-less-than-thrilled collaborator.

"It's still morning then, is it?" Fraser grumbled. "Everything go okay here overnight?" It sort of looked to Heritage like the stout lodge keeper, who resembled a logger, had just butted into the breakfast line to grab a coffee. He said good morning to one of the guests, so at least he was friendly about it.

"I think so," Heritage responded. "I slept like a time capsule." His simile sort of fell out of his mouth and onto the wooden floor and made absolutely no sense whatsoever to either of them. "Look, I appreciate the suite you've provided me, and it's a beautiful place you've got here, but so far I'm getting quite a kick out of quasi-roughing it across the way. That sense for adventure will change with the weather soon enough, I suppose."

"I see." Brad took a seat in one of the wooden chairs on either side of a low wood table, its top an eight- or ten-inch slice taken from the trunk of a tree that might have been a thousand years old. Heritage would have to count the rings some rainy afternoon. Brad continued. "No offense intended here, Mr. Carter, but I'm surprised they let a man on the island. That whole place seems occupied by disgruntled women, either done wrong by their men or not foxy enough to have interested the opposite gender in the first place. Haven't you noticed?"

"To be honest, no—I really hadn't," Heritage said, perhaps too curtly. Other than François, the drowned water taxi driver, Mac Mulligan, the RCMP officer, the coast guard captain, Lyle Hudson, and the food-sick native named Sennan, Heritage really hadn't met any truly local men, and hadn't thought to question it. "I spend most of my free time in the kayak, and don't mix with the neighbours, I guess." He was ready to move off that subject, then thought to add, "Not that it matters to me one way or the other. I get along with people and don't get too hung up on judgments."

"Yeah? Well, good on ya for that. I'll just warn you, so that I can say I did—you'll find talk around the village running the gamut saying those women over there are everything from eco-feminists to lesbians or even witches."

"My God!" Heritage exaggerated his shock. "Which of those is worse?" The men had their laugh and thankfully moved on. "I spoke with my grandfather this morning. He sends his greetings." It was a lie, but Heritage needed to prop up the premise that his grandfather was still calling the shots when it came to business.

"I hope you passed along my wishes to him," Fraser reciprocated, with a niceness that might have been a front for his own agenda. "Do we have news this morning?"

Heritage leaned in. "Let me begin by saying my grandfather and I feel our course is clear in Clayoquot Sound. Carter

Pulp & Paper is prepared to stand behind our offer to front the eighteen-million-dollar loan guarantee in exchange for access to the wood fiber resources extracted from Timber Forest License number seventy-four—up to a market value of eighteen million. Any profit realized above that is yours, Brad. It is our understanding that you plan to use that guarantee to acquire the TFL from MacMillan Bloedel, as they want out of Clayoquot Sound and after last summer are anxious to beat a hasty retreat. My role during the next several months, in addition to learning the resort business, will be to help clear the legal hurdles that will bring about provincial concurrence and the appropriate ministry approvals for this TFL transfer."

Heritage sipped his coffee. The things coming out of his mouth were like a foreign language he'd never completely mastered but at least he had been wise and sly to memorize a few of the dirtier phrases he could drop into the conversation so as to appear fluent. Rather than learn the intricacies of business grammar and the consequences of monopolistic power structures, he'd only regurgitated the clever idioms that he'd been spoon fed by his grandfather by way of Lonnie. There were times he wanted to get caught, exposed for the two-faced front man he was—but alas, his accent was too smooth and his face too damn sincere and believable.

He went on. "I don't want to mislead you, Brad. The province is not pleased with Mac-Blo's planned abandonment of Clayoquot, especially since both the 1993 Lands Use Decision and the Timber Accord were practically tailor-written to enable them to bring all the trees down and straight to market. The fact they haven't met their annual allowable cut for the past five years speaks to activist pressures, to be sure—particularly losing out on Meares Island in the '80s, but also to their less-than-aggressive presence here since the start of this new decade. I believe, and my grandfather remains optimistic, that the Ministry of Forests will not only bless the transfer of this license into Canadian hands at a bargain basement price, but will also permit the Fraser-Carter Joint Venture to harvest the balance of the 350 hectares in the TFL, plus pick up the deficits from the annual allowable cut, retroactive for the past five years. Let's face it. The new government needs these stumpage fees to balance the budget. Otherwise the New Democratic Party might as well prepare to hand the government right back to the So-Creds or the Liberals."

Heritage leaned back in his chair like he knew without a doubt he'd just earned his Oscar nomination. He smiled into the empty coffee cup he'd been using as a prop to telegraph how confident he was in his position. He knew that because he could talk the talk, he had probably made Fraser temporarily forget all about his Wickaninnish peccadillo or his Headlands takeover scheme. It was the same smooth talking that had kept his grandfather mildly impressed and hopefully indebted to his faithful envoy services, rendered conditionally and oftentimes under duress over the past couple years. Heritage dressed and breathed the part thanks to the constant grooming by his grandfather's six-figure attorney, Lonnie. But even Lonnie knew that Heritage's spunk represented the new generation of corporate law, and that when negotiating the future, it was more advantageous to send in someone who gave the appearance they might actually be alive in that future, to hold the parties to account. Now, if only Heritage could have passed the bar on his first attempt, all of Lonnie's checkboxes might have been ticked too. Sure, it bugged Heritage every time Lonnie dangled a doubt about the guarantee of his inheritance, but Tage also knew that blood was thicker than litigation when it came to his own future. If it came to contesting the unsatisfactory outcome of his inheritance, Heritage just knew that once a judge or jury heard his sad story—about the brutal and tragic loss of his parents, about the manipulations he'd endured at the hands of his psychotic, workaholic grandfather—he'd be just fine in the end. He may not have passed the bar exam on his first try because he didn't care enough about it in the first place, but he'd learned and he'd witnessed plenty in his thirty-two years to be a menace to anyone who stood in the way of what he had coming.

Whether his grandfather had finally reached the end or was still just practicing for it, Heritage realized it might not hurt his case one bit if he could seal this one deal and maybe cook in an added insurance policy of his own. With the morning's fax, he'd been given approval and the instruction to table the TFL-purchase guarantee, but what came next was total freelance. He looked at Fraser. "All we need to make this happen here is for you to sign over your half of the Headlands Lodge to me—as the company's legally appointed representative—as collateral in the event you default on the TFL guarantee. Normally, this wouldn't have been necessary, but because you have defaulted on the original loan . . ." Heritage sort of just left it there, dangling in the space between them. He knew this knocked Fraser off balance, and so Heritage chose that precise moment to scoot the twelve pages of paperwork across the table to him. "Now, do I have your agreement?"

Fraser hadn't flinched at the collateral condition but that may have had more to do with the possibility that he was not yet fully awake or hungover. He scanned the pages one at a time, then Fraser seemed to scratch out a quick calculation on the backside of one of the pages. Heritage crossed his legs to appear disarmingly at ease.

"You know, it hadn't occurred to me to pursue the annual allowable cut deficit, to be honest with you. I supposed it would be the entitlement of the TFL and the obligation of the license holder to maximize the yield in any given year, but I hadn't considered there might be opportunity for a reach back into the poor performance years. The province may be pissed-off at Mac-Blo just enough to reward its successor that added bounty."

Brad Fraser leaned back, letting that sink in. Heritage knew to hold his tongue, though his heart advanced like a stopwatch on borrowed time. Brad Fraser demonstratively skimmed each of the twelve pages a second time, spending extra time on the final one, which was sure to cause him the most heartburn. But to Heritage's concealed surprise, next to his grandfather's initials and signatures, Fraser initialed each page and signed on all four signature lines, returning the stack of papers back across the table.

Heritage broke the silence, as he countersigned and initialed each of the clauses. "Five years reach back, maximum—but that adds around another five or six million to your balance sheet, beyond the eighteen million. If you can get at that timber, that is. This isn't without risk, Brad. We only need look back to last summer's fiasco at Kennedy Lake to know the opposition this buyout will face." Heritage paused, knowing this pep-talk threatened to push Brad Fraser into gluttony overload. He continued. "Still, we feel that Fraser-Carter should take immediate steps to hire back all the Clayoquot loggers laid off by Mac-Blo to garner local support and loyalty. You get this town working again and it'll be a PR grape-stomping opportunity that will have everyone drunk with the outcome."

"Everyone except the blasted enviros that have made Clayoquot Sound quite probably the least popular drink at the bar." Fraser seemed pleased by his extension of Heritage's metaphor, but Heritage wasn't sure it made sense. Brad wasn't ready to let the analogy run dry, though. "There's got to be a way to shut the tree-huggers out of Clayoquot Sound," he continued. "Eighty-six the bastards from the club, I say!" He seemed incapable of restraining his cleverness and Heritage wondered if he might be still drunk. Heritage sat there grinning, both his hands clasped on top of his mission, very adeptly accomplished, if he did think so himself.

Heritage couldn't reveal that he was both irritated and bored by Brad's company, or that he couldn't care less about TFL 74. He had his own logjam to sort. In the intervening minutes, while Fraser devoured two croissants, Tage's brain began to wander back to the skull in Dottie's living room floor, the painted-over map in Stephanie's playhouse, and how he was going to scheme his way out of watching Aidan over the coming week in order to dart home and suck up to the patriarch maybe one last time. Heritage appeared to be jotting notes to himself when he'd actually lapsed into nervous doodles of his own trying to catalogue all the *what ifs*. What if Aidan's storytelling somehow escalated and the rumours reached his grandfather's attention? What if Dottie Bard discovered Heritage not only worked for but was heir to one of the largest forest-gobbling paper conglomerates in North America? What if Brad Fraser expressed concern to the head of Carter Pulp & Paper that his grandson might be cavorting with environmentalist lesbian witches on Wickaninnish Island? What if he didn't make a showing at Wellesley Hospital in Toronto? Would his granddad's living vendetta edit him out of his inheritance? What if he shirked his obligation to Mona to watch Aidan after garnering Dottie's personal recommendation? Could those two team up their wiccan powers to *newt*-ralize him? He underlined, then internally chuckled at the word he'd just invented in the margin of his legal pad, recalling his conversation with the librarian about newts and other spell conjuring ingredients. But this wasn't a chuckling matter; this was serious. He crossed out the word with a barrage of diagonal hashmarks.

It wasn't these individual horrors that concerned Heritage. It was the Armageddon that would ensue should there be this multi-horror pile up with everything colliding at once in some blind intersection that Heritage couldn't see coming. That scenario immobilized him in his chair as he sat across from Brad Fraser—saying nothing, but thinking everything.

He would have liked to think he'd never been more backed into a corner, and that he simply couldn't resist the jumbled challenge of trying to manage his way out of it. But the truth was that he'd been born into that corner and forced to sit there with his nose in it for thirty-two years. Close calls and precarious circumstances only served to adorn his confinement.

Brad Fraser caught his heir-apparent business partner staring out the window and took it as a compliment for the room's sweeping view. "That happens to me a half dozen times a day."

"This is a stunning spot, Brad," Heritage said, recovering. "It is such a shame my grandmother didn't live long enough to see it . . ." He trailed off.

Sitting across from a zealot like Brad Fraser, Heritage liked to think he was facing the last of his dragons. All that mattered in the weeks and months to come was being able to eventually fall asleep at night without having those fire-breathing nightmares that were so often a side effect of his grandfather's business. Some nights were easier than others.

Heritage threaded each of his rolled-up dress pant legs inside the kayak and pushed his boat off the sand below the lodge. He had been so pleased with the paperwork signing and the relief he was feeling just knowing that Brad Fraser would soon be off and out of his hair on his month-long holiday, that he hadn't taken the time to change out of the business clothes. He'd faxed the signed agreement back to Lonnie and followed up with a phone call to explain the collateral clause he'd added to the contract. He could tell that his grandfather's lawyer was beside himself impressed with how Heritage had handled matters and received Lonnie's hearty congratulations with a pride he hadn't experienced when performing his grandfather's bidding before. Perhaps he'd just proven his value to his grandfather, the company lawyer and most importantly, to himself. As scheduled, his day of housekeeping training had involved some toilet cleaning, but after a week of outhouses, Heritage sort of embraced—make that *worshiped* plumbing and porcelain in a whole new light and through himself gleefully into the work. In other words, his mood could not be dampened.

Heritage had been heading straight for Wickaninnish Island when he suddenly stopped mid-stroke in the open channel. Swell after swell barreled under him as he sat there, idle, thinking. Bobbing in the main channel above the wreckage of the *Tonquin*, he realized he had somehow managed to jam up his brain and confound all his motor skills in that moment just by thinking about François. What were success and fortune, after all, without someone to share these accomplishments with? In the first days after the hot springs, he had tried to convince himself that what had transpired between them there had been natural or circumstantial or the unintended consequence of getting stoned, and that it would be best not to overload this with feelings or expectations. He had even tried to commute the sense of abandonment he had felt during those first lonely days on Wickaninnish Island to the loss of his connection to society in general—when in reality, it was only François he missed, François he longed to reconnect with, to get to know better. But he might have screwed that up too, by not disclosing he'd been with François' girlfriend before he ever knew they were together.

Heritage drummed the side of his kayak. There was some shattered fiberglass mending between them that Heritage decided on the spot he needed to attend to. Paused there in the channel equidistant from the Headlands and Wickaninnish Island, Heritage could feel the current pulling him toward town. He took that as an omen, and decided he had tired of moping about the guy. It was time to find him.

He checked his watch. Seeing he had oodles of time, he immediately maneuvered the rudder to orient him north with the incoming tide, toward the village at the end of the narrow, crooked finger of land that formed the peninsula. As he dipped and pulled his paddle, he tried to remember if François' oyster farm schedule was eight or ten days on, four days off, or the other way around. But whether or not the object of his affection might be back from the farm, Heritage knew he'd feel better after poking around town for him. At least then he would be doing something instead of waiting for time to scab over wounds that would only keep bleeding until he either applied first aid or stocked up on enough junk food at the Co-op to get over it.

Twenty minutes later, Heritage stuck his paddle straight into the water on his right side and brought his kayak into perfect alignment along the dock just behind the Lady Slipper, a modified whale-watching cruiser that looked as though she'd been out of commission for several tourist seasons. Checking the time again, he allotted no more than an hour for his François search and rescue mission if he was to make it back to Wickaninnish before Aidan arrived home in Mason Robson's skiff from his week at school. He already knew Mason wouldn't be driving her boat since she was in Campbell River attending a poetry-writing workshop. She'd given her boat key to Mac Mulligan to make the school boat run and Mac was the first person Heritage bumped into on the dock as he was securing his kayak.

"How's her nose behaving?" Mac shouted from the back of a boat three vessels away from the Lady Slipper.

"She's good as new, Mac! Thank you again for fixing her." Heritage jogged toward him thinking he might know if François was in town or still out at the farm, but before he asked, Mac commented on how brave he was taking on two hellraisers for the weekend.

"I'm just happy I only got stuck being the boat bus driver. I'll be popping the boys over to Wick in another hour after they get sprung from school. I can take you too if you like."

Heritage sort of laughed that off saying he was looking forward to the paddle but thanked him for the offer; adding that he was just stopping by the Co-op for a few things. He was right thinking that Mac would know about François' whereabouts. Mac had last seen him a few minutes ago at the bakeshop.

Walking up First Street in dress pants and flip-flops, Heritage felt the odd man out, but he had bigger challenges ahead apparently. Nobody had bothered informing him that he'd be teen-sitting two kids instead of one for the first few days, but Mason had instructed Mac to bring both Aidan and her son Rowan over to the island on Friday afternoon at four o'clock. Having another teen underfoot actually came as a relief as Heritage had been particularly nervous about being with Aidan alone. It was just remarkable that Mason wouldn't have wanted to speak to Heritage directly before trusting her son with a stranger. Heritage hadn't met Mason or Rowan yet—but was looking forward to making as many solid impressions on the islanders as he could while expanding his network of locals, particularly if he were ever to consider making his own bid to become one of the Wickaninnish Island shareholders. Dottie had mentioned this could be a possibility—that they were always looking for new investors—and that he could maybe have his own little cottage there someday too, if he played his cards right. He hadn't known at the time, during that gut-wrenching crossing when she had dumped him on the island that by *cards* she was more likely referring to Tarot than playing.

He had since understood, through his limited conversations with Mona and even the librarian named Gillian, that there were maybe a dozen women who had shares on the island, but most of them were only around in the summer months. Mason, he remembered, like Mona, was one of the few who was there year-round, toughing it out to raise her teenage son by herself. Both their boys in their teens were known to take advantage of their mothers in the vacuum of their wild and isolated upbringings—and now, Heritage would be responsible for both of them, but Aidan, he had already been convinced, must be the gang leader, the trouble instigator, the devil's own seed. Something else was bugging him though; something Brad Fraser had said about Wickaninnish being some feminist outpost and anti-male establishment. While a reputation of that calibre would be intriguing and make for good story telling, Heritage already doubted the claim's veracity. He'd already met Lyle and the coast guard captain, Matt—both had places and at least occasionally lived on the island—plus Matt's dad lived there too, Matt had mentioned. True, he hadn't met Rowan yet—but Aidan was practically a fully-grown man in his own right. So that was five males, and Heritage made six. Even if he had been the only one, Dottie must have had her reasons for making him feel welcome and for extending the invitation for him to stay there. So far, he hadn't been eaten by warlocks or sacrificed by witches. It didn't seem his place to question the arrangements, but he would keep alert. The consequential riddle might be where all their men—the men who had been with Dottie, Mona, Mason, and Stephanie—had disappeared to. He wanted to avoid being dispatched there himself. Indeed, he was on the hunt for one of these missing fellows at the moment.

Even before Mac gave him the tip, Heritage figured the airy SunRyes Bakeshop seemed the most logical place to start looking for someone. Since stimuli and illicit treats were hard to come by in a small town, the one place you could get damaging amounts of quick fixes like coffee, gossip and sweets or a slice of pizza, would be where you could find just about anyone if you waited long enough. Sure enough, while stirring brown sugar into his coffee in the self-service area, Heritage overheard a man's accented voice regaling a small crowd in the two-story octagonal dining room. It sure sounded like François, so Heritage moved along the wall that separated them to tune in more clearly.

"And it was at da Hot Springs dat he asked to give me a blow-job," the jovial voice whispered, almost too clearly for Heritage's virgin, unsuspecting ears. "I could not believe it when he ask me dis." There was some laughter.

"What did you tell him?" a female voice asked.

"I didn't tell him nutting," he could hear François say

"So, what did the guy say next?" another compatriot asked.

"He couldn't speak cause his mout was full." François dropped a few consonants and the punch line with perfect timing. There were three seconds of silence before everyone decided to take it as a joke, awkwardly laughing at once. But Heritage wasn't laughing—he practically threw his cup and saucer into the bus tub as he stormed out of the bakery, catching François' eyes. Heritage was halfway down the sidewalk in front of the bank by the time François caught up to him in his fancy dress pants.

"Hey, what's your hurry?" François asked, out of breath.

Heritage didn't stop or acknowledge the voice he wished he hadn't recognized in the bakeshop.

François stopped on the sidewalk just beyond the Co-op grocery store and yelled after him again. "Hey, dat wasn't about you," he volleyed out into the sound.

Heritage was red-faced—enraged and feeling utterly betrayed. His stride carried him down the slope to the dock, and his pride kept him from looking back. He stepped one foot into the cockpit of his kayak, and though he should have known better, followed it with the other, promptly losing his balance. He toppled into the sea. The kayak, still tethered forward and aft, rocked itself still. The cold shock of the water's temperature stunned him and it was a second or two before he knew which direction was up. By the time he figured it out, full-on embarrassment had set in—he wished he could stay underwater, but since he had to breathe, he surfaced slowly. Concealed behind his kayak until he was satisfied there was no one racing to his aid, he worked his way around the boat and hauled himself out of the sea.

He sat there on the dock—his feet still in the water until he thought they might be going numb—momentarily unsure of what to do next. He didn't have a ready change of clothes without unpacking his kayak and rooting through the dry bags he'd packed for his teen-sitting stint, but he had the life jacket, and a Patagonia windbreaker rolled into its pouch in the front storage hatch. He peeled off the wet shirt, retrieved and then unfurled the pullover, just as François, ambled down the dock.

"Here," he said, pulling the green OSU sweatshirt over his head. "Wear dis."

Heritage stood until the two were nose to nose and eye to eye. "What was that all about back there?" Heritage asked, clearly hurt.

"You mean dat joke? It wasn't about you. It wasn't about us. Dat bunch of us, we was talking about our friend Marcel. Dat was his joke. I was telling it cause nobody has seen him for days and we was just exchanging stories, you know?" François presented an uneasy smile, that off-colour tooth looking a shade darker in the sunshine.

Heritage accepted the sweatshirt, standing there—wet and bare-chested, nipples protruding—for nearly a solid, teasing minute before pulling the green sweatshirt over his own head. He tried to control his shivering since his pants, socks and briefs were still sea-soaked. "I've worn this sweatshirt before, you know," Heritage confessed, ironing the collegiate letters with his hand. "It was in a little shed I've been using the past week and a half on Wick." Heritage paused. "But you must have known that because you got your sweatshirt back. You were there."

"Yes, I was der. I went to grab a few of my tings since I guess me and Stephanie were breaking up. I didn't know you were der or I would have gone looking for you."

Heritage needed to look away from those dark eyes. "What else did you find there, François? In that little cabin?" He was fishing another confession out of him, thinking he would discover where his new paperback novel had gone.

François took a second to bite his lower lip. "I saw da note, da one Stephanie left her Mum."

Heritage looked back into those eyes and exhaled powerfully. "About that note—"

"Don't worry. Stephanie fucks everyting. I was hurt at first but I was definitely not surprised. I'm over dat now." François gave a conciliatory smile. Heritage melted.

"And the bottom of that note she wrote . . . the P.S. about me?"

François reached into his back pocket and produced his wallet, opening it in front of him and extracting the torn bit of grocery sack that he'd carefully folded to carry around with him. "Dis?" he asked. Heritage nodded, scrunching his face into a question mark. "I took it cause I didn't want Dottie seeing dat part. Plus," he added, "I didn't have nutting from you—no telephone number, no way to know what happened to you." He held it up. "I kept dis to remember you."

Heritage didn't know what to say, but what he said next definitely killed the romance of the moment. "François, about your friend, Marcel—unless there is more than one here—"

"No. Just one Marcel. He drives da water taxi." François' face registered hope until he read the concern and dread washing over Heritage's face.

"I'm sorry to be the one to tell you this, but Marcel is dead. He drowned on Sunday night. No, I guess it would have been early Monday morning," François' eyes grew even bigger before squinting in disbelief.

"No. No. Dat's impossible." François' eyes filled with tears he managed to hold there.

"I am so sorry. His boat ran onto the rocks in the middle of the night on the west side of Wickaninnish—during that storm we had, remember?"

François was shaking his head back and forth. "I was wit him on Saturday."

"I'm sorry. I really am. I don't know what he was doing out in that storm. I was sleeping in a different cabin on the west side of the island that night. I heard his mayday on the marine radio." François sort of leaned forward into a hug and Heritage held him there, on the dock. "I tried to help the coast guard find his location, because I could see the light from his boat at first, but then it disappeared, and the maydays stopped. The coast guard arrived too late. I spoke with the captain—Matt. The next morning, they found Marcel's body. They have been trying to locate his family to let them know, before they release the information about the accident, you know, locally. This must be why you didn't know this already." Heritage squeezed his arms tighter around the distraught man. François hugged back, then pulled away.

"Marcel and I—" He stopped himself.

"Go on."

"We have been having dis affair. Stephanie caught us kissing once at dis dance out at da airport. We sort of cooled tings after dat, tinking she was going to blab to everyone."

"I see," Heritage said.

"I was supposed to be seeing Stephanie, and Marcel, he was dating da library lady."

"Gillian?" Heritage's voice went into an upper register.

"Yep. We bot of us had covers, but we were busted and Stephanie isn't known for her discretion. Marcel and me, we had to act like we barely knew each udder after dat." François looked down at the wet spots on his pants that corresponded with the places he and Heritage had touched during their hug. "Tanks for telling me."

"Listen," Heritage wasn't sure which information might help so he just started talking to feel the space between them. "There's one more thing I should tell you. I later found Marcel's wallet . . . in fact, it looked just like yours. I took it to the RCMP and gave them a statement. If I had known, I would have given the wallet to you."

François' eyebrows lifted. "You found my wallet den." He lifted the wallet he'd just tucked the paper sack P.S. back into. "Dis one is Marcel's."

"I don't understand."

"It was our way of staying connected to each udder. We switched wallets but kept our IDs. Dis way, he was always wit me and I was always wit him."

"Oh, man," Heritage exclaimed. "I wish I had known this. I could have gotten you your wallet back."

A tear escaped François' eye. "I have the wallet I want," he said. "I better go break da news to Gillian. She is gonna be wrecked."

"Are you okay?" Heritage was more concerned about François.

François gave him a quick hug. "Sure," he said, but not very convincingly.

Skimming over the choppy water between Monk's Point and Felice Island with the sun in his eyes, Heritage lowered his sunglasses and found himself intimidated by the expanse of ocean that churned between him and the navigation beacon he needed to aim for but could barely make out in front of Mona's place across the way. A raft of seagulls launched off the water ahead of him at the same time Heritage paddled, nostrils first, into a stench that was unmistakeably sewage. This, he recognized with most of his senses including a rancid taste in the back of his throat, must be the place where the village sewage outfall pipe was located. He was careful not to over-splash his paddling through this section as he glided past a used condom floating on the surface and a half stroke further past a tampon applicator. What humans were doing to this planet, he feared, would come to no pleasant end. How could the newly crowned environmental capitol of the free world still be pumping raw, untreated sewage straight into the Pacific Ocean? Why hadn't the all-politically-powerful Dottie Bard addressed this already, he wondered in disgust as he tried to hold his breath. He ruddered hard left passing by the hospital at Duffin Cove to tack along Tonquin Beach for a hundred metres further hoping he could evade the sludge, but found the stink sticking with him—or on him. He buried his nose in the sleeve of the loaned green sweatshirt and he smelled the complex fragrance that was François; part man . . . part oysters . . . part cedar campfire . . . part gasoline . . . maybe part Marcel, too. Heritage knew now that François was every bit as complex as his scent—and that he wanted to experience a fair bit more of both. He tightened his grip on the paddle and decided to just go for it and headed straight out in the channel where air quality quickly improved.

Three-quarters of the way across the channel, his dress pants and underwear still wet but warming beneath the spray skirt, he set the rudder and power-paddled through the deeper troughs toward calmer water and the afternoon shadows already draping over Mona's place. He would have just enough time to unload his clothes and the hatch full of groceries he'd liberated from The Headlands' pantry for the planned offensive, before the kids got home from school. How domestically suburban that sounded to him! How completely contrary to the hellish reality he was bracing for and anticipating—knowing what he knew about Aidan.

Heritage got to thinking he still hadn't spoken to Dottie about upgrading to the empty triangle cabin on the outside beach—or about anything, really. In his defense, he had stopped by her emporium twice, once after he'd given his statement at the RCMP and also when he picked up his kayak from Mac. She hadn't been there either time, but he'd been sure to leave word that he'd stopped by, mostly so that he could keep blaming her for making zero effort to mend the fence she possibly didn't even realize was broken between them. If he could rack up enough "honest try" loyalty points, he could easily redeem them for use of the triangle cabin, he figured. And minding Mona's kid for a week, maybe two, was going to qualify him for the bonus sweepstakes round. That's when maybe he would ascend in their estimation and get invited to buy his way onto the island and receive his own share and building site.

He paddled by the rocks with the white-painted concrete base and navigation beacon and marveled at the eel grass and kelp forest that shimmered and swayed in the soft currents swirling beneath him. In the distance, to his right, he noted a few clouds had snagged on Lone Cone peak on Meares Island, but other-wise, the reflection on the smooth water heralded the clear sky overhead. He was relieved he wouldn't have to fight the weather in addition to fighting the teenager who'd been spoiling for a row from the moment they'd met. Heritage unbraced his knees and pulled the release tab on his spray skirt. It was like taking the lid off a terrarium that had been sitting in the afternoon sun. He stopped paddling and the forward momentum glided his kayak toward a partly sandy beach just a little to the north of Mona's house. The sands received his bow with a gritty whisper that was amplified inside the hull, announcing his arrival. He was back, for his second time that day, on Wickaninnish Island.

With Dottie's place and the Headlands Lodge completely out of the sightlines from this location and with Mona's quaint little house tucked in a comma of beach that faced east to Meares Island and south maybe to Radar Hill with treed rises in topography on either side, Heritage could almost imagine he was landing on a completely different island. Here, he could start fresh, bask in the morning sunshine and contemplate the new directions his life was about to take without stressing over all the witchy dark trappings that had oppressed him on the southern end of this bewildering and definitely bewitched island. Surveying, with his hand visoring the sun from his eyes, Heritage revved the accelerator on his own designs for acquiring his share on the island. What other magical pockets like this still existed around the perimeter, he wondered? He was instantly anxious to circumnavigate its coastal entirety and stake some claim. Where could he toss up a unique, timber-framed enclave of his very own?

If . . . if . . . if. There were those nagging, conditional, speculative doubts creeping back in again! He had long hated the uncertainty surrounding his grandfather's condition and the conditions the old man had placed on Heritage's inheritance. Now, that he could almost perceive the first tremors of movement, that something might finally be about to happen in his favour, made the waiting even more urgently agonizing. He was almost there, he felt, standing on the veranda of his life's destiny, making another two-column checklist in his mind: If he could swindle the Headlands away from Brad Fraser; if his grandfather finally succumbed; if Heritage were given the opportunity to purchase his own patch of rainforest paradise; if François could get beyond his grief over losing Marcel and come to terms with settling down; if Dottie's witchcraft could be neutralized; then . . . *then*, Heritage could envision himself living large in a place like this and revelling in the string of glorious moments to come, just like this one—and be happy the rest of his days. But this was still Wickaninnish Island, he reminded himself, taking a giant breath in and bracing himself.

Heritage checked his wristwatch; it was 3:32 p.m. He had maybe a little more than thirty minutes to get settled into Mona's place, before he was scheduled to intercept the charming bundle of adolescence and his buddy, apparently, as they got sprung from their week of detention. Heritage decided to use Mona's invitation to make himself at home as an opportunity to do a little snooping around. Nothing would solve the confounding puzzle of what made that teenager tick faster than helping himself to a few of the puzzle pieces.

It was a funny cottage—more of a mini-house, really. With two unimaginative stories, it looked from the outside like it had been plucked from the cul-de-sac of a housing development anywhere in North America, except that it had been painted using the same colours as the bakeshop on the other side of the channel. And what were those shades, anyway? Eggplant with chartreuse trim? It had none of the driftwood railings or other hippie flourishes—no cargo netting, Japanese glass balls, or moon snail shells. He sort of instantly understood why Aidan might have been so quick to stir up mayhem everywhere else—home looked a little pedestrian and tucked-up when compared to the other weathered cabins he'd explored on the island so far.

Heritage pulled the kayak as far up the beach as he could before reaching a barricade of rocks and driftwood. This shortened the distance for the multiple trips he needed to make to transfer the contents of his hatches to this new cottage for his limited occupation. He muscled the sticky sliding glass door open, announcing himself in case the place wasn't empty. Entering the cottage through the kitchen, he found it stainless and sterile as a bakery, which also made some sense to him since the outside was painted to mimic the SunRyes. He walked through the kitchen, taking one step down to a living room that was either too narrow or full of furniture to be truly functional but then, Mona was a short-statured woman and until his last growing spurt, Aidan too might have gotten along just fine in this downsized space. That's when he spied the framed photographs on the floor-to-ceiling bookshelves that alternated with similarly sized narrow windows that faced the beach—photos of Aidan and Mona, some with Dottie, one with a man who could have been Lyle Hudson, but none of the man who might have been responsible for bringing precious Aidan into the world.

He didn't linger there and moved back into the kitchen and through a curtained, walk-thru pantry, into what had to be Aidan's part of the house. He based this impression on a clutter of belongings hanging from hooks on either side of a closed door with a giant letter *A* hanging on it—a pair of binoculars, a sling shot, a wetsuit, a fishing rod, some dried bull kelp seaweed, an Oakland A's baseball cap, a yellow rain coat with hunter green rain pants, and an ornamentally engraved knife with a carved wooden handle hanging from a leather lanyard that looked as though it had come from Indonesia, or Thailand maybe. Heritage removed the leather sheath and tested the blade to see if it was dull. It sure wasn't. Next he tried the door handle, but it was locked. Accepting for a moment that deciphering Aidan and his motives might have to wait for live clues, he decided to concentrate instead on Mona. He found her loft bedroom at the top of a really skinny staircase that hugged the backwall of the living room, with the door at the top landing not only wide open but missing completely from its frame. Her bed was mostly made, though the once-white duvet, now stained slightly manila-envelope-yellow, was hanging crooked on one side of the bed. After his housekeeping training at the Headlands, Heritage would notice a detail like that—but it also jumped out at him, with everything else about the room so nicely arranged and organized, as if for his inspection. Perhaps Mona had assumed Heritage would sleep in her bed during the time she was away— and possibly even snoop around, given the access. Then again, a woman riddled by cancer likely had other preoccupations.

He spied a bra hanging on the inside of the slightly ajar closet door. Feeling only a little perverse, he lifted it off the doorknob. He discovered that one of the cups had been completely stuffed and sewn shut. He hadn't known that about Mona, but with the chemotherapy and everything she had revealed about her medical challenges, it made sense. He replaced the underwear and canvassed the dresser top for photos of a man—any man. But aside from photos of the devil child taken at regular intervals in his development, no other males seemed to exist in Mona's life. On a nightstand on the far side of the bed, there was a photograph of Mona with Dottie in younger days, by the looks of hairstyles and the fuzzy quality of the photograph, probably taken with a Kodak Instamatic. They were posing in a forest, standing in front of a magnificent Sitka spruce that Heritage was able to identify by the pattern of the bark on the trunk. He studied this photograph carefully, somewhat intrigued by two things at once: there were actual photographs in the frames in this house, and the two subjects in this photo were actually holding hands. On closer examination, it seemed Dottie might have been trying to conceal that detail by jutting out one of her hips. Her expression suggested she might have opposed the documentation of what was perhaps more than a friendship. Who had taken the picture? There was either a thumb or a partial shadow of the photographer discernable at the top corner, just barely entering the frame. With the dark, heavy canopy of the forest setting, Heritage could tell that a flash bulb had been deployed to unnaturally illuminate the subjects. He figured the picture must be close to ten years old, so Aidan probably wasn't the photographer, plus the camera seemed level with the height of the women, suggesting the photographer was likely an adult. It might have been Stephanie or Mason or somebody else that Heritage may not have encountered yet. He wasn't sure why that mattered except he figured the photographer would have known the story between these two women. The more Heritage stared at the photo, the more it became a composition of their two clasped hands.

He replaced the frame on the nightstand and opened the little drawer to reveal the pharmacy that kept Mona alive or comfortable. Each of the amber containers had mostly current prescriptions. He thought he recognized a few of the drug names—Seconol, Demerol, Gravol—and tried to imagine the ailments beyond the pain or nausea they were prescribed to alleviate. He also tried to understand the decision to leave these drugs—especially the THC, which he knew to be a marijuana derivative—within the easy reach of a teenager. His stint at fathering had already started, he supposed. He backed out of the room and climbed down the narrow stairs from the loft just as his intended charge burst through the front door of the cottage.

"Hello," Heritage said, momentarily freezing red-handed on the stairs.

"What were you doing up there?" Aidan demanded. "Going through my mother's panties drawer?"

"No, Aidan." Heritage's voice was lower than normal. It was his parenting voice. He'd been practicing it off and on the past few days. He continued down the steps and turned to face the boy. "How was school this week?"

"Fuck you!" Aidan spoke slowly, scrunching up his face until the peach fuzz that grew there took on a five-o-clock hue beyond his years. He disappeared through the pantry and jammed a key into the lock of the door with the giant "A," slamming the door between them. The "A" nearly flew off the tack that held it there.

Heritage waited until the letter stopped swinging from side to side. He walked up to the door, the wood creaking beneath his feet, and cleared his throat loudly.

"I'll be sitting outside on the deck thinking about putting dinner together when you grow up." He waited a second or two. "Did you hear me?" He almost added "young man," but cut himself short. There was no answer—in fact, no sound from inside the room. Heritage turned slowly to leave, but the first creak provoked the bedroom door to open, as though cued.

"Would you like to see my room?" Aidan wore the closest thing to a smile he could come up with on short notice. Heritage smiled back and nodded his head just once before entering the dark room. He looked around, letting his eyes adjust, leaning at first on the dresser just inside the door. "I keep my underwear in the bottom drawer if you want to check mine out too," Aidan said. "Unless of course, you'd rather smell the ones I have on now."

"You're a very funny boy, Aidan. If I didn't have better things to do with my evening, I'd stay for your second show." Heritage turned and took two strides toward the door. Aidan panicked and darted across the room, leaping onto his babysitter's back. "I'm just teasing," he said, locking his arms around Heritage's neck and rubbing a knuckle into his hair. Heritage reached back with both arms to loop under the kid's legs. He adjusted the teenager's position on his back.

"Let's go make dinner together then," Heritage suggested before leaning down to allow the child to dismount.

"Only if you carry me down to the beach."

"Come on, Aidan. You're way too big for this. Get down."

"Relax. It's not like it's giving me a hard-on, or anything. I'll behave." Aidan grabbed some brown rice from the pantry and tossed the bag on the counter as they passed through. "We have to wait for Rowan. He's just dropping off his books."

"Rowan?" Heritage pretended to be surprised but was immediately relieved.

"I know you probably had your heart set on having me to yourself, but Rowan's orphaned this weekend too." He released his arms and hopped onto the kitchen floor. "You're in charge of both of us, like it or not. We'll try to go easy on you."

"I appreciate that." Heritage didn't know which of them was being more facetious, as he straightened his back, thinking Aidan probably weighed as much as he did. "I'll just make more rice."

Minutes later, Rowan bounded up the deck steps to rap on the sliding glass door. He politely and properly reached out to shake Heritage's hand. "I'm Rowan Robson."

"And I am Tage Carter. Please call me *Tage*—that's like *Page* with a *T*." Heritage cleverly swiped a line from Aidan's book and flashed a sly smile in his direction. Aidan rolled his eyes.

"Cool," Rowan said.

And that was the last word he managed to get in, as Aidan commanded the rest of the evening's Q & A over brown rice and red beans—Aidan's request. Forty-five minutes later, Heritage would regret his dinner choice as it launched an impromptu and highly competitive farting contest that soon rendered the odd little cabin a hazard to their breathing health.

The boys spilled out onto the deck, then raced ahead on a trail into the woods they'd probably used their entire lives and could likely sprint with their eyes closed. Heritage hadn't gotten over how black the forest was at night—he lagged behind, feeling his way a bit more cautiously. It was a warm evening. Heritage had left François' green sweatshirt on the sofa and was surprised he didn't need it. Any phase of the moon would have helped illuminate his path, but it was a cloudless and moonless night in Clayoquot. Stars, in the spots where the forest allowed, were the brightest he'd ever seen.

The thought of parachuting from this paradise back into industrial Toronto disturbed him. He didn't want to break his splendid Clayoquot trance with big city family matters but if his grandfather had finally pulled the sheets up on the bed he was prepared to die in, it would be worth the trip and a journey he knew he would have to make. Just at that moment, the toe of his hiking boot caught a tree root while he was looking up at the stars, and he crumpled to his knees. "Damnit," he cursed the root and then raised a shaking fist to the night sky where he half-believed his dead parents were supposed to be keeping watch over him. Even thinking about the last surviving member of his family— however much longer he had—caused him havoc and now, pain. He brushed off his knees and continued in the direction of the teenagers' yells and taunts about boogeymen. The path elevated and crossed a series of cedar shake footbridges to get over and around another promontory that lent Wickaninnish Island its measure of varied topography. Heritage had already seen higher spots and steeper cliffs in his excursions around the southern end of the island but this rise of land along the eastern shore struck him as a nice spot to build his house one day, especially if he could open up a view of Meares Island and the glaciered peaks of Strathcona Provincial Park beyond. He wasn't as sure that he wanted to be wedged in between Dottie and Mona, or that close to Aidan, though. But for ease of boating access to and from The Headlands, he already believed he wanted to be on that more protected side, rather than on the exposed outer coast that took the brunt of whatever weather the Pacific Ocean tossed at it. He thought of Marcel Labbé in that moment and remembered how permanently unforgiving that side of the island could be.

He could hear the boys shouting up ahead, or down below, but couldn't make out the reason for their second wind and sudden animation. Heritage looked in all directions and could not see the lights from Mona's cabin which he knew they'd left on, and believed he couldn't see Dottie's place from that point of eleva-tion either. He could see the lights of Headlands Lodge across the way and was grateful to see it not engulfed in flames given that both its managers were away. Heritage could also see the lights of homes and an occasional set of car headlights along the low ridge above Tonquin Beach. Between the tip of Tofino and Felice Island, where he'd paddled through the shit earlier that afternoon, he could see the string of lights from Opitsat Village all the way in the distance on Meares Island. He wondered if all those lights would dash the illusion of living on a quasi-remote island, or be the comforting evidence of a civilization-within-reach that made off-the-grid living that much more special. There would certainly be no lights to be irritated or comforted by on the west side of the island. He watched the blinking white navigation beacon in front of Mona's place, but he couldn't see her house.

He liked it up there and decided he needed to piss, to mark his territory. He was midstream, when he heard Aidan two-syllabling his short name. "Ta-age . . . Ta-age . . . Come out and play," he hauntingly sang through the trees. Heritage shook the last drops of his leak onto the already saturated moss floor and took off in the direction of the last call. Twice, he thought he was back on the trail, but he wasn't. The third attempt would have been the charm if he hadn't sunk his right boot in a fern-disguised water course of mud. He clomped into the open, out of the trees and onto the beach.

Heritage thought at first his eyes might be playing tricks. Where the waves lapped the sand, tiny flashing green lights outlined them like fairy dust in a Disney movie. He rushed to the water's edge, thinking the mirage of mini-lights would disappear. But it didn't. The teenagers were in the ocean up to their waists about twenty-five metres to his left, splashing, spinning, diving, and hollering with delight in the shallow water. As he got closer, it looked as though their movements were making the lights happen.

"Tage! Come in!" Rowan hollered. "It's bioluminescence! It's unbelievable!" He couldn't contain his joy.

"Bio-what?"

"*Bio-lum-in-es-cence,*" Rowan sounded the word out, at the top of his lungs.

Heritage glanced down at the ground, his weight sinking into the wet sand. Scanning left then right, he could make out every article of the boys' clothing strewn in every direction. He'd been in the ocean once already that day, and didn't relish a re-entry, despite the fascinating green lights.

"Don't be a pussy, man!" Aidan taunted him. "Strip down and get in!"

"This only happens a few times a year," Rowan added.

Wanting to seem cool to the kids, Heritage kicked off his hiking boots, and standing in socks first on one boot, and then the other, he got down to his bare feet and tossed his boots higher on the beach. He pulled the long-sleeved jersey over his head and his T-shirt came off with it. With his dark hairy torso unveiled, he could no longer getaway with looking like the teens, not even in the dark. Undoing his jeans, he was having about a zillion second thoughts, each overruled by some nonsensical need to be seen as fun and to establish trust with these boys, who were becoming men in spite of their feminist surroundings and lop-sided parenting. Suddenly seeing himself as the male messiah that could give them someone to emulate and admire, Heritage felt inspired to lower his briefs until he was as naked as they were, but decided against it. He rushed into the water and arched into a graceful dive just as soon as the depth was right. He opened his eyes in the saltwater. At first, they stung—but the discomfort quickly passed, and he took in the green pyrotechnics all around his fingers and arms. He surfaced a short distance away from the boys, who had begun to shake in the cold water, their bodies illuminating with every twitch.

"What causes this?" Heritage asked.

"Bioluminesence is caused by dinoflagellates moving between the surface layers of the water," Rowan explained. "It is a form of plankton."

"Shut up, brainiac, and check out what I'm doing!"

Aidan wasn't shaking because the water was cold. He was jerking off, and causing a frenzy of green light collisions a foot below the surface. Rowan began laughing and splashing his friend before joining in the plankton jerk. Heritage felt himself begin to swell and knew he needed to get out of the kiddie pool. That was no place for an adult. He dove again into the water, his white ass cheeks breaching like a humpback before trailing a green flume of bioluminescence that gave away his location no matter which direction he headed. When he came up for air and rubbed his eyes, one of four teenage hands grabbed his adulthood, and this kicked off a new game of boner tag. Heritage shouted, "That's enough," refusing to play. Rowan went next for Aidan's crotch, but Aidan pivoted and held Rowan from behind in a headlock with one arm, and maneuvered the smaller boy's waist to pull his butt against his erection.

"We've never done it in the ocean," Aidan barked like a sea lion in heat. "Wanna watch me fuck the plankton out of my little buddy, Tage? Come on! He doesn't mind. He likes it, don't you, Rowan?"

Heritage didn't believe him, but also didn't want to call his bluff, for Rowan's safety and his own twisted voyeurism. The adult said nothing as the boys grunted, yelled, swallowed ocean, and coughed and splashed. Rowan didn't seem to be protesting and Aidan didn't mind being watched. The water was achingly cold, and since Heritage was not moving around, his leg muscles began to cramp. He turned away from the humping boys and began the climb to the beach. Aidan let the insults fly.

"Oh, come on! Stay! I'm about to blow. You've watched me cum before. Why don't you turn around and show us that you don't have a hard-on!"

Heritage didn't acknowledge the insults and challenges and kept putting one foot in front of the other until he was out of the water. He wouldn't be turning around to show them anything—and not because he didn't have anything to show. "I'll get a fire going."

"Sure you will. Right after you jerk off, probably!" Aidan was hoarse and freezing and Rowan had started to whimper from the cold. Aidan released the headlock and his teen captive splash-escaped to shore. Heritage had his pants back on and fastened by the time Aidan came out of the water, telltale bioluminescence swirling in his wake. Rowan, half dressed, sprinted past Heritage, shouting something to the effect that he was going home to sleep in his own bed.

"Was that little stunt for me?" Heritage asked, without turning around to face Aidan.

"It was if you enjoyed it," Satan with an A replied.

Once they had crossed the threshold into his mother's cabin after the incident with Rowan, Aidan behaved the rest of the night. Together they lit candles in Mona's room on the second floor where the radiant heat from the fireplace below whooshed up the staircase to create a cozy sauna. On top of the bedding, the pair hung out in the toasty room beneath the slant of the cabin's roof, with a book and some homework. Heritage suspected it was a brittle détente between them, but took it as progress, if not a breakthrough. It hadn't been fifteen minutes before Aidan fell asleep with his clothes on at the bottom of Mona's bed, his homework still spread beneath him as he proceeded to drool on it.

When Heritage first stirred the next morning, he realized Aidan had maneuvered under his arm to rest his crew-cut blonde head against Heritage's dark hairy chest. He knew everything about this scene would be judged as wrong by outsiders, and still, the moment offered a glimpse of how their souls might somehow develop, fuse and manifest properly under the right nurturing and of course, disciplinary conditions. Heritage had found something so irresistibly fatherly or romantic or disturbing about the ritual of Aidan's acceptance of him, that he could scarcely breathe. At some point in the evening, with all the heat trapped under the roof in their sleeping space, they'd each peeled off their shirts but maintained their barrier-establishing briefs. The rising sun rammed its searchlight through the loft bedroom window to expose and reveal them, man to man, head to torso, innocence tucked under the arm of innocence.

No! It was *boy* to man. He was wrong to apply any grownup sense to this, but Aidan looked so entirely adult in that morning light. Heritage could even make out faint blonde hairs in the ridge between the kid's pectorals. *Stop studying! Stop justifying!* Came the shrill voice of his better nature—but not loudly enough for him to do anything about it. By the time the wind-up alarm clock had rattled them both awake thirty minutes later, Heritage felt they had connected, bonded even. But he didn't feel at ease about any of this.

In the first forty-five minutes of their first Saturday together, all the repairs that the night might have managed to knit together seemed to unravel when Heritage broke it to the teenager that his grandfather was dying in hospital and that he would need to travel to Toronto in the coming days. He added that he was already looking to find someone else to watch Aidan until he could get back—maybe even Mac Mulligan. Just as their time together seemed to be finding its groove, he really hated that he had to leave. It wasn't at all the way he wanted to handle the matter. At the news, Aidan's temper quickly rose like mercury in his cheeks, and he loudly banged his heavy spoon against the side of his porridge bowl. This would be a setback, Heritage duly noted.

Soon, Aidan stormed out of the cabin, and wasn't seen or heard from for the rest of the day. At one point Rowan had tried reaching Aidan on their walkie-talkies. Heritage followed the sounds of Rowan's trucker convoy calls to just outside Aidan's still-locked bedroom door. The other walkie-talkie was clearly on the other side. The word *breaker, breaker* was repeated a few times more before Rowan gave up. Around midday, Heritage went looking for Aidan on both of the trails he knew, but also figured there were dozens more he didn't—and probably a hundred hiding places on the island if a person didn't want to be found. Heritage ventured north to see if he could find Mason's place—maybe Aidan had gone there. But after getting almost immediately lost in the woods, he turned back, and spent the afternoon sunning himself on Mona's deck. When the tide went out, Heritage collected a hefty bucket of mussels from the rocks with a paring knife, thinking he and the boys would feast on *moules-frites* when Aidan returned. Rowan eventually showed up, but Aidan was still at large well after dusk.

"He does this," Rowan said, dismissing Heritage's concern. "Once he didn't speak to me for a month."

Heritage studied the contrast of this angelic, gentle boy, with his brown hair parted on the side and combed across his forehead like a pleated velvet proscenium theatre curtain. In his slight, long-legged, almost unhealthy skinniness, he looked like a youthful European prince who had levitated off the canvas of a royal family portrait and climbed out of its ornately gilded frame to have a go at real life. His chalk-white skin looked like it had evaded solar rays for the better part of his fourteen and a half years—making Heritage wonder if he only played in the forest, where the sun couldn't find him. More likely, he spent his life indoors, around adults and mentors who challenged him to excel academically—Rowan struck him as a bookworm. This might also be a survival tactic to avoid the abuse by his bully of a friend, and maybe attract a scholarship that would deliver him from Satan with an A.

"Rowan, are you okay with what happened last night? You know, in the ocean with the phosphorescence?"

"You mean bioluminescence," Rowan said. "Phosphorescence, even fluorescence is a reaction to light. Bioluminescence is a chemical reaction that doesn't require exposure to an external light source. Phosphorescence happens during the summer here sometimes when there is lots of sun on the water. The algae suspended in the water soaks up the sun and can later appear to be glowing in the dark when there is movement or a disturbance. Bioluminescence is different because it is made by an organism. Fireflies, which I have never seen but would love to one day— well, those are bioluminescent too."

"I see." Heritage didn't. "I was referring to what Aidan did to you in the water."

"He didn't *do* anything to me. He was faking it to shock you. It's what he does."

"I see," Heritage repeated—except this time, he did.

"Next time, you need to put cornmeal or oatmeal in a bucket of water with the mussels before you cook them. Let them soak for a few hours and the mussels will take in the meal, and when it passes through them, it will pull most of the sand out of the mussel. It's way better that way." Rowan wiped his mouth with a napkin. "May I be excused? I have more homework and my mom should be back soon."

"Of course, Rowan. Thank you for having dinner with me, and for the recipe tip."

"Sure. You're welcome." He pushed his chair away from the table. "Uh, see ya around, I guess."

"You will." Heritage smiled at the polite young man. "And you can talk to me about anything, anytime, okay?"

Rowan locked eyes with him a moment and then nodded before turning to leave through the sliding glass door.

It couldn't have been fifteen minutes later that Aidan burst into the cottage, while Heritage was doing dishes. He didn't say a word, slamming his bedroom door. Heritage could hear him lock it from the other side. Cue the silent treatment. He was being punished. Heritage hadn't engaged in such negotiating tactics since he was a teen, himself. He was ill-equipped for it as an adult. He could resort to bribes or even blackmail. Or he could wait the teenager out. He didn't need to resolve everything head-on and immediately.

It was Sunday morning when the younger teen had tapped

on the sliding glass door of Mona's cottage to pick up his friend that Heritage learned from Rowan that the boys were heading off to work on their cougar trap. Heritage had raised his eyebrows at the news, and Rowan explained that earlier that last summer, a cougar had apparently moved onto the island from the larger Vargas Island to the north. The boys had been sharpening long alder branches into stakes that they were wedging at angles into rocks and driftwood below a cliff on the west side of the island. When pressed, Rowan admitted they had not seen the cougar or any evidence that it had killed any of the deer on the island. Aidan came out of his bedroom, drank a swig of orange juice straight from the bottle and shouldered himself roughly past Heritage, who was standing in the kitchen, clearly in his way.

"I could help with the cougar trap," Heritage offered.

"No, thanks," Aidan said, glaring at Rowan for revealing their secret project. With that, the two boys disappeared on the trailhead at the south end of Mona's beach.

Heritage stood there staring across the water for several minutes with the sun warming his face and the satin OSU emblem on his chest. He topped up his coffee mug and wandered out to plant his butt in a chartreuse-painted Adirondack chair. His brain was waking up and synapsing like popcorn inside his cranium. It had been a sharpened alder stake that had pierced the roof of his loaner shed at Dottie's place. The door to that shed had been painted over with the same colour as Mona's cabin, now that he was thinking about it, which was the same colour scheme at the bakeshop. Who needed fingerprint detective skills when the prime suspect was as obvious as Aidan had been?

The next morning, Heritage offered to pick Aidan up from school so they could go shopping for dinner together, or go out for a burger, or whatever Aidan wanted. Aidan didn't respond and boarded the school boat unimpressed and without looking back. Even Mason, fresh from her poetry workshop in Campbell River, and the day's appointed school boat driver, seemed to notice the rift. Heritage held onto her hand when she reached out to greet him for the first time.

"You and Mona certainly have your hands full raising teenage boys on your own," he said. "I don't know that I could do it."

Mason leaned in, and with her Swiss-German accent, said, "I have it worlds easier than Mona." That was a statement Heritage already knew nobody could debate.

After so much progress earlier in the weekend, Aidan's snubbing had nearly shoved Heritage to compromise. He couldn't very well take the kid with him to Toronto, though the ill-conceived possibility had crossed his mind. And he couldn't ignore his grandfather's last cries for attention when they'd both engaged every greedy bone in their bodies to keep each other indentured and guessing to the very last wheeze. It would just be for forty-eight hours away, seventy-two, tops—and then he and Aidan could start over again. Children were resilient, much more than adults. Aidan had probably forgotten the whole thing by the time the boat had pulled up to the Government Wharf below the school.

But Heritage worried about it the entire day. He kept remembering how their Saturday morning had begun—his loaner son tucked under his arm. The number that did on his psyche nearly prompted him to cancel the arrangements he'd made with Mason—to cover for him while he slipped out of town the next day, provided he could get flight connections. If he could manage to side-step the snare of his own bourgeoning thoughts of fatherhood long enough to race home to bag the millions that were due him, he could afford to finally settle down, and maybe have a kid of his own one day. He shook off the thought like a chill. No heirs! That had been his motto ever since he was made to realize he was one. He didn't even like children, and if he gave it a second thought, he'd remember he hadn't trusted or cared much for Aidan after their first encounter, either.

No—he had to go to Toronto.

———

Jogging up the wide steps to the one-level schoolhouse, Heritage was nearly bowled down by the exodus of students. There couldn't have been more than a hundred of them, but they rushed past with gale-like force. He stood there, waiting for Aidan to appear. But as the last of the children either boarded the buses or rounded the corners and disappeared, Heritage found himself and the school all but abandoned. He walked inside and leaned his head into the office window. "I'm here to pick up Aidan Rye," he announced, thinking in the next second that others might find it odd that an unknown man was there to pick up one of the students. When an assistant poked her head out of an adjoining office, Heritage expanded. "I'm Tage Carter. I'm watching Aidan Rye for Mona the next two weeks."

"Lucky you," she practically snarled. "Ninnish went home sick after first period this morning."

"No." He hadn't heard what she'd said exactly, but started over again, sure she'd misunderstood him. "I'm to pick up Aidan Rye from school."

She walked directly to the window and leaned down to student height to speak to him through the circle cut into the glass. "But I'm telling you, Ninnish—I mean, Aidan—went home this morning after first period." She turned to holler into the office. "What was it this time, Andrea?"

"Bloody diarrhea," came the shouted response from the other office.

"He went home complaining of bloody diarrhea." Heritage's face registered shock, but the assistant did not flinch—like any seasoned educator. "It's nothing to be concerned about," she confided. "We keep a running list of all the student excuses as evidence so that we can say that we truly have heard it all before."

He was too much of an alarmist, especially in the realm of

blood, to just accept the news and walk away. He wanted to know where the accountability was. "I'll admit I'm real new at this, but you mean to tell me you let a kid walk out of here, bleeding between the legs, without an adult waiting to care for him? Did he see a doctor, or the school nurse?"

"You have to understand Ninnish, Mr.—I'm sorry, I didn't catch your last name."

"Carter. Tage Carter. But maybe we're not talking about the same student."

"Oh, I'm sorry," she said. "I keep using his nickname. It's a real bad habit I picked up from the other children. Aidan's nickname at school is Ninnish. Actually, Wicked Ninnish among some of his teachers. Nobody calls him Aidan. And I'll be honest with you. He is such a troublemaker at school that an opportunity, fabricated or otherwise, to send him home for the day is manna, pure manna." She gestured heavenward.

"So, nobody actually checked—for blood that is."

"Mr. Carter, I didn't bring my stool kit to school today. Now, that's my excuse. If Aidan comes to the office and isn't feeling well, we send him home. This is not an infirmary or a penitentiary." She was on the verge of becoming snooty with him. Like all school Mondays, it had been a long one. It was time to go home.

Another woman emerged from the office to intervene. "Mr. Carter, is it? My name's Madeline Broussard. I am the principal of the school. Until I checked Aidan's file just now, I wasn't aware that his mother was in Victoria for treatment again and that she'd signed custodial care over to you for two weeks. Aidan had told me he was going straight to the bakery to have his mother take him home. As you must know, the bakery is a block away. Mona Rye is extremely involved in this school. I take the responsibility for the decision to allow him to leave. I'm sorry you weren't notified."

"So, it's anybody's guess where he is now, then?" Heritage was beginning to understand the dilemma that riddled their lives every day.

"With Ninnish, it's anybody's guess. Here is my home telephone number." She wrote as she spoke. "Call me if you don't find him at the bakery or if he isn't already home on the island. You know, despite the records in this file that rather paint Aidan Rye as a troubled teen from a broken home, he can take care of himself. There aren't many of our students I can say that about. I'm sure he's fine."

Heritage wasn't appeased. He was outraged. He left the school for the bakery—never dreaming he'd run smack into François.

"Hello," Heritage offered formally, coldly, altogether preoccupied.

"I've been looking for you," François said, beaming.

Heritage wanted to take the time to sip a cappuccino and shoot the breeze, but he was a stand-in father now, and everything else came second. "Say, do you know Mona's kid, Aidan?"

"Mona—da woman dat owns da bakery? Yes, I know him."

"Have you seen him today?"

François shook his head, changing his expression to match the seriousness in Tage's face and tone. "He's not in da bakery. I was just in der. Say, do you have some time? Maybe we could talk."

"Uh, I really can't. I'm watching the kid for Mona and he left school early today, supposedly sick. I need to find him."

"I could help you." That brownish tooth caught Heritage's eye. It was truly the only distraction on an otherwise perfectly assembled man, and week-old feelings began to tickle Tage's skin just beneath the surface of his crumbling resolve.

"I have to get out to Wickaninnish Island to see if he's home. I'll have to see you another time, François."

"Let me take you. My boat is just down da street. You can be der in five minutes. If you kayak, it will be tirty minutes from here, and dat is only if you don't fall out of your boat stepping into it again." His look of concern transformed into a giant brown-toothed smile as Heritage blushed.

"All right. If you wouldn't mind popping me across to check for him, that would help a lot. Thanks." Then Heritage remembered. "Oh—my kayak is at Middle Beach. And I left the lodge truck parked in the school parking lot."

"I can bring you back here. No worries. Let's see if the kid is home, first."

With François' arm lobbed over the back of Heritage's shoulders, the two strode toward the dock without saying much, and, remarkably, without drawing attention. Reaching the boat, François engaged that green-eyed flirting gimmick of his as Heritage used his shoulder to steady himself stepping into the boat. In that moment, it seemed to Heritage they were close enough to kiss, and that François' eyes seemed to be suggesting they could— but nothing beyond their naked fencing at the hot springs really provided them the basis for such an intimate and spontaneous development in their relations.

Heritage turned his head away when it became obvious François wouldn't. He didn't understand what was going on between them, or why François' renewed interest caught him so completely by surprise. He had convinced himself that what had happened at the hot springs was nothing more than conjugal liberties, exercised by men who'd been too long at sea. In the absence of women, Heritage had heard that Gold Rush miners, soldiers, inmates—hell, even earthworms and bonobo monkeys—improvised. Heritage thought it remarkable though, that François would be so quickly over his grief with the loss of Marcel, that he would already be courting a rebound with him. He must surely have been misreading things.

Heritage sat down on the forward bench of François' aluminum skiff. François started the boat. "Dis is no problem for me, honest!" he repeated. "I'm off work for four days now."

Just great, Heritage thought to himself as the boat picked up speed and began to hold his hair back. François finally surfaces with four days free, and Heritage was contending with a blood-shitting teen and a nonstop, one-way ticket departing from Vancouver to Toronto in another thirty-six hours. An hour earlier before leaving The Headlands, he'd even booked and pre-paid his charter seaplane connection to Vancouver at Megin River Air for dawn, Wednesday.

When they were underway and Heritage was pretty sure François had plenty else to keep his eyes on, he glanced back to get a better read. The Frenchman was staring at him. The motor was too loud for conversation, but Heritage tried anyway. "Can you see past me okay?" he asked.

"If I wanted to, I could," François answered, without breaking his gaze. Heritage turned back around, with eyes stretched open into the onrushing wind. They watered up instantly. He didn't know what to do next, except look through his pack for his sunglasses. When his eye sockets overflowed onto his cheeks, he didn't wipe them away. When the smile eventually crawled like a sunrise across his face, he kept it to himself.

As they neared the east side of Wickaninnish Island, Heritage rose slightly, to point out the best approach to take, tucking in behind some outer rocks atop which the white coast guard navigation beacon had been cemented, long before either of them had probably been born—now that he was seeing its weathered-age up close. François cut and lifted the motor out of the water. Heritage pointed toward Mona's house.

"See the smoke from the stovepipe? He's there. Aidan is home. Thanks for the ride. Maybe we can talk soon."

"I hope so. I'd like dat very much. We need to pick up where we left off, don't you tink?"

Heritage kept stumbling into conversational traps. François seemed to be employing innuendo at the end of each sentence, like it were some kind of punctuation. "Well, you know where to find me now," was all Heritage could think to say.

"I sure do, so you can't hide from me anymore."

"Right. Well, I wasn't hiding from you, for the record book, but okay. Goodbye, then," Heritage said awkwardly as he leapt from the bow of the boat onto a sandbar that wasn't quite the shore. Heritage immediately noticed the deep channel of water between his little beach island and the actual beach.

"Um, I tink you are about to get wet again," François smiled, pointing out the obvious gap in his planning. "If you climb back in, I can get you closer."

Heritage—to his absolute, maximum embarrassment—reached for François' extended hand and stretched his long leg to step back into the boat. After about fifteen seconds when François refused to let go of his hand, Heritage swiveled to face François. "I won't pretend to be cut out for this boating world if you stop pretending you don't notice it."

François scratched the top of his head with his free hand. "Okay. And I won't pretend to be interested in you if you stop pretending you don't notice it."

François' sudden and eloquent command of English surprised Heritage. "Okay. No more pretending, period." François pulled him closer. This was it, Heritage thought—the blow that would knock him clean off the fence. He closed his eyes as their faces drew together.

The scruff on François' upper lip and chin acted as antennae, and from that first contact, the docking of their mouths became one controlled, deliberate, and entirely unstoppable motion. Heritage's legs quaked as he tasted François' mouth, fresh from one of those Fishermen's Friend lozenges he must have popped in earlier. His knees buckled. François' free hand moved to steady him. The kiss continued.

"Ta-age!" The voice belonged to Aidan. Heritage jerked away from the embrace, away from the kiss, away from the truth. Aidan was standing on shore amid the salal bushes, his alarmingly pale face in clear view.

"I'll be right there, Aidan," Heritage said calmly, despite his desire to throttle the spoiler. He turned back to François, who had busied himself with boat things, though he kept an eye on everything through the dark strands of hair that had escaped the elastic band during the crossing and provided a set of parentheses to his face.

"Shit!" François whispered. "Ninnish will blab dis to everyone."

"No, he won't," Heritage promised, taking off his footwear and rolling up his pantlegs. "Aidan and I have a gentlemen's agreement."

"Dat devil's no gentleman," François said, starting the motor on his boat and inching it closer to shore. His face was blank in worry, and his voice cracked in fear.

"Listen, I have to travel to Toronto the day after tomorrow for a few days. It's my grandfather. He is dying. I'll be back soon though, and look forward to seeing you the next time you come off the oyster farm for a few days?" Heritage straddled the boat rail and lowered his feet and ankles into the water, but he'd misjudged the depth and didn't touch bottom until the sea had breached the tops of his boots. "Thank you for the lift over here . . . and for the kiss, too."

François nodded, biting his lower lip. Heritage could see he was beating himself up for having been—what, exactly? Heritage wondered. Careless with his emotions? Hand over hand, Heritage maintained contact with the boat rail until François pulled it out of his reach. The suddenly too serious Quebecer gently turned the boat around. Avoiding the visible sub-surface rocks and with his motor sputtering, he navigated into deeper water without looking back, before gunning it back into the open channel.

Heritage splashed the rest of the way to reach dry sand, not completely understanding François' panic but at the same time, he was already formulating the story he would need to convincingly deliver to the kid who likely had witnessed their kiss. Heritage felt silly covering up something so natural, but even he knew that Aidan was a wild card.

He stopped by the outhouse to take a standing leak, then took a bit longer than necessary on the wooden deck surrounding Mona's cabin. He muscled his feet out of his wet socks and boots and then unfastened and lowered his pants, also wet up to the knees, and lay everything out to dry. The day's sun had already finished with this beach and deck and had moved on, slipping behind the shadow-tossing trees that towered stories over the small cabin. Heritage figured Stephanie's triangle house would be basking it its rays now. He would have liked to steal away for a nap in her loft, but needed instead to face his teen tribunal. But the longer he fussed and postponed, the more uptight he became. His briefs had been spared the sea's reach, but out of modesty, Heritage pulled his dress shirt over his head to hold it in front of his crotch, since the day's underwear choice was on the skimpy side. His heart and breathing inside his T-shirt signaled it was either now or heart attack and so he entered the Rye's cabin. The sticky sliding glass door announced his arrival with the squeal of metal on metal and the young teen spun around, his face flush, his crew-cut blond hair glistening with sweat.

"How was your day, Tage?" he asked, sternly, clearly distressed. Heritage didn't move. "I've asked you a question, Tage. How was your day?"

"My day? Fine!" Heritage finally answered. "I understand from speaking to the school that you've been feeling sick."

"Just not quite myself. No worries. Here. I've made us dinner. Sit." Aidan pulled a chair away from the table for each of them.

"Let me just wash up and—"

"Sit!" Aidan yelled at him. He brushed his hand through the crew-cut bristles of his hair with a slap, as though he'd completely misjudged the distance between his hand and his face. Growing as fast as he was, it was possible that distance was still changing.

"Please sit," he asked, more restrained, forcing a slight but no less strained smile. Heritage walked toward the table, noticing through the upper loft windows how quickly the sun had all but abandoned the east side of the island. It couldn't have been much before five, and the cabin was lost in shadows. Once he sat down, in only his undershirt and briefs, he could see that Aidan had every ground-level curtain pulled shut, with only a few candles lit. He had obviously gone to some effort, as the table was set and there were pleasant odors of prepared food that had steamed up the small space. It was hard for Heritage to stop thinking about François and the five minutes that had possibly just changed his life—but because Aidan was acting a bit unpredictably, Heritage was wary.

Aidan presented an over-filled glass of red wine. Heritage accepted it, drinking a gulp right off the top to keep it from spilling. It was bitter, but he couldn't expect a kid to know his wine or how full to fill the glass, no matter how mature he acted otherwise. "Thank you. So, you're feeling better then?" he asked, spreading the cloth napkin to cover as much of his lap as he could.

"Like I said, no worries." Aidan stressed it this time—case closed. Heritage took another drink. A plate of spaghetti with mushrooms and other not-so-recognizable chunks was placed before him, dusted quite heavily in Parmesan that must have come from a can. Aidan sat down across from him.

"You're not eating anything? It smells delicious." Heritage twirled a bite too large on his fork.

"No. I'm just going to take it easy on my stomach and drink some juice." Aidan raised a glass of what had to be the palest looking apple juice Heritage had ever seen. "To bachelors."

Heritage had just taken his first salty bite and had no room in his mouth to add wine, but raised his glass cordially. Whether he was just relieved to not have been asked about the kiss with François yet or he was really hungry, he began devouring the food on his plate. He drank the wine way too quickly. The pasta sauce was terribly salty and Heritage had already emptied one water glass before reaching for the pitcher across the table. When Aidan moved to refill his plate, Heritage thought he smelled gin—or maybe it was bourbon—on the kid's breath.

Maybe the wine Heritage had been nervously sipping was already clouding his judgment. It might have been booze he smelled on Aidan, but it could have been teenage breath, too.

He wasn't sure about much of anything except that he felt like he was becoming fantastically buzzed. He knew this was not the optimum state for a babysitter to be in, but he also knew it wasn't possible to get drunk from just one glass of wine. He accepted the next glass of wine, but silently vowed not to drink it. Aidan sat across from him, sipping his juice a little too frequently for it to have been juice alone. Heritage was going to say something but stopped himself. Aidan seemed neutral—almost chilled out, and remarkably disarmed for someone normally spoiling for his next insulting attack. It was a pleasant change. Still, it didn't make sense to Heritage to launch into a lecture about Aidan's school stunt with the diarrhea or his possible alcohol consumption. He wasn't the kid's father. Forgetting his vow, he sipped more wine to wash down the salty pasta sauce.

Aidan didn't talk. He drew on the tabletop with the tip of his finger in a small circular motion until it made Heritage dizzy. It wasn't long before the babysitter's dizziness turned to drowsiness. The need to lie down was suddenly paramount. "Do you have homework?" he asked, hopefully.

"Sure. Lots of it, as a matter of fact. Why? Do you want to nap or something?"

"Yes. I think so. Dinner was so satisfying—thank you. But all I want to do is sleep." Heritage got up and found he needed the chair to steady himself. "I'll just crash a bit over on the couch if you have things to do."

"Don't use the couch! You're too tall to fit. Use my room." He pointed to the upside-down letter A on the door across the living room. "I'll be out here if you need anything." Aidan reached for his stack of books on the table.

Heritage thought for a fleeting second that this could be a trap, but he wasn't in any condition to protest or even remain upright a minute longer. So he accepted the invitation. His heart was sprinting, and his breath was shallow. His whole body was being stormed by the rapid onset of drowsiness. This wasn't like him and he knew it but he also didn't think it was anything that couldn't be fixed by a quick nap.

"All right, then. I shouldn't be too long—twenty minutes, tops." He made his way through the narrow kitchen using every solar or propane run appliance he could put his hands on just to keep vertical. He continued through the pantry and ducked his head to enter the kid's Hobbit-like room, and partially pulled shut the door behind him. The room was pitch-black, except for a few fat candles that had been left burning, and the few centimetres of light edging through the crack at the bottom of the door.

Heritage felt his way across the room, stubbing his foot on the metal railing at the bottom of a brass bed. The candle flames multiplied their flickering flames a hundred times more in the shiny brass rungs of the head and footboards, and called his balance into question. Heritage pivoted to collapse onto the bed—it seemed to take forever before the mattress finally caught him.

When his eyes adjusted to the darkness and could focus on something, he saw a large tie-dye print stretched above the bed. It had been thumb-tacked into the ceiling. The colours were the most amazing he had ever seen. He stared into this kaleidoscope until his eyes watered, and through that fluid membrane, all the colours and patterns of the tie-dye design began to swirl and twirl above him in a prism-like dervish. He quickly shook his head, trying to clear the fuzz. He started to develop a hunch that he'd been slipped something in his food or the wine, maybe. As the intensity of everything grew and his awareness of it heightened or possibly dulled—he couldn't tell—he grew drowsier, and then groggier, and then sleepier. He sternly called out Aidan's name, but could not get enough air to pass through his vocal cords, so it came out as a whisper that reached nowhere.

He was tumbling through some new experience, in a space without gravity—or was he beginning some acid trip? Oh god, he realized. That was it! The little bastard had probably gotten a hold of some LSD off Lyle Hudson—likely stole it from his unattended medicine bag—and was experimenting with it on him. He fought the thought of closing his eyes now, giving into sleep, and this kept him delighted, amused and fixated on the kaleidoscope of a ceiling that was starting to run down the walls and turned the mattress into a pliable, sheet of intricately stained glass under his body. Heritage rocked in such a splendid state of euphoria that he no longer fought it but instead wanted to prolong this elation for as long as he could. There was no sound—not a creak in the floorboards, nor a dinner dish finding the kitchen counter next to the sink. He heard and felt nothing, but was seeing absolutely everything . . . until he wasn't.

He had been floating without landmarks, weightlessly scooping back and forth through the air like a feather in freefall, neither in nor out of consciousness, for a period of time he couldn't quantify. He didn't know how long his eyes had been shut, or if they were even closed at all. Exotic Middle Eastern music, with the most hypnotic percussion and haunting female singing, both carried and confused him, filling his ears, as thickly as the scented incense that passed in and out of his lungs. His arms, waist, and legs were useless—as though they had become paralyzed from a spinal injury he'd never had. He couldn't move or see them or use his hands to check his malfunctioning eyes that felt as though they'd become swollen shut. The pornographic sequence that jarred him from his dreaming state had tricked him into thinking he was enjoying the most amazing sex. He tried to crane his neck and strain his eyes but it was like peering through a layer of Vaseline that had been applied a centimeter thick to each of his eyeballs, and his head felt heavy as a bowling ball.

Heritage balanced on the cliff of panic but recognized that he was too engulfed in pleasurable stimuli to protest, worry, or care.

He felt the urge to giggle. Maybe he was giggling already. His normally analytic brain ran through a series of rebooting though inconclusive tests, trying to determine if his eyes were open or shut. Heritage struggled to wiggle a finger or a toe, but he could not muster any of his muscles. He tried again to lift his arms, but the blood in his veins must have been replaced with molten lead. Delightfully soothing sensations rolled under and through his body like ocean swells that had traveled partway around the globe to rock his boat gently along its journey. But to where was it headed? He didn't know but he didn't care to disembark. Next stop: the underworld, perhaps. How exciting, he thought. He'd never been there before. There was no past. He had no anxiety about the future. There was only now—a now without eyelids, without anything resembling a waking consciousness, without arms and legs or the will to snap out of whatever state or dimension he was floating inside.

He heard speaking—It wasn't Arabic, but he had heard this voice before, and this calmed him. He was concentrating now, waiting for it to speak again. He tried to remember who it was that had a voice like that. Was it his father's voice welcoming him into the afterlife? Would he see his mother here, too? Had he died?

"Is that as far as you can go? Move over, amateur, and watch this!"

There was that voice again just as a sudden warmth and familiar sensation jump-started Heritage's physical awareness with a jolt almost as though conducting electrode paddles had just been discharged on his chest, or lower, maybe. Inside his woolly cerebral cocoon flashed giant red lights on and off and on again that he took to mean . . . WARNING . . . WARNING . . . and then alarms—more mechanized than human—began to sound as though sub-woofers had been implanted inside his ear canals. And that's when Heritage realized he had an erection, and not just a casual boner, but the hardest, most throbbing Tom-of-Finland dream cock his subconscious had ever conjured. Heritage was on his way to convincing himself that not only had he mastered a state of nirvana by dreaming with his eyes wide open but that he'd unlocked the secret formula to doubling the size of his penis. But he was embarrassed at the same time, because there was no way he could face his dead mother with that gargantuan hard-on.

The alarms morphed into a new sound, distinct and apart from the music—two familiar tones: one baritone, followed by another in a lower alto register. Half a minute may have passed, or no time at all—and again, there was that same two-tone sound. It was a reference. Heritage needed only to race through his memories to connect the tones with reality, so that he could get his eyelids back and discover where he was. He focused and he concentrated.

Then it sounded again, and the answer came to him in the form of a question. Was that the foghorn?

There were more sounds now—whispering voices, panting, groaning, more feelings, and more information coming at him like bullets firing one clue after the other but from a very slow-motion machine gun that was sending data-ballistics through a room that had been diabolically filled to the tie-dye ceiling with honey. Tie-dye. There was something he was remembering about tie-dye. Then more flashes of light and the sounds of small-scale mechanization followed—the next puzzle for him to begin solving. In his delirium, Heritage was magically able to crank his head an inch or two off the floor of the boat or the gurney or the operating table. He began to make out the visage of a crew-cut blond head of a boy—a boy he recognized and who was engaged in some measure of a bobbing motion at the junction of his paralysis. There was other movement in the room too, perhaps the manifestation of a pale ghost. Was it his dead mother? Appearing first on one side of him and then on the other, and these glimpses were accompanied by more flashes of light and the sounds of small motors.

"Ya think he's bigger than the flashlight?" the familiar voice asked the room. "Let's find out!"

Oh god! What the hell was Aidan doing in his sex dream? The adult's eyelids fluttered back into full function and widened to see things he shouldn't be seeing. He opened his mouth to use language but—like his arms and legs—not every faculty had returned. Then simultaneously, the spell was broken, the anesthesia wore off and all the sensations and senses he'd always known converged in a multi-sensory pile up and his nightmare was certified.

Heritage tried to squirm and bellow, but "What?" was the only speech he could manage and when it came out, the one syllable sounded like he'd suffered a massive stroke. Had he? The screams inside his head would have been forceful enough to topple the cabin off its reinforced concrete posts if only he could get them out. His one word though, had given an arresting startle to the individuals attending to him, both of whom, nearly jumped out of their own skins.

Aidan looked up from his science project, both shocked and upset that Heritage was coming to. "Relax and enjoy this. We both know it's what you've been fantasizing about, so I'm just making it easier on you, you know, to get what you really want."

Heritage grunted but couldn't articulate his rage with words or demands. Scanning his body, sending pings to test his motor skills, he could deduct that he was tied down; each of his wrists and ankles were restrained but also his torso and waist and upper thighs were belted to prevent protest, escape and movement. With his lifted neck spasming, he could only watch and scarcely wiggle, as the teen demonstrably turned his manhood into an ice-cream cone. "I saw you with that Quebec fucker, François. I saw you kiss him," he said, as he made the head of the adult's hypnotized or drug-charmed penis disappear inside his mouth. Heritage tried to pelvis buck the kid off but only shoved his erection deeper into the teenager's mouth. But this achieved the objective as it launched the teenager upright into a choking fit. Heritage let his weighty head drop to the mattress.

———

Frustrated and wiping his mouth with the back of his hand, Aidan was shouting at him now. "You can't have him, you know. Just like you can't leave me for Toronto this week." Heritage was rocking his head back and forth as he watched Ninnish strip naked and climb onto the bed to a straddling position above Heritage's waist. The demented teen began experimenting with his position and his pain tolerance, as if he were messing again with a flashlight. "And I have thought ahead. Do you think I just cooked this up? I know exactly what I have to do." He winced from the burn of trying to force himself upon the end of his opponent.

It wasn't comfortable for Heritage either. In actuality, it was painful the way the inexperienced boy was going about it. "OWW!" he managed to communicate. Aidan got the message, loudly horked up a handful of spit from the back of his throat and slathered the snotty spit on the adult's unflagging erection. Heritage tingled like the muscles in his whole body were coming out of sleep. He moved his jaw back and forth to massage his mouth and summon his vocal cords. He craned his neck and gave it his best shot to form a sentence.

"What in the fuck do you think you're doing, Aidan? Think!" Heritage dropped his neck again and the spittle that flew from his mouth touched back down on his face. He had his speech back and he wasted no time in using it. "Don't you know about AIDS? I could have it. You don't know! Mess around like this and you could get it and die, you know."

"I'm not . . . afraid . . . to die." Aidan paused, waiting for the pain to go away. It didn't.

"Aidan, you can't do this!"

There was another flash of light but this time it illuminated the shadows to reveal that the two of them were not alone. Satan with an A had an accomplice. An accomplice meant there was a witness, and as his eyes adjusted to make out the shape of this person lurking in the dark margins of the bedroom, Heritage realized it had to be Rowan, and that Rowan was taking pictures for evidence—or blackmail—with a Polaroid camera.

"Rowan! You're in on this?"

"Shut up!" Ninnish bore down. Tears streamed from the teen's eyes and he faltered some, jolted by a minor quake of shooting pain that attempted to destroy his resolve, but of course wouldn't. He rose off his prisoner completely. Heritage exhaled in relief. Ninnish hopped off the bed and stormed through the door toward the kitchen. Heritage determined the source of his bondage—burlap ties that he couldn't break or loosen. In seconds, Ninnish returned to the bedroom with a liquor bottle and another tin of baking lard.

"Give it up, kid."

"I said shut up!" He lathered shortening between his legs and straddled Heritage again, wasting no time in getting at least as far as he had before. It was easier on both of them—not much, but easier. Ninnish took a swig from the bottle and contorted his face. Locking eyes with his prize, the boy took a giant breath, slipping down further in some twisted attempt to become a man. "Rowan, get in close with that camera!"

Heritage moaned reflexively. He craned his neck to add vision to the unspeakable experience. The kid looked uneasy, like he might have been in the process of passing out. "Can't handle it, can you?" Heritage goaded him, the sensation now edging out the last of his will to maintain a full-on protest. Ninnish straightened up and took more of him, expelling a blast of air from his teenage lungs. His face went white and it seemed he was having trouble focusing.

"Shut the fuck up!" The child gulped and then clenched his jaw. He wasn't giving up. He took another drink before throwing the bottle against the bedroom wall, where it hit with a thud but didn't break. The pain was part of him now. He placed both hands on Heritage's flat, hairy stomach and forced himself down, down, lifting back off again each time the pain became too much. Ninnish breathed rhythmically until he was able to relax some more.

A more sinister Wicked Ninnish looked into his captive's suddenly focused and bloodshot eyes without pausing as he gingerly, and with much effort, began to more firmly squat on his trophy. In that moment, Heritage realized his body was responding sexually to the child's manipulation. He was as engaged and engorged as an adult could be and just as helpless as a child ever was. The angelic looking teen appeared panicked with his mouth drooped open. The room went silent. Either the music and the foghorn had stopped or Heritage stopped hearing it. His lungs strained—his last breath lodging fast behind his sternum. Heritage fully recognized the next sensation that engulfed him—couldn't mistake its pressure. But his Protestant nature and loopy state would not allow him to believe he could physically get inside a child. A shadow moved along his left side and there was a flash of blinding light.

"Aidan! Don't! Don't do this. That's enough!" All Heritage could do was protest and squirm, still bound, still helpless, still hard. He lifted his head and could just barely make out the naked teen's fuzzy outline, just as he could also sense—with some discomfort of his own—that the stubborn, boastful boy was struggling to get past the pain. "Come on! You're just a kid."

"Could a kid do this?" Aidan demanded, short of breath, dropping his weight further down. "Make sure that camera is ready," he told Rowan.

The struggle continued, becoming even rougher on him as the kid was neither gentle nor giving up. "Aidan, listen to me. If you stop this right now, I will not mention it to anyone."

"Then. What. Would. Be. The . . ." Aidan gulped for air then held it, as he forced his hips, his pelvis, and his teenage butt all the way down. ". . . *point?*" He let all his air out in one explosive burst. He'd managed to completely capture his prize. For Heritage, there was no mistaking that the kid had succeeded. He felt the pinch and involuntarily flexed his erection, forcing even more blood into the various chambers, causing Aidan to whimper audibly. The kid wasn't remembering to breathe and had clamped every muscle in his fifteen-year-old body.

There were suddenly two or three flashes of bright light, each followed by the sounds of photos being ejected from a Polaroid camera. Heritage was temporarily blinded and couldn't tell where the camera was in the room. He lifted his head again. Ninnish—the very wicked and demonically-possessed Ninnish—had adopted a crooked, half smirk of total satisfaction. The two locked eyes and under that ocular arrest, the younger began to experiment with movement that the older could not conceal was working. There could be no second-guessing that the teenager had his babysitter right where he wanted him, and because Heritage could not help the flexing of his cock, the teenager could both read and feel that his prisoner was beginning to enjoy his captivity, whether he said so or not.

Heritage had no option but to lie there, more immobilized by the kid's weight and more helpless than he had been even seconds before. He was now entirely captured. There was no minimizing the achievement. Aidan slowly began to accept his victory and regained control. It still burned, but none of that mattered now to the boy intent on becoming a man through this semen-stealing ritual.

Heritage said, "This is not going to end well for you."

"How can you say that?" Aidan asked. "I am giving you the greatest gift—my virginity. You are the one I have chosen. Everything . . . has . . . worked . . . out . . . perfectly," he spoke in breathy, staccato, satisfying syncopation.

Heritage was stunned as he clenched his teeth together and struggled with every cell of his being to deny how beautiful the gesture and how wonderful the feeling was, as his body involuntarily barreled toward ecstasy. Aidan read the man's eyes and body and breathing and flexing like a textbook he was trying to commit to memory, and could tell, even with limited experience, that Heritage was getting closer to giving up what Aidan had been after since the first day.

———

Aidan recovered the ritual. "As long as we both live, what I am giving you right now, cannot be returned or destroyed. After tonight, I will belong to you, and you will live forever inside of me."

"Rowan!" Heritage belted out, trying another tack to frighten Aidan from completing his mission and to intimidate Aidan's accomplice. "I know you are in here, that you both have equal parts in this kidnapping . . ." He paused to moan, as Aidan was becoming more comfortable with the obstacle. " . . . and I just want you to know . . ." He tried to muffle his low-register humming sounds of enjoyment, but he couldn't jam the Morse code signal coming from his manhood. "This will not end well for either of you."

Aidan rose nearly off the mount, a flash bulb exploded, and then the teen plunged back down again, realizing this new advantage as he upgraded the torment and torture of his prisoner.

"Aidan! Damnit . . . this is serious."

The adult tried to keep his eyes from rolling into the back of his head in ecstasy, fighting the growing urge to geyser his life's resistance into the void where he didn't belong and had no business being.

"We need to make a pact, the three of us. Aidan, slow down or climb off because I'm about to shoot." Aidan instead ramped up his pogo stick animation, clearly determined to make his captive give up what he'd so far refused him.

"What is happening here needs to stop, and we need to keep this to ourselves. It can't leave this ro-o-o-o-om—fu-u-ck!" Heritage raised his head off the bed as he began climaxing inside the boy, just as the boy who wasn't a boy—and without even touching himself—began cumming too, magnificently, miraculously, onto Heritage's dark hairy abdomen and chest. Flash bulbs began popping in his face, but Heritage was neither able to stop nor strangle the photographer.

"Shit! Shit! Shit!" Aidan was chanting through laboured breathing. "Didya see that? I blew my wad without even touching myself. That's a fucking first!" He was full of himself, and full of Heritage, who throbbed reflexively like an embolism inside him.

The very wicked Ninnish, slowly and wincing at first, rose from his work to a standing position to tower over his prisoner. A mixture of sperm, shortening, and blood oozed out of the boy to run down the inside of his legs. In the candlelight, all Heritage could see, as the boy stood over him on the bed, was the pink ooze between the teen's legs against a backdrop of tie-dye that was no longer spinning. Heritage's eyes must have registered horror and surrender simultaneously. Aidan knelt back down and marveled at his own semen on the hairy stomach of his catch. He collected a finger-full from Heritage's belly button and extended it to Heritage's lips, applying it like ChapStick. Heritage did not turn his head away, even though he had regained full mobility with his neck and head. For some curious reason, he instead licked both of his lips in one circular motion, thinking it demonstrated he could not be vanquished. The taste struck him as a cross between celery and cotton candy.

Standing again over him, one leg on either side of his conquest, all sweat-glistening and lard-smeared proud, the boy gripped his hard penis in one hand and stretched his scrotum downward to exaggerate his pubescence. He toyed with masturbation to see if he could cum again before falling to his knees on top of his captive's chest. Heritage tried to heave him off but with his legs, waist, and upper torso strapped to the mattress, it was futile. Ninnish held the adult's mouth open with the finger of one hand, his own face crooked with a demonic stare, as he moved his abdomen into his babysitter's face. Heritage protested but his words were muffled though still clear.

"I'm going to kill you, Aidan."

"You're going to have to," the devil child responded, forcing his dripping erection past protesting adult lips and teeth. There was another flash of light that blinded and disoriented Heritage as he choked and tried to eject the boy.

Heritage smelled semen and shit and garlic on the boy's hands, and thought for a minute that he might throw up. Instead, he clamped down with his teeth to put an end to his unwilling participation.

Aidan recoiled, slapping him hard across the front of his whiskered face. "You fucker!" he screamed, examining himself for damage.

"Ninnish, I have to pee," Rowan timidly announced from the shadows, unintentionally wrecking the moment as he clamored out of the room.

"Aidan," Heritage said, "I don't know what kind of sick mind you've got, but it obviously hasn't thought five minutes past my getting free from this bed to beat the living shit out of you." His words were breathy but packed with anger. His head flopped back onto the bed, overcome by cramps developing in his neck.

"You underestimate me, like everyone else, and that's why it will be so easy to destroy you if you reject me." Ninnish adjusted himself to sit back on Heritage's stomach, playing with the adolescent semen that had dripped through the coarse black hair.

"What have I done to you, kid? Why your need to destroy me?"

"Because, if I didn't get your attention—" he stumbled and started again. "If I didn't get evidence that I can use against you, you'd just keep on ignoring me—which is the same as destroying me. It's that simple."

Heritage tried to wriggle out of his straddle, which only tightened on him suddenly and uncomfortably. "How so? Why do you think that I would want to destroy you? Why do you think I even care about you?" But Heritage was in no position to negotiate. He was still naked, completely immobilized. Nobody even had the decency to clean him up.

Aidan wasn't quick with a smart-aleck response this time. It took him a while to come up with something—when he did, it stung. "You give me someone to look up to and I mostly just want you to stick around. This is my insurance." He reached for the Polaroids, displaying them like a deck of cards, as though he were a magician. "I just gave you my virginity. That should give you a reason to care about me. I chose you." The kid let that statement hang in the air, then continued. "Thank you, Tage, from the bottom of my . . ." He tripped on his words. "Well, from the bottom of my bottom."

"You don't get to thank me for something you stole, Aidan. I didn't give you that. I didn't take your virginity. Nothing about what has happened here tonight came from me voluntarily—so don't thank me, okay?"

Aidan climbed off his captive and moved his crew-cut blond head within centimetres of Heritage's right ear to whisper. "I felt your cock twitching inside me. Your body doesn't lie, Tage. I know you enjoyed every second of this. And don't forget, I watched you lick my spunk off your lips. You didn't spit, you didn't struggle . . . you swallowed it. I am inside you, just like you are inside me. Nothing you say or do will change that."

Heritage tried to sound calm. "So what now?" He needed to play along if he was ever getting released.

"I'll get a washcloth. Hold on." Aidan left Heritage still erect and bound to the bed.

Heritage next heard water running in the kitchen as he stared up at the tie-dyed ceiling. His thoughts bounced around his cranium like pinballs with every blink of his eyelids acting like paddles that kept the panic perpetually moving. What in the hell would happen next? What else was Aidan capable of? Why hadn't Rowan returned? What would prison be like for a convicted child molester?

Ninnish returned to his stifling bedroom, now thick with incense and candle wax and perspiration and testosterone, looking radiantly triumphant. Heritage was sure the kid's plan, his trap, and his prey had all behaved just as he'd fantasized about. Rowan, had in fact, predicted he couldn't pull this off, and yet there Aidan stood, bathed in candlelight, gently washing the erection of the man who had just taken his virginity. Heritage began to realize how the teen's brain was thinking—semen from each of them was stirring inside their bodies, muddling with their enzymes and chromosomal histories to cement their future forever together. It was true, Heritage had to concede. This act, this spell—whatever this was—it could not be undone. Aidan's virginity, if this were even true, could not be given back.

Ninnish could not be brought down from his victory pedestal. He didn't stop bathing his prisoner and moved the washcloth to his hairy stomach and chest, where his own jizz lingered. He circled the man's nipples with the cloth and lowered his face to the man's. Heritage turned his head away. The teen kissed him on the forehead instead. "We are bound to each other now—like blood brothers, only stronger."

Heritage looked into the trancelike blue eyes of someone he believed to be utterly in love. The kid was confused and misinterpreting and misplacing feelings and affections with which he had no experience. If ever there was a time for tough love, it was now, but Heritage also needed to get free of that bed, and that room.

"Aidan, untie me and we can talk this through, just you and me. In another two years, you'll be eighteen—an adult. Then sex like this, even making love with an older man, won't carry the same consequences." It seemed to Heritage that Aidan was listening. He went on. "You do realize, don't you, that I am exactly twice your age, and right now, the law sees you as a minor? You need to think about what you have done and what has happened here. Think about what happens next. Where do we go from this moment, with everything changed between us? Think beyond yourself, Aidan. Think about what Rowan has just witnessed. Think about what happens to me if this ever gets out in a town as small as Tofino."

"No. *You* think!" Aidan's voice cracked. "Think real carefully. I just gave myself to you!"

"But I didn't ask you to. I didn't need you to. Shit! I didn't want this! Do you think this makes me happy? It doesn't!" Heritage knew he was losing any ground he'd just gained.

Ninnish turned and left the room, slamming the door so hard the upside down "A" flew off and skidded across the kitchen floor. Heritage lay there, trying to stretch his muscles, which felt as though they had begun to atrophy from being in the same position for what he guessed might have been hours. He was sluggish and struggling to keep his eyes open when Aidan burst back into the bedroom, his face reddish with rage, his teenage body outlined in a halo of light coming from behind him.

"I'll tell you what happens next," he sputtered. "You don't get to forget about this and go back to ignoring me and pretending like I don't turn you on."

"I hardly think I've been ignoring you, Aidan." Heritage stopped short.

"And you don't get to run off to Toronto the day after tomorrow like nothing ever happened." Aidan began untying one of the ankle restraints—behaviour Heritage needed to encourage if he were ever to walk free again.

"It's my grandfather. He'd dying." Heritage spoke gently, trying to lure the kid into untying more of the restraints. The fact that Heritage still had an erection was compromising his approach. It was as though after robbing a bank he still brandished the handgun he'd used as he tried to plead his innocence at the police station. He wished his weapon would go limp, but like so much else, this was not in his control.

Aidan untied the rope at the adult's waist and loosened the strap running across his thighs. "I never had grandparents; no idea who they even were." He roughly grabbed the adult's cock and studied it, as if still feeling every centimetre of it inside his bum. "I'll be better at it next time," he assured his captive. "You will teach me how to become better at it."

"Aidan, look," Heritage said. "I have to level with you. I'm flattered that you chose me to give your virginity to. That is a big deal and I have to let that sink in. Maybe when I'm not so drugged up, I'll realize how special that is, really."

Heritage had realized he needed to play into Aidan's demented scenario, or he wasn't going anywhere. He started out by trying to identify with him, lowering the temperature to meet him at his age and mentality, but then his adult took control. "This can't happen again, Aidan. It shouldn't have happened this first time given our age difference, but that's on you." He suddenly thought about François. What he would make of this? He blurted out, "I already like someone else—someone closer to my age. We need to put this behind us and go back to being good neighbours."

Aidan didn't like what he was hearing, so his alter ego, Satan with an A—or rather, Wicked Ninnish—leaned in to speak directly in his prisoner's ear.

"You don't get it, do you? I've captured you. You belong to me! Your semen is leaking out of my ass and I have pictures—proof of what you did to me. I will have you again and forever, 'cause in the eyes of anyone who I want to see things my way, you've just raped a fifteen-year-old minor—as you put it." His eyes narrowed. "Against his will." With the tip of his tongue he experimented with the taste of semen flavored Crisco, still on his own lips. Then, climbing back on the bed to stand over him naked, Ninnish let go a stream of piss on Tage's chest and stomach. "Here's another offering for you," he said. "There. You've been marked by an evangelist."

"Evangelist?" Heritage squawked, tightly shutting his eyes and mouth as the piss stream traveled toward his head.

"It's an anagram," Ninnish stated as his stream began to peter out. "Rearrange the letters and you've got *evil's agent*—at your service." Aidan shook the last of the piss into the stale air, before disappearing for several hours in search of the missing photos and the equally absent photographer.

Aidan knew there were only two places Rowan could have disappeared to when the chickenshit didn't return from peeing. Aidan first headed north in the direction of their secret clubhouse on the other side of the headland. He couldn't help his smile and even whistled as he threaded the trail between the trees in the dark from memory. Aidan figured Tage just needed some cooling off time—maybe a nap to sleep the drugs off—before he returned to untie his wrists and the ankle he hadn't gotten around to liberating. He tried to keep his butt cheeks clenched inside his shorts as he walked, not wanting to lose a drop of the magic potion he had collected. With so much air trapped inside him, the battle not to fart was everything. He had followed the magic spell to the letter, had not eaten for something like twenty-four hours, wanting to be pure, empty, and clean in order for the spell to work and the captured potion to take.

Only Ninnish knew he was following an ancient ritual first suggested and maybe even practiced by Aleister Crowley. He hadn't mentioned it to Rowan, as he would have freaked right out, as he always did at the mention of witch stuff. But Aidan had read the steps over and over again. He had long been aware that Crowley had been this eccentric priest—he guessed he was a warlock really—from the early 1900s. The guy had viewed sex as the ultimate magical power, so Aidan was fascinated to learn everything he could. Crowley had been deep into the occult and became this high-ranking member of a secret society called Ordo Templi Orientis, a sect that used sex rituals in its initiation ceremonies—often using semen and menstrual blood as the key ingredients in spells to gain supreme power over someone or to ward off evil influences. As Aidan, like most teenage boys, had been obsessed with sex and his own body's remarkable and evolving ability to reach new plateaus of awareness, stamina, and gratification, he'd been naturally drawn to Crowley's writings and teachings—a couple volumes of which anchored a quarter of the bookshelf in Dottie Bard's cabin library, where he'd often go to read up on this shit.

Thinking about sexual rituals or sexual anything had always managed to work the young man into a hormonal frenzy that essentially involved round-the-clock masturbation—usually solitary, but sometimes with a curious but reluctant and bashful Rowan. This had culminated in the past year and a half for Aidan—at least—with orgasms of his own. He could tell that Rowan had been frustrated that he did not measure up size-wise, and that he could not cum yet. In secret, Aidan had begun making his own semen offerings, as regularly as a delivery milkman, onto all sides of the massive, ancestral cedar that everyone referred to as "the Matriarch"—not far from the labyrinth at the south end of Wickaninnish Island. And each offering he made there was commemorated by another doll's limb, which he would carry there in his pocket, and pound with a nail into the base of the tree's trunk where he'd aimed his ejaculation in reverence.

He had been almost as obsessed with dolls as he was with masturbating. He had been stealing them from friends and stores and garage sales most of his life. Some of his favorites—the anatomically correct boy dolls—had been brought to him by his Uncle Lyle, and had been collected during the old man's travels around the world. One of these was his Joey doll, which Lyle had explained was a collector's item made by the Ideal Toy Company in 1976 to commemorate Archie Bunker's grandson, Joey Stivic, from the TV show *All in the Family*. Another favorite was his Baby Wee Wee, an infant boy doll from Ireland. Baby Wee Wee seemed to get this tiny boner right before he peed, and this had fascinated Aidan and given him hours and hours of play (and wet clothes) when he was only a few years younger. Both he and Rowan had role-played sucking Baby Wee Wee dry before graduating to each other. Dolls had been a ritualistic talisman and a top-secret fetish. He preferred GI Joes or Ken dolls, which he never amputated. But he settled more often for Barbies, which were easier to find and entirely disposable since they were girl dolls. Generally, they were harvested for their disembodied parts for other rituals—like ringing the lower trunk of the Matriarch. From masturbation, with and without dolls, through puberty to semen, Aidan's fascination remained dynamic, and his curiosity deformed into dangerously insatiable levels. Poor Rowan had taken the brunt of this obsession, but as of this magical evening, Aidan Rye had graduated with full honours to the adult class.

Their secret clubhouse, which was just this abandoned and dilapidated cottage that nobody could touch because it belonged to a shareholder who had mysteriously disappeared when Aidan had been quite young. Everyone warned and supposed the owner could magically reappear one day to claim it, but Aidan had only known the place as empty and hard for anyone else to get to. Aidan could tell that Rowan hadn't been there because of the strand of Old Man's Beard that Aidan always placed across the short wooden paddle that held the clubhouse door closed from the outside. The branch dangling moss was everywhere in that part of the forest. Aidan placed a new strand over the paddle after looking inside, just to be sure his partner in crime hadn't climbed through a window, given that most of them—at least on the ground floor—no longer contained glass.

Since Rowan wasn't there, he must have gone home, so Aidan next took off across the trans-island express trail. He could usually get to Rowan's cabin in twelve minutes from his bedroom, but it would take him at least twice as long trying to hold everything in. A little over halfway across the island, the sensation of needing to shit overcame Aidan's ability to keep moving, so he made a quick detour and ducked into the labyrinth. There, on top of his pyramid of dirty, mossy, doll heads, as he looked up through the forest clearing at a sky of stars, Aidan expelled the most rewarding crap of his life, into which he planted a stubby, amber-coloured pill bottle as a placeholder, since he hadn't thought to bring a doll's head along. He ambled off toward

Rowan's place, feeling at least a kilo lighter. Expecting to find Rowan asleep in his bedroom, he approached the cabin stealthily, knowing Rowan's Mom was home, most likely already asleep in hers, too. Aidan cupped his hands around his face at the window-pane and noted Rowan's neatly made bed. "That little bugger," he mumbled as he tried to figure out where he was hiding. He next thought to check Lyle's cabin on his way home. The two boys, every once in a while, had enjoyed uninvited sleepovers in the cargo net. But Rowan wasn't there either.

As he crossed back on the trans-island, he was thinking about his mum. The last time she had undergone surgery or chemo, less than a year before, he had been dragged along to Victoria. Each day she was there, Aidan would get deposited at the university library to study and be inspired by higher learning. And study he did. This is where he learned what foods would not only increase his sperm count and volume but improve the taste of the semen he was producing. Celery, fenugreek, walnuts, citrus fruits, whole wheat, salmon, all manners of shellfish, dark chocolate, garlic, bananas, broccoli, ginseng, turmeric, asparagus—these were all items that he instantly insisted be incorporated into his diet. The growing teen practically subsisted on Stromboli buns from his mother's bakeshop since most everything on his list was baked into that recipe. Before long, the disturbed pubescent scientist could see and taste the voluminous results for himself—but more recently, his obsession with semen turned into a compulsion to compare his vintage with that of others. Rowan's dry tap had been a staggering disappointment.

Bound by proximity and seeking an escape from boredom, Rowan had always shuffled alongside his buddy for the ride. Their experimentation had been extensive, uncomfortable, and often invasive. But this mission—capturing and drugging an adult male specimen—might have been a risk too riddled to carry off, and too daring to get away without punishment. Rowan was nervous and dissenting, and had insisted that he have no part in this, but Ninnish had persuaded him to watch and chronicle the semen-capturing ritual with Aidan's camera, as this would provide them the insurance policy they needed to keep the adult cooperative and quiet. But then, Rowan had disappeared to pee and hadn't returned. Aidan saw it as a violation of their pact. It had taken hours for them to get to that part in the plan where Ninnish would milk the semen from their prisoner, using his no-longer-virgin butt. Despite his skepticism, Rowan had seen with his own eyes that Ninnish had gotten the adult inside of him.

Aidan wanted to see the rest of Rowan's photos, mostly because he couldn't believe he'd managed the feat, himself. Of course, the blue diamond-shaped pills that Aidan had liberated from his Uncle Lyle's Feel Good kit—ground up into a powder and stirred into the red wine Aidan had offered Heritage at dinner—would ensure the adult wouldn't lose his erection even if he desperately wanted or needed to. He was sure that Heritage would try to sabotage him by going soft, but with the pills, he couldn't succeed. Heritage had probably wanted to squirm out from under the teenager too, but the boys had tied him down expertly. The olive-green Rohypnol capsule from his mum's upstairs pharmacy—a tranquilizer he understood to be something like ten times stronger than valium—was easier to dissolve in water, he'd determined from a quick experiment on the kitchen counter. By adding six more times the salt to the spaghetti sauce than was needed, Aidan almost guaranteed the adult would empty his water glass during the course of dinner. Rowan, for his part, needed only to wait on the driftwood below the house, watching for the kitchen light to go dark—which had been their established code that the coast was clear and the adult was out cold. Aidan knew that Rowan hadn't planned on actively participating much beyond working the camera, but in the moment, Rowan had become aroused. He hadn't seen a grown man naked before—his own father had been away in prison almost since he was born. Aidan could tell Rowan was impressed by the naked specimen, so he ordered him to "Suck it!" Rowan had shaken his head no, but Aidan had commanded his younger foot soldier to do what he said. "I dare you." Rowan gave in, taking the head of the adult's penis in his mouth. He had sucked on Aidan's penis maybe a dozen times before, and Aidan had always asked to suck his back, which he enjoyed—so this was maybe a rite of passage for Rowan, too, though he drew the line and had insisted on holding onto his own virginity a while longer.

The boys had taken turns with their mouths and hands over the course of a half hour until the passed-out Heritage was rigid as a rolling pin. That made three of them, though Rowan kept his business in his pants. Aidan had ceremonially removed everything he was wearing, and while Rowan had seen that plenty before, his only-slightly-older friend looked more like the full-grown man beneath him, and this had registered as a deep sadness, as Rowan figured he would be losing his friend that night to adulthood.

By the time Aidan returned to the cabin, empty handed and well after midnight, he calculated he'd make less noise if he snuck back into his bedroom through a secret trapdoor that he had built into the floor under his bed years ago. Like a sea otter squirming on his belly to enter its den, Ninnish slid the wooden panel aside so he could access his secret crawlspace beneath the house. There, he'd walled off and insulated a cozy nook where he'd stashed all his limbless and headless doll bodies, some men's nudie magazines that Lyle had also smuggled him, and a few odds and ends of witchcraft paraphernalia that he'd swiped from his mother or from Dottie.

Gently lifting the hatch in the ceiling of the crawlspace and moving it out of the way, Aidan emerged under his brass bed. Tage was asleep and snoring—more accurately, he'd just passed out again, sleeping deeply but entirely unresponsive to the few test touches the teen administered. Convinced it was safe to proceed, Ninnish untied the rest of the burlap restraints, before he caressingly washed the stench of urine from his victim's body, with a washcloth and soapy warm water. Turning the adult body first to one side, then the other, continuing to wash as he went, Aidan next gathered up the Crisco, blood, and sperm-consecrated bedding and the restraints coiled at the edge of the bed before snatching his walkie-talkie off the top of his dresser and retreating with these implements back through the floor, like the suddenly accomplished *Ordo Templi Orientis* apprentice warlock that he was becoming.

Rowan had dozed off in the loft of the triangle cabin, with the flashlight still on—the same flashlight the boys had used together when it had just been the two of them experimenting. Feeling profoundly sad and overly emotional, Rowan examined the collection of Polaroids that he'd just dry-whacked off to. Crying now, he realized he'd lost his friend tonight and any far-fetched notion of the two of them ever becoming boyfriends or teen lovers had been erased by Aidan's fascination and obsession with somebody new in the woods—someone with whom Rowan knew he could never compete. Before closing his puffy eyes, the teen perked up, damn sure there were droplets of what had to be his own first sperm catching the light beam on his white skin just below his belly button. He sat up like his waist was spring-loaded and looked closer. At least that was something.

Maybe forty-five minutes later, the walkie-talkie in his school backpack squawked him awake.

As soon as he had stirred from a chill and realized that his hands and feet were no longer bound to the bed, Heritage grabbed his shorts and the OSU sweatshirt and bolted out of Mona Rye's cabin and into the September night. In his lingering delirium, he had somehow overshot the trail that linked the cabins—Dottie's and the one he'd been using—on the southeast side of the island, and had ended up marooned and wandering deep in the forest. There had been a new moon—but just the tip of a toenail of one—that was just about as useless as his altered brain in helping him see a recognizable route or landmark. At some point during his flight, he understood that he'd been drugged by the boys. He kept running, though, jumping over logs and spongy bogs in an effort to work the barbiturates or hallucinogens out of his system.

The harder he pushed himself, the deeper he drove into the rainforest without a clue where he was headed. It was an island, for fuck's sake. Any minute he would reach the coastline, if he just kept moving. Heritage was driven, running from what he'd done, or rather what had been done to him, and he was slowly realizing that nobody in the world was going to believe him over the kid. There was an ache at the base of his windpipe that spread along a growing network of new cow parsnip burns and stinging nettle and salmon berry scratches that hashed and dotted his exposed legs like a crossword puzzle. When all of that combined with the cramping in his right abdomen and the constriction of his adrenalin-infused upper thighs, Heritage began to weaken. Soon, he just had to stop and hold completely still.

Heritage had raced through unforgiving brush for more than an hour before collapsing onto a bed of moss in a small clearing he didn't immediately recognize. Heaving and sweating, he pulled his lankiness into a fetal position and rubbed his wrists where the burlap had left his skin raw in places. He'd gotten himself lost— or was he found?—in a drug-laced haze that seemed to mute and blur everything but the reason he was running. That much he remembered—that unthinkable act he would probably never be permitted to forget. He did not feel safe or protected from this truth, but at that moment, he needed sleep more than redemption, and surrendered to it.

When his own shivering awakened him some hours later, the dawn had hole-punched a thousand polka dots in the brooding forest walls that surrounded him. Through the oculus in the pantheon-esque canopy overhead, Heritage rubbed his eyes to witness the dark pink start of what he already knew would be a foreboding day. He smelled urine and maybe feces and tilted his head away in favor of fresh air, only then remembering the circumstances of his predicament, and thinking that the source of the smells was him—or, rather, remnants of Ninnish, still on him. He plunged his nose and mouth into the thick moss, inhaling a dozen centuries' worth of decaying forest floor into his lungs. He exhaled with a scream of fury that emptied his chest but not his conscience. He propped up on one elbow to survey his bedroom, batting a small, green Japanese glass float across the green carpet until it bumped against a large obelisk-shaped crystal surrounded by some miscellaneous animal bones.

Heritage sat up to examine a lovely moon snail shell from among the other offerings seemingly placed at his feet by forest fairies while he slumbered. "Fuck-me!" he half-shouted, half-belched using his voice for the first time after many more than several, sedated hours. He recognized that he was positioned just off the exact center of the same labyrinth that he had accidentally encountered once before—where he'd found Marcel Labbé's wallet. He rose to sit back on his haunches to survey the tree-lined room, consisting of those concentric circles and the distinct and angled entrances leading into a pentagon-shaped core, where his traumatized body's overnight depression was still visible in the moss.

Heritage stood—and with new eyes, re-familiarized himself with the angled and interlocking entrances leading to the labyrinth's pentagon center, made, as they were, by the lines forming a star—the upside down pentagram inside two outer rings of rocks and shells and bones, too, he now realized in better light. Of course, he had already clued into the occult origins and suspected purposes of this glen—an appreciation that only intensified now, after surviving a night in the spot he would have previously believed could have killed him. Beyond the rock outlines that demarcated the boundary rings, Heritage realized there was another outer circle; this one guarded by—and he counted them—twenty giant Sitka spruces, which must have topped seven stories tall and easily 100 years of growth apiece, judging by their girth.

Heritage pivoted a full, slow rotation to focus on one tree in particular. This specimen with the straightest, most uniform trunk he thought he'd ever seen, seemed to be older, larger than the others, the closer he got to it. As he stretched open his long arms, he discovered it was possibly the most perfectly shaped trunk he had ever tried to throw his arms around. From where he was, Heritage could gauge that the other trees were spaced at nearly precise intervals—roughly the length of his own wing-span—around the outermost circle. But who could have been there a hundred years or more ago to have deliberately arranged such a magnificent garden? Heritage wondered if other trees had been removed from the centre to create this sacred spot, though he saw now evidence of stumps.

Beyond the outer ring, the forest grew thick, without symmetry or symbolic meaning. Heritage studied the inner circles again, those that had been outlined with round pebbles and sea-shells with the five breaks allowing the different paths to enter the labyrinth. The tips of crystals arranged in low clusters next to each of these entrances were now illuminated by the sunrise—a detail that he had missed during his first accidental visit when he'd encountered Marcel's wallet on that overcast afternoon. If the labyrinth were a compass—and he was only guessing now—and the largest Sitka marked true north, then these entrances seemed to be marking the four half directions: northwest, south-west, southeast, and northeast.

He returned to the center mound of offerings again—to the same spot where that wallet had been previously tucked in the moss. He giraffed his legs wide apart and bent to examine something that seemed different to him just as a waft of shit stink filled his nose and rifled the head it was attached to backwards like a hinge. It was shit! Something or someone had taken a runny dump right on the altar. "Whoa," he said, stepping back. And just like before, a crow or raven pierced he silence to rattle out a call that sent Heritage out of his skin. Pinching his nose with a thumb and forefinger, he looked around and overhead through the pixie sticks of branches and the circular wall of spruce trees but could not spot the phantom bird. When he lowered his head back down, a right-angled corner of something plastic sticking out of the shit and moss snagged his gaze. Being careful not to touch the shit, he gently brushed the moss away to expose what lay beneath. What he saw catapulted him backward.

"What the hell?"

It was a Polaroid picture, and when he flipped it around, the distorted image was a close-up photo of him . . . unmistakeably, Heritage Warren Carter the Third . . . asleep, naked, and bound . . . in Aidan's bed!

He spun around, expecting to catch the prankster or pranksters who were messing with his head. He nervously paced a half dozen steps in three different directions, not knowing what to do, where to run, how to hide. The forest was closing in on him. The raven, no longer invisible began taunting Heritage, hopping onto different branches around the circle until it dropped what it had been struggling to carry in its bristled beak. Heritage watched as the orangish object tumbled end over end, deflected off one of the tree trunks before landing in a cushion of sphagnum moss within arm's reach. Heritage and the swooping raven nearly collided as both raced to retrieve the fallen prize. The raven pulled up at the last possible second with a screech that nearly broke Heritage's ear drum, but the human already had his fist tightly around the cylindrical container. The raven let it be known throughout the hemisphere that he was pissed and had been outwitted. Heritage raised his fist in victory and the raven flew off.

He slowly opened his clenched hand as the blood flowed back into his white knuckles and fingers. It was a plastic prescription container. Whoa! He shot his hand away from his nose. There was that smell again. It was on the bottle or in the bottle, maybe. Heritage held the container up into the sunlight and could see it wasn't empty, but it didn't shake like it had pills in it. Still smelling shit, he wiped the container on the dewy moss and brought it back to his eyes for examination. The label had been mostly removed except for one strip that had the letters *Ry* (which he took for *Rye*) on one line, and *Rohy*—something on the second line. The latter must have been part of the name of the drug prescribed. He popped the childproof cap to examine the contents and found the bottle filled not with pills but with dark curly hairs—lots of them. They looked like pubic hair. But that didn't make any sense, unless—his face flushed in panic—they were his! He fumbled with the waist button on his jeans and pulled back his underwear. He'd been clipped, all right. Just above his genitals, clumps of hair had been taken. But why?

Then it hit him. DNA.

"Jesus!" he exclaimed out loud, hoping nobody other than maybe the raven was listening. The teens intended to frame him. The pictures, his public hair, and millions of his little swimmers probably still detectable in Aidan's rectum, had all been carefully collected—and for what purpose? To take him down and put him away for good. The two teens had bagged their cougar and hadn't used sharpened alder stakes to do it. This whole nightmare of this incredible incident meant he was now officially on the run, and he had to get off that island and out of the sound. There was no guessing what Aidan's next move would be. His own next move seemed clear to him. He needed to find the rest of the Polaroids on his way out.

Heritage needed to locate where Rowan lived. This was the perfect time to do that, while Mason was taking the kids to school. But he couldn't just leave this labyrinth in the middle of the rainforest without first honoring the power center it must have been for at least half a millennium. He could certainly use some spiritual help at the moment. He closed his eyes tightly, standing in the center of the island sanctum, and offered his soul and all his wealth yet to come, in exchange for deliverance from the evil and very wicked Ninnish. He opened the stinky prescription container lid and dumped the pubic hairs into his palm. He took a giant chest full of air and blew the filaments into the air. Offering and pledge made, he tucked the container back into his shorts pocket and bowed with some invented ceremony to each direction in the labyrinth.

When he turned north to head back into the forest, he halted abruptly in his boot tracks. Standing there before him, seen now in a slightly different light filtering through the canopy from a different angle, Heritage recognized, that the grandest, straightest tree he thought he'd ever seen, he had in fact seen at least one other time before. The largest tree trunk in that circle of twenty, was also the tree in the old photograph of Dottie and Mona holding hands in the picture framed on Mona Rye's nightstand. He was certain of it. That tree had the very same, distinctive junction, maybe thirty feet up the trunk, from which three or four equally proportioned trees seemed to grow independently like an upturned fork—or a trident the likes of which Poseidon was always depicted holding.

Heritage approached its primary trunk, which had to be several times his own girth, and reached his arms around it pressing his body into it. He implored the giant to absorb him into its cadmium, conceal and protect him for eternity. He didn't fully understand why, but he knew in that moment that he needed to make a connection to that particular tree—as a way to decode the mystery and history of this place. He thought again of the portrait of Dottie and Mona in front of this tree and this made Heritage acknowledge and long to understand the *her*story, that surely occurred and lingered here, too. It seemed to him that if he just continued holding on tightly until he metabolically fused as one with that tree that had been standing for a hundred, maybe two hundred years, then no mortal human being—no matter how possessed or evil—would be able to bring the two of them down.

The chill he'd felt when he awoke was gone, replaced with fire—ancient, purifying fire. He knew this was part of the deliverance he'd asked the labyrinth for, so he closed his eyes to receive it. He concentrated steadily, his fingers crawling into the reptilian bark as he detached his soul from every earthly binding he could think of: greed, gluttony, anger. He let them go. Sloth and envy followed as he recalled his university studies of Dante's *Divina*, and—just like that—they too were discharged. But he couldn't think of the final two deadly sins. Pride! That was one, and after the humiliation he'd endured the past twenty-four hours, pride was pretty much on its way out anyway. What was left for him to denounce?

He began tapping impatiently against the trunk, trying to come up with the last sin. If he couldn't think of it, he reasoned, it must not have had that much of a hold on him. He hoped the Old One in his arms would accept that feeble excuse and absorb him anyway. He braced for his full deliverance, but a sound in the forest startled him. His eyes popped open.

Something was coming toward the labyrinth.

He inched around the tree trunk until it stood between him and the noise. He heard voices but couldn't tell who they belonged to. Looking up the backside of the trunk, he realized he might be able to scramble up from there into the crotch of one of the forks. He spotted a notch carved into the tree that happened to be exactly the height of his extended arm—it became his first handhold. Pulling himself up, hand and over hand, he noticed new notches, spaced as if created for a man precisely his size. Heritage and the tree were working together. With his long legs and arms, he ascended the giant easily. But up there in the first fork, he still felt exposed, with little to hide behind. The voices he now heard were growing closer and clearer, and Heritage recognized them as belonging to his teen tormentors from the previous evening.

Reaching for branches high on the trunk to his left, he pulled himself daringly higher still. Then he noticed a moss-and-lichen covered platform another six feet above him, crudely spanning a gap between the main and one of the secondary trunks. He wondered if it could be an eagle's nest, so he continued climbing. He was already a good ten metres off the ground and began encountering more branch clutter, impeding his ascent. He stopped there, hoping his camouflage would be enough.

He held his breath. Below him, the labyrinth had pinwheeled to reveal to him the pentagram was not inverted or positioned upside-down from this vantage, with all its exquisite proportions and ridges becoming even more obvious the higher he climbed. Only when approaching the labyrinth on foot from the south or southwest—he revised since that was the half-direction he had decided the paths were orienting from—would the star seem upside down. He was impressed by the exactness of the circles and the straightness of the entrance points. He examined the precision of the outer ring of spruce—how their branches gracefully cantilevered over the clearing like giant trusses in an unfinished roof.

Ninnish and Rowan entered the labyrinth from the northwest, trailed by some distance by Mason, who was yelling at the boys to stop messing around or they were going to be late for school. Rowan made a bee-line through the clearing, and was the first to reach the other side, but Aidan lagged noticeably behind. Heritage, with his heart pounding, watched the latter bend down at the mound in the middle of the pentagon. Aidan looked ahead and behind to make sure his friend had disappeared into the trees, and that Mason hadn't quite caught up, before gingerly checking the moss with his fingers. This was where the Polaroid had been stashed before Heritage had confiscated and tucked it in his back jeans pocket. Aidan must have been the one to place it there. Heritage squinted to see if the kid would discover his theft. Mason called after the boys just as the raven returned to the clearing, this time with other black-winged friends. At the cawing commotion, Aidan rose, looking up at the birds suspiciously before he hustled off to catch up to his friend.

Heritage thought that Ninnish was walking with a hitch—not really limping, like from an ankle injury, but loping. Like maybe he was suffering from a well-deserved soreness, further up the anatomy. With a free hand, Heritage cupped his crotch defiantly—then immediately wondered why he'd done that. He was furious with the boy, but it wasn't like him to be vengeful. Still, he couldn't help feeling good that Aidan was already paying a price for his actions. As furious as he was, he was terrified, too—but that was taking a little bit longer to admit. Perhaps he hadn't jettisoned as much of his anger and pride as he'd intended while trying to make his peace in the labyrinth below.

Mason next came into Heritage's view using the northwest path, same as the boys. But she stopped at the outer circle, then deliberately walked to her left around the outside, where she touched a hand to the trunk of the tree he was in, before she entered the labyrinth from the northeast path. She didn't walk directly to the mound of objects at its center, like he had, and like Rowan and Ninnish had—instead, she walked the lines of the pentagram, one foot touching the heel of the other with each step until she'd almost traced the entire star. But then, she turned around, paused with her eyes shut and exited the labyrinth walking blindly but accurately backwards on the southwest path. When she reached the outer ring, she opened her eyes and turned back around, continuing into the woods in the same direction as the boys. That movement struck Heritage as deliberate, possibly meditative, but not the least bit spooky. That last part was a lie. Heritage was totally creeped and shaking on his stoop. He had not counted Mason to be in the company of witches, but of course she was a dues-paying broom-rider, he now realized.

She was a woman on Wickaninnish, which Heritage was learning meant she had to be at least gumboot-deep in the occult, herself.

By prior arrangement, with Mason's return, Heritage had been relieved of his Rowan-sitting responsibility, but certainly not his accountability. He decided at that moment, just as soon as he figured his way down from that tree, that he would leave Mason a note describing the emergency with his grandfather. His note would apologize but inform her he needed her to cover for him with watching Aidan, so he could fly to Toronto first thing in the morning. He'd already told her this would be a distinct possibility, so it wouldn't come as a big surprise or huge imposition. That seemed the best way for him to scoot out of there and then probably never return to Clayoquot again. That would be his deliverance—as long as he couldn't be extradited back to the scene of this non-crime that hadn't been his fault. The tree he was embracing had leveled with him—it was time for Heritage to leave Wickaninnish Island.

He looked down to judge his descent, but the notches he'd used to climb up weren't as visible on the way down. Actually, he couldn't see them at all and wondered if he had only imagined them on his way up the tree. Panic and second doubts rattled him, and the height made him woozy. For whatever ridiculous reason, he looked up—when he did, he felt better, but the rotting platform or nest above him caught his eye again. He climbed a few armlengths higher and saw—stacked atop what looked like a thick piece of plywood resting on a couple of cross timbers—a scattering of bones, algae-green from exposure in the forest and mostly camouflaged by moss, spruce needles and other debris. From the few feet he was away and out of reach, they seemed unmistakably human. A mossy mound off to one side could have been concealing a skull or a pelvis maybe. Heritage wasn't about to find out.

Again, he panicked and got dizzy looking down. Fortunately, from this slightly higher and laterally-adjusted position on the trunk, he could make out the climbing notches again. Forearms straining and his whole body quaking, Heritage lowered himself to the consecrated ground and promptly quick-stepped his trembling muscles and shattered nerves into the woods in the direction from which Mason and the teens had come.

If he could figure out which cabin belonged to Mason, traveling further north beyond Lyle's cottage, he could leave his note, sweep the kid's bedroom for hiding places, and if he had any luck with Lyle's marine radio, he could reach François for an emergency pick-up.

AIDAN'S AUDACITY

Throughout first and into second periods, Ninnish found he didn't have to dramatize some convincing, follow-up performance to top his dramatic and early departure from school the day before. It wasn't like he had to act or use his imagination at all to nail the delivery. He really was in a lot of pain down there, and while this had always been part of the plan, he had underestimated the intensity of having to sit all day in a plastic classroom chair. Finally, during reading hour he approached the teacher's desk and requested a doctor's pass. Ninnish was sent to the office.

"What is it this time, Ninnish?"

The school's receptionist, along with just about everyone else, it seemed, wanted to taunt him by using the nickname he'd had since first grade. He answered to it, but that didn't mean he accepted or embraced it. He'd just decided he wasn't going to be irritated by it anymore even though he was and couldn't wait to grow out of it. From the faculty's perspective, Aidan Rye had been sent into this world to irritate and disrupt all authority, and this was one way, perhaps the only way, for them to call him out and remind him of his place. And it seemed to work, judging by the quick wince he gave almost as automatically as a facial tic every time he heard it.

"Same problem as yesterday, only worse. I'd like to see a doctor today." He wiped the back of his hand against his nose and caught a whiff of the adult sex that had dried there—he hadn't bathed beyond a washcloth since. He sniffed again while the school worker scratched out her permission on a pad.

"Really, Ninnish. The things you come up with." Her heavily made-up eyes narrowed black as she handed him the slip.

"Fuck you," he muttered behind his still raised hand.

"What was that, mister?"

"Thank you," he said, this time lowering his hand to reveal a smirk. He walked away from the window toward the front doors of the school, thinking there wouldn't be enough time to get even with all of them.

When he walked into the doctor's office, roughly three blocks away, the receptionist was on the phone. "Oh, he's just walked in the door," he heard her say. So, she was talking to that bitch at the school. He'd used the doctor pass before and skipped. It was no surprise to him the school would track his movements. "Have a seat if you would, Aidan. Doctor McAnally is with another patient."

Ninnish had learned to go easy on his bottom during the bumpy boat ride to school and so chose the softest seat in the waiting area. He'd picked up a *National Geographic* and had just cracked the cover when the examining room door opened and Dr. McAnally walked out with François Lévesque—of all people. Ninnish lifted the magazine in front of his face. He didn't like François and had never pretended he did. François had spent far too much time on Wickaninnish Island last summer cuddling Stephanie—another person whom Ninnish never pretended to like all that much. And now that François seemed to be moving on Tage as his next conquest, Aidan had all the reason more to wish him dead, just like Marcel.

He had seen François naked once though, lying in the sun next to the blowhole on the rocky outer side of Wickaninnish. The blowhole was an ocean carved passageway through the rocks that waves got funnelled into and compressed to shoot out like Ol' Faithful into the air. Aidan and Rowan had spent countless hours placing dolls of varying sizes on the spout so they could teach them how to become astronauts. After spying on the naked François for some time, Ninnish lucked out when François started to jack off. Ninnish had jumped out of the scrub brush, brandishing a boner of his own, hoping to get a closer look and perhaps an invitation to assist. Embarrassed and surprised, François immediately stopped, grabbing for his clothes and telling the kid to scram. Ninnish begged him to finish what he'd started, promising he wouldn't tell everyone on the island what he'd seen if François would only continue. He had tried to assure him, in the next breath, that he *would* certainly blab to everyone if he didn't continue. Of course, the adult refused to be extorted. The two had snubbed each other ever since.

Dr. McAnally had a bad habit of continuing office consultations in the hallway, which was a reliable source for town gossip. "The cream should take care of the chafing, but if it doesn't . . ." He lowered his voice when François appeared panic-stricken. "If it doesn't, come back for another script," the doctor whispered.

The receptionist perked up. "You need to take Ninnish—or I should say, Aidan—next." She pointed to the *National Geographic* attached to the teenager's face. "Sorry, Aidan." She turned back to the doctor. "We need to get him back to the school before they break for lunch."

"Let's go, Aidan," Dr. McAnally exhaled, dramatically. "Can you hold on another five, Ted?" he said to the native fisherman with a slight puncture wound. The man, who had already been in the waiting area when Aidan arrived, nodded. Aidan stood to follow the doctor into the room.

"Hey Ninnish!" François hollered after him. "What are you in for?"

"None of your business."

The doctor put his hand on the teen's shoulder and led him into the room, closing the door behind them. "What's the problem?" he asked, plopping down on an adjustable stool.

"It's embarrassing for me, but I think I might have hurt myself. The last couple of days there's been blood in my, you know, my shit and everything."

"Really?" The doctor made some notes in a file.

"You don't have to write this down, do you?"

"You wouldn't want me to forget what you and I talked about, would you?"

"Oh, you won't forget this," Ninnish said, suddenly irritated the doctor might not be taking him seriously. "You won't ever forget."

The doctor set the file on a cabinet and leaned forward on his knees. "You said you think you might have hurt yourself. What do you mean?"

The teenager looked away from him. "I, well, we were kind of goofing around —my friend Rowan and me."

"Rowan Robson?"

"Yeah. We were daring each other to do things, you know."

"Things like what?" The young doctor, who was on a two-year rotation in the sound, seemed anxious to reconnect with his own adolescence through the adventures of this one.

"Well, I got this flashlight and dared Rowan to look up my butt with it."

"Okay. And then what?"

"He did."

"What did he see?"

"How should I know?" Aidan snapped at him turning red in the face.

"Then what?"

"Uh, Rowan dared me to stick the flashlight into my butt."

"And you didn't do that, did you?" The doctor shook his head from side to side.

"I did. I smeared cooking shortening all over it and I had a couple of drinks of you know, like gin or something, and then I just, well, sat on it. It hurt like hell. Rowan had to pull it out for me. At first he wasn't going to. He was too grossed out. But then I dared him to and he had no choice."

"Oh dear." The doctor's hands went to his head. "And now you're bleeding?"

Aidan nodded, still without making eye contact.

"Okay," the doctor said. "Let's have a look at the situation. Britches down."

After a moment spent considering the request and getting up the nerve, Aidan turned around, undid his jeans and shoved them down past his knees. Around the young man's rectum, the doctor saw a bruise the size of an apple. While he hadn't seen the size of the flashlight, chances were good that there was no internal damage beyond the hematoma. The doctor grinned some, but didn't laugh. Anal fascination, he had read in the *New England Journal of Medicine*, was common enough among adolescents. His patient had probably already learned a poignant lesson, so he didn't press it further with an unnecessary lecture.

"Okay, Aidan. You can pull up your pants and turn around now." Without hesitating, Ninnish spun, nearly whapping the still-examining doctor in the face with an instantly full erection.

"Well, I, uh, must say . . . that stands out just about as much as the bruise on your bum, young man. Is there something else you need or want to talk to me about?" The doctor sat up straight and made eye contact again.

"Don't you want to touch it?" Ninnish asked, thrusting his hips forward.

"Well I certainly don't need to, unless there's something wrong with your penis. It looks to be functioning just fine." The doctor leaned back in his chair and folded his arms in front of him.

"How much bigger do you think it will get? I mean, I'm still growing and everything."

Dr. McAnally stroked his chin. "Look, Aidan. I know you don't have a dad or a brother to talk about these things with, so I don't want to discourage your questions. You're what? Fourteen now?" He opened the chart. "Fifteen—you just had a birthday this summer. Your penis is going to continue to grow as you do, but part of growing up is learning how and when to use it."

"Oh, I know how to use it. Don't you worry about that."

"If it's all the same to you, I'll choose to worry about someone who doesn't know how to use a flashlight properly, okay? There are consequences to sex, Aidan. If you're going to be with a girl . . ."

"Ah, come on. I learned all this shit years ago. Don't bore me." Aidan touched himself when it became apparent his invitation to the doctor would be declined.

"And you learned about AIDS too, Aidan?"

"Yes, yes, yes. How big's the dick in your pants, doctor?" His touching had turned to masturbation as he stared at the lump in the doctor's khaki pants.

"Do you like girls, Aidan?" The doctor pulled the flap of his lab coat across his lap.

"Not much," Aidan answered, short of breath. "Are you getting hard, too? Is that why you pulled your apron thing shut?" He clenched his bottom lip between his teeth and pumped faster.

"No, Aidan. Now look. This is getting out of hand. Is there a point to this?" The doctor closed the patient file, flustered.

"I want to show you how much I can cum. I've just about got it . . . no . . . thanks . . . to you!"

"So, you prefer boys. Is that it? That's okay, too." The doctor couldn't help but watch the kid climax, as there was as much voyeur in him as the next guy. The exposed head of the teen's penis turned cherry red before giving up a few dollops of what the doctor silently figured was more than likely sterile spermatozoa.

"Huh," Ninnish grunted. "There was ten times that much last night—easily!"

"When you had the flashlight up your bum?"

"Yes."

"The flashlight was putting pressure on your prostate gland, and that forced more 'cum'—as you call it—through your urethra. Okay, show's over, Aidan. I have other people waiting to see me, and some of them actually hurt."

Dr. McAnally stood, taking one last look at his patient's genitalia. "Are those sores from masturbating, Aidan? You really need to take it easy if you want your penis to last as long in this life as you do. I mean that."

"What if I told you they were teeth marks?" Aidan asked cavalierly.

Dr. McAnally made an inquisitive face but didn't want to judge. "Then, look, I would say, if you aren't double-jointed or flexible enough to have made those marks yourself, then maybe you should have a word with Rowan about being more careful to cover his teeth with his lips, before sticking a flashlight in his mouth." The doctor stood. "Okay, pants up, young man! Now, I want you to let me know if the bleeding bum doesn't stop after today." He glanced back over his shoulder. "You can phone me with that information, in that case, and we can decide where to go next." The doctor closed the door, giving the exhibitionist a chance to fasten his pants before leaving.

Heritage had been pacing and noticed his hands were trembling.

He was so anxious to be out of Clayoquot he'd started to hyper-ventilate, fearing the RCMP would roll up any second to haul the child molester away for good. He was staring down the hour and minute hands on his watch. He was scheduled to be on a charter flight at dawn, but still needed to make it through the day and night ahead, before he was in the clear. He'd half-expected to be swamped or intercepted by that cocky coast guard captain as he crossed an astoundingly flat Templar Channel in Mona's green canoe that he'd stolen to get himself off Wickaninnish—but he encountered no one other than a pair of harbour porpoises, keen to show off their distinctive white underbellies. He had next feared that Constable Toren would be waiting with handcuffs on the beach when he landed, but the beach was empty.

Inside the lodge, Heritage was surprised to learn from Chef Solberg that Brad Fraser had apparently skipped town a few days early. Everyone had it in their calendars—and Fraser had even told Heritage that he was leaving for the Caribbean on Friday, but he hadn't shown up to the lodge on Monday—Heritage had heard from a desk clerk that Fraser had said he was making a janitorial supply run to Port Alberni yesterday, but nobody had been able to reach him and he hadn't returned with the supplies. The chef had driven by the Lodge keeper's in-town house on his way home last night and again this morning, but there had been no signs of life. Heritage sort of deputized the chef on the spot to keep an eye on the place for the rest of the week—to be the *acting*, acting general manager, as it were, while he sprinted to Toronto for a few days. The man couldn't be more than five years older than Heritage, but already had fathered four young children of his own to support, so Heritage sweetened the temporary management deal by adding a two-thousand-dollar bonus to his next paycheque. The chef's face lifted, and he quick-drew his hands from his chef's apron pockets to shake Heritage's hand. This reminded Heritage to hand over the car keys to the Jeep Cherokee and apologize that he had left the company rig in the Co-op parking lot. The chef assured him it would be no problem to pop one of the kitchen staff into town to retrieve it.

Heritage excused himself to use the phone in the back office—which he supposed was officially his now, if Fraser had really vacated the peninsula. He busied himself, perhaps prematurely, with rearranging the items on the desktop. Fraser must have been left-handed, because none of it was working for Heritage, not the stapler, not the tray of paper clips, not the phone. If there had been a window in Brad Fraser's office to stare out of, Heritage would have been fixed in front of it with a stare more blank than focused. His drug-fuzzy mind was on scramble and every so often his heart would begin racing and he'd have to work on his breathing to calm himself down again. In this uncurable hangover, it took forever for enough minutes to total one full hour passed, while he hid-out, laying low, waiting for his sky to fall.

Lust! *That* was the seventh deadly sin. Heritage thought how ironic it was that lust hadn't more automatically occurred to him—particularly after the sexual World Series of the past two weeks. Then, as he followed that thought train through the tunnel that was his head, he determined it hadn't been *his* lust; not with Stephanie and certainly not with Aidan. He might have had a minor lust flare-up with François, but even that could just as easily have been explained as circumstantial, exacerbated no doubt by the heady weed they had been smoking. The funny thing about lust, for Heritage, was he didn't often feel it. In maybe the two dozen or so times he'd had sex, it had never been something he'd initiated or really needed to happen. He always rose to the occasion, but he never really felt corporeally horny—cerebrally horny, perhaps. For example, he'd spent many a day on the island, stuck in the rain that first week thinking in great detail how he would have liked to be having sex with François—even whacked off to the steamy scenario in his head. But that didn't mean he popped an instant boner in the man's presence—though *instant* was probably being too subjective, as Heritage knew arousal would follow even the slightest suggestion, grazing touch or a shift in fabric. On this groggy day-after, his antenna was particularly hyper-receptive which underlined the running theory he'd been slipped something for that function too, by his mad-teen-scientist tormentor. Heritage reached a hand under the desk to readjust himself out of a sudden pinch, and he tried to think about anything else. He reached for the handset of the telephone.

After twenty minutes of trying and failing to connect with Toronto to let Lonnie know about his travel plans and to get an update on his grandfather, he walked the short distance from the office and emerged behind the front desk. He asked the staff if any guests had complained about not being able to phone out, since all he had been getting was a *circuits busy* recording. One of the desk clerks smiled and explained that she'd heard on the radio that the phone company had not been able to handle the call volume after Michael Jackson Vancouver concert tickets had gone on sale at sunrise.

"You're serious?" he asked.

She nodded, still smiling. "Welcome to the end of the road just beyond the last telephone pole, Mr. Carter." She put a calming hand on his shoulder just above his bicep. "This happens frequently."

"Michael Jackson concerts in Vancouver?" Heritage raised his eyebrows, facetiously.

"If it isn't phone circuits, it's the hydro that gets knocked out—and then there is no phone, no lights, and worse, there are no pumps to carry the, uh, wastewater to the main sewer line that runs under the highway. It can be a real mess. Michael Jackson is really the least of our regular concerns—but he is apparently the reason why the phones are not working at the moment."

She squeezed his shoulder and stepped away to attend to a couple that were approaching with their bags to check out. He stood there in a stupor another moment before ascending the staircase to hide out in a suite that he'd assigned himself just as soon as he'd stowed Mona's green canoe next to his kayak in the equipment shed located among the trees just off the beach below. He had decided, during the canoe crossing, to keep his distance from the kids and the island until the seaplane could carry him out of this mess and out of Clayoquot Sound and possibly for good. He was sleeping at the Headlands tonight where he could count on alarm clocks and a proper washroom. With his calling card out, he kept checking the phone like he was trying to win a radio station giveaway by being the seventh caller. He hadn't been very lucky lately. But he couldn't just give up and turn himself over to the authorities. Depending on whether Aidan was bragging, exaggerating, squealing, or biding his time, Heritage still felt he might have options to mount a defense, but running away certainly made the most immediate sense. Even if his hands had been tied (along with everything else the previous night) until he knew the kid's next move, he felt less out-in-the-open at The Headlands.

Heritage packed, became frustrated, unpacked and repacked his bags, laying out his travel clothes for the morning. He felt as though he were becoming schizophrenic, flip-flopping between analyses of what was his fault and what wasn't. He was convinced the RCMP and the Ministry of Family and Child Services were going to blitzkrieg the Headlands at any second, with Ninnish pointing straight at his abuser from a safe distance, buffered no doubt by a contingent of horrified social workers who'd swallowed his tall tale hook, line, and sinker. And what would the adult's defense be? Especially if there were Polaroids, pubic hair, sperm, DNA?

No, he had to get out of there. He'd been standing in one terrified position, staring out the window at Wickaninnish Island for so long he'd begun to spasm. He tried to walk it off a few steps in each direction, but he was a mess. He busied himself by trying the phone line again. All circuits busy.

Movement in the channel caught his eye. It was the coast guard lifeboat crossing from Tofino diagonally in a straight line toward Dottie's cove. It was the same boat that had responded to Marcel Labbé's drowning and was likely piloted by Matt Greene, with that half-breed wolf-dog of his. Heritage didn't even bother wondering if they were coming for him—he *knew* they were. Aidan must have squealed—what attention-grabbing teenager wouldn't have? Heritage ran through the most likely scenario in his head. They wouldn't find him or his kayak on the island, and so the Headlands would be the next place they would look—and perhaps the RCMP were already coming up the drive. There was a quick double knock on the door to his hotel suite that sent him out of his skin and caused him to wonder whether or not he could survive a jump off his balcony from that height. He had already waited too long to respond and when he opened the door—the staff person was already halfway down the hall. The young, pony-tailed bellman doubled back when he heard the door open.

"This phone message has just arrived for you, Mr. Carter. Your line was busy, so I thought I'd just run it up to you."

Heritage smiled, but it was forced, given his duress. He unfolded the pink piece of paper.

Grandfather released from hospital. Sends instructions for you to stay put until further notice.

"Now, that's a spot of good news to start your day off with, isn't it?" The desk clerk turned to leave. Heritage tried to conceal his escalating panic. He closed the door to his suite and walked back to the windows to check on the coast guard across the channel. The boat was still there. Heritage's heart drummed rapidly. He'd taken a scalding hot shower as soon as he'd arrived that morning, but now that the authorities appeared to be on the hunt for evidence, another shower would be insurance that none of the boy's DNA could be found anywhere on or in his body. He threw the deadbolt, stripped, grabbed his razor and stepped back into the still steamed-up glass shower stall.

The already incriminating situation and the new development that he would not be leaving Clayoquot at dawn, called for some radical manscaping, to even out the chunk of pubes that had been harvested without his consent. *Without his consent* had been the theme of that party, and given that there was a photographer present, Heritage suddenly felt compelled to more-radically alter his appearance down there and everywhere. So he shaved everything below his scalp—what was left of his bush, his chest, his abdomen with the appendectomy scar, his navel, before dropping down to the jewels. He shaved the base of his penis, his scrotum, and then behind it, before eliminating what hair he might have had between his elongated, oval ass cheeks. He shaved his already scratched up legs—something he hadn't attempted since his buddy Imogene Mantoya had taught him the elongated stroke technique. He shaved his armpits, which had been trickier than he'd ever imagined. When he looked down at his feet, he was standing in water that covered them, the drain impeded by what looked like a small cat. He grabbed a handful of his shearing and airlifted it to the toilet—visualizing the trip the flush would take the glob before it popped up on the surface of that patch of choppy water off Tonquin Beach. He thought about shaving his head, but his hair was too long for the safety razor, plus he didn't have any clippers. What he did have, when he was finished, were microscopic nicks everywhere—on top and under the scrapes and scratches from his midnight escape through the brush. They stung in the steam and water, and then red-polka-dotted the white hotel towel as he pat-dried his thrashed body. Death by a thousand cuts.

The coast guard boat had moved on or at least out of view by the time Heritage emerged from the washroom. He dressed in the same clothes he'd worn after his first shower of that strange day, taking note of the new sensation of fabrics on his hairless frame. He towel-dried his head hair and styled it with his fingers. If he weren't going to Toronto after all and if any other escape from *Clayoquotraz* were out of the question, then he supposed he needed to go about his business as though nothing had happened. This was going to place a whole new breed of demands upon his acting skills. Not only had something definitely happened with Aidan—Heritage had orgasmed, which would seem to indicate that he had liked it and couldn't help himself. Betrayals abounded! He had engaged in anal sex with a boy half his age. How in the hell was he supposed to mount a defense that pointed to anything else, otherwise?

Business as usual. Business as usual. Business as usual. He kept repeating the mantra to himself with every step down the staircase to the lobby and Stu Solberg, who was hosting a conversation with a few guests and staff below.

"I've got a phone call from the secondary school for you, Mr. Carter. You can take it at that house phone on the table," the desk clerk said, pointing.

"Thank you," Heritage said, his voice trembling. "I'll catch up to you in a moment, Stu." He walked to the phone, which rang as he neared it, causing him to jump. *Count to three.* "Tage Carter, here."

The voice on the other end sounded preoccupied, perhaps from being on hold for so long. "Oh, hello? Mr. Carter, we have Aidan Rye in the office here, and he's just returned from seeing Doctor McAnally. Aidan says the doctor is releasing him from school today. Since we've got your name on file as his temporary guardian, we wondered if you could come and take him off our hands."

"Doctor? Now?" Heritage took care not to speak too loudly. "Yes! Of course. I'll be there in less than thirty minutes. Thank you." He placed the handset down without looking and missed the cradle, then jiggled it in noisily. *This is a trap. This is another trap. The police are waiting. A medical team is on standby to compare pubic hairs and test for the last time he had intercourse.* Heritage knew he was losing it. His head began to sweat. His breathing was erratic. He was convinced a sting operation was unfolding downtown, that they were slowly reeling him in, one crank at a time. He took a big breath and walked to grab Stu's elbow at a table in front of one of the big windows where guests were reading the *Globe and Mail* and leaving a trail of croissant flakes and salal jam thumbprints on the pages.

———

"Stu, I'm actually not feeling very well today. I don't know how I thought I was going to be able to travel to Toronto in the morning, but now that I don't have to, I'm thinking maybe I should take it easy for the next day or two. If it is all right with you, I'd still like you to be in charge for the rest of this week—the bonus still holds, of course." The chef was nodding. "And while I hate the thought of losing revenue, I think I will shift into one of the forest cottages for the next few nights." Heritage was thinking out loud. "Or maybe the whole winter, now that the weather is turning—you know, something out of the way, but still reachable if something comes up." He exhaled the last of the air from his collapsing lungs against the back of the hand that he held in front of his lying mouth.

"No, of course." Stu said, already getting into full swing with his acting-acting general manager role. The chef raised his finger and called out, "Jacqueline ?" He motioned the desk clerk over, who had been tidying up the self-serve coffee and tea station nearby. "Mr. Carter has decided the Headlands will be good enough for his big city tastes after all. He will be staying the winter with us. Can you see to it he gets settled into one of the north, forest-facing cabins—maybe number six on the end, as it is the closest to the kayak shed?"

"Absolutely," Jacqueline said with a guest-first smile. "I'll be right back with a set of keys."

"And one more thing," Heritage added. "Since it would be prudent for me hit the pharmacy, I could bring the lodge vehicle back if somebody was available to run me into town now."

Stu volunteered for the task, handing the Jeep keys back to his acting boss. So much acting, Heritage thought . . . it was enough to make him really sick.

From the Co-op parking lot, Heritage intentionally drove through the alleyway behind the RCMP detachment building where every one of the two reserved parking spaces had a patrol vehicle still in it. As it was unlikely the authorities were conducting their sting on foot, Heritage decided to relax a couple of degrees without lowering the mercury completely. He headed up Third Street and pulled in front of the school.

Aidan was sitting alone on the low concrete retaining wall. He didn't recognize Heritage because of the vehicle at first, but had started to stand anyway. When he saw the driver, he smiled, reaching for the door handle. Heritage had to fiddle with a couple of switches before managing to lower the window on the passenger side.

"We play by my rules or we don't play at all," he told Aidan sternly. Aidan nodded and Heritage popped the lock. "Fasten your seat belt."

"It's nice to see you too, Tage." Ninnish jammed the seatbelt buckle into the slot. "I haven't had a particularly easy day, just so you know."

"Oh, you haven't, have you?" Heritage feigned concern. "Just shut up, Aidan. Until I figure out what I'm going to say to you, neither of us is going to say anything." Heritage flipped the turn signal well in advance of the intersection, making sure he didn't forget anything. As he waited at the stop sign, an RCMP cruiser sped out of town toward The Headlands. The blood drained from Heritage's face. Maybe the Mounties were just heading south. The Headlands was just one of about two or three dozen destination points before the highway junction that also happened to be south. It didn't mean the cruiser was going to the Headlands per se.

Heritage knew Ninnish was watching him—that he probably detected his panic and was about to exploit it. He needed a plan. So far, it seemed as though there had been no immediate repercussions from the previous evening. Aidan was calmly sitting in the passenger seat, and as long as he was where Heritage could watch him, he couldn't be off telling somebody what the big, bad adult had done to him. Momentarily relieved, Heritage started to pull onto the main road out of town when Aidan yelled. Heritage slammed on the brakes just as a white-haired pedestrian crossed in front of the Cherokee. The woman put her hand on the green hood to steady herself and looked up and into the window at the driver.

"Ha!" Aidan squealed. "It's Aunt Dottie. You should have hit her!"

"I told you to stay quiet." Heritage corrected the slight smile on his face and pushed the window button. "Dottie, I'm so sorry. You came out of nowhere."

"I thought you were Brad Fraser and I was looking forward to telling you your floating wilderness lodge application was turned down by council! What are you doing driving around in that ogre's car?"

"When did you get back? Is Mona home too?" Heritage's questions might have been too eager.

"I came back Monday night, in time for the town council meeting. Your mum has a real nice room this time, Aidan. She can see the Craigdarroch Castle from her bed."

"That's nice," Aidan said without looking up from a handheld computer game he'd extracted from his backpack.

"Why aren't *you* watching Aidan, then?" Heritage blurted out awkwardly. He instantly retracted his tone. "I didn't mean that the way it sounded."

"Yes, you did," Aidan said, still without looking up from his game.

Dottie straightened until her face was out of Aidan's sight, above the roof of the car. She gave Tage, who could see her plainly, a knowing expression that said that she empathized but she was no fool. "The fact you would ask me that only two days into your stint already answers your own question better than I could. And why aren't you in school, mister?" She leaned back through the driver's window.

"I'm not feeling well."

Heritage went pale.

"What do you mean you're not feeling well?"

"Bloody diarrhea, okay? Can we just go or are we going to sit here blocking traffic all day?" He shoved the computer game back in his pack.

"Maybe you should see a doctor then, young man."

"I already did."

Heritage tried to look around her straw-like hair for oncoming traffic. "Look, he just needs to get his rest, so I'd best get him to bed." Realizing what he had just said, how it sounded, what it implied, and how it stalled there in the air between them, caused the teenager to finally look up.

Dottie didn't take her hands off the door and instead looked Heritage right in the eyes and said, "Don't think for one second Dottie Bard doesn't know why you are driving this rig and that she knows you can't be proud of having sold your soul."

Heritage didn't know why she spoke of herself in the third person.

"Whose rig is it?" Ninnish asked—true to his usual, meddling form.

"Good-bye, Dottie," Heritage said firmly. He finally made the right turn he'd been signaling for the past ten minutes. Aidan started to repeat his question when Heritage cut him off. "Shut up, Aidan. I'll tell you when it's time to talk." And with that, the two rode in silence the rest of the short route to the Headlands Lodge.

With every click on the odometer, Heritage wrestled over whether or not to take Aidan there, mixing business with—well, whatever the hell the previous night had been. But unless he just kept driving and abducted the little shit, his new, temporary cabin in the forest next to the lodge seemed the best place for the two of them to iron out a working agreement and for Aidan to grow up real quick and face reality. If it took the rest of the week, so be it. But come Monday, he'd damn well better be out of the babysitting racket, off Wickaninnish Island, and maybe even outwardly pretend he was relocating back to Vancouver or Toronto, as far as Ninnish, Dottie, and Mona ever had to know.

He didn't see any way that he could have anything to do with Wickaninnish Island any longer—not now—not with Aidan and Rowan both able to blackmail him. If he were forced to stay longer in Clayoquot Sound—say by his grandfather's astounding resiliency and his orders to complete the takeover of the Head-lands—Heritage supposed he could adopt an even lower profile, sticking to his cabin in the forest and taking his meals in the lodge without ever leaving the confines of the designer compound. He didn't need to become a member of this bizarre community if he had no intention of staying. After the past twenty-four hours, he had new cause to be paranoid, but even before last night, he was already suspicious of the handful of townsfolk he had encoun-tered. In another, less precarious frame of mind, he might have been motivated to change that outlook and win the populace back over to his normally decent and charming side. But at the moment, with the accuser playing victim and likely still plotting in the passenger seat next to him, and with evidence mounting or missing, he was stuck, and scrambling to get un-stuck.

"I want you to sit on the porch of the last cabin at the end of this path, number six." Heritage pointed to the trailway leading into the woods. "I'll return these car keys to the front desk. Then you and I are going to discuss last night, man to man. Understood?"

Ninnish undid his seat belt, nodding his blond crewcut head of coarse hair that was already growing out again. Heritage only half-expected him to be on the porch when he got back. He knew he was taking a chance, but for some reason, it seemed a good strategy to fool the kid into thinking he trusted him. Not even five minutes later, Heritage jogged down the forest path toward his assigned cottage and found Aidan with his school backpack, sitting in an Adirondack chair. The two went inside. Ninnish tossed his backpack on the bed next to Tage's packed bags. "Is this where we're sleeping tonight? It's nice."

"Aidan, about that—"

"You can call me Ninnish. I'm used to it—and besides, I don't mind it so much when you say it."

"Fine, Ninnish." Heritage plopped down in an overstuffed chair covered in an American Southwest motif that he'd thought out of place the first time he'd been in the cabin during his property tour and walkabout with Brad Fraser. He motioned Ninnish to sit across from him, on the matching hide-a-bed sofa with a clunky pine coffee table between them. He continued.

"What happed last night is really upsetting me today. I'm very angry but I'm also very scared. I'll be leaving the sound for good on Monday."

"I have to pee. Where's the can?"

Tage's hands went to his face in frustration. He pointed past the kitchenette. He didn't know what he was going to say, but he had to vindicate himself. He still hadn't figured out how he was going to hand Ninnish off to Dottie or Mason until Mona returned from treatment, but that is clearly what needed to happen. Then there was François—that's who he'd rather be sharing these rustic-appearing four-star digs with, all things considered. Instead, he was panic-stricken over what his French-Canadian crush would make of recent events. There were often no choices in the hand you got dealt in life, he remembered his mother saying—only wrinkles. This new one was already turning out to be a doozy.

Ninnish was taking longer than a piss should have taken. Heritage went to the bathroom door and knocked. "You okay in there?"

"Uh—I'll be out in a minute," Ninnish yelled through the door. Inside, the teenager sitting on the toilet, was trying to work up enough nerve to hit himself in the nose. He needed some stage blood to work with. At his age, bloody noses seemed to spontaneously happen three, sometimes four times in a day. After a minute, Tage knocked again. Instead of answering him, Ninnish popped himself in the face with his flat hand, issuing a simultaneous groan. The tap opened, he let the nostril drain into his open hands, which he then smeared around the inside of his legs and on the toilet seat. When Tage barged in a few seconds later, the scene had been set. "I can't get it to stop!" Ninnish launched into hysterics.

"Jesus!" Heritage was not good at blood, and it seemed to be everywhere. He went to one knee and placed his hands on the teenager's bare hips, moving him slowly to the walk-in shower stall. "It's going to be okay," he reassured him in hushed tones. Heritage balanced him while the boy stepped out of the rest of his clothes. Heritage tested the water until it was comfortable, before backing him into the soft spray. "What did the doctor say?"

"That I shouldn't stick flashlights up my ass, and to come right back if the bleeding didn't stop."

A smile the turned around teen couldn't see, streaked like a comet across the adult's face but just as quickly was gone again. The RCMP hadn't road-blocked the village, and Heritage had been allowed to pick up the boy at the secondary school. Now he knew why. Ninnish was incapable of telling the truth—even when it suited his nefarious purposes. With a facecloth, Heritage dabbed at the blood-streaked legs, turning Ninnish as he worked. When the child had spun 360 degrees, it became apparent Satan with an A had worked himself into full arousal again. With his fifteen-year-old calling-card sticking straight out, once again level with Tage's face, Ninnish said, "See what you do to me?"

Exasperated again, Heritage pushed himself away, finally seeing the trail of blood coming from one of the kid's nostrils.

"No, Aidan, you do this to yourself. All of this!" He motioned to the last of the pink water swirling down the drain. He wiped his forehead with the back of his wet arm. The shower had made the bathroom humid. Heritage suddenly found it difficult to breathe or stand-up without feeling he might topple over in an exhausted heap of ragged culpability. "I'll be outside when you're finished." He left the bathroom door open and went outside on the deck.

He thought he must be going crazy. Rinsing the teenager

down and seeing the boner it gave him, had actually aroused him, too—credit was maybe more due the drug enhancements still swirling around his bloodstream—but if he hadn't left the washroom when he did, he might well have been exposed as the fraud of the century. His guilt was taking on new cargo. He'd never really thought about minors as sexual entities before—and yet, he had been a somewhat sexually enterprising teenager himself, fooling around with his neighbourhood playmates when he was about Aidan's age.

And it wasn't that being an actively sexual child was wrong. What was wrong about the whole mess had nothing to do with Aidan's hormones but everything to do with their age difference. Heritage didn't even know what the age of consent was nowadays—he'd never needed to know—but he figured in a couple more years, when Ninnish was actually eighteen, instead of just looking that age, Heritage would still be sixteen years older, but then there would have been nothing improper or criminal about engaging him or any eighteen-year-old in a sexual relationship. So, Heritage had to ask himself, now that he wasn't tied up and drugged, was the law the only thing stopping him from voluntarily having sex with the teen. He readjusted the flagging erection in his pants. Probably he hated to admit it, but Aidan was a pretty handsome and well put together man-sized kid. It was the scariest thought he'd had to grapple with in years. Yes, sex was only sex, except when it wasn't supposed to be sex at all—and that's when the forbidden became red-handled and polished-chrome irresistible. At thirty-two, he was still learning things it seemed Ninnish had already figured out at fifteen. Heritage knew he had to leave—separate himself from the boy. It had, in that moment, gone beyond being unable to trust Ninnish. Now, he needed to accept, he couldn't fully trust himself.

Ninnish stepped onto the porch with a towel wrapped around his abdomen muscle stacked waist, looking every bit like a California surfer. "I think I need to lie down for a while. Is that okay?"

Aidan was still playing his weak and wounded cards, which might have worked with somebody that didn't already know the kid walked around with a trick deck.

"There's a bed up in the loft." Heritage pointed, looking away from his charge and out through the trees toward the sun sparkling on the water. "You take that one and I'll sleep down here tonight." Ninnish went back inside and started up the ladder.

Heritage had an idea that might buy him some time. He went to the base of the ladder and looked up, addressing the climber. "I'm going to run to the grocery store to get us something for dinner. I can take you back to the island tomorrow when we're both feeling better."

Ninnish flaunted with the realization that Tage could see under his towel. "Do you have some shorts for me to sleep in? I messed up mine." He took off the towel and lobbed it on his keeper's head.

"Yeah," Heritage answered. He grabbed a pair from his packed bag that had been left on the bed by the staff, and reached up to hand it off. Next he took the ladder in both hands and unhooked it from the loft, laying it flat on the main floor and then scooting it under the main bed.

"What if I have to pee?" Ninnish deliberately hesitated to put on the shorts, making the most of another naked moment. Heritage marveled how adult the teenager looked standing up there with his hands on his hips. He would probably make a very attractive adult if he were allowed to live that long.

Heritage was doubly desperate to talk to somebody about his predicament—desperate in the first degree because this wasn't something you talked about, and desperate in the second because there was nobody in the village he was close to or trusted. It wasn't as though it was fair to pin that predicament on the small size of the town, as there wasn't really anyone in his life anywhere that he could just call up and say, "Hey, you'll never guess what happened to me last night!"

While he wasn't above walking the twenty to thirty minutes it would take him in each direction, he knew Ninnish couldn't be left to his own devices in a room full of somebody else's devices for that long. Even going back into town at all seemed—to the wised-up teen-sitter—to be living a bit on the stupid side. Still, he had to meet with Dottie to make arrangements for the immediate handoff of Ninnish, and he wouldn't have said no to another chance meeting with François at the SunRyes Bakery. Given recent developments, their reunion, when it occurred, would likely entail a hasty goodbye, and Heritage wasn't exactly thrilled about that. François would understand when Heritage revealed he wasn't cut out for a small town, since he wasn't from the sound originally, either. Heritage would just make up some totally believable excuse that the urban pace of Vancouver, Toronto, even Montreal was calling him. Maybe he'd even suggest that François consider leaving the sound with him, if the preamble to their goodbye turned out to signal their bond was perhaps stronger than the tug of the rainforest for both of them. Heritage would have loved to paint over the unfortunate episode from the previous night with a romantic what-if-future involving François, but the stain he needed to cover up first was going to take more than one coat. It would be better, he knew, if he could just disappear into the mist rising off the Pacific surf, not reflecting on or visiting this twisted place again. But he also knew he had unfinished business here for his grandfather just as his grandfather had unfinished business when it came to his final task of dying.

On the drive into town, Heritage began to realize that his planned purification by nature and the hope of adopting a new, altruistic nobility with his life and fortunes had so far been a sham. He'd arrived in the village just seventeen days earlier, chasing a higher purpose, thinking he would become some environmental messiah. But instead, he had lied at least once to everyone he had met. He was lying still about who he was and why he was really there. He hadn't done a thing to save the environment. He hadn't yet managed to survive his grandfather's ever-imminent demise to change the face of the family's pulp-and-paper ways or credibly wrest control of their hospitality arm away from Brad Fraser at Headlands Lodge. He hadn't turned out to be the kayaking enthusiast he had wanted to be. Ever since the drowning death of Marcel Labbé, the Pacific Ocean scared the hell out of him. He hadn't once crossed that channel without white knuckles and a ridiculously racing heart—even thinking about it made his paddling shoulders tense. On the plus side of the ledger—if a man were to only mark the relevance of his existence and the depth of his achievements by the number of times he'd taken advantage of sexual opportunities (and he knew men who were that way)—then Heritage practically had license to boast. In just seventeen days, he'd engaged in casual sex four times (five times if he counted the passed-out bloke in the cargo net at Lyle's dance party), including once with a minor—and that tallied more sexual partners than he'd had the whole previous year in the city. Heritage couldn't decide if this accounting signified anything that he could really hang his hat on—unlike the erection in his pants that could easily support a hat, a wet raincoat and an umbrella at the moment, too. He had most definitely been fed a teenage fistful of Viagra. It had only been seventeen days in which so much and yet nothing had happened. It really didn't amount to enough to run away from and it wasn't enough to make him want to stay.

Heritage was recognizing his whole life had been suspended in this ambivalence like a whole bunch of sliced bananas stuck in lime Jell-O. He wanted this to change. The only problem with his resolution was that he expected someone else to provoke and orchestrate that change for him. For too many years, he'd counted on his grandfather's passing to be the catalyst for his new life. *I'll do that once he's gone, and that's going to change when I start spending the bad money for good.* These had been his mottos so long that they no longer rallied his optimism. One person. Any person. That's all it would take. Any person, that is, but the one take-charge-person he couldn't be for himself.

He parked the jeep in front of the grocery store and for a few minutes couldn't corral enough motivation to let go of the steering wheel. As he idled there, he watched Dottie emerge from the store, François angry on her heels. They were clearly engaged in an argument that couldn't be settled—probably why François had said he usually tried to avoid her. Dottie had turned to walk away, François' mouth and hands still talking after her, when she suddenly turned back to wave a finger at him. "No!" Heritage had been able to read that on her lips and all over her face. This time, François turned to walk away. Heritage scrambled out of the Cherokee to catch up to him, after getting his arm untangled from the seat belt.

"Hey, what was that all about?"

Seeing Heritage, François tried to smile through his rage and a mouthful of a Coffee Crisp candy bar he'd just bitten into. "Dis is a surprise. You were supposed to be getting ready to head back east today, no?"

"My trip was for tomorrow morning, but it got canceled. My grandfather apparently left the hospital and is feeling better. Listen. I need to talk to you, but I have to catch Dottie first. Are you headed to the bakery?"

"Sure. I can be der." Heritage had noticed that François didn't wear a watch or seem to have much of a schedule on his days off from the oyster farm, since he was pretty readily found hanging around downtown. Heritage didn't even know where he lived or if he lived alone. There hadn't been enough time to find these things out.

"Ten minutes, then. Wait for me." Heritage ran down the hill, pursuing the red-faced, white-haired dread of the village, and offering to take the groceries off her hands.

"Oh, it's you. I thought for a moment that—"

"That I was François?" he offered. "I just saw the two of you being anything but friendly."

"How is Ninnish feeling?" She ignored the invitation to argue or confess.

"That's what I need to talk to you about. My grandfather has gone into the hospital in Toronto. He is all the family I have so I will be leaving the sound on Monday. I can't watch Aidan anymore."

"Your grandfather—really?" she asked, as though she suspected he was fibbing. "What's with this bloody diarrhea story of Aidan's?" They continued walking past her building toward the dock.

"I'm sure you know his scams better than I do. He's sleeping it off now and will probably be just fine once the end-of-the-day school bell rings. But I'm not cut out for this. Aidan likely needs a father figure and that's the last thing in this world I want to be for anyone. Can you please take him back until Mona returns?"

Dottie set the groceries down next to her boat. "That's not the issue here. You said you'd watch him. I think you should watch him."

"I did not say I'd watch him, actually. Mona said, *you* said I'd watch him! Aidan told his mum that I said I'd be happy to watch him, and Mona said you also told her I'd be perfect for it. I did not say I'd watch him." He inhaled dramatically to refill his chambers. So much for tamping down his defensiveness.

After Dottie stepped onto her boat she motioned him to hand her the groceries. "What I told Mona was that you were living on Wickaninnish now and that perhaps to earn your keep, you would make yourself available to help out when needed. I don't think that is too much to ask or expect. We are a collective on the island."

"Fair—okay. That's fair, I suppose. Sticking me with Aidan is not fair. Aidan needs a psychologist or a parole officer, not a fly-by-night kayak bum who hasn't taken the time to grow up himself. I can't help that I'm needed in Toronto now. Everything else is incidental to that. Family first," he added for emphasis, but even to him it sounded empty.

"Oh, I don't think so. Knowing Ninnish, he's probably got you over some barrel and you're not finding it very comfortable. Am I right?" She watched his eyes for the truth.

Except for the barrel, she was dead right. But he denied it. "No. You're wrong."

"No, I'm not," she insisted, shaking her head and looking up at him with her white hair in her eyes and mouth. "Listen, since you are here, I need a hand getting a drawer unstuck down below. Do you have a minute?"

He boarded the familiar white and blue boat without answering and ducked his head to enter the cabin. He hated it when people didn't take him seriously. Living in his grandfather's shadow, he had gotten that a lot. One of the first things he noticed below deck was a photograph of a younger Stephanie in a cheap frame that had been glued sloppily and slightly crooked to the wall with silicone. "That's Stephanie, isn't it?" Even though he knew of their mother-daughter relationship, he hadn't learned that from Dottie, but he was still surprised to have seen a photo of the crazed redhead—a little like seeing a ghost from a past that seemed longer ago than it really was.

"Uh-huh. You know Steph?"

"Briefly. Real briefly. She, uh, rescued me I guess, after you'd left me on that beach that turned out to be infested with bears. Remember that?"

"Oh, that. Infested? Really?" She exaggerated her concern, putting groceries inside cabinets. "There." She pointed to the stuck drawer.

He gave it a tug, but it was wedged tight. "Have you heard

from her yet?" He made idle chat to disguise the difficulty he was having with the drawer.

"Stephanie may well be my flesh and blood, but we've gone years at a time before without talking," she responded, with a defiant little laugh that stopped him cold.

"So, you haven't heard from her, then?" He was astonished. "I didn't know the two of you were estranged to that degree."

"Estranged is an odd term and you should probably accept that there is a lot you still don't know, greenhorn." Dottie handed him a large butcher knife—more of a cleaver. "Try this." Heritage accepted the weapon-looking-implement, and immediately suspected it had a history he'd rather not know about—a suspicion he tried not to reveal by keeping his enlarged eyes focused on the task of unsticking the drawer. "It's best you don't ask," Dottie volunteered, rather convincingly. He used the back of the thick blade to roughly tap the drawer face at the bottom and the top of each corner. This broke whatever adhesive goo had locked the seal, and when he tugged the drawer, it dropped open onto the linoleum floor of the galley, jostling the handgun and a handful of loose bullets inside.

"Whoa!" he gasped aloud.

"Relax, city boy. It was my husband's. I keep it around in case I encounter wildlife that has been hurt or suffering."

"But you didn't keep the husband around?" Heritage was fishing, having collected just enough information to be every bit as dangerous as her gun or cleaver. Brad Fraser had told him that his best friend's disappearance had been dubious and that he was certain Dottie Bard had everything to do with him vanishing.

"I lost my husband to a tragic fishing accident." It sounded to Heritage like a well-practiced line.

"You've used it then?" Heritage's hands were shaking as he tried to align the drawer back onto the rails of the cabinet. "The gun, I mean."

"Plenty," she blurted out. "Mother Nature—well, she can be a callous wench."

Heritage didn't want to let on that anything she said shocked him, but he couldn't figure out why she clearly wanted him to know the gun existed—other than maybe warning him she could fend for herself. "I came across a seal once, swimming frantically and lopsided in one direction, missing half of its belly thanks to an orca that wasn't coming back for seconds. I can't abide suffering." When she saw that Tage was still staring at the handgun, she added "It's a SIG Sauer semi-automatic, Model P225."

"If you say so," Heritage shut the drawer, acting disinterested, and stood back on his feet, still ducking his head to fit inside the cramped space. "Stephanie—I'd asked if you'd heard from her since she left?"

"Why the concern? Did you fuck her?"

"Pardon me?"

"I'm sorry if that was too direct. It's just that my daughter screws everybody. It would have been remarkable if you had been spared. So, did you have a sexual encounter with my daughter?"

"It's more like the other way around. She gave me a lift to Ahousaht and then split overnight. I was more stranded there than I was on the beach with the bears. If it hadn't been for François—" He cut himself short, having exacted his intended blow.

"Don't mention that man's name on my boat or anywhere in my presence. We are at war." She slammed a can of tuna on the countertop before closing her eyes, possibly to count to ten.

"War? I thought he was Steph—your daughter's boyfriend." Heritage wondered if he might be able to antagonize some useful information out of her. "I didn't know that at the time, of course, or I would have . . ." He trailed off, not sure what he would or wouldn't have done differently.

"Stephanie was only dating him to spite me, and none of my repeated warnings and not-so-subtle attempts to sabotage their relationship seemed to be working."

"I see. And by *sabotage* I suppose you mean you cast some wicked spell on François?" That unintended statement was out of his mouth before he could get grab it by the leash and jerk it back. She stopped what she was doing and fixed a laser stare on him that could have split an atom. "Oh yeah, I've been through your glass library, Dottie—just like you went through my books on this dock the day I arrived. I see what you're up to."

"No, you don't" she snapped back. "You can't see. You're not a seer. That bothers me about you."

"I'm not even sure what that's supposed to mean." Heritage didn't speak mystical or hippie or occult.

"If you were a seer, you would have seen to stay clear of my daughter and that hippie François. You would have seen a path of nothing but trouble where Mona's son is concerned. If you were a seer, you would have seen that I am your only true ally. But you don't see. You're too busy feeling." She sounded disgusted, like *feeling* was the dirtiest word she'd ever conjured. It was one of those criticisms he didn't mind hearing if it distinguished him from her. He didn't want to be like Dottie Bard. He barely knew her, but he knew that much. And she was right about him. He had several feelings about her.

"I don't know your history, Dottie, and I don't want to know. I just wanted to get along in this town but if that means you expected me to take on your enemies and your baggage to win your favour, well I'm just not that desperate for your kinship. I have a mind of my own, eyes of my own and yes, feelings that are just mine. I rely on these for my survival, whether you have any use for them or not." He took a breath to assess where that left her. "If you won't take Aidan off my hands, I'll ask Mason. My grandfather is dying. I'm returning to Toronto after this weekend, one way or the other." Everything seemed to him to be coming out of his mouth in a disjointed way but perhaps he'd made his point. Heritage didn't do confrontation well.

"Well." She gently stacked the tuna on the shelf and secured the cabinet door. "That's a real shame." She left the cabin for the deck and began fiddling with the outboard primer button. He followed her outside. "A seer would have realized that I have just outfitted my boat for an extended trip up the coast and away from the village, so, no, I can't take Aidan off your hands. Good luck with that, though." She half-waved, half-dismissed him as he stepped backward off the boat and onto the dock. "Say, do you suppose on your way out of our lives, you could untie my bow?"

If his guilt-complex hadn't been so thoroughly pummeled by the Aidan incident, she might have had a chance to finish him off. But there was nothing left to even bruise. He was desperately down for the count, and after the coming weekend, everyone would have to settle for a piece of the memory that was Tage Carter.

"Well, I guess this is good-bye, then?" He said. Her boat motor was loud and spitting puffs of white smoke on the surface of the water. "Bon fucking voyage," he tossed after her as she was pulling away, knowing she couldn't have heard a fighter jet over the sound of her boat motor.

Heritage bolted up the dock ramp as he had a tight schedule to keep if he was still to speak with François and race back to the lodge before Ninnish sacrificially threw himself from the loft, or perhaps the cliff for even grander dramatic effect. His calves took the brunt of the steady, three-block slope that rose from the water to the bakeshop, while his head, probably still half-suspended by wine and drugs, throbbed twice for every thud of his booted feet. He fingered the prescription container still in his pocket, not sure why he had carried it around with him all day. Its residual potency was more psychologically lethal to him than it ever had been when it was full of medicine. On the practical side, he just hoped he didn't drop dead on the sidewalk before he'd had a chance to tuck it away for safe keeping as evidence and proof.

Heritage spotted a native man jaywalking in a way that suggested he was heading straight for him and indeed, he was.

"Your last name's Carter, isn't it?"

Heritage didn't know why, but he tried to make a joke. "Depends on who's asking. I'm Tage." He offered his hand to the man while simultaneously realizing that this could be the start of the police take-down and apprehension of the accused child molester. His hand was rebuked so he put it back in his pocket.

The man—who wasn't an arresting officer—was wearing a nearly full-length, yellow, oilcloth slicker, plus gumboots and a rain hat—even though there wasn't a single cloud in the sky. The hat was tied under his prominent, clean-shaven square chin and his skin was smooth and brown—without wrinkles, which Heritage would note, applying his dead mother's life principles. He was shorter and a bit stockier than Heritage. His bottom lip was quivering as he gained the nerve to speak.

"I know who you are and where you come from. You are not welcome here. I don't want you on Wickaninnish Island."

"I'm sorry." Heritage took a step backward taking his hands out of his pockets in case he needed them. "And you would be—who?"

"Your grandfather," the man half-stuttered, "has been raping this rainforest. This has been the home of my people for more than one hundred centuries. You have no business here. Go home!" As he spoke, his temper rose in his face, a face Heritage thought might crack under the awkward pressure. "Go back, please, to where you came from. You are not welcome here."

He pushed past Heritage as he continued down the hill toward the dock, walking away with a slight hitch in his step. Heritage's heart beat faster than his breathing. He'd just been served notice—hastening the departure he needed to get more deliberately underway.

Heritage checked his wristwatch as he passed the Co-op realizing he needed to save his quick grocery shop for after his chat with François.

Rising from the table he'd taken next to the door, and looking around first, François rather tenuously hugged Heritage, pulling back quickly with that brown-toothed smile of his. Men apparently weren't normally huggers in that salt-calloused sea town, Heritage deducted. "You survived da Dragon Lady?" It was one of those questions that didn't require an answer beyond the raised eyebrows that accordioned Heritage's forehead.

"For some reason, you are not her favorite person in the village," Heritage said.

"More dan one reason for dat, I'm sure." François pushed his cheese bun to the middle of the table, suggesting they share it. "I ask too many question dat make her uncomfortable—plus I had sex wit her daughter, just to get closer to da trute—and still," he continued after swallowing a bit of cheese bun, "I have way more questions dan answers."

"Well, I had sex with her daughter once too, so she couldn't have been all that loyal to you anyway." Heritage felt this had been covered off before in earlier confessions, but he wanted to be clear. "Or really, she had sex with me, but we already talked about this, right? And you're cool with that?"

"Yeah, sure. Anyway, I tought so, as soon as you two showed up at da dock in Ahousaht, I could tell right away." François lowered the hand from his mouth briefly. The brown tooth making him self-conscious, Heritage figured, at the same time it made him exotically sexy. His smile was so perfectly contained, tacked to high cheekbones, snap-buttoned inside dimples that were there whether he smiled or not, and tethered by laugh lines to a y-shaped cleft in his chin that, had he been a movie actor, he could have visually covered roles that ranged from playing a James Bond villain to Jesus Christ, especially with his long, dark hair and redemptive green eyes. In fact, if it hadn't been for that off-colour tooth, and the almost comical Québécois accent, François made a decent doppelgänger for Christ Almighty and probably inspired his own share of Second Coming anxiety.

"You said you ask her too many questions. About what?"

"Her past. I don't tink some women like to be asked about der past."

"That goes for some men, too." Heritage said it a little too defensively.

"Maybe," was all François could say. "I asked her about my fadder today. Dat was da fight I tink you maybe saw as we were coming out of da Co-op."

"What about your father?" Heritage took his first nibble off the cheese bun.

"He's been missing since I was twelve, I tink, maybe eleven, I don't know." He crinkled up his face and reached into his back pocket to extract a black leather billfold which Heritage now recognized as having belonged to Marcel. "Da last time I heard from him was dis post card from Kamchatka—you know, dat place across the ocean from here, in Russia." He handed the folded and worn card to Heritage for his inspection. Heritage took the postcard but his gaze could not be pried from the wallet.

"Wow. I have to say that does look almost exactly like Marcel's billfold." Heritage couldn't help but comment before scanning the post card, and this made his friend's normally chipper face fall into a narrowed-eye, bit-lip sadness, brown tooth front and off-centre. "This reminds me that I wanted to ask you about the wallet I found, the one that you said belonged to you, but that Marcel had been carrying. Do you know why Marcel had the empty wrapper of a condom tucked inside?"

François blushed and started to respond but stopped himself. He and Heritage locked eyes, green to hazel, and something in that gaze compelled him to come out with it. "Dat wrapper is from da rubber I used to fuck him . . . it was his first time and I tink he wanted to remember dat always." François eyes watered and Heritage reached his hand beyond the plate with the split-in-half cheese bun and squeezed François' balled up fist. François sniffed the runny snot back into his nose and cleared his throat, stretching his torso back in the chair.

Heritage waited a minute then picked up the postcard,

flipping it over to read the backside. "I'm afraid my French isn't what it should be."

François took the card back. "It says, *La Cathédrale Saint Basile-le-Bienheureux de Moscou dans la nuit*. It basically says I have been to St. Basil's Cathedral at da Kremlin. I will return to Canada on a Russian fishing troller to work off da coast of Vancouver Island for some month. Perhaps one day you will be old enough to come to da end of dat road der and wave to me on my boat. I will always be waving back at you, son. With love from your fadder—Lucien Pelletier."

"Is that your last name?" Heritage suddenly realized he hadn't known that.

"No. My last name is Lévesque, after my mother's second husband." He folded the postcard in half twice along the creased lines and tucked it inside the billfold that really belonged to Marcel.

Heritage grabbed the wallet from his hands. "Let me see your driver's license. I want to see how that last name is spelled."

"Eh!" François made an attempt to grab it back, but Heritage moved it out of his reach. Heritage opened the billfold and recognized the border of a British Columbia driver's license, liberating it from the split-pockets in the leather. Heritage recognized a CIBC bank card and a long-distance calling card. And when he removed the driver's license, there was a powdery dried-out condom flattened behind it—long out of its wrapper.

Heritage's hands began to visibly tremble as he realized what he was looking at. "I have so many questions for you right now."

"Here's da ting," François started in, before clearing his throat again and leaning in to whisper. "Marcel and I were having dis relationship dat nobody knew not'ing about. I already told you dis but, I was in love wit' him, but he didn't tink he was wired dat way. I knew he was having sex wit da lady from da library—and wit Stephanie, too, I was sure dey had been sleeping togedder. Da first time, Marcel and me, we uh, you know, make love, I told him he should use dis condom. So he opened da package but den he say, I trust you, François. Save dis, he tell me, for somebody you don't trust." François paused. A tear fell to his cheek but was wiped away instantly. "Now, you know da whole story. What I said before, dat I used a condom for Marcel's first time—it wasn't da trute. We had unprotected sex. He kept da condom wrapper in his wallet, I kept da unused condom in mine, but when you put da two togedder, den you know our secret."

"That's beautiful," Heritage said. But he was thinking a hundred different things at once.

François was biting his lower lip again. "Dis town is nasty wit rumours, you know? Someting like dis gets out and it destroys people. I kept dis for me because I wanted someting from Marcel. I have notting. Der was no evidence of our relationship. We had to be careful about dat. I also didn't want da librarian to find out dat Marcel was screwing around wit Stephanie—and well, with me, mostly because dat library lady—she was in love wit Marcel too. And she has it worse dan me, cause she's pregnant."

"Marcel's?" Heritage asked more with his face than with words.

"Tink so." François wiped another escaping tear with the back of his hand. Heritage could see how deeply wounded his hot springs buddy was grieving this loss. From habit, Heritage looked at his wristwatch, simultaneously panicked by the amount of time that had elapsed since leaving Aidan alone at The Headlands. Ninnish quite possibly had burned down the whole place already—but with François' revelation, there was just no way he could stand up and leave now.

"You mean the other red-headed woman named Gillian, right?"

"Yep. Dat's her."

Heritage reached for what was left of the cheese bun, but his hand kept traveling to quickly and discretely pat François' hand again. He needed to connect with him physically in that moment—to communicate that he understood, and that he had feelings for him, too. That was a lot of messaging to fit into one quick hand pat. François' face indicated that he'd understood but needed a moment to compose himself.

The windows of the octagonal seating area at the SunRyes Bakeshop were probably always this steamed up by the ovens, the side-by-side coffee machines, and the humidity escaping the regularly rain-wet clothes of the chatting patrons inside. That reminded Heritage of the native man in full rain gear who had just confronted him on the street, in the middle of a sunny day, and in that moment, Heritage thought to glance outside and was astonished to see that storm clouds had moved in. The blue sky had been upstaged up by a menacing dark grey curtain. That inhospitable man had been wrong about Heritage's intentions there, but he was bang-on right about the weather.

Heritage continued. "I had hoped we would have had time to hang out like this together, you know, but these past two weeks have been crazy stupid. I didn't know how to reach you, and, of course, at the time, I had no idea you were connected to Marcel." Heritage paused. "I already told you I was there, on Wick, the night he died. I radioed the coast guard from Lyle Hudson's cabin, but the storm was too bad and they didn't get there in time. I am so sorry."

François pulled his hair back from his face. "I will never know why he was out in dat storm at dat time of da night. I have been going crazy in my head trying to figure dat out."

Heritage had more puzzle pieces than François realized but didn't want to overload the moment so kept the additional information about Marcel's attendance at Lyle's dance and drug party to himself. He was torn between his desire to be compassionate and his obligation to say goodbye. He wasn't needed or welcome in Clayoquot Sound now. It wasn't safe for him to make a go of things. Not on Wickaninnish Island, and not, he was really sad to accept, with François. The confrontation with the native fellow on the street had revealed to him that secrets didn't stay secret for long. His identity would get out—apparently already had. He thought to ask François if he knew who the rain-geared native man was, but decided it didn't matter, since he wasn't staying.

"Can I ask you someting?" François leaned over the table.

"Of course." Heritage smiled in a way that François took as flirtation and so he smiled back with those dark green Messiah eyes of his. Under his breath, behind his teeth, and without moving his lips, Heritage was thinking, *Fuck.*

"What do you dream about at night?"

"What do I dream about?" Heritage repeated the question for no other reason but to buy time while he rooted around for an answer. He knew that in that crowded dining space, the potential for eavesdropping was acute—not that he was about to disclose a particularly steamy sex dream, though he had had plenty of those since meeting François. "If I am being honest, I haven't been sleeping much. I am supposed to be babysitting Mona's kid, Aidan, but I am not doing a very good job of that either. What do I dream about? I guess I dream about falling in love and building a house in the rainforest at the edge of a cliff overlooking the ocean."

He stopped just short of describing his dream man to share it with—terrified to think he might be sitting across from him at the very moment he'd decided to walk away from this place.

"What do *you* dream about, François?" Heritage cupped his chin in his hands with his elbows on the table, and knew he probably looked like a smitten cheerleader in the presence of the football team captain.

"I used to dream of finding my fadder, you know." François paused to decipher the slight but detectable disappointment in the face of his companion sitting on the other side of the table from him, and then added, "Lately, I dream about you."

Heritage blushed, and after a considerable stare, finally blinked and relinquished a smile. "I can't decide if you are an angel or the devil! So, you have traveled to the end of the road to wave at your father's boat, but you haven't seen him? What did Dottie Bard know about him?"

"Dat's just it. She said she didn't know anyting about him, didn't know who he was. And den she just got mad, impatient with me for asking, you know?"

"Like she was hiding something?" Heritage asked, intrigued.

"Oh, she knows," François said. "She knows my fadder. I am sure of dis." He pushed the last bite of the cheese bun toward Tage, who seemed determined to finish it piece by piece. "And da lady here, at da bakery. She knows, too. My fadder, he was here. I don't know what happened to him, but he was here."

Heritage suddenly recognized the music wafting over the din of a dozen conversations, and wondered if it had been playing all along. He swallowed the last of the bun and washed it down with a gulp from François' coffee. "Whoa! That's a lot of sugar! And your mother?"

"She lives in a place called St. Boniface in da Red River Valley of Manitoba. She's Métis—a direct descendent of Louis Riel."

"Really?"

"My fadder never married her, as she was underage. I barely know her myself." Heritage raised an eyebrow. "I was sent to an orphanage in Montréal. I don't even remember da name. And later to a public, all-boys' school named Urgel Archambeault. After I turned twenty-four, I was told my mudder's identity, and so I traveled to meet her. She had her own family by den. I don't interfere."

"But she told you about your father."

"Yes. And gave me dis postcard he'd sent to me from his travels. I've been looking for him off and on for da past four years."

"Do you have a picture of him?" Heritage believed he could now make out some of the Métis features, the cheekbones and great round eyes set wide apart. It made him look even more exotic than before. Louis Riel? The only man ever hanged by the government on Canadian soil, he recalled from history lessons. Now that was something, he thought as he glanced again at his watch. Ninnish had been left unattended for one hour exactly. Heritage thought he might push that another thirty minutes, but knew he didn't dare go beyond that. Plus, he hadn't been grocery shopping yet—he'd have to wrap things up with François or drag him along to the grocery store.

"I had hoped Dottie Bard might have an old picture of my fadder, as I don't know what he looked like. My mudder's parents destroyed everyting but her memory when dey discovered she was pregnant." François looked up and acknowledged another fisherman that he knew, gesturing with his chin and smiling with his eyes.

Heritage lowered his voice to a whisper. "So why do you think Dottie Bard holds the answers to your father's disappearance, way out here on the other side of the country?"

"I heard a rumor once dat in da past she was, uh . . . how should I say dis? *Une filles da rue* for da fishermen on da foreign boats. Supposed to be dis is where her money came from—and Stephanie too, many years later."

"You mean a prostitute? Stephanie told you this?"

"Yes. Stephanie didn't know her fadder, same as me. So today I asked Dottie Bard if she ever heard of my fadder. She lied to me."

"Interesting. Why would Dottie deny that, I wonder?" A moment passed. "She has something to hide," the two men said, practically in unison. Heritage thought about that some more and added, "Oh, she has plenty to hide. I can tell that by the lines on her face."

"What can you tell by da lines on my face?" François said, grinning.

Heritage narrowed his eyes to study him. "Hmm, I can tell that I've sat here too long admiring you, and now I have to get back." He slowly stood, waiting to be coaxed back down. Instead, François stood with him and the two left the SunRyes Bakeshop together. As they walked past the bank and across Campbell Street, Heritage recalled the native man that had accosted him there.

"Say, do you know an older native man who maybe lives on Wickaninnish Island? Says his ancestors have been here ten thousand years?"

François gave Heritage a look. "Dey all say dat." He laughed.

"But der's only one native guy on Wick and he isn't from here. I tink he is from Ontario."

The two waited for a beat-up white pickup truck to clear the intersection before crossing. "What do you know about him?" Heritage asked.

"Not much. He is an environmentalist. Lives off da land with his wife and four kids. His oldest boy is Matt Greene, he's da captain of da coast guard station here. I know more about him dan his Dad."

"Ah, okay," Heritage made the connection. "I met Matt. He came to Lyle's cabin the night Marcel, uh, well . . ." He stopped short. He didn't want to leave François on a sad note.

"Matt's okay. A bit full of himself, like his Dad. Walks around here like he owns Clayoquot Sound. Wanted to be an RCMP Mountie but couldn't pass the qualification tests cause he was homeschooled by his crazy Mudder. So he went into da coast guard instead."

"But they aren't local natives then?"

"Nah. Ojibwa, I'm pretty sure. Transplanted."

Heritage stopped and said, "I'm here," pointing to the green Cherokee with the Headlands Lodge logo and name on the two door panels.

François quickly looked around, then planted a quick kiss on Heritage's mouth. "I like your dream," he told him. "Be nice to be part of dat."

When the pair reluctantly parted company a minute later, Heritage ducked into the grocery store for a ten-minute power shop. He had not told François goodbye. He hadn't mentioned anything about having to leave for Toronto—that he had been thinking he might not return to Clayoquot Sound. Most pressing for him, he hadn't said a word about the predicament he faced with Ninnish. His formerly full and troubling slate had been erased mostly clean the second François placed his chalk mark in the column next to Heritage's rainforest cliff-house dream.

Driving back to the Headlands, at first tapping his hands on the steering wheel to the radio before clenching them into a crippling jumble of white knuckles as he neared the lodge, Heritage knew almost instantly that he would help François find out what happened to his father, and that his allegiance probably had more to do with bringing down Dottie Bard than with arranging his new boyfriend's family reunion. He would first have to neutralize the threat that Ninnish posed, though. The question wasn't so much how Ninnish planned to assassinate what was left of his good character as it was when. Heritage decided he would give it a day or two more for the nasty chapter with the teenager to resolve itself, while letting Ninnish think he was returning to Toronto for good, because he wasn't cut out for small-town life in the rainforest. At least one of those two components had a good chance of proving true. He could certainly stay out of sight at the Headlands for a week, making the kid think he was gone. Once the extortionist realized the futility of trying to blackmail someone who had already left, he would abandon his obsession and move on to terrorizing somebody else—the poor soul.

Heritage pulled into the manager's parking spot next to the main lodge, relieved to see the place still standing. He returned the jeep keys inside, though Stu Solberg had already told him he didn't really use the lodge vehicle since everything he needed was delivered two or three times a week. Heritage performed a cursory check on the staff in the kitchen before walking through the woods to his new cottage, embracing a new defiance as he prepared to confront the boy. He glanced high into the giant trees and took in two lungs full of the sweet-smelling cedar decay. He wasn't running away from this, he decided silently. He would plant his stubborn flag in the ground to claim this utopia for himself—and maybe for François too.

While looking into the towering canopy he missed the tree root that sent him tumbling horizontally into the salal off the edge of the path on the downslope side of the steep hill. He skidded dramatically to a stop at the base of a large hemlock with its swirling bark pattern that had defied gravity by growing on the very edge of the cliff above the rocks and surf below. Groceries tumbled out of the trio of bulging plastic bags and scattered down the slope to create an impromptu Easter egg hunt among the ferns and salal cover. Heritage used a tree trunk to right himself, but he had badly twisted his left ankle. He raised a fist to curse the blasted rainforest and his ongoing love-hate relationship with it, and vowed he would overcome this setback too. He gingerly placed his weight on his foot, then stepped in each direction, as though he were negotiating his way out of a minefield that had been booby-trapped in every direction. The metaphor summed up his first seventeen Clayoquot days and nights.

Heritage heard the television before he limped into the cottage to find Ninnish lounging on the first level in Heritage's shorts and green OSU sweatshirt, splayed out on the southwestern-styled sofa like he'd been poured out there in liquid form to re-solidify from slimy amoeba into teenager again. The ladder to the loft was upright and leaning against the second floor.

"Oh, good, finally. I am starving!" said Aidan, with no explanation for why or how he was on the main floor. On second examination, Heritage realized now that the loft was directly above the queen size bed that made a logical landing pad below for a teen not to be caged or easily defeated.

Heritage hobbled into the room, struggling with the torn bags. "I'm afraid half the groceries are scattered down the hill below here. I just took a tumble and twisted my ankle pretty bad." With that, sweet, kind Aidan jumped off the couch and came to his rescue. Heritage never knew which Aidan he was going to get but knew not to trust any version since it could mutate in a blink. This Aidan, who was maybe just ten or twelve centimetres shorter than Heritage, worked his head and shoulder under the adult's armpit and helped him hop to the sofa. Aidan next asked which ankle before removing both hiking boots and socks, taking extra care with the left foot.

"Oh, yeah, ya did," Doctor Aidan confirmed with one look at the redness and swelling. "Let me get you some ice."

"I'm more concerned about the groceries down the hill. Can you take a quick look before the ravens do? I bought a half dozen Coffee Crisps for you, but only managed to retrieve one of them."

"Gross!" Aidan made a face. "Coffee in a candy bar? That's child abuse."

Heritage held his tongue thinking the teen's comment poignant given the adult abuse he'd recently been subjected to by the child, but yes, he could see that he'd misjudged the teen's tastes as not quite adult yet. Suddenly the fitter and more agile of the two and not at all appearing to be suffering from his possibly fabricated bum issue, Aidan bounded out the cabin door and disappeared into the woods below the path. Heritage propped a sofa pillow under his foot to elevate the ankle. When Aidan had been gone for ten minutes, Heritage began to think he'd stupidly just helped his prisoner escape. This daydream morphed into the relief he would feel if the kid had decided to run away—like, far away, choosing this moment to leave town to find his way in the world.

Heritage heard a short burst of clicks and beeps, coming from the loft. The sounds became a voice.

"Aidan . . . you out there? Aidan! It's Rowan, over."

Forgetting his ankle, Heritage stood too quickly and the rush of pain that resulted nearly knocked him back down. He hopped the short distance and pulled himself up the ladder to the loft where he saw Aidan's open backpack on the mattress there, the antenna of a play walkie-talkie sticking out of the opening. Heritage pounced on it, depressed the voice transmit button, then covered his mouth with the other hand, said "Yeah, what's up?" Then he thought to add, "Over."

Rowan bought the disguise and answered right back. "You on the island right now?"

"No," Heritage muffle-responded.

"K," Rowan replied, then paused before continuing. Heritage was trying to think of something to say that might provoke the accomplice to spill the beans about the Polaroids. The radio was silent and Heritage knew that Aidan was going to barrel through the door any second and catch him in the loft going through his things. He could feel sweat forming on his forehead as he imagined the ticking sounds coming from the time bomb he was holding in his hands. "You take care of the pictures?" Heritage asked in his best teenage voice, thinking for sure he'd just flubbed it, before descending the ladder to resume his elevated ankle repose.

He waited just shy of forever and then the radio crackled: "Yep. In the skull box like you said. Over."

BY A THREAD

"Now, tell me again. You have paddling experience, right?" Heritage was badly limping on account of his ankle and shouting back into the wind as Ninnish followed, holding the other end of the green canoe, as they made their way back down the short beach to the spot where Heritage's kayak was already lined up and ready to launch.

"I told you yes before." Aidan was unapologetically curt, having woken up on the wrong side of the loft after the previous evening had turned sour. Heritage knew it was only a matter of time before Aidan's nursing turned from *Nightingale* to *Ratched* again, but they did manage nearly two hours of civility, watching TV and eating mostly junk food together. It was predictably short-lived and Wicked Ninnish wasted no time barging back onstage once Heritage refused to let him share his bed and sent him fuming up to the loft. There, the possessed teen's head nearly started spinning and puking green vomit when he discovered from his loft perch that Heritage had shaved off his body hair. He had shouted down to him with so much rage, that Heritage had felt the spittle hit his face, saying something to the effect that he had no interest being with a teenager and demanding to know why Heritage had shaved off the hair that had made him such a sexy adult. He was crinkled right out of shape that morning and dying to have Tage ask him why—but Tage was not about to give him that satisfaction. They hadn't said more than a dozen words to each other after the blow-up over sleeping arrangements and manscaping. But Heritage was encouraged to have confirmation that the teen didn't find him as enticing without his fur. That should fix him, he'd thought foolishly.

With Rye Family canoe that was twice as wide as Heritage's sleek kayak, lined up parallel to his boat, Heritage surveyed the water. Ninnish shoved his backpack of schoolbooks and dirty underwear under the front seat of the canoe, pulled it and then pushed the nose into the water where the surf lapped at the protected sands. He climbed in the back of the canoe and clenched the paddle waiting impatiently for Heritage to finish fussing with his array of bungees, a new compass, dry bags, and accessories. Heritage stepped into his spray skirt and donned a life jacket. Ninnish had refused to zip his up, because he said it stunk of mildew. Heritage didn't bother arguing because he knew it was true, from the moment he liberated it from the nail sticking out of the wall of the equipment shed where the boats had been secured. At this point, Heritage didn't care if the life jacket smelled or even if it had any flotational properties left to it.

The flat all-sand shelf of Middle Beach below and just to the north of the lodge was a private—and in Heritage's experience, made for a usually simple—beach to launch from or land on, as it was mostly protected from the open ocean by Wickaninnish Island across the kilometre-and-a-half-wide channel.

"Okay, Ninnish. The wind is going to be pushing against us

and there's likely to be some pretty intense chop in the middle. We stay together. Understood?"

Ninnish nodded, but then struck out immediately on his own. Heritage, who was still fiddling with his spray skirt and would have preferred to lollygag on the beach reading the water, testing the wind with a wet finger, and running through his two-column checklists, had to take a few safety shortcuts to catch up to the kid. As they left the pocket and passed the headland, the winds and tide began pushing them north toward town. It had rained through the night, and Heritage hoped for a weather break, but a fairly steady rain started out of nowhere, and an uneasy feeling found its way inside all his protective gear. In the next seconds, the elongated expanse of Wickaninnish Island was erased from sight like a bleep on a radar screen that had just gone dead. The foghorn at the lighthouse on Lennard Island blared. *Fuck me, not again!* Heritage was cursing to himself.

The acquisition of the compass was so recent—a find from the lost-and-found box behind the front desk at the Headlands—that Heritage had forgotten to record their starting position before paddling into the void. He straightened his back and assumed perfect textbook paddling posture—which was code for fear and signaled he was nervous. Heritage power-paddled to get within a dozen feet of his partner's boat and yelled. "You okay?"

Ninnish nodded without looking away from what he assumed was still straight ahead. Without Wickaninnish as a landmark, they could have been paddling in figure eight formations for all they knew. They shoveled through the chop another ten minutes and found themselves in swells so steep they often disappeared from each other's view. Heritage knew it was no longer wise to turn back—they'd been on the water too long and had to be more than halfway across. As long as Aidan was keeping water from spilling into the open canoe, they could do this, he felt. They kept paddling, waiting for a break in the rain or a parting of the mist curtains. Heritage kept the foghorn on his left side and paddled stronger on his right to veer west and north. He tapped the compass face.

The needle was stuck. In fact, the compass was broken—likely the reason it had been discarded.

Wickaninnish was such a long island, even if they overshot their preferred landing site at Mona's cabin, it would be an easy paddle back along the shore. If they had become somehow disoriented southward in the near zero visibility, and if the tide were going out, it was conceivable they could overshoot Wickaninnish and the adjacent Echachis Island without even knowing it. It would be open ocean beyond those safety barriers, and with sea conditions wholly different from what they were experiencing in the channel.

Heritage watched Ninnish closely. His strokes seemed strong, deliberate. He couldn't see his eyes beneath the brim of his baseball cap but could guess Ninnish didn't know fear enough to show it. After another few minutes and with his nose running, Heritage felt they had to be nearing the far side. The Pacific barreled into and out of the sound through Templar Channel—it was usually in the middle of it that Heritage had experienced a maximum of animation during his daily commutes back and forth to the lodge. He had come to terms with the notion that the Tla-o-qui-aht and pirate poltergeists from the *Tonquin* battle must be haunting the waters in that stretch for all eternity, since only once had he found the water in the middle of the channel calm. If the pair was more than halfway across—that was good.

"We gotta be almost there," he hollered encouragingly to Ninnish—who didn't respond and actually appeared for the first time to be flagging.

Just then, a glimpse of dark land mass flashed between the sheets of rain and cloud. They were on target! Heritage's kayak passed Ninnish and the stronger paddler slacked some to compensate. "Let's keep going, bud," he coached. He hadn't used that term since high school. *Bud?* Where had that even come from?

A swell rose like a wall between them and there was a slap

like a paddle hitting the water sideways. Heritage pivoted to look behind him, nearly losing his balance. "Fuck!" he exclaimed.

The kid had gone over and he hadn't rolled back out of it. Ninnish was in the water, the canoe upside down. Heritage had never experienced a successful roll in the wild himself, having done it a couple times in the shallow end at the Vancouver Aquatics Center, in order to pass his kayak paddling certification course. But that was with a kayak and a spray skirt. There were ways you could right yourself in a proper kayak, he knew, but in that open washtub of a contraption that Ninnish had been paddling, a body was just contents to be dumped into the sea, like refuse. Heritage frantically reversed his paddling to reach the upturned and badly dented underside of the green canoe. He screamed into the wind and rain for Aidan to surface on his command as he rode the swells, mindful that he wasn't completely out of the main channel's rollercoaster yet.

"Aidan! *Aidan!*"

The water was just as cold as Ninnish thought it would be. He'd been in the ocean—well, pretty much wet and waterlogged—his whole life. He was mostly impervious, he figured. He had anticipated the lung-gasping shock of it for the past six hours since coming up with the plan to get back at Tage for the three things that had infuriated him the most lately—threatening to leave him for Toronto, refusing his request to sleep in the same bed, and discovering (when Tage had emerged from the washroom) that he'd shaved off all his body hair. Why in the hell had he done that?

Aidan could hear his name and the panic behind the shouting, which was exactly what he had wanted to provoke—concern and compassion—proof that Tage cared for him, liked him a little, and maybe could one day love him.

What surprised him most was how dark things were under the aluminum canoe where he was hanging onto the crossbar that spanned the middle section. He could make out strobes of daylight when waves lifted the bow or stern out of the water, but with the sun veiled by clouds, it wasn't much. He'd slipped out of the canoe as it rolled over, letting go of the paddle but holding onto the lip of the canoe until his wrist twisted and he had to break his grip. His unfastened lifejacket had easily slipped from his shoulders and had risen to the surface by design. It had been a momentary struggle to come back up under the canoe instead of somewhere alongside it or worse—separated from it altogether. He'd bumped his head with a solid thwack as the upturned boat caught air on one end, just as a swell slammed it back down on the other. Throughout his morning planning, he knew he couldn't afford to lose physical or visual contact with the canoe. He also knew he needed to time his moment when they were more than three-quarters of the way there, so he could swim the rest of the way to the island if Tage, for some reason, was unable to rescue him. Holding onto the cross bar, with his head poked into the pocket of air trapped inside the canoe, he was able to extend the illusion of his apparent time beneath the surface until Tage was good and panicked. That time should have passed by now. He was ready for his superhero rescue.

Heritage was hoarse by the time he paddled up next to the hideous hull of the upside-down wide boat. Only one image from his entire life could compare to this terror that spiked him in the eyes like a sharpened alder stake. That had, of course, been the indelible, brain-branded memory of discovering his dead parents upstairs in their blood-splattered bedroom after they'd failed to pick him up at Pearson Airport that Christmas Eve. They had been dead, of course—days dead. He had arrived much too late to save them. But Aidan—troubled, wicked Ninnish, if he could find him, could still be saved. It had only been a minute or two. He drummed the bottom of the upturned canoe with his paddle and continued to scream out his name, as he scanned the surrounding water for any flash of the kid's red life- "FUCK!" There it was, about five metres away—the red lifejacket without a teenager's body in it. The longer he yelled and the more time that passed, the less he could hold his optimism, and the faster he burned through his adrenaline.

He braced his paddle against the lip of the canoe, extending it flat onto the constantly changing surface of the water like a training wheel. With his other hand he reached down to grab anything he could touch. Just before he and the capsized boat drifted into calmer waters, one last swell passed beneath him, causing his balance to teeter. The sensation that he was going over intensified. In that tipsy second, he gasped, stretching his lungs full of air until his chest pained him. He steadied himself, then let the air out before plunging his free hand back into the water. That time he caught the rim of the canoe, and with a tug beyond his normal strength, he flipped it right side up.

Ninnish was not with his boat. His backpack, all contents of the boat, including the paddle, had been emptied and were gone.

For a moment, Heritage couldn't think what to do next. His eyes darted over the surface of the water and strained to see into it, but as more and more time elapsed, a very dark reality began to sink in. It had been four, maybe five minutes by now. Heritage realized in the weight of that grim reckoning, that Ninnish might have perished. Perhaps that damned labyrinth had heard his contrition and was making good on a promise to restore tranquility and peace to his life, he thought guiltily. The muscles in his shoulders suddenly relaxed a little. With Ninnish gone, in the freakiest of accidents, Heritage could stay put in Clayoquot

Sound, pursue whatever developed with François and never worry about some psychotic teen holding him hostage again.

He took air back into his lungs and began to formulate how he would report this to the authorities. He looked toward Wickaninnish Island, which had completely reappeared through the barely drizzling rain now. He was surprised to see it much closer than he expected. He would continue on to Wickaninnish, and radio the coast guard from Mona's cabin. That would give him time to get his story straight. He reached toward his forward hatch for some rope—and heard and felt a thud. Simultaneously he spotted the green OSU sweatshirt bobbing face down, immediately off his port side, the one place he hadn't looked.

"Jesus!" he exclaimed aloud, jeopardizing his balance all over again as he struggled to get a grasp on the hood of the sweatshirt. "Jesus!" he repeated, his heart trying to bust out of his ribcage. It had been so much neater ten seconds earlier, when he thought he could just paddle away, leaving the body at the bottom of the channel with the spoils of the *Tonquin*, never to be recovered. Now things were complicated again. Now there would be an autopsy or an inquest, and it would probably be discovered, upon examination of the child's injured bum, that he'd had anal intercourse within twenty-four hours of his death. And when the hair fibers or the semen results happened to match the man who had recovered the body, the authorities would be handed their lucky break in what they would quickly proclaim an open-shut homicide case.

No, he decided, without benefit of a clear, calm, or rational mind. Things all around would be better for him without the body. He was shocked to even be thinking this way, but over the past forty-eight hours he had been more scared than at any other point in his life.

He secured his paddle under a shoelace of bungees on the front deck of his boat. All he could think was that he had to get François' sweatshirt off Ninnish and let the ocean do the erasing for him. He'd tried to get the teenager out of the sweatshirt last night, but that and everything else had been a losing battle from the first skirmish. Heritage was sick and tired of losing. Holding onto the canoe for leverage, he reached again for the hood and tried to haul the water-weighted body onto his kayak. He had to suddenly correct his balance as Ninnish forced his kayak to roll over to the left. He scooted his butt and legs right to pull the boat back down, but his sprained ankle couldn't take the pressure, as he tried to jerk the body further out of the water. Heritage misjudged his strength, and the dead boy's head slammed against the side of the very boat that had failed him. The smack was brutal—like a kettledrum in its thudding resonance. Heritage felt genuinely bad for the first time since the accident had occurred. He rolled Ninnish toward him and water streamed out of his almost angel-ic-looking mouth to pool on top of Heritage's still-taut spray skirt. The boy's blue eyes were open, and his long eyelashes were moist-ened together, appearing darker and no longer blonde.

The young man had never looked more still and innocent to him. Heritage could see stubble where Ninnish had been shaving his fuzz. The temptation to touch his paper-white face—to once again capture the attention of those almost alien blue eyes—strangely consumed him. Almost involuntarily, he hinged at his waist and lowered his face toward him, until their lips brushed slightly. How perfectly natural that seemed. When Ninnish wasn't spouting off, actively defying him or acting like, well, a teenager—when he was more like dead—he actually looked like a young man to whom Heritage might have been attracted under different circumstances.

Instead, he was a dead boy with very dead secrets.

When Aidan sensed the canoe being lifted off him, he seized his nerves, grabbed a breath and went under. Ducking, then crawling hand over hand beneath Heritage's slim kayak until he reached its rudder, he surfaced quietly near the kayak's stern on the port-side. He silently sucked in another breath, his hand still gripping the black metal rudder, before posing with his face down in the water, for full heart-stopping suspense. The same fifteen-year-old heart that felt as though it might have stopped when he had first hit the frigid water had since slowed to barely keeping a discern-able rhythm. He was entering the trouble zone. His circulation no longer bothered making the trip to his extremities which were turning all tingly. His quick sips of oxygen were playing havoc with his brain. His muscles began shutting down. He soon couldn't kick his legs or tread water with his arms, but he kept a hand on the kayak's rudder for reference. The lifejacket would have kept him on the surface—kept him from slipping under until the prank was finished. But he'd let that go.

Ninnish hadn't factored on being in the water that long, and though his body was probably slipping into hypothermic shock, he could sense that he was still breathing—that he was still alive, still pretending to be drowned—until his head thwacked against the boat, knocking him clean unconscious. He didn't know where his brain had gone next—but it was gone for several minutes. When his focus returned, he could see and feel Tage moving above him, struggling to get the sweatshirt off his shoulders. He had watched as Tage's face came very close to his own, but he couldn't speak, and he couldn't let him know he needed help. *Did* he need help? It was peaceful lying there, not feeling anything, not having to do so much as blink. He could see that Tage had propped him up—felt some rough tugs as the sweatshirt he was wearing was being pulled off for some reason he didn't understand. That was when Tage's face came so close to his that it blurred.

For one or two seconds he felt weightless, unattached to everything—but that passed in a splash. Why was he back in the water? His body revved to life, in coughing spasms and flailing limbs. The water was freezing now, and he could feel it. That wasn't his plan. He tried to scream but instead gulped seawater.

Heritage was paralyzed. Not one motor response seemed useful to him in that moment of reality-flipping surprise. His eyes were dispatching live images to a brain not at all prepared to interpret them. His breath was trapped in his windpipe, unable to reach his lungs or leave his gaping mouth. In his panic, he abandoned his newly thought-out scheme. He couldn't stick to it.

His hand, dispatched by reflex, grabbed the choking kid's wrist, and jerked the body back onto his kayak with a pull that nearly dislocated both their shoulders. Ninnish was wriggling, and his fighting resistance nearly defied his rescuer. The boy was not nearly as manageable as he had been before. The instability of the kayak and Heritage's exhaustion threatened his own safety now, too. Heritage knew it was imperative for him to stay in his boat if he was to be any use to either of them and prevent this from becoming a double tragedy. The muscles in his arm and fingers gave out and the boy slipped back into the sea. Without a life jacket and without energy or will, Ninnish surrendered and began to sink.

In that instant, it came to a death-or-life choice for Heritage. But it was no choice at all. He wasn't *that* monster. Heritage could not sacrifice the boy, even though the thought of holding him under with the edge of his paddle had rattled the more primal and vindictive lobe of his hypothalamus. With the aluminum pole and one end of his paddle wedged under his left underarm, and the other paddle blade hooking under one of the riveted seats of the canoe, Heritage fashioned an outrigger giving himself a steadier and wider platform. In the next movement, Heritage's right hand plunged into the water like a cormorant to grab for the back of the boy's sinking white neck, barely visible beneath the grey slate surface and fading by the second and centimetre. He made contact and clutching him there by the scruff like you would a puppy, Heritage one-handed the boy back to the surface bringing his head above the water between the two boats. Ninnish was unresponsive. Heritage needed to figure out a way to get him back onto the deck of his kayak so he could try to pound the water out of his lungs, but before he could work something out, his powerful shoulders and long arms had already accomplished the task. The teenager's upper body landed roughly but more squarely over the skirted cockpit of Heritage's kayak this time, and Heritage quickly maneuvered to distribute their combined weight so they didn't tip over. Then by grabbing the waist of Aidan's jeans, Heritage craned the boy's midsection and legs out of the water and pushed his feet over his paddle and into the canoe so that his body laid crosswise on the two boats. He forcefully turned the lifeless boy on his side toward his own torso and began thumping him violently on the back with an open hand. After several thuds, each harder than the last, Ninnish miraculously began to choke up water that pooled on the top of the spray skirt.

The beautiful boy's wet eyelashes fluttered, and his eyes rolled back into place. Heritage was as elated as he was exhausted. He accepted that his emotion came from someplace where he had no control. Tears began tumbling out of his hazel eyes to fall on Aidan's face. But in the next minutes, Ninnish turned hypothermic. His lips turned as blue-gray as his eyes, and his body began to tremble, then quake in convulsions he couldn't control. Heritage hinged at the waist and tried to warm and pin the shakes out of him with his upper body, rubbing the kid's head and face rapidly to generate heat. But this made them unstable. It was impossible to properly hold him—to bring his body temperature up without upsetting the kayaks. Heritage realized he could just as easily lose him now, out of the water, as he might have minutes ago beneath it.

"Aidan, listen to me. Can you hear me?" The child gave no indication he could. "We need to get you warmed up and to the island. You're going to make it, you little shit!"

He repeated the pep talk over and over again while he worked. He took off his own lifejacket and then his windbreaker. Ninnish was acting as a brace between the two boats. They were floating together into calmer waters and when Heritage looked for his bearings, they had drifted nearer the shore than he'd realized. Heritage threaded his light jacket over the teen's head and torso, not bothering with the arms. He then maneuvered him into his own, slightly larger lifejacket, securing it as tightly as he could by the straps—like a straightjacket that would secure him if there were further struggle. He tugged the hood of the jacket over the crew-cut blond head and pulled the drawstring as tight as he could until the blue angel's face momentarily disappeared, except for the nose.

Heritage couldn't paddle with the kayaks positioned as they were—and besides, Ninnish was lying on top of his paddle. Not a single boat had passed them. It was up to him to be a hero, however reluctantly. He had to get Ninnish into the bottom of the canoe so he could paddle-tow him to the island. He leaned forward again, sandwiching the trembling body as he foraged through his forward compartment for rope. He came across an extra zip-up fleece he'd forgotten about, and wrestled Ninnish into it, life jacket and all. By that time, Ninnish was still shaking quite violently, and his teeth were chattering, but his eyes—when Heritage peeked inside the cinched hood—seemed to be tracking. Heritage took that as a good sign. He was only slightly concerned about having immobilized the boy's arms inside layers of jackets in case they ran into more trouble but for now, it would both restrain him and conserve heat.

Heritage measured out a section of rope so that Ninnish would be a safe distance back and out of the way of his paddling. He told Ninnish everything he was doing, making most of it up as he went. He had never towed another kayak before—in fact, he didn't know the first thing about it. He couldn't reach the stern or bow of his kayak from where he sat, so he tied one end of the rope around his own waist, thinking as he knotted it off that it was probably not his best idea. He needed to get Ninnish into the canoe and there was just no dainty way to do this, so he apologized at the same time he lifted and shoved the teen off his kayak and into the canoe. It worked, but with a thud and that thud was Aidan's head hitting the metal seat in the aft of the canoe.

Shouting, Heritage tried to coach the kid to "scrunch up, tuck into a fetal position!" but he couldn't get Aidan to respond or cooperate. Heritage was aware the knock to his head may have conked him clean out leaving his brain unconscious, but it was the best he could do.

He stowed the wet green sweatshirt between his legs under his spray skirt, then carefully, passing the canoe hand over hand, he reached the front toggle and tied the other end of the rope to it. Letting Adian's boat drift behind him until the rope was taut and pulling at his waist, Heritage began inching forward one power stroke at a time, reading the tree and shoreline to take the most direct route to Mona's cabin.

Ninnish had blacked out from the blunt force trauma of hitting his head, but in that unquantifiable space and time, his quaking lessened to shivers and as his body temperature began to rise. In several more minutes, he became more primitively aware in his dark, floating womb. He could tell he was lying in water—maybe a few inches of it—but the more he breathed out, the warmer his insulated world became. He sensed he was in motion. He felt as though he were being jerked along and figured this to be Tage out there in front of him, paddling them to safety. He knew that this latest stunt would have consequences. His riskier ventures always did. But he had succeeded in provoking Tage to demonstrate that he cared about him—enough to save him from death. This would bring the two of them inseparably closer. This bond—this lifesaving moment—would prove that they belonged in each other's lives.

Wicked Ninnish used his recovery time, curled on the floor of the canoe, to plot his next move. He needed a showstopper. He needed a huge trick. It would have to top all the others in his shrewd bargaining for Tage's attention, detention, and eventual affection—the ultimate prize. And if he failed—the thought stopped him cold, still shivering. If he failed, there could be nothing left of Tage for him to obsess over. Nothing.

Ninnish felt the bottom of his canoe scrape across the tops of barely submerged rocks. They had made it into more protected water. The hero and object of his obsession had succeeded. His shivering had mostly stopped, and it wouldn't be long before he was nearly restored, and then completely resurrected, ready to face whatever was left of his nine lives.

He licked the salt from his lips.

Heritage had not said more than five words since the sea-ravaged pair had beached just below Mona's cabin on Wickaninnish Island. And those five words weren't the least bit ambiguous: *I'm leaving for Toronto Saturday.* There had been no discussion and no opportunity for recourse. He had stoked the fire in the wood stove at Mona's house, moved the wicker couch in front of it, and mummy-wrapped a naked, stripped-to-the-boner Ninnish in a bundle of quilts. Heritage could only shake his head at the boy's youthful virility. He'd upset a sewing basket that had been left on an edge of the couch, getting the bundle of testosterone in front of the raging fire. But he couldn't be bothered to pick up the mess of buttons and thimbles that had scattered everywhere. He snatched his windbreaker and left the cabin with an unintended smack of the sliding glass door, to make the necessary arrangements with Mason while Aidan recovered and Rowan was still in the village at school.

Though he hadn't been there before, Heritage had learned from Rowan that the Robson cabin was the next cabin north of Lyle's place on the outside coast. He figured the best way to reach it would be on the Trans Island Expressway as he'd heard the kids call it—or the TET as it had been labeled on the map on the back of the A-frame door—that is, until it had been painted over. He hobbled along the beach to get to the trailhead, not certain at all that his ankle was up to this. But he had returned them—at greater risk than he'd even anticipated—to the island for a reason; a mission really—and neither a sprained ankle nor weather nor witches, not even a teen-rumoured cougar roaming the woods were going to discourage or dissuade him. He didn't really have the time or the ankle strength for the long way— which he was more familiar with but would have sent him around the mostly perimeter coastal trail. He left the beach taking a right turn straight into the rainforest.

Since discovering the labyrinth and several of the cross-island network of trails that seemed to intersect there, Heritage was beginning to believe the four cottages—Dottie's, Mona's, Mason's, and Stephanie's out at Big Beach—were somehow linked by back trails that led to and through the labyrinth—possibly to facilitate ceremonies and the commerce of witches. He wasn't sure why he thought that, and he recognized that he may have been layering on the mysticism or fabricating an occult out of thin air. Maybe the shells and stones in the forest clearing had been nothing more than a bored child's art project and maybe Dottie's library was just for intimidating show.

Just as he'd achieved a half-hitch stride that favoured his ankle, Heritage hit a dead-end in a particularly dense section of woods. He hadn't realized how aggressively he had been plodding along until his stillness gave him a chance to monitor his chest-heaving and a heartbeat that seemed to emanate from his bad ankle. How odd that the trail would just end at the tree in front of him. He poked his head around the sizeable trunk of the tree that wasn't just any tree and was surprised to discover he'd reached the edge of the labyrinth and was standing at the very Sitka he had climbed. He would have sworn he'd been cutting straight west across the middle of it.

He brashly took a few steps inside the first circle, fuming that his earlier supplication to the spirits that he be delivered from the very wicked Ninnish had been ignored. He was still stuck with the teenage burden and still limping—though now literally and not just figuratively—along this hazard-strewn obstacle course that was leading him anywhere but out of these dark woods.

"What gives?" he screamed out, turning as he yelled.

A raven or crow answered him but from which branch, Heritage could not tell. There wasn't time to practice patience with the spirits or try to understand the planetary energy vortexes he might be up against, standing in that spot. But he'd also matured to face this stretch of rotten luck, and in his introspection that followed, Heritage realized he needed to crowbar open his cynicism to receive some positive healing energy and try a different, less antagonistic approach to the intermeddling forces at play. For all he knew, the labyrinth may have heard him the first time, may have arranged his deliverance through the drowning of Ninnish, but then he had been the one to intervene and screw everything up. He stepped gently back across the outer circle of rocks and shells, and took a deep, cleansing breath, exhaling slowly. Continuing this elongated mode of breathing, Heritage moved around the left side of the largest Sitka to enter the path from the northeast, being careful not to step over the lines irreverently, but following the lines and honouring the patterned entrances—much like he'd seen Mason walk the pentagram. The star traced, he knelt down in the exact center, lifted his head and gaze north to the multi-forked Sitka spruce—the one he knew cradled the ancient bones of somebody's ancestor. He squeezed his eyes shut, and then tried to relax his face and posture to assume some measure of calm contemplation so the healing and rebirth mumbo-jumbo could get inside and really take hold this time. Heritage needed a divine intervention to break the demonic chain of events.

Starting with the throbbing in his left ankle, he focused his mind to travel around his anatomy—visiting what he remembered of his chakra locations, inviting the purification of his body and intentions. Continuing his deep breathing, Heritage opened his eyes to meditate on the monolithic Sitka towering before him. He scanned that massive, perpendicularly perfect trunk, first, visualizing its roots down deep, then traveling up to the forks and then up one side—not the trunk he'd climbed, but the other one, which contained the bones.

"Who did you belong to?" he called up into the branches. The pesky raven squawked back at him from a different tree, one Heritage hadn't been paying attention to, though the raven— ever opportunistic—was paying attention to him. Heritage looked to the forest floor around his knees, scattered with shells and Japanese glass floats—and suddenly realized he hadn't made a physical offering. He had *taken* things from it—the wallet, the prescription bottle with his own public hair. And he had asked the labyrinth for deliverance from the teenage evil—had bargained his soul even. But he hadn't sacrificed anything. No wonder his request hadn't been granted. The raven cawed again for attention or confirmation—Heritage could not be sure since he wasn't fluent in *Corvus* behaviour or language.

He searched his pockets for valuables, but he was not one to carry cash or wear jewelry aside from the wristwatch he couldn't give up. He fingered the Gerber knife always attached to the belt around his waist. Just another frivolous purchase that had been hyped by the Mountain Equipment Co-op eco-pushers—only once had he used one of the knife's twenty-six blades, when he cut that authenticating gash across the top of his hiking boot. He ran his finger over that superficial cut on the boot's leather that contained his swollen ankle. Oh, and the mini-scissors, he recalled, when he cut Stephanie's note from the grocery sack so he could trace the map from the door onto its backside. Sure, the knife was designed for scaling fish or quartering musk ox, but he hadn't encountered anything he needed to stab or filet, so he had mostly forgotten about it on his belt altogether, except when it got hung up as he entered and exited the cockpit of his kayak. That was a pain he would be happy to be rid of as he'd mostly tired of cursing it each time it clunked the fiberglass. Otherwise, he really only remembered it when he changed pants—which, incidentally, didn't happen as often as it had in the city, where he had been satisfied just looking the wilderness part, instead of smelling it.

He undid his belt. Why not? It had been a hundred-and-fifty-dollar knife. That was value. That was sacrifice. That was his offering and he held it high to catch the sun's ray and the raven's watchful eye. "Good luck carrying this off, Warlock!" He'd momentarily lost his Zen state. But just in case he decided he wanted the knife back—say, if deliverance never came—he tucked it under the mossy carpet, out of sight and off to the side of the altar. He dropped his head, paying reverence somewhat superficially, and was on his feet again. Rethreading his belt, he thanked the labyrinth for almost killing Ninnish, which would have taken him off his hands—but reminded the spirit energies there that they hadn't quite finished the job and that he would no longer stand in their way. He thought about this heartless stance and then refined it, thanking the labyrinth anew, and ever so reluctantly, for also bringing the little shit back to life.

Heritage turned around to back out of the labyrinth, just as he'd seen Mason do, bowing and then saluting the raven still overhead on the branch. Heritage wondered how long it would be before the bird couldn't resist the shiny pocketknife. Walking backwards, Heritage realized his ankle was no longer aching—in fact, wasn't bothering him at all anymore. He tested his weight on it, he had miraculously recovered his range of motion. It was good as new, which freaked him out all over again.

Since he was there at the blessings dispensary and curious to see what the raven would do, Heritage decided he would take a closer look at the bones in the tree. Using the hidden notch system, he climbed the trunk, this time choosing the fork he hadn't climbed before—the one with the platform. The last ten feet or so had been hacked limbless, though nowhere near recently, and he had to inch his way upward by straddling it with his arms and feet, like a koala bear. He edged his chin high enough to be able to see over the top of the platform, where he found himself surely looking into the eye sockets of what was left of a skull. He gently touched its mossy surface, then nudged and pushed it around to get a look on all sides. There was a section on the back where moss didn't grow, because there wasn't anything to grow on—a sizeable chunk of the cranium was missing. This made the second human skull Heritage had come face to faceless with on this island, the other being in the box cut into the floor of Dottie's cabin. He could almost hear the click of the light switch that just turned on for him. Skull . . . box . . . skull box! Rowan had said he'd stashed the Polaroids in the skull box, just as Aidan had instructed him to. Heritage almost lost his grip in that moment of revelation. He better positioned himself, shimmying even higher up that fork in the trunk to grab onto a branch to steady himself, his torso just cresting the edge of the platform, where he could conduct a better examination. The other bones were not at all even roughly where they should have been if a body had been hoisted and placed in the tree, on the platform, intact. The platform was a puzzle of bones that Heritage doubted he could ever reassemble based on his limited understanding of anatomy. Beyond that, his forensics skills were—well, weren't.

Still, he was fascinated. He pulled his head back to bring

something into better focus. He saw what looked like the pattern of a denim belt-loop sticking out of the moss. He gently pulled, and along with it came the partial waistband of what was once a pair of jeans. Sure enough, the leather trademark of Levi's was still barely traceable, as were the waist and length measurements of 34 and 36, respectively. Heritage's premise that these were native bones from a century or more ago were dashed. He ventured that the skull must have belonged to a tall and moderately slender man—a contemporary, since denim wasn't an aboriginal fabric, and 36 was the length of a modern man's legs. It was exactly the measurement of his own inseam, in fact. He shook the waistband slightly to free it from the dirt and moss. What looked like a bronze coin dropped from the mostly decayed clump onto the platform before bouncing or rolling off the edge out of sight to drop the ten or so metres to the labyrinth floor below.

Heritage nearly snapped his neck trying to see where it landed but got dizzy looking down and had to accept he'd lost sight of it the moment it deflected off the platform. He scanned the branches above and across from him for any other clues. Finding none, he hurried down the trunk of the tree like a fireman to find the coin just as he heard and from the corner of his eye, spied the raven enter a diving scream to the same hallowed ground below, first prodding the moss where he'd stashed the pocketknife.

"Hey!" Heritage shouted, missing a foot hold and momentarily dangling from his handhold still an uncomfortable distance from the ground. "Get away from there . . . SHOO!" He once again bestraddled the trunk and managed to descend two more metres before dropping the rest of the way into the moss. He worried that this had just messed up his ankle all over again, but it seemed to be okay as he rushed the raven with his arms flailing. The raven lifted into the air, but just switched places with Heritage, lighting in the moss near where he though the coin might have fallen. Heritage reversed direction, more concerned about not losing the coin than his knife.

A date on the coin could provide a clue—if it was a coin at all and not just a grommet from the Levi's. On his hands and knees, and with the raven chatting and clucking near the altar, Heritage systematically searched the outer perimeter of the labyrinth beneath the tree. For five minutes he ran his fingers over the moss and through the grass and mulch, until he took a splinter or thorn into his knee and had to suspend his search. He hiked up one leg of his kayaking pants to work on the microscopic barb—salmonberry or Devil's club, he suspected.

He returned to searching the moss and wondered if the island's rumoured and collective intolerance of men had anything to do with the bones on the platform. He had to question everything, since nothing and nobody—except maybe François—had been what or who they seemed to be. Was that man—those were men's jeans, after all—sacrificed here and left to preside over the labyrinth, or had he gotten himself up there accidentally? Both theories struck him as preposterous.

Heritage cocked his head suddenly to one side to place a far-off sound that wasn't a raven. Someone was approaching.

He scrambled to his feet and dove into the chest-high salal and waited, crouched down, eyes wide. The random snapping of twigs grew louder until Dottie Bard, of all deceptive people, emerged onto the path and proceeded in an obvious hurry, without stopping, cutting straight through the labyrinth southeast to northwest. Shockingly, she gave no indication in her stride that the island's spiritual center or the pentagram pattern in the pathways held any mystique for her. She dislodged a Japanese glass float with the toe of a gumboot without stopping to reverently replace or even kick it back. Maybe the labyrinth had been established—even overgrown—long before she'd been introduced to the island. Still, he expected her to know enough about it to warrant a bow or curtsey. Likely she was hell-bent on one of her missions and just not paying attention, and then again, perhaps she wasn't the practicing witch he'd believed her to be, and that library collection of books in her cabin had either been inherited or was there to intimidate the crap out of trespassers. If so, that had worked on him.

She hadn't been able to take Aidan off his hands because she was leaving on a planned boating trip up the coast, eh? That treacherous bitch, he thought to himself as he felt the mercury in his thermometer redden his face and threaten to blow his head off the stump of his neck. He almost Jack-in-the-boxed right out of the salal bushes to confront her as she passed within metres of his hiding spot. But he wasn't buying it. There could be no way she was oblivious to the labyrinth, unless she were a fake witch—a spell-casting imposter or conjurer just for show. Even a greenhorn like Heritage, (isn't that what she'd called him once?) with his miraculously cured ankle, knew the labyrinth was special—sacred, and not something to dismiss, discount, or mess with.

There was a lot more that he still didn't know about the rest of the purported, nearly all-female population of Wickaninnish Island. Sure, if he were staying, and interested in mischief, he could have advanced Brad Fraser's crazy-ass rumour—and for some, it would have seemed rather believable—that the coven of scheming, man-hating witches on Wick Isle had actually sacrificed a man in some purification ritual—maybe even Dottie's husband who had been Fraser's best and missing friend. Heritage didn't know this to be true, but maybe a sacrifice had been necessary to bring the elements of earth, air, fire, and water back into alignment. There were a lot of questions he could ask, if he had the time and weren't leaving for Toronto by the end of the week. Then again, in his current fix, he'd do well to keep his mouth shut and hope others did the same.

He was leaving, anyway, just as soon as he could pawn off the kid—which reminded him he had been on his way to see Mason. But, wait—wasn't Mason's cabin in the same direction Dottie had just headed? He forgot about the coin he'd been searching for but superstitiously replaced the green glass ball that

Dottie had kicked, before easing his way, facing backwards, out of the labyrinth. It was time to pursue and stalk the queen of his growing league of nemeses to uncover what urgent business had prompted her sudden return from what she said had been a planned multi-day boating trip upcoast and the all-too-convenient reason why she couldn't take Aidan off his hands—unless and of course she'd lied about that too.

Sticking to the path and doing his best to quiet his steps, Heritage got to thinking, that could not have been Dottie Bard's first time to the labyrinth. She'd likely made the same cross-island march a hundred times. Maybe the labyrinth only held Wiccan powers at night, or on full moons, and was just a clearing and shortcut during daylight. Maybe the witches only really used tha clearing in the trees for male sacrifices, high ceremonial incantations, or testicle-grinding rituals. Still, Heritage couldn't see how the circle of ancient Sitka trees wouldn't have demanded pause and curious wonderment each and every time one saw them. Dottie seemed to have all but snubbed the landmark—which probably meant she was either impervious to spiritual influences, or she was being carnivorously consumed by them.

Dottie was in a frantic hurry having worked herself up overnight into an anxious mess. She had been hiding out on her boat, laying low in God's Pocket, anchored next to Mac's oyster farm in one of the many coves of Meares Island, when it hit her. Tage had been serious about leaving Clayoquot Sound and he was going to follow through with it unless she stopped him. She needed to reach Mason before Tage got to her. She needed to ensure that nobody would be available to take Ninnish off his hands. He couldn't leave if he couldn't pass that brat baton. Somehow, she'd gotten her wires crossed and thought Mason was still at her poetry workshop in Campbell River. Mac had told her over a pasta and merlot dinner on her boat last night, that Mason was back—that he'd only had to drive the kids to the island after-school once, before she returned to take over the runs. It was odd that Mason hadn't checked back in with Dottie when she returned—unusual for she and Mason, especially at a time like this, when Mona was away from the island for treatment and Ninnish was being watched by others. Understandably, Mona's jealousy had not made it easy for Dottie and Mason to attend to their fledgling and highly secretive affair.

Mason had lived with her biologist husband, Clive, on the outer coast of the island —some 400 meters north of Stephanie's triangle cabin—longer than almost all of them, except for Sharon Greene. Mason, who was the *wood* in Dottie's pentagram, (Mona the *fire*, Stephanie the *water*, Sharon the *earth*, and Dottie the *metal*) had homeschooled their only child, Rowan, during the mid-eighties while she and Clive took on just about every environmental issue in the hemisphere. Stephanie babysat Rowan on several occasions while his parents were either in court or jail for civil disobedience. Meanwhile, tensions in Clayoqout Sound had very short fuses after the group of environmentalists (that included a rollcall of almost every shareholder on Wickaninnish Island) had successfully blocked chainsaws from reaching Meares Island in '84 and then halted a logging road from being blasted through Sulphur Passage in the late spring of '88. So, by the time an overloaded logging truck came barreling out of the mountains near Bridal Falls toward the end of that year, relations and patience between enviros, loggers, the Mounties and the governments that were sanctioning the wholesale destruction of the rainforest—were collapsing and at a breaking point. The logging truck rounded a blind corner traveling too fast toward the Kennedy Lake bridge, when it encountered Clive Robson standing in the middle of the road holding up a STOP LOGGING NOW placard. The truck driver, who was from Ucluelet and someone Clive knew, lost control and careened over the right bank to avoid hitting Clive—but was killed instantly. Mason's husband and Rowan's dad was made an example to pestilent environmental activists everywhere, and was put away for eighteen to twenty-five years for involuntary manslaughter.

Dottie had wasted no time then—like she was wasting no time now—rushing into the void to console and convert Mason over to her dark and manipulative side. For Mason, without her husband, the mounting loneliness combined with the perils of raising a boy on her own and off the grid had made the coven not only attractive, but essential for her survival, and as for the proper development and socialization of her son, she had reluctantly sent him off to public school after second grade. Dottie had influenced and reinforced Mason's decision-making every chance she got—something she did not just with Mason, but with all the women on Wick. That had included Stephanie until her daughter started breaking away. Halfway through the previous summer's War in the Woods when Mason had been hauled off the blockade by over-zealous RCMP officers still carrying a five-year vendetta for the killed logging truck driver, her wrists and ankles inhumanely zip-tied together, it was Dottie who had insisted Rowan would fare just fine under Stephanie's care during Mason's three-month detention at the Nanaimo Correctional Centre. And especially since Stephanie had babysat him off and on most of his life already anyway. Mason, again had been played, and again she reluctantly agreed, and then Dottie informed Stephanie about the arrangement she'd brokered, not considering for a minute that this would be the last straw for her daughter and herald the rift that so far, couldn't be repaired between them.

This had required Dottie to focus all her less-than-super and anything-but natural occult powers just to hold relationships, her businesses and her master plan to re-develop Wickaninnish Island together—and for the most part, Dottie had believed she was making headway. It had always been unfortunate that both

Mona and Mason were raising sons and not matrilineal daughters, but Dottie figured brainiac Rowan was going to grow up to be a rocket scientist or brain surgeon and that would take him far away from Wick. It was really only Ninnish she needed to neutralize. For the longest time, she'd been pretty sure Aidan was going to recklessly do himself in, but as the kid went crashing pell-mell through puberty, Dottie needed his adolescent sights trained on finding his ticket out of Clayoquot Sound.

Then, lo and behold, handsome, charming Tage Carter wanders into the rainforest, instantly snagging Aidan's attention. Dottie knew two things. Tage Carter wasn't cut out for remote living and wouldn't stay, and Ninnish—once he set his obsessive mind to something, like a pit bull with a porkchop, just wouldn't be able to let go. That's why Dottie couldn't let Tage leave for Toronto—not without taking Ninnish with him. That's why she'd gotten Steve Greene to phone the Headlands Lodge pretending to be someone from Carter Pulp & Paper back east, to leave the message that Tage should stay put—that his grandfather was suddenly improving. She and Steve had been in cahoots since the early eighties. When he told her that his coast-guard son, Matt, had encountered Tage during official business at Lyle's place and had later run his name and ID on the Canadian Police Information Centre, connecting him to the behemoth paper company, Dottie knew who and what she was up against. She smelled money and lawsuits and a financial future for Aidan once sweet Mona relaxed her grip on this life. She just needed to keep the teenager and the interloper in her little island petri dish long enough for the chain-reaction to commence.

Mason was pure. She was innocent, without a mean or vindictive corpuscle in her body. It helped that like her time-serving husband, she too was a trained scientist—an astro-physicist, with a knack for automatically boiling bones to essential broth—and expediently getting to the facts of any matter. She didn't get hung up in feelings like Mona did. Her one indulgence that wasn't science was the astral plane, and by extension the studies of Theosophy and Rosicrucianism. Her remarkable belief that the world had an esoteric order made her a natural Wiccan with unique insights into nature, the physical universe, and the spiritual realm. Dottie had been drawn to her because Mason rounded out the essentialism that Dottie didn't have the patience to research, study, or possess. Mason therefore conducted most of the rituals and taught alchemy and mysticism to the relatively newer Wicca recruits like Gillian, from the library, and Samantha, one of the nurses from the hospital.

Since sex was power, and spirituality was often disguised as power that led to higher purposes—according to Aleister Crowley—Dottie had used both on Mason. Sure, all the women on Wickaninnish were sisters, and linked in the Wiccan sense. Even some of the men, like Steve Greene and the Greene children, had dabbled in the dark crafts, observed sabbat eight times a year, and cloaked themselves in the mossy island vestments as though it were the only basis for their existence—when, in reality, it was the only way they could tolerate each other's idiosyncrasies and self-serving biases. Dottie—not a fan of labels—didn't like to think of herself as a lesbian or a witch, unlike some of the others. For her, both the lore and the lure of a reimagined *Wicca*-Ninnish Island—a result of her own marketing—had become amusingly exaggerated over the years, mostly by her own tireless promotion but with lots of assistance, too, from the village's rumour mill. But with Mona's health and powers beginning to flounder, Dottie both counted on and courted Mason, who had been the final heart to be won over in the shareholder skirmish that flared up every time Dottie began pushing that capital venture and master plan for the island. She'd only recently secured Mason's pledge to vote favourably, but only after Mona had passed. Dottie knew she needed to continue servicing the Mason account until that island consensus transpired but she also sensed it wouldn't be much longer now. May Mona rest in peace, she prematurely whispered to herself.

Dottie respected and was attracted to a self-made type—a heartier caliber of woman, like Mona, like Mason, like Sharon Greene. She'd harboured such hopes for Stephanie to step up, but she'd been disappointed by her free-spirited, antagonistic, and often sabotaging ways. She had needed to accept years ago that her daughter wasn't dependent enough on anybody to gain strength and sustenance from the Wicca collective. Fearing her daughter might be a lost cause, since she hadn't needed these supports or rituals or costumes or pageantry to know who she was as a woman, Dottie needed to find others. It was strong women like that that Dottie admired most and wanted to recruit to her island and to her feet, as the high priestess-apparent—once Mona, the elder, had passed this mantel to her on her way to the next realm in the astral plane.

Dottie sensed that Mason's allegiance to her had always been tentative if not conditional and that Mason probably knew this went both ways. She'd had to accept that Mason likely feared her more than she loved her—which only stung a little. Dottie also knew that it hadn't helped that Mason stubbornly believed it had been Dottie who had anonymously leaked the information about Clive's journals that had led to the discovery of pre-meditated evidence against her husband during his trial for involuntary manslaughter. He had penned an entry a few weeks before the accident, saying that someone probably needed to get killed in order for the country to take the spiraling fate of the planet seriously. Dottie hadn't been entirely responsible for that trial's outcome, and so went to great effort to convince Mason she had nothing against most men—only certain ones.

Dottie expelled an *umph* immediately chased by a raucous "Bloody Hell!" Just as she'd rounded the standing wall created by an upended cedar's jumbled roots, her left gumboot found air—not the trail and not the regular footbridge that spanned this spot. Her right foot followed and together her legs sank with a squish about a foot deep into a mud pot, and the suction, when she tried to jerk it free, pulled her foot right out of her sock. The sock had stayed inside the rubber casing, and the boot stayed in the ground. Her bare foot, only momentarily free and clean, had nowhere to go but back into the same mud pot. She exhaled audibly, like that was the last thing she needed in her day. She wasn't even supposed to be on the island—now she was stuck in it!

Heritage had been having a rough go of it—catching up to Dottie on a mission was an endurance sport—but he could tell by a faint trail of her perfume that lingered in the air and was getting stronger, that he must be getting close. She'd already taught him an easier route to get around the backside of Lyle's cottage, and that saved him climbing up the steep rise and down the cliff. It astounded him how much wetter things became on the open ocean side of the island, which, at most, couldn't be more than a kilometre and a half wide to begin with. Heritage would have kept right on death-schlepping through the mud until he'd run out of island had he not heard Dottie scream for Mason. That shriek stopped him in his tracks, or else he might have rounded the upended tree in front of him to fall right on top of that mastodon in the tar pit.

"Ma-son! It's Dot."

Heritage could hear Dottie cussing and struggling. He held onto a root in the wall that separated them, not sure whether to laugh or help. He did have to pee, so he needed this to resolve quickly or he was going to burst.

"Dottie?" Mason hollered back. "Are you out there? Come in if you are. I'm just putting the finishing parmesan touches on some delicious homemade minestrone soup."

"Mason, I need help!" Dottie called again.

Heritage was afraid he'd pee his pants if this slapstick routine between those two continued much longer. He crouched on the trail and sat back on his calves, trying not to laugh as he envisioned Dottie at La Brea in her final throes. He suspected it was rare for Dottie Bard to be immobilized or idle. She seemed like a shark to him that way—if she stopped, she died.

Inside the cliffside cottage, Mason put her spoon down on the counter and opened the screen panel of her sliding glass door. "Dottie?" she yelled toward the forest.

"Yes, it's me. I'm afraid I am stuck in the mud and could use a tug out." Dottie spotted a Tahitian carved Buddha stuck between the roots of the upturned tree off to her left side. "I'm down by that Buddha you brought back from Phuket," she yelled.

"Coming, Dot. Let me just turn off the stove," Mason hollered back.

"Mason? What is taking you so long?" Dottie was nearly screaming now. "*Mason!*" Dottie's baritone voice sounded a new alarm that rattled the tree trunks and surely disturbed the mud surface she was trembling in. This time, there was a slam of the screen door and Mason bounded down the steps of her wide porch.

"Sorry, Dot." Mason was on her way to the rescue. "I just finished making a lovely soup. You have time for a cup or bowl while it's hot?" There was a half-minute gap in the conversation until Mason rounded the curve in the trail, and then, "Oh heavens, Dottie, you *are* in a fix!"

"Obviously! Now brace your legs and lend me your arm." Dottie couldn't help directing even her own rescue. "What happened to the little bridge that used to span this hazard?" Dottie suddenly spotted what she'd missed earlier, the remnants of that bridge turned up on its side and at least a couple body lengths out of her reach. "I'm so glad you were home! It's almost as though somebody didn't want anyone approaching your house, Dear."

"Oh, that's Rowan for you, always setting booby traps! The monsters in his imagination must be hyperactive!" Mason giggled. "Or maybe it's just hormones."

"I need to hose off my legs and borrow a pair of your gumboots, it looks like," Dottie said.

Heritage deducted that her boots mustn't have come out of the mud with her feet. He listened as their two voices carried on, moving away from him now and toward Mason's place. Heritage poked his head around the root wall and could see the mud trap and that the women had moved on ahead and out of sight. Hanging onto the upended roots, Heritage traveled around the obstacle like it were a climbing wall that delivered him to where the trail picked up again, but he knocked off the Buddha statue and it did a double somersault dive with a possible twist before landing with a splat in the mud. The last thing Heritage needed was any more bad karma, so he repositioned his boots and grabbing onto a lower root in the knotted wall, he plucked Buddha from the mud and lifted him back to his shelf. With the day's second rescue completed, Heritage spanned the mud mote with his long legs and rejoined the trail on the other side, sneaking carefully along it until he spotted the four-by-four stilts and deck railings of Mason's place.

There, just outside the home, he could see they were using what must have been a creek-fed garden hose, as Mason washed the mud off Dottie's bare foot, then together they tugged and pushed on the mud-caked boot that Dottie had managed to hold onto. It let go suddenly with a loud suction noise that sent the two of them sailing backwards onto the wooden decking in laughter.

Heritage cozied up to a tree he could lurk behind and pivoted his feet to face the ocean, which he could see below him between the trees. He relieved himself unceremoniously on a patch of moss—still within earshot thanks to the breeze that carried their words to him. He zipped and moved closer and could see Mason and Dottie embracing on the deck. He could tell that neither seemed particularly anxious to pull away. He crept closer to see what he could learn firsthand. Edging along one side of the cabin, he moved within a half dozen feet of the conversation but gave up his sightline in the maneuver. He could hear the women's muffled voices and needed to get closer to make out what it was they were talking about. He tucked under the cottage and deck that was almost elevated enough on posts for him to stand upright in the space underneath . He moved to the stacked firewood pile and determined he was pretty close to being directly under the chatting women.

He wasn't catching every word, but he got the gist of their conversation. Mason was saying she had been worried about her boy, who seemed more despondent the past few days since she'd returned from her poetry workshop. She had become concerned that he might be depressed and was thinking she might talk to the doctor about it. Maybe he was just being more bullied by Ninnish than usual, or was having a harder go at puberty than most, without a father around to clumsily talk him through it. She said she knew that the same birds and bees message coming from her would fall flat and carry zero credibility. That's when she mentioned that perhaps she could ask Tage if he'd mind having that talk, man to man. He seemed to be making some progress with Ninnish. She and Mona had discussed how very grateful they were to have Tage spending time around their boys as they turned into men.

"Actually, Tage is why I'm here to talk to you, Mason. I'm afraid this is a bit delicate." She paused, unknowingly giving Heritage just enough time to climb higher up the stack of firewood so he could hear them better.

"Is it bad news from Mona, Dottie?" Mason asked, sounding quite concerned.

Heritage could hear the scooting of a chair on the wooden floor above his head and imagined Dottie must be leaning in for a spot of added drama. "It's not good, Dear. She's having adverse reactions to this new chemo and I'm afraid her latest CT shows the cancer has spread to her pancreas."

Heritage covered his ocean-facing ear to test if he could hear them better. It helped a little but even though he was just centimetres away, it wasn't as good as being in the same room.

Dottie looked around Mason's U-shaped kitchen and marveled that the sun pouring through the windows made it possible and even necessary to keep her sunglasses on. It was rare the sun brightened her corner of Wickaninnish, given the east facing orientation of her heavily forested share; a spot her adversaries claimed—usually, but not always behind her back—sat under a cloud of evil tethered to her dark soul. It wasn't that. She just hadn't built at the water's edge and out of the trees in the open because she didn't want peepers or trespassers.

Mason saw Dottie looking at her kitchen and must have felt the urge to justify the mess. "I apologize for the disarray, Dottie. I was canning a batch of Clayoquot mud masks, thinking you could use the inventory for your store with the holidays coming up."

"Those jars are my best sellers." Dottie turned to affectionately embrace the lady of this house. When Dottie, who was always the first to pull away, stepped back, she saw it. Mason was wearing a new necklace. Dottie recognized it immediately. It was a magic word square written on consecrated parchment, hanging around her neck on a single strand of white thread. White thread was Mona's signature—she used it in most every pagan ritual she performed or presided over. Dottie also recognized, having once snooped through Mona's copy of *Book of Shadows*, that the arrangement of the letters T, A, H, C, A, L in a box was meant to protect the wearer against bewitchment, lift hexes, and ward off the evil eye. Seeing this around Mason's neck, Dottie could only confirm what she'd suspected of Mona's interference. Yes, Dottie's campaign to develop the island had intensified, and Mona, no dummy, could see that Dottie had resorted to taking her relationship with Mason to an intimate level—the one place where Mona would be shut out and couldn't meddle. Mona must have suspected the two were getting closer and that must have been why she'd given Mason the necklace—to protect her and protect Wickaninnish Island from Dottie's development plans. It was damn true, Dottie could admit. When it came to that obsession of hers, presented with even the slightest opportunity, Dottie found she could cuddle, write poetry, hold hands, or even invoke the triple goddess of fertility incantation during the vernal spring equinox from memory if need be—all to win Mason over and secure another consensus vote before the next annual general meeting of the island's shareholders.

Dottie hit herself on the side of the head with an open hand. It had been Mason's birthday that past weekend. Not only had she forgotten it was coming up until Mona had reminded her during their drive to Victoria, but she'd been so anxious to clear the village and get on her boat and out of Tage's reach when he came looking for a substitute Aidan-sitter, that she'd walked out of her office, leaving the antique chalice with the ruby inlaid Eye of Horus sitting gift-wrapped on her desk. So many things had gotten clogged up in her mind. Dottie Bard had always had far too much on the go and she was going to drop from a cardiac arrest one day—but even then, she would probably just pick herself up, brush off her pants, and walk herself up the hill to the hospital. She had kept promising herself she was going to take a break—a vacation even—to clear her mind. But it hadn't happened. Every year she vowed she would be truer to her mantra, written in fancy calligraphy on a folded index card and kept next to the alarm clock on her in-town nightstand above the shop—a quote from Helen Keller: *Life is either a daring adventure or nothing at all.*

Mason ladled minestrone into medium sized bowls for each of them, re-joining Dottie at the small round dining room table.

". . . which brings me to Tage and the reason I've urgently needed to speak to you. Aidan can't get abandoned twice. He's about to lose his mum. He can't lose Tage, too."

"Oh, I know. It has been so good for the boys to have an upstanding, stable man around. I really like the influence he's been having on Rowan who perks up when he talks about him." She tested the temperature of the soup. "Can you believe that Tage had never heard of or experienced bioluminescence until Rowan explained it to him?" Mason slurped from her soup spoon.

"But I lately get the sense from Tage that he's dead-set on returning to Toronto, as soon as this weekend," Dottie reported. "He hasn't had an easy go of things with the rains and well, let's be honest, with Aidan so far."

"Are any of us really surprised by that?" Mason lifted another spoonful to her mouth.

Dottie realized it would be rude not to even try the minestrone, so she gave it a taste, finding it delicious. Hungrier than she realized and not even remembering if she'd had anything for breakfast that morning, she raised another half dozen spoonful's of the warm homestyle goodness to her mouth. While her friend ate, Mason continued the conversation. "At first, I thought you were going to tell me you were going to ask Tage to leave Wick—your general intolerance of men and all." Mason put it out there, befuddled as usual about Dottie's true intentions.

"No, nothing like that." Dottie half-smiled. "I actually don't mind the guy but I have a feeling Ninnish is about to run him off for good, which is the opposite of what Aidan wants and what this island needs right now." Dottie put the spoon down, and it wobbled back and forth across the half-empty bowl.

"Does it need more salt? How about some bread, dear?" Mason offered. Dottie faced both of her palms up, signaling that she and the soup were just fine.

"I get the sense from Tage that something has happened to make him want to leave here without ever looking back." Dottie leaned back.

"Hmm." Mason paused to think. "Rowan was in one of his funks yesterday morning when I boated the boys to school—you know, one of his silent phases he gets into sometimes when Aidan has been bullying him." Mason held that thought a moment to see if Dottie was becoming impatient, as she did sometimes. Dottie tilted her head up in encouragement, so Mason went on. "It hadn't been planned in advance and it must have happened after I went to bed, but I assumed Rowan must have decided to spend the night with Ninnish and Tage at Mona's as I didn't hear him come in. But sometime before breakfast, both of the boys were here and getting ready for school, which I found odd, given that Tage was supposed to be watching him. Then, after school yesterday, only Rowan came back to the island with me. He said Aidan had left school not feeling well and that he was staying on the village-side with Tage so he could be close to the doctor or the drugstore, or something like that."

As she spoke, it occurred to Dottie that Mason was stringing the chronology together like a bracelet, but that she was coming up several beads short.

"And your point, Mase?" Dottie prompted, at last revealing her trademark impatience. They'd advanced to the pet-name stage in their clumsy intimacy earlier that summer and had been referring to each other since as Mase and Dot, testing if that would stick. Dottie still vacillated, questioning whether her heart was really into this romantic tactic to get her friend on her side.

"Last night, while I was making dinner, I heard Rowan on

his walkie-talkie trying to reach Aidan, so I asked him how he thought it was going with Aidan and Tage, you know, while Mona is away. And that's when Rowan sheepishly related that Ninnish had tried experimenting with his mother's medications—on Tage."

Dottie let a laugh explode past lips that had tried to be serious. "Well, now that is interesting because Ninnish asked me the other day which of his mum's prescriptions was most likely to knock someone completely out, if you can believe that. I pressed him about the *someone* he had in mind, but he said he said *something*—not someone, and that he was referring to that cougar the boys are so convinced is on the island."

"Well, I haven't seen a cougar and I'm always here."

"Me either," Dottie continued with her side of the story. "Of course, Aidan already knew about his mum's white-hot panic over needle injections and IVs, but I accidentally let it slip that she sometimes takes a sedative called *Versed* to conk out before any procedure requiring needles. I told him she comes right back out of it in fifteen or twenty minutes. But he wasn't satisfied with that for whatever reason, so I did mention another drug called *Rohypnol*, a stronger tranquilizer I know Mona has taken before, around the time she had her mastectomy. I told him I was pretty sure that would send even the biggest cougar into a deep, long nap. I also said he could always ask his Uncle Lyle, since he's a doctor and practically a pharmacist."

"Oh Dottie, you don't send a teenager asking about drugs to Doctor Feelgood, for heaven's sake!" Mason laughed awkwardly, then raised her hand to her mouth to gossip. "I don't know if you heard this, but Samantha at the hospital told me that Marcel Labbé's blood had LSD levels that were off the charts, when they performed his autopsy. You don't have to think too hard about where he would have gotten drugs like that," Mason leveled with her.

"No, I hadn't heard that about Marcel. Just tragic, his drowning," she tossed in.

"And that it happened very close to here, even more so tragic.

Rowan and I must have still been away school shopping with Mona in Vancouver the night it happened." She was shaking her head, but then snapped out of it. "But back to the boys, well, okay then," Mason, said. "Putting your conversation with Ninnish together with what Rowan told me about the experimentation the other night, that would make sense then, but I don't think it had anything to do with that cougar."

Dottie shook her head and lipped the word *no*.

"What do you suppose Ninnish did while he had Tage drugged?"

"That's a question maybe for Rowan if he was in on it, but knowing Ninnish, I doubt he's passing the time reading comic books." The two women laughed uncomfortably, yet almost too knowingly. "At any rate, Tage is suddenly trying to pass Ninnish off on you or me, like the kid's got the plague or something."

"Or something, is right," Mason interjected. "Well, better with a stranger than with my son, but I will tell you, Rowan would have had nothing to do with a dangerous stunt like that. He is just too responsible. Though I will say, the way Ninnish bullies my boy makes me sick in my soul. I have mentioned this to Mona, but she just doesn't see it. That's all I can say."

"Don't worry about Ninnish, Mase. It's all part of my plan. Don't think I don't know Mona plans to leave Aidan the bakeshop and her share of the island, and has me named as his legal guardian to boot. I'll be sending him to some all-boys prep-school so fast . . ."

"Well, that would make him happy, you know. All boys."

"Precisely. Give Aidan what he craves, and it should straighten him out, pardon the pun—or the double entendre, I guess. Which is why I dropped everything to rush over here in the first place. Tage plans to hit you up —to get you to take over the guard, as it were."

"Well, he already did. I was supposed to watch Ninnish last weekend because Tage had to get back to Toronto on some family emergency."

"Oh really?" Dottie adjusted her weight in her chair, scooting it back from the table with a screech. "Well, I've come to terms with Tage being here—on the island for now, even though he is just like the others—men, I mean. Turns out he had sex with Stephanie inside the first thirty minutes after meeting her, of course. You know how that kind of sexual power trip disgusts me!" Dottie grimaced and stared out at the sun's glare on the water.

Mason might have wondered who in Clayoquot Sound (and all of Patagonia by now) had Stephanie not had sex with, just as she also might have wondered who Dottie was referring to as the initiator in the sexual power trip. But she didn't dare utter either question.

Dottie rose to take the two soup bowls to the sink, where she rinsed them without soap and set them in the drying rack. "Tage is definitely headed off the edge, all right. Whether he's pushed, trips, or he freely jumps remains to be seen. My guess is he'll take Ninnish over the side with him—that kid is smitten. So don't you dare take that teenager off his hands, Mase, until they're good and dirty." That came out wrong. "Tage's hands, I meant. We need him to stay here—for the good of the boys' development."

At that moment, a radio squawked, and Heritage realized he wasn't alone under the house on that bluff overlooking the sea. Rowan had snuck up on him, though perhaps not intentionally. But with a hand over one ear tuning out the surf and his other ear tickled by spider webs, trying to tune in to the conversation overhead, Heritage hadn't heard or seen Rowan approach. Then again, the kid was so skinny, he could have been standing sideways and been mistaken for one of the support posts holding up the deck and house. Only the radio gadget he carried had given him away—and that might have gone unnoticed if Heritage hadn't just pulled his head out of the rafters after a chair on the floor above his head pushed back suddenly, nearly deafening him with its piercing screech.

"Rowan—" Heritage tried to manage a nonchalant whisper.

"Oh, hi, Tage. Don't worry. This is how I get the information I need, too. Say, I can't get Aidan to answer me on our walkie-talkies. Is he okay? Is he on Wick at his house?"

Heritage lowered himself off the woodpile and brushed off his kayak pants with his hands. "Uh, right," he was whispering. "Well, we encountered a spot of bad water as we were paddling over here this morning and Aidan's backpack got spilled with all his school books inside and sank in the channel. If he had his walkie-talkie in that bag, it's gone. Aidan's just fine and he's recovering in front of the woodstove at his place."

"Cool. Thanks." With that, Rowan scurried out from under the house. He paused at the bottom of the front steps and hollered inside the cabin. "I'm home from school, Mom. Mac got tied up with something so I got a lift over here from Captain Matt who just dropped me at Big Beach. I am going to meet up with Ninnish to give him his homework assignments, and uh, Tage is here to speak to you." Rowan gave what looked like a half salute to Heritage before bounding off into the forest.

Mason appeared on the porch just after Heritage had popped out from under the house to appear as though he'd just gotten there, too. "Ro-wan?." She yelled at the tree line knowing it was pointless. Then she turned to greet Tage. "We were just talking about how brave you are to take on Ninnish."

"I don't think *brave* is the word for it, Mason." He saw Dottie behind the screen door. "Hello, Dottie," he said, sternly—still not over the terse conversation they'd had at the dock the previous day. Heritage had to think quickly for an excuse to be there. "Even though it's a school night, I thought I'd stop by to see if Rowan wanted to spend the night with Ninnish— I mean Aidan and me. No doubt Aidan's grown bored of my company. All I do is read, I'm afraid." He thrust his hands into the pockets of his kayak pants, ramming his middle fingernail against a metal object that his fingers quickly worked out must be a coin, which was curious since he never carried cash. His brain scrambled to resolve how a coin found its way into his pocket . . . unless, instead of falling to the ground as he'd presumed, it fell from the platform and straight into the wide opening of his pant pocket. Maybe his luck was changing. He couldn't resist pulling it out for examination. He looked down from his conversation with Mason to examine the stylized capital letter M and what looked like Greek or maybe Russian writing that encircled the letter. He safe deposited the coin back in his deep pocket and put a foot on a higher step leading to the deck. Mason seemed on the verge of giving her permission for the sleepover when Dottie cut her off.

"Actually," Dottie said, "Mason and Rowan have asked me over for dinner tonight, to celebrate Mason's birthday." Heritage watched surprise register on Mason's face, and knew Dottie was bullshitting. But she continued. "There is supposed to be quite a meteor shower tonight, and we have plans to watch it from Cormorant Rock." Mason's reaction telegraphed that Dottie might have been a better on-the-spot liar than even he was.

Heritage waited for an invitation to join them for the celebration, but it wasn't forthcoming. "Okay, then. Thought I'd check. Hey, have a good night. Sounds like fun." Heritage made sure to make eye contact with Mason, who wasn't up to bearing the burden of Dottie's lie. "And happy birthday to you, Mason."

Mason silently mouthed the words *thank you* with exaggerated big eyes that communicated it was very much a surprise birthday party.

Heritage jogged his way back along the bypass trail that Dottie had revealed to him when he had clandestinely tailed her to Mason's place. At first, he thought he needed to get right back across the island to check on Ninnish. Then he remembered that Rowan said he was heading there to hang out with his buddy. This bought Heritage some more time to think and to plot. He hadn't succeeded in dumping the teenager on Mason. Dottie being there had blocked that. He was still reeling from the morning's near-drowning incident and the drugging incident before that—plus the Polaroid evidence that he still needed to recover and destroy. On top of this, though the least of his immediate worries, he still didn't know what to make of Brad Fraser's disappearance, and he had not received an update from Lonnie or Monica on his grand-father's condition. With all those spikey, lead-weighted balls in the air and any one of them lethal enough to strike him in the temple or take out an eye, Heritage was just grateful to have this time alone while he figured out how best to juggle his demons.

The trail was taking him through the forest, but with so much on his mind, it seemed he had already traveled well beyond what he thought should have been a righthand branch in the trail that lead to Lyle's cabin. If it was there, he must have missed it. He wasn't heading to Lyle's anyway, but he would have liked the map in his head to reveal some accuracy on the ground, and so far, the two versions weren't meshing. Thinking he was on the same trail that would take him back to the labyrinth he spotted an orange float hanging from a short rope partway up the trunk of a Douglas fir. He stopped, looked around and there, on his right, was the righthand branch in the trail, he would have defi-nitely missed had it not been for the marker. He turned onto it and the trail narrowed significantly but ten metres later, didn't deliver him to Lyle's. Instead, the foliage on either side of the trail suddenly peeled back and the path ended at the edge of a cliff he'd not been to before—and one he might have strode right off of had he not been paying attention. To his right, was a somewhat natural-looking bench that was comprised of a gnarled but still living tree with some man-made flourishes. It was pretty clear that the tree had been forced by the relentless winds coming off the ocean to grow backward and somewhat horizontal to the ground. At some point in more recent years—by the look of the hewn wood—someone had added a stump for support and a decorative backrest and arms. Sitting on the makeshift bench faced you southwest into the sunset—when you could catch one.

With his hair held back by a prevailing wind, Heritage sat on this throne at the edge of the cliff and daringly overlooked a cauldron formation in the black rocks that was some twenty-five metres deep. At its roiling bottom, water whooshed in and water drained out in a constant cycle that must have been naturally carving out this vertical depression from the cliffs over centuries or more likely millennia. Heritage was no geologist, but the formation reminded him of the crater of a volcano—not that he'd seen one of those except on television. It occurred to him that this might be the ideal repository for things you wanted to get rid of for good. And that made him think of Ninnish—how he'd almost lost him that day in that same sea. It was the same ocean that had taken Marcel away from François, and perhaps had swallowed up Dottie's husband, Johnny, too—before leaving his ghost boat adrift for days.

As Heritage sat there contemplating the countless number of souls that must have perished beneath the surface of an ocean that large, a cormorant entered the cauldron from the north, followed in by two more cormorants through a narrow passage in the cliff where the waves, too, appeared as though they needed to hang an almost ninety-degree right-turn to enter through the breach they had eroded over time. The sleek black birds looked like they were covered in oil, but weren't of course and only refracted light that way because they were wet. They short-flapped to land on outcrops of rocks that formed multiple ledges across from him and disappeared there, black on black. This must be Cormorant Rock, Heritage realized—a nesting place and refuge for these seabirds—the spot from where Dottie had said she and Mason would be watching the meteor shower later that night. More seabirds came and went. The ocean churned, and every once in a while, a larger wave whooshed into the chasm, tossing mist up and into his face. Heritage found himself fretting about Ninnish. The teenager, likely recovered, was no doubt getting right back into mischief with Rowan again—setting the next trap to spring on him. Heritage couldn't take another drugging and would be making his own food between now and the moment he left for Toronto.

He ran back over how the teenager had drugged him in order to rape him—and rape is what it had amounted to, though Heritage knew he would never be able to convince a judge or jury or anybody else to believe that. Learning, with his ear to Mason's floorboards, that Dottie had been aware of what Ninnish was up to and didn't deter or stop him—in fact, had helped him narrow down which of Mona's many pills to use—incensed him. This reminded him of the prescription container and the funny-looking coin still in his pocket. He took both of them out to examine them in the sun while he sat there on that funky bench. He'd kept the half-labeled container with him at all times, even transferring it to different pants when he changed clothes, to remind him to make a list of the other medications in Mona's nightstand, thinking he might find a match. The coin, on closer examination, seemed to have Russian Cyrillic writing that banded in a circle around the large M. It took his brain less than a minute to hatch a wild theory of how a coin from Russia might have found its way onto a burial platform in a giant Sitka tree on Wickaninnish Island.

There was a sudden woosh of waves in the cauldron below him. Heritage checked his wristwatch and made a mental note, underlining once again, how Cormorant Rock would make a good place to get rid of things for good. He popped the lid on the medicine container to drop the M-coin inside it for safe keeping but noticed a nest made from several of his pubic hairs still stuck in the bottom. He carefully placed the coin next to him on the bench, stood and braced his footing. Then, holding his arm way out over the edge of the cliff, he shook the container and watched the wad of curly filaments scatter downward until the pubic nest began to tear apart and get carried back up to him on a hefty breeze blowing straight up the rock face. His left hand rested on his lower stomach, where the stubble from his recent sheering irritated him most. He stepped back from the edge, suddenly uncomfortable with the precarious height. He blew the last of the little hairs out of the container, retrieved the M-lettered coin from the bench to pop it inside before he snapped the lid back on tight and dropped the container back in the deep pocket of his kayaking pants.

He couldn't help thinking he should wait there, in the scrub brush, to nudge Dottie Bard over the side later that evening during the meteor shower. His callousness and ruthlessness suddenly bothered him. He tried to pinpoint the moment he might have lost Dottie's favour. But that required determining when he could have gained it in the first place. Rising from the bench, Heritage felt the Polaroid picture crinkle and crackle in his back pocket, reminding him there was more evidence he needed to feed to the roiling cauldron below. He pulled it out to look at one more time, his nakedness, his hard-on, and all the places he'd been tied down, all visible in the photo. At first, he thought about keeping it for evidence, but evidence of what? It wasn't even taken from a decent or remotely flattering angle and he looked more dead than aroused. Besides, Heritage knew there were other Polaroids, more evidence he needed to get his hands on before somebody else did. He tried to tear the flimsy plastic frame in half, but it resisted. It seemed almost indestructible. The first time he could have made real use of his fancy pocketknife, he didn't have it on him. He had to settle for a short stick that he used to scratch the image unrecognizable before tossing it underhand like a frisbee, off the cliff. It spun, plummeting out of his sight.

He turned away from the cliff to attempt to pick up the main trail again, if there even was such a thing on this densely forested island where everything seemed to be constantly shapeshifting to keep him guessing and confused. As just one example, the orange buoy float hanging on the tree trunk—when he was able to find it again after much hunting—was only visible if you were traveling south from Mason's place. It wasn't visible and the fork in the trail leading to Cormorant Rock was completely concealed by foliage if you happened to be traveling north. It was this confounding jumble of secret passages, dead-ends, fallen trees, paths that were either washed-out or submerged and the varying shadows created by the forest giants at different times of the day, that conspired to make sure you never, ever quite traveled the same way twice.

He'd been on the island almost three weeks, hardly enough time to have cultured an enemy but Heritage was constantly looking back over his shoulder, paranoid enough to believe he had already amassed several adversaries who were out to get him, and that he had maybe only one friend on his side—though François was a tap that ran cold more than hot. Earlier, while under Mason's house, he'd heard Dottie tell Mason that she had plans for him that sounded altogether nefarious to Heritage. She said she would use him as a means for getting Aidan off the island and out of the way, too—almost as though she were laying a premise for killing two birds with one rune stone. Was he a step ahead of her or a generation behind, he wondered? As he continued to mount his own defense while simultaneously building his case against Dottie, he couldn't help dwelling on that photograph of her and Mona holding hands in front of the unknown photographer who was clearly privy to their intimacies. Had Mason been that photographer? There was that, plus the prolonged hug he'd seen Dottie have with Mason on her deck just minutes ago. That photo and that embrace seemed to suggest to him, that lesbianism might have been just as common as Wicca on Wickaninnish Island. Now, Heritage didn't have the same issues or recoil from lesbians as most gay men he knew (which wasn't many, but he'd learned not to get Imogene Mantoya going off about dykes) but he'd long been aware that straight men found lesbianism an irresistible fantasy. Weren't they always bragging about how they coveted the act of having sex with two lesbians as the equivalent to winning the Stanley Cup? An only slightly more intriguing subject for their locker room banter around the topic of how mysterious and beguiling women could be was to elevate them to tricksters or witches with magic, hypnotizing or destructive powers over them. Even the slightest mention of witchcraft had been the taboo that had gotten Brad Fraser trash talking Wickaninnish Island in front of him during their first in person meeting. Broom riding lesbian witches didn't personally do anything for Heritage, but that might have been another reason Brad Fraser had questioned Heritage's involvement with the island.

And just like, that, he was lost again, staring at a junction in the trees he'd never seen before. For fun—because wasn't that what Wickaninnish Island was all about? —he kept to his left to hopefully learn a new route, to where? Well, he had no clue. His ankle felt good-as-new as he jogged, zigged, zagged, sloshed, tripped, and leapt the thousand or so metres from one side of the island to hopefully get to the other. After ten minutes or so, Heritage could begin to make out the water through the trees ahead but needed to bushwhack with his arms to get through the last overgrown several metres. He could see the problem with the new route was that it had dumped him considerably north of Mona's cabin where he thought he was headed, and onto a mounded white sand beach oriented almost northward looking toward Stubbs Island with a cloud-topped Lone Cone Mountain looming behind it. Heritage left tree cover to wander out into the open on the beach. He could see the one-level Tofino General Hospital across the way with its orange windsock moving in the breeze. This is how he knew he was north of Mona's place, but when he walking to the water's edge to look south, another rocky promontory blocked him from catching a glimpse of Mona's cabin or the navigation beacon that he knew was positioned further out in the water, though he could just make out the roof of the Headlands from that angle.

Turning back around to face the forest from which he'd emerged, he saw what he'd completely missed seeing before, even though he must have come out of the bushes right next to it. There, situated at the south end of the sand bar, at the edge of the tree line—or more accurately *under* the limbs and branches of that treeline, was a dilapidated, two- or three-story cottage, the collapsed porch of which looking as though it may have one time straddled the orangish-brown stream that came gurgling out of the forest. The little creek braided through the sand to reach the ocean next to where he was standing. The neglected wooden structure didn't just look derelict and abandoned, it was. Looking all creepy and haunted, Heritage thought it should have been condemned, but it wasn't like the island fell under any village building inspector's jurisdiction, being off the grid and all.

He heard a boat motor behind him and crouched down on the sand with his hand over his eyes in time to see Dottie's white and blue cabin boat make a beeline for town. So, she wasn't staying at Mason's for dinner or stargazing. Another lie. That's all people did here—lie and double-cross. All the way back to Chief Wickaninnish pretending the Tla-o-qui-aht had changed their minds about selling fur pelts to the *Tonquin* only to murder nearly everyone on board instead, to Brad Fraser, Dottie, Stephanie, Ninnish. Everyone had lied to him.

Of course, Heritage had lied to everybody too. Maybe he belonged here, after all.

Daylight was dwindling by the time he had bushwhacked through some of the densest underbrush he'd ever encountered and soon the east side of the island would be heading into *le crépuscule*. It had taken Heritage forty-five minutes to crawl less than a quarter of a kilometre over the imposing, brush and tree tangled headland that separated the sandbar on one side from the front steps of Mona's cabin tucked back in a cove just on the other side. No wonder Heritage had never seen or been to that falling-down shack or beach before. He took a pitstop in the outhouse without a door, where he did a quick assessment of his stinging cuts and bruised legs while in his sitting position. From there, he could see Mona's Boston Whaler still anchored a short canoe paddle beyond the rocks and a straw of blue-grey smoke issuing out of the stove pipe of the cabin. So, Ninnish hadn't taken off on him. He was relieved.

All he wanted was a warm shower—a hot one being completely out of the question on Wick since anyone with a shower had them al fresco on their breezy decks, letting the water drain through the deck boards and onto the mossy rocks below. He supposed he could have drained Mona's propane tank by heating the gravity-fed creek water. But that was too much work to fiddle with the diverter valves and pilot light. Heritage needed a shower to clean his cuts and scrapes, and since it was getting dark, he figured he could manage it without attracting anyone's attention, despite the waxing moon that was cresting from behind Mount Colnett on the other side of the channel and beyond the tidal mudflats that Heritage knew existed there between Tofino—a half dozen smaller islands—and Meares Island. The shower started out warmish thanks to the long garden hose that had been sitting in the sun but soon the shower water turned icy which made for a jerky, soapy rinse-and-dash—all in under sixty seconds. He was as quiet as he could be so as not to disturb a hopefully still-sleeping, still-recovering Ninnish. Then he panicked, remembering that Aidan was supposed to be hanging out with Rowan, and the two of them doing anything quietly was inherently suspicious.

He soon discovered that Ninnish was gone and there was no trace of Rowan either. There was something safety-pinned to the blankets where Heritage had left him sleeping in front of the woodstove. It wasn't a note as much as it was a penciled map showing the route to the labyrinth and a diagram of the labyrinth itself. In the center of the two concentric circles was the carefully sketched outline of a body, arms and legs splayed out like DaVinci's *Vitruvian Man* except all its appendages, even the penis, had been drawn to appear as though they had been separated from the torso. The figure overlayed the pentagram but in a way that still looked every bit the shape of a star. The safety pin pierced the figure's phallus, which had been drawn with much more care and detail than the rest of the crude map—a testament, no doubt, to the artist's obsessive preoccupation. Heritage held the drawing up to examine it closer and discovered the safety pin was tied to a long strand of white thread. The still-burning coals in the stove glowed orange through the lined notebook paper. Heritage couldn't tell from the drawing if the person lying in the labyrinth was supposed to be Ninnish, himself, or some other man, but starkly, with all its limbs lobbed off, the fellow, whoever he was, couldn't be in the best of shape. The words carefully penned at the top of the page were less vague than the artist's rendition, in all capital letters: *YOU CAN'T RUN AWAY!*

"Ninn-ish!"

Heritage's primal yell threatened to pop the glass panes from their sills. He tossed his wet shower towel on the kitchen counter and jumped into a pair of jeans, thinking they were his. They weren't, but he managed to pull them on anyway. He grabbed the toasty green OSU hoodie from the chairback next to the woodstove, coaxed his sore feet back inside his Timberlands and walked outside, gathering the white thread in his hands as he went. He yelled again.

"Aidan!"

With the drawing still in his hand, he paced a minute on the cedar decking. He decided to interpret the note the only way he could, as yet another cry for attention. But then he realized with a panicked exhale that everything in the past weeks—from the exhibitionism to the drugging to the near-drowning that he no longer suspected had been an accident—it had all been one long wail for attention, for help, for deliverance. What he didn't know was whether he or Ninnish was screaming it the loudest.

He leapt from the deck to the beach, reeling in the thread as he went bounding back onto the path as the thread instructed, navigating by the light of the late-September moon as it ascended the night sky and began to illuminate his progress through the forest canopy above him. He trotted in and out of the tree line along the eastern shore, drumming over sections of boardwalk, dispatching avalanches of sand and pebbles as he cut through pocket beaches, still collecting the thread that ballooned like a judiciary wig in his hands. He had forgotten to grab the flashlight off the shelf, but remarkably, the thin white thread nearly glowed in what scant moonlight there was.

As he hurried along the trail, he decided he was going to march Ninnish directly over to Mason, in the middle of her so-called stargazing birthday dinner party, if that's what it took to get him off his hands for good. Between Dottie's cabin and Stephanie's shack, where the path lined with empty green wine bottles hung a right turn into the forest, he momentarily lost the white thread that had either run out or broken. He knew his way to the labyrinth, of course, but the white thread had somewhat reassured him he wasn't wasting his time and had been on track to catch the spider who'd spun this web. There was something deliberate and intentional about that white thread. Heritage didn't want to screw anything up or arrive without collecting every centimetre of evidence that Ninnish was certified and should be institutionalized. He widened his eyes at the same time he ran right into the thread again. He tied the broken ends together with a knot —though he didn't know why he was doing this—and quickly continued on his course, shouting out all the variations of the kid's names.

It wasn't a new feeling, but Rowan certainly felt cast aside since his buddy's focus had pivoted from hanging out with him to entrapping Tage—the biggest predator to hit the island since the cougar—which neither of them had even seen once—but strategizing the hunt had helped pierce their boredom. It was probably just the same when it came to Tage. Aidan would tire of that too and move on to terrorize the next thing that came along or more likely return to just hanging out—just the two of them together again. At the same time, he also felt tremendous relief to no longer be the object of his older friend's experiments and bullying—even if it was temporary. Sometimes—well, usually, Aidan just took things too far. Like the other night when he put those drugs in the meal he cooked for his babysitter. Rowan was definitely not okay with that which is why he sat that part out, down on the beach. He wasn't really okay with the rest of it either, but because he didn't believe Aidan would actually go through with everything that he talked about doing, Rowan wanted to be there to witness the fail and tell him he'd told him so.

At the last-minute tonight, though, he'd chickened out of the latest scheme. He'd helped Ninnish set the stage in the clearing, but just didn't have the stomach to stick around like some geek taking Polaroid pictures again. Rowan had made an excuse that he was late for dinner to celebrate his mum's birthday but promised to circle back to check on Ninnish in case his plan went sideways—which he was sure it would. The latest trap would be a modification of a dare Ninnish had first proposed earlier that same summer: if Ninnish could endure two hours tied naked on the forest floor, in the center of the witch's labyrinth that had freaked them both out since they were children, Ninnish would get to stick his boner up Rowan's bum. If he didn't last the two hours and begged to be untied, Rowan got to do the same to Ninnish.

That was the way they played, Aidan's rules. Dares were always dead serious stuff and they were always sexual.

But all of that changed once Tage came along.

After bringing every candle from both of their houses, Rowan had mostly done his part and had been hurtfully dismissed. "Tie your own damn hands, then" he'd told Ninnish as he stormed out of the candlelit clearing and headed home.

While lying in wait, Ninnish prepared himself to sacrifice everything in order to keep Tage from leaving. He'd never felt that way about anyone. That very morning, he had been willing, almost eager to die because of it. He felt the same way still, lying on a bed of spruce needles, moss, and jagged moon shells. It would be his sacrificial altar, if it came to that. He knew Tage didn't take him seriously, but he also knew that could change with time. On the other hand, he was running out of time, and would lose Tage forever if he didn't do *something*. He turned his head to one side—he still had seawater in his ear. He had adjusted the ropes one last time before settling deep to wait beneath the perverted moon already peeping on him between the trees. The steel of the ornately engraved athame, on which his naked body lay, had been cold at first but quickly warmed in the hallow between his shoulder blades. His head was gently propped on a fresh blanket of moss that he'd cut from the forest floor and carried like a roll of shag carpet to cover the altar of doll heads plus the stench of his two-day old shit. The ropes around his ankles were tied securely in place. Those at his wrists looked tied but weren't so that he could turn his body over when the moment came to offer up the tunnel of the oracle.

He had accused Rowan of double-crossing him, maybe wrongly and maybe rightly, but someone or something had removed his offerings made to the spirits of the labyrinth—the wallet and the prescription container. He had been furious to find them gone, and suspected that must have been why his incantations had not succeeded in eliminating François and compelling Tage to fall under his love spell. Rowan had denied taking what he had referred to as "his stupid offerings" and even confessed to stashing one of the Polaroids in the mound of doll heads for safekeeping—but that Polaroid was also not where *he* left it. He accused Aidan of removing that. This caused an argument and distrust between them and Rowan had decided to walk away rather than put up with Aidan's accusations.

Maybe it hadn't been Rowan's fault. As he lay waiting, Aidan thought there was a possibility it might have been Matt Greene's wolf-dog, which considered the southern half of the island its marked territory. Or it could have been either Matt's weird dad or his siblings, who lived nearest the labyrinth and couldn't keep their noses out of the island's business. Of course, it could have been Dottie, or half a dozen other islanders who happened upon his treasures and made off with them like the trickster ravens and thieves they were. Any moment now, none of that would matter. Aidan had already begun to detect the soft tugging of the white thread tied in a double knotted bow wrapped around his genitals three times. Ninnish would soon open his blue eyes to gaze upon Tage's handsome face. He clenched his fists to ward off the cold and tried to slow his breathing.

As Heritage neared the labyrinth, he began to notice flickering lights that turned out to be candles scattered around the clearing. The sight curbed his pace and quickened his heart. In the middle of the woods, the outer circle of the labyrinth was outlined in candles, and more were positioned in lower nooks of trees and on branches, glowing with the spookiest and most incandescent light Heritage had ever seen.

At first, he didn't see Ninnish lying naked in the center of the labyrinth—just as the teen had depicted himself in his drawing, except all his appendages were still attached. Heritage's feet continued walking forward, though his mind was frozen in suspended awe. There Ninnish lay naked on his back, his limbs extended to mark the half-directions of the labyrinth, and tied with long lengths of rope to four stakes pounded at sharp angles into the earth. Heritage stopped abruptly, his hands full of white thread, taking the vision in, and unable to utter a sound. He saw the pentagram in flickering candles around the boy's still and translucent body. His angelic head was raised on a flawless sphagnum pillow, his closed eyes' blond eyelashes were like fiber optic filaments that caught the candlelight. The white thread that had brought the adult to this ceremony was tied in a bow around the boy's scrotum and an ever-ready erection that stood perpendicular as the ring of Sitkas.

Was he dead? With that boner, Heritage knew better.

"This is beautiful," he spoke with a reverence the space commanded. "But what is it all about?" Heritage was smitten by the grand visual feast, but it didn't change the sour reality at its core— an acutely disturbed child he couldn't rescue or save any longer.

Ninnish slowly raised his eyelids like the curtain on an opening number. "I want you to take me. Like I had you the other night." Aidan's lips were chalk-white with dryness, and Heritage thought the colour really hadn't returned to his face after the near-drowning. Aidan was not blinking, his blue gaze welded in time, his heart beating for one purpose only.

"This is your chance to get even with me. I gave you my gift. You give me yours."

Heritage looked away. The child's skin was suddenly too blinding. He glanced to the platform in the forked tree to the north and wondered what the spirit of the bones made of all of this. "I don't want to get even, Aidan. I just want to get away from here, off this island. It's—it's become more than I can handle. *You* are more than I signed up for."

"I can't accept that. If you go—" Aidan's dry throat cut off the words and he swallowed.

"If I stay," Heritage insisted, "I'll destroy you." That didn't come out exactly the way he meant it, though he supposed it was the truth.

"If you leave, you destroy me." Ninnish spoke clearly and unflustered. His intelligence, like his appearance, camouflaged his youth.

Heritage didn't know what to say. He tried to come up with something mature, but he drew a blank, like a child. "I'm sorry, Aidan. Let's get you back home. You've had enough excitement for one day."

Tage deposited fists full of bunched thread to cover the teen's impressive nakedness, and shifted the weight of his crouch to work on the knotted rope at the young man's ankles. The knots had been tied very tightly by someone who knew knots. Heritage remembered the knife he'd jettisoned as an offering to the labyrinth. He searched the softly illuminated moss for a break in the earth. He spotted it and hopped once like a bullfrog to retrieve it. He unfolded the main and longest blade and the candlelight reflected off it into Aidan's troubled blue eyes just as a branch snapped behind them. They both jerked at the noise but Ninnish seemed to take that as his cue and maybe confirmation that Rowan and his trusty Polaroid camera were lurking in the brambled thickets.

"Tage! Wait!"

Ninnish screamed so suddenly and dramatically that Heritage fell out of his balance, having to employ his arm as a kickstand to keep himself from toppling over. "I'll do whatever you say!" he screamed again. "Just don't use the knife. I'm sorry. I'm sorry!" He was out of his mind with hysterics and Heritage wasn't at all sure he should be untied at all.

"What is your problem?" Heritage demanded in a frantic

whisper, trying to ascertain what had provoked the escalation in the child's voice. Maybe it was the sight of the knife. He set it to the side of his boot and tried the knot again with his hands. Ninnish began to struggle against the ropes, loudly and frantically whimpering. He thrust his pelvis into the air, as though he was convulsing. Heritage suddenly wondered if his hyperactivity might have been misdiagnosed epilepsy.

"Hold on, dammit!" Tage yelled when Ninnish kicked his hand, jamming a few of his fingers back. "Hold still, you little shit!"

The reverberation of his deep voice in that clearing surprised him. Ninnish fought him violently. Heritage tried to hold him down with one hand on his stomach while the other hand worked on the knot. Ninnish was screaming and writhing like he was possessed—Heritage was shouting back, trying to settle him down. Once he got him untied, Heritage was sure his panic would subside. And then another thought flashed into his mind like ice water in his face. What if Ninnish had gotten into some of his mother's drugs or had taken something he'd stolen from Lyle, and this episode was the bad reaction?

Maybe he was not dealing with a hyperactive teenager but one under the influence of something other than hormones. He most certainly was not acting like the kid he thought he knew. Of course. That made sense! He had free access to anything from his mother's dresser, which practically constituted a fully stocked pharmacy. But he had also been hanging around the margins of Lyle's house party that day, when drugs had been on full display. Marcel had taken so much he had passed out buck-naked on the tree limb, and hours later, was likely still so high he thought he could plow his boat back into the fury of a storm, to go hunting for his missing wallet. Heritage began thinking Ninnish was maybe on acid, and it had either amped his adrenalin or triggered his paranoia—or both.

The screaming, spitting, and kicking was not letting up. Heritage managed to get one loop of the double knot undone before

Ninnish jerked for the knife. It happened so quickly, Heritage didn't have time to question how he'd undone his wrists or if they had truly been tied at all. Ninnish had the knife and was squirming like a snake that had just been halved by a power lawnmower.

"Not my nuts," Ninnish pleaded, holding the blade to his scrotum amid the pile of white thread. "Don't cut my nuts!" His voice seemed loud enough to travel across the channel.

"Ninnish—goddammit!"

Heritage tried to get the knife out of Aidan's hand, but it wasn't his pocketknife. He looked off to the side where he saw his Gerber resting after having been evidently deflected out of his hand. He looked back at the much longer dagger in the kid's hands. "Hold still god damnit—"

And whoosh! With one spectacular moonlit flash of steel, all oxygen was siphoned from the clearing, the night went instantly still. Sounds vacated their ear canals like the universe had tripped a circuit breaker. Four hands glistened red in the muted candlelight. A kilometre of white thread turned pink in an instant. Aidan's face registered one fixed look of horror before his blue eyes rolled into his cranium and his head dropped back onto the moss. Behind them there was a thud followed by a symphony of crashing branches that were accompanied by one long whoop sailing through the forest.

"*No-o-o-o!*"

Rowan Robson was screaming out more than he could breathe in as he clicked on and tried to keep his headlamp trained on the trail that raced beneath his suddenly very clumsy, fourteen-and-three-quarter-year-old feet. He didn't even realize he was instinctually cupping his own genitals as he tore through the wooded night in terror.

What he'd just seen from his lookout stoop in one of the Sitka trees on the edge of the labyrinth didn't register with anything he knew—but he was smart enough to fear for his own balls and his own life. He ran faster, sure that Ninnish was already dead or bleeding out. It wasn't enough to reach their cabin where he'd left his mum squealing to open the giftwrapped package that Dottie had just returned from town to give her. No. Tage knew where he lived and would come there next to cut his nuts off, too. Instead, Rowan veered through the trees barreling toward the ocean, racing for Cormorant Rock, thinking the two were likely already watching shooting stars from the sunset bench. He ran faster but thought to stop screaming, since that might give away his position if he was being chased by a killer—or the cougar.

He fully assumed Tage was on his heels, right behind him it sounded like, as branches he'd bent in his locomotive push forward snapped back, some breaking behind him. In fact, he was sure of it. Ninnish was for sure dead already—he'd seen the blood gushing from between his friend's legs with his own eyes—and unless he could outrun the murderer, he'd have to kill again to eliminate a witness. If he was going to get away with this, he'd have to silence Rowan too. The trail took several illogical jags, right then left. Frustrated, Rowan hopped a fringe of salal to run along a short beach at low tide. He ducked back among the trees and the trail began its climb to the cliffs of Cormorant Rock. Instead of slowing in his ascent, he managed to push harder.

As he neared the top of the cliff he yelled for his mother. Mason stood next to where she'd been sitting with Dottie on the tree bench to receive her panicked child, who burst out of the brush like a lightning bolt, knocking her off-balance. Dottie tried to grab her, but Mason was already in motion and Dottie only managed to connect with the collar of Rowan's jacket. Dottie jerked him back, causing him to choke and tumble backward into the salal.

Without a scream, without the slightest bit of resistance, the birthday girl vanished off the side of the cliff, into the frothy cauldron below Cormorant Rock, surely impaled on the sharpened alder stakes that the boys had set in the rocks below to trap their cougar.

Rowan threw his hands over his ears and squeezed shut his eyes. Dottie, with her own breath caught in her throat, waited, begging the goddesses to hear Mason's cry for help—but instead she heard the distinctive crash of a wave as it cannonballed around the corner and against the face of Cormorant Rock. The effervescent sound of millions of salty bubbles in retreat, amplified by the concavity of the rock cliff, seemed to pop like corn inside Rowan's tormented ears. He pounded his head against the ground until he realized that wouldn't change what had happened. He gazed through his tears into the speckled black sky. Two stars shot across the giant screen at the same time, in different directions. The night returned to complete silence but for the wailing sobs of Rowan Robson and the foghorn off adjacent Lennard Island, which suddenly pressed into service to insensitively toll the danger of the coast's foreboding rocks.

Heritage tilted his head toward the bellowing sound. He couldn't guess how far he'd traipsed through the woods, carrying the limp body of the badly bleeding boy. He honestly didn't remember the last fifteen minutes, but there Ninnish was in his cramping arms as he headed across the island, so he must have been thinking rationally enough to know he needed to get medical help for the boy. He also had enough sense to carry him away from Mason, who would have responded irrationally to Rowan's account of whatever it was he'd thought he'd just seen. As Heritage rammed his way through the forest, taking branches in the face, he struggled with the decision: should he attempt to doctor Ninnish himself, with first aid supplies he suspected he wouldn't find at

Dottie's cabin? Or could he possibly make it to Mona's cabin, where there was a marine radio? Either way, Ninnish was at grave risk and was no longer even moaning.

Though he didn't have much in the way of his own lung capacity or even optimism, Heritage kept telling Ninnish to hang in there—that he wouldn't let him down. When the two reached Dottie's dark cabin, to his total surprise since he'd watched her return to town, Heritage spotted her boat moored ten or fifteen metres out in the cove. His back and arms were very near failing and he was at risk of dropping Ninnish, so he took a gamble and scrambled to the rusted rowboat he knew was stashed in the trees just above the high-tide mark. He'd earlier thought about using it to collect rainwater—before he realized rainwater was not in short supply. He put Ninnish on the rusted floor of the row-boat, François' green blood-soaked hoodie still tourniquet- tied between and around the teen's legs. He dragged and splashed the rowboat into the water.

He climbed in and quickly faced backward, using his right foot to put pressure on Ninnish's crotch. He was worried about the amount of blood the boy had lost. He was panicked there might not be a key in the ignition of the boat when he got there. He hadn't even gotten to the question of whether or not he could figure out how to start and drive the damn clunker. He would row all the way to the hospital if he had to. The boy was already unconscious, so there wouldn't be the usual struggle. There was only so much his limited first aid could accomplish for him now. And since he was being honest with himself, it was a bit late if Heritage thought he could still be a hero and save Ninnish all by himself. It was going to take a team of experts —medical and psy-chological. The best Heritage could do was expedite the delivery.

They reached Dottie's boat in the time it had taken the fog-horn to complete two cycles of its two-tone dirge with a pause in between—Heritage figured they were about two minutes apart. He heaved the teen onto the siderail and balanced him there while he climbed onto the larger boat himself. Easing the boy onto the floor, Heritage noticed how the moon lent a surreal blue glow to the boy's skin and how the major veins just beneath the surface looked like purple yarn coated by a thin and even layer of Elmer's glue that hadn't quite dried. Satan with an A looked peacefully and deceptively angelic in unconscious repose.

Heritage grabbed a ratty floater jacket from the cramped single berth, and unzipped it open on the floor of the boat. He lifted Ninnish into it and did his best to zip him back up. Heritage tried to remember what little he had once known about running motorboats from the dozen summers he had spent in Ontario's Lake Country with his parents and grandparents at the Carter family's compound. With bloody hands, he pulled the anchor off the bottom of the shallow cove. He shoved the rowboat as hard as he could, thinking it probably would sink before drifting out of the cove anyway.

The key was there, attached by ball chain to a painted piece of foam rubber. He turned the key, and the boat sputtered, sending plumes of light-grey exhaust into the night. Heritage put the boat into gear and headed through the narrow cove opening before punching it into the channel, aiming for the village at the end of the peninsula on the other side. He could see a bank of fog moving in from the open ocean over his right shoulder, but managed to scoot ahead of it—following the choppy swath of light cast by the three-quarter moon that was about to be swallowed entirely by the fog. His only thought now was arriving at the hospital with the boy still alive. He turned on the boat's radio, gave his mayday and asked for an ambulance to be waiting at the First Street dock. A minute later he heard the siren and saw the lights of the ambulance leaving the hospital. Nobody had to tell Heritage Carter the Third that his version of the wickedly unfolding story wouldn't be remotely persuasive without corroboration from a victim he urgently needed to survive.

DEPOSING THE DAMNED

Heritage didn't see how the interrogation could have been any more cliché, unless perhaps *Street Legal*'s Leon Robinovitch himself had been sitting across from him, asking the same irritating questions over and over. Heritage fidgeted with his wristwatch. That wasn't a good analogy, Heritage sort of remembered, since Eric Peterson's character, Leon, had been a lawyer, and not a criminal investigator. He perhaps should have gone with a character from *Hill Street Blues*. It didn't matter, of course, and this officer was probably only deploying a textbook questioning technique that he had picked up at the RCMP training academy in Regina. But Heritage was trained—though not quite yet licensed—as a lawyer, himself, and was certainly smart enough to know he was being asked the same questions, just worded differently. He tried to vary his answers without changing the facts, so the officer had something new to write down.

He'd been sitting in that musty room down the hall from

the public complaint counter for nearly an hour, staring at the lime-green algae that had established a stronghold in the corner of the concrete floor opposite him. He had repeatedly asked for an update on Ninnish's condition, until he realized it might have made him seem obsessed over the victim. When he first reported to the front counter at the RCMP detachment feeling drained and hypoglycemic in the middle of a post-adrenaline crash, he had expected to be heralded by trumpets as a hero, and not a criminal, though he suspected Dottie Bard had something to do with the way he was being handled and processed. She had arrived by coast guard lifeboat clutching Rowan's hand about the same time the EMTs had finished transferring Aidan by stretcher into the ambulance. That had seemed oddly quick to Heritage for Dottie to have gotten from there to here without her own boat, which he'd stolen, unless Captain Matt Greene had also been in attendance at Mason's surprise-to-her birthday party. Rowan was looking particularly traumatized and much, much paler than usual. He sure felt for the kid, given what he must have thought he witnessed from up in the tree above the labyrinth. He started walking over to give Rowan a reassuring hug, but within five seconds, Dottie dropped her mind on the dock and the scene mostly went bat-shit-crazy from there.

Heritage's first impulse had been to high-tail it up to the hospital where he could monitor and get updates on Aidan, but when he saw that was where Dottie was going too, he turned on his boot heels and walked instead to the RCMP detachment where he'd expected to be met with less irrationalized drama and fewer accusations. So far, though, he'd been less than impressed by the treatment he was receiving. He had asked for something to eat and was brought a leftover cake donut in an otherwise empty box from Tim Horton's. Tofino didn't even have a Tim Horton's, so the thing was especially stale—and regrettably inedible. For reasons he didn't know, but suspicions that were starting to creep in, Heritage began to believe that Dottie was possibly feeding a counter-narrative to a different RCMP officer at the hospital and had probably already divulged a dozen ways to incriminate him by now. Otherwise, he should have been thanked for his time and for voluntarily coming to the station. That was just not the way his night was unfolding.

It was the third time he'd been asked to start from the beginning. For the third time he told them what little he knew of Aidan Rye, and some, but certainly not all, of the events that had occurred during the twenty-odd, very odd days he'd known him. So far, he hadn't had to disclose to the RCMP who he really was, momentarily forgetting that they'd likely worked up a whole profile on him when he'd turned in Marcel's wallet. He'd used the name Tage, that visit. He didn't have any identification on him this evening, and it was midnight in the seaside town. Toren, the officer he'd interacted with before, didn't seem to be on duty, so nobody who could vouch for him was really reachable. He'd dropped every local name he could think of, and had explained how he had been left responsible for the safety and well-being of a minor who was a notorious troublemaker—something well known to everyone in this town but him.

"Yes, I was there when the accident happened. I've already told you all of this."

He knew the whole thing looked bad—and while he wanted to cooperate, it wasn't like he had nothing to hide. No matter how much he'd practiced denying his affiliation, he was still Heritage Carter's grandson and there was still a handful of Polaroids out there in the sound somewhere, so yes, he was sweating bullets, he was agitated and his forehead glistened under an unkempt flop of curly brown hair. Even more incriminating, he'd had anal intercourse with the barely fifteen-year old in question. The situation could not have been more delicate.

"I've already told you. I don't know if Ninnish was really fifteen. I think he said he was fifteen once but then in the next minute he seemed to remember he'd just had a birthday at the end of the summer. But hey, I wasn't here when he was born, so I'm not the one to ask. The kid could have been fifteen, maybe held back a year or two in school. I don't know."

The balding Mountie stared at him, tapping the eraser tip of his pencil on his front teeth. "You speak of him in the past tense, as though he might be dead. Do you think you killed Aidan Rye?"

"No," Heritage answered, perhaps too emphatically. "I don't think I killed anyone." As soon as he said it, Heritage was sure one of the officers was going to seize on the word *think* and he kicked himself for not using a more definitive choice, like *know*. He quickly followed up, having remembered the officer's name he'd spoken to a week or more ago. "Look, is Constable Toren not working tonight?"

"You've had a run-in with the police before?" The balding Mountie tried to knock him off his measured balance.

"I turned in a missing wallet," Heritage said, glaring at the officer. "Is that a run-in?"

"Mason Robson is dead," the second officer blurted out. "The coast guard managed to grapple her badly beaten body from the water around Cormorant Rock about forty minutes ago."

"What? No!" He dismissed, knowing that just could not be possible. The two officers didn't speak but stared him down, maybe thinking he would crack. Heritage did start to launch from his chair knocking the table with his knees, but he didn't achieve lift off or he would have blasted the hell right out of there. "Well I certainly didn't kill her," Heritage exclaimed, more shocked by the news than their implication that he might be involved.

"Did you rough her up?" the other Mountie asked. "I'm told she had a nasty pair of puncture wounds to her torso."

"No, I most certainly did not!" Heritage was far too spent by this rapidly compounding ordeal to think clearly, to speak rationally or even to really sit upright. He hadn't slept well the night before with Ninnish letting him know with every huff and puff that he was bent out of shape for being banished up there in the loft in the cabin at The Headlands. He'd performed a mid-sea rescue of a drowning child who later tried to kill himself. He then carried said stabbing victim across an island and raced him to the hospital before voluntarily, on his own accord and volition, presenting himself at the RCMP station to make a statement. It had been one hellish long day and he was beyond tired. "Look, can either of you level with me? Is Aidan Rye going to be okay?" He looked the younger, balding Mountie directly in his very blue eyes and for a second, for whatever reason, the officer stopped chewing on his pencil.

"Word is, he's lost a shitload of blood and it looks like he might lose a testicle, but the doctor thinks he was able to save the penis. They won't know for a good little while how this will affect him sexually in his later years."

Heritage wanted to say hopefully it might slow him down, but he thought better of it, choosing not to say more until he'd met with a lawyer. Ninnish was alive. Heritage exhaled and his aching shoulders relaxed. For several minutes the three of them just sat in that moldy space in silence. After a while, the younger officer motioned with his chin and the two Mounties left Heritage in the concrete bunker or a windowless room. Heritage looked at his fancy sea diver's watch. He was nineteen hours and thirty-eight minutes into a day he was mistaken to have started quite so opti- mistically, if at all.

Dottie knew better than to question the reasons behind tragedy. She'd seen—hell, she'd caused—more than her share of grief and tragedy in a lifetime. She rubbed her eyes. The clock above the hospital receptionist's desk had helped her keep track of the unreasonable time she'd been kept waiting. The receptionist on duty was also the part-time librarian. Dottie knew her as

Gillian—but for some reason, always struggled in the moment to remember her name—often greeting her as Lillian, which had been her maternal grandmother's first name. This evening, Dottie noticed the bump for the first time and wondered if the poor dear was pregnant. She had been Marcel Labbé's girlfriend—there was another tragedy for you.

Behind the bank of three leatherette chairs where Dottie sat in her pink sweatpants splattered with mud, was a bronze plaque with raised letters. It recorded the generous funders of the village hospital. Her name was second. She'd brought the village water. She was working on a waste sanitation proposal that would end decades of dumping it untreated into the sound. She'd been a village councillor so many consecutive terms she had a special, high-back chair installed in the chamber room, even though it didn't match any of the others. Nobody ever asked her why her chair was taller than the mayor's. Nobody would have dared. Dottie knew she was untouchable. No matter what people may have thought of her personally—and those feelings ran the gamut—no one could dispute the modern conveniences she had brought the village during her two-decade reign.

Everybody but Samantha Campbell, the already on-duty night nurse, had been called in from home for this triple emergency. Sam had been looking forward to another uneventful evening of working her word search puzzles in between med rounds. It was easy money, with decent benefits that allowed her to raise her kids during the day. Of course, she knew all the victims, and she knew Dottie Bard. Everyone knew Dottie. Ninnish—well, there wasn't anybody he hadn't terrorized, and she was mildly surprised he'd lived this long. She'd always said hello to Mason Robson in the co-op, which was the only place she really ever ran into her other than during the various Wheel of the Year events on Wickaninnish, like Litha solstice and the Ostara equinox. But those weren't really speaking occasions where you got to know a priestess better. She had been looking forward to Mabon in a few weeks where she'd see Mason again. Now, she was in the morgue at the end of the hallway.

The victims were never faceless or unknown in a small town. Everybody knew everybody, whether you sold them their beer on Friday nights or sewed their penis and scrotum back on after a knifing. From where Sam observed the sleepy goings-on, behind the nurse's station, there were no secrets. She knew the town drunks and the village hypochondriacs—sometimes it even felt as though she'd dated half of them. And she knew the town snobs who always acted like they couldn't be bothered to return a hello, until something like this forced them to come into contact with the working class.

She could tell by the way Dottie Bard kept fidgeting, that she was feeling put out by the whole thing. She supposed she could make things easier for her—offer to check for an update on either of the children. But she found the moment too equalizing to mess with the fleeting balance.

One of the double doors squeaked open and the hospital's senior ranking nurse, Sherri Remington, began her well-practiced code blue walk, from the emergency room down the short corridor to the reception area. Sam had seen the walk plenty. With a penchant for hogging authority and a talent for exaggerating every situation without saying anything, Remington's hips swiveled like Marilyn Monroe's, whether she was in the hospital or the hardware store. And it snagged gazes and raised eyebrows everywhere she went. From the way she walked to how she always let just enough of her frosted hair poke out of her surgical cap, Remington was probably trying to attract Doctor McAnally, who was one of maybe four gainfully employed and eligible bachelors in the village. Sherri Remington was a piece of work—another snob, really, who was too good for this town, and, as a recent divorcee, just happened to have to rely on a regular job—just like Sam. That was equilibrium at work too, in Samantha's mind—which was why she could always greet her with a smile and a hello, whether it was reciprocated or not.

"We're running short of B-Neg," Sam told her supervisor on arrival. "We possibly won't need more before we transfer the patient to Port Alberni, but just in case, we should contact the Royal Jubilee in Victoria, where they have the boy's mother in oncology."

"No," Dottie Bard—who had only been pretending to be minding her own business—piped up. "Mona's in no shape to be getting news like this. Besides, she's not B-Negative."

"Oh?" the nurses asked, in unison.

"Ninnish was adopted. I'm B-Negative."

"Oh?" Nurse Remington moved closer, perhaps wondering if that was a connection or nugget of gossip worth investigating. "Well, we should tap you for half a litre if you're feeling up to it, Dottie. It's better to be safe, you know." Dottie gave a single, dignified nod. "I'll get my kit."

They couldn't hold Heritage without evidence. They had probably already detained him longer than was warranted, considering he was the one who delivered the teen to the hospital and that he had come to them voluntarily—and for the second time. Given the inaccessibility of Wickaninnish Island at night, and with the apparent victim not able to speak and the only witness incapacitated by his own trauma, they thanked Tage Carter for his time, and for his willingness to come forward.

The RCMP officers didn't know what to think. Without checking the casebooks, they were pretty sure they were dealing with the first near-castration to be investigated in Clayoquot

Sound. Figures it would have happened on Wickaninnish Island, they joked uneasily. Being men who had fathered, the whole incident came wrapped in a disturbing poignancy neither of them could easily shake. Short of murder, robbing a boy of his only ticket to becoming a fully functioning, procreating man, was probably the sickest crime either of them could imagine. So far, though, there was no telling if what had happened to little Aidan Rye really was a crime at all, and not just a case of self-mutilation, as Tage Carter claimed. Both officers had heard their own kids tell stories about this boy everyone called Ninnish, and while nobody wanted to accept deviance and wickedness in a child, their training reminded them that anything was possible, and that the best and worst of adult criminals had begun their lives as children.

Heritage left the RCMP detachment on foot. Since his attempts to hand off Ninnish to Mason or Dottie had not succeeded, he supposed the mixed-up teenager was still his responsibility. He walked back to the hospital where he'd been taken. It had been absurd to think he'd run into François at one o'clock in the morning, but he hoped for it desperately. He didn't know anybody else he could talk to. Under a streetlight, he examined the blood on both sleeves of his shirt and was amazed the RCMP had released him looking the way he did, after the story he'd told. He had promised to take them to Wickaninnish Island first thing in the morning to recover the dagger and show them where things happened. He'd also told them he was managing and staying at the Headlands if they needed to ask him more questions. He supposed it helped that he had been a law student and could speak their language. It also helped that he was telling the truth, he had to remind himself.

Heritage walked through the entrance of the hospital and was immediately accosted by Dottie Bard, who tried to block him before Nurse Remington could pull her back. She had a hypodermic needle stuck in her arm and dangled a half bag of blood from it as she shook her finger at him.

"You have no business here, Tage Carter. No business."

Without addressing the mad woman, he turned to the receptionist, who he knew from the library, smiled, and asked about the boy he'd brought in earlier. Gillian was more intent on putting Dottie in her place than upholding the hospital policy that reserved the release of information to immediate family only. She told him what she knew and went on to explain that Ninnish had a rare blood type, which was why Miss Bard was donating, just in case they needed it. Again, Heritage looked at the blood on his sleeves as he leaned on the front desk. Rare blood type, he thought to himself. Yet Dottie Bard just happened to be a match. What were the odds of that, in a village of 1,100? Obviously higher among family relations, he deducted.

Dottie demanded that somebody phone the RCMP to have him removed.

"Don't bother, we're already here." It was officer Luis Toren with one of the other Mounties Heritage had just interviewed with at the detachment. "Hello again, Mr. Carter," the blue-eyed bald officer greeted him. "Had we known you were headed here, we could have offered you a lift."

"I'm just checking on the status of the boy." Heritage held up both arms in their blood-stained sleeves, palms facing the officer. He figured they'd deliberately followed him there, which told him he was still their only suspect in what they still assumed was a crime—maybe two crime, with Mason's apparent death figured in. So much for his ability to speak their language.

"Say, Jeff," said Toren. "Why don't I pop Mr. Carter out to The Headlands? I can be back here in ten."

The other officer turned and said, "Good idea." He turned to Heritage. "You can't do anything more for the kid here tonight.

Go and get yourself cleaned up. Get some rest. I have a feeling tomorrow's going to be a long day."

Heritage nodded and thanked Gillian by name, hoping to demonstrate to everyone within earshot just how local he'd become in such a short time. She smiled politely, flattered. He followed the uniformed man out the hospital doors. When they reached the white vehicle with yellow, blue, and red stripes with the buffalo on the seal, Heritage didn't know if he was supposed to ride in the front seat, or in the back behind the grate. The question must have been easily read on his face.

"Up front with me is fine," Toren told him. They both climbed in and fastened seat belts. "You know, Tage, if you wanted to talk—you know, off the record—I'm happy to listen."

Heritage thought about that for a moment. "Thanks," he finally said. "I'll remember that." He was quiet for the rest of the drive and said goodnight as he shut the passenger door.

Heritage hadn't been able to tell if they'd taken shifts, but an RCMP cruiser had been positioned in the parking lot all night. He hadn't been able to sleep, and had sat at the table in his cabin for hours, two-column-strategizing on a legal pad. Every hour or two, he'd step outside, sneak quietly along the forest path just to confirm the Mounties were still on the clock. They obviously thought him guilty and a flight risk to boot, or they wouldn't be parked outside. Heritage knew how much trouble he was in, but he also knew the truth. He knew it would take some pretty slick evidence or a confession from Ninnish or Rowan to get him off this grappling hook.

By early morning, he'd been able to finally accept that all of the boy's desperate actions stemmed from a crush that had turned into an unrequited obsession. In the absence of a father,

Heritage rationalized, the boy gravitated toward the first male figure that had wandered into his woods. Not having been socialized with men, Ninnish had behaved naively and inappropriately. Heritage would later go back to his notes to cross out the word *naively*. The kid knew what he was doing.

Heritage couldn't remember a point in his own childhood—or in his life, really—when he'd been as desperate as Ninnish seemed to be. And then he thought about François. Though it hardly classified as an obsession, he was indeed lonely for his lanky friend from Quebec. He knew when—not if—this episode with Ninnish got out, François probably wouldn't have anything to do with him. And that snubbing—while truly sad—would be nothing compared to the showering of rebukes, penalties and consequences that would rain down on him from his grandfather's sanctimonious pedestal on high. Heritage had needed a fresh tablet page to sketch out a separate two-column checklist just to forecast *those* dream-altering damages. And this brought him to the realization, that when it came to his inheritance, he had been every bit as desperate and obsessed as Aidan.

While he'd arranged to meet Toren and he assumed other officers too, outside of the Headlands at nine o'clock, he didn't think he'd specified that he wasn't staying in the main lodge. So when he opened his cottage door at five minutes to, he was surprised to find Officer Toren on his porch just about to knock.

"Good morning, Tage."

"Good morning." Heritage was a little relived that it was Officer Toren since the two of them had some measure of rapprochement and he wasn't a stranger.

"We hope we're not rushing you," the younger, balding officer with the blue eyes from the previous evening said.

"Not at all."

"We wondered if we might take a look at your identification," the younger officer inquired. "You didn't have it with you last night."

"Yes. Of course. Uh, let me find it. Come in, if you'd like." He wanted to show he had nothing to hide, but inwardly he cursed himself. In fact, he had much to hide—and he hadn't remembered to hide it. In his delirium, he had forgotten to factor the issue of his full identity into his all-night strategy session. As he rifled through packed bags, which couldn't have done anything to discourage their suspicions that he was a flight risk, he panicked all over again about any of this reaching his grandfather. His ID would be the surest way the sordid details would bullet-train across the country, once the connection was made. He wanted to one day be proud of his name, and what he'd done with it. The problem was he couldn't do anything with it until the man who'd pioneered it, finished pioneering. This Ninnish fiasco jeopardized everything.

"Going somewhere?" the younger of the two officers asked, looking around at the packed bags.

"Yes and no," Heritage answered, as honestly as he could. "I had planned to fly to Toronto this past Wednesday. My grand-father was in the hospital. Then, then . . ." He was stuck. *Then, Ninnish drugged and sort of raped me*, he wanted to say, but didn't. "Then I received word he'd been released from the hospital in Toronto, and for me to stay put. I'm doing some legal paperwork and business auditing for Brad Fraser. I think I mentioned that last night."

"You didn't," the balding officer said.

"He mentioned this to me," Toren revealed, "when Tage came to the detachment to turn in Marcel Labbé's wallet."

The younger constable wasn't satisfied. "What kind of legal work?"

"Does it really matter?" Heritage tried to make light of the rather heavy situation.

"No, I suppose it doesn't matter. Just making conversation." The officer smiled in a way that Heritage understood as meaning he wasn't 'just making conversation' at all. He removed his driver's license from the credit card pouch and reached it over the sofa to the officer. "Heritage, huh?" he asked, before passing the identification to Officer Toren.

"Yes, sir."

"Please," Toren objected. "No need for *sir*. Neither of us have been knighted by the Queen. Not yet, anyway. The Third?" he was studying the driver's license. "Your ill grandfather would be the—"

"First," Heritage volunteered.

"And your father?"

"The second," Heritage said. "And dead."

"Oh? Your mother?"

"Also dead." Heritage looked away.

"I'm sorry," Officer Toren thought to say, writing the particulars from the ID in a small notebook.

"Thank you," Heritage replied but looking at the balding officer when he said it, as if to communicate that a little kindness could go a long way.

The message was not received, or if it was, it backfired. The balding officer looked up at the loft. "You sleep in both beds last night," noting that neither had been made.

Heritage stammered. "I . . . I've been here several nights, and the cottages are self-contained and don't regularly come with housekeeping."

The younger officer was looking around. "These cabins are pretty nice," he commented. "Would you call this a cabin or a cottage, do you think?"

Heritage wanted to know what the hell it mattered but said, "I think they refer to them as cottages in the brochure."

The Mountie approached the ladder leading to the loft. "Mind if I take a look?"

"Be my guest," Heritage regretted the words as they rushed past his lips, but the officer was already halfway up, anyway.

Toren returned the driver's license to Heritage and announced, "we should get a move on."

———

The officer in the loft said "Um . . . there's some blood on the pillowcases up here."

Heritage went flush as a breath got caught sideways in his throat. He coughed and said "Pardon me?"

"And some schoolbooks . . . *Intro to Social Studies* . . . *Algebra Explained.*"

Heritage was silent, having assumed the crew of the *Tonquin* had been the recipients of Aidan's schoolbooks.

"And there's this," the officer displayed the walkie-talkie in his hand, pressing its squawk button, which was answered by static.

"Those," Heritage had no choice but to explain," belong to Aidan Rye. As I explained last night, his mother Mona asked me to watch him during her cancer treatments. It was too stormy the other night to get back over to Wick so we stayed here."

"And the blood?" he asked as he prepared to descend the ladder, books and walkie-talkie in hand.

"Beats me," Heritage lied.

"Shall we, then?" Toren motioned for the door.

The three of them left the cabin, and walked down the pebble pathway to the beach below the Headlands where Heritage normally kept his kayak. There, an RCMP zodiac and two other uniformed men waited to whisk them to Wickaninnish Island.

Nobody really said anything until they neared the east shore of the island. Heritage pointed when asked where they should make landfall, and on his advice the boat tucked between two rock groupings, into a little bay—Dottie's—no larger than a couple of zodiacs placed side by side. It was remarkably sunny for the third week of September, one of the officers remarked. The others nodded.

"Do you remember," one of them broke into song, "the 21ˢᵗ night of September?"

"Earth, Wind and Fire! Love that song!" Constable Toren, exclaimed, naming that tune.

"First day of Autumn," said another, hoisting several cameras and equipment bags onto his shoulder.

"Autumnal equinox," Heritage added, being the first out of the boat, hopping from its rigid, inflatable side to a rock draped with a strand of slippery bull kelp. He motioned for the pilot to toss him the rope, which he tied to a gigantic chunk of drift-wood that was going nowhere. The suspect guide waited for the four policemen to coordinate their field packs and cameras. Toren changed into hiking boots. Heritage offered to carry something for them, but they declined, possibly sensing it would have been a little like asking Jesus to carry his own cross. Up the rocks, past Dottie Bard's cabin and the pathway lined with wine bottles, they disappeared into the forest—Heritage reluctantly leading the way.

Daylight diminished inside the forest and Heritage was both surprised and impressed he'd been able to negotiate the rooted path the previous night, especially with a badly injured Ninnish in his arms. The further he penetrated the twisting maze of ferns and low branches, the more unbelievable his story became, even to him. Spiderwebs broke across his face every few steps, as though no one had passed through there in days, maybe months. He wanted to get inside the heads of the police so he could figure out what to say that would make them believe his incredible story. But in the next minutes, he had a sinking feeling he'd missed a turn in the trail.

He'd only really come across the labyrinth on purpose once. Each of the other times, he'd practically tripped over it trying to get somewhere else. Remarkably, he had gotten the party of investigators lost and had to admit it. The ferns gave way to kel-ly-green moss that covered round cross-sections of a tree that had been sliced to line that section of the trail. Shockingly bright orange chanterelle mushrooms polka-dotted the green carpet.

Heritage now knew he was on the wrong path, but felt he could still steer them south again, toward the labyrinth. Soon they passed a giant cedar that had toppled probably a half century ago, erecting a barricade of sod and root as tall and wide as a house. The quasi-trail they were on wound around it, and Heritage could not conceal his awe. The roots were knotted on the underside, like Medusa's hair, imprisoning hundred-pound boulders in its intricate cage. The divot of earth that had been peeled back when the tree had toppled over had filled in with marvelous moss—a zillion sprigs of what looked like restaurant parsley standing on end but was actually licorice fern. They next passed another tree—a nursery log—that had fallen before any of them had been born, that now had seven full-size trees growing right out of it. Heritage could have almost forgotten he was leading a criminal investigation team and not a rainforest interpretive walk. But he was lost.

"Look," he finally admitted it. "I've got us lost. I know the labyrinth is around here somewhere, but we must have gotten off the trail. We can either double back or I can push on through and try to find it."

One of the older officers, with the photography equipment, was panting too hard to speak. Heritage had not been mindful of his age—it looked like he could use a rest. Toren offered him some water from a canteen he'd packed around his waist.

"How did you find your way last night, in the dark?" The officer he hadn't met before and who had driven them in the boat asked what the others were probably wondering.

"And back out again—packing a teenager?" the crime scene photographer piped up after lowering the canteen from his face.

"God—I forgot to mention it, before! There was this white thread. A trail of it." Heritage became excited by the potential of the detail he'd inadvertently left out. "Ninnish had attached one end to the map he'd left for me in his house, and the other end he'd, uh—"

Heritage paused to consider what he was about to say, so it didn't come out wrong or hurt his case. "The other end was tied to him when I reached him. I followed the thread, gathering it as I walked. It led me straight into the labyrinth."

———

Heritage tried to read their blank faces. It took a minute, but then Toren spoke. "Correct me if I have this wrong, but in Greek mythology, didn't the daughter of King Minos do the same thing to help Theseus find his way out of a labyrinth after he'd killed the Minotaur?" After a moment of disbelief, his partners broke out laughing. Toren continued. "No, she did, I swear! Ariadne left a trail of thread so Theseus could find his way back to her."

"You tell me, brainiac," the still-winded policeman asked. "And some fifteen-year-old kid is supposed to know all that?"

"He's at least fifteen, but looks older," Heritage corrected.

"Last night, you weren't sure how old he is. Today you're sure, Tage?" The balding officer stroked his unshaven chin.

"Yes, I am sure," Heritage said. "I can't confirm your Greek mythology, and I may have gotten us momentarily lost, but I'm sure about Aidan's age."

"I'll have to look the Minotaur story up when I get back to a computer," Toren said, "but my daughter just did a book report about it. At any rate, we can take a few minutes here while Heritage gets his bearings."

Heritage walked about six metres in every direction, trying to see a landmark—a depression in the earth or a clearing in the trees that might have indicated the position of the labyrinth. He was learning that the great outdoors, except in wilderness guidebooks, never looked the same way twice. Unfortunately, this lesson would come at the cost of his credibility if he didn't get the group back on course. After five minutes, the group resumed its march and followed Heritage in a direction he suddenly felt confident about, and within thirty metres they were standing in the company of Sitkas on the edge of the pebble and shell-lined outer circle. The four ropes still trailed toward the center, where Ninnish had been tied. Seeing the scene gave Heritage a quick chill that he couldn't help but shake off visibly, catching the attention of Officer Toren who had been watching him closest.

"So, this is the place, then?" Toren surmised. Heritage nodded, brushing the hair off his forehead with his hand. He knew it didn't look good. The whole labyrinth had given him a creepy, evil feeling the first time he'd seen it, too, and he was seeing it that way again through the eyes of the officers. He started toward the center, but Toren held out his arm.

"Thanks. We'll take it from here. We won't be but a few minutes."

Heritage stepped back and crossed his arms. He scanned the forest floor in the inner circle for his knife. When he didn't see it, he widened his eyes-only search to the outer circle. Still, he couldn't see the knife from where he had been asked to stand. In their skirmish, Heritage couldn't even remember if he had been the last to hold it, so he didn't know where it had ended up. He also couldn't make out the other dagger with the longer blade— the one he figured had been the same knife in the engraved leather sheath hanging on the door to Aidan's bedroom. Heritage was sure that had been the knife Ninnish had used to injure himself.

Standing there knowing his goose was cooked, he just knew it was only a matter of time before someone at the hospital realized Ninnish had been anally violated. Ninnish would probably be the one to tell them, too. He wondered what the teen would tell the authorities when he started talking, and what he'd already told Dottie Bard. And what about Rowan Robson?

"What about Rowan Robson? Is he talking yet?"

Nobody answered him. As he stood there, he remembered to look up, high in the granddaddy Sitka, to the platform that held the remains of the mystery man in the Levi's. *What the hell?* The bones were gone! At least from that angle, it looked as though the platform had been removed. Heritage moved a few steps to his right to get a better view. Sure enough, somebody had completely dismantled the platform in the last twenty-four hours—but who? He thought about mentioning it to the RCMP, perhaps to draw the focus of the investigation away from him—but he couldn't be sure it wouldn't backfire on him, too, just as everything else had. He wished he could remember seeing the platform in the tree the previous night. It had been there yesterday afternoon for sure, when he'd watched Dottie cut through the labyrinth. He supposed anyone could have taken the bones down from the tree—including Ninnish himself, if he were trying to cover up another of his stunts. Who else could have suddenly needed them removed? If he could reveal and solve that mystery, he might gain some credence for his own alibi.

While the photographer and investigators worked the scene, Heritage was left unattended at the edge of the labyrinth. He moved as nonchalantly as he could to get multiple looks into the forest canopy. He wanted to be completely certain the bones and platform had been taken, not just relocated to another tree. He also wanted to be certain that he had been looking up the right tree in the first place. He stepped behind the Sitka and his eyes locked on the first handhold notch in the trunk at roughly the height of his extended hand. Unless they'd used a ladder or step stool, whoever had climbed that tree to take the bones had to be as tall as he was, or they couldn't have reached the first notch.

Heritage had military-grade fireworks going off in his cranium. He recalled the waist and inseam measurements on the Levi's tag—the same as his, likely the same as François since they were the same height—though he'd never seen him wear Levi's. The waistband remnants that had been up in the tree had belonged to an adult. And there was still the matter of that Russian-looking coin that he'd at least had the good sense to pop back inside the plastic, amber-coloured prescription container, still at the bottom of the front pocket of his kayaking pants, wadded up on the cabin floor with his bloody shirt, back at The Headlands.

Officer Toren approached his suspect. "Well, I'm afraid that's all we can do for now. The knife doesn't appear to be here. We'll have to come back with a metal detector, most likely." Soon the photographer, the balding officer and the RCMP boat driver joined the huddle, with their plastic Ziploc bags of bloody moss and rope samples. Heritage kept tally: the bones, the burial platform and both the knives had gone missing. So far, he hadn't been arrested, which meant they didn't have enough, if anything, on him specifically. "If you would be so kind to lead us back to the zodiac," Toren said.

"Of course. Didn't you want to, uh . . ." He paused. "Didn't you want to see Mason Robson's place while you're here?"

That was an epic slip up, he realized even while he was suggesting it. *Why don't I show you where I beat her up and tossed her body off the cliff, too?* He knew that's what they must have taken it to mean. Regardless, they declined his offer with an explanation that the coast guard had taken over that branch of the investigation since the body had been recovered from the water. Heritage led the investigative party directly back to Dottie's cove, this time without getting lost.

Waiting impatiently on the front deck of her cabin, Dottie Bard avoided Heritage's stare as they shuffled past.

"We'll be with you in five minutes, Dottie," Toren said, waving. Heritage suddenly knew why his expert assistance was no longer required. Dottie Bard was taking the second tour shift. The officer that had driven them over piloted the zodiac back to the Headlands while the key suspect watched from the pontoon as Dottie took the remaining three investigators back into the woods, in the direction of his loaner, A-frame shed.

"I don't check references," she told them. "I have lived my whole life on the basis of my exceptional good judgment of character." She held the cottage door open. "Obviously, my judgment failed me in this instance."

Toren suppressed his smirk. He'd had plenty of dealings with Dottie Bard's shameless ego over the years. Her brashness and aggrandizing ways no longer surprised him. "So, you invited him to live on Wickaninnish Island in this—what do you call this? A cottage or a shed?"

"It was my daughter's extended bedroom and play cottage when she was younger, before she built her own cabin at Big Beach and before she left for Patagonia." Dottie always volunteered more information than had been requested. It was her impatience, mostly. She never understood why people didn't bundle multiple questions together. It seemed such a waste of her time.

"Have you heard from Stephanie?" Toren asked, fondly. He'd gone to secondary school with Dottie's daughter until she'd dropped out suddenly in their tenth year. Some said that was to complete a pregnancy, but he hadn't been sure.

"Not yet," Dottie said. "It's only been a few weeks, really."

"Hey, Jeff. Take a look at this." The photographer pointed to a pocketknife on the rough wood dining table. "Could be the one." They bagged and marked it. Next Toren found a notepad, commenting that whoever used it last sure pressed hard on the paper—they'd made a clear impression on the blank page beneath it.

"Can we maybe get a lead pencil rubbing?" The balding constable, asked.

"Easily," Toren remarked, holding the pad up to the window. The investigators worked their way around each other in the tight quarters, taking photographs and bagging evidence as they processed the small, one-room cabin. When it seemed they might miss it, Dottie pointed out a length of coiled rope on the floor next to the wood stove. It seemed, at least to her, to be oddly placed. After discussing it briefly, the RCMP decided it could well match the rope samples taken at the clearing in the forest, and bagged it for comparison.

"Do you know, Dottie, if this cottage is generally locked at all times?" Toren asked.

Dottie started to chuckle but then turned somber and acted serious. "Only one cottage on this island has locks, Luis, and that's Mason Robson's—or, I should say, it *was* Mason Robson's.

Her jailbird husband insisted on it before he went off to prison. The rest of us are—well, trusting, shall we say?"

"Maybe a little too trusting, as you've already established you might have been with Tage Carter," the older officer with the camera suggested, a bit sarcastically.

"Perhaps," she said, humouring him.

They left the cottage and walked the short distance to join the primary trail north. Dottie recapped the details she'd already provided them regarding Mason Robson's accidental death. On the question of where her son, Rowan, had been taken after he'd been released to Dottie's custody earlier that morning, Dottie was uncharacteristically tight-lipped.

"The boy is in no condition to talk to anyone yet. He's in a safe place. Don't you worry." She was not about to relinquish control of her island. She would present Rowan to the authorities when she was ready, and it would have little or nothing to do with Rowan's state of recovery.

This hadn't impressed Luis Toren. "The boy's a witness, Dottie. We'll have to speak to him as soon as possible, while things are still fresh in his head, you know." Toren would be going straight across the channel from Wickaninnish to the hospital, and he would have liked to have had Rowan's testimony before he questioned Aidan Rye. Ninnish was a tricky one. Toren remembered the school fire a few years back—Ninnish had been one of the last seen leaving a stairwell before flames had broken out, eventually destroying the audio-visual storage closet. Ninnish had told Toren straight to his face that nobody could prove he'd ever been in that stairwell. He hadn't said he didn't start the fire. He had said nobody could prove it. And indeed, nobody could.

Just then, a call came over the police radio. Toren responded—it was the main detachment office with news that Social Services was at the hospital and ready to speak with Aidan Rye. As the RCMP had requested first crack at Ninnish, that meant they had to race back to the village or risk the evolution of a protracted testimony—which, with Ninnish, could be disastrous.

"I want to talk to Rowan Robson, Dottie. I want to talk to him by tomorrow. Please don't put yourself in a position where you'd appear to be obstructing this investigation." He smiled. She didn't smile back. The zodiac returned from The Headlands, after dropping Heritage on Middle Beach, and the RCMP packed up and left Wickaninnish Island.

The hospital was practically Toren's second office. He was sure he spent as much time there as at the detachment between the dozen or so water mishaps and the monthly car accidents that plagued their isolated village at the end of a treacherous logging road that happened to have been paved but not much improved since the '70s. He didn't recognize the face of the new caseworker from the Ministry of Children and Family Services, but he recognized the look. Nobody dressed up in the village for anything. Toren often joked that a person could look under the pews at either of the two village churches and find more gumboots than heels on Sundays—and there didn't even have to be a rain cloud in the sky. It wasn't a particularly funny joke, but Toren wasn't known for his sense of humour. With his straight face and darker features, he might have made a better mortician, had the village been large enough to require one. Case in point: Mason Robson's body was just the latest corpse en route to Port Alberni over that paved logging road that linked Tofino to civilization.

He introduced himself to the caseworker and thanked her for waiting.

"Shall we?" she asked. The two entered the hospital room together.

"Hello, Ninnish," Toren said, before catching himself. "Hey, Aidan. Luis Toren, here. How ya feeling, chief?"

Ninnish turned his head toward them but didn't speak. He appeared greatly weakened. A saline IV dripped into the vein in the top of his hand from a special blue pump that clicked with every delivery.

"Aidan," said the caseworker. "My name is Kari Washbrook, and I'm from a provincial agency called the Ministry of Children and Family Development. Together, Officer Toren and I would like to ask you a few questions, if you're feeling up to it—okay?" She made a sweeping motion with her head and her long dark hair swung behind her right shoulder. Toren couldn't tell if she was trying to be sexy in front of the teenager, or trying to impress the uniformed adult. Toren was bad with flirtation—reading it, giving it, and receiving it.

Ninnish opened his mouth to speak but was quite dry. He cleared his throat. "I'm really tired right now," he struggled to say. "Maybe a little later."

Before Toren could impose his authority, Washbrook had relented. "Sure, Aidan. We'll come back," she said using her nurturing baby voice.

Toren added, "In fact, we'll be just outside in the hall when you're ready."

The caseworker smiled as she touched the boy's forehead before turning to leave the room. Toren knew Ninnish was manipulating them. He wouldn't have allowed him to get away with it, but the provincial bureaucrat had answered first. He had never had a great rapport with the reps from social services. It seemed they always had the attitude that whatever it was that they were called to mop-up should have been prevented by the local RCMP in the first place. He would not have been the least bit surprised, if her paperwork and final report wrangled the details and made a play on community emotions, until Ninnish's loss of his right testicle was revealed to have been the RCMP's fault. That was how these investigations involving kids seemed to play out. He deeply resented the interference of outsiders who thought they understood his community's issues and challenges. He couldn't yet admit to himself that perhaps he had missed the signs that might have prevented this. He didn't yet know enough about the newcomer, Tage—Heritage Carter—to have given him the benefit of the doubt. But knowing what a storytelling expert Ninnish was, he wanted to believe the adult. That kid was a pack of trouble who should have been watched more closely. Toren had felt for the kid, his mum riddled with cancer like she was, no clue who his father might have been. There really was no one in his life to set an example. That saddened the policeman—himself the young father of three highly promising children.

"Hey there, James!" Toren's deep voice slid down the shiny waxed floor of the hospital's short hallway. The lanky young doctor, who was not only a friend but also the crooning centerpiece of the Swell Buoys, Toren's locally cultivated and well-rehearsed jazz combo, reversed direction to greet him. The two men came together in a soulful handshake that probably only reinforced what the Victoria-based social worker had already been thinking was too eerily familiar and nepotistic about small towns. Luis caught her rolling her eyes.

"Can I talk to you about Ninnish a bit?" Toren asked his doctor buddy.

"Uh, sure. I can give you five or ten minutes, I suppose." The light-haired doctor gave a nod to the caseworker, who hadn't been introduced.

"Kari Washbrook," she volunteered.

"MCFD, right?" McAnally guessed. There was an unwritten dress code around town, suggesting dresses were only appropriate for one event a year—the annual veteran's drag show fundraiser at the Legion, which he'd won two years in a row. Any other time, a person figured someone in a dress had to be a Jehovah's Witness, pushing bibles. "Follow me," he said, leading the pair to his office where Toren and Washbrook took seats at the doctor's desk while he closed the office door behind them.

"So, what do you think we have here?" Toren was leading the doctor with his question.

"Well, I am concerned," the doctor leveled with them. "Ninnish lost quite a bit of blood and I have thirty-eight stitches holding him together down there waiting for orders to transfer him to Port Alberni Regional, where they can pop a prosthetic testicle in his scrotum for appearance-sake. If he was attacked or victimized or whatever it is we want to call this, he's damn lucky he didn't bleed to death. If he did this to himself—and to be honest with you, knowing what I know of Aidan Rye, it's possible—then I think we're dealing with a mildly psychotic child."

"What makes you think a fourteen-year-old boy would attempt to castrate himself?" Washbrook asked, her face scrunched up in utter disbelief.

Toren looked at McAnally and then just came out with it. "He's fifteen and sexually precocious, and you just have to know Ninnish. That's all." Toren and the doctor had a quick, uncomfortable chuckle.

The doctor rolled his stool closer to the desk, adopted a more serious look and opened a file on his desktop. "And my best guess would be he's more likely *six*teen," the doctor theorized, reading from the chart. "There has always been some discrepancy in my mind with his records." His off-the-cuff comment was met with two sets of raised eyebrows on the other side of his desk, so he continued. "Physiologically, he seems older. And since he was adopted and the adoption records aren't with his file, I've always had my doubts about his birth date—never mind his birth location, listed as northern Alberta. I've requested adoption records from the Province of Alberta, but no file has ever been located."

"That's interesting, Doc," Toren said. "I didn't realize Ninnish wasn't Mona's. I wonder if the Canadian Police Information Center database would have anything useful here."

Doctor McAnally shook his head. "With no record of who his mother or father was, your looking into an empty file cabinet. It is a non-starter. I've discussed this with Mona . . . that's his adoptive mother." He glanced at the social worker. "She was very tight-lipped about the circumstances but indicated that she was approached anonymously by a woman whom she'd never seen or met before. She wasn't at all sure about what year this was—but the woman said that she couldn't care for her infant child, and that she respected Mona's standing in the community. She begged Mona to get him the care and family he needed. The woman handed Mona the crying child and just vanished."

"Wait a minute," Kari Washbrook interjected. "Surely, Child Protective Services was contacted and has records?"

"You tell me," the doctor said. "Mona said that she had wanted a child so desperately, but she'd apparently had some medical risks and an emergency hysterectomy when she was a teenager. This mystery woman from Alberta magically appearing out of the mist seemed to Mona to be some divine sign that the universe intended for her to raise that child—so that's what she did."

"And there's no paperwork, no report of an abandoned child, no process undertaken for formal adoption?" Kari Washbrook was growing incredulous.

"I didn't say that," the doctor objected. "I said I have never seen anything in the medical records."

"And the other boy," she inquired. "The one who lost his mother in the fall?"

"Rowan Robson," the RCMP officer said.

"He was held for observation under light sedation overnight and released to the care of his guardian this morning," the doctor reported.

"His guardian?" Toren and Washbrook asked together.

"Dottie Bard," the doctor replied.

Again, Toren raised his eyebrow. "So where is Rowan now?

I took statements from Dottie on the island this morning and Rowan wasn't with her."

"I wouldn't know," the doctor admitted. "Listen, I need to get back to the clinic. I have appointments this afternoon." He rose from the desk. "Oh, another thing about Ninnish—er, Aidan. Just the other day—Tuesday, it was, he was sent by the school nurse to the doctor's office. He was bleeding from, well—his bottom. I'll admit I don't see that every day with a teenager. He had inserted a flashlight up his own bum and evidently tore or grazed part of the rectal wall."

"You didn't tell me this," Toren interjected, almost immediately realizing that this would have fallen under patient confidentiality anyway.

"I hardly tell you everything," the doctor replied—half coldly, half teasing.

The social worker was growing disturbed by the pair's coziness. "And did it occur to you, doctor," she said, "especially now in light of this attempted castration, and the introduction of an adult suspect, that the boy may have been raped?"

"Hold on!" Toren felt obliged to leap to the doctor's defense. "Ninnish is always crying wolf."

"Why do you call him that?" she asked.

The two men looked at each other. Finally, Toren spoke. "Ninnish, uh, well—to the best of my memory, his classmates started calling him that because he lives on Wickaninnish Island and boats to school. Adults, mostly his teachers at the secondary school, who have had the opportunity to deal with him over the years, just expanded the nickname to Wicked Ninnish because of the trouble that seems to precede and follow him. This latest incident won't change that reputation." Toren looked to McAnally while the caseworker finished her notes.

It was the doctor's turn to raise his eyebrows—not sure what to make of her presence and line of questioning. These visits usually amounted to an inspection of the yokels—to make sure they were adhering to the provincial standards of child welfare. He supposed the thought of anal penetration by something other than the purported flashlight would have to be considered and hopefully eliminated. If what she suggested actually happened, then he had erred by not pursuing the examination when Ninnish had first been sent to him. There had been the whole masturbation stunt too. The doctor hadn't mentioned it, because he thought the boy was fine—over-stimulated, perhaps, but fine.

Toren shifted in the chair. He'd passed Ninnish off all these years as a potential nuisance, but only to himself. He couldn't imagine Ninnish being a victim of anything but his own boredom. But then he was always taken by surprise when anything devious took place under his watchful guard. What the social worker seemed to be implying was that they had really fucked up if this kid was being abused by an adult in their jurisdiction and they had missed the signs.

"I'm going to insist I have the opportunity to question Aidan alone," she announced. "If you two are as dismissive with a fifteen—pardon me, or maybe sixteen-year-old—as you have been with me, it's no wonder he hasn't talked. May I?"

"Absolutely not! I'm sorry, Miss—Kari, but I can't permit you to, in any way, coach his statement. We'll talk to him together when he's ready. If it's me to whom you've taken this exception, I'll happily assign another constable to accompany you." Toren was red-faced. She'd taken it too far.

"Has he had other visitors this morning?" she asked the doctor.

"Just Dottie Bard—a close friend of the family."

"And was she chaperoned by Officer Toren?"

"No, but—" McAnally knew he wasn't helping the situation.

"Thank you." She stood to excuse herself. "Gentlemen."

Toren didn't pursue the tug of war. The two men held silence long enough for the click of her city heels on the linoleum tiled floor to dissipate a safe distance away.

"Let me walk you to the clinic." Toren offered, and the two

left the hospital together. As they walked up the hill on the asphalt sidewalk, Luis was thinking this warm, sunny weather was the delayed summer they hadn't had.

"Anything stand out as odd to you in this case, Jimbo?"

"Well," the doctor started, then paused. "That's tricky for me to say. And I probably shouldn't, on the record."

"But, we're best friends here. That social worker from the ministry could easily make us look backward or negligent if we don't get on top of this fast—both of us." Toren motioned his head in the direction of the crosswalk.

"Okay, two things," the doctor said. "The angle of the laceration to his groin is consistent with self-infliction. But it could have been just as possible that your suspect was leaning over the kid's head and torso—you know, like down on all fours—and pulled the knife upward himself."

"Okay, and the second thing?" Toren wasn't exactly feeling vindicated so far.

"Maybe unrelated, but Ninnish has a rather rare blood type—B-Negative."

"Yeah, so?"

"Guess who else has the same type?"

The RCMP officer wasn't in the mood for riddles. "The social worker? I don't know!"

McAnally paused, knowing he was stepping way out of bounds. "Dottie Bard."

"Interesting odds, I suppose. But what does it mean?"

"Maybe nothing." The doctor leveled with him. "While blood type isn't always passed from parent to child, in some cases, such as in rare blood types, the type can carry, or maybe skip a generation before showing up again."

"Are you saying Dottie is Aidan's mum?"

"Or grandmother, perhaps."

Luis stopped walking. "You mean Stephanie? Jesus Christ! Well, let's just check hospital birth records."

"I did," the doctor confirmed. "Ninnish wasn't born here."

"So where was he born? Wait. You said that Mona had told you the woman that gave her the infant for adoption was from Alberta."

The two started walking again, the doctor in more of a hurry than the policeman.

"I don't know if that's true either, since Alberta hasn't been able to provide any records." McAnally flipped it back to his friend. "What do you know about your suspect?"

"Not a lot," Toren hated to admit. "His name is Heritage Carter the Third. He goes by Tage." Toren had to glance at his pocket notebook to get the right names in the right order.

"What do you know about Heritage Carter the First?" The doctor enjoyed playing detective as much as his detective friend occasionally thought he knew more about medicine.

"Nothing yet, why?" Toren hated having things pointed out to him, and he had a feeling his friend was about to point.

"Dottie Bard says he died the day before yesterday, and that he was the senior Carter of Toronto's Carter Pulp & Paper Corporation."

"Dottie told you this? That's funny. She gave me this act that she didn't know thing-one about the man when I questioned her this morning."

"She also told me that Carter Pulp & Paper has almost half ownership interest in The Headlands."

"What the hell?" Toren stopped walking again, but they'd arrived at the clinic and he knew his time with the good doc was up. "This fellow seems to have gotten his fingers into a lot of pots here in our tiny town."

McAnally put a hand on the policeman's shoulder. "Let's hope it's just his fingers in pots and there isn't something more disturbing that happened here," he said ominously before disappearing through the clinic door.

Dottie didn't want to upset her in the middle of her treatment, but Mona needed to know what had happened and it would be better if the news came from her. Dottie picked up the phone and dialed the Oncology Department nurse's station at Royal Jubilee Hospital in Victoria. The past twenty-four hours had seen such an illogical chain reaction of tragedies that Dottie hadn't had time to process all of it for herself. Yet she was about to lay it all on the shoulders of a woman whose body could not bear the weight of an eagle feather. Dottie was still in crisis mode and this was just another box needing to be ticked.

"Mona Rye's room—please, and thank you."

She really needed this to be one of Mona's coherent moments. The medications they usually gave her to counter the chemo whacked her way out of her senses, and there was no telling what state she'd be in now.

"Mona? It's Dot, dear. How are you feeling today? That's good to hear, dear. Listen, Mona—there's been a few accidents I need to tell you about. Last night, Ninnish got into an argument with Tage and a knife was pulled. Ninnish was cut pretty badly." She paused. "He's stabilized in the hospital and the doctor says he'll be well enough to be released in a few more days," she fibbed that bit. "They've taken Tage in for questioning. Now, I don't want you to worry. I have everything under control. You have enough you need to be concentrating on right where you are, without having to worry about this . . . well, I'll tell you. It seems everything is pointing to Tage having attempted to castrate Ninnish. I know that sounds positively draconian, but Doctor McAnally says he's managed to save most of it, and that he has every expectation that Ninnish will still be able to function in that way."

Dottie had hoped to avoid the surgical details, but Mona pressed her for them. "And there's one more thing I need to tell you. Oh—well, Rowan Robson witnessed the altercation and will be able to testify against Tage. And remember what I told you that Steve Greene had told me about Tage—what he'd researched about him? Well, his grandfather died two days ago in Toronto, so we'll be able to go after Tage for everything he's got. Ninnish will never have to worry about money, and I—*we* will be able to keep Wickaninnish Island just the way you wanted it."

That last part was a crock of steaming bullshit, and they both knew that Dottie would do her own thing the moment Mona passed. But Dottie continued. "Well, there's another accident I need to tell you about. You don't have to worry about Mason now. She's dead, dear. I know it comes as a horrible shock. Last night, after Rowan witnessed the attack on Aidan, he went running through the woods for help. Mason and I were at Cormorant Rock watching the meteor shower. No, Mona—it was not a romantic night! I had gone to their place to have dinner to celebrate Mason's birthday." Dottie switched gears. "It's amazing to me how you can reserve energy for jealousies when you don't have the strength to sit up and go to the washroom by yourself. Anyway, Rowan came thrashing through the trees and ran smack into his mother, knocking her off balance at the edge of the cliff. She tragically fell to her death, Mona. The coast guard retrieved her body early this morning."

There was a silence on the line and Dottie gave her a moment to process that. She knew it was a hefty shock but didn't suspect that Mona would actually be too upset by the news, considering Mona's long-held suspicion that Dottie and Mason had been secret lovers. Then Mona came back on the line with an apology that she'd had to put the phone down while the nurse changed her IV to her right hand, as the chemo drugs seemed to have collapsed the veins in her left. She'd missed the whole last part of Dottie's story.

Heritage headed straight to the main lodge along the forest path with the intention of phoning his grandfather for an update, and to falsely reassure him he was making progress on the Headlands front—but the staff pounced on him the moment he walked through the door. Employees were frantic as they had not received their paycheques and payday was two days ago. Stu Solberg emerged from the kitchen relieved to see him, saying he had been trying to track him down but that he hadn't found him in his cabin any of the times he knocked and none of the staff had seen him in the main lodge during the past few days. Stu went on to say he had taken more heat from staff over their missing money than the kitchen had ever given him. Before disappearing, Brad Fraser had assured Stu that he had set up payroll with the accountant to be automatic while he was away in the Caribbean, but when the cheques weren't delivered to the front desk on Tuesday, and Stu contacted the accountant, the bookkeeper told him there weren't sufficient funds in the account to cover payroll, and that she had been trying to reach Fraser to arrange an emergency transfer of funds, but that he hadn't responded to any of the messages she'd left on his home answering machine.

It occurred to Stu and some of the staff that Fraser might have skipped town with the money meant to cover their salaries, and Stu wanted to phone the police. Heritage managed to calm everybody down with the explanation that he had already been talking with the police—not a lie—and that he would immediately cover their salaries by the end of the day after he made some phone calls to Toronto.

Behind closed doors in Fraser's office, Heritage panicked. "Shit, shit, shit, shit!" He didn't need this on top of everything else. He turned on the desktop computer, waiting for it to boot up. He gave the rolodex a spin to the C tab, and dialed the Tofino branch of the Canadian Imperial Bank of Commerce, asking to speak to the manager.

Luis Toren put the cruiser in reverse and backed out of the Headlands parking lot. "I appreciate your willingness to come back into the detachment for some follow-up questions. I know it's been a long stretch for you. Have you gotten any sleep?"

"No," Heritage answered, having anxiously paced the balance of the afternoon away.

In the awkward silence that followed while Toren was driving down the gravel patch of road to reach the highway leading back into town, the officer thought he would offer his condolences. "Say, I heard about your grandfather this morning. I'm so sorry."

"You heard about my grandfather? What did you hear?"

Oh, fuck, Toren thought. He didn't know. "Well, nothing—aside from his passing, I mean."

"My grandfather died?" Heritage couldn't believe what he was hearing—and he couldn't believe he hadn't remembered to phone Toronto in the middle of trying to straighten out the payroll issue.

"I'm sorry, Tage. I assumed you knew."

"I didn't know. I had received a message at the Headlands on Wednesday morning that he'd been released from the hospital, and for me to abort my planned trip home. Now, you're telling me he's dead?"

"You know what? I might be getting bad information. It did come to me second-hand."

"Who did you hear it from?" Nobody local, he had believed, knew about his grandfather.

"Tell you what, I'll let you use the phone at the detachment. You can call and get the details for yourself."

"Thank you." Heritage stewed. With so many developments during the past forty-eight hours, he was conditionally relieved to finally hear that his grandfather's death had been one of them and that his grandfather would be spared whatever bad press, bad blood came from the predicament he found himself in now. Still, he needed to understand why he'd been told his grandfather was fine, when clearly he wasn't. He needed to make that phone call.

———

Inside the RCMP offices, he was directed to the same drab room where they'd questioned him the previous night. A telephone was brought in and plugged into an outlet just above the lime-green algae in the corner. "Thank you," Heritage said.

"Dial 9 to get out," Toren instructed. "I'll give you some privacy."

Heritage waited for the call to connect. The answering machine picked up, which was not overly surprising, given the news. The message had been altered from its normal corporate greeting, and it confirmed what Toren had just told him. His grandfather had died, and the offices of CPC would be closed for the remainder of the week to allow family and employees time to mourn his loss and attend services. *Family*, Heritage scoffed. He was the dead man's only living relation, and he had been left in the dark, perhaps intentionally. He hung up the phone and pulled out his credit card folio where he kept his driver's license, credit cards and a laminated list of important telephone numbers and dialed Lonnie's home telephone. His grandfather's attorney would have an explanation. Whether he'd part with it was another matter.

"Lonnie? It's Heritage here. I've just been told my grandfather died two days ago. Is this true?"

The attorney seemed caught off guard, and instead of answering, asked where Heritage had been for the past week. Heritage was annoyed. "What do you mean, where have I been? I was ready to fly home on Wednesday morning when I got a message at the Headlands that I had assumed came from you—it said grandfather had been released from the hospital, and for me to stay on the assignment here." Heritage stood and began to pace. "What do you mean, the message didn't come from you?"

The attorney explained he had waited for two hours at the airport Wednesday night and finally had gotten the airlines to verify passenger lists when Heritage hadn't arrived as scheduled. Lonnie confirmed that Heritage's grandfather had passed away later that same evening, and in the shuffle of making the necessary arrangements, he hadn't been able to start phoning until early yesterday, when he began leaving messages for Heritage at the Headlands.

"What is going on here?" Heritage asked in an insinuating tone. "I've just come from the Headlands and nobody mentioned that there were any messages for me. And another thing—" He'd need access to his grandfather's bank account to square things with the staff. "Brad Fraser has gone missing and seems to have made off with all the cash in the bank accounts. Vanished to the Caribbean, apparently. I need to cover their salaries, or there's gonna be a mutiny on the Bounty." Lonnie tried to explain that all personal assets had been frozen and that Carter Pulp & Paper's board of directors was doing its best to reassure investors that they had prepared for this and were instituting transition measures. "Transition to what?" Heritage asked. "Don't I have a say in what happens next? To put it more bluntly, isn't everyone, including you, working for me now?"

Turns out it was a fair bit more complicated than that, but Lonnie said he preferred to discuss those matters in person. He did agree to advance Heritage a hundred grand from his trust fund so that he could keep the Headlands running, but the details around what would happen next would need to wait for the will reading and probate.

"When are the services?" Heritage asked. "Where? I'll be there. Thanks, Lonnie."

Heritage hung up the phone. It was done. Heritage Warren Carter the First was no more going to be directing how he lived his life—for the first time in his life. He stepped into the hallway to let Toren know he had completed his call. But Toren wasn't waiting in the hall or eavesdropping on him—probably because the room and phone was already tapped. Heritage walked down the hall toward the public counter until he heard voices, then stopped. One voice belonged to Toren. The other was a woman's voice he couldn't place.

———————

"I don't know what you plan to do with this," she told him, "but I intend to push this until we have a conviction and he's put away. The child could scarcely speak about it, he's so traumatized. I'm telling you—I want your suspect brought up on charges and off the streets of this village by the end of the day."

"I'll talk to the boy myself and I'll ask our 'suspect,' as you put it, about the specifics Ninnish mentioned to you, according to this report." He backhanded the sheets of stapled paper she'd presented to him. "But you don't convict without evidence, and you don't rush to accuse a man based on one statement—especially when that statement comes from a known liar. I told you I needed to be there when you talked to him. You may well have spoiled the one chance we had to get him fresh and un-coerced. So far, after speaking with Dottie Bard and now you, he's already rehearsed his story twice. He's probably going to be real good at it by the time I'm allowed to question him."

Heritage could tell the conversation was ending and slipped back into the interrogation room, where he elected to stand, trying to calm his breathing and lower his temperature. He was being framed. He would need a good defense lawyer.

Toren entered the room. He motioned Heritage to sit at the table and closed the door.

"Would you be surprised if I told you that the coast guard found footprints in the mud on the cliffs of Cormorant Rock that, at least from first glance, might just match the tread and size of the bottoms of your boots?" The policeman pointed to the boots Heritage was wearing.

"No, it wouldn't surprise me because I was at Cormorant Rock earlier yesterday." Heritage waited for him to produce samples of his pubic hair they'd probably found on the cliffs, since they'd obviously been very thorough. The detective held his questioning until Heritage became visibly nervous and began to fidget.

"Ninnish is talking, Tage."

"I'll just bet he is," Heritage deflected before apologizing. "I'm sorry. This is starting to get to me. I've just learned my grandfather is dead. The memorial service is next week in Toronto." Heritage looked down while fingers from one hand removed the dirt from under the nails of the other. It occurred to him the debris was likely a mixture of blood and dirt—evidence was everywhere—though he'd showered almost too carefully for a trace so obvious to still be detectable. He moved his hands under the tabletop.

"Let me tell you what we have so far and maybe you can help me with it." Toren scooted closer to the table and opened his notebook that had grown into a full-size file folder overnight. "I am sorry about your grandfather and the way you had to hear this news." He paused for that to sound sincere. "Now, Ninnish has said you pulled the knife on him last night, that you said you were going to castrate him when the two of you first started arguing. We have recovered the pocketknife with Aidan's blood on it from your cabin on Wickaninnish Island." Toren watched Heritage's face for reaction. Listening to the litany of their discoveries, Heritage sort of left his body for a moment. "Also, there in that cabin or shed or whatever you call it, we discovered a coil of rope which matches the rope left behind at the scene—the same rope, which was apparently used to tie Ninnish down on the forest floor."

"No. That's not right," Heritage objected, but to a point made a minute earlier. "You said you found a pocketknife in that A-frame with Aidan's blood on it?"

"That's right."

"Impossible! This is how I know I am being set up." Heritage straightened up, suddenly inspired to play detective himself to find out who was framing him. "Can I see this pocketknife, please?"

"I'm afraid it's secured in the evidence locker, and I can't—"

"In this building?" Heritage pressed. "Is the evidence locker in this building?"

The constable was becoming agitated. "I don't see why this is important to you and for reasons you can surely understand, we don't bring weapons used back into the interrogation room—for our own safety."

Heritage was becoming insensed. "Is that what this is, Lance— an interrogation?" He'd let the porn name slip from his lips.

"My first name's Luis," the constable at least wanted that record straight.

Heritage raised a hand to his mouth to conceal his embarrassment and apologized. "You remind me of a Lance I once knew," he fibbed. "I apologize, Luis—or rather, Constable Toren."

"I don't mind if you call me, Luis, but I can't show you the pocketknife."

"Fine. Is it a multi-blade Gerber?"

"Yes, I believe that is the brandname."

"Then, that is definitely my knife, but it wasn't the knife used in the labyrinth last night. Aidan had brought a larger dagger with him. He had been laying on top of it, pretending to be tied up. Only his ankles were tied. His wrists weren't. My pocketknife was there, because I stashed it there—not because I ever intended to use it, but because I had been spooked into thinking I'd been cursed since arriving here in Clayoquot Sound. I was reading up and finding all these spooky things, you know, like human skulls and books on witchcraft and other bones and shit." He stopped. Even to him he was sounding like a lunatic, now. "I sacrificed my pocketknife as an offering—a gift to settle the spirits that had been sending nothing but bad luck my way."

Toren's eyes had grown to the size of loonies and he'd stopped taking notes. "O-kay, he tried to regain control of the interview. "Let's move on from the pocketknife for the moment. We can always come back to that." Heritage nodded his agreement and the constable continued his questioning. "Now, you told me earlier this morning that you did not tie up or restrain the victim." He stopped when that sounded too technical, even to him. "Aidan,

I mean. You said that you followed a string or white thread, and found Aidan in the clearing already tied down."

Heritage nodded. "Except for his hands, like I just said. They weren't restrained. The ropes were just wrapped around his wrists but not tied there."

"Right. We have also acquired this notebook from that same A-frame shed, and a slight pencil lead rubbing reveals a perfect match to this map drawing that we extracted from your hoodie sweatshirt pocket." Toren scooted a clear plastic Ziplock bag across the short distance of the table that separated them.

"I don't need to see this again," Heritage turned the bag upside down and scooted the evidence back, noting the paper contained within was badly stained by the blood from Ninnish. He also saw that the underside of the bag was marked with the words *EVIDENCE* and *PREUVE* in block letters—just as he remembered the same officer using when he had turned Marcel's wallet over to him, which had probably also ended up inside the same evidence locker, he presumed.

"Of course, we also retrieved the pencil next to the pad on the table, and the prints we lifted from that as well as from the knife we suspect will match yours, if you'd be willing to be fingerprinted. Of course, you've already told us the knife belonged to you and it is not surprising that you may have used a pencil in a cabin you were known to be occupying."

That was interesting, Heritage thought silently to himself. He wasn't being booked for a crime, or the officer would have automatically taken his fingerprints as part of that process. Suggesting, rather, that if he were *willing* to provide a fingerprint sample, revealed the RCMP either had their doubts about Aidan's story or knew something he didn't. "Is there only one set of fingerprints on these items?" Heritage was sure his accuser's prints would be everywhere.

"There are other smudges that might or might not belong to someone else. We just can't tell."

"Have you printed Ninnish?"

"We have Aidan's prints on file as part of a school identification program. So far, we haven't found a single print matching his anywhere in your cabin, or on any of this evidence."

"I am definitely being set up here," Heritage finally blurted out.

"By a fifteen-year-old?" Toren sounded cynical, but was prepared to go there if Heritage could back it up.

"No." Heritage knew somebody else was manipulating evidence and it was the same someboy that had removed the burial platform and bones from the Sitka. Granted, Ninnish could have stashed the notepad, pencil, and rope in his cabin before the incident at the labyrinth, but he couldn't have carried the knife back there since they hadn't stopped at his cabin while evacuating Ninnish to the hospital. The knife hadn't walked itself back, and Ninnish had been with him or in the hospital since the accident. Mona was in Victoria. Stephanie was in Patagonia. Mason was dead. So it had to be Dottie. It had to be Dottie who removed the bones and the platform from the northernmost Sitka in the labyrinth too, but when?

Heritage was about to voice his suspicions and name his primary suspect when he realized, if it wasn't Dottie, it might have been Rowan Robson carrying out Aidan's beckoning. It could have been anybody, except everybody, it seemed, was pointing their fingers back at him.

"Officer Toren, I know it looks bad, but things happened last night exactly the way I told you. I am wracking my brain—just as much as I hope you are—trying to understand how this evidence has so conveniently accumulated inside that little shed on Wickaninnish Island. I don't have any experience with understanding Aidan's age group, aside from the time when I was part of it myself—but I don't underestimate him anymore. He is either a very intelligent boy or a normal teenager with an adult-sized imagination. He is the damaged and dangerous one here, not me."

Toren looked up from the file. "I have to ask this—and I hope you'll pardon the intrusion—but are you gay, Heritage?"

Heritage didn't answer right away—but not because he was embarrassed. He wasn't sure. "I'm not really anything," he finally said. "I've slept with a few women. I've slept with a few men. Sex isn't really my bag, though. I don't seek it out. I really don't need it, like other men do. I don't know why that is. That's just me."

"Fair enough." The officer took a deep breath. "I ask because Aidan Rye says you raped him a few nights ago—you know, anally. According to this report, he told a social services caseworker that three nights ago you slipped him something in the food you prepared for him, and that this knocked him out, and that when he came to again, you had him tied down and were, uh, already inside him, having intercourse. He told the caseworker you didn't use a condom, that you also forced your penis inside his mouth. He has described your genitalia as larger than normal, circumcised, with a small mole on one side of your penis and a scar on your hip that runs into your pubic hair."

Heritage was very careful not to explode. He wanted what he said next to ring with truth—because it was the truth. He wanted to connect in a very genuine way with that particular RCMP investigator. He needed to be believed.

"A few aspects of that are true," Heritage started to explain. "I have a surgical scar from an appendectomy when I was nineteen and I am circumcised. But I need to make sure you understand precisely what happened, who got drugged, and who raped whom, and then try to understand why I didn't come forward with this before now. I have to also take you back to the first time I met Ninnish. Are you willing to hear me out?"

"That's what I am here for. Do you mind if I take a few notes?"

"As long as we understand each other—this is an expanded explanation for what I already told you last night. *Not* a confession."

The investigator nodded, leaned in, and flipped to a fresh page of his investigation pad. Then, methodically, chronologically,

Heritage laid out nearly every detail of his relationship with Ninnish—from the outhouse to the labyrinth. He was emphatic: he hadn't volunteered to babysit Aidan Rye—he'd been tricked into doing it by Dottie. When he learned that his grandfather was dying, he couldn't get Dottie Bard or Mason Robson to take the teenager off his hands. That shocked him—since they were both mothers, and best friends of the boy's sick mother. He talked about Ninnish jerking off in front of him, how the teenager seemed radically oversexed, but that he had only discouraged that type of behaviour, telling the kid that he wasn't interested, because that was the truth—he wasn't.

Officer Toren took notes while also consulting the caseworker's report. "Ninnish says he told you that he didn't like hairy men and that the next time he saw you, you had shaved your entire body to surprise him, to please him, and to entice him into fooling around with you sexually." Heritage shook his head, with a hand over his mouth. The officer went on. "Would you mind lifting your shirt for me?"

Heritage stalled. "Look, I am a hairy guy—but I was so disgusted after being drugged and waking up to find I'd been used as some sort of sex experiment by these two teenage boys, I, uh—I shaved. I don't know why—maybe to purify myself when it seemed soap was not enough to erase the, uh, indignity of it."

"Whoa. Back up. You said you were part of an experiment by these two teenage boys. Are you saying that Rowan Robson was involved the night your penis found its way into Aidan Rye's bum?"

"My penis didn't find its way there! It isn't a garter snake. Aidan sat on me after I'd been drugged. But yes, Rowan was there."

"How is it—" Toren stopped to rephrase his question. "Look, I'm a guy, too, okay? I know how guys' bodies work. If you aren't really into sex, as you already stated, how do you explain being aroused enough that a teenager could force himself to sit on what had to be an erection?"

"Seriously, you're asking me that question? Haven't you ever heard of Viagra? There are ways to get and keep an erection without being aroused. They must have slipped me something like that at the same time as the other drug."

"And do you have a theory of how teenagers would have gotten their hands on drugs like these—in Tofino?"

Heritage pondered the usefulness of bringing Lyle Hudson into the story but decided to reserve that as it would provide an opportunity for a whole new line of questioning. "Have you seen Mona Rye's medicine collection?" he asked. Officer Luis Toren's face indicated maybe he had, so Heritage continued building his defense. "I believe it was one of Mona's prescriptions, something that begins with the letters *R O H* maybe?" Heritage was struggling to remember the right letters in the right order. "Anyway—the drug I think was used on me by the kids was her prescription. I found an empty container—"

He cut that sentence short, not meaning to be *that* helpful. He realized that Mona's prescription arsenal wasn't going to account for the erection dysfunction medicine. This was the obvious redirect the officer across from him must have already been formulating. So, Heritage spilled it. "I can also tell you that there have been other drugs on that island. Do you know Lyle Hudson? Has a cottage on the west side high up on the rocks?"

"I know the name, but I don't think he's from here. What can you tell me about him?"

"Not much," Heritage answered honestly. "But he must be a retired doctor or a pharmacist the way he dispenses medicine." Heritage realized that wasn't going to be sufficient, so he went on. "While exploring the island maybe a week ago, I, uh, I stumbled upon a party at his place. There were drugs—plenty of them, including Viagra. And I saw Aidan Rye there, poking his head out of the forest from time to time. He seemed very curious. And why wouldn't he be? There was probably more excitement on that island than he'd seen in his lifetime."

"Tell me more about this party," Toren seemed intrigued and

Heritage was relieved to be on a topic that steered the conversation away from the sexual act with the teenager. "What kind of drugs? Did you take anything?" the officer asked, pen poised.

Heritage was seeing how this worked. His cooperation was getting him deeper in the quicksand. "Let's say that I was made to feel welcome. In the city, we would have called it a dance party. There were only men—mostly from a British dance company that was on tour and had performed in Vancouver the night before, I think. The weather was warm and the music was pretty decent, so there were a lot of shirts and pants off. And everyone, mostly, was, you know, just dancing."

"What kind of drugs?" Toren said again.

"I'm not an expert, but I imagine there was Ecstasy, maybe some LSD. Everyone seemed to be having a pretty great time."

"And did you see this Lyle character giving or selling drugs then?"

"Yes—but not selling. Lyle seemed to have put himself in charge of making sure everyone was enjoying themselves. It was the first time I'd met him, but it was his place, so he was playing the good host, I guess." Heritage wondered if he should mention Marcel Labbé, but decided against it.

Toren was busy writing and Heritage realized he had been talking for a while so he considerately let the officer catch up. "And these drugs . . ." Toren said after a moment. "Did you take anything from Lyle?"

"Oh, right—you asked me that. Sorry. Uh, yes—I took some Ecstasy, I think, and with a Viagra chaser."

"You *think*?" Toren raised an eyebrow.

"Based on when I have experimented with before, you know, at dance parties in the city—yes. I'm pretty sure I was feeling the effects of Ecstasy. Limitless energy, super keen hearing and vision, just an all-around good feeling in my body. Everything looked and sounded, well—beautiful." He almost sounded like he was selling it.

Toren looked up from his notes. "And what's a Viagra chaser?"

"Well . . ." Heritage knew he was starting to sound like an expert, which he realized wasn't going to help him, but he had to lay the groundwork that made it plausible that Ninnish had been in proximity to the party and possibly had stolen the Viagra from Lyle's copious supply. "A Viagra chaser is like an insurance policy that your body will function—you know, sexually—in the event the other drugs you're taking start to interfere with arousal." Heritage paused to see if he was losing his audience or forfeiting his case.

"Would you say you experiment with drugs on a regular basis, Mr. Carter?"

"Look, I know that didn't come out right, but the answer to your question is no. I don't even really drink, beyond an occasional beer or glass of wine. I was just trying to fit in and interact with some local adults—people my age. I'm new here and don't know many people yet."

"Do you think you'll be staying?" The officer had stopped writing.

Now that was a good question, and Heritage said as much. "It's getting off to a pretty rough start, so I don't know the answer to that yet." That was true. He'd obviously alienated himself from the Grand Dame, or head witch, or whatever the hell Dottie Bard was—something even Brad Fraser had warned him against. Mona Rye wasn't likely to trust him again with so much as a cheese bun. François was running hot and cold—affectionate in private but cautiously distant in public. Heritage didn't know what was going to happen next—or what he even wanted to happen next.

To Heritage, Toren seemed satisfied with how the questioning was going, though he'd just more formally referred to him as Mr. Carter. Everything he'd told the officer was true and could be backed up, he supposed, with witnesses—Lyle Hudson, Rowan Robson, the dancers from the ballet troupe—if they were cooperative, reachable, and willing to tell the truth. Heritage went on to defend himself even more forcefully—after all, he had saved the kid's life not once but twice in the past forty-eight hours. "If I had a secret to bury—say, that I was into young boys and that I had molested him—don't you think I would have let him drown in the channel or bleed to death in the forest to protect myself? Do you think I would have voluntarily presented myself here, at the RCMP station, if I had done anything wrong?"

Toren put his pen down. "You present a good argument, counselor. I mean, I can't forget that debate is your gift—your law-school training, right? Still, I find myself wanting to believe you in spite of the evidence. Unfortunately, the soon-to-be-proven medical fact that you had your—uh, your adulthood up a teenager's butt isn't going to play well in the minds of my superiors . . . and, God forbid, your future jurors, if this comes to that, though I expect it won't. While this falls into the bizarre bin, there isn't any evidence of a crime. Even if you had fooled around with Mona Rye's kid, he is above the legal age of consent, which happens to be fourteen in British Columbia—all of Canada, actually." Toren closed the file and scooted away from the table. "Will you be traveling to your grandfather's memorial service then?"

"If I'm free to go, yes. I would very much like to be there." Heritage was surprised to learn the age of consent and surprised that his mobility wasn't being restricted.

"When do you expect to be back here?"

Previously, when he'd been trying to get the hell out of Clayoquot Sound, there had been no return ticket consideration. He had wanted to clear out before the shit hit the fan. But now that it was everywhere, he was already feeling drawn back to the place to clean things up and have another go at it. With his grandfather dead, Brad Fraser missing, and the Headlands without a captain's hand on the wheel, he was being presented with his opening—the eco-dream he'd come here to realize in the first place.

"I can be back here a week from today, as long as I can get flight connections. I fully realize this case needs to be resolved, and that Ninnish needs to get the psychiatric attention he clearly, desperately requires. I want to be part of that solution if I can." Was that even true? Heritage silently cross-examined his own statement. He had been trying to strike a balance between revealing that he cared about the kid's welfare, and appearing to care too much. He realized why he struggled with this—he *did* care. Aidan Rye had somehow managed to grow on him. The two of them had been through a lot of life together in the past few weeks. There was something flattering about having been someone else's obsession. It hadn't come from the adults he had desired, but it was still nice.

Toren stood and a coin dropped from the upturned file to roll on the table toward Heritage. "Oh! I'd forgotten to ask you about that. That was also in your sweatshirt pocket, along with the map."

Heritage reached for the coin. "It's my good-luck charm," he said, thinking he'd better lie—and for the first time that day, too. Secrets, he was learning, were good as currency, if you could keep them. He had forgotten that he did have it with him, for the next time he ran into François.

"You better hang onto it, then. You never know—" Toren cut himself short, smiled and turned to open the door. "Do you need a ride back out to the Headlands?"

Heritage shook his head, dropped the coin into his shirt pocket, and thanked the officer.

"I'm good," he said, and then headed straight for the bank to make arrangements to cover the payroll.

TOKEN TELLS

Twenty-four hours later, Heritage had once again sat in the co-pilot's seat, next to his pilot, Jason, on a seaplane flight back to Vancouver. After deplaning at the docks of the seaplane base on the Fraser River, and during the short walk from the seaplane base where he was told he could catch a shuttle bus to the main YVR terminal for his nonstop to Toronto, Heritage kept turning the coin over and over in his front pocket.

Between the two engraved circles on the coin were two words which looked Russian to him, but he didn't know what they meant. He didn't think about the coin's origin again until he was passing an Aeroflot ticket counter on the way to the concourse and the gate for his departing flight in Vancouver International Airport. On a whim, he took the coin out of his pocket and walked up to the agent.

"This is a subway token for the Moscow Metro," she said, with her Slavic accent. "But it's an old one. It is probably worth about fifty kopek." She smiled, revealing a residual streak of red lipstick on one of her front teeth. "I haven't been back to Moscow in years, so it may be worth more now—maybe less?"

"Really?" Heritage remembered François' postcard, from a time when his father had visited Russia. "I think it is worth a lot more than that," he said, smiling back. "Thank you very much."

Heritage hurried through the terminal to reach his connecting gate. Riding a moving sidewalk, he glanced several passengers ahead and thought he recognized a woman's crazy hairdo from the back. He wondered if it could possibly be his old drag queen friend, Michael Rozzeau—aka Imogene Mantoya. He watched to see if she would give him a flash of her sideways profile. She did, but it wasn't Imogene. He moved a few steps ahead on the rolling sidewalk and said her name.

"Stephanie Bard?"

Stephanie spun around just as the auto-walkway ended and the conveyor belt disappeared inside its housing. She lost her balance and toppled over the carry-on suitcase she was standing behind. Heritage was the next domino and he fell on top of her and her suitcase. Passengers stacked up behind them tried to help them to their feet. Embarrassed, they shuffled their suitcases off to the side.

With a hand over his mouth, Heritage apologized, saying "I am so sorry!"

"Oh," she replied, as he held her forearm trying to help her steady herself again. "Hello there, uh . . ."

"It's Tage. We had a—a moment on your zodiac earlier this month."

"Right. A thing, yes." She subconsciously rubbed her belly, causing Heritage to look down at it. Was she putting on weight?

"I thought you were exploring Patagonia this whole time," he said. "What are you doing in Vancouver?"

"Yeah, about that . . . I got down there and the company I was supposed to kayak guide for had folded . . . gone out of business. I've been hanging low at my uncle Lyle's townhouse in Gastown."

"And where are you off to today, then?" He was beyond flirting and small talk, and was going to be late boarding his own plane if he wasn't more expedient.

"Edmonton," she said, still rubbing her stomach. "I'm pregnant with the most wretched morning sickness."

The blood flushed from Heritage's face.

"*Pregnant?*" he asked as though he were hard of hearing.

"Yep. That's good ole fertile *moi*." She laughed awkwardly. "Just introduce the slightest bit of semen anywhere around me and I'm planted."

"You've gotten pregnant before, then?" He was fishing.

"Yes, several times," she confessed. "Even had a kid when I was fifteen, but gave him up for adoption. Had to, my mother told me. She handled all the arrangements. She could still tell me what to do back then."

"Whatcha going to do this time?" Heritage asked, pointing rather crudely at her abdomen, which she hadn't stopped rubbing.

"Well, assuming it is François' I guess I need to get around to seeing if he wants to be a father. Regardless, I'm thinking that maybe it's time for me to get serious and be a mother this time, as long as the baby seems healthy and everything. But I'm taking some time for myself—you know, away from my mother and the sound's rumour mill. To sort shit out."

"And if François isn't—"

"What? Ready to be a father?"

"No. What if François isn't the father? What if it is somebody else?"

Stephanie's brain raced ahead to see where he might be going. "What do you mean? It's not like I was sleeping with men up and down the coast." She faked offense. Heritage had been told of her promiscuity but figured that was another matter, for another time.

———

"You had sex with me. I came as I was struggling to pull out." He hated having to spell out the obvious.

"Well then, do you feel like being a father?" Stephanie drove the point home.

"No!" Heritage said quickly and with perhaps too much animation. "I don't," he added, more quietly. "How old are you again? Is it even safe for a woman your age to carry and give birth?" He was toying with her a bit, but there was a reason for the question.

"I am thirty-two, fuck you very much, and in the optimum age range to be having a child. Nobody is putting my ovaries out to pasture."

Heritage was busy doing math in his head—something he usually tried to avoid in the age of calculators and computers. If she had a child when she was fifteen and she was thirty-two years old—just like him, then her first child—a son, she'd just said—would be seventeen by now. A seventeen-year-old boy—nearly a man himself. Just a year older than Satan with an A.

Then, the other shoe dropped, and Heritage's mouth dropped open with it. What if Ninnish turned out to be older than Heritage thought? What if Dottie Bard had handled the arrangements with Stephanie's first-born, and had cooked his birthdate so that her only grandson wouldn't ever get smuggled too far away from her? What if—fuck! His brain was exploding. It would be twisted, he realized—but what if Stephanie was Aidan's biological mother? Who had been the father that time? Why had Mona agreed to go along with the deception? Unless even she had been double-crossed and fooled by Dottie Bard, too.

"Look," Heritage said. "Good luck in Edmonton. I am running late for my plane."

"Say, how do I contact you if this heads in a direction where, I don't know, maybe I might need you to take a paternity test?"

"Why don't you start with François, since there are probably multiple chances he holds the winning ticket? I'm heading back to Tofino after attending my grandfather's funeral in Toronto. I won't be hard to track down. You'd just have to come back home."

And with that, the two of them parted—no goodbye, no condolences for his dead grandfather, no apologies for potentially screwing up his life with her runaway fertility.

His grandfather's will had been no contest. When Heritage swooped in out of thin air in time for the much-publicized memorial service, there wasn't a paper, magazine, or television station that hadn't profiled Toronto's newest, richest, and most available bachelor. Heritage the First had in fact left everything to his grandson—who, it appeared, he had trusted just a smidgeon more than his corporate attorneys, who had been scheming to protect their own interests. Heritage managed to keep his two lives separate for the forty-eight hours he was allowed to bask in the Toronto limelight. Carter Pulp & Paper's shares had taken a dip on the TSE following the news of its founder's death, but the overnight popularity and media fascination with its successor saw them rebounding by the end of trading the following Tuesday.

Heritage had swiftly engaged one of his law school lawyer friends in Vancouver, who had been working at the environmentally minded Sierra Legal Defense, to personally oversee his transition to power, codify his first executive order authorizing the operation of Carter Pulp & Paper to remain status-quo for the remainder of the fiscal year. In addition, Heritage and his lawyer formalized a provision that operations be driven by its board of directors (of which Heritage had just become chairman) for the next ninety days, ordered a freeze on all mergers and acquisitions during the same period, and made arrangements for his ailing bank account to ail no longer. By the time Heritage Warren Carter the Third and Only left Toronto late Wednesday afternoon, he'd added a dozen new entries in his portfolio of important contacts—none of whom could deliver him from the mess waiting for him back in Clayoquot Sound.

And there to remind him of that was Constable Luis Toren, standing next to his cruiser on the First Street dock as the float-plane glided toward him on the day Heritage returned to the scene of the—what? It hadn't been a crime, he needed to keep reminding himself.

"You look no worse for wear," Toren said when they met on the tarmac, shaking Heritage's hand. "Welcome back."

"What, no marching band?"

"Didn't you get enough of that fanfare and attention these past few weeks in Toronto?" Toren joked as the two moved toward his vehicle, parked diagonally on the red-railed dock. Heritage, in his blue-plaid sport jacket, dress slacks and fancy shoes, took a spin around as though he were a fashion model at the end of the runway, taking it all in as he inhaled the crisp sea-air into his lungs. He was back in Clayoquot Sound, on different footing, since his first arrival. While the place didn't seem at all like it changed, he sure had.

"To bring you current with the situation here, Ninnish stands behind his original story to the caseworker. He's back in the hospital, by the way." Toren reached for the hanging bag slung over Heritage's shoulder and tossed it in the back seat of the cruiser. "He had some complications after returning last week from the regional hospital and surgery centre in Port Alberni. They'd implanted this silicone superball in his scrotum, but his body seems to be rejecting some of his stitches." Toren stopped. "Probably more than you needed to know."

"I'm still allowed to ride up here, right?" he asked. Toren had been acting familiar and not at all indifferent, so Heritage assumed he wasn't a prisoner yet.

"Of course." Toren started the vehicle and turned his

headlights on, even though it was the middle of the day, "There have been a few developments I should warn you about."

"Sure." Heritage remembered to fasten his seatbelt. A small penlight mounted above the onboard computer illuminated the underside of Toren's square chin. The day's sun angled through the driver-side window to light up the officer's thin blond whiskers. The policeman's sea-blue eyes reminded Heritage of the glass marbles he'd collected in primary school—blue, always blue. Had he not been anxious, even apprehensive about returning, Heritage might have wrung a fantasy crush out of the whole Constable Toren experience. Heritage had changed. He was feeling much more confident and sexually decisive and liberated since his grandfather's passing—that was for certain. He had nothing to hide from the old patriarch anymore. He could pursue whatever and whomever he wanted in this new future of his—just as soon as he could mop up the Ninnish spill.

"For starters," Toren said, "Dottie Bard wants you crucified, and Mona has returned from her cancer treatments early to be with her son. Together, I think they could take you in an alley if you're not careful. And believe me, they're more than motivated to do so now that everyone's heard and can smell that you've come into money. Second, the caseworker from social services has had her hands full trying to get Rowan Robson to talk. But he won't—he has been clinically mute since the tragic and traumatizing accident with his mum. When the caseworker learned you were returning, she only relented on her demands that you be held in custody pending a trial when I gave her my assurance you would be under twenty-four-hour surveillance."

"Am I?"

Toren let slip a chuckle. "We don't have the resources. Plus, you've more than demonstrated you're no flight risk. Hell, you came back, which is more than I think I could have done in your shoes—which are pretty fancy I have to say, and yes, I noticed."

"Well, I'm honest if I'm anything," Heritage acknowledged.

"But I thought with the whole age of consent thing, we agreed a crime hadn't been committed."

"Well," Toren leveled with him, "the allegation of rape is still a crime, whether the victim is of age or isn't."

"The victim?" Heritage let that roll around in the space between them a moment. "The victim here is me! I'm the one who was drugged, tied down, and raped. He doesn't get to play the victim card." Heritage's temperature was rising at the very notion someone would believe Aidan Rye over him.

Toren checked his mirrors before backing into a three-point turn to navigate around a wall of stacked crab traps, while leaving the dock. "Things have changed here with the notoriety surrounding your identify and inheritance. People here, even the government—particularly the Ministry of Children and Family Development—everyone really, is acting differently about this situation now that it's widely known that you've got money. Money changes things."

"It shouldn't change the truth, Officer Toren." Heritage fixed a stare through the windshield, biting his tongue.

"You're right. It shouldn't, but that's my job here—to uncover new details or get a confession."

"Confession from whom?" Heritage was defensive now. "I have nothing further to say on this matter."

"Calm yourself. I wasn't referring to you. We still need to see if we can get Rowan Robson to corroborate anything that you've told us."

"Plus, he has the Polaroids." As soon as he said it, Heritage realized he had let his temper get the best of him.

There was silence, except for the sound of the turn signal as Toren pulled up to the only stoplight in town and prepared to turn left onto Campbell Street. "You failed to mention this before. There are photos?"

Heritage bit his lower lip. "There are photos."

"You've seen them?" Toren drove past the RCMP detachment

building, which Heritage noted as proof he wasn't being taken into custody or more interrogations.

"I saw one photo—found it in the labyrinth actually and of course destroyed it. But I heard other pictures being taken . . . you know, the mechanical sounds a Polaroid camera makes?"

"And you're saying Rowan was the photographer."

"Yes," Heritage stated with full confidence.

"Interesting," Toren replied, managing to reveal the slightest lift of a grin that could have easily transformed into a grimace—the look could go either way, Heritage figured. But this also reminded Heritage what he'd thought he'd heard Rowan transmit over the teen's walkie-talkies the night he'd brought Ninnish from school to his cabin at the Headlands . . . and that was *skull box*. He still didn't know what that meant or if he'd even heard the radio transmission clearly.

"Sounds like Rowan is key here," Toren said, gently. "We need to create space for the cat to let go of that kid's tongue." The pair left the downtown core of the village, heading toward the Headlands. "Oh, and one more development to pass along to you. Interpol is working on an arrest warrant and extradition order for Brad Fraser. The problem is, they can't locate him. They have no idea where in the Caribbean he's hiding, or if he just said he was heading there to throw us off his scent."

"Then you likely already know that my grandfather's company—*my* company—owns the Headlands Lodge." He watched the officer for confirmation, and he got the nod. "My forensic auditors have confirmed that Fraser had completely liquidated the operations and reserve accounts of all the funds that had built up there. My grandfather had suspected Fraser was embezzling from him, and that's why he had sent me here to catch him in the act and then wrestle full ownership of the lodge back from him."

"Well, I didn't know that last part," Toren admitted.

"Our lawyers and accountants are already cooperating with Interpol and have requested he be brought up on charges, but we don't have any real expectation of recovering the funds." Heritage was no longer a corporate parrot just talking the talk. He was the person in charge of the message, and the president and chairperson accountable for the outcomes. He had been groomed and he was ready for this.

Toren signaled the cruiser was turning right off the highway onto the gravel road that would soon join asphalt again just before reaching Mackenzie Beach and then gently curve northward to wind its narrow way through the rainforest to the front steps of a four-star lodge that Heritage now owned—well, almost. There were still some technical hurdles that seemed to rest on Brad Fraser's arrest and extradition back to Canada, but his team had assured him, it was good as done.

"Now I have a couple of developments to spring on you," Heritage said, figuring it was time to work more collaboratively with this RCMP officer he was learning he could trust.

"You've been doing your homework then, too?" Toren asked with a grin.

"No, I've been doing yours." Heritage returned the grin with one raised eyebrow. "Do you know François Lévesque?"

Toren nodded.

"Has he ever asked you about his father, a fellow named Lucien Pelletier?"

"Yes, as a matter of fact. He told me his father had suspiciously gone missing over a decade ago and that all traces of him had led here to Clayoquot Sound."

Heritage was nodding. "Right. Well, I think I've found him, or what's left of him. But I want a chance to talk to François first, alone."

"Okay," Toren said, hesitating. "Do you know how to reach him?"

"I only run into him at the SunRyes bakeshop. He doesn't have a phone, as far as I know."

"I might be able to pick him up on marine radio if he's anywhere around his boat. I'll give it a try. I can bring him to you, but it's not such a good idea for you to wander around the village looking for him. This is the reason I met your plane. Both Dottie and Mona are sticking around town for Mason Robson's funeral, which is tomorrow morning. Under the guise of protecting them from you, I'm really trying to protect you from them—if that makes sense." Toren pulled the cruiser into a vacant parking space outside the main lobby of the lodge. He turned off the engine and the headlights.

"I appreciate that." Heritage undid his seatbelt. "Anyway, I am pretty sure I accidentally uncovered the remains of Lucien Pelletier's skeleton up in a tree over on Wickaninnish Island—before someone went back in and removed the bones after the knife incident with Ninnish in the labyrinth. I want to break this news to François myself, and then I will give you the details and location."

"That sounds intriguing. You're saying the bones were there and then they weren't."

"Yes, that's what I'm saying."

"I'll check to see if a missing person report was ever filed, but it didn't ring any bells when François asked me about his father, maybe a half a year ago now. To be honest, other priorities intervened. I just didn't remember to look into this for him, but I will now if you think you have physical evidence that he's dead."

"Right. So, if we can find the bones again, you could have them analyzed to see if there is a family match, and from that we could work to confirm the identity." Heritage was getting excited by the prospect of solving this mystery for François.

"Well, I think you have watched too much television. This will surprise you, but we don't have that technology here in Tofino. We'd have to call a team in. If the skeleton is contemporary, they might be able to match dental records."

"Hmm." Heritage paused. "I don't remember any teeth being part of the skull."

"Well then maybe your John Doe is older—much older."

Heritage shifted his butt to better face the driver. "I don't think so. Kinda tangled up in the bones was a frayed waistband from a pair of Levi's jeans. The leather tag sewn to the waistband indicated a waist of 34 and an inseam of 36. That's the same sizing measurement as mine, and François Lévesque is easily as tall as me."

"But no teeth—?"

"Maybe the guy didn't floss? I don't know." Heritage liked making the officer smile. "My second hunch is this. I have reason to believe Ninnish is older than he claims to be. I have reason to believe he is seventeen, not fifteen. Don't think for a minute I'm not hoping he turns out to be well above the age of consent so he can be questioned as an adult for the stunt he pulled. But I don't think Ninnish knows how old he is, or who his biological mother was. That may be part of his confusion, and the reason he lashes out at the world. You'll need to trace his birth records—and while you're at it, you should know that Mona is not his biological mother. She had mentioned to me something about having an emergency hysterectomy in her teens, something like twenty years ago. It didn't register when she said it, so I forgot about it, but I have a feeling you'll discover Aidan's birth mother is actually—"

Both men said the name: "Stephanie Bard."

"Jesus," was all Toren could say next, though he expanded on that. "I have been trying to work this out in my head. One of the doctors at the hospital mentioned to me the rare blood type that Aidan Rye has, and that Dottie Bard—of all matches—turns out to have the same type, even donated blood in case Aidan needed a transfusion. You wouldn't know this either, but I am from here originally. I even went to school here, the same time as Stephanie Bard. She was a grade or two younger than me, but I remembered this tenth grade rumour when Stephanie got pulled out of school in the middle of the year—that she might have gotten pregnant. I also knew that Mona Rye had needed to have her uterus removed in her late teens when they first discovered she had cancer. Quite the survivor story, that one!"

"Well, I happened to run into Stephanie at the Vancouver

airport a few weeks ago," Heritage said. "I was on my way to Toronto. Turns out, she went to South America but bailed . . . had to come back and was on her way to Edmonton when I spoke with her. She told me she was pregnant again, and that she'd gotten pregnant more than once before, and even had a son seventeen years ago that Dottie had forced her to give up for adoption." Heritage let that sink in, then continued. "There's one more thing." He waited for Toren to be ready for this. "I want access to Ninnish in the hospital."

"Oh I don't—" Toren started to protest, but Heritage held firm.

"I want to go in with a wire, and I think I can get him to tell you the truth. He won't do it if you or the caseworker or anyone else is there. If you can get me in, after visiting hours when the place is dark, I am confident I can deliver you the truth. Now, if you can't get me this access, I'll have to trust you to find the truth out by yourself. But I'm not sure either of us can afford that much time—given the RCMP's limited resources here, and all."

Heritage could tell that Toren was pondering his unthinkable suggestion that flew in the face of protocols and was definitely way outside the box. He knew this because the officer's hands still grasped the steering wheel, though they'd been parked there with the engine off for five minutes. Heritage hoped that everything in the Mountie's gut was telling him to trust his passenger who might be on the verge of something big. Surely, the nice and decent treatment Heritage had received from Constable Luis Toren from the start had to suggest he must have had his doubts about the accusations. Heritage knew he had to come off as too clean and genuine to have been the sexual pervert the women and children were making him out to be. For Toren to entertain his scheme to coerce the teenager to talk, he'd have to first take a giant leap and accept the notion that a child could sexually abuse an adult.

Toren was shaking his head now. "I would have to get approval from the higher-ups for such an undercover operation," he said, taking his hands off the steering wheel and turning his upper body.

———

"This won't surprise you, but we don't have the equipment here to fit you with a wire. We'd have to bring in a team from Victoria. I do appreciate your conviction, though. I'd even like you to be right, to be honest with you. So, I'll ask," he promised, smiling.

"Thank you. I guess the plan would be for me to wait here, then, until I hear from you?" Heritage opened the passenger door, and started to exit the cruiser.

"With the curtains pulled!" Toren smiled at him as he waited for Heritage to grab his travel bag from the backseat, before starting the souped-up engine and putting the squad car in reverse. "Oh, you know what I found out?" he added as he opened the window. "That Greek minotaur connection, you know, with the thread—it panned out. I got my daughter to dig up her school report. But get this: I went poking around Mona Rye's cabin over on the island the other day, and there, inside this wicker sewing basket—under all kinds of thread—curiously none of it white, I uncovered a mythology textbook. And the chapter, you know, about Theseus and Ariadne? It was bookmarked with a piece of black thread."

"That's significant, isn't it?" Heritage leaned through the window frame.

"It is and it isn't," Toren said. "You had access to Mona's house too. I can't prove it was Ninnish or Mona or Santa Claus that bookmarked that passage in the book." Luis scrunched up his forehead and said, "Welcome back, Mr. Carter," as he rolled up the window between them.

Heritage walked into the lobby of the Headlands to check his messages, and was intercepted by Chef Stu Solberg and quickly joined by the full complement of staff—housekeepers and gardener included—who had been waiting for his return and began applauding on cue. "Mr. Carter, welcome back." Stu reached his hand out, and they shook. "Again, we are very sorry to hear about your grandfather, and also pleased you've chosen to return to the Headlands so soon. We have upgraded your cottage to the Cliff Suite indefinitely, and hope you will find it fully appointed to your satisfaction."

"Stu, it's just me. Thank you, everyone." He looked out at his staff, before turning back to the chef and saying, "I don't require all this fuss." Heritage blushed, expressing his gratitude as the applause died down and staff returned to work. Heritage was pleasantly surprised to see the chef and staff acting as though they hadn't heard about his recent tangle with the children and witches of Wickaninnish. He wondered how it was even possible in that small town that the rumours hadn't caught up to him at the Headlands. But he was grateful for it.

"But you're CEO of Carter Pulp & Paper now," the chef said. "The Headlands is surely to be yours soon—once the bounty hunters put down their rum and cokes and get around to arresting Brad Fraser wherever he is. That warrants a celebration and some distinction in how you get treated around here. Let me pamper you, please, and make you feel welcome."

"Of course, Stu. Thank you for this. Thank you for being the rudder on this crazy ship the past few weeks—maybe months. Who knows how much of the real responsibilities of running this place Fraser had already dumped on you before I put you in charge? Thank you, sincerely." Heritage let the gratitude swell there for a moment before asking, "Are there any messages for me?"

"A stack of them. Faxes, too. We have them waiting for you in your room. May I show you the way?" Stu took the hanging bag off Heritage's shoulder.

"Certainly." The two began ascending the grand staircase. "Say, Stu, I have been puzzled by the message I received a few weeks ago before my grandfather passed. You remember—the one that said my grandfather had been released from the hospital and for me to stay put here? I don't suppose you have any indication who might have called that in, do you? Male or female, young or old?"

"I wouldn't have been the one to take the message, as I am usually in the kitchen with my fat head in a stew pot—but I will look into it for you. Perhaps the desk clerk who took it will remember some of the details. It does seem a strange message, now that you mention it."

The chef walked him upstairs to the end of the hallway—and to Heritage's relief, didn't linger after presenting him the key. The room was indeed posh as he remembered, with a gigantic spray of white gladiolas, lilies, fern fronds, and salal arranged on the desk in an oversized vessel that was more bucket than vase, with a sympathy card that had been signed by all the lodge's employees.

Heritage tossed his bag on the king-sized bed and plopped into one of the two swivel chairs that faced the French doors to his private balcony—with a view of Templar Channel, and Echachis and Wickaninnish islands beyond that, currently looking connected by a low tide. Aside from the handful of nights he'd used the suite, he had to wonder how many times this palatial treasure had actually been occupied, and about the identities of the guests who had been able to afford the staggering nightly price tag.

Keeping in the hyper-wood theme, the room glowed in rare yellow cedar and ewe—two of the most endangered softwood species in the rainforest. The unapologetic indulgence of that four-star resort had started to carve deep trenches in Heritage's reborn eco-conscience. He was glad the message on top of his incoming pile was from his green-minded Vancouver attorney. It wasn't too early to begin charting the controversial retrofitting and transformation his company would have to undergo—from ceasing the liquidation of old growth forests to embracing agri-pulp and purpose-planted second growth timber for the fiber his mills needed to remain operational.

Before he began working through the messages, he checked the small telephone book for the SunRyes Bakeshop. It had been a long travel day and it was already four-thirty in the afternoon—seven-thirty Toronto time—and chances were the bakery had already gone to its abbreviated winter hours and was closed. But he had to try. He wasn't a very patient junior detective. A woman answered, sounding too much like Mona—he wasn't ready for that confrontation yet, so he hung up the phone. It rang again so instantly he was momentarily afraid to answer it—he'd was still *that* paranoid.

Thankfully, it was François. Toren had reached him by marine radio on the company skiff where he was working late repairing a net. He only had to walk a few metres to the payphone on the dock to give Heritage a ring at the RCMP's request. Heritage asked him if he could land his skiff on the small beach below the Headlands, and François said he could be there in twenty minutes to pick him up. Heritage hung up, making sure the Russian metro token was in his pocket. After changing from city shoes to wilderness boots, he left his suite to negotiate the rocky trail down to the beach.

Toren really hadn't had much opportunity to make high-stakes requests of his regional superiors, since nothing much ever happened in the sound. He'd never seen anything as high-tech as a miniature wire microphone anywhere near their detachment, and couldn't remember if they'd even received a surveillance demonstration during their Mountie training at the depot in Regina or at any of the annual recertifications or specialty courses they were endlessly subjected to just to stay on top of the latest technologies and ever-evolving procedures.

As soon as he reached his office, he put in a call to the regional chief constable at home, and after much persuasion and risking his professional reputation on a hunch, he received the go-ahead, with the condition that social services came on board to support an interrogation approach that would not be without some risk. Given the rapport Toren had already failed to establish with Kari Washbrook, he knew that gaining her support would require the combined charm of both him and Dr. McAnally. He phoned Victoria to put in his surveillance team request, and then drove to McAnally's townhouse overlooking the harbour.

François was in an instant good mood. He'd been thinking about Tage for the past several weeks, and had just returned to the village from his oyster farm rotation when the RCMP officer had radioed him the message. He had been anxious for news and of course had wanted to have it confirmed that Tage was planning to return to Clayoquot Sound. He knew it was way too early, but he was tired of being sad, grieving Marcel's death. He just wanted to give into the feeling that he and Tage could maybe be at the edge of romantic discovery. But he was still hurting—still piecing back together his broken heart after the tragic end of his secret love affair with Marcel. He knew about the dangers of rebounding. Maybe it was too soon to feel anything again. Still, he zipped around Monk's Point and flew past Tonquin Beach with new hope that seemed to have turned his aluminum skiff into a hovercraft.

In his adrenaline-fueled enthusiasm, François daredevil-gunned the skiff onto the beach, cutting and yanking the motor up with precision as he sand-braked to a stop just a little over a metre short of where Heritage was standing, waiting for him. François sort of amazed himself and wondered why he didn't just deliver oysters to the Headlands this way all the time. It would sure save him the hassle of unloading the boat, loading that stinky truck, and fighting the tourist-choked highway twice a week.

Heritage hopped aboard the beached vessel, and the two men

hugged for several minutes. Neither of them said anything. Neither of them had to. The afternoon skies had turned overcast, and the evening was feeling October brisk. Even at the ocean, the smell of autumn hung, suspended like strands of cedar smoke from campfires and chimneys, creating an artificial ceiling low enough to jump up and touch.

At least until the winter rains arrived any day now to wash it from his senses, François reveled in the change of another season. The holidays were coming, and there was now a chance he'd have someone to share them with. That hadn't really happened since he was a small boy. For some reason, he hadn't gotten around to making his usual travel plan to leave the sound for the off-season, and suddenly the prospect of staying put through the winter thrilled him. The rains were usually guaranteed to drive him landward, and with his paycheques from the oyster farm tucked nicely away in the bank to get him through the dark grey months, the winter was all his—and now it might be all theirs. This hope filled his stomach with big-winged monarchs, tickling his insides with anticipation. A few of them managed to escape in a spontaneous giggle, which prompted Heritage to pull away.

"What's so funny?"

"Nutting. I'm just happy."

Heritage took his hand. "Here, I want to show you something" he said, plunging his hand deep into his front pocket.

"I've already seen it," François joked with him. "Da hot springs, remember?" The Quebecker giggled some more. But when Heritage sat him down on the skiff's bench and placed the coin in his hand, François asked, "So what is dis?"

"François, it's a metro token from the Moscow subway—in Russia. I think it belonged to your father." Heritage sat on the back of his calves so his face was even with his friend's. François' mouth fell open as he stared at Heritage. Heritage went on. "What size was your father? Was he tall like you?"

At first François didn't speak. He was thinking. "Of course, I only remember him as being a giant, since I was so small. Yes, I suppose he would be my size. Where did you get dis?" He angled the coin to catch the cloud-filtered light as all of Clayoquot Sound was about to be plunged into *le crépuscule*.

"I found it on Wickaninnish Island. Among some bones, stashed high in a tree."

"And you tink it is my fadder?" François' face fell some—even though he had accepted long ago that his father was likely dead.

"With the bones I found, François, there was part of a pair of jeans. Levi's. It was the part here at the waist." He motioned to the Levi jeans that François had on—that he'd never seen him wear before. "It still had the leather patch attached that says, you know, what the measurements of the jeans are." Heritage reached to move François a quarter turn where he was sitting to examine his Levi's patch. "They were a man's measurements—thirty-four inches at the waist and thirty-six inches long—exactly the same as these jeans. That would be a man my size, or yours. When I discovered that this coin came from Moscow, that made me think . . ."

"And deese bones, were dey close to Dottie Bard's cabin?"

"Well, they were there a few days ago. But they've been removed. Someone has taken them."

"Will you show me dis place? I want to see da exact tree for myself."

"Of course." Heritage was unsure what the tree had to do with it—but it was François' right to see it.

"Can we go der now?" François stood, raising Heritage by the elbows to a standing position.

Without further discussion, the two shoved the boat back into the water and they sliced across Templar Channel in the skiff, shoulder-to-shoulder just like that first rainy day, except without that sick native chief on the floor of the boat at their feet. Heritage didn't relish retracing his steps on Wickaninnish—but with François, he could face any demon . . . or witch . . . or murderer.

After getting the RCMP investigators lost, Heritage wasn't

even sure he could find the blasted labyrinth without the thread. He figured his luck would improve if he could use the trail he knew best—the one that started by the back of Stephanie's little shed, not that far from Dottie's cabin. As they snooped around the opening of the cove, they could see no signs of occupation. No woodstove smoke, no kayaks, no anchored boat.

Dottie's coast seemed clear, so they pulled in and anchored by the buoy-tethered rowboat that had been recovered and returned to its mooring after Heritage had used and abandoned it after getting the hemorrhaging Ninnish from shore to Dottie's motorboat. Heritage and François gingerly transferred into the smaller boat and Heritage rowed them to the beach, trying not to make a big deal about the half-litre of bloody water he saw swirling at François' gumbooted feet. The pair dashed into the woods, using a flashlight from François' boat that was flickering near dead by the time they reached the clearing. Standing near the mound of the labyrinth, Heritage was able to point to where the platform had once been positioned, high in the largest Sitka tree. After a minute or two staring up into the gracefully swooping branches, François broke down into sobs as giant as the trees that ringed that possessed clearing.

Heritage pivoted to hold him, and François completely relinquished all emotional control in his arms. It had been more than the latter could bear. He'd spent the last two years in the sound convinced his father was there. He'd experienced the same prophetic dream—three, sometimes five nights a week—with a very specific tree in it. He now realized he had lived most of that past summer in an on-again, off-again relationship with Stephanie—within several hundred metres of that same tree from his dreams, now towering before him. He didn't have to be told that those contorting limbs had held the remains of his father. He already knew that, somehow. This was just the hallowed defeat that signaled the end of his life-long search and extinguished the last hope of ever finding his father alive.

———

When he could speak, François said, "Dis is da tree. My fadder was definitely der." He pointed up into the first fork of branches ten metres above them. Heritage coaxed him to sit in the moss at the edge of the labyrinth.

"Tell me about your father again," Heritage said, inviting the memories into that sacred place.

François spoke. "My fadder was a horrible man, says my mum. He slept with utter women, lots of dem. I had a sister, but my mother says he abused her, too, so she ran away. None of dis mattered to me. To me, my fadder was just like God—someone I could see but never touch. When he left home for good, I was six years old. I said den dat I would sail around da world until I found him." He held the metro token at the end of his long and outstretched arm. He examined it in the heavy dusk's diminishing light. "Now, I found him. Dis is where my fadder's journey and my search for him ends."

Heritage cupped François' angular face in his hands and gently dabbed his wet cheeks with his thumbs. "I think you are right," he said. Heritage traced François' new moustache and the slight goatee it grew into—new growth since they'd last seen each other that only made him look even more like the contemporary renditions of the Christian messiah. This reminded Heritage of his own body hair, that had mostly grown back in the weeks since they'd been apart. Heritage touched those quivering lips, behind which lurked that brown miscoloured tooth that Heritage longed to see through a smile that was likely going to be delayed awhile longer. A debate was firing back and forth across Heritage's brain like a game of ping-pong. He wanted to comfort his aching friend, but his friend needed to know everything first. "François, there's something else that took place here. I need to talk to you about it. Tell me if now is not the right time. I know this is difficult."

"No, tell me. Never have I had ears for hearing da truth like I have right now. My ears hear so much from dis place. It is da perfect time for revelations. Tell me, please." When Heritage hesitated and his eyes revealed the fear inside him, it was François' turn to hold his friend's face. "Find da beginning and just tell me," he said—so reassuringly that the words began to fall from Heritage's mouth until they'd piled up around them in the cushioned moss.

Heritage found the beginning, navigated through the choppy, whirlpooled middle and had given François an end. On their way back across the island, Heritage also remembered to mention that he'd bumped into Stephanie in the Vancouver Airport, and that she had told him she was pregnant again. François, with no trace of panic in his smile, replied, "I have no worries der. I always used protection with dat woman, because da word was out dat she slept wit everyone." It was Heritage's turn to panic.

The sun was long gone, and the moon was waning crescent again, rising from behind Meares Island, as their boat—with Heritage's covertly recovered kayak and paddle laying crosswise—skipped back across the channel to the peninsula—like a flat rock tossed underhand.

Constable Toren and Dr. McAnally had not succeeded in convincing Kari Washbrook nor her Victoria-based superiors at the Ministry of Children and Family Development that keeping the teenager in his hospital recovery bed the extra few days that it would take them to get set up for the wire-tap was a good idea. Aidan had gotten well enough to be scheduled for release the next morning. McAnally had said as much earlier in the day himself. "Absolutely not," had been Washbrook's response. She did agree to look into the possibility that Aidan Rye's birth date had been incorrectly reported.

"Look. The kid has fully grown pubic hair, at least a four-o-clock peach fuzzed shadow, and can reach productive orgasm when masturbating." The village doctor had pulled out all the stops to underpin the duo's many runaway theories.

"We also need you to doublecheck your database in BC and Alberta for a child born in 1977 to a birth mother with the name of Stephanie Bard," Toren added, and the doctor nodded his support of that suggestion.

Kari Washbrook cleared her throat before speaking. "I have already checked medical records in both provinces. Stephanie Bard's medical history does indeed confirm that has the same rare blood type as her mother—and the same rare blood type as Aidan Rye. We have every medical reason to believe that Ninnish could be seventeen years old, and I can even concede that chances are that Stephanie Bard is the boy's biological mother." The caseworker then looked each of the men straight in the eye. "What does any of this change for the boy if you're right?"

"It gets the boy one year closer to being a man," Luis Toren stated, for the record. "And then we can dismiss all this pretense that we've been dealing with a defenseless child. "It's that simple." He paused. "Plus, it gets you home in time for your weekend."

REAL TO REEL

Aidan was achy and swollen around the groin but had run out of sway with the nursing staff that had grown resentful the round-the-clock menace hadn't been discharged already. The teenager had been using them like a vending machine, inventing cravings for Cheezies and even sweet-talking Sherri Remington into smuggling him a couple of his favourite candy bars when she'd come on shift an hour earlier—he'd developed a taste and appreciation for Coffee Crisps, of all the disgusting, adult-tasting things.

The teenager was bored. He'd watched more TV than he could take, especially since the Tofino General Hospital didn't even have cable. He'd been stuck with three channels, and one of them French. At least the hospital in Port Alberni last week had the Discovery Channel, MuchMusic, and HBO. He'd earlier overheard the doctor talking to a day nurse in the hall and he was certain that he'd been about to be discharged. But then there was a shift change, and it was suddenly nighttime again and he was still in his hospital bed, the orange telltale stains of Cheezies on the scratchy white linen sheet that covered his chest. Below that sheet, he'd been playing with himself, mostly to verify that everything still worked—and so far, it did. His first boner after the slashing came on like a miracle after he'd been stitched up and left alone for a few minutes that first night. And then again, last week, just hours after regaining consciousness following the surgery in Port Alberni where they'd popped his new fake nut inside his ball sack, he got his boner back, and while his body was still swimming in a pool of pain killers, he managed to cum too—a large, somewhat yellowed load, but cum all the same. He was working out another offering to the horned gods right now, beneath the sheet.

The lights in the hallway outside his room had been reduced, and he'd heard the clamour of activity as the visiting hours ended and things started getting locked up for the night. The day nurse had already left, and it was just that slutty nurse on duty and maybe the librarian who worked reception sometimes. It was stupefying that his wrist hadn't snapped, with all the jerking off he did. While it made no sense in the world to him, cumming had even gotten better since the accident.

There was all kinds of action happening under the big top when Aidan heard a noise in the hall that stopped him midstroking. He was sure it was that damn nurse again. She was so crazy full of herself that she must have thought he enjoyed being flirted with, and that all her *big-boy-like-you* innuendos were getting him hot and bothered or something. They weren't. He was so over it. But there was someone moving down the darkened hall, so he withdrew his hands from under the bedding and folded them to lay over the top of his erection.

The lights and TV had been turned off in his room so he could concentrate and conjure up the fantasy in his mind that he could jack off to. So at first he couldn't tell who the shadow belonged to. But someone had slipped quietly into his tiny hospital room.

"Hey, buddy," Tage Carter whispered in his ear. "It's me, so don't freak out. I am not here to hurt you, but I've been so worried about you, you know? It's been killing me not to see you. I've been dying to know you are okay, and that you've forgiven me for having to go to Toronto. I want to let you know that I am back now. I'm not leaving again. I'm home."

Aidan's heart was tripping over its own ventricles and atria. He reached in the dark for Tage's hand. Finding it, he brought it back to his thin sheet covered hard-on and said, "I've missed you too. Go ahead. Feel how much I've missed you, Tage." He felt the adult-in-the-room's fingers squeeze him gently, fondly there. When he didn't retract his hand, but instead leaned over to plant a soft kiss on Aidan's forehead, the latter swooned. The man must have come to his senses and realized by his absence and maybe the number of times he'd almost lost Aidan, how much he really cared. His heart must have grown fonder, like they say.

"I forgive you for going to Toronto," Aidan whispered, putting a free hand on top of Tage's hand that was still cupping him there. The kid squeezed, then drove the adult hand back and forth to massage him there. "Do you forgive me for drugging you, tying your down and sitting on your cock, Tage? Have you forgiven yourself for loving every second of it?" Satan with an A was elated, throbbing and so very proud of himself for finally bagging the prize and at last, capturing his cougar that had been evading him. He extended his arm, the one with the IV needle still dripping the antibiotic and saline cocktail into a vein on the top of his hand, and he found Tage's hard-on and gave a squeeze there. "I knew you hadn't gotten enough of me and that you would be back for more," the teen confessed. "Whadya say you bust me out of here and we hide out on Wickaninnish until everything settles down? I've already been promised—that as soon as I'm better—I can move into Stephanie's pyramid cabin at Big Beach while she's away. And I am better. I am *definitely* better now," the kid emphasized.

<hr>

Then the lights came on, and there were suddenly other adults in the room. One carefully removed a long black wire from inside Tage's windbreaker and Tage was escorted out of the hospital by policemen and ripped once again from his life.

MONA'S MOMENT

A subpoena was not the ticket Heritage thought he would be using to return to Clayoquot Sound, but Luis Toren had tracked him down, and three and a half months into his new role as president and CEO of the Carter Pulp & Paper Company, he'd just been served. He had erroneously and perhaps too optimistically believed that his time spent there, on the left side of the country, would have been washed away by the winter rains, or that his mercurial ascendance as one of "Canada's Top 40 Under 40"—according to the *Financial Post*—had provided him a Teflon suit where nothing stuck except his streak of good luck. CP&P's international board of directors had installed the grandson to bring stability to the company's volatile share prices, since most of them had stock options and therefore a reason to cozy up to the heir who didn't have a business or even a science degree, and hadn't bothered to finish law school. Heritage would have thought he was the least likely candidate to carry the company name forward—but he would have been wrong about that too.

Since his grandfather's funeral and after the quick return trip he'd made to Tofino to satisfy his promise to the RCMP, Heritage Warren Carter the Third had returned to Toronto to take up residence in the family's not-so-modest mansion in Hogg's Hollow—in the Don River Valley, on Knightswood Road. Heritage had many fond memories of playing explorer in the sprawling backyard that bordered the heavily treed Paddington Park. It was there that he first fell in love with trees at a time when the world had held more wonder. His own father had been the forestry student and the business law graduate his succession-minded grandfather had desired—but his brain had been wired funny, too. He could pioneer and patent new ways to maximize a tree's cellulose properties, but he couldn't cope with his wife's demands for basic intimacy. After Heritage graduated from Upper Canada College and shifted westward for university, his father's relationship with his mother soured. He had frozen her out, and she retaliated by taking a lover—the certified public accountant who had done their taxes for years. The accountant was to be the only one who survived that decision, after the reconciling events just before Christmas Eve, 1988.

Jason, his half native floatplane pilot, had selected a different, more northerly route this time, to give his repeat passenger a view of the Comox Glacier atop Strathcona Provincial Park. Like before, Jason narrated their route like a seasoned museum docent. "A geological survey done in the '70s counted around 170 glaciers on Vancouver Island. Now, there's maybe five left." He pointed to the patch of snow reflecting the sun back at them. "The Comox Glacier over there is the largest remaining, at about a square kilometre. Scientists at UVic have predicted these five will disappear in the next fifty years. The earth, she's getting hotter. I see it with these glaciers. I didn't used to see all these rocks sticking out of the snow when I started flying twelve years ago. Nobody's listening to me, but it's happening fast."

The pilot had learned a fair measure more about his passenger's identity in advance of their third trip together courtesy of some gossip his auntie—who was also his booking agent—had overheard at the liquor store. The whole town seemed to be talking about Brad Fraser's vanishing act, and the thirty-something multimillionaire who had rescued the four-star resort and its twenty-eight full-time jobs from certain receivership. With a wealthy celebrity onboard, Jason deliberately chose a northern transect from Vancouver, based on what he thought his passenger's interests were—more industrial than touristy.

Not so subliminally, the pilot also wanted to expose Heritage Carter the Third to the clear-cut patchwork of destruction his grandfather had been responsible for. The timber forest licenses hadn't been in his name, but the Carter Pulp & Paper Company had created the Canadian market for cast-off fiber, which had kept the chainsaws buzzing up, down, and across Vancouver Island for the past several decades. Cast-off tree fiber didn't yield merchantable lumber but could be turned into cardboard—and with insane amounts of bleaching, into photocopy and toilet paper.

Heritage had received the message loud and clear, and was growing more and more disgusted by his grandfather's footprint. He had already vowed to walk more lightly, but after seeing the clear-cuts on this flyover, he would return to Toronto and begin by throwing his newfound wealth around to source fiber from second-growth, purpose-planted tree farms, and somehow funnel profits to replant the forests and restore the ecosystems on Vancouver Island.

Heritage was embarrassed that he kept forgetting the pilot's name, and this marked his third trip with him too. But as a new CEO, he'd met so many people whose names he'd had to memorize and remember, that his Clayoquot contacts had been mostly deleted to make room for the new data that had become necessary for his day-to-day corporate existence. "Hey . . . you know I don't think I mentioned this to you, but I ended up spending some time on Wickaninnish Island last fall . . . W . . . I . . . C . . . K . . . " Heritage started to spell the name out loud, but stopped himself. "Telling me that it was spelled exactly like it sounded on our first flight together came in handy. So thanks!"

"Oh yeah?" the pilot asked him. "There has been this Bermuda Triangle of bad luck surrounding Wickaninnish Island lately. A good friend of mine, Marcel Labbé, was killed there after his boat wrecked on the rocks. Then a really sweet woman, Mason Robson, fell off the cliff near Cormorant Rock, leaving her only son orphaned, since his dad was already in prison for murder. They say things come in threes, so—" The pilot cut himself off—he'd made his point.

"Believe it or not, in my short time here, I had already met the two of them—Marcel and Mason," Heritage said, leaving out that he'd seen both of them alive on the days that they ended up getting killed. Maybe he was the bad luck charm. This made him squirm some in his co-pilot seat.

"Wow, that's something," the pilot said. "I don't have much connection or business with the folks on Wickaninnish Island, but I talk pretty regularly with Matt Greene from the coast guard station. His pop, Steve, seems to always be up in arms about something over there."

"I met Matt and his dad, too." Heritage wasn't bragging—more coming to terms with the small size of the place, and how everyone was interconnected. "I was made to feel very unwelcome by his father one day on the street outside the Co-op." Heritage didn't know why he threw the last bit out there. Maybe he was still bitter about that exchange, and fishing for something.

"That sounds like Steve. Not a warm fuzzy person. Acts like he owns the place—always flexing his native muscle, like he or his ancestors are from here, or something."

"Well—he is native, right?"

"Sure. Algonquin, maybe. But definitely not Tla-o-qui-aht or Nuu-chah-nulth. He has pissed off most of my family, coming off, like he does, as an official native voice when he isn't from here—you know, like when he speaks to the media from the blockades he's always organizing."

"Interesting," was all Heritage could think to say. The western coastline of Vancouver Island came into view. During the hour-long flight, they had already cleared the larger mountains, and the pilot hung his turn left, pointing to the hot springs below. "Oh cool," Heritage said. "Yes, I've been there with my friend, François." Heritage was intentional about dropping that name—he was still fishing for something maybe he didn't know.

"Oh yeah? I know François. Cool guy. Has his head on right, even though his heart seems pretty broken up. Came here to find his father, but hasn't had much luck."

Heritage casually reached into his front pants pocket to finger the very expensive vintage, Russian rose gold men's bracelet he'd purchased on a whim, with François and their upcoming reunion weighing very heavily on his heart and mind. François had tried to give him the metro token back the night before he'd left Clayoquot this last time, as a demonstration of his trust that Heritage would return to help him recover his father's remains and as a way to keep them connected through the unavoidable string of weeks to come when they would have to be apart. Heritage had known that he needed to return to Toronto to address the company's leadership transition. But once there, he quickly became consumed by his new powers and the demands on his time. François' tender gesture had cattle-branded Heritage's heart with François' initials, but he'd insisted François keep the metro token. After the first month away, he had tried to get a message to François to let him know he'd been detained, and even tried to invite him to spend some time with him in Toronto instead—but his messages and offers of airplane tickets had not been returned or accepted.

He turned to ask his pilot a question. "You grew up in Clayoquot, right?"

"Hold that thought one minute." The pilot pressed a button to communicate on the radio. "This is Jason with Megin River Air. I'm about ten minutes out from Tofino Harbour with one passenger . . . request landing clearance and approach coordinates." Heritage could hear the same static in his headset while they waited for a response. While they waited in silence, descending in elevation, Heritage was tring to commit the name *Jason* in his head so that he would remember it this time.

"Roger that, Megin River Air. Continue southeast and stand by for landing instructions. We have a med-evac underway which I expect should clear the hospital heli-pad in the next five minutes. Copy?"

"Copy that, Tofino." The pilot paused and turned to Heritage. "Hmm. Never good news, since you almost always know the person being evacuated. Yes, I was born in Tofino General. I grew up here. My father is Chief Sennan of the Hesquiaht."

"No kidding? I met your dad. François and I gave him a lift to Hot Springs Cove from Ahousaht in September."

"See how small this world is?" the pilot chuckled as the pair soared above the white sand beach that outlined the half circle that was Cow Bay on Vargas Island. *"Hishuk ish tsawlk,"* he said, and then translated. "We are one and all interconnected."

Heritage smiled. He could see Tofino a short distance beyond. The pilot pointed at the helicopter that had just lifted off and was turning south.

"Megin River, this is Tofino Harbour. Continue to Lennard, then bank left and you are clear to land heading northeast in the direction of Catface Mountain. Watch for harbour traffic."

"Megin River Air copies and will continue to Lennard, banking east for a harbour landing in the direction of Catface," Jason repeated. He glanced as his passenger and picked up the conversation. "What didya think of my pops?"

"Sennan? Well, he was pretty seasick when I met him. Not very talkative."

"Oh yeah, that sounds about right. His given name in Nuu-chah-nulth is Tukuuk Naqmiihas. It means thirsty sea lion—or, maybe more appropriately for my Dad, one that doesn't like the taste of saltwater."

"What is your given name?" Heritage asked.

"Are you ready for it?" the pilot asked with a smile. "It's Pisat-ukma Waaxnii. It means playful river otter. Don't ask me why."

"Okay," Heritage replied with a laugh and a wink. "I won't ask."

It hadn't taken Stu Solberg more than fifteen minutes, from the time he received the call, to arrive at the dock with a different green Jeep Grand Cherokee—a souped up version with all the bells and whistles that had been sitting in Brad Fraser's double garage—a vehicle that had become, ipso facto, a Headlands Lodge asset with the innkeeper's disappearance. Heritage suspected the vehicle had been purchased with funds skimmed from the lodge in the first place, but details of Fraser's embezzlement activities over the previous decade would be what the court case was expected to uncover. It wasn't the only reason Heritage was back in Tofino, but it was the more urgent and court-ordered one that he couldn't put off—unlike having to face the other local characters who had left their unique scars on his psyche. He really needed to slip in, then slip back out of town with the least number of run-ins with the locals as could be managed. He did harbour one wish, though, and that was that he wouldn't be leaving alone, that François could be compelled to return to Toronto with him. That was the job of the bracelet in his front pocket—to signal a new start with all of its possibilities and all of his aspirations for the company and for the planet. He wanted to ask François to be a part of that.

He wanted François to love him and be loved. Heritage was more invested in what money couldn't buy than he could be tripped up by all the things it suddenly could—like the bracelet. This was a long shot that grew even longer when his messages to François hadn't been returned, but Heritage was ridiculously hopeful.

In the correspondence accompanying the subpoena that had been served to him in his new top floor corner office at CP&P, the prosecuting attorney had indicated that it was widely held that Heritage had been the last person to see Brad Fraser alive. While nobody seemed to be suggesting Fraser was dead, as the senior representative of the Carter empire—owner of fifty percent of the Headlands—Heritage was identified as someone they wanted to hear from as they examined all future financial and operational scenarios for Headlands Lodge. Heritage, of course, had his own ideas and motivations. As the new CEO and president of Carter Pulp & Paper, he was prepared to buy out the multiple liens and heavily leveraged operation in order to gain complete ownership, but there was one big caveat: Heritage needed to determine if there was a future for him personally in Clayoquot Sound. If that love boat had already sailed off into the sunset with François at the helm and without him aboard, then Heritage was only there to get the company's fifty percent out of the lodge. After that, he'd walk away for good.

In other words, Tofino was getting a second tryout for his affection and his company's investment.

With his luggage loaded in the back, the newly bearded chef and acting manager from the Headlands Lodge got both the Cherokee and their conversation rolling down the road.

"Listen, Tage," the chef started. "I really appreciate you stepping in like you did with the cash to cover staff salaries and bills, and for underwriting the new employee health and dental benefits and of course, I want to thank you for your trust and for naming me as the general manager."

Heritage knew the gratitude was genuine. He'd just helped

Stu become a decision maker in an arena with bigger consequences, and Heritage suspected this was new territory for the
thirty-three-year old—who would turn thirty-four in another
month. Heritage had only just recently learned they were nearly
the same age, though Stu had been born a year earlier, in 1961.

"You are welcome, Stu. And the beard looks great on you. Not
everyone can pull off facial hair. I for one, look like Sasquatch if
I miss a day of shaving."

The chef laughed the compliment off and said he grew one
every winter—for better or worse. Stu Solberg easily had a decade
of hospitality experience on Heritage, and the new lodge owner-
in-waiting knew this only too acutely—which is why he'd made
the interim position permanent. Heritage also knew he was the
one who should be thanking the chef for getting him out of his
tight spot—enabling him to attend to his grandfather's funeral
service and hastily escape the complications that had flared up
more locally with the teenager. He was grateful that none of that
sordid affair appeared to have spilled over to contaminate the
business. Brad Fraser had already done enough damage on that
front. Heritage would reserve an earful for Brad Fraser if he ever
had the chance to testify against him—but he was doubtful they
would see justice served. Stu indicated as much, saying the local
bookkeeping accountant was still working the numbers, but that
it appeared Brad Fraser had walked off the edge of the earth with
hundreds of thousands of dollars in cash.

Heritage was pleased to see the place all dolled up for
Christmas and that the Lodge had not been run into the
ground in the past two and a half months. Stu had been the
right person to leave in charge, and Heritage had been smart to
put up $100,000 of his own money to float operations. There
would be an influx of revenue in the coming weeks, with the
Christmas break. With a few staffing cutbacks in January, and
by hibernating the stand-alone, fair-weather cottages until spring
break, Heritage could see the cash-flow projection carrying the

Headlands well into the new year. By then, he would either need to get his money back out of it, or plow more of his grandfather's capital into renovations and securing it for keeps. Which of these outcomes stuck depended almost entirely on the reception he received in the next several days. Because he'd already been forewarned that Councillor Dottie Bard would be involved, he was expecting it to be chilly at best.

François would factor into his decision-making, if he wanted to be factored in. But without any attempt by François to return Heritage's messages or accept his invitations—if he'd even received them—Heritage was steeling himself for the unpleasant reality that the bracelet in his pocket might have to settle for the real estate around his own wrist.

In the schmozzle of whole new experiences he'd had to untie and sort since his grandfather's death, determining the company's future involvement with the Headlands was the most personal, given his history in that place and his grandfather's sentimentality around these thirty-five hectares. His granddad had originally intended to retire out west and share this slice of paradise with Heritage's grandmother, Margaret, before she'd been diagnosed with the MS that had all-too-expediently ended her life and scuttled his retirement dreams. Instead, his grandfather vowed to work to death, and then stubbornly kept that promise.

Heritage the grandson had never been in a place where the people he didn't want to see or run into so greatly outnumbered the ones he did—which is why Tofino was so tricky for him to navigate. That ratio and those odds just didn't happen in big cities like Toronto or Vancouver, where there was a myriad of ways to keep anonymous. In the short three and a half weeks in September that he'd been in Clayoquot Sound, before the last ten-week time period he'd stayed away, Heritage had managed to make and collect history and enemies and almost land criminal charges—though that, gratefully, hadn't materialized much beyond the hysteria that eventually died down. He and his actions barely made ripples in the Toronto pond—now that the news cycle had moved on to showcase or expose bigger newsmakers than he would ever be. Here, he stood out like a neon-outlined Christmas tree shooting Canada Day fireworks out of its death star of Bethlehem—in the middle of an otherwise pristine rainforest. Now that he had returned, he was self-conscious about the target on his back. Heritage simply couldn't know if his scheduled appearance at the court would be a get-in / get-out scenario or a dig in / weather the storm and stay-for-good proposition—and this perfectly summed up his quandary with Clayoquot Sound. In the meantime, something had been bugging him as he stared from his suite across the channel to Wickaninnish Island. With hours of daylight still left in this remarkably sunny December Tuesday, he changed into kayaking clothes.

In many respects, time seemed to stand still in Clayoquot Sound. Trees that had taken hundreds if not thousands of years to grow were in no rush to change the world or make a profit or drop their needles for attention. The Pacific Ocean would slosh its tides high into the fjords and estuaries and then suck them back out again in cycles that repeated twice every twenty-four hours—whether Heritage Carter was there or not. It would be easy to feel insignificant—like one person in a city of millions. But Heritage had also seen evidence of how one person could change the landscape and alter natural systems in ways that would never be the same again. That one person had been his grandfather, and the scars of that man's ninety-two-year existence could be seen from space—or at least from a seaplane.

His eco-brain was on fire and Heritage was thinking his business model needed a green make-over. He was making two-column checklists in his mind as he pulled his signal-yellow kayak from the equipment garage next to where the trees stuck some of their roots into the sands of Middle Beach. He wondered what would happen if he were to boldly announce to his board of directors, shareholders, and staff that CP&P was going to replant one million hectares of forest by the year 2020—just twenty-five years away. And why did toilet paper have to be white? People everywhere had made the switch to brown bread. How would a naturally coloured toilet paper and paper towel fare in the marketplace? Heritage absolutely needed to find out. He would make the Headlands Eco-Lodge (which he would also rebrand) ground zero for his green market research.

Simultaneously, he wanted to roll out an environmentally-friendly guest housekeeping program. People didn't really need to have a maid clean their room or cottage every day. Bedsheets and towels didn't get changed every day at home. He would commit to diverting ten dollars to local recycling efforts and conservation groups each time a guest declined housekeeping. That would add up over time and make a difference, he bet. Dottie Bard had been involved with a blockade or protest on the day he had first arrived in Clayoquot Sound, and some organization must have been behind the War in the Woods the previous summer. In his perfect world, there would be an organized nonprofit she wasn't already involved with, where he could make a big financial splash. Otherwise, he would funnel the money into a school conservation field-trip program.

With the nose of his kayak pointed to the cut between the islands of Wickaninnish and Echachis, Heritage zipped across the channel as though he had wings instead of a paddle. Whether it was the fresh air, the abundance of sunshine, or a passionate resolve to turn over a greener leaf, Heritage was buoyed with optimism. He was reconnecting with his original plan for coming to Clayoquot Sound in the first place. Before all of this, everything had been theoretical and far-fetched. But now it was real—within reach, and likely necessary for his well-being.

A paddle blade clipped a swell and splashed a bit of saltwater on his face. He tasted it on his tongue. The tide was in. That meant there was enough water that Heritage could paddle through the cut between the islands—something he had never done before, but the shortcut would hopefully get him to Big Beach undetected. Since it was a Tuesday afternoon, just after the lunch hour, Ninnish and Rowan should still be in school. Mona—if she were feeling well enough—would be at the SunRyes Bakery. And Dottie—hell, Dottie could be anywhere. But Wick was probably out of her range on a weekday.

Heritage paddled almost competitively and with renewed confidence on the water. As he neared the shores, he watched the ocean floor rise up beneath the white keel of his boat gliding gracefully over the crystal-clear shallows. Starfish, sunfish, urchins, and anemones—in purple, orange, red, and mint- and lime-green decorated the rocky, submerged tide pools. It seemed like he was snorkeling without getting his hair or face wet. The passageway was like a chute in a water park and Heritage felt the swells swoosh him along. Ahead, he could see the breakers, and the open Pacific beyond them. This was new paddling territory, and his heart began accelerating inside his chest driving adrenaline into his arms. He dragged a paddle blade to slow his speed, so he could study how the breakers were interacting at the west entrance to the cut—how the water rose and then retreated, exposing rocks and then an advancing water wall, with the next one loaded and barreling in right behind. Heritage wanted to time an incoming wave to stay off the rocks, but needed to quickly power through its retreat, to ride and slice into the next breaker coming at him. If the next wave crested and fell on the tip of his kayak before he reached it, he feared it could push him down and possibly hold him there.

He saw his opportunity and paddled like mad, ejecting into the open water without scraping or getting turned crossways in the waves. It was so exhilarating that he couldn't help but issue a full-throated "Woo-hoo!" which he hoped was drowned out by waves hitting the black rocks on either side of the entrance. Beyond the wave break, the sea's surface transitioned into deep troughs. Heritage hung a right with his rudder. Staying on the far side of the breakers, he paddled north, looking for his next available right turn into the cove at Big Beach. He passed a ridiculously large house on a low promontory to his right. Heritage hadn't seen this house before, but deduced that it must have belonged to the Greenes. He had only met the oldest son, Matt—the coast guard captain—and his dad, the cranky native man who had confronted him on the street outside the Co-op. He'd heard mention of Sharon, but had never encountered her in person.

A wolf-like dog appeared on the deck of the house and began to bark at Heritage. He remembered that dog accompanying the coast guard captain the night he rode out the storm sleeping in the cargo net at Lyle Hudson's cabin. Heritage kept his head lowered, avoiding eye contact with the animal, paddling steadily, observing from the corner of his eye that no humans seemed to be appearing in the windows or on the deck. He didn't want to give the impression he was snooping or had any purpose other than taking a leisurely paddle, circumnavigating Wickaninnish Island—something he'd thought about but still hadn't done.

The barking dog faded with distance and the noisy ocean. In a few more strokes, Heritage spotted Stephanie's lookout cabin on the cliff on the far side of Big Beach. But he could not see the beach for the wall of sea-scrubbed black crags on his right, which sheltered it from view and the ocean's fury. He had remembered that, just like the cauldron at Cormorant Rock, there was a hidden entrance at the northern end and that was what he'd come for and where he was aiming the nose of his kayak now. In five more strokes, he veered inside a gap in the rocks, and Big Beach opened up before him.

He oriented his boat perpendicular to the beach, though the waves inside the rocks weren't likely big enough to dump him if he got caught sideways. Still, he wasn't in the mood to get wet. There was a sandpaper sound as his bow came to a rest. He climbed out of the cockpit and hauled the boat high onto the beach, and then tucked it among some sizeable lengths of driftwood, silvered with age. He stomped the sand off his sandaled feet and headed into the woods to pick up the trail that was supposed to express-deliver him to the labyrinth.

Except he couldn't find that trail. Or any trail. But he could swear he had first accessed Big Beach from the labyrinth on a trail. How could it have been erased?

The forest floor was thickly mossed, with no signs of foot traffic. Heritage stubbornly expanded his sweep, veering more and more south toward the Greenes' compound of houses and satellite cabins. He didn't want to arouse suspicion, and certainly didn't want to encounter that wolf-dog, which was larger and more menacing than a German shepherd.

Heritage was back on the cursed island to work through a shopping list of hunches. First up: find out if the bones he believed had belonged to Lucien Pelletier had been returned to the Sitka tree at the edge of the labyrinth. In his pocket, he nervously fingered the different sized links of the Russian rose gold bracelet as a talisman or a rosary—depending on which gods or goddesses might be paying attention. With any luck, divine or even occult intervention, and maybe some cutting-edge forensic science, he could link the bones to the metro token to the bracelet he wanted to put around François' wrist. And then, if the man belonging to the bones had been murdered, they could work together to uncover the identity of the killer. They were long odds, but the island had already taught him to anticipate the incredible, and to never underestimate the breadth and depth of its wickedness.

There was a sudden growl close behind him, and he jumped, then spun around to make eye contact with the dark furred, black-headed wolf-dog.

"Hey, boy. It's okay."

"The dog isn't stupid," a male voice in the forest ahead of him said. "He knows you aren't okay, and that you aren't welcome here. This is private, sacred ground."

Heritage slowly turned, having recognized the strange speech syncopation in the voice. Steve Greene had popped out from behind a cedar trunk three metres in front of him, while the dog continued to snarl behind him. He was boxed in and hadn't heard either of them approach.

"Look, Steve. I've met your son, Matt. I know Stephanie and Dottie and Mona and Lyle, and I knew Mason. I am not a stranger trespassing here, so you can drop your intimidation act." Heritage was trembling, but hoped it didn't show in his loosely fitting kayak pants. "And can you call off the big, bad wolf?"

Steve Greene didn't say anything for a minute. All of Heritage's name-dropping had sort of wrecked his authority. "I warned you that you aren't welcome here. I don't care who you've met or who you know. I want you to leave this island."

"I'm not leaving until I get what I came for," Heritage said—though he had no idea where he was going to take that statement next.

"Well, you are on my wife's land. This southern part of the island from Big Beach to Echachis Island belongs to us. We are a private people, and I don't want you here."

Heritage thought about the island. If what Steve Greene said was true, then that meant the labyrinth belonged to Sharon Greene. It wasn't property in common with the other islanders, or some spiritual center for a coven of novice witches. He maybe had that wrong in his head, then.

"That maze or labyrinth thingy in the clearing, somewhere around here—that's yours, or your wife's?"

"There is no maze. No labyrinth. Now go!" Greene said, rushing a metre toward him.

"But there was a labyrinth here two months ago. And in a tree on the edge of it was a burial platform—a wooden raft wedged high in the trees. It contained human bones. Bones belonging to a contemporary human—a man about my size, who wore jeans from Levi Strauss." It was Heritage's turn to close the gap between them, and he moved closer. Steve Green took a cautious step backward. Heritage continued. "The dead man in the tree had this coin—turns out it was a metro token from the Moscow subway, in Russia. The token must have been in his jeans pocket but the jeans had mostly decayed away. Since this is your wife's land, perhaps you can answer some questions about this man's identity. His remains were there in the tree on her property, as you claim. I climbed that tree and saw them for myself. But they were gone a few days later—the day after Mason Robson was knocked off balance by her son, Rowan, at Cormorant Rock. Rowan had been frightened by something he witnessed that night at the labyrinth—the same labyrinth you say doesn't exist anymore. I was there at the labyrinth that night too, and so were the bones of the man in the tree platform. The very next day, when I brought the RCMP into the woods to show them the labyrinth, the bones and the platform were gone."

Heritage swallowed, but wasn't finished. "At first, I suspected Dottie Bard had something to do with the labyrinth, and that maybe she had climbed that giant Sitka tree and removed the bones and dismantled the platform. Except she was at the hospital that entire night with Mona's kid, Ninnish. I doubt she could climb a tree, anyway, since she's not in the best of shape. You could climb a tree, though, I bet." Heritage pointed his finger at the man and moved a stride closer, causing the dog to bark and lunge forward, though it kept its distance and waited for a command. "You seem remarkably fit for a man your age. You must work out with your son, Matt. He's muscle-bound too, isn't he? Looks fiercely handsome in his coast guard uniform, with all those dark features he must have inherited from you."

"It is time for you to leave this island," Steve Greene said.

"Why don't you come with me? I'm heading straight to the RCMP detachment after this conversation, to tell Officer Luis Toren about the skeleton I found in a tree on your wife's land—with a sizeable hole on the back of its skull."

"I'm warning you. Don't make this any business of yours, or there will be trouble."

Heritage chuckled dramatically. "There has been nothing but trouble since the moment Dottie Bard introduced me to Wickaninnish Island. If I could reverse that history so that I never stepped foot on these shores, believe me, I would. Now, call off your wolf dog and I will leave."

Heritage looked over his shoulder—and standing there, holding the dog by the scruff of its neck, since he didn't wear a collar or have tags, was Steve Greene's son, Matt—out of uniform but wearing camouflage army pants and matching tank-top, and glistening with sweat like he'd just walked off the set of a *Rambo* movie.

"What's going on here, Father?"

"We have a trespasser who won't leave when he's been asked to."

"Seriously?" Heritage said. "I just told you I am leaving. Now, if one of you very friendly men could point me in the direction of Big Beach, where I left my kayak, I'll get off your *wife's* land."

Matt moved forward. "Mr. Carter. I didn't recognize you at first. I thought . . ." He paused. "Hell, we *all* thought that you had disappeared right along with Brad Fraser and François Lévesque. All three of you vanished at the same time. There's been so much loss and mystery lately, and it seemed such a coincidence that you would all leave at once."

"My grandfather passed away. I was in Toronto, taking care of the family business. I didn't disappear. There is no mystery with me."

"Well I wouldn't say that," Matt circled around him to stand on the same side as his father. "We didn't know that we had a multimillionaire in our midst. It seems to me you were downplaying that. Now it turns out you are half owner of the Headlands Lodge. And you're on my mother's land, where I assure you that you have no family business. You are not without your own mystery, Tage— or should I refer to you as Heritage Carter, now?"

Heritage felt like he'd taken a sucker punch to his gut with the news that François was gone. "Look, like I told your Dad, I am leaving. I came here looking to construct an explanation in my own mind around the things I saw and witnessed here. Things that are no longer here, according to your dad—"

"What things?" Matt stepped closer to him and puffed up his chest. "What has been removed—other than our neighbour Mason, and my friend Marcel? Huh? You were here, on our island, the night both of these people perished. From where I stand, you are jinxed, and you have brought a curse to this place. Like my father told you, you are not welcome."

"Fine. Point me to Big Beach and I will remove myself and my curse from your lives—and your mother's land."

"Big Beach is that way," Steve Greene extended his arm and an arthritic-looking finger.

Heritage turned. The wolf-dog circled around him widely to rejoin Matt. Heritage expected a bullet or an arrow in his back, or for a mossy skeleton to fall from the limbs above, to knock him out cold. Instead, he simply walked away toward the sound of the ocean, without turning to look back.

He awkwardly dragged his kayak to the water and hoisted his spray skirt up around his waist. Sitting in the cockpit, he arm-walked the boat into deeper water before paddling like the Dickens to get the hell out of that cove, and through the cut. Suspecting he was being watched by at least one pair of eyes in the forest, he made like he was paddling back across the channel, but after about a dozen strokes, he ruddered a hard left and sprinted back to Dottie's cove. He hadn't finished his hunch list.

Heritage powered the last few strokes to drive the bow of his kayak into the sand. He released the spray skirt and scrambled out of the cockpit, dragging the kayak higher up the beach to stash it behind a Jurassic-sized chunk of driftwood. He made a beeline for Dottie's cabin. Over and over in his head, he'd been playing back the clue that he thought Rowan might have accidentally transmitted over the walkie-talkies. Heritage had long thought he had said the words *skull box* but hadn't made the connection. Heritage had only seen two skulls in his whole lifetime, and both of them on Wickaninnish Island, but only one of them had been in what might be considered a box . . . the secret trap door under Dottie's futon sofa.

Heritage let himself in, saying "don't mind if I do," out loud as he crossed the threshold. With the shattering news that François had left Clayoquot, his first order of business was to place the bracelet from his pocket on his own wrist. He fiddled with the clasp, having to use his chin to hold the two ends in place. It was a shitty, disappointing consolation prize, but Heritage needed to face new music, if he was getting out of Clayoquot Sound alive.

He lifted one end of the futon and pivoted it forty-five degrees. He braced his nerves for the giant spider that could scurry out when he lifted the lid. But there was no spider. There was no skull. There was only his paperback book—*The Discovery of Heaven*—inside that box in the floor. Heritage reclaimed what was his.

When he found what had been stashed between the pages of the thick volume . . . nineteen Polaroid photographs, he claimed those as his, too.

It had already been revealed and introduced into evidence that Brad Fraser had been embezzling from Heritage's grandfather for half a decade. That had been squarely and forensically established by the financial wizards at CP&P, who had amassed enough spreadsheet and bank record evidence even before his grandfather had sent his grandson, Heritage, to ratchet up the pressure. It had worked. Fraser had realized the jig was up, and had stolen away to Aruba, one of the only Caribbean islands that didn't have an extradition treaty with Canada. It had been one of Luis Toren's buddies at Interpol who had verified that the former hotelier had reunited with his pilfered proceeds and the mother of his two children. All were living quite comfortably in a pocket-size mansion on the outskirts of Orangestad.

Heritage's court-ordered appearance at the travelling inquiry was a formality. His Toronto lawyers had filed the takeover bid and moved the necessary buyout funds into a trust account well in advance of Heritage's testimony. The proceedings would be an open-and-shut formality, after which the Headlands would belong entirely to him—his own personal investment in Clayoquot Sound—lien-free, unencumbered, fee-simple title, independent, and wholly separate from CP&P.

Heritage sat confidently at a long table with the company's primary lawyer, Lonnie and his grandfather's accountant, both of whom had traveled to Tofino separately as part of longer vacations they would be commencing with their wives—all of whom were already ensconced in suites at the Headlands, courtesy of its new owner. Heritage had retained his grandfather's accountant out of decency and deference to his departed mother, whose affair with the man had left Heritage an orphan. Heritage knew that his sweet mother had caused at least a few of the wrinkles around the man's eyes, and that together, they'd experienced happiness and cheated life—and their spouses.

The CP&P team, with Heritage seated in the middle, were dressed in tailored suits and polished dress shoes. They were seated directly across from the journeyman judge who was occupying Dottie Bard's council chamber seat, since it had seemed the most authoritative piece of furniture available in the commandeered village council chambers. The judge and his stenographer had made the journey by car from Victoria—an operational decision they made whenever their schedules allowed as a means of reinforcing the notion that justice could take place anywhere, and not just in the provincial capital. Gillian from the library observed the inquiry from the public seating area—she was three months closer to giving birth now. She was also moonlighting as a reporter for *The Westerly News*—the third part-time job the single mother-to-be needed to hold in order to assure the extra health benefits she would shortly require. RCMP constable Luis Toren was also there, partly at Heritage's request, and partly as a security presence, should matters become contested or heated. Nobody anticipated they would. Still, it was Tofino—and only a year after the War in the Woods, so authorities were right to be on guard.

Heritage watched the clock's second hand round the bend and climb to the top of the hour. The magistrate banged his gavel, which seemed to cue the council chamber door to fly open on its own. In filed Dottie Bard, Mona Rye, a repatriated Stephanie (looking twice as pregnant as when she and Heritage had tangoed in the airport), Steve and Matt Greene (the latter out of camouflage and back in his coast guard uniform), followed by Stu Solberg from the Headlands. Next to wander in through the council chamber door—on "Tofino time," which basically meant he was late—was Mac Mulligan, looking particularly ragged as he'd just come in from his oyster farm. He flashed a smile and a chin-up greeting to Heritage as he sat next to Dottie, and made a public display of taking her hand and holding it on her lap. Heritage watched Dottie squeeze his hand, but then return it back to rest on his own lap. Were they dating still, or not? Heritage figured Mac was probably wondering the same thing in that moment.

The magistrate was about to call the proceeding to order but there was one more arrival. Last through the door, and to Heritage's utter surprise, swaggered Aidan Rye, looking like Billy Idol circa *White Wedding*—1982. In his dramatic entrance, you could hear the crowd gasp, as every head, including Heritage's, snapped to attention. Looking handsomely adult, with longer and spikey blond hair and visible facial scruff, he seemed, at least to Heritage, to have metamorphosed—filling out and possibly even maturing. Had it only been three months? Maybe Ninnish was working out with Matt and Steve Greene. The two adversaries locked eyes, blue to hazel, and Heritage's heart raced as though he were sprinting toward a hundred-metre tape stretched across the edge of a precipice—a vivid image, with Mason's tragic death still fresh in everyone's memories.

Acknowledging the public gallery, the magistrate cleared his throat.

"We are three minutes past the top of the hour and this proceeding will commence. I will politely assume that everyone in attendance today has a vested interest in the matter before this court, which will attempt to determine the abandonment and possible criminal embezzlement of monies from the Headlands Lodge, owned jointly by Brad Fraser, who is missing and not present, and the Carter Pulp & Paper Company, represented here today by its president and CEO, Heritage Carter. The court recognizes the pre-filings in this case—namely, the forensically audited financial statements and the takeover bid and proposal by Mr. Carter. The court believes this will satisfy the creditors—namely, the Canadian Imperial Bank of Commerce and the employees of the Headlands Lodge. The court also wishes to recognize the $100,000 in bridge funding provided personally by Heritage Carter—this money, I understand, has sustained the operation of the lodge during the past three months since Brad Fraser left the country. Now, I understand and have reviewed evidence that suggests Headlands Lodge is an economic driver in this community, that it employs twenty-eight workers, and that it accommodates members of the traveling public, who journey here to experience or to do business in Clayoquot Sound. Also before this court is a report filed by RCMP constable Luis Toren and corroborated by the International Criminal Police Organization, otherwise known as INTERPOL, that substantiates evidence that Brad Fraser appears to have fled the country with pilfered funds from Headlands Lodge, with the intent of defrauding both his business and his business partner, Mr. Carter. Mr. Carter has answered a court-ordered subpoena and has traveled from Toronto and is present with us in these chambers today, while Mr. Fraser is apparently in hiding somewhere in the

Caribbean—the Island of Aruba, I believe. Mr. Fraser has not complied with Interpol or RCMP warrants or demands that he return to Canada to cooperate with the courts and there is, I understand, no extradition treaty between Canada and Aruba."

The magistrate paused to take a sip of water from the clear glass that had been filled to the brim for him. He ironed the frilly white shirt beneath his open black robe with his hand, and then continued.

"Normally, in matters of fiscal and physical abandonment of a business, particularly when substantiated fiscal impropriety has been involved—and certainly with a generous acquisition and back-up offer on the table that would retire the remaining debt and satisfy all known creditors—I would be in a clear position to more automatically rule in favour of Mr. Carter's proposal. However, given the public's clear interest in this matter, demonstrated by the number of you in attendance at this inquiry this morning and from what I understand has been a rousing bit of activity in your local paper's opinion pages over the past few months, I am going to open the floor to hear from those who might wish to enter a comment for the record with regard to this takeover bid by Mr. Carter, first. Does anyone wish to provide comment at this time?"

Every muscle in Heritage's well-tailored body clenched in anticipation of the barbs about to fly. He listened to the ticking of the large, round clock that hung above but off-center from the framed photograph of Queen Elizabeth II. There was a loud scooting of a chair and Heritage looked in the direction of the noise. It was Stu Solberg, standing to speak.

"Your Worship, my name is Stuart Solberg, and I have been the executive chef at the Headlands Lodge since it opened in 1992. For the past three months, following the disappearance of Brad Fraser, I have been proud to have been named by Mr. Carter as the interim general manager of operations. I wanted to convey my opinion and the feeling of the rest of the staff that I . . . *we* feel that Headlands Lodge, under the full ownership of Heritage

Carter, will provide us and the visiting public with the financial stability to maintain the first-class accommodations on which this business's fine reputation rests. On behalf of the hard-working staff at Headlands Lodge, we wish to endorse Mr. Carter's take-over bid. Thank you." Stu lowered his head but kept his eyes on his very grateful boss. Heritage nodded his appreciation.

"Thank you, Mr. Solberg. Are there others, who—" The magistrate cut himself off, seeing that Dottie Bard was already standing.

"If it please Your Worship," she began. Her formality made Heritage want to gag up his buffet breakfast.

"You may proceed," the magistrate said.

"Thank you, Your Worship" Normally the most outspoken dissident in the council chambers, Dottie cleared her throat and moved with impunity toward the magistrate as she prepared to disqualify the man who thought he should own Headlands Lodge. "It is my opinion and the feeling of many who have taken time out of their personal lives to assemble here today, that Heritage Carter is not morally fit to own a business in this community. He is the opposite of upstanding, and in fact misled many of us, misrepresenting his intentions when he first arrived here in September. Beyond these completely sufficient reasons for denying his buyout and takeover bid of Headlands Lodge, this man should be in custody awaiting trial for the brutal anal rape of a male child in this community, if the local RCMP detachment were even remotely capable of doing its job." She paused, but not long enough to sustain an objection or receive the daggers that Heritage and Officer Toren were shooting at her. "I have evidence your worship should review before rendering your judgment in this matter. May I approach the bench?"

The magistrate had not—and frankly, could not, in his wildest imagination—have foreseen this wrinkle. He wasn't sure what was appropriate. The accusation she was making against the man's character was appalling and seemingly incredible—and yet, she said she had evidence. He looked to the uniformed RCMP officer, standing near the door at the back of the room, for some indication of the woman's sanity or bias. Toren sent his eyeballs to the top of his crewcut and exhaled loudly.

"Ms. Bard, if you have evidence in what you suggest might be a criminal matter, then I would recommend, even urge you to turn it over to the RCMP investigators with jurisdiction over such matters. This is a public inquiry to determine the future ownership of Headlands Lodge and the suitability of Mr. Carter's takeover bid."

Dottie took a measured step forward. "There is no suitability here, Your Worship. Tage Carter is a predator—a predator of children and a predator of vulnerable, small business interests. You invited comments from the public. I have made my comments. I will thank you for your better judgment in this matter."

"May we get your name for the public record, please?" The magistrate signaled with his chin to his administrative assistant to make note.

"Dottie Bard, local business owner and senior city councillor for the Village of Tofino," she said—then thought to add, "you're sitting in my chair, Your Worship."

The traveling judge wasn't sure what to make of her, but gave it his best shot. "Ms. Bard, I thank you for your comments and for your service to this community. I hope you will understand that I am unable to receive evidence that does not pertain to the matter before this inquiry. Now, I would ask if there are others who have comments they wish to have added to the record—pertaining to the matter before this inquiry." Heritage shifted weight in his chair.

Steve Greene stood and exchanged spots with Dottie. "I would first like to acknowledge we are gathered here today on the traditional territory of the Tla-o-qui-aht Peoples of the Nuu-chah-nulth First Nation. The word, Nuu-chah-nulth, means *all along the mountains*. Heritage Carter's company—the Carter Pulp & Paper Corporation—has destroyed much of the ancient forests and watersheds here, all along these mountains. After raping our lands, the man before you making application to buyout and own the Headlands Lodge came here to rape our children!"

Heritage sent an elbow into his corporate attorney's ribs. Lonnie let out a startled sound that he masterfully turned into the word "Objection!" Steve Greene held his tongue, waiting for the magistrate to weigh in. Lonnie stood. "Your Worship, my client, and the applicant in this inquiry, is neither a rapist of the lands nor of this community's children. We object to both this inflammatory characterization of my client and to the offensive language being used by this member of the public. My client has been made a recent target by a small handful of misinformed activist citizens, operating, in my opinion, without any access to facts, and, I would suggest, without any vested interest in the business matter before this inquiry."

The magistrate took off his eyeglasses, which he had been wearing far down the end of his nose. "Listen, I am going to abbreviate this period of public comment and turn instead to the applicant so he can make a statement in support of his application. Mr. Carter?" The magistrate leaned back in his chair.

Heritage scooted his seat backward and stood. He had nothing prepared to say. His case for the business takeover had been deemed by the football-size team of CP&P lawyers back in Toronto to be ironclad. The inquiry had been believed by most to be a formality. Heritage realized it wasn't the magistrate he needed to address. It was the people behind him in those borrowed council chambers.

Heritage Warren Carter the Third raised one shoe to its Italian leather toe and pivoted around to face these more fearsome judges. He named his accusers from his right to his left. "Steve, Matt, Mona, Dottie, Mac, Stephanie—welcome home by the way, Constable Toren, Chef Solberg, and Aidan . . ."

The rugged beauty of the boy with the spikes of blond hair, who had metamorphosed into a man faster than a caterpillar becomes a butterfly, tripped him up. The newly minted multimillionaire paused to recover his breath along with his composure.

"Aidan Rye, also known as *Ninnish*, also known as *Satan with an A*." Heritage smiled a toothy, young Kennedy grin. Ninnish found himself bound by the spell, and could not possibly help but smile right back. Heritage went on. "I know you. I know all of you. And each of you, if you are honest with yourselves, know me, too. I have not hurt any of you. I have not disrespected any of you. I have not caused harm to a single person in this village—*not one of you* have I hurt, put down or defrauded in any way. I am petitioning the court to purchase Headlands Lodge, to erase this business's substantial debt to its creditors, to secure full-time employment with benefits for twenty-eight employees, and to invest in the future of this community and its growing tourism economy. Your community . . . my community. It is not by accident that I am here. Whether I chose Clayoquot Sound of Clayoquot Sound chose me, I am here." He faced Ninnish and closed with a promise made personally and deliberately to him. "And I am home to stay." Heritage turned back to face the magistrate. "Thank you."

On an impatient whim, and needing to blow off steam after the inquiry, while Lonnie and the chief financial officer sorted out the successful paperwork filings, Heritage slipped out a side door and decided he'd walk away from the downtown commotion and head to the Headlands on foot.

After about a kilometre of walking in dress shoes that pinched his toes, suit jacket slung over his right shoulder, he had the impulse to stick out his thumb to see if he could snag a ride. He admired his vintage Russian rose gold bracelet at the end of his arm and wished it were magic, that it could just conjure up François chugging up behind him in his oyster delivery truck, slowing to offer him a lift that would last the rest of their lives. But that was a mirage from another time, and Heritage needed to accept that. He could see the Esso gas station in the distance and tried to guess how many minutes walking it would take to reach it. He had seen the surfers hitchhiking with their boards, but had no personal experience or evidence that hitchhiking really worked—that people were trusting or lonely enough to pick up just anyone on the side of the road. But maybe even an alleged child molester—who dressed well—could get a ride in this free-wheeling-hang-ten culture.

Sure enough, the first car to come up behind him actually stopped to give him a ride.

"Hop in." It was a woman's muffled voice, barely audible through the closed door, and it sounded insistent. Heritage opened the car door and stooped to climb in. It was Mona Rye. He froze.

"I said, get in!" she said again, impatiently.

"Look, this is not what either of us needs right now. I can walk."

"You can do a lot of things, mister —or so I'm finding out. I want to talk to you. It's not about Aidan."

Heritage slowly lowered his butt into the car seat and shut the door. Mona eased the car onto the highway heading out of town.

"So talk," Heritage said, fastening his seat belt. "I'm going to the Headlands, by the way."

"I know where you're going," she told him. "First, I'll say I'm not surprised by any of this. Second, this conversation never happened, and I'll go to my grave —probably sooner than anyone thinks—denying it. Are we understood?"

"Understood."

"I won't waste your time telling you things you've already figured out. You're a smart man, Tage. And I'm a sick woman, desperately short on time. There are things that have happened on Wickaninnish Island that would have us all sharing a jail cell together, if the truth ever got out. I'm not here to suggest these things should be known, but I'll tell you the whole story and you can decide what you can use and what you can't in building your own defense—and more importantly, finding your way around here."

She took a deep breath. "Here goes. Seventeen years ago, there was a murder. I suppose I had a hand in covering it up, but the deed was done before I became involved. Dottie's then-boyfriend—and incidentally, your friend François' father—took Stephanie into the labyrinth and raped her there. She was three weeks away from turning fifteen. He said he did it to keep her from becoming a witch, like the rest of us. He didn't understand the covenant. Really, none of us understood it back then. It was a hobby that happened to exclude men. That's all that mattered. We'd all been somewhat recently burned by the men in our lives, and we all had been bedded and then scorned by Lucien Pelletier, who—unbeknownst to any of us—had a secret mission to impregnate as many women and girls on the planet as he could."

"Jesus!" Heritage exclaimed. "Sounds like quite the Casanova!"

"His complex, exactly. He was a Casanova-Jesus, and we all fell for it, or threw ourselves on it over the course of two consecutive summers. He had these messiah-like qualities that made you think he was worth following and falling for—that he only desired you. He played us all, even uterus-deficient me." She winced at the self-deprecating joke. "And he played us against each other. I was gobsmacked that he wanted me. He infected us all with the same delusion—that we were the only ones he found attractive." She changed the position of her hands on the steering wheel. "Like I said, we threw ourselves on it."

Mona signaled to turn right while Heritage let that sink in.

"But back to the witchcraft school," she continued, once they'd transitioned onto the gravel road. "It was bonding and it was therapy and it was deliverance. Of course, Stephanie fared worst, and became pregnant—I think you've already figured out that's where Aidan came from." Mona paused and glanced sideways to her passenger. "Dottie went berserk with rage, of course. She got Lucien drunker than all get-out one night at Big Beach. As they were stumbling back across the island, she shot him in the back of the head. But what's worse is what she did next."

———

"What's worse than cold-blooded murder?"

"She strung him between four trees in the labyrinth—just like you found Aidan, I understand. And she quartered him there." Mona wasn't paying much attention to her driving and drifted into the loose gravel, overcorrecting with a jolt.

"She *what?*" Heritage couldn't believe what he was hearing.

"She cut him into four pieces —or tried to, I should say. One offering to each of the four mystic and ancient elements: fire, water, air, and earth. Oh, shit! I got that backwards. No, first, she took a pitchfork. Right. That came first. The pitchfork was important, because it was meant to represent the sacred triple-phallus symbol—otherwise known as a trident. If you didn't know—in witchcraft, the trident is normally displayed by any male deity whose sole function is to copulate with the triple goddess. Again, more information than you probably need. But she took the pitchfork and stabbed his groin but apparently missed, so tried again, but her aim wasn't as good with a pitchfork as it had been with the revolver. And after he'd bled out, she tried to quarter him with a saw and a butcher knife."

"Christ!" Heritage shook off a sudden chill down his spine.

Mona held her hand out to indicate there was more. "According to the sacred prescripts from *Malleus Maleficarium*, the witch's bible we used back in the day, Dottie felt she had to carry out the complete ritual and so proceeded with disembowelling the poor sod before she decapitated him. After that, the covenant sort of intensified."

"No shit," Heritage offered, a bit cynically. "And what became of the body?"

"Well that's where things got interesting." Sitting sideways in the passenger seat, Heritage let go a burst of air between his lips and raised an eyebrow. "I know," Mona acknowledged, before going on. "Because Dottie had forgotten the step that required the body be hanged, and because the head had already been removed and there was nothing really to hang him by, she had to involve Steve Greene. Together, they rigged a platform high in the biggest tree in the labyrinth, and with a pully that Steve had in his shop, they pulled the arms, legs, and torso up to the platform. Dottie said that part constituted the hanging."

"And Lucien's head?" Heritage asked, just as Mona turned onto the paved driveway that wound between the trees for another couple kilometres through the woods.

"Steve Greene had put it inside a plastic Co-op grocery sack, tied it to his belt loops, and climbed the tree to place it on the platform."

"And his guts?" Heritage could complete the rest of the blanks for himself, but wanted to give Mona the chance to get this off her lopsided chest.

"His heart was buried, wrapped in a tea towel, in the mound at the centre of the labyrinth, and the rest of his entrails were left as an offering to the wildlife of Wickaninnish Island. Then, Dottie called the coven together. At the time, it consisted of me, Mason, Sharon Greene—who was still active with us at the time—and Stephanie, though the latter was a rather unwilling, traumatized, and noncommittal spectator. Anyway, that doesn't matter, since Stephanie was mostly just out of it. Dottie explained to all of us that she felt Lucien's spirit needed to forever preside over the coven, and protect it and all of us from other men, forever."

Heritage was processing all he was hearing as he spun the Russian bracelet around his wrist like he was trying to get a lid off a jar. Mona pulled up to the main lodge entrance and turned off the engine.

"I remember, that Dottie had sketched her rendition of the ceremony on a sheet of parchment. We kept it for ages, and pulled it and the reliquary out for ceremonies on the anniversary of his death for years after that. I think I had it last, pressed between the pages of an old Greek mythology book. I was pretty sure I must have destroyed it sometime since, but then Aidan seemed to get his hands on it."

"Wait. What's a reliquary?"

"Embarrassingly, it was just a mason jar—you know like you'd use for canning dill pickles? A reliquary holds a relic—which in this instance was Lucien's pickled penis."

An explosive laugh cannon-balled out of his esophagus at that. "You have got to be pulling my leg now."

Mona gave him a look that communicated she wasn't pulling anything. "Before too long, Dottie began to fear the law of three, which in Wicca-speak applies to any act good or evil."

"I don't understand."

Mona undid her seatbelt and turned her body to continue her explanation. "Anytime someone uses white magic to perform a good deed, that goodness is paid back three times in that person's lifetime."

"And every time someone uses black magic to perform an evil deed . . ."

"You got it," Mona said. "Internally, Dottie couldn't decide whether what she had done to Lucien was good or bad, white or black, so she didn't really know what to look forward to. The uncertainty began to eat at her. Certainly, Stephanie's pregnancy couldn't be good, so immediately following the sacrifice of Lucien, she sent Stephanie to her Uncle Lyle's house in Vancouver, to continue the pregnancy away from Clayoquot. Stephanie stayed with him for three years, even after she'd given up the baby Ninnish at birth. She had not resolved her anger with her mother. By this time, Dottie was convinced she was being paid back for having committed evil. She figured bringing the child back to Wickaninnish Island would be a good act, whose own law of three would counter the bad she was already receiving. When the baby Ninnish was presented by Dottie to the covenant, and to me as the new mother—all without Stephanie knowing because she was away in Vancouver—Dottie asked us to seal our vow by agreeing to be tattooed. Crazy, right?"

"What isn't crazy, in this context?" Heritage stated more than asked.

"I had already been so scarred by surgeries and cancer that

there wasn't much available canvas. But Dottie, Mason, and I, with the newborn Ninnish in my arms, trotted into a tattoo parlor on Commercial Drive, and we got branded—all with the same symbol of our secrecy and devotion."

"That symbol being . . . ?"

"This." Mona opened the first two buttons on her blouse, and spread the shirt open to reveal a bluish-green sea monster of sorts, wrapped around a rust-coloured trident, positioned on the exact center of her chest.

"How appropriate," Heritage commented, also noting her size-able mastectomy scars. "All three of you have this tattoo?"

"No. Dottie talked Sharon Greene into it and then, even Stephanie, too, before she would allow her to return to her home to Wickaninnish Island. All five of us have this tattoo. We are wood, fire, earth, water and metal. We complete the pentagram—or the pantacle—as Aleister Crowley referred to it."

Heritage struggled to recall if he'd seen the tattoo on Stephanie that day in the zodiac. No. She'd worn her t-shirt.

"Dottie was counting on Aidan as something of a male warlock deity, thinking he would grow up to be the reincarnation of Aleister Crowley, that the rest of us could turn to—the overlord of the pentagram. But that doesn't appear to be working out."

"No, I don't suppose it does. And at some point, you decided to turn back the clock on Aidan's birth date. You cooked the theory he was eighteen months younger than he really was so that the math could never reveal that this adopted bun had come from Stephanie's oven."

"That was Sharon's contribution. It was a stroke of genius, really. Poor thing, though. She didn't know it yet, but she had also gotten pregnant—not by Steve, the Grand Chief of All Things Native, but by Lucien Pelletier, too." Mona waited for that to sink in before continuing. "Sharon needed to conjure up another white lie, so all of a sudden, she up and disappeared to Southern California to take care of her aging mother. That was code for living out her pregnancy without anyone up here finding out about it. I think she thought she would give up her baby for adoption, too. Except that giving birth at her age had jumbled up her emotions and hormones, and really did a number on her brain wiring. She sort of lost it and could never get it together again to return back here."

"Wait." Heritage needed clarification. "Steve, even Matt, seem to be pretending that Sharon, Matt's mom, is still here. That doesn't make sense. I was told by Steve that I was not welcome on his wife's land, that it was her property I was trespassing on—like she was busy inside making cookies, or like she might walk out of the house and tell me to fuck right off. I kept waiting to see her on the island, or have her pointed out to me in town, but—"

"But she's not here, and she's not coming back here—ever. Steve is in denial, and has brainwashed the kids to believe that as soon as their mama is well again—as soon as that psychiatric hospital says it's safe for her to travel—she'll be back."

"That's pretty messed up," Heritage said, when something else hit him. "Wait, I just realized this means that Aidan and François Lévesque would be half-brothers."

"Aidan likely has enough half-siblings to square off against each other in a hockey match," Mona squared with him, but she wasn't finished. "Some years back, I began to wrestle with my conscience, and with the control Dottie seemed to have over me. No doubt, I worried myself sicker than I'd ever been. I needed to get out from under, if you know what I mean."

"I more than know." Heritage thought of how he'd only recently been liberated from his grandfather's control, himself.

"I came up with a plan to shift Dottie's allegiance, ever so slightly. It was a long shot, but when Mason's husband's court case went to trial, I got my break. I was having tea one afternoon at Mason's, trying to help her work through her anxiety. After a spell, she drifted into a nap, and while she dozed, I came across one of her husband's journals. One entry was dated just before the accident with the logging truck—I don't know how much you know about the manslaughter charges against Clive, but long story short, he was standing on an active logging road when a truck came around the corner and had to veer off the hillside to keep from hitting him. The journal entry, written roughly a month earlier, said something to the effect that somebody was going to have to be killed before the environmental movement could gain any public or governmental attention. In a big way, he was right. I stuffed the journal behind the waistband of my pants and smuggled it off the island. Later, when I was in Victoria for the last days of the trial, I slipped it in a plain envelope addressed to the prosecutor's office."

"What was that supposed to accomplish?"

"I wasn't entirely sure, to tell you the truth. I thought Dottie had become rather partial to Mason in the months after her husband's accident. While that should have made me—oh, I don't know, jealous or something—I was actually relieved. The trial had been heading for a dismissal of charges—you know, he was the father of an infant boy and the sole wage earner for the family. I needed him out of the way so Dottie could assume his place. That's what I mean by a long shot, but it worked like a twisted dream. The prosecutor saw the journal entry as premeditation. To set an example to environmentalists province-wide, the judge and jury charged him, and it stuck."

"And Dottie took up the slack at home?"

"Like a soldier. That is, until she realized that Mason wasn't going to hand her the island either."

"Hand her the island?"

"Dottie wanted to expand the coven—or so she claimed. What she really wants is to make a load of money by parceling off the island to other fierce women—a new generation of independent feminists who stand up to men and chart their own destinies. I said no. Mason said no. I probably don't have to tell you I'm the next best thing to dead. And Mason—well, coincidence or attrition? I wasn't there when she plunged off the cliff. But what I do know is that I am now the last of Dottie's breathing resistors."

"What about Steve and Matt Greene? And Lyle? How are these three men permitted to live in this Wiccan female utopia? And why did Dottie invite me to the island?" Heritage undid his seatbelt, though he had no intention of going anywhere.

"Right. I guess I left out that part." Mona cracked her driver door window, and Heritage did the same. "Lyle is easy to explain," she said. "His unbreakable allegiance to Stephanie—and vice versa—is way stronger than Dottie's relationship with her own daughter. Stephanie turned her back on Dottie once, and it nearly destroyed her. Dottie tolerates Lyle, because it protects the tentative relationship she has with Stephanie. Coast guard captain Matt— Dottie recently gave him a real estate tip that Strawberry Island would be coming up for sale, and that he would be smart to work with the owner to obtain it without involving a realtor. This was meant as a gift or professional advice, friend to friend, but Dottie just wanted him off Wick." She took a sip from her Nalgene water bottle that looked like it had enough bits of bread dough stuck to it that she could have made a Stromboli bun. "The drugs they have me on make me so dry. It's like a drought in my body these days."

"And Steve Greene?" Heritage asked.

"Steve Greene is in cahoots with Dottie, plain and simple. He shares and protects her biggest secret. If you're looking for who stashed the knife and the rope in that garden shed of a cabin that Dottie stuck you in, my bet would be that was Steve Greene."

"The bones of François' father have gone missing, and the platform in the giant tree above the labyrinth has been removed. Would this be Steve Greene's doing, too? And where do you think they are now—the bones, I mean?"

Mona nodded, and then shrugged. She had worn herself out, and Heritage could sense their conversation nearing its end. "Perhaps you should check out Lucien Pelletier's cottage, just north of my place around the headland. The house may have been used by

Ninnish and Rowan as a play fort or something, but since you really can only get there by boat, unless you want to bushwhack . . ." She trailed off, reaching again for her water bottle. "I imagine the place has barely been touched since Lucien's execution."

Execution. Heritage thought about that term a moment. "I don't suppose you know what happened with François—where he might have disappeared to when he left Clayoquot—do you?" Heritage had nothing to lose by asking—Mona had seemed to be in a mood to help him.

"I don't. But Dottie might. I know she and François had words a few months back that had left Dottie shaken, even weeks after."

"Any mention what the argument might have been about?"

Mona shook her head. "Dottie said she was too upset to even talk about it."

Heritage was trying to figure everything out at once. Just when his own act was coming together, his long-range plot to find everlasting happiness on a cliffside home at the edge of the rainforest—and someone to share it with—was sort of falling apart. He gave the bracelet on his wrist a spin and opened the passenger door.

Folding at the waist to lean his head back inside the car, he said "So, aside from your creepy party tattoos, I still really have nothing in the way of proof, do I?"

"It depends on what you're trying to prove, doesn't it?" she asked with a smirk. "There's one more thing you need to know." She reached her hand toward him.

"What's that, Mona?" He took her bony hand in his own.

"About my son, Aidan—"

Heritage tried to take his hand back in protest but she clamped a grip on it.

"He turns eighteen in early October . . . and he's some kind of wicked in love with you." She let go of his hand and refastened her seatbelt, turning the key in the ignition. "Nice speaking with you, Heritage . . . and good luck with everything."

———

LUCIEN LIVES

Heritage had worked himself up into a mental pretzel that was causing his heart to race. He knew his brain could use unknotting as he lay on his bed, propped up by a mountain of high-end pillows. He has spent nearly two hours stewing and rehashing the day—the drama of the inquiry, seeing a grown-up Ninnish for the first time since he'd coerced the teen he'd left behind to make a confession on tape, and then, all the information that Mona Rye had dumped on him. What *was* he trying to prove? He knew he urgently needed to figure that out, but nothing was sorting for him.

And then, like magic, the moon on the water was showing him the path. It was real, laid out right there in front of him just outside those giant bay windows. He traced the swath of moonlight in a direct line from Middle Beach to the mounded white sand beach on Wickaninnish Island that was glowing like a lightning bug—or bioluminesence, just north of the blinking navigation beacon near Mona's place, leading precisely to where she had suggested he might find some answers—in Lucien Pelletier's old cabin. He could think of nothing more exhilarating than the sheer concentration and nerve it would take to go paddling at night—something he had never done before, or even imagined doing. The cover of night would make for a spooky crossing, but the ability to see smoke from stove pipes and lights in windows would also allow him to know who was home on the island, and who wasn't. This seemed an advantage in his ongoing skullduggery, so with a pirate's "Arr, matey," he was out of the room like a bolt.

Studying each black swell as it came barreling toward him, holding his breath as each humpbacked sea monster lifted and passed under his kayak, Heritage settled into a cadence, concentrating only on rhythmically paddling and keeping his kayak in the path of moonlight. In his front hatch he'd stowed his sleeping bag, a headlamp, a flashlight, and some leftover muffins from that morning's buffet, just in case he got marooned. He was learning—evolving—to anticipate the unexpected in Clayoquot Sound. It had become clear that mayhem came with the territory—and remembering Chief Wickaninnish and the wreckage of the Tonquin somewhere in the depths beneath him, he thought perhaps it always had.

The sound of each paddle blade as it dipped into the cold, dark water struck Heritage's ears as music. There was no other sound as he approached the middle of the channel. He lowered his pulse and breathing to a near-Zen state—though he had no life experience with this, and no concept of what Zen really was. His vision, hearing, and olfactory senses were heightened to super-human levels in the pitch-black voids on either side of the moon path. As far as he could tell, he was still aligned with the mounded sand beach he remembered sticking out from Wickaninnish Island's east coast like an elbow. The seagulls and eagles were sleeping. The great blue herons, with their lanky legs and massive wingspans, were folded up inside their twig nests, high in the dead snags of trees. Seals were hauled out on outer rocks and sea otters were rafting, and tucked in the shadows for the night.

There was no phosphoresced plankton in the water, but Heritage flashed back to the night he first learned about the phenomenon, remembering Ninnish play-humping Rowan in the water. Had it really been play? He still wondered about that, smiling in the moonlight. Heritage shifted his butt in the plastic seat to accommodate, of all things, a sudden swelling in his groin under the spray skirt. He paddled on, settling on the notion that he was finding himself turned on by the exhilaration of being in nature, and alone on the ocean at night. His paddling sprint had peaked, getting him through the barrel swells of the main channel.

As he settled back into a more sustainable stroke, he heard a motorboat off to his left coming from the direction of the lighthouse. He strained his eyes into the abyss but could see no running lights. The motor was getting closer—Heritage realized he wasn't visible either. He stopped paddling, and leaned his long arms forward to try to fish his headlamp or his flashlight out of the front hatch. He could hear the slapping of the bottom of the motorboat as it hopscotched from swell top to swell trough. Heritage was still a half-kilometre from reaching the more protected waters along the eastern shore of Wickaninnish—he was still very much situated in the main boat channel. He could see lights on at Mona's cabin but could not find his own lights.

The sound of the motor seemed nearly on top of him. He was afraid he was a sitting duck. Who in the hell would be on the water after dark without running lights? Well, except for him. He straightened and raised his paddle straight up. Then, like a metronome, he waved it maybe thirty degrees back and forth—until, at what seemed like the last moment before certain collision, the boat's motor cut out. Heritage hadn't realized how rapidly his heart was thumping until he was back in silence.

"Hey," he yelled, hopped up on adrenaline. "I didn't know if you could see me."

"Tage? Is dat you?" A familiar voice volleyed back from the darkness, as the speaker's face drifted closer into the moonlight.

"François? No shit, it's you!" Heritage exclaimed. "I was told you had disappeared, that nobody had seen you for weeks—no, months." Heritage grabbed onto the side of the skiff and pulled his kayak parallel to it. In his oversized floatation jacket, François crouched down so the two were more face-to-face. But the face that Heritage was looking into seemed skeletal, gaunt. François looked like crap—like he had let himself go, or had been wandering in the wilderness in search of food or something. He looked like a ghost. That's what it was—though Heritage had never seen a ghost just like he'd never once experienced Zen.

"Oh, man . . . you don't look so good."

François just stared, zombie-like, back at him, and then looked away. "It's dat I'm just not in a good place right now. I did disappear. You didn't see me tonight." François was nervous, rambling. His regularly gorgeous hair looked matted and unwashed. There were some scabs or pimples on his nose and face, and his usual effervescence was flatter than flat.

"What happened?" Heritage reached to grab the open collar of the man's float jacket, but reflexively, François pulled back and stood up. Heritage went on. "What are you doing out here, at night, without lights on your boat?"

"Look," François snapped. The stench of gasoline or maybe diesel oil that emanated from him stung Heritage's nostrils. François threw his arm back, lazily pointing toward Wick. "Since dat day when you showed me dat place over der, where you say my father's bones were up dat tree, I tink I became crazy, you know? My fadder, he now haunts me in my sleep, so I don't sleep. I have so much rage inside me dat I can't be around people right now. I need to go."

"Wait!" Heritage pleaded. "I am going to your father's place right now. Did you know he had a cabin on Wick? I just found this out today. The cabin's still there. Come with me!" Heritage was so excited, thinking he could save François from his demons.

François shook his troubled head even before Heritage completed his invitation. "I just gotta go," he kept saying over and over, as he moved with one long-legged stride toward the back of the skiff. He restarted his engine—Heritage could not be heard over the noise, so he let go of the skiff and pushed his kayak clear of the boat. François did not look back at him as he gunned the skiff away into the night. Heritage sat there, bobbing up and down in the wake, in shock, thinking he might have just seen a ghost for the first time.

The sound of the boat's motor diminished like an excruciatingly long fade-to-black at the end of a really sad movie. Heritage realized that is what he was, too—profoundly sad. His tragically fallen messiah had looked more like a brutally battered Jesus coming straight from the crucifixion. François was visibly and perhaps mortally damaged. He seemed too far gone to be reeled back into a saner, happier, more promise-filled future. And as Heritage thought about the crock of malarkey that happily-ever-after never was, he couldn't blame François for running. It sent an ache through his heart that called into question what he was doing there, what he needed to prove, and where the whirlpool he was spinning in would take him next—if not down the wicked drain, too.

Heritage drift-paddled past Mona and Ninnish's place, looking for any signs of movement. They must have been home, as nearly every light was blazing on both floors—a luxury that could only have come from a two-day recharge of the solar panel's batteries. He rounded the rocky point with the flashing navigation beacon and encountered stronger currents and a headwind that required him to pull harder with each dip of the paddle. His destination— the white beach with its steep underwater drop-away shelf—was truly glowing now in the moonlight, and loomed like an over-stuffed feather pillow another hundred metres ahead. He pulled harder on his left side and foot-pedaled the rudder accordingly.

He would need to ram the steep beach at full paddle to get high enough in the sand that he didn't have to get his feet wet when climbing out. The decision to wear hiking boots was incontrovertible evidence that he was getting smarter. Wearing sandals in the dark would only have invited more cuts and scrapes and blood offerings to an island that had already exacted enough from him.

Noting that there were no lights in the dilapidated two-story shack that squatted in the shadows under the edge of overgrown trees like it had gone there to take a dump, Heritage put his back into his strokes, and surely tested the strength of Mac's fiberglass repair job on the front underside of his kayak as the momentum scooted him uphill to a stop. He scrambled out of his boat, grabbed the rope and wood handle, and dragged the kayak high onto what must have been considered Lucien's beach. It's not that the ground was consecrated, but the hairs on the back of Heritage's neck told him it might still be haunted, and was most assuredly hexed by the coven of witches that the Quebecois Casanova had harmed with his womanizing ways.

Heritage retrieved the headlamp and stretched the band around his head, adjusted the straps, and moved his thick hair out of his eyes and under the elastic. He kept the light off, so as not to attract attention from anyone across the channel, in their fancy homes above Tonquin Beach; or from any crazies who happened to be driving their boats around in the dark without running lights. He looked toward the gap between Felice Island and the tip of Tofino at the end of the crooked-finger peninsula to mark in his memory the direction he'd last seen François headed. He would have given anything to understand who or what he was running from, or even what he was chasing. But lowering his shoulders, Heritage settled into the premonition he might not ever know or see François again. A tear, and then two escaped his eye. François was gone, with legions of hellhounds nipping at his heels. It had been a fanciful fling, and a loose end Heritage had thought he was returning to Clayoquot Sound to tie up in a bow—with a bracelet he'd have to grow accustomed to wearing himself. He was finally figuring out that François had a perpetual funeral going on in his heart—a round-the-clock double requiem for his father and Marcel—a ritual so somber, so dark, that new love and promises could not disrupt it.

Heritage smeared the tears from his cheek with the palm of his hand that continued to comb through his wavy hair. He pivoted around in the sand. If he hadn't come back for François, then why in the hell was he there at all? Was there another tangle he had yet to unknot? Mona's words came back to him in that instant. *It depends on what you're trying to prove*, she'd told him earlier that afternoon.

Heritage reluctantly approached the house, locating a rotten and moss-slippery set of stairs on the left side. They had been cleverly camouflaged by cedar branches that grew that way in the caretaker's absence. Every step creaked, and the cottage let out a moan under Heritage's weight on the porch. The place felt very precariously held together, like it might come apart and collapse in a moldy heap at any moment. He reached for the doorknob, and the wood around it further disintegrated until Heritage withdrew the suddenly liberated hardware in his hand. Momentarily clicking his headlamp on, he found the hook clasp that had held the door shut from the outside. There was no padlock, no slated-for-demolition notice, and nothing stopping him from entering.

He stepped inside and placed what was left of the doorknob on a kitchen counter. Without the moon and under the trees, Heritage could not have managed without the headlamp, so he left it on. The reflection of the light and the outline of his own body in the one piece of glass that was cracked but not broken out like the rest, across the room gave him a start. The headlight in the center of his forehead was joined by the spare flashlight in his hand, and together, the beams bounced around the room— from the scattering of open Playboy and Playgirl magazines, to the girly pin-up calendars thumbtacked to the walls. A dirty, stained mattress, no larger than double size, was half on the floor, and half propped inside a bed frame that had collapsed—from overuse, or from weather and time. It smelled mildewy and damp and his nose was beginning to react when his headlamp focused on what looked like the green OSU sweatshirt wadded up with several pairs of Heritage's underwear, encrusted with what he could only guess was Aidan's jizz. Near the sweatshirt were more Polaroids, all turned face down. Heritage's hand shook as he prepared himself to flip them over, like he was Vanna White on the *Wheel of Fortune*. One by one, he uncovered a study of portraits, all of his slumbering and drugged-out face. One shot included someone's fingers—he guessed they were Aidan's—holding his eyelids open to reveal his hazel eyes. There were similar photos of his teeth, with the corners of his cheeks being held apart. And then there were close-up photos of his hairy chest, his nipples, his belly button, the trio of moles below one of his underarms, and then the photos closest the balled up underwear, were of his penis—flaccid, semi-erect, and then four photos from different angles that showed him at full mast, with another mole on one side of his erection. Heritage gathered up all the photos and stuck them in the back pocket of his kayaking pants. He didn't know what to do with the sweatshirt and the underwear, but supposed there was no way they could be linked back to him. The sweatshirt wasn't even his. He had only been wearing it because he believe it belonged to François.

The photography was Rowan's handiwork, and that abandoned house must have been his second hiding place—and, given the volume of pornography, his and Aidan's jerk-off headquarters. These photos did not include any trace of Ninnish, beyond the fingers in the one shot that could have been his or Rowan's. These were a separate batch distinctly different from the more incriminating shots that had been stuffed between the pages of his paperback—photos that, had they been submitted to the police, could have put him away for life.

Wait. He stopped breathing. Was that the evidence that Dottie had in the file folder that she tried to introduce to the magistrate earlier? Did she have photocopies of the photos?

"Fucking hell!" Heritage said to the spiders. But that wasn't the half of it. Heritage began to recognize the books from his own library, the ones he'd been compelled to put on display on Dottie's dock that first day he'd arrived—books he had thought were still being stored at Dottie's kayak and book emporium in town. But here they were: some on the table, some on the floor. He checked the inside covers, and each one of them had his signature, Heritage W, Carter III, cursively autographed on the top of the first page. Only Dottie knew about his book collection. Only Dottie had said she would safeguard them for him until he had gotten settled. Only Dottie could have moved them to this dilapidated cabin.

Heritage expelled two lungs full of air through lips he hadn't fully opened. The headlamp beam revealed the next horror. Headless and limbless doll torsos were lined up on the windowsills and shelves. Spread open on the lopsided table was last year's annual report, and audited financial statements from Carter Pulp & Paper. So was the torn-off portion of the grocery sack with the scribbled note from Stephanie to her mom, bragging about her sexual conquest of the newcomer, and describing the size of his penis.

That entire cabin had been someone's stash—Dottie's, Aidan's, Rowan's maybe? The whole place had been staged to frame him—not for Heritage to find, but to provide a giant lead in any criminal investigation. Steve Greene came to mind next. Coast guard Matt's dad had told Heritage he wasn't welcome there, and told him that he knew who he was and where he'd come from, and that no good could come from him staying. With the pornography and pinups everywhere, the scene seemed to have been set by a man. Heritage picked up a magazine to check the publication date, and was shocked to find it to be August 1977. The other magazines were from the same era. They must have belonged to Lucien Pelletier. He didn't even need to wonder if Ninnish or Rowan knew about the place, as they had likely masturbated on every square centimetre of the island.

Heritage rose from his squat to a standing position, and his flashlight beam illuminated a large mason jar in the main living room. He moved closer, walking across the carpet of moldy porn magazines whose pages had been cemented together ages ago. Heritage raised the jar with the reddish-brown fluid to his face, and held the flashlight to the glass bottom of the jar. What in the hell was that? His face scrunched up and his eyes narrowed as he turned the jar with one hand. Its pickled contents were white as Caspar the Friendly Ghost, but more elongated. A sea cucumber, maybe? Heritage had seen, even touched the species before in a tide pool tank at the Vancouver Aquarium. His focus shifted, like he was adjusting a camera lens, blurring what was inside the jar to focus on the folded piece of wax paper it had been sitting on like a coaster. He set the jar on the windowsill and unfolded the parchment.

It was the diagram—the original, not Ninnish's replication on the page from the notebook—showing the quartering of Lucien Pelletier. Heritage looked again at the mason jar and remembered the reliquary that Mona had told him about, and the relic she said it contained. Heritage's hands were trembling.

She had said the original plan existed for years on parchment paper. Heritage studied the drawing. The arms and legs were certainly disarticulated—but so was the head. And there was an angrily drawn gash at the point between the victim's legs, where his . . .

In that instant, Heritage had no doubt what was in the mason jar: Lucien's pickled dick.

It must have been spared Dottie's pitchfork. This was the penis, if the legend was accurate, that had impregnated so many women in addition to François' mother—Stephanie, Sharon Greene, and others, he supposed. He held the jar up again. It was a damn impressive sea cucumber, even after seventeen or so years in that suspension. The life and pleasure and havoc it must have brought into the darkest corners of the galaxy made it worth preserving. Heritage marveled that the member in that jar was the legendary instrument that had helped create Ninnish, just as it had helped create François and at least one other kid, who was probably running around Southern California. Three half-brothers, ricocheting through their lives without a clue that they had sprung from the loins of the same man. Through them, and quite possibly through a squad of others, Lucien Pelletier lived on, regardless of Dottie Bard's enraged attempt to put an end to him—to erase all signs he'd ever been there or existed. For some reason, Heritage realized Dottie Bard was trying to eliminate him now, too, by planting evidence and sticking him with Ninnish. He sneezed three times in a row. The mold was getting to him.

Before deciding what to do next, he realized he couldn't leave without checking the upstairs. He found the staircase, testing each tread for rot as he went up. Weary of a trap—like everything had seemed to be since his arrival in Clayoquot Sound—Heritage stood at the top of the stairs and surveyed what the headlamp and flashlight revealed. The room was one open space with a steeply pitched ceiling. The windows were blacked out from the inside, the glass panes painted black to match the walls, the ceiling, and—

"Fucking Christ!" Heritage stammered and began trembling uncontrollably. There on the floor, in silver spray paint, was a replica of the labyrinth—the outer rings, the pentagram, the entrance points from four directions, and the mound of muddy doll heads, stacked in a domed sculpture of moss, mud, and plastic eyeballs that caught the flashlight's beam in the pentagram's centre.

Heritage gulped, from a swallow that had gone down sideways, causing him to cough. At the top of the pentagram was a toothless human skull, and a crooked line of neck and vertebrae bones. The femur and tibia bones had been laid out to flare in the same directions as each of the stars' bottom points. In that context, the stacked pile of doll heads corresponded with the skeleton's pelvis, which was either buried under the doll heads, or missing. The radius and humerus bones, and some of the phalanges, were assembled to stretch the length of the pentagram's lateral points. The scapula, clavicle, and some of the ribs were roughly in the positions an amateur coroner would have guessed they should be.

Still quaking where he stood, Heritage, for some zany reason, flashed back to that scene in *The Goonies* where Sean Astin's character suddenly comes face to face with the skeleton of One-Eyed Willie. Heritage introduced himself using a variation of those lines. "*Bonjour,* Lucien . . . I'm Tage Carter . . . you've been expecting me."

With both light beams trained on the skeleton, Heritage had completed the puzzle. The mound of dirty doll heads looking into the world with sleepy eyes from the centre of Lucien's groin, represented the children that had sprung from there. What Heritage could not know without delving further, was that each of the thirty-two doll heads in that mound had a single tooth from Lucien's jaw buried in it, and held in place with mud and who knew what else?

"I did this."

Aidan broke the silence beyond Heritage's audible heartbeat, speaking calmly, but with authority, from his position at the top of the stairs.

Heritage's boots left the ground with the startle but his voice wasn't working.

"I moved the labyrinth here." Ninnish moved into the black room to be with Heritage. Heritage's headlamp acted as a follow spot. "I figured out that Lucien was my father. I know that François and I are half-brothers. I've heard rumours that there are many other children from this man—my father."

Ninnish kneeled opposite Heritage, with the pelvic mound separating them. "I am not stupid, and neither are you. We both know that Dottie Bard killed my father. We both know that she and Steve Greene want to destroy you, but they somehow think they can get their hands on your money first." Ninnish paused to swallow. "We both know the real reason you came back to Clayoquot Sound, Tage—it's me."

Heritage shifted uncomfortably, but said nothing. It was a good thing, too, because Ninnish was just getting started.

"I don't think I hide it very well, but I have been obsessed with you since that first day on the dock, when I smacked into you on purpose. From the moment our bodies first touched, I changed. I don't know if it was chemistry or witchcraft—believe me, I have placed a shitload of spells on you, mister. But the truth is, I have not been the same since you got here."

"Are you in love with me?" Heritage took that moment—the eye of what he was sure would soon be a storm—to cross-examine.

"What do you think?" There was a silence between them while a breeze outside sent cedar limbs tickle-scratching the rusted metal roof over their heads.

"There are some of my personal things downstairs," Heritage said, "and the pictures from that night at your place, when Mona was away."

"Sure. Some of these things I swiped from you, and some of them Dottie Bard gave me. Like your books." Heritage was nodding, and Aidan went on. "I was supposed to deliver those books to you—she'd given me twenty bucks to do it, but instead I read them because I wanted to know about everything inside your head."

"But what I don't understand is what all my things are doing here, in this house. And the Polaroids, Ninnish—those could destroy me."

"Exactly—that's why they are here. I came here to burn this house down tonight, with everything in it. My Mum came home this afternoon and told me she had her conscience-clearing conversation with you . . . that she told you about everything, and Lucien's house. I knew you couldn't resist seeing it for yourself, so

I've been waiting for you. I don't blame you. As you can see, it's quite the museum."

"And so it is your plan to set the place ablaze?"

"With or without us in it, depending on—" Ninnish cut himself off, not wanting to seem overly dramatic, and suddenly acting adult enough to know the difference.

"Depending on me, Ninnish? Depending on whether or not I agree to stay for good this time, and make some promise about loving you back? Is that it?"

Ninnish smiled, running his hand through his much longer blonde hair like he were posing for a Hollywood headshot. "At least you know what you'd be getting yourself into, since you've been into me before." There. That was the flash of adolescence that Heritage had been on the lookout for—some trace of the kid Ninnish used to be, in the middle of an otherwise very adult conversation. He was shocked that nobody had dropped their pants or dared the other to jerk off yet. Perhaps Aidan had grown out of that stage in their odd relationship.

"Look, with François out of the picture—"

Heritage interrupted. "What do you mean, out of the picture?"

"This afternoon I was talking with François at the dock. Nobody had seen him around for months, and for some reason, he all of a sudden decided to act like I was worth talking to. I don't know why, but I ended up blurting out everything I knew about his father. He asked if I knew who killed his dad, and I said, sure. It wasn't my secret to keep, so I told him Dottie Bard, that's who. Next thing I know, he pats me on the shoulders using both hands, and thanks me for being the first person in Clayoquot Sound to be honest with him. Then he jumped in his boat and took off in the direction of that oyster farm he works at."

Heritage shifted weight from one leg to the other, wishing he could transfer from this life to another. How had he gotten into this mess? What was he really feeling about the things Aidan was telling him—about Aidan's declaration of love? How had Aidan grown up in just three months' time? And then he remembered that it hadn't been just three months. It had been three months plus eighteen. When Heritage left for Toronto, he had believed Aidan was probably at least sixteen and not the fifteen he'd been told. He had returned to learn that Aidan was less than a year away from turning eighteen. This was a broad psychological leap for Tage's brain and jumbled feelings to make, but he was doing his best to square this new, matured version of the child he'd left behind with the young man standing before him now.

"I just ran into François, on the water, during my paddle over here," Heritage said, pausing as he choked up. "I am almost completely certain that this amounted to his final goodbye to me and to Clayoquot Sound, and that I will never see him again."

Ninnish stood, and moved around his facsimile of the pentagram, Heritage's head lamp serving as a follow spot. "I came here from the labyrinth," he said, "stopping at home for some matches and gasoline first. I guess my talk with Frenchie must have set off this chainsaw of events—and I say chainsaw, because he got ahold of one. It must have been a really big one, too—cause sometime this afternoon—probably while we all at the hearing with the judge, he came over here and cut down every last Sitka tree around the edges of the labyrinth. It's one giant mess down there at the other end of the island now. The labyrinth, and about 10,000 years' worth of trees—well, they are no more. Completely wiped out. Good thing I already relocated the labyrinth here."

Heritage wondered whether or not François had enough rage in him to pull that off. The answer instantly came to him when he remembered the terrorized face he'd just seen on the water: *yes.* "Where did you find the bones then? You weren't the one to take them out of the tree platform. You were in the hospital when they went missing."

"Oh, these?" Ninnish pointed to the floor. "The bones were exactly where I knew I would find them—in a tote just inside Steve Greene's firewood shed. I'm sure he got this panicked call from Dottie saying something like the police were on their way over, and to make them vanish, like real fast." Ninnish motioned toward the stairs. "Shall we?" he invited Heritage to follow him downstairs, and Heritage did.

An old-fashioned kerosene lamp had been lit while Heritage had been preoccupied upstairs, and when he left the bottom step to enter the room, he saw Ninnish raising one of the pairs of Heritage's underwear to his face. "I've missed you, Tage. You may never appreciate or know how much." Heritage probably blushed, but it was still too dark inside the house to be noticed.

In the distance and across the channel, multiple police and fire sirens began to wail. "I bet that's François now," Ninnish said. "That would be my cue to get things underway here." Ninnish put the underwear on the chair arm and noticed a Polaroid that Heritage had missed as it had fallen between the arm and the cushion. He chuckled, extending the photo to Heritage, to complete the collection Aidan suspected was in Tage's back pocket. "You know, I heard it from that librarian in the bakeshop the other day, that somebody—she didn't know or say who, but I'm sure it was Dottie—someone left one of the Polaroids behind, on the copy machine at the Co-op." He laughed some more. "I guess it was one of the nuns, Sister Greta maybe, had gone to the Co-op to photocopy the Saturday mass bulletin, and found the Polaroid still on the glass. I have no idea what the photo was of, but we can imagine, right?" Ninnish was still laughing just as Heritage felt like puking everything out of his stomach.

"Hey, look!" Heritage pointed through the window, toward a large orange glow that seemed to be coming from the lower part of downtown Tofino.

"Yep," Ninnish said. "I would have bet my doll collection and all my porn that Dottie Bard would be the second stop on François' revenge tour. Looks like I was right. And that really is my cue to get things going here. You should take off." He poured out all the orange fuel from the kerosene lamp, dowsing the ratty armchair.

"Ninnish, what are you doing here?" Heritage's voice leapt to an upper register.

"It's called a purification ritual, and it needs fire—shitloads of it. If I do it now, it will get added to Frenchie's rap sheet, and not mine. Now, get going!"

Heritage moved toward Ninnish and the armchair, and lingered there a few seconds, though he wasn't sure why—perhaps, in the hope of giving him a hug. That may or may not have been a good idea, but since it didn't come, there was no foul. Instead, Heritage covertly palmed the mason jar containing Lucien's penis from the windowsill, and worked it under the waistband of his briefs, behind his back and out of Ninnish's sight. He didn't know why he wanted that curio, but it seemed like good insurance in the event Ninnish succeeded in torching the waterlogged museum of horrors to the ground. Upon reaching the door leading to the porch, Heritage turned back, thinking to offer Ninnish his headlamp. But the armchair was already engulfed in flames and Ninnish was tossing gasoline in every direction.

Outside, Heritage wrapped what remained of Lucien in a spare fleece, tucked him into the front hatch of his kayak, and dragged the boat to the water's edge, then panicked about the long divot line he'd left in the sand. He quickly backtracked and frantically kicked sand, trying to erase his beach prints as the beach began to turn orange and red.

Sirens were still filling the night air as the arc of orange across the way had easily and madly doubled in size, giving the volunteer fire department—and likely the coast guard crew as well—a conflagration that would forever help them remember just how 1994 had ended. By the time Heritage climbed into the cockpit and attached the spray skirt to the front lip of his kayak, he could discern a new path on the water in front of him—this one flame orange, coming from the crackling and glass breaking commotion behind him and stretching in the direction of Headlands Lodge. He had been shown the way in both directions.

Heritage's soul was at peace, bathed by divination and dancing to its deliverance. As he paddled along that orange trail growing more brilliant with each stroke, he had no need to look back—only ahead to what would come next. Given everything he'd learned, and accepting there was much he would never understand, what he did know and what he could finally accept was that absolutely everything—but the double-bladed paddle—was out of his hands.

A RYE FOR A RYE

Tage's hands ran over the cuts left by François' chainsaw. It hadn't been an easy job, he could tell by the uneven ridges that marked each new pass of the grinding teeth. He could feel where the chainsaw had become stuck, and where François had needed to reverse the blade, retreat, and try his pass over again.

That stump and the nineteen other tombstones that ringed what had been the labyrinth, were each larger than the dining room table in his grandfather's Toronto mansion. What had been a moss-carpeted natural-looking clearing, a sacred ceremonial place and a crime scene, at least twice, had been rendered most unnatural, even stripped bare by François' vandalism. That gaping wound in the forest canopy was still bleeding pitch, exhalation, and history, and Heritage didn't know how to bandage up the pieces to heal the spirits of these massive beings. In his silly helplessness, he couldn't resist hauling himself onto the stump's tabletop, laying himself out flat, and stretching his long arms and legs. He already knew he would not be able to touch the edges, but he tried anyway. He'd twice climbed that tree—the same tree that had cradled Lucien Pelletier's bones along with some of the island's very darkest secrets. Ninnish had been accurate when he'd reported François' destruction had brought an end to 10,000 years of living when these twenty giants were mowed down in their prime.

Tage flipped over onto his stomach and started to count the rings, but grew more depressed by the time he'd reached the halfway point—about 300 years. In the exact center of that mammoth altar, François had placed the Russian subway token as his calling card, returning to the tree the treasure it had hung onto for seventeen years or more. What else had this tree held? Plenty more secrets, to be sure—like being the backdrop for the photo on Mona's old nightstand, featuring Dottie tentatively holding Mona's hand. They were both gone now, Dottie having preceded the cancer-riddled Mona by nearly seven months, and it still hadn't really sunk in for Heritage how those other losses in the past year—his own grandfather, Marcel, and Mason too—had affected him.

Dottie Bard had met her rocky end—dragged until drowned behind her own boat. Her body had eventually been found near Grice Bay, floating face-down with her feet and ankles horribly tangled in a fisherman's net that had either been attached to or gotten snagged on two of the cleat ties on her boat, which had wrecked on an exposed shoal during a falling tide. The nylon ropes had cut such deep, mangling lacerations into her ankles that investigators had a devil of a time trying to determine if it had been an accident. As she had been found just a day after her store and office building had been torched to the ground—even the supporting piers had burned right down to the tide line—it seemed unlikely that her death was accidental.

As for poor Mona Rye, she had returned early in that new year to the cancer ward at Victoria's Royal Jubilee Hospital—but it would be for the last time. She came home to Clayoquot Sound three months later in an unmarked urn. The SunRyes

Bakeshop had been closed for three weeks out of respect for the hardtack and sometimes sourdough broad who had been mothering, feeding, and funding environmental activists for the better part of two decades.

Heritage flipped back over, face up in the sun. As he lay there—sprawled out like a tabby cat presenting his belly for a rub—a variety of differently shaped clouds traveled across that expanse of jean-blue sky overhead. His never-idle brain was busy taking roll call of the dead—Mona, Dottie, Mason, and even Marcel, whom he'd never known but whose presence and physique he'd admired at Lyle's dance party. Each had loomed larger-than-life in one moment, only to be robbed of their lives in what seemed like the very next.

And then there was Rowan.

Rowan Robson was the one soul who wouldn't be the same, as there would be no miracles for the boy who was convinced he'd accidentally killed his mother. With his father, Clive, in prison, and his mother dead, Rowan had not been able to see his way forward. On a breezy Friday afternoon, only weeks after the commotion in the labyrinth and the fire at Dottie Bard's shop, and with school out for the weekend, Rowan had hitched a boat ride with Mona and Ninnish to the island for a scheduled weekend sleepover. After supper, Rowan asked politely if he could be excused from the table, and then calmly announced he was going to take a walk. Mona had pushed Aidan to go with him, but Ninnish was stubborn and not in the mood, and so Rowan had set off by himself.

He walked across the trans-island express trail, and without entering the house full of memories he couldn't bear to face, he tossed a yellow rope over a truss under the deck, tied the long end to the closest post next to the stairs, and then tied the short end around his neck, while balancing on a wobbly piece of upturned firewood. With tears gushing out of his eyes and with the rope around his neck already too tight, Rowan's feet pushed the firewood away. The hand-split log tumbled off the side of the cliff, bouncing and flipping before splashing, just like his mother had, into the ocean below. Rowan Robson swayed there, back and forth in that breeze, for what had to have been the first peaceful night of his life.

Stephanie Bard had stayed behind to fill her mother's Birkenstocks, and somehow found the money her mother hadn't left her to expand the kayaking company, become a Patagonia clothing store outlet, and take on two other recently newborn children inside her in-store daycare. Gillian the librarian's baby boy and Stu Solberg's new daughter got along just fine with Stephanie's boy, who she'd named and christened *Rowan*. That had been Aidan's idea, as a way to pay tribute to his childhood buddy. The new Rowan's paternity was still a mystery to everyone, including Stephanie. Unlike her mother, she'd decided she was better off *not* knowing everything. Gillian's curly red-haired son was a chip off his old man's block, according to those who remembered Marcel Labbé. The two infant boys, who shared a playpen during their mother's workweeks, had so many similar characteristics and mannerisms, that when combined with the general knowledge about town that Stephanie, in her younger years, had more-than gotten around the sound—it was widely believed that Marcel had been the father-in-common; motoring around, as he did all those years in his trusty water taxi. Some even said that he was, always trolling—never too far behind and apparently unable to resist a woman's wake.

And then there was Ninnish . . . Aidan . . . Satan with an A.

He would have never been able to forgive the conspiracy of adults who had smothered, coddled, and deceived him. So it was best for everyone that he hadn't needed to. The fire that leveled Lucien Pelletier's cabin on the other side of Wickaninnish Island had been instant—out of control almost from the second the match hit the kerosene. Ninnish had popped back upstairs to start a second fire in his relocated labyrinth, but there hadn't been time for him to get out. The place had gone up like a bomb—and with good reason. Lucien had stored a crate of unexploded ordnance leftover from World War II beneath his living room floor. Ninnish could not have possibly known that about his father or his father's cabin. Nobody did. But in 1930, the HMCS Thiepval had sunk, maybe twenty nautical miles south of there in the Broken Island Group, and Lucien had purchased the crate of explosives off of a salvage fisherman as a novelty sometime in the '70s. He'd built his cabin right over the top of it. It had always been his plan that if the authorities—or more probably, the jilted women—ever came after him, he would fire bullets through the floor until the dynamite blew him into the stratosphere. It's just that Dottie Bard's bullet had beaten him to his own punch line.

Heritage had heard and felt the shockwaves from the explosion, of course. The blast had concussed his ears and affected his hearing for the next several days. It echoed off the rocks around him for the next several minutes. Looking back over one shoulder and then the other, he could see nothing but red-hot, fire-orange apocalypse. Gods and goddesses bless that horny heart of his, Heritage remembered praying as he kept paddling, afraid that Ninnish had not been able to get out of that house in time.

And he hadn't. The seventeen-year-old's heart had stopped beating the instant the shockwaves hit his chest . . . only to miraculously restart again thirty seconds later when his over-developed teenage body landed with a thud ten metres away on the beach. It had been the jolt of hitting the ground, after his ever-so-brief stint as an astronaut, that had kick-started his not-so-damned ticker again. When the wind had returned to his lungs, Ninnish sat up in the sand, pretty certain he was dead. He was deaf, which disoriented him, but there were no burns—not a scratch or broken bones. But there was also nothing left of the house—so how in the hell could he have survived that? Without sounds, he became convinced he was already in the afterlife, or stranded somewhere in the in-between. He raced over the headland, using his secret shortcut through the salal, and burst into Mona's cabin, demanding to learn whether or not she could see him or hear him. She'd been sleeping, and had taken one of her special pills to keep her sleeping, so she was slower than usual to arouse to even semi-wakefulness. But after a few minutes of screaming and heavy stomping, Ninnish was able to satisfy himself that he had, in fact, survived the un-survivable. Mona had slept through the explosion, which was a testament to her medications. The stunt had left Ninnish with a headache, temporary hearing loss, and a bit of an immortality complex. But other than that, Satan with an A was neither more nor less, but he was alive and would live to torment another day.

Tage adjusted his butt cheeks on the stump to keep them from falling asleep, and he raised his knees by pulling his feet in closer. He pleaded with the tree's ghost to placate him, to regenerate everything that had been lost by growing itself back and right through his body if necessary. Heritage knew the tree wasn't a starfish that could simply regrow its limbs after they'd been bitten off. Still, he imagined somehow lifting the severed tree, scattered on the ground with the others, like Greco-Roman columns after the Persian sacking of the temple, and then steadying it above him, meticulously realigning the girth and grains from the top part of the tree with the stump beneath him. And then, as he balanced the trunk there on his belly, with everything lined up perfectly, he would pull his hands away from the upper trunk and the tree would fuse back together with its lower self, using his sacrificed essence as glue to hold everything together as it was. And if he could put *that* tree back together, maybe he could put the other trees back together, too. And if he could restore that sacred clearing, then maybe that circle of Sitkas would breathe their ancient breath back into the collapsed lungs of the island's lost souls.

But Heritage didn't have superpowers. He didn't know if he even had the guts to stick it out until his boyfriend and the other guests had arrived. But a late-autumn memorial service had been his idea. It would seem inauthentic for him to not be there to play host when everybody began to arrive. He glanced at his fancy diving watch. It wouldn't be long now.

Heritage Carter the Last shut his eyes, and it wasn't long before had gently drifted off.

A hand squeezed his shoulder and a familiar voice invaded his tabby catnap. He opened his hazel eyes and spotted the Russian rose gold bracelet around his boyfriend's wrist sparkling in the sunshine that filtered through the expanded hole in the canopy.

"Well, hello, handsome."

Tage craned his neck for a greeting kiss. "This came for you today." He sat up.

"What is it?" Tage asked, squinting at the silhouette hovering above him, while his eyes adjusted in the sun.

"Well, by the looks of it, I'd say it's a postcard from Kamchatka. By the read of it, I'd guess it was sent to you by François—my half-brother."

Heritage studied the image of what looked like a volcano peak on the front and tried to read out loud the words "Kamchatka Petropaviovsk Kamchatskiy" on the back, but butchered the pronunciation comically. The postcard was addressed in block letters to TAGE CARTER, GENERAL DELIVERY, TOFINO, BC V0R 2Z0, CANADA. The message was as contrite as it was brief. It read: *Sure hope you weren't blamed for my actions.* And it was signed by a sloppily scrawled letter *F*. There was no return address, of course, and no way Tage could communicate back to the correspondent to let him know that the season for blame had passed.

"Hmm," Tage purred while his boyfriend scratched him behind the ears. "How were things at the bakeshop today?"

Aidan hopped up on the stump and sat down next to Tage. "Oh, you know," he replied. "Same old, same old. My mum had always made baking seem so easy. But I am pretty proud to announce I think I mastered her Stromboli bun recipe this afternoon!"

"Hey, good for you . . . did you bring me one?"

Aidan patted his lover's belly and whispered, "You are already becoming my Stromboli bun." Tage brushed his nose against his lover's, and the two kissed there in the sun.

Aidan finger combed Tage's nap hair. "I can report that Mac Mulligan and his boatload weren't far behind me leaving the dock," he warned. "Everyone else will be arriving here very soon."

"Say, here's a question for you. I've just been laying here, you know, thinking—"

Aidan cut him off. "Thinking? I caught you sleeping!"

"You know that I make lists in my sleep. What if we turned these fallen Sitkas into lumber and built our very own dream house out of these trees, right here on Wickaninnish? You know that spot where we picnicked the other week—high on that promontory between your Mom's cabin and Dottie's place?"

Aidan smiled the devilish smile that had first slayed Heritage that day when he'd caught him in the outhouse. "You mean the expansive, two-floor house with the oversize kitchen, sunken living room and a crow's nest lookout tower jutting through the green metal roof, with two stories of giant picture windows facing Meares Island?"

"That's the one!" Heritage exclaimed and the two embraced as voices were heard in the distance, approaching through the forest. "And another question I was pondering, you know, while I was thinking here . . ."

"What's that, Tage?" he asked, fingering the dark hair on his true love's chest.

"I was wondering why you nailed all those doll limbs around the base of that grandmother of a cedar, not far from here."

"Oh yeah?" Aidan smiled again, gathering his long blonde hair off his forehead with his fingers. "I did it to see if anybody would notice . . . and in all those years, only you did. That's how I know—how I've always known—that you are the only one for me."

"Hey, get off the furniture, you two!" Mac Mulligan play-scolded, as he entered the labyrinth looking all Captain Highliner-like and carrying Dottie's ashes in a recycled bait jar. Stephanie and Gillian followed Mac, both schlepping their infant boys in over-the-shoulder slings that cradled their offspring on their breasts and bellies. The librarian's tattoos were on full display as she handed off the red jerrycan with Marcel's remains inside for Stephanie to hold, while she adjusted her boy's weight so that he rode more comfortably. Then Stephanie did the same, revealing a flash of her own chest tattoo, as she lifted Lil' Rowan out of his sling. Matt and Steve Greene entered the clearing from the opposite side, with what looked like matching hand-carved cedar boxes that held the cremated remains of Mason and Rowan. Aidan reached into his dry sack to extract the whole-wheat flour bag that contained his mother's ashes. And to everybody's surprise, Lyle Hudson ambled into the sanctuary from the north end, carrying his vintage black leather doctor bag, and wearing an original hand-painted Greenpeace T-shirt—which everyone agreed was probably the most appropriate vestment anyone could have worn to an affair like that.

Everyone had assembled for one last ritual in that unholy and unconsecrated spot, to pay their respects and return to Wicka-ninnish what had always belonged to the island. In five, carefully poured out piles of ash, one on each of five stumps between which you could have traced a pentagram—wood, fire, earth, water, metal—their departed were strewn to rest. Not the least bit surprising, everyone had something to say. Even Matt Greene's wolf-dog barked up a rousing benediction when he got into an argument with a raven that had arrived just in time to preside overhead.

Just as they'd arrived on that path through the woods that started just past the wine bottles at Dottie Bard's old cabin, the funeral party departed back into the woods, and Aidan took a short cut home to start dinner preparations.

Purposely the last to leave, just as he'd been the first to arrive, Tage had wanted one last moment alone in that resting place—now sacred, now consecrated anew. He walked back to his meditation and napping stump to add the postcard from Kamchatka to the metro token shrine. He reached behind the stump to extract the glass jar with the reddish-brown fluid that suspended Lucien Pelletier's sea cucumber in a state of perpetual inanimation. He belonged in this cemetery as much as the others did—maybe more so, since his life had abruptly ended here.

Heritage placed the jar on top of the postcard and the metro token on top of the jar's lid. He hefted his body back onto the stump and thought about François Lévesque and that brown-toothed smile of his. That misguided messiah was probably still out there at the other end of the ocean, searching for any traces of his father—that Casanova-Jesus who maybe did and maybe didn't know another one of his bastards had in fact been hiding, out in the open, on Wickaninnish Island the whole time.

From that severed rump of a towering relic that had once been so tall it snagged the clouds, Tage's hazel gaze visually walked the pentagram one last time, starting first, with Marcel because he had been the first to leave this realm. His ashes had been given the northern most stump in the circle deemed most appropriate for a man who had been a mariner navigator. It wasn't the tree that Heritage had first mistaken as north, the one that had contained Lucien's bones, the stump of which he stood on top of now. It was actually the tree two stumps to his right that marked true north. Gillian—the librarian, hospital receptionist and newspaper reporter—had explained in her short speech just a few moments earlier, that a reversed or upside down pentagram, with two points projecting upwards, was a symbol of wickedness, because it flipped the proper order of things and emphasized the unholy triumph of matter over spirit. She had said it was the goat of lust attacking the heavens with its horns. Heritage had to smile, because that perfectly summed up Lucien, François, Marcel, and his own Ninnish—all goats of lust who rammed their way through life, leading with their horns.

TOFINO TIME

A bruise.

A little more than ten years on, that is exactly what the jigsaw puzzle piece of crimson and purple and rose-coloured sky reminded Aidan of as he gazed heavenward through the mist and cobwebs and the old man's beard that dangled there like dirty lace in the surrounding old-growth canopy. His head rocked almost hypnotically back and forth on the mossy sphagnum pillow that now cushioned the entirety of the table-sized tree stump on which the boy-turned-man-turned-hapless-cynic lay, sprawled out in his mushroom-fueled stupor—thank you, Uncle Lyle.

He had wandered into this sanctum, to this man-hewn alter, with increasing frequency as the days grew cooler and shorter, and his memories began to ache within him. With Heritage more often than not away from the sound, tending to corporate business or making appearances around North America on his popular speaking tour as an environmentally-focused CEO renegade wunderkind, Aidan was left in charge of keeping the home fires stoked in Clayoquot Sound—both at the SunRyes and the Headlands. The long-ago loss of his mother and Rowan still weighed on him, but he'd secured Tage's heart and devotion, so all was not lost—in fact, he'd never been happier or felt more alive. Part of that was due the psilocybin, no doubt.

This day, October 4, 2005, marked both his twenty-eighth birthday and his wedding day—an event he never really dreamed would be possible in a year he never thought he'd live long enough to see. And yet, there he was, stoned and killing time before the ceremony at four-o-clock on Big Beach. He was twenty-eight years young, according to a recently surfaced birth certificate that had been emailed to him by the British Columbia Bureau of Statistics. It didn't concern him in the least that the old man he was marrying in another half hour was forty-three. Aidan was content with the balance of his life, his official age and his new birthday—never having been thrilled with a summer celebration that always seemed to get lost in the shuffle of holidays and sunshine. October was perfect for him—smack in the middle between Mabon and Samhain on the Wheel of the Year and being a Libra suited him, too. His birthday horoscope that morning predicted he was very different from the rest of the people born under the same zodiac sign and that being born on this date suggested he could be a rebellious soul. "Ya think?" he just shouted up through the hole in the canopy at that bruise formed by a kaleidoscope of psychedelic popcorn clouds.

The Clayoquot sun scarcely levitated above the tops of centuries-young cedars now as it undertook its abbreviated stroll across an autumn sky—an expanse which, at least today, seemed just as foreboding and raggedly tattered as that wicked bruise overhead. Far too much had happened in this clearing now overgrown with salal, ferns, chanterelles, and salmon berry. It had been like wading through chest deep water just to reach this stump his half-brother had acrimoniously exacted from the gods and goddesses. Aidan no longer had to answer to these deities or demons, but he would catch hell from his betrothed when he emerged from the woods onto the beach with his cheesy white tuxedo suit polka-dotted with green, orange, and banana slug slime stains. He'd been commanded, as he left the house, not to get dirty.

He and Heritage had awoken to pink and red skies that morning, entangled in each other's arms and legs on the other side of the island in the master loft bedroom of their sunrise-facing dream house on a cliff at the edge of the rainforest. Red skies in the morning was a maritime caution for sailors to heed warning, and as if to substantiate that myth, the weather had not been looking great for the ceremony and beach salmon barbecue reception that would follow. Tage was stressed out beyond words, and back at the house pacing. But not Aidan—thank you again, Uncle Lyle. Yet that bruise overhead perturbed him. It was one hole in the coniferous ceiling—a blemish hardly worth noticing, had it not been so ferociously exacted from the lower-middle of the narrowest point of Wickaninnish Island, in a place now protected as a UNESCO World Biosphere Reserve, and revered the world over for its remaining stands of ancient trees.

Of course, this spot had been the execution and resting place of a father he'd never known, and the trunks of the trees mowed down here now formed the upright supporting beams that ringed their round, three-story deluxe treehouse that squatted on the promontory south of his Mum's old cottage. This castration of Nature, like the loss of his own testicle in this same clearing, had also borne the incisive scars of Man's delusion—for what had been gained from the felling of those twenty giants could not have possibly compared to what had been lost in irrevocable totality.

And what had become of his half-brother who had cut them down, who would also one day—maybe had already—become one with a decaying forest floor in the end? What had become of all of his half-brothers and maybe half-sisters too? Ninnish traced his own scar with his hand down his pants. Was this the end, he wondered, as he adjusted his butt to keep it from falling asleep on the altar. No. It may have well been the bruise that foretold it, but it was not yet the end. With his other hand, he burrowed his fingers under the moss and rubbed his fingertips uneasily across the weather-smoothed tree rings, convincing himself that they felt forgiving.

In his twenty-eight years on Wickaninnish Island, Ninnish had paddled or motored his many boats throughout most of Clayoquot Sound and had seen whole stands of old growth obliterated by industry, exposing more sky than his eyes could stand. Often, in the middle of such desecration, a single tree was spared. Perhaps it had been recognized as culturally significant—stripped of a portion of its bark centuries ago, by indigenous people who had needed the fibre for shelter or clothing or fuel. Maybe a solitary tree had been selected as the one cone tree that was unrealistically expected to re-seed the entire clear-cut. Either way, the tree had been deemed important and spared. Significant, but condemned all the same to tower there by itself—a resilient speck of green piercing an otherwise unchallenged sky, almost begging the wind to drag it down and end its loneliness. It had taken him nearly three decades, but at last he knew that a solitary tree left in a ravaged clearing like that could be just as wicked a bruise as the one he stared into now.

His blue eyes watered as he refused to blink until the other trees began to frolic, stories above him, their cone-laden limbs exaggerating the sea breeze's gentle tugs. He shut his eyes tightly to meditate or hallucinate—depending on the strength of the mushrooms he had ingested forty-fve minutes earlier—until he could feel the stump, reborn, piercing his stomach and other guts, to imprison his legs and outstretched arms, arresting his activist-come-lately soul in agile, swirling grains that recorded not only time but its disappearance. The very ghost of this tree's spires materialized in his hallucinogenic gaze, to blot out the bruise like cheap make-up, applied several shameful layers thick.

And when at last he opened his eyes again, the forest had healed over—and time, for the wicked, had been restored.

Dunlap
(117)
Robert Pt
Eugvik Rk
Lone Cone
753
Maurus
Elbow
Bk
Channel
Rassier Pt
2
Kakawis
10
Opitsat
24)
Heynen Channel
10
5
Stubbs
56
Duffin Pass
5
Tofino
1)
2
76
Templar
(1)
09
2
(50)
5 (10)
inish
(50)
(50)
(1)
43)
(2)
37
(50)
10
(5)
Rf
(7)
27
Nob Rk
(50)
Lennard
(4)
(09)
(27)
Fl 10s 35m 17M
42
16
30

AUTHOR'S NOTE

The author wishes to respectfully acknowledge that the setting for this work of fiction—Clayoquot Sound—is part of the traditional territory of the Nuu-chah-nulth People who have continuously occupied and plied these coastal waterways, gently harvesting its bounty for a period of time many believe stretches back more than 13,000 years.

European contact here, beginning with Captain James Cook's exploration of the west coast of Vancouver Island in 1778, brought diseases, new customs and commerce which disrupted the harmonious balance with nature, decimated the Indigenous populations and changed forever the symbiotic relationship between the First Peoples and their surrounding environment. The region's wealth of natural resources was further discovered (and plundered) during the fur, fishing and whale trades of the past two centuries. Its exploitation has continued to modern day with industrialized clear-cut logging, mechanized over-fishing, fin-fish open water aquaculture and now, unbridled eco-tourism which attracts upwards of one million visitors annually.

In the Summer of 1993, more than one thousand rainforest-defenders faced off against the government, logging companies and the Royal Canadian Mounted Police, to stage a summer-long blockade of a bridge and logging road located just south of Tofino. Their unwavering sacrifice illuminated for the world the eminent threat facing this rare coastal temperate rainforest and resulted in the arrest of more than 900 protestors—many of whom faced trials, incarceration and the life-long stain of criminal records. This watershed event—this *War in the Woods*—also provoked and inspired a scientific panel in 1995 to develop 127 unanimous recommendations that underpinned the creation of the Clayoquot Sound UNESCO Biosphere Reserve in January 2000.